PRAISE FOR JASON MATTHEWS

PALACE OF TREASON

"*Red Sparrow*, Jason Matthews's debut thriller, is a challenging act to follow. *Palace of Treason*, the sequel to *Red Sparrow*, does not disappoint. The book is enthralling. Matthews deftly weaves in enough backstory to hook both new readers and those returning. *Palace of Treason* shimmers with authenticity. The villains are richly drawn . . . the scenes of them on the job are beyond chilling. Whether in Vienna, Moscow, or Washington, Matthews's scene-setting is superb, and he has a fine eye for telling details."

—*The New York Times Book Review*

"As authentic a spy novel as you are ever apt to read, rendered in exciting prose by a master who helped craft the rules by which spying is conducted. A ten-cloak, ten-dagger read."

—*The Washington Times*

"On a scale of one to five stars, *Palace of Treason* is a six. With *Palace of Treason*, Jason Matthews has resurrected the spy novel from the doldrums of silly car chases, martinis shaken not stirred, and dubious tradecraft to reflect the deadly serious stakes of the new Cold War."

—*New York Journal of Books*

"Like the first novel, [*Palace of Treason*] is as suspenseful and cinematic as the best spy movies around. Matthews knows his tradecraft, and he knows his writing craft, too."

—*The Philadelphia Inquirer*

"[*Palace of Treason*] is every bit as good as [*Red Sparrow*]. Authentic tradecraft, a complex plot that steadily builds tension, and credible heroes and villains on both sides make this a standout."

—*Publishers Weekly* (starred review)

"You'll never see Vladimir Putin in the same light after reading this chilling portrait. Matthews's characters seem to leap out of the page; his firsthand familiarity with the toys and routines of the spy world is a definite plus. VERDICT: Seldom is a sequel as stunning as the original, but this one absolutely triumphs."

—*Library Journal* (starred review)

"Matthews's latest is an extraordinarily commanding, acidly relevant, and unrelentingly suspenseful tale of espionage, brutality, and conscience."

—*Booklist* (starred review)

"Matthews's vast experience working in the shadowy world of espionage and spycraft lends an authenticity to his story that few can equal. And it doesn't hurt that he can write. . . . This is another must-read for fans of the spy genre."

—*Kirkus Reviews* (starred review)

"Jason Matthews has an amazing feel for the insider lingo and relentless intrigue of the spy's life. *Palace of Treason* is a harrowing look into the lives of spies. . . . This is stay-up-all-night reading, and we're pummeled by hair-trigger actions on every page."

—*BookPage*

"His real-life experiences in the shadowy world of spying make the story fresh, timely, and nearly authentic. . . . A sophisticated, behind-the-scenes, powerful story . . . Well written, creative."

—*Missourian*

"The world of a spy is unique and claustrophobic, but this bold tale captures its every nuance with expert precision. A tantalizing premise, and a heroine who's an alpha female, forge a piece of thrilling entertainment that does not disappoint."

—Steve Berry, *New York Times* bestselling author of *The Patriot Threat*

RED SPARROW

"A primer in twenty-first-century spying . . . Terrifically good."

—*The New York Times Book Review*

"A smart, intriguing tale rooted in his own experience . . . Fans of the genre's masters including John le Carré and Ian Fleming will happily embrace Matthews's central spy."

—*USA Today*

"You, too, may also conclude that *Red Sparrow* is the best espionage novel you've ever read."

—*The Huffington Post*

"[A] sublime and sophisticated debut . . . *Red Sparrow* isn't just a fast-paced thriller—it's a first-rate novel as noteworthy for its superior style as for its gripping depiction of a secretive world."

—*The Washington Post*

"This debut novel from a thirty-three-year CIA veteran delivers action as pulse-pounding as it is authentic."

—*New York Post*

"Matthews's exceptional first novel will please fans of classic spy fiction. . . . The author's thirty-three-year career in the CIA allows him to showcase all the tradecraft and authenticity that readers in this genre demand. . . . [A] complex, high-stakes plot."

—*Publishers Weekly* (starred review)

"An intense descent into a vortex of carnal passion, career brutality, and smart tradecraft, this thriller evokes the great Cold War era of espionage."

—*Library Journal* (starred review)

"A compelling and propulsive tale of spy versus spy . . . *Red Sparrow* is greater than the sum of its fine parts. Espionage aficionados will love this one."

—*Booklist* (starred review)

"Features enough action to satisfy even the most demanding of adrenaline junkies . . . The author's CIA background and the smart dialogue make this an entertaining tale for spy-novel enthusiasts."

—*Kirkus Reviews*

"Not since the good old days of the Cold War has a classic spy thriller like *Red Sparrow* come along. Jason Matthews is not making it up; he has lived this life and this story, and it shows on every page. High-level espionage, pulse-pounding danger, sex, double agents, and double crosses. What more can any reader want?"

—Nelson DeMille

"[Jason Matthews is] an insider's insider. He knows the secrets. And he is also a masterful storyteller. I loved this book and could not put it down. Neither will you."

—Vince Flynn

"The spy thriller is back in full force thanks to newcomer and CIA insider Jason Matthews. . . . I have not read a more exciting, gripping novel in a long time."

—Doug Stanton, *New York Times* bestselling author of *Horse Soldiers*

"All the tradecraft and cat-and-mouse tension of a classic spy thriller—a terrific read."

—Joseph Kanon, author of *Istanbul Passage*

THE RED SPARROW TRILOGY

Red Sparrow

Palace of Treason

The Kremlin's Candidate (forthcoming)

PALACE OF TREASON

A NOVEL

JASON MATTHEWS

SCRIBNER
NEW YORK LONDON TORONTO SYDNEY NEW DELHI

SCRIBNER
An Imprint of Simon & Schuster, Inc.
1230 Avenue of the Americas
New York, NY 10020

This book is a work of fiction. Any references to historical events, real people, or real places are used fictitiously. Other names, characters, places, and events are products of the author's imagination, and any resemblance to actual events or places or persons, living or dead, is entirely coincidental.

First Scribner trade paperback edition June 2017

SCRIBNER and design are registered trademarks of The Gale Group, Inc., used under license by Simon & Schuster, Inc., the publisher of this work.

For information about special discounts for bulk purchases, please contact Simon & Schuster Special Sales at 1-866-506-1949 or business@simonandschuster.com.

The Simon & Schuster Speakers Bureau can bring authors to your live event. For more information or to book an event, contact the Simon & Schuster Speakers Bureau at 1-866-248-3049 or visit our website at www.simonspeakers.com.

Interior design by Maura Fadden Rosenthal

Manufactured in the United States of America

10 9 8 7 6 5 4

Library of Congress Control Number: 2015017172

ISBN 978-1-4767-9374-0
ISBN 978-1-4767-9376-4 (pbk)
ISBN 978-1-4767-9375-7 (ebook)

To my brother, William,
with admiration.

PALACE OF TREASON

1

Captain Dominika Egorova of the Russian Foreign Intelligence Service, the SVR, pulled the hem of her little black dress down as she weaved through the crowds of pedestrians in the red neon, pranging chaos of Boulevard de Clichy in the Pigalle. Her black heels clicked on the Parisian sidewalk as she held her chin up, keeping the gray head of the rabbit in sight ahead of her—solo trailing surveillance on a moving foot target, one of the more difficult skills in offensive streetcraft. Dominika covered him loosely, alternately paralleling on the dividing island in the center of the boulevard and drafting behind the early evening pedestrians to screen her profile.

The man stopped to buy a charred kebab skewer—typically pork in this Christian quarter—from a vendor who fanned the charcoal of a small brazier with a folded piece of cardboard, sending an occasional spark into the passing crowd and enveloping the street corner in clouds of smoke fragrant with coriander and chili. Dominika eased back behind a street pole: it was unlikely that the rabbit was using the snack stop as a way to check his six—for the last three days he had shown himself to be oblivious on the street—but she wanted to avoid his noticing her too soon. Plenty of other street creatures already had watched her passing through the crowd—dancer's legs, regal bust, arc-light-blue eyes—cutting her scent, sniffing for strength or frailty.

In two practiced glances, Dominika checked the zoo of faces but did not get that tingle on the back of her neck that meant the start of trouble. The rabbit, a Persian, finished tearing the strips of meat with his teeth and tossed the short skewer into the gutter. Apparently this Shia Muslim had no compunctions about eating pork—or slathering his face between the legs of hookers, for that matter. He started moving again, Dominika keeping pace.

An unshaven and swarthy young man left his friends leaning against the steam-weeping window of a noodle shop, slid in beside Dominika, and put an arm around her shoulder. *"Je bande pour toi,"* he said in the crooked French of the Maghreb—he had a hard-on for her. Jesus. She had no time for this, and felt the smoldering surge in her stomach running into her arms. No. Become ice. She shook his arm off, pushed his face away, and kept walking. "*Va voir ailleurs si j'y suis*"—go somewhere else, see if I'm there—she said over her shoulder. The young man stopped short, made an obscene gesture, and spat on the sidewalk.

Dominika reacquired the Persian's gray head just as the man entered La Diva, passing through the scrolling lights framing the dance hall's entrance. She drifted toward the door, noted the heavy velvet curtain, and gave him a beat to get inside, this diminutive man who held the nuclear secrets of the Islamic Republic of Iran in his head. He was her prey, a human intelligence target. Dominika ran the edge of her will rasping across the whetstone of her mind. It was to be a hostile recruitment attempt, an ambush, coercive, a cold pitch, and she thought she had an even chance to flip him in the next half hour.

Tonight Dominika wore her brown hair down around her shoulders, bangs covering one eye, like an Apache dancer from the 1920s. She wore square-framed tortoiseshell eyeglasses with clear lenses, a Parisian Lois Lane out for the night. But the typing-pool effect was spoiled by the low-cut black sheath dress and Louboutin pumps. She was a former ballerina, her legs shapely and knotted in the calves, though she walked with a nearly imperceptible limp from a right foot shattered by a ballet-academy rival when Dominika was twenty years old.

Paris. She hadn't breathed the air of the West since she returned to Moscow after being exchanged in a spy swap on a bridge in Estonia months ago. The images of the exchange were fading, the sound of her long-ago steps on the silver-wet bridge increasingly muffled, draped in the fog of that night. Returned home, she had inhaled the Russian air deeply; it was her country, *Rodina*, the Motherland, but the clean bite of pine forest and loamy black earth was tainted by a hint of liquid corruption, like a dead animal beneath the floorboards. Of course, she had been greeted back home enthusiastically, with florid kudos and good wishes from lumpy officials. She had reported for work at SVR Headquarters—referred to as the Center—immediately, but seeing her colleagues in the Service once again, the milling herd of the *siloviki,* the anointed inner circle, had collapsed her spirit. *What did you expect?* she thought.

Things were different with her now. Exquisitely, massively, dangerously different. She had been recruited by a CIA case officer—with whom she had fallen in love—then vetted, trained, and directed to return to Moscow as a penetration of the Center. She was learning to wait, to listen, to appear to be a wholly quiescent creature of the mephitic atmosphere of her Service. To that end, she had demurred when several idiotic headquarters positions were offered to her—she would wait for a job with the kind of access CIA really wanted. She feigned interest in the process and otherwise took the time to attend a short course in operational psychology, and another in counterintelligence: It might be useful in the future to know how mole hunters in her Service would be hunting, how the footsteps in the stairwell would sound when they came for her.

She bided her time by looking into their souls, for Dominika was born a synesthete, with a brain wired to see colored auras around people and thereby read passion, treachery, fear, or deception. When she was five years old, Dominika's synesthesia shocked and worried her professor father and musician mother. They made their little girl promise never to reveal this soaring precocity to anyone, even as she grew accustomed to it. At twenty, Dominika was lifted on maroon waves of music at the ballet academy. At twenty-five, she calibrated a man's lust by his scarlet halo. Now just past thirty, being able to divine men's and women's spirits just possibly would save her life.

There was something else. Since her recruitment, Dominika had been visited by images of her late mother, a benign chimera that would appear by her side to offer encouragement and support. Russians are spiritual and emotional, so fondly remembering ancestors was not at all creepy or demented. At least Dominika didn't worry about it, and besides, her mother's spirit fortified her as she resumed her double life, a shimmering hand on her shoulder as she stood at the mouth of the dark cave, smelling the beast inside, willing herself to get on with it.

On her return to the Center from the West, there had been two clearance sessions with an oily little man from counterespionage and a saturnine female stenographer. He asked about the *ubiytsa,* the Spetsnaz assassin who had almost killed her in Athens, and then about being in CIA custody: what the CIA men had been like, what the Americans asked her, what she told them; Dominika had stared down the stenographer, who was swaddled in a yellow haze—deceit and avarice—and replied that she told them nothing. The bear sniffed at her shoes and nodded, apparently satisfied. *But the bear was never satisfied,* she thought. *It never was.*

Her exploits, and near escapes, and contact with the Americans cast suspicion on her—as it was with anyone returning from active service in the West—and she knew the liver-eyed lizards of the FSB, the Federal Security Service, were observing her, waiting for a ripple, watching for an email or postcard from abroad, or an inexplicable, cryptic telephone call from a Moscow suburb, or an observed contact with a foreigner. But there were no ripples. Dominika was normal in her patterns; there was nothing for them to see.

So they placed a handsome physical trainer to bump her during the "mandatory" self-defense course run in an old mansion in Domodedovo, on Varshavskaya Ulitsa off the MKAD ring road. The moldy, spavined house with creaky staircases and a green-streaked copper roof was nestled in an unkempt botanical garden hidden behind a wall with a crooked sign reading VILAR INSTITUTE OF OFFICINAL PLANTS. A few bored class participants—a florid Customs Service woman and two overage border guards—sat and smoked on benches along the walls of the glassed-in winter garden that served as the practice area.

Daniil, the trainer, was a tall, blond Great Russian, about thirty-five years old and imperially slim, with sturdy wrists and pianist's hands. His features were delicate: Jawline, cheek, and brow were finely formed, and the impossibly long lashes above the sleepy blue eyes could stir the potted palm fronds in the winter garden from across the room. Dominika knew there was no such thing as a mandatory self-defense class in SVR, and that Daniil most likely was a ringer dispatched to casually ask questions and eventually elicit from an unwary Dominika that she had colluded with a foreign intelligence service, or passed state secrets, or seduced multiple debauched partners in hot upper berths of swaying midnight trains. It didn't matter what transgressions they harvested. The counterintelligence hounds couldn't define treason, but they'd know it when they saw it.

She certainly was not expecting to be taught anything along the lines of close-quarters fighting techniques. On the first day, with dappled sunlight coming through the grimy glass ceiling of the winter garden, Dominika was intrigued to see a pale-blue aura of artful thought and soul swirling around Daniil's head and from the tips of his fingers. She was additionally surprised when Daniil began instructing her in *Sistema Rukopashnogo Boya,* the Russian hand-to-hand combat system, medieval, brutal, rooted in tenth-century Cossack tradition with mystical connections to the Orthodox Church. It was normally taught only to Russian military personnel.

She had seen the Spetsnaz assassin use the same moves in the blood-splattered Athens hotel room, not recognizing them for what they were, but horrified at their buttery efficiency. Daniil spared her nothing in training, and she found she enjoyed physically working her body again, remembering the long-ago discipline of her cherished dancing career, the career They had taken away from her. *Sistema* put a premium on flexibility, ballistic speed, and knowledge of vulnerable points on the human body. As Daniil demonstrated joint locks and submission holds, his face close to Dominika's, he saw something in her fifty-fathom eyes he wouldn't want to stir up unnecessarily.

After two weeks, Dominika was mastering strikes and throws that would have taken other students months to learn. She had initially covered her mouth and laughed at the bent-leg monkey walk used to close with an opponent in combat, and the swirling shoulder shrug that preceded a devastating hand strike. Now, she was knocking Daniil down on the mat as often as he dumped her. In the dusty afternoon light of the room, Dominika watched Daniil's back muscles flex as he demonstrated a new technique and she idly wondered about him. The way he moved, he could have been a ballet dancer, or a gymnast. How had he gotten into the killing martial arts? Was he Spetsnaz, from a *Vympel* group? She had noticed, with the eye of a Sparrow—a trained seductress of the state—that his ring finger was significantly longer than his index finger. The likelihood existed therefore, according to the warty matrons at Sparrow School, of above-average-sized courting tackle.

Estimating the size of a man was not the only thing Dominika had learned at State School Four, Sparrow School, the secret sexpionage academy that trained women in the art of seduction. The classrooms and auditoria in the walled, peeling mansion in the pine forest outside the city of

Kazan on the banks of the Volga were in her mind still. She could hear the droning clinical lectures on human sexuality and love. She could see the jumpy, roiling films of coitus and perversion. The lists of sexual techniques, numbered in the hundreds, endlessly memorized and practiced—*No. 88, "Butterfly wings"; No. 42, "String of pearls"; No. 32, "The carpet tack"*—would come back to her, uninvited thoughts of the numb days and evil nights, and everything sprinkled with rose water to cloak the musk of rampant male and lathered female, and the dirty-nailed hands squeezing her thighs, and the drops of sweat that hung from the fleshy noses that inevitably, unavoidably, would drip onto her face. She had endured it to spite the *svini,* the pigs, all of them, who thought she would lie on her back and open her legs. And she would now show them how wrong they were.

Calm down, she told herself. She was fighting the building stress of being back in Russia's service, in the embrace of the Motherland, the start of an impossibly risky existence. There was additional anguish: She didn't know whether the man she loved was still alive. And if he was still breathing, her love was a secret she would have to guard to her core, because there was the small detail that he was an American case officer of CIA. She waited for the overdue start of Daniil's sly elicitation, plausible after the earned familiarity of fourteen days of physical training. She would have to be exceedingly careful—no baiting, no sarcasm—but it was also an opening for a well-timed bit of *dezinformatsiya,* deception, perhaps a sly hint about her admiration for President Putin. Everything she told Daniil would go back to the FSB, and then the Center, and be compiled with all the other pieces of the "welcome home" investigation, and ultimately determine whether she would retain her status as an *operupolnomochenny,* an operations officer. But my, those eyelashes.

Dominika held her head erect, elegant on a long neck, as she pushed through the musky velvet curtain into the La Diva club. The bouncer at the inner door looked with professional approval at her little black dress, then glanced briefly into her tiny black satin clutch, barely large enough to hold a lipstick and wafer-thin smartphone. He pulled the heavy curtain aside and motioned her to enter. *No weapons,* he thought. *Mademoiselle Doudounes, Miss Big Chest, is clean.*

Captain Egorova was in fact more than able to dispense lethal force. The lipstick tube in her purse was an *elektricheskiy pistolet,* a single-shot electric gun, a recent update from SVR technical—Line T—laboratories, a new version of a venerable Cold War weapon. The disposable lipstick gun fired a murderously explosive 9mm Makarov cartridge accurately out to two meters—the bullet had a compressed metal dust core that expanded massively on contact. The only sound at discharge was a single loud click.

Dominika scanned the black-lit interior of the club, a large semicircular room filled with chipped tables in the center and tired leatherette booths along the walls. A low stage with old-timey footlights stood dark and empty. Her target, Parvis Jamshidi, sat alone in a center booth pensively looking up at the ceiling. Dominika did a second quick scan, quartering the room, focusing on the far corners: No obvious countersurveillance or lounging bodyguard. She weaved between the tables toward Jamshidi's booth, ignoring the snapped fingers of a fat man at a table, signaling her to come over, either to order another *petit jaune* or to suggest they go together for thirty minutes to the Chat Noir Design Hotel down the block.

She was keyed up as the familiar feel of the hunt, of contact with the opposition, rose in her throat, tightened across her chest, and switched on the glow-plugs in her stomach. Dominika eased into the booth and put the little clutch down in front of her. Jamshidi continued looking up at the ceiling, as if in prayer. He was short and slight, with a forked goatee. His El Greco hands were folded on the table, long-fingered and still. He wore the requisite pearl-gray suit with white collarless shirt buttoned at the neck. A small man, a physicist, an expert in centrifugal separation, the lead scientist in Iran's uranium-enrichment program. Dominika said nothing, waiting for him to speak.

Jamshidi felt her presence and his eyes lowered, appraising Dominika's figure—the slim arms, the plain, square-cut nails. She stared at his face until he stopped looking at the blue-veined cleft between her breasts.

"How much for one hour?" he said casually. He had a reedy voice and spoke in French. In the club's musk-cat air his words came out milky yellow and weak, all deceit and greed. Dominika noted with interest that the ultraviolet light in the club did not affect her ability to read his fetid colors. She continued to look at him mildly.

"Did you hear me?" Jamshidi said, raising his voice. "Do you understand French, or are you a *putain* from Kiev?" He looked up again at the ceiling, as if in dismissal. Dominika followed his gaze. A Plexiglas catwalk hung suspended from the rafters and a naked woman in heels was dancing directly above Jamshidi's head. Dominika looked back at his preposterous goatee.

"What makes you think I'm a working girl?" said Dominika in unaccented French.

Jamshidi looked back down, met her eyes, and laughed. It was at this point that he should have heard the rustling in the long grass, the instant before grip of fang and claw.

"I asked you how much for an hour," he said.

"Five hundred," said Dominika, brushing a strand of hair behind her ear. Jamshidi leaned forward and made a further obscene suggestion.

"Three hundred more," said Dominika, looking at him over the tops of her eyeglasses. She smiled at him and pushed her glasses back up. As if on cue the stage footlights came on and a dozen women trooped out wearing nothing but thigh-high vinyl boots and white peaked caps. Filtered spotlights dappled their bodies with pink and white stripes as they gyrated in formation to blaring Europop.

Jamshidi originally had been spotted in Vienna by the Russian Rostekhnadzor representative in the International Atomic Energy Agency, who noted the Iranian's after-hours predilection for the leggy escorts who sipped sherry in the bars of the Gurtel district. The IAEA lead was passed to the Vienna *rezident* who in turn reported it to Moscow Center, SVR Headquarters in Yasenevo, in southwest Moscow.

A vigorous debate in the Center ensued regarding whether Jamshidi was a valid recruitment target. Pursuing an official from a client state was unwise, some said. The old techniques of blackmail and coercion would not work, others said. The risk of blowback and damage to bilateral relations was too great, still others said. A single department head wondered out loud whether this was a too-convenient opportunity. Perhaps this was a provocation, a disinformation trap somehow hatched by the Western services—CIA, Mossad, MI6—to discredit Moscow.

This *zagovoritsya*, this dithering, was not uncommon in SVR. The modern Foreign Intelligence Service was as riven by fear of the president of the Federation—of the blue-eyed X-ray stares and back-alley reprisals—as the NKVD was of Stalin's rages in the 1930s. No one wanted to validate a bad operation and commit the ultimate transgression: embarrassing Vladimir Vladimirovich Putin on the world stage.

Alexei Ivanovich Zyuganov, chief of the Counterintelligence Department of the Service—Line KR—was first among many who declared Jamshidi's recruitment too risky (chiefly because the case was not his). But the president, a former KGB officer himself (his service record, including a torpid foreign posting to Communist Dresden in the late 1980s, was never discussed, *ever*), overruled the too-timorous voices in SVR.

"Find out what this scientist knows," Putin ordered the SVR director in Yasenevo over the secure *vysokochastoty* high-frequency line from the Kremlin. "I want to know how far along these Iranian fanatics are with their uranium. The Zionists and the Americans are losing patience." Putin paused, then said, "Give this to Egorova, let her run with it."

It normally could be considered a towering compliment when the president of the Federation specifically designated an officer in the Service to manage a high-profile recruitment operation—it had happened occasionally in the past with old KGB favorites of Putin's—but Dominika was under no illusion about why she had been selected. She had not even met the president. "It's a great honor," said the director, when he summoned her to his office to inform her that the Kremlin had given instructions. Khuinya, *bollocks,* thought Dominika. *They want a former Sparrow to run this pussy snare. Very well, boys,* she thought, *mind your fingers.*

Her selection did accomplish one thing. The palpable weight of the FSB counterintelligence reinvestigation was lifted. All the games stopped: The tinted-window Peugeot was no longer parked outside her apartment on Kastanaevskaya Ulitsa in the mornings and evenings; the periodic jovial interviews with the counterespionage staff trailed off; and *Sistema* workouts with the toothsome Daniil ended. Dominika now knew she had been cleared—certainly Putin's impatient orders had hastened the process, but she was through. She savored the irony that President Putin himself had just put her, the fox, in the henhouse. But the savored irony soon turned into a thin white line of anger in her stomach.

Things moved rather quickly after that, including her assignment to Line KR, the counterintelligence staff. Alexei Zyuganov summoned her and without emotion informed her that the decision had come down from the fourth floor that she was to manage the operation against Jamshidi from Line KR. His demeanor was sour, his voice contemptuous, his gaze indirect. And beneath the façade, in the few seconds of direct eye contact, she saw demented paranoia. He sat in a swirl of black as he spoke. He droned that the resources of his department were to be used to ensure that her planning was sound, and that there would be no flaps—none whatsoever would be tolerated. Zyuganov's deputy, Yevgeny, in his thirties, scowling, stout, and broad, dour as an Orthodox deacon and impossibly dark, from thatched hair to woolly eyebrows to orangutan forearms, leaned against the office doorjamb behind Dominika, listening, while appraising the curve of her buttocks under her smooth skirt.

The truth was that Zyuganov was furious at being publically overruled regarding the recruitment of the Persian. The poisonous and diminutive Zyuganov—he was just over five feet tall—was doubly stung by the case being handed to Dominika Egorova and not to him, was *trebly* stung by the fact that the president of the Russian Federation knew of and had an eye on a mere captain, his new subordinate. Zyuganov appraised this *shlyukha,* this trained whore, from the sodden duck blind of his mind.

She was the rare, ridiculous female *operupolnomochenny,* operations officer, in the Service, but with a pedigree and an unassailable reputation. He had heard the stories, read the restricted reports. Among other accomplishments in her young career, she acquired the information that led to the arrest of one of the most damaging penetrations of SVR, veteran Lieutenant General Vladimir Korchnoi—a traitor run for *a decade and a half* by the Americans—ending a mole hunt that had lasted years. Zyuganov had managed part of the search to unmask Korchnoi, and had not succeeded where this bint had. Then she had been wounded, captured, and held briefly by CIA, returned from the West in triumph to Yasenevo, given a meritorious promotion to junior captain, and now, peremptorily, was assigned to Line KR to work a director's dossier case.

Zyuganov, who started his own venomous career during the precursor KGB years as an interrogator in the Lubyanka cellars, could not oppose her personnel assignment. He dismissed Egorova and watched her go—she was forced to squeeze by an unmoving, smirking Yevgeny in the doorway. The operation against the Persian was too important to scuttle, but Zyuganov's Lubyanka instincts stirred in another direction. He could take control and earn high-profile credit for bagging the Persian if Captain Egorova were out of the picture. He sat back in his swivel chair thinking, his little feet dangling, and looked at the dark-browed Yevgeny, daring him with a gassy stare to say anything. *Vilami na vode pisano,* the future is written with a pitchfork on flowing water. No one knows what's going to happen.

Outside the club, Dominika led Jamshidi by a clammy hand through the thick haze of nighttime traffic, dashing across Place Blanche and then more slowly downhill a half block to the little Hotel Belgique with its blue-striped canopy over the door. A bored *ubiytsa* behind the counter, a bruiser with big arms in a dirty T-shirt, threw Dominika a key and a towel.

The door opened a foot before it hit the metal frame of the bed as Dominika pushed into the room. They had to squeeze past the cracked dresser. The screened toilet in the corner of the room was ringed in rust stains, and a large mirror, spotted and smoky, hung over the headboard by a dangerously frayed velvet rope. Jamshidi walked to the toilet to relieve himself. "Take off your clothes," he said over his shoulder, splashing liberally outside the porcelain. Dominika sat at the foot of the bed with her legs crossed, bouncing her foot. For five kopeks she would put her lipstick tube against his forehead and push the plunger. Jamshidi zipped and turned toward her.

"What are you waiting for? Strip and get on your stomach," he said, slipping out of his suit coat. He hung it on a nail on the back of the door. "Don't worry, I have your money. You can send it to your momma in Kiev—that is if she's not working next door."

Dominika leaned back and chuckled. "Good evening, Dr. Jamshidi," she said. "I am not from Ukraine."

Jamshidi's head came up at the mention of his name and he scanned her face. Any Iranian nuclear scientist violating sharia and furtively tomcatting in Montmartre quickly sniffs danger. He didn't ask her how she knew him.

"I don't care where you're from," he said.

So educated, thought Dominika, *and still so stupid.* "I need a few minutes of your time," said Dominika. "I assure you it will be of interest to you."

Jamshidi searched her face. Who was this tart with the Mona Lisa smile? "I told you to get undressed," he said, stepping toward her, but unsure about what was happening. His ardor was running out of him like the sand in a broken hourglass. He snatched at her wrist and pulled her to her feet. He stuck his face close to hers, drinking in the scent of Vent Vert, searching her eyes behind those incongruous glasses. *"A poil,"* strip, he said. He squeezed her wrist and watched her face. He got nothing. Dominika looked him in the eyes as she put a thumbnail between his first and second knuckle and pressed. Jamshidi jumped with the pain and jerked his hand away.

"Just a few minutes," Dominika said, with a little lead in her voice, to give him a hint, a taste. She spoke casually, as if she had not just lit up the median nerve of his right hand.

"Who are you?" said Jamshidi sliding away from her. "What do you want?"

Dominika put her hand on his sleeve, pushing the limits, the man-woman Islam thing. Not so big a problem with this educated Persian who lived in Europe, this whoreson with a taste for redheads.

"I want to propose an arrangement," said Dominika. "A mutually beneficial arrangement." She left her hand where it was. Jamshidi threw it off and turned for the door. Whatever this was, he wanted out. Dominika stepped smoothly in front of him and Jamshidi put his hand on her chest to push her aside. Slowly, almost tenderly, she trapped his hand tight against her breast with her elegant fingers, feeling his moist palm on her skin. She applied light downward pressure and stepped into him—Jamshidi's face contorted in pain—forcing him nose-first onto the ratty bedspread. "I insist you let me tell you," Dominika said, releasing his hand.

Jamshidi sat up on the bed with wide eyes. He knew all he needed to know. "You are from French Intelligence?" he asked, rubbing his wrist.

When Dominika did not react he said, "CIA, the British?" Dominika stayed silent and Jamshidi shuddered at the worst thought, "You are Mossad?"

Dominika shook her head slightly.

"Then who are you?"

"We are your ally and friend. We alone stand with Iran against a global vendetta, sanctions, military threats. We support your work, Doctor, in every way."

"Moscow?" said Jamshidi, laughing under his breath. "The KGB?"

"No longer KGB, Doctor, now *Sluzhba Vneshney Razvedki*, the SVR."

Jamshidi shook his head and breathed easy; no Zionist action team, praise Allah. "And what do you want? What is this nonsense about a proposal?" he said, confidence back now, his yellow stronger.

Zhaba, *you toad,* thought Dominika. "Moscow would like to consult with you; we would like you to advise us on your program." Dominika braced for the indignation.

"Consult? Advise? You want me to spy on my own country, on my program, to compromise our security?" Jamshidi the righteous, Jamshidi the patriot.

"There is no threat to Iran's security," said Dominika evenly. "Keeping Moscow informed will *protect* your country against its enemies."

Jamshidi snorted. "You are ridiculous," he said. "Let me up now; get out of my way." Dominika did not move.

"I mentioned that my proposal would be mutually beneficial, Doctor. Wouldn't you like to hear how?"

Jamshidi snorted again but stayed still.

"You live and work in Vienna, accredited to the International Atomic Energy Agency. You travel frequently to Tehran. You are the leading expert in your country on centrifugal isotope separation, and for the last several years have directed the assembly of centrifuge cascades at the Fuel Enrichment Plant at Natanz. Correct so far?"

Jamshidi did not respond but looked at her as he kneaded his hand.

"A brilliant career, steady success in the program, in the favor of the Supreme Leader, and with allies in the Security Council. A wife and children in Tehran. But as a man of exceptional needs, a man who has earned the right to do as he pleases, you have made acquaintances—both in Vienna and during these occasional furtive and unauthorized weekends in Paris. You appreciate beautiful women, and they appreciate you."

"May *Shaitan* take you," said Jamshidi. "You are a liar."

"How disappointed your friends would be to hear you disavow them," said Dominika, reaching for her clutch. She took out the phone and held it loosely in her hand. Jamshidi stared at her. "Especially your friend Udranka. She has an apartment in Vienna on Langobardenstrasse, very near your IAEA office. You know it well."

"You fucking Russians," said Jamshidi.

"No, actually, you are fucking a Serb. A quite innocent girl, I might add. Udranka is from Belgrade. You've seen quite a lot of her."

"Lies," stuttered Jamshidi. "No proof."

Dominika swiped a slim finger across the screen of her phone to start the streaming video and tilted it toward Jamshidi so he could see.

"Your most recent visit, August twenty-third," narrated Dominika. "You brought candy—Sissi-Kugeln chocolates—and a bottle of Nussberg Sauvignon. She broiled a beefsteak. You sodomized her at twenty-one forty-five hours, and left fifteen minutes later." Dominika tossed the phone onto the bedspread, watching the brutality of her words work on him as the tinny video continued. "Keep it, if you wish." He looked once again at the screen and slid it away from him.

"No," he said. The color around his head and shoulders was bleached out, barely visible. Dominika knew he had already calculated the unspoken threat. The mullahs would execute him if his twisted little habits were exposed, if his prurient misuse of official funds was revealed, but especially if his *stupidity* at being blackmailed was brought to light. "No," he repeated.

Ran'she syadyesh, ran'she vydyesh, thought Dominika, *the sooner you get in, the sooner you get out.* She sat beside him and started talking softly, concealing her contempt. He was a beetle in a matchbox, with nowhere to move—Dominika didn't let him protest or feign ignorance. Instead she firmly told him the rules: He would answer her questions, they would meet discreetly, she would give him "expense money," she would protect him, and (with a subtle nod) he could continue taking his pleasure with Udranka. They would meet in Vienna, at Udranka's apartment, in seven days' time. He should reserve the entire evening. Dominika asked whether that was convenient, but got up before he could answer. He had no choice. She walked to the door, opened it a crack, and turned to look at him sitting small and quiet on the stained bedspread.

"I will take care of you, Doctor," she said, "in all things. Are you coming?"

They left the room and descended the narrow staircase with peeling paper and creaking treads. The *ubiytsa* came from around the counter and stood at the bottom of the stairs. "Fifty euros," he said, arms across his chest. "Entertainment tax." A brown haze floated around his head: cruelty, violence, stupidity. Uncomprehending, Jamshidi tried to squeeze by him, but the man pinned him to the wall with a meaty forearm under the chin. His other hand brought up a cutthroat razor. "One hundred euros," said the man, looking up at Dominika. "Prostitution tax." Pinned by the neck, Jamshidi could only goggle as she stepped off the last stair and drew close.

Dominika was partially conscious of a faint annoyance at being interrupted, nettled at an outside interference. Her vision was acute and ice clear in the center, but hazy around the margins. She smelled the thug through his shirt, smelled the brown animal essence of him. Without a break in stride, Dominika pushed right up to him, through his brown cloud, and grasped the back of his greasy head softly, lovingly. Her other hand clamped onto the side of his face, her thumb at the hinge of his jaw. She pressed violently in and up—she felt the temporomandibular joint click under her thumb pad—and the brute's head came up and he howled in pain, the razor falling from his fingers. In a cloud of funk and perfume, Dominika pulled his smelly hair and yanked his head back. An instant flashing thought: *What would* Bratok, *big brother Gable, one of her CIA handlers, think about this temper of hers?* Then, electrically, a second thought: *What would all her Americans feel as they watched her in this reeking stairwell doing* this— Her focus snapped back and she struck the bruiser once with the open web of her hand, very fast, in the windpipe. The man grunted once as Dominika pulled him violently backward, hitting his head against the wall to the sound of crunching plaster. He lay on the floor and didn't move.

Dominika bent, picked up the straight razor, and folded it closed, stilling an impulse to reach over and drag the edge heavily across the unconscious thug's throat. Jamshidi had slid slowly to the floor, gasping. She squatted beside him, her dress riding halfway up her thighs and revealing the lacy black triangle of her underwear, but Jamshidi was staring only at her luminous face, a strand of hair bedroom-sexy over one eye. Slightly out of breath, she spoke softly, straightening her eyeglasses. "I told you we support our friends. I will protect you always. You're my agent now."

PORK SATAY

Marinate thin strips of pork in a thick paste of sesame oil, cardamom, turmeric, pureed garlic, pureed ginger, fish sauce, brown sugar, and lime juice. Grill over cherry-red coals until pork is caramelized and crispy.

2

Three a.m. and the fourth arrondissement was dark and quiet. The Louboutins were pinching as Dominika walked through the narrow streets of the Marais back to her boutique hotel near Place Sainte-Catherine. *Tant pis,* a shame, but one does not go barefoot on the sidewalks of dog-loving Paris.

Finishing her encrypted text to Zyuganov as she walked, Dominika did a quick appraisal of the pitch. Stepping over the unconscious thug, a bewildered Jamshidi had stutter-stepped into the night, nodding vaguely at Dominika's sweet whispered reminder to meet in a week's time. The yellow fog around his head was starched almost white with shock. She reported the results of the Jamshidi pitch modestly to the Center—and to a skeptical and resentful Zyuganov—as a provisional success. As in all intelligence operations, she would not know whether Jamshidi was fully cooked until and unless he appeared at Udranka's apartment in Vienna in a week, docile and ready to be debriefed. The continued lollipop promise of the 1.85-meter-tall, magenta-haired Serb, now a Sparrow under Dominika's direction, would be an incentive for Jamshidi to behave. Dominika commiserated with her Sparrow, shared an occasional glass of wine with her, paid her well—solidarity between sisters. Most of all, she had listened to Udranka's canny assessments of Jamshidi, every detail, the better to stopper him in the recruitment bottle.

As she walked along the deserted street she checked her six for trailing surveillance, unlikely at this hour, by crossing the street and taking half-second snap glances in either direction. She was escorted first by one, then two, then three, street cats, tails high and trotting serpentinely around her ankles. Dominika thought that Sparrow School had wrought one elemental change. Her life had been forever altered when she was directed against an officer of the American CIA—specifically Nathaniel Nash—to unman him, to compromise him, to elicit the name of his Russian mole. But the whole operation had turned out differently than her SVR masters planned, hadn't it? She was now working with CIA, spying for the Americans, she told herself, because Russia was rotten, the system was a canker. And yet, what she was doing, she was doing *for Russia*. She had thrown in with CIA, *she* had become the mole. And she had fallen into Nate's bed against all logic, against all prudence. She closed her eyes for a second and whispered to him, "Where are you, what are you doing?" One of the French cats looked over its shoulder at her, and gave her a *qu'est-ce que j'en sais*? look. How should I know?

That same minute, in the deserted offices of Line KR, Zyuganov fumed in his darkened office, the light of a single desk lamp highlighting Egorova's text-message report of the successful Paris recruitment approach to Jamshidi at the Pigalle nightclub, forwarded a few minutes earlier via encrypted email. The terse report detailing the episode stared up at him, mocking him. Egorova was a direct threat to him, her facile management of the operation making him look plodding and trivial. Zyuganov scanned the short paragraph, weighing risk and gain. *She's done well, flying solo, this well-titted-out upstart,* he thought. The Paris *rezidentura* had been totally cut out of the operation—no need for additional, local colleagues shouldering up to the trough. He reread her message—clipped, balanced, modest. Zyuganov squirmed in his seat, his envy overlaid by annoyance that built into a gnashing anger, fueled by fearful self-interest.

Her Jamshidi approach up to this point had been a precise operation, and she managed it with relentless thoroughness in a short time. *Damn it,* thought Zyuganov. Egorova had researched the target, conducted surveillance in Austria and France to determine his patterns, and then meticulously concocted a classic *polovaya zapadnya*, honey trap, using a primal, leggy Slav as a nectar bribe to lure the goateed physicist into the snap trap of a chintz-upholstered Viennese love nest that kept his *khuy* in a perpetual state of leaky anticipation. *Invaginirovatsya.* Jamshidi had been turned *inside out*. And tonight she had stage-managed the Paris pitch—playing the hooker, naturally. Zyuganov calculated: Egorova was returning to Moscow from Paris tomorrow. His crawly mind raced as he searched through papers on his desk to find the name of her hotel—Paris can be a dangerous city. A very dangerous city. Zyuganov picked up the phone.

The cats had deserted her. Three thirty in the morning and a bird was trilling in a tree along Rue de Turenne as Dominika turned into the dimly lit Rue de Jarente. There was a single lamp burning over the door of the Jeanne d'Arc; she'd have to buzz the night porter to get in. She was nearly to the entrance when she heard footsteps coming from across the narrow street, from behind the parked cars on the right curb. Dominika turned toward the sound while leaning on the night-bell button with her shoulder blade.

A man was approaching—a large man with black, shoulder-length Fabio hair and a leather coat. From her left, a second man rounded the corner of a side street and walked toward her. He was shorter but thicker, balding, and wore a padded vest over a work shirt. She saw a wiggly leather sap in his right hand. They both looked at Dominika with dull, wet-lipped relish. *Not professionals,* she thought, *not from any intel service. These were gonzo bullyboys high on absinthe and blunts.* Dominika leaned on the bell again, but there was no response from inside the hotel, no lights, nothing stirring, and she backed smoothly away from the entrance, hugging the wall, her red-soled Louboutins rasping on the pavement. She kept facing the two men, who had now converged and were walking shoulder to shoulder. She backed into another side street, Rue Caron, which opened onto tiny Place Sainte-Catherine—cobblestoned, tree-lined, stacked café tables darkly sleeping. *Two fights in one night: You're pushing your luck,* she thought.

With the extra room, the men rushed her, hands out to grab her arms, and as the sap came up Dominika touched off the lipstick gun in her bag, the metallic *click* of the electric primer muffled by the disintegrating satin clutch. Close range, point and shoot. There was a puff of goose down as the bullet hit the vest just above the shorter man's right nipple and its metal dust core expanded inside his chest cavity at three times the rate of a copper slug, vaporizing the vena cava, right ventricle, right lung, and the upper lobe of his liver. He collapsed as if spined, and his chin made a *tok* as it hit the *pavès* of the square. The black sap on the cobbles looked like a dog turd.

A two-shot *lipstick gun,* she thought. Fabio was on her now, a head taller. A streetlamp lit up his red-rimmed eyes, and the air around his head was swimming yellow. As he reached to grab her, a not unpleasant scent of leather came off him. She gave him a wrist, which he took, and she trapped his hand and quickly stepped into him, leaning him back on his heels. Dominika hooked her calf slightly behind his leg and pushed with her shoulder, applying torque to his knee. He should have gone down and given her time to put the heel of her shoe into his eye socket, but he grabbed the plunging front of her dress and pulled her down with him, tearing the material and exposing the lacy cups of her bra. They hit hard together, and Fabio rolled Dominika over onto her back, the Louboutins flying off, and he was on top of her—she smelled his leather jacket and the stale-cake bloom of week-old shirt—and she was using her hands to try to reach something, eyes, temples, soft tissues, but there was a singing bang and her head rocked, and maybe she could take one, two of those punches, but not many more.

The weight was off and Fabio was standing over her; she covered up but he kicked her ribs once and was measuring the distance for a big-booted neck stomp when a blessed street cleaner holding a power nozzle connected to a little bug-nosed water truck with a merry revolving orange light entered the other end of the square and started hosing down the cobbles. Fabio kicked Dominika again in the ribs, a glancing blow, and ran. She lay on the ground for a second, feeling her ribs for damage, watching the sweeper truck wetting down the far end of the square. She turned her head and saw the body of the man she had shot, lying small and facedown in a pool of black blood. *The sweepers would have some extra spraying to do,* she thought. *Now get out of here.* Stifling a groan, Dominika rolled to her feet, gingerly retrieved her shoes and glasses, and limped around the corner to her hotel, holding the scraps of her dress together with her other hand. She was quite a sight: She'd tell the night porter she was through working conventions—the hell with fertilizer salesmen from Nantes.

She left the room lights off and went into the bathroom, peeled off her torn dress, and examined the bruises in the mirror—red now, the eggplant purple would come tomorrow. Her cheek ached. She put a cold cloth on her eye, then eased herself with a groan into a hot tub, thinking about the towering coincidence of being mugged in Paris, about the pitch to Jamshidi.

And about Zyuganov. *Yadovityi,* poisonous. One of only two men she had ever known who showed not color but black foils of evil. She guessed that he betrayed without conscience, and would in turn expect and watch for betrayal. She knew he would consider Putin's heavy-lidded attention to her a serious threat, as if she were stalking him with a knife. And an operational triumph—such as recruiting Jamshidi—would be equally threatening to his standing. So if she failed, or if she was injured—say, *mugged on the street*—Zyuganov could take over management of the operation and personally carry the sensational intelligence reports to the fourth floor of Yasenevo and to the Kremlin.

It was the familiar, acid taste of double cross, the usual knife-across-the-throat treachery, and Dominika weighed her grim determination to fight them, to burn down the Service, to damage their lives. She considered reactivating contact with the CIA and Nate now, this very evening. Her assignment to Line KR and the Jamshidi case would potentially provide magnificent access, stupendous intelligence. They would marvel at her accomplishment in so short a time. She sank up to her neck in the hot water. She had six hours before her flight to Moscow.

It wasn't her mother this time. Marte had been a classmate at Sparrow School—corn-silk blond hair, blue eyes, and delicate lips—who, driven mad by the salacious requirements of the school, had hanged herself in her dormitory room. Dominika had been very sorry at the time, then furious: Another soul consumed by the Kremlin furnace. Marte sat on the rim of the tub and trailed her fingertips in the bathwater. There's time enough later for the Americans, said Marte; you have to go back now and put the noose around the neck of the Devil.

Dominika returned to Moscow on the morning Aeroflot flight from Paris sore and stiff, one raccoon eye throbbing. A car brought her to Yasenevo directly, and before she could report to Zyuganov, a waiting aide whisked her into the elevator and up to the executive fourth floor, past the portrait gallery of former directors, bushy-browed and wearing their medals on the lapels of their Savile Row suits, their rheumy eyes following the familiar figure of Dominika Egorova along the cream-carpeted hallway. *Hello! You again. Have they caught you yet?* the directors asked her as she passed. *Take care,* malyutka, *be careful little one.*

Pushing through the door of the director's suite, then passing through the lush-carpeted reception area and into the office brought back a flood of memories, of when she had been manipulated by her uncle Vanya Egorov, then first deputy director of SVR. Dominika and her dear uncle had quite a history together: Vanya had used her as sexual bait in a political assassination, then recruited her into the Service, then packed her off to Sparrow School—Whore School—for professional instruction in the carnal arts. She knew his yellow halo of deceit and puffery all too well, and didn't blink an eye when he was removed from the fourth floor, dismissed from the Service, pension forfeited.

Ancient history. Now as she entered the bright office, one wall of windows looking out onto the pine forest around the headquarters building, the doughy, distracted director rose from his desk, fussed, looked at his watch, and grunted at Dominika to follow him. To see the president. They rode down to the underground garage and into an immense black Mercedes redolent of leather and sandalwood cologne. They careered north through Moscow in the VIP counterflow lane, the emergency blue *migalka* flasher on the dashboard lighting up Dominika's black eye, which the director occasionally glanced at with faint interest.

The car shot through the Borovitskaya Gate—suddenly filled with the kettledrum notes of the tires on the Kremlin cobbles—and past the yellow and gold Grand Kremlin Palace, around the ivory Cathedral of the Archangel, and through the arch into the courtyard of the green-domed Senate building. Dominika shuddered inside. The Kremlin. Majestic buildings, gilded ceilings, soaring halls, all filled to the rafters with deceit, rapacious greed, and cruelty. A Palace of Treason. And now Dominika—another sort of traitor—was coming to the palace, to smile and lick the impassive face of the tsar.

A quick tug at her skirt and tuck of a strand of hair behind her ear as they heel-clicked in unison down the corridor. They waited under the vaulted ceiling in the grand reception hall in the Kremlin Senate, a room so large that the colossal Bokhara carpet on the parquet floor seemed like a prayer rug. Dominika could see the bloom of green around the director's head, and she was surprised that he was nervous, even fearful, of the interview with the president. Putin's *chef de cabinet* came out a door on the far side of the room and walked with muffled footsteps toward them. Brown suit, brown shoes, brown aura. Closed down and proper, he bowed slightly as he addressed them.

"Mr. Director, would you take advantage of the opportunity to call on the minister? He would be pleased to welcome you in his office." Another door opened and a second aide stood with his heels together. The message was unmistakable: Putin would see Egorova alone. The director of SVR nodded to Dominika and watched her dancer's legs as she crossed the room toward the massive twin doors of Putin's private office. *Just like in the old days,* he thought—*how long would this one remain in favor?*

Putin's aide stuck out a protocol arm and led her across the warmly paneled office of the president to another door, knocked once, and opened it. A small sitting room, blue flocked wallpaper bathed in afternoon sunlight, richly carpeted, a satin couch in celeste blue beneath the window. Outside, the copper spire of the Troitskaya Gate was visible over the Kremlin garden trees. The president came across the room and shook her hand. He was dressed in a dark suit with a white shirt and deep blue silk tie that matched those remarkable blue eyes.

"Captain Egorova," Putin said, referring pointedly to her new rank—a stunning promotion after her return. No smile, no expression, the unblinking stare. Dominika wondered if he chose his neckwear to match his eyes. He gestured to her to sit, and the satin brocade sighed as she sank into it.

"Mr. President," said Dominika. She could be phlegmatic too. He was bathed in a turquoise-blue haze, the color of emotion, of artistry, of intricate thought. Not the yellow of deceit nor the crimson of passion—he was deep, complex, unreadable, never what he seemed.

Dominika was dressed in a dark-gray two-piece suit with a navy shirt, dark stockings, and low heels—thank God for that; she would not tower over the president. Her brown hair was up, the recommended style in the Service, and she wore no jewelry. Standing, Putin continued looking down at her, perhaps measuring the depth of her blue eyes against his own. If he saw her black eye he gave no indication. An aide came in silently from a side door with a tray that he set down on a small side table. The president nodded at it.

"I have called you to the Kremlin during the lunch hour, for which I apologize. Perhaps a snack?"

An exquisite fluted Lomonosov porcelain serving dish in the cobalt net pattern first used by Catherine the Great held glossy sautéed mushrooms and greens, swimming in a mustard sauce. Silver spoon and toothpicks. Putin bent and spooned a dollop of the mushrooms onto a toast point and held it out, actually held it flat in his palm, to her. *Eat kitty, won't you taste?* Dominika thought of politely refusing, but accepted. The president watched her chew—the dish was mushroom earthy and complex, the sauce smooth and rich—as if he were assessing how she ate. He poured mineral water. This was madness. The blue haze behind his head and shoulders did not change. Bozhe, *God, eating appetizers in the Kremlin,* she thought. *What next, perhaps he'll offer me his toothbrush?* She shifted slightly to ease the throbbing in her ribs.

"I am glad you returned safely from Estonia," Putin said, finally sitting down beside her on the couch. "The information you acquired was instrumental in unmasking the traitor Korchnoi. I commend you for your coolness and fortitude."

SVR General Korchnoi had spied for the Americans for fourteen years, the best Russian agent in the history of the Game. The general had been her protector, like a second father, when she entered the Service. After the general's arrest, CIA had concocted the swap to exchange Dominika for him, simultaneously saving the general and inserting Dominika as the new CIA supermole in Moscow. But something had gone wrong—she didn't know what. Someone had been hurt on the bridge after she crossed the midpoint and was back in Russian hands—through the night fog she had gotten a glimpse of a body on the ground, had heard a man bellowing. A monstrous double cross? And the man sitting next to her had certainly given the order. It could have been Korchnoi crumpled on the bridge roadway; it could even have been Nate. Nate could be dead, and all along she had been thinking about him as if he was safe. *He could be dead.* At the thought she tamped down the cloying taste of mushrooms in her mouth, swallowed the mustard sauce in her throat.

"*Spasibo,* thank you, Mr. President," said Dominika. "I only did my duty."

Not too much sugar, she thought; *just a teaspoon.* "I regret that the *izmennik*, the traitor, found refuge in the West, that he did not pay for his betrayal."

Putin's blue halo flared. "No, he was destroyed," he said bluntly, without inflection. Through the shock Dominika thought, *Nate is safe.* Then, *They killed the general.* Silence in the sun-drenched room. "Now you know a secret," Putin said, one corner of his mouth curling a fraction. This Putin smile surfaced from the mineshaft of his soul, a mortal threat all the same, and the bitter revelation bound her to this new tsar, this *imperator*, her neck in the noose and the bit in her mouth. But he had just confirmed it: They had killed Korchnoi on the bridge, meters from freedom. The old general had dreamed of retirement, of a life without risk, devoid of fear.

Dominika breathed through her nose and looked at Putin's impassive face. Out of some obscure memory, Dominika recalled that Khrushchev's favorite Cold War threat had been the earthy, peasant curse *Pokazat kuz'kinu mat'—I'll show you Kuzka's mother*—which meant *I'll annihilate you. Well, call Kuzka's mother, Mr. President,* thought Dominika, *because I'm going to punish you.* Over the taste of copper in her mouth, the edgy secret that soared above it all, the ice-cold diamond in her breast, was that she was CIA's new penetration of her service. Not even this blue-eyed python knew that.

"You can depend on my discretion, Mr. President," said Dominika, returning his unblinking stare. He cultivated the image of a clairvoyant, the inescapable reader of men's minds and hearts. Could he see into her soul?

"I look forward to excellent and speedy results in the matter of the Iranian scientist," said Putin. "The Paris operation was satisfactory, the debriefing next week will be critical. I want regular progress reports from you." Obviously he already had been briefed. Zyuganov. *You swivel-eyed dwarf*, Dominika thought. *Did you also tell Putin how I got this black eye*? Putin's stare never left her face. "Of course, you will work under the guidance of the director and Colonel Zyuganov," he said. His meaning was clear: He was ordering Dominika to work within the hierarchy of the Service, but also expected her to report directly to him, a vintage Soviet tactic to drive wedges between and place informers among ambitious subordinates. The cerulean cloud above his head blazed in the sunlit room.

CIA's beautiful mole inside the Russian Foreign Intelligence Service nodded, counting the pulses pounding in her breast. "Of course, Mr. President," she said. "I will keep you informed of everything I do."

KREMLIN MUSHROOM APPETIZER

Aggressively sauté thinly sliced mushrooms in oil until brown around the edges. Add greens (spinach, chard, or kale) and capers, and cook until wilted. Season, then stir in mustard and vinegar and let thicken, spooning sauce over mushrooms and greens. Serve lukewarm or cold.

3

The endless buzz of Athens traffic on Vasilissis Sofias Boulevard was audible through the grimy windows of the CIA Station, windows that had been shuttered and curtained since the bureaucrats cut the ribbon on the chancery in 1961. Athens Station, a warren of interconnecting offices, hallways, and closets, had not been repainted since then: An Electrolux canister vacuum from the 1960s lay forgotten in the back of a coat closet beside a 1970 Martin flattop guitar with no strings that generations of officers assumed had a concealment cavity for bringing documents across borders, but no one could remember how to open it.

Deputy Chief of Station Marty Gable walked into CIA case officer Nate Nash's small office. Nate had half a *tiropita,* a triangular cheese pie, on his desk that he had bought on the street for breakfast, and he brushed the flaky crust off his pants as he stood up. Gable reached over him and took the last half of the pie, popped it into his mouth, and chewed, while looking around Nate's new office. Gable swallowed, picked up a framed snapshot of Nate's family, and held it to the light. "This your folks?" Nate nodded. Gable put the photo down. "Handsome looking bunch. You're adopted then, or what, forceps delivery?"

"It's great being in your Station again, Marty," said Nate. He respected the stocky Gable, maybe was even fond of him, but he wasn't about to say that out loud. Nate had started his third tour two months ago in the bustling anthill that was Athens Station, happily again under the sponsorship of urbane Chief of Station Tom Forsyth and his cynical, profane deputy.

The three of them had been an effective team, having run several world-class operations over the last years. In Moscow during his first tour, Nate had handled MARBLE, CIA's best clandestine agent in Russia, until the general was shot during the spy swap they had arranged to rescue him. During his second tour in Helsinki, Nate had recruited young SVR officer Dominika Egorova—code-named DIVA—and together with Forsyth and Gable had engineered her return to Moscow as CIA's next generation mole in the Russian Foreign Intelligence Service.

The loss of MARBLE to the Kremlin's treachery had affected them all, but Nate most of all had changed since that evening when he cradled MARBLE's head in his lap, watching his agent's blood ooze over asphalt wet with the Estonian fog, shimmering in the reflected light of the spotlights. He normally was nervous and earnest and ambitious. But Nate now had become darker, focused, less concerned about managing his career, about detractors and competitors.

"Fuck 'It's great being in your Station again, Marty,'" said Gable. "We got a walk-in downstairs; Marine Guard just called. Let's move."

As he bounded down the stairs beside Gable, Nate's brain geared up. *A walk-in, an unknown person off the street. Go. The clock started the minute the walk-in arrived. The marines in the embassy foyer would have checked him for weapons, taken any packages from him, and buttoned him up in the walk-in room, a windowless, tech-filled interview suite with video, audio, and digital transmission equipment.*

Go. A walk-in, could be anything: A madman with aluminum foil inside his hat to ward off alien radio beams, an undocumented exile pleading for a US visa, an information peddler who that morning had memorized a newspaper article and hoped to serve it up as secrets worth a few hundred dollars.

Go. Alternatively, a walk-in could be a bona fide volunteer—foreign intel officer, diplomat, scientist—with colossal intelligence that he was willing to pass to the Americans for money, or because of a crisis of ideology, or to exact revenge against a tyrant of a boss, or to spite a system in which he no longer believed.

Go. A good volunteer is a free recruitment, access established, intel ready to harvest. Volunteers over the years were the best cases, the ones they carved in stone.

Go, go, go. Find out who he is, do a lightning assessment, flip him, arrange recontact, and get him out of the embassy as soon as possible. If he's Russian, North Korean, or Chinese, he's on a clock, his embassy counterintelligence watchdogs will note how long he's unaccounted for. Thirty minutes tops.

On the embassy ground floor, Gable nodded to the marine standing outside the door and they pushed their way inside the room. The fish sauce smell of vomit hit them in the face. Sitting in a plastic chair at the small desk was an old bum, his rumpled suit coat wet down the front with puke, trousers spotted and dusty. He probably was in his sixties, with gray stubble on his cheeks, eyes red and rheumy. He looked up as the two CIA officers came into the room.

"Christ," said Gable. "Like we have time for this crap. Get him out of here." Gable gestured toward the door, signaling for Nate to call the marine. They'd walk the old drunk to the basement garage and ease him out via the loading dock. Stop the clock. False alarm.

Nate quickly assessed the man. He didn't look like an old Greek coot: hands strong and nails trimmed. Shoes muddy but expensive. Disheveled hair cut short at the ears. He sat straighter when they entered the room, not like a drunk. A little wind chime tinkled in his brain. "Marty, wait a minute," said Nate. He sat in the chair beside the old man, tried to breathe through his mouth to avoid the cat urine smell of him.

"Sir," said Nate, trying English, "what can we do for you?" He heard Gable shift his feet impatiently. The old man looked up into Nate's face.

"Not good English," said the old man, but his bass voice was strong. More wind chimes. "I give informations," he said softly, as if the words caused him pain.

"We already got the recipe for muscatel," said Gable, crossing his arms.

"Not understand," said the old man.

"Sir, who are you?" said Nate. The old man blinked and his eyes filled with tears. Gable whispered, "Oh for Chrissake." When the old guy wiped his eye, Nate saw his wristwatch: steel link band, heavy case, "*pobeda*" (victory in Russian) written on the dark face. Soviet army watch? He remembered Russian Afghanistan vets wore them.

Nate held up his hand. "Give him a minute," he said.

"My son dead, Ossetia, bomb." Nate recognized the cadence and accent—a Russian?

"My daughter dead, *gerojin*." Russian for "heroin," thought Nate.

"My work closed. I come to Greece, *izgnanie*." Russian word for "exiled." What the fuck? Gable had shut up by now, and Nate leaned forward, forgetting the stench.

"Sir, who are you?" he asked again.

"*Govorite po-russki?*" the old man said, do you speak Russian? Nate nodded, and looked over his shoulder at Gable.

"Do you know *Glavnoye Razvedyvatel'noye Upravleniye*, the GRU?" said the old man in Russian. He had straightened in his seat, his eyes darting between Nate and Gable.

"What?" said Gable. "What?"

"I am from the GRU *Generalnyi Shtab*, the GRU of the General Staff."

"What office?" asked Nate, holding up his hand to fend off Gable for a second.

"Ninth Directorate of the Information Service, under Lieutenant General S. Berkutov." He raised his chin and his voice boomed.

"Holy fuck, Ninth Directorate, GRU," said Nate out of the side of his mouth.

Gable leaned over. "Identification, documents," he said.

The old man understood the word *dokumenty*, and pulled out a faded red booklet. "*Voyennyi bilet*," he said to Nate.

"Military ID card," said Nate, looking at the bio page. The sepia-tone picture was attached to the page by a grommet. "Lieutenant General Mikhail Nikolaevich Solovyov," Nate read, emphasizing the rank. "Born 1953, Nizhny Novgorod." He flipped to the second page. "Here it is, Directorate Nine, GRU." He handed Gable the booklet. Gable went to a small cabinet in the corner of the room, unlocked the doors, and fired up the digital equipment. The old man's ID booklet would be copied, the images encrypted and transmitted to Langley in the next fifteen seconds. Gable also texted the Station upstairs to start traces—they would be listening in real time to the audio of this interview.

"What did you mean when you said 'exile'?" said Nate in Russian. The old man's eyes flashed.

"I directed the Ninth for three years," he said. His words came out rapid fire now. "Do you know the work of the Ninth?" He closed his eyes as he recited. "Analysis of foreign military capabilities. Clandestine acquisition of technology to counter adversary weapons systems. Coordination with our domestic armaments industry." Nate translated for Gable.

"Yeah, what's he doing in Greece?" said Gable. The old man nodded, guessing what the question was.

"There is a struggle inside GRU now. Putin"—he spat the name—"is placing his people everywhere. There are many contracts to exploit, many rubles to siphon off. I opposed changes in my Directorate, exposed corruption." His voice dripped with contempt. "I was reassigned to the Russian Embassy in Athens. In the military attaché office, subordinate to a colonel. They may as well have sent me to the camps."

"And you came to us," said Nate, knowing the answer.

"I have given thirty years to the service, to the country. My wife is dead. My son was in the army; he was killed six months ago, a needless civil war. My daughter died alone in an abandoned Moscow tenement with a needle in her arm. She was eighteen." He was sitting up straight now, as if giving a military briefing. Nate was still, letting him talk, for the next step was the critical one.

"Last night I drank vodka and walked in the street. I am a lieutenant general. I wear the *Zolotaya Zvezda,* the Golden Star. Do you know what that is?"

"Hero of the Russian Federation, replaced the Soviet star," said Nate.

The old man's eyes narrowed, surprised that Nate knew. "And *za Voyennye Zaslugi,* the medal of Military Merit, and *Orden Svyatogo Georgiya Pervol Stepeni,* the Order of St. George, First Class." He looked back and forth between Gable and Nate, wanting them to be impressed.

"I have a lifetime of information," he said, tapping his forehead. "I am still in contact with many loyal officers working in secret projects in Moscow and elsewhere. My duties allow me to make inquiries, to request data. I will educate you about GRU, the technology-acquisition operations, about Russian weapons systems." Nate translated.

"Get him to tell you why," said Gable softly. Despite not understanding Russian, he was reading the old man as well as Nate now; he knew how close they were.

"Why? Because they have taken everything from me: my children, my career, my life. They ignored my worth and discounted my loyalty. Now I will take something from them." Steel in that voice now, determination. Silence in the room, the CIA officers letting him roll.

"I know you are wondering, it is the question with every *dobrovolets,* every volunteer. What do I want in return? My answer to you is this: Nothing. You are professionals, you will understand." More an order than a request. Nate glanced at Gable—revenge and ego; control the former and feed the latter. Time check: twenty minutes. Set the recontact, someplace secure, someplace they can watch for ticks. Get him out the door.

"I will meet you"—he pointed at Nate—"in two days' time. You will want *dobrosovestnost,* bona fides. I will pass the performance data of the Sukhoi PAK FA, the T-50, including the new wing-leading-edge devices—you in the West have nothing like it."

And on a rainy night two nights later, on a muddy path in Filothei Park, CIA's new penetration of GRU, freshly encrypted LYRIC, did exactly that.

In the years since Nate had joined CIA, he had acquired an appreciation of the villainy of the Russian Federation, and of the dissolute external intelligence service, the SVR, twisted progeny of the old KGB. What fueled this Kremlin kleptocracy, what motivated it, was not to bring back the Soviet Union, nor to reinstill the worldwide dread generated by the Red Army, nor to formulate a foreign policy based on national security requirements. In Russia today, everything happened to maintain the *nadzirateli,* the overseers, to protect their power, to continue looting the country's patrimony. Nate wanted to devastate the opposition, to avenge MARBLE, to take away their power.

Nate was dark—black hair and straight eyebrows—of medium height, and slim from varsity swimming in college. What colleagues and friends noticed however, were darting brown eyes that read faces, weighed gestures, and narrowed with quick comprehension. On the street, those brown eyes scanned ahead, watched the wings, picked up the peripheral anomalies before there was movement. During surveillance exercises as a CIA trainee, instructors noted, first with skepticism, then with approval, that Nate was always switched on. He seemed to sense the pulse of the street—whether it was a Washington, DC, boulevard or a teeming European avenue—and he blended into a crowd, something that taller, or gangly, or redheaded trainees could not do.

His early fear of failing at his job, despite the signal successes in his young career, simmered alongside his determination not to return to the bosom of his family—father, brothers, grandfather—in Richmond, Virginia. Lawyers who were clannish, boorish, patriarchal, violently competitive, and invidious, they had not individually encouraged Nathaniel in his application to CIA, and had collectively predicted he would be back to the family law practice in a few years. There would be no pill more bitter than to separate from CIA and return home.

But as the steel was honed, as Nate accumulated experience and concentrated on operations, there was the remaining ache, the one that wouldn't fade. It had been more than nine months since DIVA went back inside; she had not agreed to resume operations with them, furious at being manipulated into the spy swap. Nate had agonized every day, every week, waiting for her sign-of-life signal. CIA Headquarters waited patiently for her to change her mind, waited for the alert on the worldwide SENTRY phone system she would make when outside Russia. Her call would instantly dispatch handlers to meet her in whatever city she designated. But the call had not come—they hadn't heard from her, didn't know whether she was working, or in prison, or alive or dead.

Soon after DIVA's recruitment, Nate had committed the unthinkable operational transgression by sleeping with her. Risking everything. Risking her, his agent's life. Risking a career that kept him whole and independent, risking the work that defined him. But her blue eyes and edgy temper and wry smile had blinded him. Her ballerina's body was matchless and responsive. Her passion for her country and her rage at those who coveted power had him in awe of her. And he could still hear the way she said his name—*Neyt.*

Their lovemaking had been drastic, clutching, urgent, guilty. They were professional intelligence officers and both knew how badly they were behaving. Typically, Dominika didn't care. As a woman, she desired him outside the limits of the agent–case officer relationship. Nate could not—would not—commit to such an arrangement, for he worried about his standing, about operational security, about tradecraft. The irony of the situation was not lost on either of them: The hidebound Russian was more willing to break the rules to feed their passion than was the informal, loose-limbed American. But until she reappeared, until he knew she was still alive, Nate had a new Russian to handle.

Nate slid down the rocky embankment, raising a cloud of dust. Dirt filled his shoes and he cursed. He was in the pine and scrub forest of the hill country around Meteora, Greece, the region of towering rock monoliths hundreds of feet tall, the largest of which were topped by squat monasteries. He looked at the GPS compass in his TALON, the tablet-sized handheld device just deployed to overseas stations from the Directorate of Science and Technology, and slanted left through the trees. There were only six TALON sets in use globally, and the S&T boys had sent one of the first ultralight units to Nate in Athens Station because of the shit-hot agent he was handling. In several hundred meters he intersected the mountain stream—milky turquoise and running fast—which he followed for another hundred meters.

Around a sharp bend in the stream he saw the man he had come three hundred kilometers from Athens to meet, after an epic surveillance detection route. Three vehicle and two disguise changes later, his countersurveillance team signaled that he was black. Eyes burning from the colored contacts, gums sore from the cheek expanders, scalp itchy from the Elvis wig, Nate removed the last disguise, ditched the car, and made his way to the meeting site, forcing himself to focus. Their smelly walk-in, Lieutenant General Mikhail Nikolaevich Solovyov of the GRU, Russia's military intelligence service, now codenamed LYRIC, stood on the elevated opposite bank, holding a fishing rod. Cigarette hanging from his lip, LYRIC did not acknowledge Nate, but continued casting his fly into the water. Cursing again, and feeling like a first-tour rookie, Nate looked for a shallow stretch in the brook where he could cross. He concentrated on stepping on the slippery rocks to cross the stream.

LYRIC had stopped casting and was observing Nate's progress with grumpy disapproval. Tall and ramrod straight, LYRIC had a round head with a high forehead, and thin white hair combed back tightly over his skull. The ironic mouth beneath the straight nose was small and thin-lipped, soft and pursed, not like the rigid, two-star rest of him. As Nate made it across the stream and clambered up the bank, the general took the cigarette out of his mouth, pinched the hot ash end off, and ground it under his shoe. The stub of filter went into his coat pocket, the habit born of a thousand parade-ground inspections.

LYRIC checked his watch—early on he had actually suggested to Nate that they synchronize watches until the young officer showed him the clock in his TALON device, slaved to the atomic clock in Boulder, Colorado, which displayed twenty-four international time zones, and was accurate to two seconds per decade. LYRIC had huffed and never suggested synchronizing watches again.

"If you had not arrived in the next five minutes," said LYRIC in Russian, "I was prepared to abort the meeting." His voice was a deep bass note from inside his chest.

"*Tovarishch,* General. I'm glad you waited," said Nate in fluent Russian, knowing the "comrade" form of address still used in the army would please him. He also knew the agent would have waited half the night for him. "This remote site makes timing difficult."

"This site offers excellent security, with admirable access and egress routes," said LYRIC, putting down his fishing rod. It was he who had first proposed the Meteora meeting site.

"*Konechno,* of course," said Nate, trying not to antagonize the old soldier. Keep the agent happy, start him talking about the secrets he has in his head. He casually tapped the screen of the TALON, activating the recording device. "I'm glad you had time to meet. We appreciate your unique insights." LYRIC's lofty general officer's ego was immovable, fueled by years of Soviet bluster and Slavic certainty that the enemy was at the gate, and foreigners were plotting against the *Rodina* at every turn. Washington's bilateral reset policy with Moscow had run aground on these very same xenophobic rocks, never mind that the State Department had misspelled the Russian word for "reset."

"I am glad your superiors find my information of use," grumped LYRIC. "At times it seems they underestimate its value." Nate, not for the first time, noted that LYRIC overlooked the fact that he had volunteered to CIA, that he had been a walk-in.

The afternoon light was low in the pines. They sat on the riverbank watching the sun sparkle off the rapids. The general, an old campaigner, pulled a package of butcher paper out of his pack and unwrapped a dozen chunks of lamb he had bought in a nearby village. Two sprigs of wild oregano lay atop the meat. Nate watched fascinated, delighted, as LYRIC gathered dry tinder, scraped a small flint, and started a fire. "GRU survival kit," said LYRIC offhandedly, handing Nate the steel. "The best. Magnesium."

He stripped the oregano leaves and threaded the chunks of lamb onto the woody stems, then pressed the oregano onto the meat, and handed one kebab—he called it *shashlik*—to Nate. Together they grilled the meat over the open flame, chuckling, trying not to burn their fingers. When the meat was charred deep brown—LYRIC examined Nate's *shashlik* critically—a lemon was cut to be squeezed over the sizzling kebabs, eaten with alternating bites of raw scallion.

"I used to cook like this for my children on leave," LYRIC said, turning his skewer sideways to bite a piece of lamb. "It is good to share food now with you." He looked down at the fire. In a rush, Nate registered that this relationship was fueled by more than revenge for Russian beastliness. It was more than an intelligence operation, more than the start of a priceless penetration of Moscow's vast military tech transfer establishment. This old man needed human contact, kind consideration, metaphysical needs somehow to be addressed while CIA debriefed him like a rubber squeeze toy. *Will he survive,* thought Nate, *or will he end up like Korchnoi?* He gritted his teeth at the memory, mouthing a silent vow to keep him safe.

"General, it is an honor to share this food. And it is a privilege to know you," said Nate. "Our work is just beginning, but it has been spectacular."

"Then let's get to work," said LYRIC, straightening and avoiding Nate's eyes. "Turn on that infernal machine of yours while I brief you." They sat on a log and LYRIC talked nonstop, a palette of variegated subjects, precisely remembered, meticulously ordered, the baritone words measured, unstoppable. Important points were signaled by a raised finger, an arched eyebrow. Occasionally there would be a personal digression, the grieving, lonely old man would be briefly revealed, then the ramrod general would resume the debriefing.

Nate was thankful for the TALON balanced on his knee—there was no way he could have kept up by taking written notes. LYRIC was still a new asset, so he let him orate; the stuff was pure gold anyway. Tech-transfer operations, thrust-vector research, the new PAK FH stealth fighter, target-acquisition radar on the BUK SA-11 used by Ukrainian separatists. Specific military reporting requirements were being codrafted with the Pentagon, and Nate would have to handle the general's steely pride and galloping ego when the time came to direct him to actively collect specific intelligence.

"Your superiors in Langley must plan ahead," lectured LYRIC, looking over at Nate. He fired up a cigarette and clicked his lighter shut. "Right now they are exulting and wallowing in the initial deluge of my information. Those who crave credit are preening before a mirror. There is excitement, a rush to standardize production of finished intelligence, the inevitable debate about how to handle the new source." LYRIC tilted his head up in contemplation, pausing as if giving dictation.

"You and your chief in the station in Athens properly should rebuff any attempts by Langley to assume control of the case. If you need ammunition, you have my permission to tell them the agent—what is my cryptonym by the way?—refuses handlers from Washington. Do not tell them I refuse to speak to anyone *but you*—that is one of the hallmarks of an operations officer fabricating a case. Simply say that I want only locally assigned handlers with superb area knowledge." LYRIC looked over at Nate as if he were a clerk in a Dickensian counting house.

"I am your case officer," said Nate. "And you met the deputy chief of Station, who can act as backup."

"A pity he speaks no Russian." LYRIC sniffed, looking down and flicking ash off his sleeve.

"I'm sure Gable deplores not speaking Russian as much as you regret having so little English," said Nate. It was time to touch the brakes, lightly, and bleed some speed off LYRIC's ego. The old man looked up sharply at Nate, wordless, then smiled faintly and nodded. Message understood, a page in the agent-handler dance card turned, respect given and received.

"And my cryptonym?" asked LYRIC, once again the curmudgeon spy.

"BOGATYR," lied Nate, who had no intention of telling the bombastic LYRIC his compartmented CIA crypt. *Bogatyr,* the mythical Slavic knight of the steppes around LYRIC's birthplace, Nizhny Novgorod.

"I like it," said LYRIC, breaking down his finished cigarette and slipping the filter into his pocket.

"What kind of bullshit is that?" said Gable. He and Nate and COS Tom Forsyth were sitting in the ACR, the acoustically controlled room-within-a-room inside Athens Station. They sat hunched around the conference table, Nate's TALON in front of them, connected to a laptop. Nate had been translating highlights of his two hours in the Meteora woods with LYRIC.

"*BOGATYR,*" said Nate, "like a Russian samurai. He's got a heroic image of himself. I made it up on the spot."

Gable shook his head. "Okay," said Forsyth, already five steps ahead. "Keep him happy, keep him talking. A general officer can be tough to handle. Delicate balance. Headquarters is strong on the case. Traces confirmed everything about him; LYRIC's the real deal, and the intel so far is giving the air force wet dreams."

When Forsyth spoke, Nate listened. He knew Forsyth's record was every bit as spectacular as Gable's—but different. While Gable was killing snakes with a tire iron, Forsyth had been drinking wine in Warsaw with a well-known Russian stage actress—coincidentally the mistress of a Soviet Northern Fleet admiral—who had photographed the fleet's readiness and deployment schedules for the coming year in her boyfriend's office bathroom. Forsyth had given her the palm-sized Tessina camera months earlier and she brought the microcassette of film out past customs wrapped in a condom hidden where only her gynecologist would have thought to look. Forsyth had accepted it with aplomb. Gable and Forsyth: Natural-born operations officers, and they both knew what they were talking about.

To Nate's perceptive eye, the relationship between Forsyth and Gable was a pragmatic alliance tempered by years of working together. Forsyth was the senior, but there was never a thought of him ordering Gable to do anything. Gable knew what to do; if he disagreed he'd say so, then follow instructions. Gable acknowledged that Forsyth sometimes thought he was undiplomatic, but they both knew that golden-boy Forsyth had at various times in his career himself gotten into serious bureaucratic trouble by speaking his mind, once memorably to a member of Congress visiting Rome Station on an endless string of summer recess Congressional delegations—they were called fact-finding trips for the benefit of the taxpayers—during which Forsyth noted that she was three hours late for her Station briefing, pointedly looking at the half dozen Fendi, Gucci, and Ferragamo shopping bags carried by her chief of staff. Gable had not been present, a small blessing, but Forsyth was in the penalty box for a year after that.

Nate saw mutual respect, knew there was loyalty, guessed at comradely affection. The COS and his DCOS watched each other's backs; they naturally sensed what the other was thinking, and they knew what came first: operations, which informed everything they did. Everything. Nate did not know it, but Forsyth and Gable had argued with Chief of Counterintelligence Simon Benford over the issue of Nate's intimacy with Dominika. In the Agency it was an infraction of the highest order: Previously other officers had famously slept with assets and been separated from the service. But even as Forsyth scolded, and Gable threatened, and Benford raved, Forsyth convinced Benford to give young Nash a break. It was not because Nate had handled MARBLE, DIVA, and LYRIC flawlessly; it was not because they recognized in Nash an exceptional internal ops talent; in the end, it was a veteran assessment that the greater good was being served by ignoring for the moment the lesser transgression. But they would never let Nate know.

The TALON recording of the meeting suddenly was interrupted by three woman's screams, high, strident, one after the other.

"Fuck's that?" said Gable. The screams repeated over the sound of LYRIC's voice.

"Peacocks," said Nate. "Two of them came out of the woods and started calling. Scared the shit out of us."

"Peacocks! Jesus wept," said Gable.

Forsyth started laughing. "Make sure you tell Headquarters about the birds when you forward the digital file. The suits will think you brought a woman to the debriefing for the general."

"Not a bad idea, but where would Nash find a woman?" said Gable.

They were gathering up papers when Gable told Nate to sit back down. Forsyth waited by the soundproof door, his hand on the latch. They would not talk about LYRIC, refer to him or the case, or even mention the cryptonym, outside this Lucite-walled room. No exceptions: Moscow Rules. The case was already in compartmented, Restricted Handling channels in Headquarters. Not more than fifty people at Langley read incoming LYRIC cables.

"As much as it pains me to admit it," said Gable, "I want you to know I think you did a fucking great job when LYRIC walked in."

Nate shifted a little in his seat. Gable was not one to give out compliments.

"I would have thrown the pukey old man out of the walk-in room. You followed your instincts, nailed your hunch, and we got a platinum case on the books. Good job." At the door Forsyth smiled.

"Now comes precision, now comes focus. I want you to run this agent as tight as a bar hostess in Vientiane," said Gable.

"I'm not sure I get—"

"I'll explain it to you when you graduate high school," said Gable.

"I'll look forward to it," said Nate.

"That don't mean you can skate," said Gable, "especially at the start of this tour. You haven't done squat on your own power since you got here. I'm watching you, Nash."

Forsyth chuckled. "Nate, I think Marty's trying to tell you he likes you," said Forsyth. He popped the latches on the ACR door.

"Jesus wept," said Nate. A moment of silence, and then the sound of Forsyth's laughter boomed down the hallway.

During their previous time in Helsinki, DCOS Gable had watched over young Nate, had kicked him in the ass, and had taught him valuable lessons: Always protect your agent, never trust the flatland cake eaters at Headquarters, make the hard operational decisions, and don't worry about the fucking politics.

Gable was fifty-something, a knuckly, leather-faced, crew-cut case officer who carried a Browning Hi Power in a Bianchi belt-loop holster, and had made his bones in every backwater capital in Africa, Latin America, and Asia. He had recruited sweating, chittering equatorial ministers, passing a bottle of Ugandan scotch back and forth inside a sweltering Land Rover. He had debriefed a Burmese four-star while holding a roll of toilet paper and watching for blue-scaled pit vipers in the buffalo grass as the general squatted, stricken with dysentery. And Gable had carried his agent out of the Andean jungle in a tropical downpour—the first ever penetration of the Shining Path in Peru—after the case went bad.

The three of them—the senior, placid Forsyth; the china-smashing Gable; and the resolute Nate—were each of a different grade and temperament, but in traditionally rank-neutral CIA they were a crew, bound by the rigors of past operations and the unacknowledged brotherhood of working together in their clandestine world. And now Nate had his assignment to Athens and they were back together. All except Dominika, who was unaccounted for, out of contact.

In Helsinki, Gable had coached him while Nate recruited Dominika, a spectacular success for a junior CIA officer. But Gable also quickly sensed that Nate and his agent had been intimate. "Are you fucking nuts?" he had raved at Nate. "You're jeopardizing her life, your agent's life." Nate had tried backpedaling until Gable shut him up. "Don't fucking deny it," said Gable. "Your only job is to protect her, not because you love her, not because it's regulations. You fucking do it because she agreed to produce intel for you and put her life in your hands to do it. And you sacrifice everything to make sure she stays alive. Nothing is more important." Nate remembered the words even as he thought about Dominika, somewhere in Moscow.

Then–Chief of Station Tom Forsyth, also around fifty, tall and slim, with salt-and-pepper hair perpetually tousled by reading glasses pushed up and on top of his head, had agreed with his deputy. But unlike the swift ass-kicking promised by Gable, Forsyth had called Nate into his wood-paneled Helsinki Station office and delivered an hour-long high mass of agent-handling rules so nuanced, so brilliantly clear, that Nate hadn't moved in his chair. Preserving the intel flow was his duty, Forsyth had said; it's why he was a case officer, and if he couldn't control personal urges, well maybe they should have another discussion about what Nate might like to do for the rest of his life. Not daring to breathe, Nate looked at his hands. He raised his head, looking for permission to speak. Forsyth nodded.

"Tom, what if my being with her is what she *wants*. What if it makes her a better spy?"

Forsyth pushed his glasses on top of his head. "It's not without precedent, giving agents what they want," he said. "We've fed agents' heroin habits to keep them reporting. I remember a porn-addicted Chinese minister who wouldn't make meetings unless we had the fuck films rolling when he walked into the safe house. And the shoes, boxes of them, for the Indonesian president's wife. Jesus she tried on every pair, with me on my knees, working the shoe horn. But we're not talking about that, not exactly." Forsyth swiveled in his chair.

"A million years ago, my first tour, I recruited a code clerk from the Czech Embassy in Rome," Forsyth said. "Cute little thing, shy, couldn't go out on her own. Cipherines, they called them, had to have an accompanying escort all the time: an older woman, an embassy wife.

"We had an Italian support asset young guy, sold stereos, but looked like a movie star. Over the space of six months, he seduced the older lady, so every time the two women came out on Saturday afternoon, the escort would sprint up the Via Veneto to get to Romeo's apartment, leaving our little flower alone. And I was there. Took another six months, but she started bringing out copies of cable traffic, intel service details, counterintelligence stuff, correspondence with Moscow, some pretty good East Bloc intel—back then Headquarters was nuts for it. Fucking Cold War."

"How did you recruit her?" asked Nate. "Sounds like she would have been terrified."

Forsyth spun back in his chair. "It took a while; we walked in the park a lot. I heard about the older brother in the army a hundred times. Started talking about her life, and her dreams—she was twenty-four for Christ's sake. When she began talking about her work at her embassy, about her code books, it was done, my first recruitment. But it didn't last."

Nate waited: Forsyth wasn't done. "We were both kids. We had been sleeping together, it's how I closed the deal," said Forsyth, looking at Nate evenly. "I had genuine feelings for her, but I also told myself a lovesick girl would do more for me. I got emotionally involved and I took my eye off the ball. And she tried smuggling out a reel of crypto tape to surprise me and they stopped her at the front door. Romeo's girl told him the whole story. Czechs caught her and sent her home, maybe prison, maybe worse. We never heard."

Nate didn't say anything. Cars on the boulevard outside were honking at something.

"My chief in Rome didn't fire me," said Forsyth, "and twenty years later I'm not going to fire you . . . yet." They stared at each other for ten seconds, then Forsyth pointed to the door. "Go out and start stealing secrets. Protect DIVA. Run her professionally. It's ultimately your decision."

LYRIC'S SHASHLIK-KEBABS

Cut small cubes of lamb and marinate in lemon juice, oregano, olive oil, salt, and pepper. Thread lamb on skewers and grill until crispy and brown. Slather with thickened yogurt. Serve with onion and cucumber salad.

4

Colonel Alexei Zyuganov had neither the sophistication nor, frankly, the inclination to win Egorova's loyalty. Personal relationships were not important. No one knew his early history; no one knew anything about his childhood. His father, a prominent *apparatchik*, had disappeared in the early sixties, at the tail end of the Khrushchev purges. His mother was Ekaterina Zyuganova, a well-known figure in the old KGB. Ekaterina had sat on the KGB Executive Council, then as KGB liaison officer in the Secretariat of the Central Committee, and finally on the Collegium of the KGB. Short, mustached, bosomy, with fantastic upswept hair, Ekaterina had worn the *Orden Krasnoy Zvezdy*, the Order of the Red Star, awarded for her "great contribution to the defense of the USSR in war and peacetime and for ensuring public safety" until things changed and it no longer was *modnyi*, fashionable, to continue wearing the red ceramic device.

Nineteen-year-old Alexei was brought into the Service by *bonna*, maternal patronage, but failed to make an impression in various low-level assignments. Bad tempered, at times irrational, and occasionally prone to displays of violent paranoia, Alexei was going nowhere in the bureaucracy: Everyone knew it, but supervisors' instincts for self-preservation prevented them from recommending he be cashiered. No one dared defy Madame Zyuganova; Ekaterina protected her son with implacable determination. Then Zyuganov disappeared from the corridors of Headquarters: Momma finally had found sonny boy an assignment for which he was singularly qualified.

Zyuganov was read in as one of four subcommandants of the Lubyanka prison, a formal KGB position title sufficiently anodyne to discourage public scrutiny, with no paperwork or records required. In reality he had joined the small staff of present-day Lubyanka interrogators, experts in *chernaya rabota*, black work: liquidations, torture, and executions. They were the successors of the *Kommandatura*, the coal-black department of the NKVD, which was the instrument of Stalin's purges and had eliminated White Russian émigrés, Old Bolsheviks, Trotskyites, and, in twenty-eight consecutive nights in the spring of 1940, seven thousand Polish prisoners in the Russian forest of Katyn. In four years Zyuganov was promoted as Lubyanka's second chief executioner and, when the chief executioner—a patron and protector—faltered, he had reveled in the career high of putting a bullet behind his boss's right ear. Zyuganov had found a home.

The dissolution of the Soviet Union in 1991 brought an end to unrestricted wet work. Part of the KGB morphed into the modern SVR; the Lubyanka cellars closed and the building now belonged to the internal service, the FSB. Zyuganov could have made the lateral move to SVR Department V, colloquially still referred to as the *Otdel mokrykh del,* the department of wet affairs, as one of the "wet boys," but his mother, Ekaterina, knew better and wanted to forfend his future. She had by that time stepped down from her last position in the Collegium, and a cushy if inconsequential retirement assignment to Paris as *zampolit,* a political advisor to the *rezident,* had been arranged. Mother's last act from Headquarters had been to place Zyuganov as third chief in Line KR, the counterintelligence department. Alexei would be safe there and could work his way up. It was all she could do for her murderous little boy.

The psychopathy of not feeling pity, mixed with innate aggression fueled by sadism, leavened by the utter inability to relate to others' emotions, had been singularly well suited to Zyuganov's ingenue career in the cellars. With the passing of the Lubyanka salad days, when an executioner could be as busy as he wished, the post-Soviet era was a definite disappointment. Things had picked up with President Putin, however. Splashy overseas operations—Yushchenko in Ukraine, Litvinenko and Berezovsky in the United Kingdom—had settled the hash of noisy exiles, and domestic troublemaking journalists and activists—Politkovskaya, Estemirova, Markelov, and Baburova—had been obliterated. But for every one of these high-publicity actions there were dozens of lesser bugs that needed quiet squashing: independent provincial administrators, military logistics managers who did not tithe sufficiently to Moscow, uppity oligarchs who needed a reminder of how Russia worked now. All these and more eventually found themselves in the basement medical wings of either Lefortovo or Butyrka prisons.

Defendants would be remanded to Colonel Zyuganov after extended sessions in the procurator's office, denying scattershot accusations of fraud, or bribery, or tax evasion. This is when trouble would start. Whispered rumors in Yasenevo held that once Colonel Zyuganov inhaled the bloom of the clammy drains in those desperate subbasements he changed—literally and figuratively—insisting on taking over and directing the interrogations personally, but only after having buttoned the vintage Red Army field tunic he favored while working: a brown-speckled coat, stiff and cracking with blood, reeking of pleural or vitreous or cerebrospinal fluids, all grudgingly spilled by enemies of the State.

They were already guilty—Zyuganov's head swam with impatience to inflict pain, he could taste it—and his instructions were to extract a confession—*prisvoenie,* embezzlement; *vzyatochnichestvo,* bribery; *khuliganstvo,* hooliganism; *nizost',* turpitude; whatever—by means of increasingly vigorous levels of physical discomfort: Levels One through Three. There occasionally were accidents—*when they would not listen, or refused to comply*—and Zyuganov's vision would clear in time to see guards wheeling broken bodies out of the interrogation theater on gurneys draped with rubber sheets. Zyuganov couldn't help that: Instruments sometimes slipped, arteries were nicked, and dislodged hematomas would cause the brain to swell.

Occasionally, a prisoner's real or imagined potential for embarrassing, resisting, threatening, thwarting, or plotting against President Putin made him or her *inconvenient.* Colonel Zyuganov would receive the vintage "VMN" code-word call on the prison administrator's *Kremlovka* line direct from the commissariat of the president. VMN, *Vysshaya Mera Nakazaniya,* Supreme Degree of Punishment, from the old Article 58 of Stalin's state penal code. It meant that the citizen should disappear, and that Zyuganov could indulge himself during an interrogation. He could splinter the bones of the legs and pelvis of a prisoner with a heavy baton—bendy steel reinforcing bars worked best—then walk around to the head of the table, sit on a low stool, stick his face close, and breathe in the shivering groans, watch the rolling eyes, and listen to the silver thread of spittle hit the slippery tile floor.

A year earlier there had been official trouble—recriminations—during the interrogation of two *Chornye Vdovy,* two Chechen Black Widow suicide bombers. The women had been arrested as they were boarding a bus in Volgograd; the bombs around their bellies had not detonated. A directive from the Kremlin secretariat—essentially instructions from the president himself—took primacy away from the internal security service, the FSB, and *by name* designated SVR Colonel Zyuganov, veteran KGB and Lubyanka executioner, responsible for the women's interrogation. Zyuganov's swamp-water heart nearly burst with pride: He would not fail the president.

As chief of Line KR, Zyuganov knew counterintelligence information was urgently needed: the Chechens' cutouts, bomb making confederates, and urban safe houses had to be identified. His impatience to extract the info, more to please his leader than to protect and preserve the Motherland, put a ragged edge on his already ragged soul.

At the start of the first session, the stronger of the two girls—Medna was her name, she was dark, thin, vital—spat on Zyuganov's vintage Red Army tunic. This was a serious infraction, massive impertinence. The scaly rage that lived in Zyuganov's intestines roared up and out of his mouth. Before he could stop himself, he dogged the knurled handle of the high-backed garrote chair Medna had been strapped to one turn too far, and the mechanism that had been slowly choking her instead collapsed her trachea with an audible pop, obstructing her airway and resulting in a noiseless, blue-faced death in thirty seconds. *Shit,* thought Zyuganov—one potential source of tactical intelligence was gone. That *suka,* that bitch, had cheated him.

The second Chechen prisoner clearly was terrified. Her name was Zareta, and she was thinking about the day a middle-aged woman came to her parents' house in the capital city of Grozny, spoke quietly to her mother, then took Zareta into the bedroom for an hour of mesmerizing, overwhelming, hypnotizing conversation. *That recruitment afternoon had been the beginning,* she thought, *and now this is the end.* Through the sour hood over her head she could hear shoes squeaking on floor tiles around her and the click of a snap hook on the wire that bound her wrists behind her back. Her legs shook with fright and she breathed hard into the cloth hood. A ratchet sound began and her arms were hoisted behind her, higher than her waist, forcing her to lean forward, her shoulder tendons screaming. If they had been conversational, Zyuganov could have told Zareta that *strappado*—suspension by the arms—was used by the Medici family in Florence as early as 1513. But Zyuganov didn't have time to chat.

Screaming into the hood, Zareta could not immediately identify what was being done to her—it sufficed to know only that her body was engulfed in pain, serious pain that was elemental, sharp, and electric, beneath her skin, deep in her vitals. Her legs shook and she felt her urine on the floor under her bare feet. Then the questions in Russian began; each was repeated by a female voice in accented Chechen. In thirty minutes, Zareta had stuttered the names of the woman who recruited her and the head and number two of her training cell, as well as the location of two training camps in Chechnya, one in Shatoy, seventy kilometers south of the capital at the end of the P305, and another east of Grozny, in Dzhalka, off the M29.

It was infinitely more terrifying not to be able to see, not to be able to anticipate each assault on her nervous system. She screamed out the name of the young man who assembled the suicide vests in Volgograd, and that of the boy who had strapped the tape-wrapped explosive sausage around her waist, snug under her breasts. He had smiled at her through his beard. If he wasn't dead already, she had just killed him.

The woman's voice came to her again, in the strange accented Chechen, asking about Black Widow operations in Moscow. Zareta knew one name and one address, but was determined not to betray these last colleagues. The Chechen voice was replaced by the Russian voice, reedy and harsh—it barely sounded human. Even though bent over double, Zareta could feel the person next to her. Someone slapped her on the back of the head. She felt fingers fiddling with her hood and it was roughly whisked off. The sudden white light of the laboratory made her wince, but it was nothing compared to what was in front of her, a foot away. Zareta screamed for three minutes, seemingly without taking a breath.

Medna's body was upright in the high-backed chair. She sat regally, hands wired to the armrests, head held upright by a strap around her forehead. Her face was a mass of purple bruises. She stared at Zareta through half-closed lids, her mouth barely open. Dried blood trails on either side of her mouth and nostrils completed the war-paint look. The real horror, the Zyuganov touch, was that Medna sat in the chair with her legs delicately crossed, as if at the theater, with the little toe of the foot closest to Zareta's face snipped off. Zyuganov clapped his hand over Zareta's mouth to stifle the paroxysm of screams.

"Look at her," Zyuganov said. "She's telling you to live." He grabbed a handful of Zareta's black hair and shook her head. "Live, and survive, and return to your parents. You have been deceived and used by these animals. All I require is one name and one address. Then we are done." As if to demonstrate, he lowered Zareta's arms until she could stand upright and wobbly, unclipped the hoisting rope, and snipped the wire off her wrists. She bowed her head, unable to look at the ruined envelope of her friend, unwilling to contemplate her own surrender.

She looked up at Zyuganov and hesitated, then whispered the name of the controller in Moscow and the address of an apartment in a high-rise building in the southern Moscow suburb of Zyablikovo. Zyuganov nodded and clasped Zareta's face and squeezed her cheeks, a "that's a good girl" gesture. He then walked to a stainless-steel table against the wall. Zareta, the busty matron who spoke Chechen, and the uniformed prison guard in the corner of the room all watched as he pulled a large gray handgun from under a towel, turned, and walked back to them. Zyuganov raised the pistol—an MP412 REX revolver loaded with devastating .357 magnum cartridges—and shot the already-dead Medna in the left temple from a foot away.

Zareta looked at Zyuganov with horrified disbelief. The guard held his hand over his mouth. The matron had turned away, clasping her stomach, and was vomiting on the floor. The hydrostatic shock of the bullet had tipped Medna and her chair over and the blood left in her body was spreading out in a black lake over the white tiles, migrating slowly toward the large central drain. *Normal'no,* just right, thought Zyuganov. This was just the kind of ogre's party he liked.

"Her mother can stuff her head with newspaper, to fill out her *kozhukh,* her head shroud," said Zyuganov in a voice that seemed several octaves too low, as if the devil had suddenly started speaking. Hands trembling, Zareta blinked away the blood from her lashes and wiped her sticky face, seeing the horns and yellow goat's eyes and the cloven hooves, and wondered how she would ever erase the memory of this brilliant, white-tiled room, or this *chort,* this little black devil with the foul jacket, or how she could return alive to Chechnya, where there would be a reckoning with the council for her betrayal and with her parents' shame. She could see their faces, but she would be alive, and she told herself that she wanted to live.

Zyuganov motioned for the guard—the soldier's face was gray—to take

Zareta away, and as she turned toward the door and shuffled past him, Zyuganov put the muzzle of the revolver behind her left ear and pulled the trigger. Zareta dropped in a heap and lay on her face, the prison smock up around her hips. *No dignity in death,* thought Zyuganov, *the little provincial slut.* The guard howled in fright—he had been splattered with something out of the girl's head—and the matron began vomiting again in the corner. Zyuganov surveyed the pink and dripping room for a second, then hurried out to draft his interrogation report for the internal service—but really for Putin. He wanted to report success and the vital CI information promptly.

Days later, prison administrators submitted a written complaint, requesting that Colonel Zyuganov be censured for excessive brutality and criminal acts including torture and homicide, but the complaints evaporated in the blue-eyed blink of an eye. The president had given him a task, and Alexei delivered. To the grousing officials Putin was reported as saying, *Delat' iz mukhi slona,* don't make an elephant out of a fly.

Young Alexei had surprised himself by doing well in the distrustful peat bog of SVR counterintelligence, and in time was promoted to the chief's position. His paranoid grain was well suited to the work. Zyuganov had learned much during the formative Lubyanka years—cunning overlaid his crusty homicidal urges—though his instincts were still firmly in a Soviet Jurassic zone. He understood the politics a little better. He missed the excesses of the Soviet years, and the president was Russia's best hope to reclaim the majesty and power of the Soviet Union, to restore the red-toothed fury and jaw-breaking brutality that had made former enemies cower.

Very few of the officers working in Line KR could in clinical terms define the worm farm that was Chief Alexei Zyuganov's brain. A trained psychologist in SVR's Office of Medical Services perhaps would classify Zyuganov's monstrous urges as patent malignant narcissism, but that would be like calling Dracula a melancholy Romanian prince. Zyuganov was much more than that, but all his subordinates needed to know was that the whiplash sting of the bantam centipede could come without warning, rages triggered by a perceived slight, an omission in work, an urgent tasking from the fourth floor, or, especially, opprobrium from the Kremlin—disapproval from the other diminutive narcissist who ruled behind those red walls. People in Line KR paid for any mistake that might even remotely make their chief appear lacking to the president. Zyuganov worshipped Putin like an Aztec worships the sun.

Zyuganov's deputy, Yevgeny, had been working largely unnoticed in Line KR for three years by the time the toxic dwarf arrived. Zyuganov had kept his eye on him, looking not for talent or initiative, but for unmitigated and abject loyalty. Overly ambitious deputies were a danger: Executioners tend not to trust people standing behind them. Zyuganov tested his hirsute deputy-designate early on by sending a number of ringers into him, some with offers of employment elsewhere in SVR, others to dangle bribes or commissions. The most important tests were the *malen'kiye golubi,* the little pigeons who whispered slander against Zyuganov himself, or who proposed plots against him. Yevgeny reported them all to Zyuganov, promptly and without omission. After an interim year of tests and snares and traps, Zyuganov was satisfied and promoted Yevgeny to be his deputy in Line KR. Yevgeny worked hard, kept his mouth shut, and did not care about his boss's sweet tooth for the cellars, straps, and syringes.

Now, Zyuganov sat slumped in his seat in the Line KR conference room, peevishly watching as Dominika—just returned from Paris—made her report on Jamshidi. She willed herself not to wince when she moved, for her ribs were on fire. She briefed four SVR managers—the chiefs of Lines X (technical intelligence), T (technical operations), R (operational planning), and KR (counterintelligence). Line X would prepare intelligence requirements on Iran's centrifuges for the upcoming meeting with Jamshidi in Vienna.

Dominika gently rejected the Line X suggestion that she include a nuclear-energy analyst during the upcoming debriefing. Jamshidi was untested and would be too skittish to accept a new face this soon, she argued. She assured the gathered chiefs that she could manage the initial technical details until the case was *utverdivshiysia,* more completely institutionalized, with Jamshidi completely under the yoke. They grumpily agreed to wait, for the sake of the operation.

Zyuganov looked past the chiefs at her, appraising, weighing, calculating. Of course she wanted to handle Jamshidi alone. She was monopolizing the case; she would in turn trot over to the Kremlin with the intelligence, soliciting—*ensuring*—Putin's favor. He contemplated the delicate situation. Egorova was essentially untouchable. He would have to be careful—ordering the unsuccessful Paris attack to disable his statuesque officer had been a calculated but risky action. She didn't seem to be badly damaged—despite a doubtful report from Paris to the contrary—and in fact had demonstrated that she had her own claws. He had already given follow-up orders to cauterize that operation: Fabio would be floating buns-up in the Canal Saint-Martin by now, his long hair fanned out in the sewage.

Dominika saw the hooked-talon bat wings of black unlimber behind Zyuganov's head. She sensed his agitation; she knew he was watching, assessing, calculating. Assuring him of her loyalty was folly: He did not expect it, and he would not believe it, from her or from anybody. She would not antagonize him, even though she was certain he had ordered the mugging in Paris—about which she said nothing on her return to Moscow. It showed what Zyuganov was capable of, how far he would go. How little the Service had changed since the purges of the 1930s and 1950s.

In Line KR, there was no specific group dedicated to offensive operations—the Jamshidi Iranian case was an example—so Egorova had conveniently been tucked away and assigned responsibility by default. Zyuganov wanted her occupied, kept in the dark. She would not be included in the other work of the department; he and Yevgeny would see to that. Not so easy keeping her penned up. Not easy at all. *Shilo v meske ne utaish,* you cannot hide an awl in a sack.

With the dim intuition of a sociopathic paranoid, Zyuganov acknowledged that he repulsed her, but that did not bother him. He did, however, want to establish alpha-wolf primacy. So after the briefing, Zyuganov had insisted she accompany him to Lefortovo to observe an interrogation. "You need to learn this work"—he had smirked—"for when you conduct your own investigations."

"Of course," said Dominika, determined not to show the panic she felt at returning to Lefortovo. She had been imprisoned there herself and "interrogated," but she never confessed, never gave in, and was released after six weeks of agony. She had endured refrigerated cells, electric shock, and nerve manipulation, but in the end she had looked into the eyes of her interrogators, read their colors, and knew she had won.

She followed Zyuganov's black fog as he scuttled along the same Lefortovo basement corridor she herself had been frog-marched down, the splintered wooden cabinets at each corner still there, into which prisoners would be shoved and locked to prevent them from seeing another passing prisoner, to starve the soul and deny human contact. Dominika kept her face impassive—Zyuganov was sneaking looks at her—and forced herself to keep walking on nerveless legs. The dwarf hurried forward with his nose up like a bird dog in a wet field. They passed the familiar steel doors with the spalling paint, the ones that hid the drains, hooks, and horrors, and rounded a corner. Zyuganov motioned for a guard to open a separate steel door, then continued down the corridor with solid doors on either side. There were none of the familiar prisoner screeches and bellows from behind these doors, no animal eyes peering out from the narrow food hatches. It was utterly silent here.

They stopped at the last of the doors in the corridor and Zyuganov hammered on it with his fist. A steel slat banged open, eyes briefly appeared, then a steel bolt shot and the door opened. Zyuganov bustled in, nodding at a plump prison matron in a too-tight uniform coat. Dominika followed Zyuganov inside, hearing the door slam closed behind her. It was an interrogation room unlike any she had ever seen before, more like a surgical theater. The room was brilliantly lit in a gassy white haze from overhead tubes that cast no shadows. Three-inch square white tiles covered the floor and continued up the walls to the ceiling. The air was thick with fumes that stung her nose and throat—the wall tiles had been mopped down with ammonia. Zyuganov turned to her to gauge her reaction, breathing in the air as if he were in a rose garden.

Along the wall, stainless-steel tables had tools and instruments laid out. A larger table was in the center of the room, beneath a canted surgical light head. A drainpipe ran from one corner of the table into the floor. Zyuganov took off his suit coat and draped it over the back of a chair. He took a brown coat off a hook on the wall and put it on, buttoning the bottom buttons but leaving the tunic top unfastened. Jaunty, with a barnyard smell. He looked at his watch and turned to the matron.

"Ring for the tray before we begin," he said.

She walked to the wall, pressed a button, and in a minute there was a knock on the door and a second matron entered carrying a tray covered by a cloth napkin. She set it on the stainless table over the drainpipe for bodily fluids and whipped the cloth away.

"*Selyodka,* Captain," said Zyuganov, "we haven't had lunch yet." Dominika, standing just inside the door to the room, could smell the pickled herring and onions over the tang of the disinfectant ammonia. She shook her head and sat in a chair away from the table. Zyuganov was enjoying himself.

"Fetch our guest," he said to the guard, his mouth full of herring.

They waited two minutes in silence, apart from the wet noises Zyuganov made while he ate. Looking at the back of the dwarf's little head, Dominika focused on the depression below the back of his skull and just above the start of the cervical vertebrae, the spot she would choose to plunge one of the stainless-steel surgical chisels set out on the side table.

The door opened and the matron pulled a woman into the room. Her hands were handcuffed behind her and she wore only a dirty prison smock and felt slippers.

"*Gospozha* Mamulova," Mrs. Mamulov, said Zyuganov, wiping his mouth with a napkin. The matron pushed the woman into a steel chair, which Dominika noticed was bolted to the tile floor, and stood behind Mamulova, her hands casually on her shoulders. Zyuganov dismissed both matrons with a wave and turned to Dominika.

"Captain, come here and hold her shoulders." Dominika frantically thought of some excuse to refuse, but was determined not to falter in front of Zyuganov. She could feel the slight woman trembling under her hands, and wondered what she had done. Zyuganov pulled up a chair to sit facing the woman, their knees almost touching, and leaned forward till he was inches from her face. There was a faint crackling sound when the dried gore on his jacket flaked off. Dominika breathed through her mouth to avoid the smell while trying to recall how she knew the name Mamulov. Who was this woman?

Irina Mamulova was in fact the wife of Russian media tycoon Boris Mamulov, whose communications empire included print and broadcast holdings. Mamulov had massively defied the Kremlin: His reporters had assiduously covered current Russian politics, running successive interviews with dissidents and rival political figures, including the telegenic members of the punk-rock protest group Pussy Riot after their release from prison. Mamulov's public opposition to the reelection of Vladimir Putin naturally triggered an investigation into his taxes and overseas bank accounts, which in turn led to the inevitable charges from the Moscow Procurator's Office of corruption, tax evasion, and theft. The blue-eyed scorpion's tail was rigid, curled forward, waiting to lance into flesh.

Mamulov knew what happened to people who defied Putin—prison terms, traffic accidents, cardiac episodes, fatal muggings—and chose not to return to Moscow after a business trip to Paris. He sent urgent word to his wife, Irina, to gather her sable coat and jewelry and meet him at their antiques-filled apartment on the Avenue Foch. Irina was detained at Vnukovo International Airport thirty minutes before departure to Orly and driven to Lefortovo in a closed van. As she was processed into the political prisoners' block, no property inventory was completed. Her fur and jewelry disappeared as completely as President Putin's previous enemies had.

Putin had called Zyuganov on the *Kremlovka*—the direct line from the Kremlin—and, with a straight face, directed him to request that Mamulova kindly detail her husband's overseas holdings, including the numbers of the accounts, to be able to clear him of the charges of corruption. Zyuganov was also directed to ask that Irina please convince Boris to return to Moscow from Paris as soon as conveniently possible. Putin told Zyuganov he had full confidence that he would satisfy the investigative requirements with discretion.

The *Kremlovka* needn't have been encrypted, for Putin's sly requests were clear. Irina was a hostage, bait to draw Boris back to the *Rodina,* and if black eyes, or loose teeth, or tissue hematomas—Level One injuries—inflicted on his young wife did not hasten his return, well, there were Levels Two and Three to consider.

Irina Mamulova was in her early thirties, with black hair to her shoulders. She was of medium height and slim, with Slav cheekbones and large brown eyes. She had met Mamulov when she was twenty-five, while working in one of his radio stations, and, despite her new life of private jets and yachts and penthouses, the pretty young Mrs. Mamulov was sensible and perceptive. She had been in Lefortovo for a week already and knew what was happening. She had resolved not to cooperate. Her husband, Boris, must stay out of Russia.

Dominika stood inside the green bloom around Irina's head—she was terrified, anticipating discomfort. Zyuganov's black wings overlaid her color as he leaned close, breathing pickled herring in her face.

"I was eager to come today to see how you are," said Zyuganov. "We have heard that your husband is quite concerned for you, is contemplating returning to Moscow to settle these legal troubles." Irina's head came up and she searched Zyuganov's face. Her eyes dimmed when she realized he was lying.

"When Monsieur Mamulov returns, this unpleasant interlude can end," said Zyuganov. *Monsieur? Interlude?* marveled Dominika, trying to imagine the oxidized circuits in this little man's brain. Zyuganov moved so their knees touched, and Irina cringed. Zyuganov looked up at Dominika without expression, as if checking whether she was still in the room.

"I heard a story yesterday," said Zyuganov conversationally. "*A woman came to the police. 'Please, help, my husband is missing. Here is his photo and personal information. When you find him, tell him that my mother decided not to visit!'* "

Zyuganov looked up again at Dominika, as if to confirm she had liked the joke. Irina stared motionless at him. Russians had long been programmed to get the message. Irina's mother's neck was in the noose next.

"We should tell Boris that your mother decided not to visit," whispered Zyuganov. "Maybe that would reassure him." He got up, went over to a side table, and came back with a short leather sap in his hand—flat black stitched leather, weighted at either end. Irina closed her eyes. Her hair fell on either side of her face, the tips of her locks trembling.

"Open your eyes," he said, and when she did, limpid eyes opened wide, Zyuganov struck her right shin with a downward snapping motion. The woman's head went back and she hissed with the pain, but did not cry out. *She chooses to fight them,* thought Dominika, holding on to her heaving shoulders. "And there is the little matter of the bank accounts, the numbers," Zyuganov said.

Zyuganov hit her right shin again, then reached across and instantly struck her left shin. Irina cried out, then bit her lip to stop herself. Her head came down and her shoulders shook under Dominika's hands. Zyuganov said nothing more; there was plenty of time. He reached down and tugged the felt slippers off Irina's cringing feet.

The dwarf looked at Dominika with a lifted eyebrow, and raised the truncheon delicately in both hands. "Shins and the soles of the feet are well-known areas to exploit," he said conversationally, "but I have identified alternate areas, such as the heel and behind the knee, that are most effective. I have recently obtained excellent results—quite unexpectedly I might add—with strikes to *the tips of the toes.*" He leaned down and swung the truncheon parallel with the floor to jam the tips of Irina's toes—the tops of her bare feet were already black-and-blue. She screamed and hunched her shoulders involuntarily. Her legs jerked spasmodically. Zyuganov inhaled her groans as if from a bottle of perfume.

Dominika fought down her nausea. She considered walking around the chair, twisting the sticky leather *dubinka* from his hand, and beating his frying-pan face into a paste. Irina raised her bowed head. Her cheeks were wet, and she looked vacantly at Zyuganov. *It is time to signal Nathaniel; it is time to start working again with CIA,* Dominika thought.

"Captain," said Zyuganov, holding the *dubinka* out to her. He expected her to stand shoulder to shoulder with him and beat the woman. This was a test; he was pushing her. Dominika knew she could not refuse—it would jeopardize her by showing him weakness, revulsion. She came around the chair and took the leather thing from his hand.

"Colonel," said Dominika confidentially, crowding him. "I cannot hope to duplicate your expert application. But something occurs to me, an idea that may bring results, especially after your preliminary efforts have shown the prisoner the realities of her situation."

Zyuganov looked at her sourly. "What idea?" he said.

"I wonder if you would indulge me this little experiment," said Dominika. She was keeping the anger inside her gut, and she tried to control her voice. "Can you leave me alone with her for five minutes?"

"Regulations are for two people to be in the room at all times," said Zyuganov.

"Certainly you determine the rules in this place," said Dominika. "And if we can achieve quick success, wouldn't it be worth the experiment?"

Zyuganov looked at Dominika, then at a weeping Irina, whose head was down.

"Colonel, give me five minutes." She reached over to Irina and squeezed her face, shaking it lightly, mostly to hide her own trembling hands. "We'll get on very nicely together."

Zyuganov's eyes narrowed. He was both suspicious and provisionally interested. He wondered what sugary, girl-on-girl pain Egorova had in mind. He would have liked to stay, but he was intrigued and knew he could watch the action on the monitor in the guards' room. He nodded and left the room. The door clicked shut, and Dominika turned and walked toward Mamulova.

There were two of them watching from the corner of the room, her two friends: blond milkmaid Marte, and Junoesque, hazel-eyed Marta, veteran Sparrow and her confidant in Helsinki, who had defied the Service and disappeared one winter night without a trace. Her friends watched her cross the room, telling her with a look to hurry and to be careful.

Dominika put her face close to Mamulova's, pulled her head back by her hair, and whispered into her ear. She was risking it all in the next instant. "*Sestra,* sister, you have about three minutes to listen to me," Dominika said. "Will you pay attention?" Mamulova stared at her, not understanding. Dominika hit the leg of the chair with the sap, hoping that on the video monitor it would appear that she was hitting the woman. Irina stared at her in amazement. Dominika looked at her significantly, and swung again at the chair leg, the sound of the leather hitting steel mimicking a pistol shot. Dominika leaned over her again and grasped her face in one hand.

"Listen carefully," she hissed to the woman. "They'll permanently cripple you, then throw you in an asylum. Your mother will be put in a refrigerated cell." She pushed Irina's face back farther, putting her lips close to the woman's ear. "Tell them the account numbers; it's only money. They will let you loose for a time, free to contact your husband, so they can listen to the call. While they wait, you'll be able to get out. You and your mother."

Irina looked at her through a swirling green fog, and shook her head slightly. She didn't believe her. Dominika swung the sap sideways, as if to strike her shoulder, but instead hit the back of the chair. Irina flinched and gasped—a good-enough reaction. Dominika's own bruised ribs were alight with pain from swinging the thing, but she stood over the woman, brought her face close again, and whispered, "Do you ever want to have children? Do you want to see Boris again? Give them what they want. All of it."

Dominika bent closer to her, visualizing what it must look like on the video monitor.

"Hand over your husband's ledgers, the ones with the foreign account numbers. Give them the keys to the overseas bank boxes. Show them where the safe is in your house. Promise to get more from your husband. Then get out, with your mother. Can you arrange it?" Irina hesitated, nodded once. Not surprising—she probably had access to Mamulov's well-paid lawyers, second-country passports, business jets. Getting out of modern Russia would be relatively easy for her, if she planned ahead this time.

"You are one of them," Irina said, wondering. "Why?"

The sound of the latch of the cell door caused Dominika to stand up, and as Zyuganov poked his head in the door, Dominika slapped Irina hard across the cheek, turning her face and cutting her lip. Nothing a little bacitracin in Paris wouldn't smooth out.

And I'm not one of them, Dominika thought. Perhaps one day they would meet for tea in Paris at Le Procope, alligator bags and suede gloves on the table between them, and Dominika could explain it all. Sure. *Kogda rak na gore svistnet,* when the crayfish whistle on the mountain, when pigs fly.

"Tell him," said Dominika to Irina, tilting her head toward Zyuganov. "*Tell him.*" She looked at Irina, the green halo of fear and indecision swirling around her. Would the little twit decide to save herself? Zyuganov looked at Dominika, then back at Irina.

"I . . . I will give you the account numbers," Irina said, eyes downcast.

Zyuganov, impressed, looked back at Dominika, who held up the sap and delicately ran a slim finger around the edge like an antiques dealer examining an objet d'art.

"You'll concede perhaps that a woman knows best what another woman fears the most," Dominika said. "Mamulova did not want to test your patience further. Congratulations, Colonel."

This was all nonsense. But was it? Zyuganov contemplated the most interesting epiphany that perhaps a woman could torture a woman better than a man could; something about getting into each other's heads, knowing their own bodies. Egorova certainly hadn't been sickened by the tableau. *Bah,* Zyuganov didn't know what to think, but he knew Egorova had given him a gift, a victory for the president over Mamulov, whose accounts would be siphoned dry in an hour of cybertheft. This would put Zyuganov at the top of Putin's New Year's Favorites List. But there had to be a trap: A gift from Egorova was poison, for she would use it against him; she would find a way to take advantage, to show him up. And President Putin would notice.

As Mamulova was led out of the room, Dominika shoved the white tile walls, the surgical lights, and the sticky truncheon out of her mind, and huffed to clear her nose and mouth of the smell of pickled herring and ammonia disinfectant. With a hard swallow, she then realized she was due back in Vienna in a few days for the follow-up meet with the Iranian. And she would see Nate again.

LEFORTOVO SELYODKA-PICKLED HERRING

Line a deep dish with trimmed pieces of boned and skinned herring, cover with vinegar, olive oil, sugar, and chopped dill. Chill for several hours. Serve on squares of brown bread, topped with translucent thin slices of onion.

5

Simon Benford was the chief of CIA's Counterintelligence Division. Short, paunchy, and jowly, with gray-streaked hair in constant disarray thanks to his habit of gripping handfuls of it while screaming at cringing subordinates—or at anyone from the FBI's Directorate of Intelligence, or the Defense Intelligence Agency, or the State Department's Bureau of Intelligence and Research, or the Department of Homeland Security's Office of Intelligence and Analysis, or any other government entity with "intelligence" in its title whose factotums, Benford raved, knew nothing about classic human espionage and operations, were ill prepared and unsuited to collect or analyze foreign intelligence, and, more abstrusely, were all "jacking off with oven mitts."

Besides being an enfant terrible and a misanthrope, the cow-eyed Benford was a legendary mole hunter, strategist, operational high priest, and savant who was considered the scourge of inimical foreign intel services: more treacherous than the Russian SVR, more inscrutable than the Chinese MSS, more elegantly devious than the Cuban DI, and twitchier than North Korea's RGB. Those CIA officers closest to Benford privately described him as "bipolar with a sociopath vibe," but secretly worshipped him. Allied foreign-liaison services loved him and hated him and listened to him: Years ago, Benford had helped the Brits uncover an illegals network run by Moscow for fifteen years in the House of Commons by following, Benford explained to the scandalized Joint Intelligence Committee, "the last heterosexual in Parliament directly to his Russian handler." The Britons were not amused.

Benford had called COS Athens Tom Forsyth on the secure line to congratulate them all on the acquisition of LYRIC. Preliminary assessment of the general's early intelligence was favorable, and Benford approved of Nash's handling of the case to date.

"I am anxious to hear from DIVA," Benford said over the phone.

"We all are, Simon," said Forsyth. "Nash is ready to go to her the minute she signals she's out. He's got a bag packed."

"There is no reporting on her status, no gossip, no sightings. No announcements in *Rossiyskaya Gazeta.*" He meant no obituaries, like former Soviet watchers would pick up in the old *Pravda.*

"She's resourceful," said Forsyth. "A tough cookie." The decision to send Dominika back inside had been Benford's, and Forsyth knew the feeling of waiting for word from an agent who was back inside and out of contact. It didn't matter where: Cuba, Syria, Burma, Moldova. "All we can do is wait," said Forsyth.

"Yes, Tom," said Benford. "I fucking know that, goddamn it." Had Forsyth been a GS-13 duty officer in Headquarters, Benford would have burst a blood vessel screaming into the phone, but one doesn't yell at a senior officer, especially not at Tom Forsyth.

"The minute she shows a feather, Nash is there," said Forsyth soothingly. "We're ducks—calm on top, paddling furiously underwater."

Benford groaned into the phone.

The morning after her return from Moscow, Dominika lay on the floor in her underwear in the tiny living room of the Vienna apartment on Stuwerstrasse, several blocks from the Danube and a quarter mile from the elegant curved towers of the International Atomic Energy Agency on the east bank of the river. The apartment windows were open to let in the summer breeze. To the south, the giant Ferris wheel of Prater park was just visible in the haze—at night the boxy cars on the wheel were trimmed with white fairy lights.

Dominika did incline push-ups on the floor, her breasts flattening on the carpet with each downward repetition. She exhaled on each slow press, feet planted high on a chair from the dining table. When her chest screamed for mercy, she shifted to the chair, hands on the seat and legs elevated on a small couch, and did slow dips—twenty, pushing to thirty—until she could do no more. The telephone in the kitchenette trilled. Breathing hard, she walked across the room to answer it.

She recognized Udranka's throaty voice. "*Devushka,* hey girl," said Dominika panting into the phone. *Sign.*

"*Devchonka,* you slut," said Udranka in Russian. *Countersign,* all normal. "Why are you panting into the phone? What are you doing? It's nine in the morning." *Mention of time: I need to see you, one hour.*

Sparrow tradecraft—trashy and quick and foolproof. A quick shower and six stops on the U-Bahn to Hardegasse, then up four flights on the immaculate staircase in the quiet Austrian apartment building. Udranka opened the door before Dominika knocked. The cramped apartment was a riot of color: mirrors on the walls, bright pillows on the couch, the impossible pink bedroom—ruffles and fringed lampshades—visible through an open door. All courtesy of SVR, including the video and audio pickups in every room. Udranka extended her albatross-wing arms in welcome, her crimson aura, as usual, blazing like a banked coal fire.

Not your typical Sparrow, thought Dominika, hugging her. This creature was not the usual perfect Slav snow queen, overbred to anorgasmy, with rouged nipples and a French wax. No, taken separately, Udranka's parts did not define libidinous beauty. She was scarecrow thin and 1.85 meters tall, with corresponding angular elbows, knees, and hip bones. Her breasts lay flat against her chest—she would not contemplate implants. She had a faint pencil-line scar running from the left corner of her mouth to her left ear, a childhood memento left by a paramilitary trooper with a stockyard whip. Her hands were long-fingered and restless, with short nails painted hibiscus red. Endless, long legs ended in large feet and red toenails. This morning she wore small drop earrings of orange coral, and a short hot-pink kimono that stopped precariously high on her thighs.

Her flaming magenta hair—the shade must be called Balkan Rust—was cut short and close to her head. Her mouth was extreme—a candy dish of large white teeth—and in constant movement: smiling, pouting, tongue wetting full lips, clucking in disapproval, open in uncontrolled laughter. Udranka's large eyes were light green with dark flecks, like ice cream with chips in it, and they could transmit, in the time it took for her pupils to expand, ineluctable sexual desire.

Udranka was a voluptuary, a natural. The spotters at Sparrow School recognized it when they saw it; the training staff had known how to refine the raw instinct, and operations officers like Dominika knew enough to point the cannon, light the fuse, and step back. Dominika had never seen anything like it—this woman could transform her striking but decidedly unglamorous persona into something captivating, using that dugout canoe of a body to mesmerize, paralyze, *devour* her Sparrow targets.

A decade ago, the leggy Serb had filled a backpack and gone to Moscow, a teenager looking for work, baby-giraffe tall with a booming laugh. She started modeling for low-end fashion houses, mostly shoes and jewelry. She went through the requisite relationships with ad execs, government ministers, and a musician, but by age twenty-six the modeling was over. Heads would turn when she entered a Moscow restaurant, eventually including the pear-shaped head of the Italian ambassador (short and stout, a count and a descendant from the Barberinis of Palestrina), who was tantalized by her toothy, high-voltage smile and transfixed by her height. The diminutive Italian had never made love to an extremely tall woman, and he couldn't wait to see how the parts would fit.

The ambassador was generous and considerate and loquacious, and kept Udranka secret from his wife. The FSB soon identified the count's leggy illicit companion. In a year's time Udranka had been recruited by the FSB as an access agent, and then highjacked by SVR and sent to Sparrow School. She needed money; they threatened to send her back to Belgrade, and she would have comfortable apartments to live and love in. Why not?

Three years later, Captain Dominika Egorova, looking for *primanka* in the Jamshidi case—bait so extraordinary that the Persian would forget the rules and his religion and put his neck on the block—came across Udranka's *delo formular.* Her service record rated her among the best of SVR's trained Sparrows, with evaluations of "excellent" in tradecraft and elicitation and "accomplished" in what State School Four called "seduction art." Udranka was assigned detached duty; Dominika assessed the hollow-cheeked Serb as cynical, dour, resourceful, a survivor. They got along, especially since Dominika treated her decently—she knew the burdens of being a Sparrow.

It had been a simple matter of trolling her in front of Jamshidi—a transparent little scenario was staged during which Udranka ostensibly had her purse snatched by a motorbike thief outside a Viennese bar with the Persian as a chance witness. The grateful acceptance of Jamshidi's offer of a taxi ride home followed, as did Udranka's demure invitation upstairs for coffee. Once inside her kaleidoscope apartment—silently covered by Line T's lenses and microphones—Jamshidi pushed past her maidenly reluctance, triumphed in her eventual swooning surrender, and relished her shuddering climaxes—two faked, one real—during which the fine-line scar across her cheek darkened with the flush of orgasm. Jamshidi's sewer-pipe mind turned to round two and variations best known to Tunisian towel boys. He expected struggles and howls of pain from this shy giraffe—which was the appeal, after all—but he could not have anticipated her response, nor did he register that she must have been trained to be able to make a man lose his mind like this, like Jamshidi did sometime during *No. 73, "Enter the Kremlin via Nikolskaya Gate."* From that evening on, Jamshidi was reeled in as surely as a record-book Volga carp that is prehooked to President Putin's fishing line.

"Come on," said Udranka, motioning Dominika to a small table in the sun-splashed kitchen, canary-yellow tiles on the walls and a lime-green teapot on the stove.

"How do you not go blind in here?" said Dominika.

The girl shrugged. "Belgrade was always gray to me. Moscow is too," she said. "A whorehouse should not be drab." Her crimson halo expanded as she laughed, incandescent. Her front teeth flashed between full lips.

"How's your *sych,* your horned owl?" Dominika said.

"Some progress," said Udranka. "Maybe something important." She got up from the table and opened an upper kitchen cabinet, easily reaching a squat bottle with a gold-colored cap. As she stretched, the kimono parted an inch, and Dominika caught a glimpse of her breasts, sleek against her body. *Mine are bigger,* thought Dominika, instantly feeling ridiculous.

"*Srpska Sljivovica,* plum brandy from Sumadija, in Serbia," said Udranka, pouring two small glasses.

God, thought Dominika, *it's ten in the morning.* She clinked glasses and sipped, while Udranka threw her head back and refilled her glass.

"What?" asked Dominika. Her instincts twitched in this color-soaked little love nest. She looked into Udranka's eyes, watching her swill brandy, watching her face.

"Mr. *Sych* came to me last night. He acted normally. He was not angry; he wanted to make love." Dominika had warned Udranka that Jamshidi might accuse her of setting him up for the pitch in Paris. Not a problem, Udranka had said; Sparrows were trained in professing their innocence in many things.

"Did he say anything about being approached, about cameras in the apartment?" Dominika asked.

"Nothing. It seems he does not blame me. He was very excited, impatient. That ridiculous goatee twitched up and down when I did 'hummingbird wings.'" She said it flatly, an emotionless technician discussing her trade.

"Number thirty-three," Dominika said, remembering, repeating the long-ago memorized, Soviet-clunky Sparrow rules of sexual techniques, *"overwhelm the nerve endings with unceasing stimulation."*

"That's right, you remember," said Udranka dully, as if she did not want to talk about it. "If you miss the old life, we could take him to bed together."

Dominika laughed. The kitchen table was bathed in summer sunlight, the bottle of *Sljivovitsa* on golden fire.

Udranka started laughing too, then stopped, bit her lower lip, and looked at Dominika, who also stopped laughing and reached across the table to briefly squeeze her hand—long bony fingers and bright-red nails. Her color, always bright and pulsing, slowed and faded.

"You should try him," said Udranka dully. "He likes to bite. Wants it only one way. He likes to hurt me. I hope he's worth it."

"He's worth it," said Dominika, not intending to tell Udranka how really important this was. Udranka stared at her and grunted. Her head went back and she refilled her glass again. They didn't talk for a minute.

"The most important thing," said Udranka. "He told me he wants to use this apartment for an important meeting. Two nights from now. *My apartment.* Cheeky bastard."

Dominika nodded her head. That was it. He intended to show up for the debrief.

"I assume the meeting is with you," said Udranka. "I'll let him in, then leave."

"No, I need you to stay close in case he decides to stop talking. You'll be a reminder he has to behave."

"I'll wear something tight," Udranka said, deadpan, her crimson halo coming back, flaring. "The man might not listen to me, but the bald one with the turtleneck always does." Dominika suppressed a laugh. She had not heard that phrase since Sparrow School. Udranka refilled both their glasses.

"After this is over, I'm getting you out," said Dominika. "Not just Vienna, completely out."

"Of course you are," said Udranka pouring another glass. Sunlight in the canary-yellow kitchen and the burned caramel whiff of brandy in the still air. Their eyes met. "I can't even get drunk anymore," she whispered.

Dominika got up from the table and put an arm around the shoulder of her Sparrow, the long-legged destroyer of men with the piano-key smile that could light up a room, whose silent, slow tears wet the front of her handler's shirt.

Vienna in summer: leafy parks and mustard-colored buildings with the gravitas of past empires in their façades, pitched roofs all of intersecting angles, trolley tracks joining and separating, polished brass door pulls, the loamy smell of endless coffees, and the sugary crunch of cakes and breads tumbled on trays set in café windows with gold lettering. And under the ubiquitous violins of Strauss in every doorway lingered the memory of the faded bass notes of tank treads from less happy times. Vienna.

Dominika was back in Vienna, with a briefcase of Center-drafted nuclear requirements, two lipstick guns, and her heart in her mouth. The upcoming debriefing with Jamshidi made action urgent. It was time to trigger recontact with CIA—and Nate. The prospect of seeing Nate again swelled in Dominika's chest until she could hardly breathe. She didn't know if he would be different toward her, didn't know how it would be between them. Her Russian pride and cross-grainedness would not let her again be the first one to make a move. She would not throw herself at him, she would not ever again watch him retreat behind regulations or security requirements or a guilty conscience. She heard the calm voice of the SENTRY operator on the line as she repeated her security code, used the identifier alias, mentioned the city, and designated the city park and clock tower brief-encounter site. Now it was time for business, her business.

It took Nate twelve hours to get to Vienna after the SENTRY system automatically cabled Athens Station to inform them that Moscow-based, Russian asset GTDIVA had called to trigger contact. Vienna, Stadtpark

Clock Tower, starting tomorrow, every day at noon. Nate took the first flight to Munich, then the train to Vienna. They always added a rail leg to tweak ops security: Once inside the European Union with common, permeable borders, there was no paper trail, and light disguise took care of ubiquitous security cameras in the terminals. Gable followed through Prague—he would back up Nate because he was a case officer Dominika had trusted—and they booked a suite at the Schick Hotel Am Parkring, on the margins of the park.

Nate stood in the suite looking out the French doors at the Viennese skyline, knowing she was under one of those peaked slate roofs. Dominika had called; she was out. It felt like she had been back in Russia, status unknown, for ten years. Nate's guts skipped as he tried to order his thoughts. Intel requirements, communications, access, security, signals, sites—the list was endless. Nate knew that this recontact with Dominika was critical; it was the first time she would be met since recruitment. Despite her call out, would she be willing to continue? The case officer in him knew that the case must be maintained on a professional basis. He would stay professional at all costs. This was espionage.

She wasn't at the RDX the first day—a bit worrying—but Nate slipped into case-officer mode and watched the rendezvous site and waited. On the next day, from his vantage point on a bench behind a low hedge, he saw her walking down the gravel path bordered by linden trees, the familiar slight hitch in her stride. She looked as he remembered her—ever so subtly older perhaps, features more sculpted, but the blue eyes were the same, the head still held high. He let her go by, checking her status, and let her wait at the ornate marble balustrade at the base of the clock. She looked at her watch once, briefly. Nate stayed still, watching for casuals, to see if anyone lingered in the shadows under the far-off trees.

After four minutes—the standard meeting window for SVR too—she began walking, not obviously looking for coverage, but he knew she saw everything. Nate walked behind her at surveillance distance for a while—he felt black, there were no repeats—watching her pinned-up hair and strong legs. She slowed to look at a statue and Nate passed her and continued walking toward the white bulk of the hotel, visible over the trees. She turned and followed him.

They were alone in the elevator, standing in opposite corners of the car, looking up at the floor numbers on the display. Nate looked over at her and she met his gaze. His purple halo was unchanged, strong and constant. The catechism stipulated that they should not speak in the elevator, but Nate had to say something.

"I'm glad to see you," said the CIA officer to his Russian agent. Dominika looked at him, blue eyes giving nothing away. She said nothing as the doors opened and Nate walked ahead of her to their room and tapped softly. Gable opened the door and pulled Dominika into the center of the room—cream carpet, dark-green couch, open double French doors with a view of the sand-drip castle spire of St. Stephen's in the distance.

"Nine months. You kept us waiting long enough," said Gable, smiling. "You okay?" His purple mantle was the same, too, pulsating, raucous, circular.

"*Zdravstvuy Bratok*, hello big brother," said Dominika, shaking his hand. She had started calling him *Bratok* after her recruitment in Helsinki, a sign of affection. She turned toward Nate.

"Hello, Neyt," she said, but did not extend her hand.

"It's good to see you, Domi," said Nate.

"Yeah, well, now we're all glad to see one another," said Gable. "Before I start weeping, let's hear what you've been up to. How much time do you have? All day? Okay." Dominika sat on the velour couch with Gable. Nate pulled up a chair.

"Let's get something to eat first," said Gable, bounding up. "Nash, call room service—never mind, give me the phone." He looked at Dominika while waiting for the operator, hand over the mouthpiece. "You look too skinny. You been sick, or just missed us?" Dominika smirked and leaned back on the couch, starting to relax. She avoided looking at Nate. She had forgotten how smooth and professional these CIA men were, how much she liked them. They were purple and crimson and blue, strong and reliable.

Gable ordered so much food they needed two trolleys to bring it all: smoked trout and salmon, beet salad, Olivier salad, poached chicken, fresh mayonnaise, runny Brie, Gouda, a crusty loaf of bread, iced butter, cucumber salad, sliced ham, two different mustards, lamb kabobs, yogurt sauce, two strudels, palatschinken with brandy apricot jam, a tray of Austrian chocolates, ice-cold Alpquell, Grüner Veltliner Sauvignon, and yellow-gold Ruster Ausbruch.

They talked for four hours. They let her do the talking; she didn't need prompting. She knew what was important, what to include, what to leave out. She spoke in English—sometimes Nate had to help her over a word in Russian, but she talked in whole paragraphs. Her return to Moscow. Promotion to captain. Assigned to Line KR under a new boss, Alexei Zyuganov. Interview with Putin. Mamulova interrogation in Lefortovo. The limited hard intel she had gleaned from KR—SVR foreign operations, counterintelligence leads—would come later.

"Hold it," said Gable. "You got in to see Putin?"

Dominika nodded. "Twice. He congratulated me on exposing General Korchnoi," she said softly, looking down at her hands. "He said Korchnoi was destroyed. I'm sure he gave the order. I thought I saw something on the bridge, but couldn't be sure. Is it true?"

"They shot him from across the river, at the end of the bridge," said Nate. "He was home free and they shot him." His voice was even, emotionless.

"I will never forget him," she said. Her eyes glistened. They sat in silence for a while, the faint buzz of traffic on the Parkring coming through the open French doors.

"It is why I made the call for you to come," she said finally. "I was not sure I would ever work with you again. But the *siloviki,* the bosses, have not changed, it is as bad as ever. Worse than before."

"We're glad you came back out," said Gable, reaching for a plate. "I *knew* you would. It's in your blood. Sweet pea, we're back together again."

Oh shit, thought Nate, and he held his breath.

"What is this 'sweet pea'?" said Dominika casually, putting down her wineglass. It was the moment when someone yells "Grenade" and everyone hits the floor.

"It's like *baloven,*" said Nate hurriedly in Russian, "something a big brother would say. 'My pet,' like that." Dominika blinked, only half believing him, only half placated. Oblivious, Gable slathered mustard on a piece of ham.

Back to business. Nate's business: internal operations, the science, art, and necromancy of meeting agents in denied environments such as Moscow, Beijing, Havana, Tehran. Running agents in the most dangerous counterintelligence states imaginable. Meeting spies inside was like wading through a tannin-black, piranha-infested pool with infinite care, trying not to stir up the bottom. In Helsinki, Nate had rebelled at the thought of putting Dominika in danger by running her inside Russia. Now, after Korchnoi, he told himself they all had to get on with it, whatever the cost, but he felt his pulse in his jaw, seeing her on the couch, legs crossed, that habit of bouncing her foot.

"Domi, we have to talk internal ops, how we're going to communicate in Moscow," he said. "If you can arrange foreign travel, we'll rely on every opportunity to meet outside. But something could happen, a fast-breaking issue, or an emergency, or a travel ban or anything, and then we need a way to meet inside."

Dominika nodded.

"We have covcom for you," said Nate, "covert-communications equipment, very fast, very secure. You can send abbreviated messages, we can direct you to new sites, we can plan face-to-face meets. You know all this.

"The first challenge, the danger, is physically getting the covcom set to you. We have to dead drop it—a longtime cache is no good. We want you to retrieve it within a day, a few days at most, of our putting it down."

What he did not say was that her life depended on the tradecraft of the Moscow Station officer assigned to load the DD, and on the perspicacity of the chief of Moscow Station in validating and approving the officer's ops plan. If the young American spook did not accurately determine his surveillance status during his surveillance-detection route, if he blundered through his run on that future fragrant night with the summer twilight silhouetting the Moscow skyline, it would be the end. If FSB surveillance saw him load a site, they would set up on it and wait for weeks, months, a year, to see who came to unload it. Dominika would never know the sequence of events that killed her.

"It will be possible," said Dominika evenly. "Line KR has access to all *nadzor* assignments and schedules. I will be able to determine surveillance deployments throughout the city—FSB, *militsiya,* police, our teams. The first exchange will be dangerous, but we can do it."

"We take this slow," said Gable. "We fucking take everything slow. There's no use getting you comms if we can't do it securely." He poured more wine into Dominika's glass.

"Remember when we talked in Greece?" said Gable. "In that little restaurant on the beach? I said you should establish yourself, take your time, create a reputation, find a good assignment, start pushing your weight around."

Dominika smiled at him.

"Well, you done all that and more. I'm proud of you."

Nate thought Gable sounded like a parent dropping his kid off at the prep-school dormitory with the engine running, but Dominika knew what he meant. She patted him on the arm.

"Well, *Bratok*, I have done something else that you both need to know about," said Dominika, picking up her wineglass. She ran her finger around the wet rim, raising a single lonely note.

"I have approached an Iranian nuclear expert; the case is brand-new. His name is Parvis Jamshidi. He is here in Vienna, in the IAEA." The CIA officers looked at each other; they didn't know the name right off, but he sounded like a target that would be high on the list.

"I gave him some bad news—how do you say, compromised him—and convinced him to cooperate," said Dominika. Gable, the legendary recruiter, the grizzled scalp-taker, cocked his crew-cut head. He wanted to hear more.

"Compromised him how?" asked Gable. Dominika looked at him as though she were a cool gin and tonic.

"I provided him a Sparrow," said Dominika. Fingers circling the rim, letting the note hang in the air. She was playing it coy, teasing them.

"What Sparrow?" said Gable.

"My Sparrow. In an apartment about ten minutes from here, close to his IAEA office." She took a sip of wine.

"And you convinced him to cooperate how?" asked Gable.

"I showed him streaming video of himself breaking the rules of sharia." She bounced her foot.

"Meaning . . ."

"Ramoner," Dominika said in French. "Sweeping the chimney, all the time, quite oversexed."

Gable started laughing, unable to talk.

"And what exactly has he agreed to?" asked Nate.

"He has agreed to a meeting, a debriefing on his country's nuclear program. He is hostile, will doubtless try to withhold some details, but he will cooperate in the end." Dominika reached for a chocolate and started unwrapping the foil.

"A debriefing where?" asked Nate. The two Americans were now both leaning toward her.

"At my Sparrow's apartment," said Dominika, popping the bonbon into her mouth.

"And when does this debriefing take place?" asked Nate.

"Tomorrow night," said Dominika.

"Tomorrow night?" said Nate.

"Yes," said Dominika, "and you're coming."

"Jesus wept," said Gable.

OLIVIER SALAD

Boil potatoes, carrots, and eggs. Dice vegetables, eggs, and dill pickles into quarter-inch cubes and place into a bowl. Similarly dice boiled ham or shrimp, or both, and add to the bowl. Add sweet baby peas. Season aggressively and add fresh chopped dill. Incorporate with freshly made mayonnaise.

6

Gable later said he had never heard of such an operational gambit: DIVA, a recruited Russian agent, proposing that Nate, her CIA handler, impersonate a Russian nuclear analyst from Line KR and together meet DIVA's unilateral Iranian source. If they could pull it off, CIA would essentially get a secret drop copy of all the intelligence generated by the case that was being sent to the Center in Moscow, a priceless look inside the Iranian program.

"Jesus H. Christ, it's the damnedest false flag op I ever heard of," said Gable, throwing clothes into his suitcase. He had passed Vienna Station a summary of Dominika's proposal for forwarding to Langley, and was immediately returning to Athens to talk to Forsyth. What the CIA officers did not tell their captivating Russian agent was that they would begin examining covert-action possibilities with the supersecret Headquarters component called the Proliferation Division (PROD) whose virtuoso officers conceived, developed, and executed operations to combat weapons of mass destruction (WMD) programs around the globe. It was an eclectic division, populated by quirky officers—physicists, operators, engineers—a number of whom were relatively normal: The extroverts in PROD were the ones who looked *at your shoes* when they spoke to you. On his way out, Gable stopped at the door and turned toward Nate.

"I have no authority to do it, but I'm green-lighting this without Headquarters' approval. No risk aversion, no politics, no lawyers. Forsyth and COS Vienna will back me up. But that means no fuckups tomorrow."

He stuck his ruddy face into Nate's. "Listen up. Nash, you have to be as smooth as you ever dreamed of being. Tomorrow night. No rehearsals. When you walk into that apartment with Dominika, that Persian dickwad has to believe you're a fu . . . a Russian. Any mistake and he's going to squawk to his people about the third man—the analyst—in the room, it'll get to the Center in five minutes, and Domi's in the wringer. Remember what I told you in Athens? Tight as a Laotian bar hostess? Do you not understand *any* part of what I just told you?"

Dominika looked back and forth at the two men. "Does he always speak like this?" she said. "What is this about Laos?"

Gable turned to her. "I already told you how glad I am to see you. Right off the bat, you bring us this once-in-a-decade lead. You've outdone yourself, but I don't want you to get careless. I want to eat room service with you for the next five years."

"Thank you, *Bratok*. For my organization, this is not so much, just a simple *maskirovka*, a deception. We Russians are good at it."

Gable looked at Nate and Dominika, shook his head, and went out into the corridor, the door closing behind him.

Dominika and Nate stood in the middle of the ruined suite, which looked like Sunday morning after Saturday night, plates stacked everywhere, napkins on the floor, wine bottles upside down in sloshy ice buckets.

"What did *Bratok* mean about Laos?" Dominika asked casually, stacking plates.

"Let's get out of here," said Nate. "Give them time to clean up."

Dominika looked at him calmly. "Laos?"

"It's not Laos," said Nate. "It's about an operation being run carefully, everything thought out, no mistakes."

"With bar girls?" said Dominika, putting the dirty plates on the wheeled trolley.

"No, it's an expression describing close coordination, like hugging a girl. Jesus, Domi, I can't explain it now."

"You're quite the *muzhlan*," said Dominika dryly. "How do you say this in English?"

"Sorry, I don't know that word," said Nate. *Who's she calling a bumpkin?* he thought.

"A pity to leave this, but we need to plan for tomorrow night," she said. "I want to show you Line X requirements. I will be speaking to the Persian in French, but you must speak only Russian. He probably speaks English—most scientists do."

"How many pages of requirements are there?" said Nate. "Did you bring them yourself?"

"There are forty pages, some with diagrams. Of course I brought them myself. We are not going to transmit them through the *rezidentura* in Vienna; this case is *razdelenie*, strictly compartmented."

Nate shook his head. "You carried intel requirements with you on the plane? That's not very professional. What if you lost them?"

Nate hadn't meant to criticize Dominika, but he worried about flaps. One accident and Langley's covert-action possibilities would be lost. But he saw her eyes flare: Gable once told Nate that there is not an intelligence officer in the world who does not bristle at being accused of shoddy tradecraft. Tell him there's a nickel parking meter beside his sister's bed, but don't impugn his tradecraft.

Dominika's voice crackled like hoarfrost on a windowpane. "I do not lose documents," she said. "And do not lecture me, Mr. Neyt, on techniques. Your agency's professionalism is no better than ours."

Nate swallowed the "So who recruited who?" because he knew it wasn't fair, and also because he'd very likely get a slap across the face. *Agent handling, Mr. Case Officer,* he thought, *leave it alone.*

Dominika wasn't through. "Russians invented spying," she said, waving a fork at him. "Do you know *konspiratsiya?* Operating secretly, not being detected, what you Americans call tradecraft, we invented it."

Invented spying? How about the Chinese in the sixth century BC? Nate raised his hands in mock surrender. "Okay, I just want us to be careful."

Dominika looked at him sideways, reading his purple halo, steady and bright, and decided that (a) he wasn't disparaging her, and (b) she really did love him. "So you want to study the notes?"

"Yeah, I'll have to memorize the Line X stuff. Gable won't have time to send our requirements before tomorrow night," Nate said. *The Center's nuclear requirements alone will be golden intel to analysts in Langley,* he thought.

"We have a lot of work," said Dominika. A pause.

"And we can't be seen on the street together," said Nate. More silence.

"We could use my safe apartment," said Dominika. "To continue the operational planning."

"More discreet than this hotel room," said Nate. "You go ahead. I'll come over in a half hour. What's the address?"

"Stuwerstrasse thirty-five, apartment six. Come in an hour."

"I'll see you soon," said Nate, his throat closing.

"Ring two short, one long. I will buzz you in," said Dominika, who could not feel her lips.

"Roger," said Nate idiotically, sounding like a test pilot.

Dominika looked at him as she opened the door. "And Neyt," she said, "I think it is all right for you to be a bumpkin."

When she was five, Dominika began seeing the colors. Words in books were tinted red and blue, the music from her mother's violin was accompanied by rolling, airborne bars of maroon and purple, and her professor father's bedtime stories in Russian, French, and English flew on wings of blue and gold. At age six, she was—secretly—diagnosed as a synesthete by a psychologist colleague of her father's, who also observed the rare *additional* ability in Dominika to read people's emotions and moods by the colored auras that surround them.

Her synesthesia made her one with music and dance, and she catapulted through the Moscow State Academy of Choreography, destined for the Bolshoi. A rival broke the small bones of her right foot, finishing her ballet career in an afternoon. Vulnerable and drifting, she was recruited into the SVR by her scheming uncle, then deputy director of the Service. He had pitched her to join the Service during the funeral wake for her beloved father.

That was about the time when the other began, the *buistvo,* the anger, the rage, the temper that would surge through her in reaction to deceit and betrayal at the hands of her Service and against the swollen bureaucrats who appropriated and encumbered her life. Dominika had long ago lost the patriotic idealism of her youth. The anger was overlaid by sadness and grief, as only a Russian could mourn, broadly and dark as the steppes, as she saw how the successors to the sclerotic Soviet Politburo—the cashiered KGB hustlers, and the thirsty oligarchs, and the crime lords, and the poker-faced president with his trademark sidelong glance—spindled Russia's potential, sold the future, and squandered the magnificent patrimony of Tolstoy, Tchaikovsky, Pushkin, and Ulanova, the greatest ballerina ever, Dominika's childhood idol. It was all done behind multiple curtains, masquerading as a government, a sovereign state, all behind Kremlin curtains.

Her parents had embodied Russian soul—her father a professor of literature, her mother a concert violinist—but they had been ground down between the Soviet mortar and Stalin's pestle, confiding only in each other, out of young Dominika's earshot, walking gingerly through life just as citizens now walk on Moscow streets, different but the same, wearily paying bribes and boiling their brown tap water and, outside Moscow, dreaming of milk, and waiting for meat, and hoarding the dear little tin of caviar for *Maslenitsa,* the end-of-winter holiday—a celebration as old as Russia is old—which brings the springtime promise of sun, and warmth, and food, and change, which never comes. It never comes.

As she sailed through SVR Academy, then inhaled the disinfectant stench of Sparrow School, then was assigned the delirious first overseas posting to Helsinki, Dominika's synesthesia became an operational asset. She could read the deceptions and suspicions in her own *rezidentura.* When she met the unflappable CIA officers who handled her after her recruitment she read the haloes of constancy—the same royal purple as her father's—and in the case of Nathaniel Nash, the luminous purple of passion. Passion for CIA, for his country, and perhaps for her.

They had fallen into their affair, pushed together by the strain of Dominika's spying, by Nate's dread for her safety. They made love against the rules, against good sense, flaunting every tenet of security. Dominika rationalized that she was already committing espionage—the second bullet behind the ear for sleeping with the Main Enemy wouldn't much matter. When Nate hesitated, retreating behind his regulations, worried about career dislocations, Dominika's anger and pride would not forgive him.

Nearly a year later, things had changed. Her disgust with the *zveri,* the animals in Moscow, was renewed. She knew that Zyuganov would just as soon liquidate her as look at her, but she knew that Putin's wet-lipped patronage of her would keep him at bay, at least for a time. She wondered quite seriously whether she would have to kill Zyuganov before he killed her. And her fury at the thought of Korchnoi, gunned down a few meters from freedom, swirled unchecked and unabated in her breast. She supposed it was inevitable that she would gravitate to her CIA handlers—and she suspected that those smiling professionals always knew it. She was satisfied with the recontact with CIA and Gable; he was right, she missed the game. And she had done a lot of thinking about Nate—the last thing he told her before she went back inside Russia had been that he cared about her. Fine, but she would not offer herself to him again.

She combed her hair in the little bathroom with the long-handled antique tortoiseshell brush that once belonged to her *prababushka,* her great-grandmother, in Saint Petersburg. She had brought it with her to the Academy, then to Sparrow School, and on her first tour in Helsinki. It was one of the few mementos from her family. She looked at the brush in her hand. The elegant, curved handle had helped her unlock—unleash—her nighttime adolescent urges, without shame. As she entered young womanhood, she noted the emergence of her "secret self," another part of her, sexual and edgy and questing, that lived quietly in the deeply barricaded hurricane room inside her—that is, until she opened the door. She set the brush down and asked herself what she expected from a life of espionage on the brink, from Udranka holding on by her fingernails, from earnest and conflicted Nate, from herself.

The street door intercom buzzed *dit-dit-dah.*

They worked until nightfall, then quit. The table was covered in paper. Two water glasses had made rings on the pages of SVR Line X requirements concerning temperatures of the thermal gradient in the gas rotors of Iran's centrifuges at Natanz. Dominika got up from the table, brushed the hair out of her eyes, sprawled out on the little couch in the corner of the room, and kicked off her shoes.

"We have an excellent chance of success tomorrow," she said.

"If Jamshidi hasn't changed his mind," said Nate from the table.

"He will not change. He cannot afford the scandal. And he cannot resist Udranka. His lust is stronger than his fear."

"If he refuses to cooperate, would you make good on your threat?" asked Nate. "Would you feed him to the mullahs?"

"Of course. I could not be seen to bluff." She lifted her chin and pointed it at Nate. "You would not? What would you do if he refused to cooperate?"

"I don't know. Try to persuade him, appeal to his reason as a scientist."

"And if he still refused?"

"Then we'd try to get him kicked out of IAEA over some minor charge."

"To let him return in good standing to his country to continue his destructive work?" Dominika wiggled her toes and stretched her legs.

"Dominika, in CIA we don't eliminate a recruitment target when the pitch is refused," said Nate. "We wait and watch, and come back in a month, or a year, or five years. Besides, we don't pitch someone until we're nearly sure of the outcome." The wiggling stopped.

"Were you sure about me? Did you know my response before you asked?"

"I wasn't sure; I held my breath when I started talking to you about working together. I thought I knew—hoped I knew—what your response would be." Nate started shuffling the papers on the table. "Then things became complicated . . ." *Time to shut up. Jesus.* Her toes started wiggling again.

"And the other," said Dominika, "was that part of the operation, my recruitment?" Nate's upper lip was a little wet, and the papers were sticking to his hands.

"What do you mean 'the other'?" said Nate.

"What do you suppose I mean?" said Dominika. "When we made love."

"What do you think, Domi?" said Nate. "Do you remember what I said to you in Estonia before you crossed the bridge back to Russia? I said—"

"You said we didn't have time for you to tell me you are sorry for what you said to me, no time to tell me what I meant to you as a woman, as a lover, as a partner, no time to tell me how much you will miss me." Silence and the sound of a car horn on the street below. Dominika looked down at her hands in her lap.

"Have I remembered correctly?" she said softly.

"How lucky for us, on the eve of our meeting with Jamshidi, that your well-known memory hasn't failed you," said Nate. He stopped gathering the papers and looked into her eyes. "I meant what I said."

Her mouth twitched, suppressing a smile, or perhaps some other emotion. "Well, it is good to be working together again," she said quickly. The bubble popped; they both knew it. It was the only way.

"Are you hungry?" she said. "Do you want to go out for one of their beastly sausages and kraut?"

"What's wrong with sausages? I like that stuff," said Nate.

"*Protivno,* disgusting," said Dominika.

"I suppose you think *salo* is better?" Dominika sat up and squared her shoulders.

"*Salo* is a delicacy," she said.

"It's fatback bacon, and you Russians eat it cold and raw, the more fat the better."

Dominika sighed and shook her head. "*Nevinnyi,*" she said, "how little you know, almost childlike."

"Maybe we should stay off the street," said Nate.

"I know a restaurant with a covered garden, the Good Old Whale; it's in the park. We can stay away from downtown," said Dominika, seeing him hesitate. "Come on *dushka,* I will watch for trouble and protect you." Dominika knew she was good, but she also knew that Nate was twice the street operator she was.

Nate pushed open the door to the apartment building and they stepped onto the sidewalk. Neither of them consciously registered that each simultaneously looked across the street and scanned both wings as they turned to walk toward the Prater, crossing busy Ausstellungsstrasse, using the double-lane boulevard to look both ways and check for trailing coverage again. They left the traffic behind and walked down pedestrian, tree-lined Zufahrtsstrasse, now inside the park, past the booths, the funhouses, the fairy lights, and the big Prater Ferris wheel always visible above the tree line, its bread-box cars picked out in white bulbs. Dominika took Nate's arm as they strolled through the smells of the confections and cakes and roasted meats, and they mentally cataloged the faces and the jackets and the shoes, to be able to recognize repeats later on.

The summer evening was cool and pleasant. Dominika's bare arm was relaxed and warm and Nate felt the familiar constriction—desire, tenderness, lust—in his throat, and he looked over at her classic profile, reflected in a hundred spinning lights, and she caught him looking at her and yanked his arm to behave, and pulled him toward the tables of the restaurant under the linden trees, Der Gute Alte Walfisch—the Good Old Whale—and they ordered sauerkraut balls with mustard, sauerbraten and red cabbage for Dominika, and *Nürnberger Rostbratwurst* with horseradish cream for Nate, and a bottle of Grauburgunder, but Dominika shook her head and refused to toast when Nate held up his glass.

Nate put down his glass without taking a sip. "What's up?"

Dominika made a sweeping gesture at the plates on the table. "This. In Russia the only people who eat like this are the *siloviki,* the fat cats licking their paws and purring when our dear president scratches them behind the ears," she said. "They are in their dachas and villas and seaside resorts—do you know about Putin's palace in Praskoveevka on the Black Sea? He stole hospital funds to build it."

Nate picked up his wineglass again. "Well, then, confusion to the *siloviki,*" he said. "Dominika Egorova will keep them awake at night, like the Russian household demons—what do you call them?—that live under the floor and knock all night."

Dominika raised her glass and touched the rim to Nate's glass. "*Barabashki,* the pounders, the bad demons, the *domovye.*"

Nate sipped. "That's you, the *domovoi* in Putin's palace, under the floorboards. He just doesn't know it's you."

"Thank you very much," said Dominika. "*Domovye* are smelly and ill behaved."

"You're certainly not smelly," said Nate.

"Funny," Dominika said. "Are all the men in your family as charming?"

Nate held up his hand. "Let's not go there. Talk about pounders and knockers."

"What?" Dominika said.

"Forget it," said Nate.

Dominika leaned forward. "No, you cannot refuse. Now I am curious."

"Let's talk about something else," said Nate. He poured both of them some more wine.

Dominika kept looking at him, even as he avoided her eyes. "You're supposed to keep your agent happy and motivated. Tell me."

Nate took a deep breath. "Not so dramatic. Two brothers, both older. Partners in the family law firm. My father is a lawyer, my grandfather a judge. Great-grandfather started the firm. In Virginia, Dinwiddie County, near the capital of Richmond. The Old South, you know what that is?"

Dominika nodded her head. "Your Civil War. Abraham Lincoln. The film *Blown with the Wind,* yes I know."

"That's right, good movie." Nate patted Dominika's hand. "It was pretty competitive growing up. In school, sports, my brothers especially, we were always fighting. They like to win, like my father and grandfather; the whole family likes to argue, all lawyers. The only thing I did better than they did was swim, and one summer I pulled my oldest brother to shore after his sailboat flipped. I guess I saved his life, but when we got to shore he started wrestling me—I was smaller than him—and he threw me back into the lake and walked up to the house. I guess thanking me was out of the question. He had to win.

"My brothers married respectable girls from old Southern families. Obedient and genteel. Everything the way it had been for four generations. Always winning. My exhausted sisters-in-law got by on pills and bourbon. I found out that my oldest brother's wife was getting back at him by sleeping around fraternity row in Richmond. I could have thrown it in his face, payback for all the thumping, but that would be losing—for the whole family—so I skipped it, and went off to school.

"My father wanted me to be a lawyer too. When I studied Russian instead, and then picked another career, it was a serious crisis. They bet that I'd fail and be back home in two years."

Dominika took a sip of wine. "Instead you are here, and you have me, and we are daring and desperate and dangerous operatives, saving the world and planning the destruction of evil."

"*Imenno,* exactly," said Nate. "Do you want this last sauerkraut ball? I'm tired of talking about me."

"Go ahead," said Dominika. "But tell me, Neyt, you don't hate your family, do you? You must never forget your family. They will always be there to help you. Like my mother is always there when I need her."

"I thought your mother passed away a few years ago," said Nate.

"She did. But she is always close by."

"You mean her memory? Of course you remember your parents. We all do," said Nate.

"Yes, but more than a memory. I can sometimes see her; she talks to me."

Nate sat back in his chair. "Like a ghost?" Would he have to draft a cable to Headquarters documenting DIVA's episodic schizophrenia?

"Stop looking at me that way," said Dominika. "I am not *sumasshedshiy,* crazy. All Russians feel a closeness to their ancestors and friends. We're spiritual."

"Uh-huh. Comes from the bottle of vodka a day," said Nate. "Do you see other ghosts?" He kept his tone neutral.

"There was a girl at Sparrow School who died, and my friend in Finland, the one who disappeared." Dominika looked down at her hands.

"She was the former Sparrow?" said Nate.

Dominika nodded. "I know the Center eliminated her."

"And they *talk* to you?"

Dominika leaned forward, chin in her hand. "Do not worry, Dr. Freud, I am not raving. I just remember my friends. They are with me in spirit, and they help me survive the days when you are not here. For me, they are like our *Rusalki,* the mermaids who sit by the river and sing."

"I read about the *Rusalki,* Slavic folklore," said Nate. "But don't they sing to men to lure them to the water and drown them?"

"They sound dangerous, don't they?" said Dominika, a trace of a smile on her lips. "But they are not here tonight, because you are here." She reached for his hand and gave it a squeeze.

A blond waitress in a dirndl, a traditional peasant skirt, came to clear the table, bending to gather plates and silverware, taking her time, looking at Nate as she reached for the mustard pot. The traditional bodice was low cut and her blouse was strained tight. One arm balancing plates, she managed to fluff her hair and ask Nate in German if he wanted anything else. Nate smiled and simply made the universal signing gesture for the check. His smiled faded as he turned back to Dominika. Annoyed. Cossack displeased. White sparks from an arc welder.

"Oh, come on," he said. "I thought we were dangerous operatives saving the world."

"Do you love me?" asked Dominika, switching to Russian.

"What? What's that got to do with this? She's just a cute waitress."

"You know the Danube is not that far away," said Dominika. "I know *Rusalki.* They will drag you—" She stopped talking and looked over Nate's shoulder.

Nate knew not to look, ingrained training, but watched her face, waiting.

"Two men, short sleeves, one tall, one fat," Dominika said in a low voice.

"Stupid Tyrolean hat on the short one?" said Nate.

Dominika's eyes searched his face, impressed. "*Very good.* They were ahead of us when we walked through the park."

"Then they stopped at a food booth to let us go by," said Nate.

"And they walked past us as we sat down here," said Dominika.

"What are they doing now?"

Dominika shrugged. "Walking back up the lane, eating ice cream."

"Three hits. Time for a loop out of the park," said Nate.

They paid and unhurriedly walked in the opposite direction onto looping Messestrasse, stopping at the Hotel Messe bar for a drink, exiting through the hotel garden, crossing over into Messezentrum arcade just before closing, moving counterclockwise around the hall until they came to the exit onto Ausstellungsstrasse, then sprinting across the road against the lights and stair-stepping into Dominika's neighborhood. They had seen no extraordinary movement in response to their provocatively aggressive movements, no scurrying or obvious parallel coverage, either foot or vehicular. And no Mutt and Jeff with the hat. They stopped again at a schnaps bar on Arnezhoferstrasse, sat, and looked out the plate glass, tired and a little winded, but stoked with the pulse of the street, with the aphrodisiac of sound, movement, and car exhaust. The adrenaline high of possible unseen opposition in the shadows faded: There was no feel of coverage, no nibbles from the street. Dominika wondered whether he was as "agitated" as she was, and whether he would try to take her to bed. She ached for him, but she would not suggest it first.

"Are you nervous about tomorrow?" she said. Their shoulders were nearly touching, and she could feel his body heat through her shirt.

"No, I think we'll be fine. You?" said Nate. The purple halo around his head pulsated.

"I expect the Persian will try to dance around a bit, but there's no way he can refuse us. I will have my Sparrow at the apartment," said Dominika. "She will make an appearance, as a reminder of what a *shalun,* what a naughty boy, scientist Jamshidi has been."

"Have you considered," said Nate, "that if our little operation hits a bump, if Jamshidi starts squawking, the Center's eventually going to want to know if your Sparrow was part of this false flag op, how much she knew. If this goes badly, they'll chop her into little pieces."

Dominika wondered how many pieces they would get out of Udranka's 1.85 leggy meters. "She's got nowhere to go," said Dominika. "She has nobody."

"I think we should include her in a contingency exfiltration plan if we have to bug out," said Nate.

Dominika looked at him in the dark bar. "You would do that?"

"She's part of the operation now," said Nate. Concern for the benighted girl was not the whole story, thought Nate. If they had to withdraw, getting the Sparrow to safety would cauterize any flap. Still, Dominika was visibly touched. She smiled at him.

They looked at each other across the little plastic table, half of their faces faintly illuminated by the light behind the bar. They didn't touch; they didn't speak. Dominika could feel the electrons jumping the gap between them, could feel them in her heightened heartbeat. Her eyes darted over his face—his mouth, his eyes, the lock of hair on his forehead. He was looking at her, and she imagined the feel of his skin against her. She told herself she would not start anything—*she would not*—even though she needed him. She needed him to ease the burden that came with her new life as a mole, a betrayer of her country, living one step from the execution chambers. But she would not.

Nate looked at her, saw her lips trembling. In Helsinki he would have gathered her up and taken her to bed. Not now. She had reemerged from Moscow, was willing to resume work as their—his—penetration agent. Nate would not jeopardize it, would not disrespect MARBLE's memory. As he looked at Dominika's backlit hair, Nate thought of what had to be done.

His purple aura, normally steady, always constant, suddenly wavered in the night air. In a flash Dominika's remarkable intuition told her that he still struggled with his professional discipline, even as he fought the passion she could see in his eyes. She knew she could not again bear to see the light fade from his eyes as they lay beside each other in bed.

"We will talk about taking care of my Sparrow later," said Dominika. "Right now, we both need some sleep."

"Do you want me to stay with you tonight?" said Nate, thinking operationally. Dominika knew what he meant. The fizz had gone out of the evening.

"I think not, Neyt," said Dominika.

They paid the bill and walked down quiet streets to Dominika's front door. Nate looked at her and the case officer in him knew what she had decided and precisely why. Correct. Prudent. Secure. Dominika gave him a light kiss on the cheek, turned, and went inside without looking back at him.

In her apartment, her eyes closed, Dominika stood with her back against the bedroom door, her arms wrapped around herself. She listened for some sound from the street below, the sound of him buzzing to be let in, so she could throw open the door and wait for him to come bounding up to the landing, into her arms.

She kicked off her shoes, pulled her dress over her head, and flopped onto the single bed, sinking into the plush comforter, trying not to think about Nate, or the bastards in the Center, or tomorrow's operation with Jamshidi, so very risky, or her itchy scalp and the wet between her legs that wouldn't go away. Dominika rolled over with a groan, hesitated, then reached for *prababushka*'s brush on the nightstand beside the bed. Great-grandmother's brush. She held it in her hand, familiar yet forbidden. She knew that in three minutes she could be shuddering, eyes rolled back white behind fluttering lids, and then asleep two minutes after that. She looked for one of her friends in the dark corners of the room, but there were no mermaids tonight. Only the memory of Nate, and of his earnest, pained expression when talking about himself, and of his darting eyes when they were walking along dark streets, and of his expression when he looked at her.

With another groan she tossed the hairbrush clattering into the corner of the room, turned over onto her stomach, and contemplated a restless night.

PRATER PARK SAUERKRAUT BALLS

Sauté onions and minced garlic in butter, stir in minced ham and flour, and cook till browned. In a bowl, mix drained sauerkraut, egg, parsley, and beef stock, then add to the skillet and cook into a stiff paste. Cool. Roll into balls, dip in flour, then egg wash, then bread crumbs, and fry till golden brown.

7

Nate had taken some care with his disguise as an SVR Line X nuclear analyst. Disguise for close-up use is as much art as science, less a matter of a false mustache or colored contact lenses than a limited number of minute details taken together that give an impression, establish the visual image that lets the observer's mind take over and complete the illusion. At dusk they met at the rendezvous point. Dominika closely inspected the finished product.

She approved the haircut he had gotten that morning, short and high on the sides. The plain three-button jacket was in vogue from the Alps to the Urals. The necktie he had chosen was all wrong ("No Muscovite would wear such a thing"), so they decided he would simply wear his light-blue shirt with the long-point collar unbuttoned. The shoes were Polish, with flat, squared toes, purchased at a discount shop ("Revolting," said Dominika. "Make sure he sees them") and the eyeglasses had clear lenses and cheap gold metal frames. She was satisfied with the look.

That afternoon Nate had met a Vienna Station officer for a thirty-second timed meet to be passed a street-expedient disguise kit from the Office of Technical Services. The OTS kit contained a gold tooth overlay crown, silicon rolls to lift the cheekbones, wedge inserts for inside a shoe to create a limp, hair-coloring wands, mustaches and spirit glue, a stick-on face mole, and a small bottle of a chemical (with applicator) that temporarily would create a port-wine stain on the back of a hand or the side of the neck. Nate decided to use only the last of these.

"Nothing distracts quite as effectively as a small detail," Nate told a skeptical Dominika, who looked at the spidery purple splotch on the back of Nate's left hand. "You guys missed *glasnost* because you were all staring at Gorbachev's head for three years."

"*Nekulturny.*" Dominika sniffed as they turned toward Udranka's apartment. They both automatically, wordlessly, walked a looping route, glancing up and down the street as they crossed, finding a double corner and watching for any reaction, and finally nodding to each other that both were satisfied they were black. On the street Dominika worked hard, but with a little envy saw that Nate was consistently flawless in this environment.

As they silently climbed the darkened stairs in Udranka's building, Nate reached out and caught Dominika by the wrist. He pulled her to face him, halfway up the curved staircase. Faint noises from behind apartment doors floated up the stairwell.

"Before we go in," he whispered, "I want to tell you how good it is to work with you again." He still held her wrist in his hand. She said nothing, unsure of what to do, of what this meant. "This operation, with the Iranian, is inspired. If it works we can change the whole equation." He smiled at her like a schoolboy, his purple halo around his shoulders. *Seal this with a kiss?* she thought. No, she was not going to risk her pride anymore.

"And I like working with you," said Dominika, lifting up his hand and looking at the colored blotch, "even if you look like a *napevat,* a troll living under a bridge." She gently freed her hand from his grasp. "Come on, we have a half hour before our horned owl arrives."

In the apartment Udranka silently appraised Nate with an eye that took in his slim figure, his hands, the line of his jaw. A Sparrow assessing an earthworm. She looked significantly at Dominika as if to say, "How is he in bed?" Udranka wore a rust-colored minidress, tight across the chest and around the haunches, and black heels that made her even taller. As Dominika fiddled in the concealed cabinet to dismantle the Center's video and audio equipment, Udranka sat down beside Nate on the couch.

"You are from Moscow?" she asked in Russian.

"Yes, I arrived last night," said Nate. He had memorized the Aeroflot schedules that morning, anticipating that Jamshidi might ask the same question.

"And you have worked with Egorova before?" she said. Udranka did not know Nate was an American case officer. It was prudent that she never know.

"No, this is the first time." Nate was about to compliment Udranka on the job she had done with the Iranian but stopped himself. No mere SVR analyst who was focused solely on the upcoming debrief would dip into such operational details.

Udranka looked him over from her seat on the couch. She crossed her legs, the muscles of her thighs moving, the start of the seductive swell of her bottom just visible beneath the dress. "I would have guessed that you two know each other," she said, looking up at Dominika, who had come back into the room. "The way you walked in together, I don't know."

"Let's leave the guessing games for later, *devushka,* girlfriend," said Dominika, smiling.

"Well, I like him," said Udranka. "He's got a good face."

"Do you think so?" said Dominika.

"Of course, don't you?" said Udranka. Nate unzipped his satchel, avoiding her eyes.

"But a studious expert from Moscow?" said Udranka, looking at him with a sideways glance. "I think not."

"Stop talking and fetch the tray," said Dominika.

Udranka smiled and went into the kitchen. She returned carrying a tray with glasses and a bottle of scotch. She leaned over the low table in front of the couch to put it down, giving Nate a prolonged look right out of the playbook. He suddenly understood what it must have been like being a Christian in the Colosseum of ancient Rome, waiting for the lions. Dominika saw it all, one Sparrow to another, and looked at Nate.

"Once a *vorobey,* always a Sparrow," she said, and Udranka laughed, straightened, walked back into the bedroom, and softly closed the door. *These Russians know their business,* Nate thought, *harnessing this elemental force of nature.* He thanked Christ that they'd soon be operating. Just then there was a soft knock at the door.

"Gotov?" whispered Dominika, ready? Nate nodded and began studiously looking at the notes set out on the table.

They had been at it for two hours. Dr. Parvis Jamshidi sat on the couch, his shirt collar unbuttoned, leaning forward with intensity. A briefcase lay on the cushion beside him, unopened. He had arrived angry, petulant, full of indignation. He had been prepared to have a tantrum when he saw Nate sitting there, but Dominika in two smooth sentences assured Jamshidi that sending an analyst was a vast compliment, Moscow's acknowledgment of his towering talent, and the Persian accepted the flummery without a blink.

Still, Jamshidi nursed an attitude—arrogance springing from fear—and

Dominika, sitting on the couch beside him, had begun harshly establishing control. Nate's French was basic, but he saw how Dominika brought the scientist from resentment to grudging acceptance of the situation by stroking his professional pride. He reveled in it, talking science, of the inevitability of Iranian success in the nuclear program, his brilliance in full cockatoo display. Dominika understood him, played him minutely, tied him up tightly.

After the first fifteen minutes, struggling with nuclear technical terms in French, Jamshidi sat back, looked at Dominika.

"You speak English?" he asked.

"Yes, of course," said Dominika.

"What about you?" Jamshidi said, looking at Nate. Seated in a chair on the other side of the coffee table, Nate did not react, and continued writing in a notebook.

"Unfortunately my colleague speaks only Russian," said Dominika. *Careful here,* thought Nate.

"I expected as much," said Jamshidi, looking back at Dominika. "I know someone who can treat that blemish on his hand," he said suddenly, his eyes darting over to Nate. Willing his hand to stay still, Nate continued writing.

"Let's continue," said Dominika in English. "You were describing the centrifuge halls at Natanz."

"Three separate halls, designated A, B, and C," said Jamshidi. "Twenty-five thousand square meters per hall. Covered by a reinforced roof and earth to a depth of twenty-two meters." Dominika translated. *This is encyclopedia bullshit,* thought Nate, checking the Line X requirements and wishing he had notes from PROD. Time to pull Jamshidi's goatee. He spoke to Dominika in Russian.

"We are aware of the configuration of the fuel-enrichment plant," he said brusquely, a little impatience bleeding into his voice. "We are aware of only two halls, however. Ask him about the third hall; that's new."

Dominika asked. Jamshidi leaned back and smiled. "Halls A and B have approximately five thousand machines each. Only a fraction of these large cascades are operating with any regularity." Nate made himself wait to consult his notes until Dominika finished translating.

"What are the problems with these large cascades?" asked Nate.

Jamshidi shrugged. "We have been converting from early Pakistani machines, P-1s and P-2s. We are learning as we go. Our own IR-1 centrifuges are vastly superior, but we have encountered problems operating the cascades for extended periods." Nate waited for the translation, then waited some more.

"We sustained a cascade crash last year because a technician assembled a machine without sterile gloves." He looked over at Dominika. "The bacteria on his hands, which had been transferred to the inner tube, was enough minutely to unbalance the mechanism. At speed the tube crashed. I suppose I do not have to describe the domino effect within a cascade accident.

"There have been other problems. Supply of uranium hexafluoride feed stock is uneven, other operating difficulties," Jamshidi said.

"Such as?" said Dominika.

"We are beset by problems from outside Iran. Embargoes of strategic materials. Computer viruses from the Zionists and the Great Satan." He looked over at Nate, as if he suspected something. "Unknown saboteurs three months ago destroyed five high-tension pylons in the desert outside the plant."

"And what about the third cascade hall?" asked Dominika.

Jamshidi sat up. "It is my personal project; I conceived it. The hall is being constructed in total secrecy, to exact specifications. It is separated from the other two halls by a tunnel and three blast doors. We are installing seismic-reactive floors. Filtered, controlled atmosphere. It is impregnable. IAEA inspectors are unaware of it." Jamshidi stuck out his chin in pride. Nate did not react, even after Dominika had translated. *This is intel; it's heating up.*

"Continue," said Nate. "Describe the function of the hall."

Jamshidi looked at them, smiled, and almost imperceptibly shook his head no. "This is my project. You go too far." Nate saw Dominika's blue eyes flash. Her voice was honey with a vinegar chaser.

"Doctor. We've discussed this already. You simply cannot stop now. We were doing so well. We are your allies, and we want to protect Iran against those outside forces you describe, that would deny you your work." Dominika put a hand in a pocket and thumbed her cell phone.

Jamshidi continued, smiling. "If you want to help my country, then you should conclude this charade. You're asking the impossible," he said.

"What can I do to change your mind?" said Dominika. "The bonds between our two countries run deep."

"Of course they do. Russia has been meddling in Persia for centuries," Jamshidi snorted.

Nate had conducted coercive debriefings with difficult agents before. He had seen Marty Gable lift a little Chinese attaché by the lapels and actually plant his butt on the mantelpiece of a safe-house fireplace, his legs dangling, and tell him he couldn't come down until he started cooperating again. Not exactly accepted technique, but it pushed some Asian button of shame or saving face or something, and the little guy was back in his chair in two minutes, pounding mao-tai with Gable, and singing like a soprano.

But this was different. All agents have internal barriers, and Jamshidi apparently had fetched up against one of his: He would give up the larger program, but he wasn't going to talk about his personal project within that program. It defined him. The door to Udranka's bedroom opened, and Udranka walked into the room, luminous, magenta-haired, her little dress moving like snakeskin over her body. Nate thought he could see the heat-shimmer in the air above her head. As Udranka passed him, Nate could smell her scent, Krasnaya Moskva, known in Europe as Moscou Rouge—the infamous Red Moscow perfume created in 1925, the same year Stalin's OGPU sent families to the first of the gulags.

Jamshidi glanced at her guiltily, then looked away. *He's going to bluff through it,* thought Nate. Udranka passed in front of the couch, towering over Jamshidi, who refused to look up at her. She went into the kitchen, trailing a bloom of coriander and jasmine. Jamshidi continued looking at Dominika.

"Doctor, we are all human, we all have desires and needs," said Dominika with a stone face. "I make no judgments. But I fear members of your own community would not so readily endorse your activities. Don't you think so?"

Jamshidi kept staring at her.

"Much less those rather stuffy graybeards—I don't mean to be disrespectful—on the Supreme Council," said Dominika. "And think of how disappointed the ayatollah would be. And how he would censure you. And what you would *forfeit*."

Jamshidi's face was pale.

On cue, Udranka returned with fresh glasses, bending to put the tray down with a metallic thump. Incongruous beside the scotch was a dish of golden cakes dotted with raisins—*shirini keshmeshi*—that Dominika had asked Udranka to purchase from a Persian bakery in town. Jamshidi goggled at the pastries: Here he was, sitting with a blackmailing Russian intelligence officer, spilling his country's secrets, and this prostitute was serving him the confections of his childhood.

Udranka sat in another chair, directly opposite Jamshidi, and crossed her legs. The Persian physically twitched, refusing to look, but reduced to fluttering and guilty glances. Nate wondered how things looked from Jamshidi's vantage point, head-on.

"Think of the furor in your offices at IAEA if Udranka, missing you, unwisely paid a call, asking for you by name," said Dominika. "These things are so much better managed in discreet venues, like this little apartment."

Udranka leaned over to take Jamshidi's glass and poured two fingers of scotch. She took a sip herself and handed the glass to him. He looked at the tangerine lipstick mark on the rim and closed his eyes. Dominika saw that his yellow aura was faded, diluted.

Sparrow manual: *No. 44, "Maximize lascivious impact with incongruous visual, aural, olfactory shock,"* thought Dominika, watching Udranka walk behind the couch, dragging a hand across Jamshidi's shoulders. Trailing scent like a destroyer escort putting down smoke, she melted back into the bedroom with clicking heels. Nate shifted in his seat, studiously looking at his notes. *God what an engine,* he thought.

Silence in the room. Jamshidi looked at Nate, and then turned to Dominika, glowering, seething, fearful. Dominika's cobalt eyes held his without blinking.

"The function of centrifuge Hall C . . . ," said Dominika, as if the feral charms of a 1.85-meter SVR Sparrow had not been flashed in Jamshidi's face in the last thirty seconds.

What does the Iranian fear most, Nate wondered, *exposure to the mullahs or losing off-shore drilling rights with Udranka?* Gable once told him that FEAR stood for "fuck everything and run," which is what Jamshidi must be feeling right now.

"Enrichment production generally is mired at the two to five percent level," Jamshidi said woodenly. "The yield to date is approximately six thousand kilograms of low enriched uranium-two-thirty-five. For forty-eight months I have pushed toward the next step in enrichment, thrown all our resources toward making the critical jump to twenty percent. Our uneven technical expertise has been a hindrance. Assassination of key program scientists at the hands of the Zionists has delayed the push. We have been able to produce only about one hundred ten kilograms of twenty-percent uranium-two-thirty-five." Jamshidi reached for his scotch, paused for a beat to look at Udranka's lipstick mark, and took a swallow. He exhaled into the glass, exhausted and beaten.

Nate looked at Dominika to see if she saw the same thing.

"And what does Hall C have to do with this?" said Dominika, relentless.

"I received permission from the Council to assemble ten cascades—seventeen hundred machines—in a separate hall. Hall C is a technical marvel, precisely designed. New machines are being brought in. Quality assemblage, the best technicians, a goal to manage a modest cascade with utterly reliable, uninterrupted performance." Dominika repeated this to Nate.

"Ask him for what reason," said Nate to Dominika in Russian.

Another sip of scotch. "We are attempting to boost our limited quantity of twenty-percent enriched stock to ninety percent, even if it is enough for only a single weapon. When Hall C is complete, we are going to push production. In industrial terms, I am commencing a production dash, a *hojoom,* to enrich to weapons-grade uranium." He lifted his head and pointed his goatee at Dominika. "While the world inspects our facilities and Tel Aviv and Washington and London calculate the months and years it will take the hapless Persians to achieve success in their program, Jamshidi in Hall C will deliver enough material for a weapon, perhaps two, in a very short time, Allah willing." Dominika translated for Nate, and he could hear the timbre of her voice, unsettled, forcing control.

"When does the dash begin?" said Nate to Dominika. *This intel is going to rock the Intelligence Community,* he thought. *And the politicians in the White House and on the Hill will be wetting their seat cushions, frantically calculating the ramifications.*

"The *hojoom* cascade will be tested in stages—primary, secondary, tertiary ranks. We will evaluate individual performance characteristics of the new machines as they are brought online, as well as their collective ability to operate at peak efficiency in a cascade for extended periods of time. This will take a month or two after construction is complete."

"Ask him if he has current performance figures for each machine," said Nate. He glanced down at the Line X requirements, way down the list of questions. "They're measured in separative work units. SWUs, pronounced *swooz.*"

"I do not have the figures at my fingertips," said Jamshidi. *Bullshit,* thought Nate. *A scientist—whether Iranian or American—could recite the numbers from memory.*

"Doctor," said Dominika, the acid drip in her voice, "can you give us an estimate?"

Jamshidi looked at them both, his face dark and mottled. He opened his briefcase and took out a slim laptop, put it on the table, and lifted the screen. "I may have some figures in my files." The laptop emitted a faint whine as it powered up.

Wonder what else is on that hard drive, thought Nate. *It must be loaded. Maybe time to try something tricky.* Unbeknownst even to Dominika, his TALON device had been recording the entire debrief from inside a slim courier-style strap bag hanging off the back of his chair. Langley wanted it all, the intel, the voices, the Russian requirements, the Sparrow, even how well their own asset DIVA debriefed an agent. Nate felt slightly guilty at deceiving her—especially since this false flag debrief was her idea in the first place—but this was, well, *work.*

Nate reached into his bag as if rummaging for a pen, activated a function on the TALON, and put the courier bag on the table, taking care to align the bottom of the bag to be facing and close to Jamshidi's laptop. If he'd done it right, the TALON would interrogate and download the hard drive via infrared link through an IR transparent acrylic strip along the bottom of the bag. Jamshidi, oblivious, was reading the screen and mumbling.

"I will have to gather SWU values. I do not have them summarized in these files," he said quickly, unconvincingly. *That's okay, brother,* thought Nate, *we have them already.*

"Next time, then," said Dominika. "You won't forget, will you, Doctor?"

Jamshidi shook his head.

"Of course you won't," said Dominika. "But let me repeat the question. When does Hall C come online?" Jamshidi's yellow halo was alternating weak and strong. *He's conflicted,* she thought, *every fact revealed is causing him physical pain.* They could not continue to squeeze him much longer. He was fading. She began thinking about a second session.

"I will not commence full operations in Hall C without a test period while we integrate the entire cascade. The seventeen hundred machines are too valuable, our best cascade array," Jamshidi said. "We still must acquire specialized structural equipment to ensure a stable floor." Dominika translated this.

"Details," said Nate to Dominika.

"We are only in the first stages. Procurement agents from our Atomic Energy Organization of Iran are canvassing industry sources." Nate almost looked at Dominika, who shot him a glance.

"Who are these AEOI reps? What countries? How long?" asked Dominika. Jamshidi abruptly closed the screen of his laptop.

"No more for tonight," said Jamshidi. "I need to collect more notes, to gather the information you ask for." *A temporizing delay, but acceptable for now,* thought Dominika. She looked over and nodded at Nate. An agent operating under compromise was delicate, brittle, especially in the early stages. They wouldn't push him further tonight. Nate nodded back. They had gotten a lot.

"Very well, Doctor," said Dominika. "We specifically request this information on future procurement of structural equipment. We will meet in seven days, at this apartment, at the same time. Is that convenient for you?"

Jamshidi scowled and muttered, "I suppose so," stuffed his laptop into his briefcase, and rose from the couch. Nate and Dominika stayed seated—no deference, no respect, keep him down—as he headed to the door.

Again on cue, Udranka came out of the bedroom and helped him shrug on his suit coat. From the entryway, Nate and Dominika heard her low tones and hot-velvet chuckle, telling him in syrupy French that she would see him tomorrow night, make him forget this beastly business; they'd play a little of his favorite game, all right? More laughter, a whisper. Jamshidi said good night and they heard the apartment door close, then the click of Udranka's heels as she came back into the living room. She poured three fingers of scotch and took a long swallow. She heeled out of one shoe, then kicked off the other, and stood barefoot in front of them, expressionless, her legs elegant and slim in a model's hipshot pose. If she had been a smokestack she would have been trailing a plume of live steam.

"Guess," Udranka said to Nate and Dominika. They looked up at her.

"He wanted to come back tonight, late. Can you imagine?"

"It must have been all the talk about enriching uranium," Dominika said.

SHIRINI KESHMESHI-RAISIN CAKES

Thoroughly mix flour, sugar, melted butter, vegetable oil, and eggs. Add saffron diluted in warm water, small raisins, and vanilla extract. Blend well. Put dollops of dough on parchment paper–lined sheet pan and bake in a medium oven until golden brown.

8

Dominika traveled to Moscow the next morning, and Nate flew to Athens the same afternoon. A day later in Athens Station, three twitchy analysts from PROD—none older than twenty seven—had reviewed the (successful) IR download of Jamshidi's laptop, along with the translated transcript of the debriefing. DCOS Gable, COS Forsyth, and Nate sat in the Station's acoustically shielded enclosure, on one side of the table, listening to their preliminary readout.

"Some of this is going straight into the President's Daily Brief," said an analyst named Westfall. He swallowed approximately once every three seconds, his Adam's apple bobbing each time. "You have a lot here: production values, enrichment rates, feed stock numbers. PDB lead item for sure. The download of his laptop was awesome."

"The intelligence about the production dash in Hall C is going to shake up our assessments from Washington to Tel Aviv," said Barnes, another analyst. "The Israelis will be pleased. This vindicates their estimates." The wrapper of a candy bar stuck out of his shirt pocket. He pushed his glasses up his nose.

"We've prepared follow-up requirements for next week's meeting," said the third analyst, clicking her pen incessantly. Her name was Bromley and she had red hair and green eyes. *She would be pretty if it weren't for the adult braces,* thought Nate. Her face was shiny with sweat. Gable scowled at her.

"You want to stop with the pen, hon?" said Gable. "It's gonna combust any fucking minute."

"Sorry," said Bromley, red faced.

Beside her, Westfall swallowed and said, "Claustrophobia."

"What?" said Gable.

"Fear of confined spaces," said Barnes.

"I know what claustrophobia is," said Gable.

"Bromley doesn't like closed rooms," said Westfall, looking at the Lucite walls of the ACR. "This room makes her nervous." Bromley reached again for her pen, but stopped at Gable's glance.

"What about airplane toilets?" said Gable, looking at Bromley.

All three analysts shook their heads. "Definitely not," said Bromley.

"I guess that rules out the Mile-High Club," said Gable. The analysts looked at one another.

"Forget it," said Gable.

Forsyth rustled some paper. "Guys, can you highlight the most important questions Nate has to ask the source? What are the missing pieces?"

"Reliability of the seventeen hundred machines working in a cascade. That's the key," said Barnes. "Performance test results."

"Or possibly enrichment curves, once the cascade begins operation," said Westfall.

"Possibly," agreed Barnes, "but don't forget SWU values." Nate could feel Gable swell in the seat beside him.

"In fucking English, please," said Gable.

Westfall sat up and swallowed. "Think of a centrifuge cascade as a dense forest of six-foot tubes, thousands of tubes. Each centrifuge is enclosed in an outer casing, and inside it spins at a screaming seventeen thousand revolutions a minute, perfectly balanced. Gaseous, radioactive feed stock is pumped in, and the centrifugal force separates lighter uranium-two-thirty-five, which is pumped out and fed to the next centrifuge in line and so on, in a repetitive, purifying cascading process. The purer the uranium-two-thirty-five, the more enriched it is. In a big cascade, the percentage of uranium enrichment rises constantly, through two, twenty, eighty percent. Ninety percent enriched is weapons grade, material ready to be used in a device."

"Device, as in a nuke?" said Gable.

Barnes nodded. "The whole process is a little more complicated, because you have uranium hexafluoride and uranium-two-thirty-eight and—"

Gable held up his hand. "Stop. I got everything I need to know."

"So what's critical with this new development, this secret Hall C of Jamshidi's, is the rate of enrichment it can manage, right?" said Forsyth.

"Nope," said Bromley, leaning forward. It seemed she had forgotten her discomfort. "There's something special; they're building it differently from the other halls." The other two analysts looked at her and nodded their heads.

"He mentioned an advanced design," said Barnes.

"He wants Hall C to be reliable, no production interruptions," said Westfall. "Based on what the source told you during the debrief, they're including a seismic floor."

"What's a seismic floor?" asked Nate.

The analysts looked at one another, smiling slightly, as if he had just asked what video games were.

"A cascade hall has to have a floor that's both level and flat to within one ten-thousandth of an inch over many square feet," said Bromley. "The cascade also has to be isolated from vibrations caused by earthquakes."

"Natanz is in an earthquake zone," said Barnes.

"The Kazerun Fault area," said Westfall. "We researched it."

"It's a strike-slip fault zone," said Bromley. "That means—"

Gable held up his hand. "Do you guys have a recipe for cherry pie?" The three analysts looked at one another to check, then shook their heads.

"Keep going," said Gable.

"After we read Jamshidi's downloaded data, we started looking into high-tolerance, reactive industrial flooring," said Bromley, looking at Nate. "It's pretty sophisticated, built for labs and missile silos and precision machine shops."

"Tell us," said Nate.

"To simplify it," said Westfall, looking sideways at Gable, "there's a framework skeleton of aluminum beams under the honeycomb floor that's controlled by piezoelectric strain gauges, which measure structural deflection—"

Gable ran his fingers through his brush cut. "Cherry pie, guys," he said. "Keep it simple."

"Computerized sensors detect shifts in the earth and minutely move the aluminum beams and joists to keep the floor level," said Barnes. "Frost heaves, small tremors, or major quakes, the floor adjusts, stays level; the cascades in Hall C keep spinning."

"How long for Iran to get one of these floors and install it?" asked Forsyth.

"Depends on a lot," said Bromley. "We have to find out where the Iranians are shopping—they're good at hiding their procurement activity—and identify the specific company that's manufacturing the floor." She clicked her pen as she thought. "At the factory they'll probably have to assemble and test the floor, then take it apart, pack it, and ship it."

Nate looked at Gable, thinking that DIVA would have to try to find out what they needed. "How big a shipment?" he asked.

"You'd need to ship by sea," said Bromley. "Hall C will be eighty thousand square feet, something like the area of twenty-five tennis courts. Flooring, beams, sensors, wiring—it all makes a big package. Not so much heavy as bulky."

"Okay, so we find the company building the floor for the Persians," said Forsyth. "What then?"

"We prod them," said Bromley, looking delightedly at her colleagues. A bursting noise of stifled laughter came from Barnes.

"What the fuck are you guys talking about?" said Gable.

"We prod them," giggled Bromley. "Prod? As in, Proliferation Division? PROD?"

"It's an inside joke in the Division," said Westfall. His face was red.

Gable scowled.

"We mean that we get to the shipment at the factory or in the warehouse and alter the equipment before it even gets to Iran. We PROD them," Bromley said with a grin. Her smile looked like a maritime knackers' yard.

"'Alter' means what, exactly?" said Forsyth.

"It's pretty technical; we've been thinking about something complicated," said Bromley.

Gable leaned forward. "Honey, there are three kinds of people: those who are good at math, and those who aren't. Keep it simple." Nate watched the techs to see who would ask the inevitable question. Gable was floating the old conversational trick used by case officers to measure an interlocutor's rapidity of mind.

"What's the third kind of people?" asked Barnes. Bromley put her hand on his arm and shook her head.

"Look, since the late eighties, Iran got smart," said Bromley. "They've stopped buying computers from the West. They inspect everything they import from the outside. What they can't fabricate in-country, they procure on the sly." She started clicking her pen again, oblivious to Gable's baleful stare.

Bromley's eyes glazed over as she fixed them on a spot on the Lucite wall above Gable's head. "They're putting everything deep underground, immune from bombs, unaffected by satellite telemetry or other radio commands," she mumbled. "Hall C is behind blast doors, the air is controlled and filtered, seventeen hundred centrifuges are humming, and enriched uranium is flowing through the pipes. And the whole thing will be on an aluminum floor that is almost a living thing, moving and shifting imperceptibly, keeping the cascade plumb level. They're making a nuclear weapon." She stirred and looked at Gable, blinking her eyes. "They're making a nuclear weapon."

Gable's eyes narrowed. "Welcome back. Have a nice trip?" he said. Bromley stared at him.

"We get the picture," said Forsyth, "but what do you guys have in mind?"

Westfall swallowed a couple of times. "We're still discussing it, but we're thinking of substituting some of their under-floor aluminum beams with our own. We'd want to do it at the factory before everything is wrapped for shipment."

"Substitute how many beams?" asked Nate, immediately thinking about the logistics of getting into a warehouse.

"We'd have to calculate it," said Westfall. "Maybe a hundred out of thousands. Floor like this, each beam is four feet long and very light."

"So, what, we saw them through halfway, and our beams bend and fuck up the floor?" said Gable.

Westfall shook his head. "The Iranians will inspect every part, every fitting, every sensor—X-rays, spectroscope, weight comparison. The substitute beams have to be identical." His expression indicated that sawing the beams was, quite frankly, inappropriately primitive, sort of like Gable.

"Talking to you guys is like interviewing Uighurs in a yurt," said Gable, who actually had interviewed Uighurs in a yurt. "Can you tell us about the substitute beams in the next forty minutes?"

Barnes was doodling on a sheet of paper. "We were thinking about casting the substitute beams with an amalgam—that's a mix—of aluminum, scandium, and white phosphorus, with the same weight as the factory-made beams. Scandium to provide density to match that of the original beams, white phosphorus to create a fire."

"Willy Pete?" said Gable quietly. He had seen white phosphorus in use in Laos.

Barnes kept doodling. "WP has a very low ignition point—about eighty-six degrees Fahrenheit—but it burns at five thousand degrees." He looked around the table. "Aluminum burns at forty-five hundred degrees. It would act as fuel in a WP combustion."

"That's gonna take a pretty long fuse," said Gable.

"The scandium will raise the WP ignition point to safer levels—around two hundred degrees—but the beams are going to have to combust without outside command," said Westfall. "No timers, no software, no TOW switch—"

"TOW switch?" said Nate.

"Time-of-war switch, you dumbass," said Gable. That was one thing he knew.

"So the Persians install the floor after inspecting it. What makes it catch fire?" asked Forsyth.

"The S waves of an earthquake. God's detonator," said Barnes.

"Try shorter syllables," said Gable.

Westfall's smile was lopsided. "We've been reading up on earthquakes, too. Seismic shocks are either deep P waves or surface S waves. Both occur during an earthquake, but S waves are what really shake things." He looked over at Barnes, who was doodling wavy lines. "The strain gauges that detect seismic movement are essentially electric transducers. S waves will make them spark—producing the electricity that's normally part of the reactive, flexible floor—but in our hundred amalgam beams, the sparks will begin the ignition of the white phosphorus. All the aluminum turns into fuel, including centrifuge rotors and casings."

"Structural steel, wiring, piping, concrete, desks, chairs . . . and people all turn into fuel," said Barnes, putting his pen down.

"Hall C becomes a barbecue pit half as hot as the surface of the sun," said Bromley in a small voice.

No one spoke for a minute. "How did you guys come up with this?" said Forsyth.

The techs looked at each other. "It was basically her idea," Westfall said, looking at Bromley.

"Bottom line is that the inside of Hall C looks like a Jackson Pollock," said Nate.

"Jackson who?" said Bromley.

"You know," said Barnes, "the guy in the nuke shop at Department of Energy."

"That's Johnson at DOE," said Bromley, "not Jackson."

"It's okay, guys," said Forsyth, smiling.

"My vote is to drop you three inside the fence line at Natanz," said Gable. "Iran would surrender in about three fucking minutes." The analysts looked delighted at the compliment from this gruff ops guy.

Gable looked over at Nate. "You get how important this is? Iran's nuclear program, right? Enough HEU, highly enriched uranium, for a bomb potentially in a year. You make sure that billy goat tells you where they're shopping for this equipment. Nothing less."

Nate nodded.

Barnes took a candy bar out of his pocket, peeled the wrapper, and took a bite. Gable looked across the table at him.

"You three done good. Gimme a piece of that."

The Restricted Handling Headquarters cable to Athens Station drafted by Simon Benford in his trademark narrative—a style once described by an analyst in the Directorate of Intelligence as "Victorian stroke novel"—arrived several days after the PROD analysts had returned to Washington.

> 1. Kudos to Station and case officer Nash for significant first debrief of Iranian scientist Jamshidi. Intelligence on the Natanz nuclear facility and AEOI plans for centrifuge project acceleration briefed to senior policymakers.
>
> 2. Urge Station to ascertain Iranian construction time lines and report any pending international purchase of seismic-reactive flooring. Potential covert-action opportunities are being examined, and available technologies are being reviewed. Covert-action project has been encrypted BTVULCAN and is compartmented in Restricted Handling channels.
>
> 3. Headquarters is well pleased with GTDIVA recontact. Commend GTD for her vigilance and initiative in recognizing the operational potential in BTVULCAN. While it

```
is imperative that DIVA not rpt not jeopardize her secu-
rity, her reporting on high-level government of Russia
(GOR) players and their plans and intentions would be of
critical interest.

4. Anticipate time-sensitive intelligence as DIVA
becomes privy to GOR decisions and actions, necessitat-
ing internal handling of asset in Moscow. Given DIVA
continued presence in Europe for the next week, C/CID
requests meeting in two days in secure Vienna location
with asset and handlers. Request Vienna Station support.
```

Three days after she returned to Moscow from Vienna, Dominika was taken in an official Mercedes at speed on the Rublevo-Uspenskoe Highway west out of Moscow. Zyuganov sat on the plush rear seat beside her, filling the interior with a soot-black cloud of resentment and bile that should have been spiraling out the windows of the vehicle as if the upholstery were alight.

Dominika's preliminary report from the Jamshidi meeting had been enthusiastically received by science Line X, which forwarded highlights to the Kremlin, the Ministry of Defense, and the nuclear specialists at Rosatom. As no recording of the meeting had been made—every experienced field officer knew you don't spook a new source with a tape recorder, concealed or otherwise—Dominika had to present the results personally. Kremlin bigwigs—ministers, generals, and bureaucrats—were smitten by the blue-eyed spy. She had created quite a sensation.

Zyuganov seethed as Dominika had been called several times to the director's office, once without him. Then came this summons from the president's *sekretariat. Thank God Zyuganov was included,* thought Dominika. She could feel the dwarf's resentment smoldering like a hot brick wrapped in wool.

Driven by a uniformed farm boy with red ears, the car careered off the Rublyovka at the town of Barvikha, past the iron gates of the famous sanatorium, pounded smoking dust down a country road that bordered a lake, past a score of wooden dachas among the trees, and finally slowed at the gatehouse to Barvikha Castle, one of the summer residences of the president.

They drove more slowly down a leafy lane until the pink-stone-paved drive emerged from the forest, and skirted a small formal garden with a single fountain. A light misting rain darkened the gray conical turrets of the castle—more a château than a castle, thought Dominika—as they stopped at an entrance at the base of one of the turrets. A white-coated butler waited at the top of the steps. There were a half dozen black cars parked in the front drive: Mercedeses, BMWs, a shark-nosed Ferrari. Zyuganov fussily got out of the car and unnecessarily said "Come on" as he climbed the steps. His black bubble was pulsating with excitement.

The dwarf was dressed in an ill-fitting brown suit, tailored as if to hide a hunchback. A cream-colored shirt, a carelessly knotted brown tie, and brown shoes completed the hedgehog look. Dominika said a word of thanks that she was not wearing brown herself. She had chosen a navy suit and low heels as a safe compromise. *We're not going to be asked to play croquet,* she thought. As usual she wore her hair up. The only jewelry she wore was a thin wristwatch on a narrow black band.

They walked on squeaking antique parquet floors down a brightly lit hallway into a small reception room, opulent with a spectacular Kashan carpet, a crystal chandelier, raised wooden wall panels, and heavy club chairs with massive curved arms, upholstered in rich green brocade flecked with gold. Podletsy, thought Dominika, *villains; the inheritors of modern Russia still decorate their palaces like the tsars.* The aide left them alone, with the door to the hallway open. There was the sound of another door opening nearby, and the buzz of men's voices drifted out, the shuffle of footsteps filling the hall. Then President Putin entered the room, followed by a short man in a tussore suit. The president was dressed in his usual dark suit, brilliant white shirt, and robin's-egg-blue tie.

"Colonel Zyuganov, Captain Egorova," said the president, shaking hands. The same ice-blue aura, steady, dramatic. He did not introduce the other man, who was jowly and had a hooked nose, dark eyebrows, and wavy gray hair. He looked about sixty years old; his perfectly cut, crème-colored suit mostly hid what appeared to be a prodigious belly. He stood quietly to the side, his hands behind his back, a filmy yellow mantle about his head and shoulders. Deceit, greed, *obzhorstvo.* Gluttony.

"I have read your report about the debriefing of the Iranian," said Putin to Dominika. "A good first meeting." Dominika could feel Zyuganov stir beside her.

"Thank you, Mr. President," said Dominika. "Colonel Zyuganov's operational guidance was essential in teasing the information out of him." She did not look at Zyuganov.

"I'm sure it was," said Putin, glancing in Zyuganov's direction. "I want you to follow up with this scientist in the matter of the specialty floor for their secret centrifuge hall."

"As of today, it's a priority, Mr. President," said Zyuganov, stepping forward. Dominika wondered why the president was involving himself in purely intelligence matters, and, more pointedly, why he was talking about operational details in front of a stranger. To question him, however, was unthinkable. Zyuganov apparently had no such reservations about speaking in front of an outsider.

"Line KR will determine what sort of equipment the Iranians require, and with whom they are negotiating," said the dwarf.

"Of course. I can tell you that we would like to examine this procurement activity closely," said Putin. "If we can determine Iranian intentions, perhaps there is a commercial opportunity for Russia," he said.

Ochevidno, obvious. Dominika instantly understood. Putin intended to use SVR intelligence to attempt to secure a big equipment deal for a crony—a hefty slice of the transaction would be tithed into one of Putin's swollen foreign accounts. His blue halo was steady. Guilt did not intrude into his calculations.

"I present Gospodin Govormarenko," said Putin half turning toward the short man. "He is associated with Iskra-Energetika. Colonel, I want you to assist him in gaining contact with AEOI representatives." Dominika recognized the name, a former Leningrad party boss, a Putin ally, now with a personal worth of ninety billion rubles. A Paris suit, London shoes, and, undoubtedly, stained undershorts. His yellow fog drifted around him like cigar smoke in a closed room.

"Of course, Mr. President," said Zyuganov, nodding at Govormarenko.

"We can make contact quickly through the Iranian Intelligence representative in Moscow. I have a direct connection with MOIS."

"Do it any way you like," said Putin, "but prompt action is critical."

"Excuse me, Mr. President," said Dominika. "I suspect that there is scant time for Gospodin Govormarenko to satisfy Iranian requirements for sophisticated building materials. They are in a rush."

"Thank you, Captain," Zyuganov said, stepping in to block her from Putin. "I'm sure we can make those determinations in Moscow."

"If there's no time to satisfy these Persians," said Govormarenko, looking at Dominika, "what would you suggest?" His voice was gruff and scratchy, etched by decades of fusel oil in bathtub vodka. Zyuganov stiffened beside her—this was his account—and she could feel the wet flapping of his black bat wings.

She glanced briefly at the little man who had discovered that striking the tips of a woman's toes created more pain, whose face was now wet with the urgency of the sycophant, and knew he too had been involved in Korchnoi's assassination. In a flash, Dominika decided to spare them all nothing. She looked at Putin with ice welling in her throat, remembering what her grandmother told her the serfs used to say to one another: *Da pozabyl tebe skazat, zhena tvoya pomerla vesnoi,* oh, I forgot to tell you, your wife died last spring. Disaster has befallen you—you just don't know it yet.

She took a breath. "I say only that the Iranians will not wait for equipment to be manufactured in Russia," said Dominika. "If I can extract the information about where the Persians are procuring, then perhaps Russia can purchase the foreign equipment on their behalf, and transfer it to Tehran." She did not add "for a profit." Zyuganov fussed at her insolence. Putin saw his agitation, instinctively sought to drive a wedge.

"What would be the advantage to Iran to purchase, say, German equipment from Russia, rather than directly?" He turned to Zyuganov, but Dominika stepped on his halting reply.

"Mr. President," she said offhandedly, "the procurement could be kept secret, which will appeal to the Persians. The equipment is quietly diverted, international sanctions and embargoes are circumvented, a most attractive element for the Iranians, even at double the cost. And Russia—you, Mr. President—gains influence inside Iran and by extension in the region." Dominika saw Putin's blue halo pinwheel like sunbeams: the tsar of all Russia, the unchallenged master of the *Turniry Teney,* the Tournament of Shadows, the Great Game.

"You see, Vasya," said Putin, turning to Govormarenko, revealing by the familiar diminutive his given name Vasili. "The strength and utility of intelligence is unquestioned. Our Service is without equal." He turned to look at his two spooks. "Now it remains to be seen which approach brings us the results we need: Zyuganov and you through official channels, or Captain Egorova through clandestine means." He turned to Dominika. A corner of his mouth turned up and he nodded—high praise from the president. She could hear Zyuganov breathing through his nose.

They had remained standing throughout the exchange and now Putin motioned them to the massive armchairs around an ornate table. A waiter brought a crystal chill bowl with four glasses and a bottle of vodka. A tray of toast rounds topped with glistening tapenade was set beside it. Govormarenko's eyes lit up and he quickly poured four glasses and proposed a toast to future success. The vodka burned in Dominika's chest. Govormarenko shoveled a piece of toast into his mouth and chewed vigorously. He nodded to Dominika, grinning, to try the appetizer, presumably so he could have more. Food was caught in his teeth. *Meshchanin vo dvoryanstve.* He was a mud-splattered villager turned gentry. She reached, took a toast point, and tasted the *zakuska,* the hors d'oeuvre. Eggplant, rich and savory, with a hint of sweetness, a hint of spice.

She looked at these men under the crystal chandelier in the wood-paneled room. This castle at this moment was filled with other Putin cronies, the usurpers of Russia's patrimony. They were gathered here under the standard of the president to hatch new schemes to stuff their pockets and their bellies, while perishable foodstuffs—eggs, milk, and meat—were scarcely available outside Moscow. She had seen what was possible in the West.

A fine gathering: Govormarenko swilling vodka in his urine-yellow haze; Zyuganov, the beater of women, his black veil pulsing, staring at the president like a hound waiting for a whistle; and the president, sitting back in his armchair, not drinking, his half-lidded eyes fixed on Dominika. He was blue and chilled, like the barely touched vodka in the shot glass before him. Their eyes met and the corner of his mouth twitched again.

He knows what I think of them all, thought Dominika. *He knows how he makes Zyuganov crazy with the dangled promise of recognition; he knows what he's doing pitting me against my boss.* Chaos, jealousy, and betrayal were his tools.

The Kremlin curtains parted for a second: Dominika's sudden intuition was that the blond, blue-eyed president slouched across the table from her was a predator—a snake coiling to envenomate something small and furry. Then a second epiphany overlaid the first: *Putin covets.* He wants what others have. And the *taking* of something from someone is the ultimate delectation.

Her recruitment as a CIA asset had many components: personal choice, revenge, holding the icy secret in her bosom, her respect for the Americans, her love for Nate— She caught herself, *love for Nate*? She supposed so. But to these she now added her renewed determination to thwart the designs of these *vyrodki*, these degenerates, to make a wheel come off the cart. She looked at the president again. He was still staring at her and a shiver ran up her back. Could he tell? Could he divine her secret? CIA's reactivated penetration agent of SVR in the new Russian Federation—code-named DIVA—unconsciously bounced her foot under the table as she dared him to do something about it.

EGGPLANT ZAKUSKA APPETIZER

Broil eggplants until soft and blackened. Scoop out flesh and mince finely. Sauté diced onion and red pepper in olive oil with tomato paste, then add vinegar and sugar, and season. Stir in minced eggplant, moisten with olive oil, lower the heat, and reduce until thickened and glossy. Chill and serve on buttered toast with chopped raw onions sprinkled on top.

9

Over the course of his career, Alexei Zyuganov did not normally have developmental lunches with contacts, nor was he particularly attuned to the nuances of joint operations with liaisons—allied intelligence services working in concert with SVR toward a common goal. Nevertheless, Zyuganov felt the urgency of the task before him. The president had in essence fired the starter's gun in a race between him and Egorova in the Iranian equipment matter. He had to get that fat oligarch Govormarenko together with the AEOI Moscow representative as soon as possible to lever the procurement requirements out of him and arrange a deal. Today's lunch was the critical first step.

Zyuganov fumed. The winner would have the president's ear and favor. It was more than the prospect of promotion or position. He would be in Putin's inner circle; he would wield influence, command respect. Zyuganov was gripped by a paroxysm of need. He had to win. And he knew exactly how. The audacity of his plan twitched in his wormy brain.

Other thoughts: Govormarenko would be a useful patron as well. Hitching his star to the oligarch would bring rewards. While most people assessed new acquaintances in terms of personality, or appearance, or sexuality, Zyuganov secretly categorized people using a different scale. *Govormarenko would be a blubbering, cowering subject in the interrogation cellars,* thought Zyuganov, *with a low threshold for pain and a pervert's fear for his private parts.* He tore off a piece of bread and started chewing.

Zyuganov was sitting at a quiet side table in Damas, a small restaurant on Ulitsa Maroseyka, three blocks from Lubyanka Square. The inner dining room was done in Damascene decor with white walls, ceilings with geometric soffits, and square-backed chairs with mother-of-pearl inlays. The restaurant was not busy. Zyuganov's thoughts cleared as he watched the head of MOIS—the Iranian Ministry of Intelligence and Security—in Moscow, Mehdi Naghdi, walk across the tiled floor. Zyuganov got up as he approached.

"*Salam,* peace be upon you," said Naghdi in nearly perfect Russian.

Zyuganov thought he looked the same since he had last seen him: average height, close-cropped wiry black hair, a fringe beard at the jawline, thick black eyebrows over penetrating eyes. He wore a dark suit and plain white shirt buttoned at the collar. Naghdi always seemed on the verge of exploding into a rage, those basalt eyes looking for insult or blasphemy. Zyuganov had met him only twice before, but he disliked this simmering southerner.

"It has been some time since I have seen you," said Zyuganov, tamping down his disdain. "I trust you have been well?"

Naghdi looked back at him unblinking, impenetrable. "Yes, well enough," said Naghdi. *He couldn't care less,* thought Zyuganov. *All right,* dolboeb, *fuckhead.*

"I have been asked by the highest authority to contact you to begin a discussion of grave strategic importance to both Russia and Iran," said Zyuganov. "There is some urgency in the matter. There is also a commercial component of distinct advantage to both our governments."

"I listen with great attention," said Naghdi, glaring. *It would take all week to get this one to scream,* thought Zyuganov; *he would be a real challenge. I'd start with electricity, to extinguish the fire in those angry eyes.*

Zyuganov outlined the proposal quickly: Govormarenko; a meeting with the AEOI Moscow representative; perhaps participation by officials from Tehran and Russian nuclear-energy authorities at Rosatom. Naghdi listened without comment, then stirred.

"And what would be the goal of bringing our respective energy officials together?" asked Naghdi.

"It would be for the subject experts to discuss acquiring specialized equipment," said Zyuganov. "To discuss methods to divert embargoed technology through Russia to Iran, to circumvent sanctions."

"At advantageous terms to your masters, of course," said Naghdi.

Pyos yob tvoyu mat, thought Zyuganov, *a dog slept with your mother.* "The advantages would be significant for both sides," said Zyuganov, already tiring of the filigree nature of the conversation. Dealing with these Persians was a nuisance.

"And can you tell me, *tovarishch,*" said Naghdi, "how the Russian Federation, and SVR, has come to believe that Iran is looking to purchase such equipment?" *How convenient,* thought Zyuganov, *the question he was waiting for. Time to set the clockwork gears in motion.*

Zyuganov had formulated his plan after the meeting with Putin and Govormarenko at Barvikha Castle. He would not be bested by the coolly competent Egorova; he would not allow it. Egorova was too good, too sharp. Getting the intel from Jamshidi would be the simple matter of an additional debrief. He, on the other hand, would have to endure the prolonged, coy waltz of bringing these bearded owls together with greedy, headstrong Russians, all of whom would have competing agendas. Time would be on Egorova's side.

No, Egorova was going to experience a setback. An operational flap. And this animal molester sitting across from him was going to be the fuse.

"In the interests of fraternal assistance I will be glad to tell you," said Zyuganov, showing his tent-peg teeth. A waiter put down a dish of fried chickpeas redolent with cumin and garlic, and hovered. Zyuganov waved him away: This was too delicate a moment to be interrupted. "We know Iran is looking for embargoed equipment, specifically for your nuclear program."

"And why would you believe such a thing?" said Naghdi. *Amateur,* thought Zyuganov, *such games. Time to rip down the curtain.* Naghdi did not move.

"I believe you have a problem. We have indications—sources must remain unidentified for the time being—that an opposition service has compromised a ranking member of your nuclear program." Zyuganov held up his hands and smiled. "Yes, I know how this may seem to you, so sudden and all, and how worrying it is to discover a traitor in your midst. We all have such problems occasionally."

Naghdi's eyes never left Zyuganov's face. "Is this all you can tell me?" he said. "It's worthless information—less than worthless."

Zyuganov smiled again. "I understand your frustration," he said, as if reconsidering. "This is strictly unofficial—between us. Our intercepts reveal an upcoming meeting, in three days' time, between the opposition service and your official."

"This is still worthless information," said Naghdi, barely concealing his fury. This little Russian *teeleh,* this dwarf, was playing with him.

Zyuganov looked down at his hands, as if considering whether to violate the rules and pass a secret. He looked up. He had decided. "Strictly between us, agreed?" They both knew there were no confidences, ever, but Naghdi nodded, eyes blazing. "And we can move ahead in facilitating the meeting between our officials?"

Naghdi nodded again. His lips were quivering and Zyuganov contemplated stringing him along a while longer, but decided against it. "You will do well to look in Vienna. It appears that one of your esteemed nuclear officials there has strayed somewhat. The opposition service is particularly adept at compromising otherwise honorable people. You know what I mean."

"Zion," spat Naghdi. Zyuganov let the word drift in the air. If the Persians wanted to shit in their pants over Israel, they were welcome to do so.

"I would suggest you begin any counterintelligence operation discreetly," said Zyuganov. "The opposition is usually very good at detecting security problems and dangers." He daydreamed about a pair of ratchet bolt pliers crushing Naghdi's forefinger at the second knuckle.

"You needn't concern yourself with our tradecraft," said Naghdi. It was apparent he wanted to leave, without lunch.

"Of course, you know your own methods best," said Zyuganov. Naghdi pushed away from the table, nodded, and walked out of the restaurant.

Zyuganov leaned back. Naghdi would pursue this lead like the fanatic he was. It had occurred to Zyuganov to add the bit about intercepts, so the MOIS would not conclude active SVR participation. The Iranians' predilection for automatically assuming Mossad involvement would further obfuscate the issue. In the end, Egorova would be waiting for Jamshidi in that safe house for a long time—the scientist would be on a plane to Tehran long before the meeting, the case ruined, the intel flow dried up. It would make a fine scene, Dominika standing in front of the president explaining how her agent was a no-show and how her case had collapsed. The operational field would be open to him.

Nate and Dominika both returned to Vienna on the same day. After nightfall Nate slipped into Dominika's apartment to review plans and to organize the intelligence requirements for the upcoming debrief the next evening. They were sitting next to each other on the couch in the tiny living room, papers spread out on the coffee table before them. Nate reviewed new Line X requirements from the Center, copying them into his TALON. Dominika was sitting back on the sofa, looking at him work. His face was intense.

"I presume this time you have your own requirements from Langley," said Dominika. Nate looked up and nodded. A touchy moment: strictly speaking, DIVA should not be allowed access to American intelligence requirements. *She* was the *agent* who provided information. The intel flow was one way. Nate hesitated, tapped the screen, and spun the TALON device slightly so she could read it. He was not going to jeopardize this operation just to keep PROD requirements away from her. Agent or not, she was a partner in the upcoming false flag session. The only information she would not see, under any circumstances, was the covert-action aspect to modify the seismic flooring destined for Iran.

Besides, thought Nate, *what's she going to do, return to Moscow and say she acquired American intel requirements? From whom? the Center would ask.*

She edged closer on the couch to read off the screen. "Thank you for sharing Langley's requirements with me," she said quietly without looking at him. "I know it is against the rules. I know it required great moral courage, as my handling officer. I appreciate that you are risking all by doing this. Even if it means the end of your career, it will be useful for me as we talk to the Persian." She glanced sideways at him. "You can trust me *dushka;* I will not tell anyone."

"I trust you," said Nate. He saw she was in a naughty mood, dripping with sarcasm.

"Do you trust me completely?" said Dominika. They were still sitting close together on the couch. Nate's purple glow enveloped them both.

"I trust you completely," said Nate, "even when you're having a tantrum."

"What is this tantrum?" said Dominika, eyeing him sideways.

"*Vspyshka gneva,*" Nate said. "Total loss of control."

"Would you like to see a real tantrum?" said Dominika. She was enjoying this. She flashed to them mock fighting, grappling, rolling around on the floor, her skirt up around her hips, mouths crushed together, a quick delicious surrender. *Stop,* she told herself.

"Ah yes," sighed Nate, "the familiar and inevitable loss of reason. Sooner or later, the well-documented *besnovati* emerges, the demoniac." Nate looked at her mouth, dead serious. She was trying not to laugh.

They sat beside each other, nose-breathing, hands moist, pulses elevated, and she looked at his halo, and he looked at the blue of her eyes, and they were different now—they both knew it of themselves and of each other. Calm down. They had work tomorrow, perhaps a second day, then Dominika would return to Moscow to resume spying, and Nate would return to Athens Station to continue his personal battle against the Center, to continue handling LYRIC. And he would see DIVA once a year, maybe twice a year, and Moscow Station would assume direct handling responsibility for her. Nate turned and started closing down his TALON device. Dominika straightened.

"Wait," she said. "I forgot to mention something. It's important. You will want to put this in your notes." She nodded at the TALON. "You are not the only ones interested in the Iranians buying sophisticated equipment." She told Nate about Putin, Govormarenko, and Zyuganov. "They want to sink their claws into the deal. The *svini* are thinking only about their bank accounts."

Holy shit, thought Nate. *Heads in PROD and Headquarters are going to explode with the possibilities:* Clueless Russia buys PROD-modified machinery and provides it to Iran at an exorbitant price to circumvent international embargoes. Twelve months after delivery from Moscow the seismic floor—the expensive gift to the mullahs from President Putin—ignites from within, and the seventeen hundred centrifuges of Hall C turn into radioactive slag for the next twenty-five thousand years. Tehran will demand answers from Moscow, Putin will be humiliated, and Zyuganov fed to the wolves in Siberia. *Holy shit,* thought Nate again. Dominika read his thoughts.

"Zyuganov is working with Govormarenko to propose the deal to AEOI," said Dominika. "It will take them longer to sit down with the Iranians than it will for us to squeeze the details out of pepper-pants."

And that's the problem, thought Nate. *PROD is going to need time to substitute the parts. If Dominika delivers Jamshidi's intel in two days, we won't have enough lead time to swing the covert action.*

"We're not going to squeeze that intel out of Jamshidi, or at least you're not going to report it to the Center," said Nate slowly, looking into her eyes.

He couldn't manipulate this triple cross without her knowing why, without her being aware of the covert action. Which was impossible. Blasphemy. Forbidden. A firing offense. There was no time to cable Headquarters; a phone call to Gable and Forsyth in Athens would be insecure. Besides, Gable would tell him to make up his own mind, take action, goddamn it, and risk the consequences. "Life's a bitch," Gable once told him, "and Life's got a lot of sisters."

"And tell me why, please," said Dominika. That tone like mercury running uphill. She was waiting to become furious, for real this time.

And Nate did, crossing the boundaries, breaking half a dozen rules. Dominika listened carefully, stayed silent. *Shit. I just told an agent, a Russian SVR officer, about a covert-action op.* He was already thinking about the interview with Office of Security in Headquarters.

"I will do this," said Dominika.

"What?" said Nate.

"Your plan. It is *genial'nyi,* ingenious. Think of the Supreme Leader's displeasure, and how embarrassed Vladimir Vladimirovich will be. And poor Zyuganov: He'll be tasting his own rubber truncheon."

FRIED CHICKPEAS

Drain canned chickpeas and thoroughly pat dry. Fry in hot oil (they may splatter) with unpeeled cloves of garlic and sage leaves until the chickpeas are crispy and the garlic is golden. Blot on paper towels, then toss with cayenne and paprika. Serve at room temperature.

10

Dusk. Nate and Dominika walked in separately on the way to the meeting with Jamshidi. They came from different directions, checking their sixes, using the lengthening shadows on the street for contrast and to pick out repeat pedestrians and vehicles that didn't belong. Nate had to loiter at the far end of Langobardenstrasse to wait for Dominika—she'd had to build in an additional loop to her surveillance-detection route to clear a "possible" and it took an extra half hour. Nate watched her approach from halfway down the block, his TALON in a strapped case over one shoulder.

He knew her elegant stride, the nearly undetectable limp, how she held her head straight, how she wore her hair pinned up. She didn't look around, but he knew those blue eyes didn't miss much on the street. Nate was dressed as he had been before—nondescript and neutral—but she was dressed in a dark pleated woolen skirt with a belted tweed jacket over a black blouse. She wore black suede ankle-high boots with a low heel, not her usual style. He looked at the boots as she approached.

"What?" she said, noticing his look.

"Nothing," said Nate.

"You are looking at my shoes," she said. She may have been a spy, a mole, a clairvoyant synesthete, but she also liked shoes.

"They're nice," said Nate.

"What do you mean 'nice,'" said Dominika. "What is wrong with them?"

"Very stylish," said Nate. This was insane: Two spooks headed to a clandestine, coercive debrief with a hostile agent, and they were standing on the sidewalk arguing about shoes.

"You're obviously quite the expert. I will have you know they are the latest style," said Dominika. "And Line T has modified them."

"Your shoes have television reception?" said Nate.

"*Nevezhda,* ignoramus. Steel toes. For self-defense. Shall I kick you to show you?"

"Look, they're very nice. You look very nice. Do you mind if I ask you whether you're clear?" Dominika looked down at her shoes, then at Nate, and nodded. He looked at his watch. "We're running late; let's go. Our boy may be there already." Dominika walked beside him.

"That is okay. Udranka can relax him before our arrival."

They entered the apartment building and walked silently up the curving staircase, both using supinating, heel-to-toe steps on the landings, to ease past the closed apartment doors without a sound. Second floor, third floor. Small bulbs in wall sconces in the stairwell had come on, casting shadows against the marble walls.

"I just cannot believe you do not like these boots," whispered Dominika, half turning toward Nate as they climbed the last flight of stairs.

Her key was in the lock and they entered the apartment—lamps were already on and soft music came from the bedroom. They had assumed their operational faces, but that ended when they saw the flies on the walls—lots of flies, the wall was black with them—and the leading edge of the blood pool coming out of the kitchen. Dominika grabbed Nate's arm and sidled up to the kitchen doorway and they looked in. Jamshidi was lying on his back, half under the table, his head propped upright against the wall, which was covered widely with blood spray. His face looked like dropped pie: Half his skull was gone, hollow and rimmed with bloody hair. The other side of his face was intact, but his remaining eye was filled with blood in an eight-ball fracture. Blood had come out of his mouth and down his chin, soaking his goatee and shirtfront. He lay completely in a pool of black blood around the edges of which settled scores of flies, drinking until they fell over onto their backs.

Nate bent to look at Jamshidi. There was no question about feeling for a pulse. He flicked open his suit coat, patted the pockets. He shook his head at Dominika: nothing.

"Weapons," he whispered, and Dominika quietly pulled open a kitchen drawer and took out two thin-handled steak knives with serrated edges. She tucked one into the belt of her jacket—like a blue-eyed pirate, thought Nate—and handed him the other knife. They straightened and Dominika tapped his arm and pointed toward the stove. The merest plastic corner of something stuck out from under the appliance. Dominika stepped over the blood and eased it out. Jamshidi's laptop case. Had it slid under the stove when he had been shot? They looked at each other. The laptop was inside. Had he brought what they had asked for? Missing data on the Hall C cascade? Procurement plans for the seismic floor? No time to check now. Dominika put the strap around her neck and across her chest.

Music playing; no other sound. Dominika nodded toward the living room and the bedroom beyond. "Udranka," she whispered, eyes wide, fearing the worst. Nate motioned with a downward palm—go slow—and they inched along the living-room wall and peeked around the corner into that implausible pink bedroom. They stood stock-still. Dominika put her hand over her mouth.

Songs for Swingin' Lovers! oozed out of a player in the corner of the room. A small electric fan, also candy pink, oscillated back and forth, stirring the pink fringe on the two lamps that cast an even pink glow on the bed and across Udranka's naked body. She was on her back, with the top half of her body hanging off the end of the bed, head upside-down, arms trailing on the floor, eyes staring at the far wall. The graceful curve of her neck was marred by a knotted cord—Dominika recognized it as the belt to that ridiculous pink kimono—cinched tight across bulging veins, which had turned her face purple and her scar white. Her mouth was narrowly opened, those remarkable teeth partially visible. When the little fan pointed at her, loose ringlets of her paprika-colored hair moved slightly. Her breasts and stomach were crisscrossed with red welts—they looked like burns, but Nate saw a wire hanger that had been unfolded straight into a buggy whip lying discarded on the rug.

Dominika's breath caught as she noticed the bottom of a wine bottle protruding between Udranka's wide-spread legs. Dominika bent to take it away. Lips compressed and white, she flipped the bottle into the far corner of the room, where it bounced off the wall and spun on the carpet. She loosened the belt from Udranka's neck, brushing the hair off her mottled forehead, but her hands were shaking and the knot was tight. She took one of the Sparrow's trailing wrists.

"Neyt," she whispered, "help me lift her onto the bed."

This is bad, thought Nate. *We're in a red zone.* They had blown Jamshidi up, then gone into the bedroom, tortured Udranka, raped her with the bottle, then bent her back off the bed and strangled her. Russians? No. Iranians? Who else? How long had they worked on her and Jamshidi? What questions did they ask, and what answers did they get?

"Neyt," hissed Dominika, "help me with her."

Most important, thought Nate, *where the fuck are they now?* Did they just leave? Do they know the laptop is missing? Do they know there are two intelligence officers in the mix? Or did they back off and are waiting for round two?

"Neyt!" said Dominika. "Lift her up." Nate took a cold wrist and they lifted Udranka up and onto the bed. Her head flopped toward Dominika, as if asking her what came next, and Dominika's trembling fingers worked at the knot around her throat. She drew the kimono belt from around her neck and covered her with a blanket. Udranka's red toenails and the top of her magenta hair stuck out at either end. Nate stood in the entryway until Dominika came out of the bedroom, eyes red. He held her for a second, one ear cocked toward the door and the stairwell. He didn't know how much time they had. He put his hands on her shoulders.

"Listen to me," he said. "We've got to get clear of here."

Dominika looked at him blankly. "I say we wait for them," she said. Her voice was uneven and gritty, like a cracked piston.

"Wait for them with steak knives?" said Nate, knowing she was serious.

"They'll be back," she said, "for this." She touched the strap of Jamshidi's laptop.

"Which is exactly what we're going to give them," said Nate. "We copy what's on his hard drive, and we leave the laptop where we found it. The Iranians must think that no one has seen their plans. We need time for our covert action. You have to return empty-handed. You have to let Zyuganov win this one."

"Zyuganov. This was his work," said Dominika. "He killed Udranka." She searched Nate's face, weighing his willingness for revenge. His purple halo was pulsing, but not for blood, she knew. He was thinking furiously.

"Give me the laptop," said Nate. He set it on the coffee table, turned it on, and aimed the TALON infrared reader at the remote USB port on Jamshidi's computer. Fourteen seconds later, an LED winked on the TALON. Nate stuffed the laptop back in its case, went into the kitchen, stepped over the blood pool, and replaced it under the stove, careful not to smear any gore. Flies were everywhere; he brushed them off his sleeve like blue bottle snow. When he came back out Dominika was standing at the doorway to the bedroom, looking at Udranka's covered body. Nate turned her by the shoulders to face him.

"We've got to get out, now," Nate said. "Is there anything you need to take out of here?" Dominika shook her head.

"We walk away together," said Nate. "If things feel right after an hour, we can split up. But only if we're black. No taxis, no trams; we've got to clean ourselves on foot first. All right?" Dominika nodded again.

Nate shook her gently. "Domi, focus. I need you with me out there," said Nate. "I don't know what we're up against." Dominika closed her eyes and took a breath.

"We're on the wrong side of the river," she said. "This is Donaustadt; the area is part residential—houses, buildings, alleys—and part industrial warehouses."

"We don't cross the river until we know we're clean," said Nate. "You can't go back to your apartment if we're still covered in ticks. And if the Iranians find out who you are, and that there were two of us at the debriefing, you cannot go back to Moscow." Dominika looked back at the bedroom.

"There is a bridge with a walkway," she said absently. "But near the river there is, how do you say, *bolota*?"

"Marshes?" said Nate. "We'll have to wade through them."

"I was going to get her out after this," said Dominika. The hand that brushed a strand of hair off her forehead shook.

"Listen, there may be a whole team," said Nate, ignoring her. "They'll want to identify us."

"She wouldn't tell them anything," said Dominika. "She was too strong." Dominika remembered the brandy and tears. "She would send them to hell."

"Worst case, they may not care where we're going," said Nate. "They may just want to finish what they started here." Dominika turned and walked back into the bedroom. She lifted a corner of the blanket and looked at Udranka's face, then laid the blanket over her again.

"Domi, we have to move," said Nate. She walked back to Nate as he opened the door a crack and peeked down the hallway. Dominika pushed the door closed.

"Before we go . . . ," she whispered, and put her arms around his neck and kissed him. Her mouth collapsed and she buried her face in his shoulder. After a minute she lifted her head and wiped her wet cheeks. "If they get close enough, they will pay."

Nate hugged her again. "Listen to me. We have one objective: to get clear of here and get black."

"Two objectives," said Dominika. Nate's face darkened, and his halo flashed. He eased her up against the door and pinned her arms at her sides. She had never seen him like this. His voice was steady, but it was not his own.

"I'm telling you this once," he said. "Stop being a Russian. Be a professional. Maybe we'll survive the night."

"What do you mean stop being a Rus—"

"Zatknis," said Nate softly. Shut the fuck up. Dominika saw his eyes; she didn't have to read the colors. She tamped down her anger and nodded at him, registering that she loved him even more than before.

As if to announce their departure, the front door of the apartment building squeaked when they opened it. Both spies used one-second eye shifts to check either side of the street. *Are you bastards there? We're coming out.* They turned right immediately and moved down the sidewalk. Nate kept his hand on Dominika's arm and reined her in from walking too fast. Nothing triggers the pack-pursuit instinct of a surveillance team faster than a rabbit bolting. Keep it slow, consistent, and reassuring.

There was a chill in the air—or was it them shivering?—and the night sky was covered in clouds bleached chalky by the mild city-glow of Vienna. It was relatively early, the streets not quite empty—a car passed, and a few last pedestrians hurried home. Lamplight from apartment windows cast inky shadows between the cars parked tightly along either curb. Dominika squeezed Nate's arm and unobtrusively pointed her nose at a man walking slightly ahead of them on the other side of the street. No bells went off—it was the way he walked, the set of his shoulders—and Nate shook his head slightly. *A casual; drop him.* They continued walking straight, shielded by parked cars and the loom of middle-class apartment buildings. Nate wanted to walk straight—no turns, no reverses, yet—to lock in whoever was following and stretch them out.

Nate's thoughts raced. If there were Iranians out there—had to be them—it would be a special surveillance team, maybe Qods Force or that

Unit 400, which did its own version of *mokroye delo,* wet work, for the mullahs. If they were going to try something, it wouldn't be before they verified who Nate and Dominika were, and that would be the end of DIVA's career as CIA's penetration of SVR.

Time check. Almost 2300. The street grew quiet, and there were fewer lights on in the buildings. Nate walked, listening for footsteps on the pavement behind them, for the soft squeal of tires ahead at the next corner, for the ill-timed scratch of a match ahead of them. Nothing. He could see Dominika spotting to her right and left, quick glances made without turning her head or shoulders. He caught her eye; she looked worried. Nate was worried. They had been out for fifty minutes, and they hadn't seen what top pros call anomalies—not a single demeanor error, no car caught out of position, no three men smoking on a street corner then hurriedly separating, as if strangers. The trouble was that Nate and Dominika both knew what they felt: There was coverage out there. And two dead people in that candy-cane apartment, with the blood, and the flies, and the lampshade fringe stirring. And the nuclear secrets of Iran in the tablet around Nate's neck. And Dominika's single-shot lipstick gun effective out to two meters, first developed on Stalin's orders in 1951 to shoot an East German traitor in Berlin. And two cheap steak knives.

They approached a corner—Langobardenstrasse and Hardeggasse—and the shadow of a man stepped out of a doorway and walked ahead of them, keeping a half-block distance. At the next corner, he peeled off down a cross street and disappeared. A woman with a long coat and head scarf hurried past them on the opposite side of the street, and Dominika whispered without moving her lips that the woman carried no purse, or string bag, or parcel. *Maybe we're stretching them a little,* thought Nate, *and they had to throw some feet closer in.*

They picked a narrow little street—Kliviengasse—that ended in a set of steps down to a path through backyard gardens. Nate stopped Dominika with an arm, and they stood in the shadows and listened. Nothing. They were tight with the tension, weary from the stress. The night wind had come up a little and there were wind chimes on someone's back porch, and a dog barked, and a wooden gate swung in the breeze, clattering as it hit the latch. Nate looked at Dominika and she shrugged, *I don't know.* He leaned toward her and put his mouth next to her ear.

"Time to go provocative," he whispered. Ratchet up the pace, complicate the route, make them choose between hanging back, staying discreet, and losing the eye, and moving closer and showing themselves. Dominika turned her lips to his ear.

"How provocative?" she said. It was insane to be flirting out here, with some amorphous black beast stalking them, but the tension was making her jittery. Nate's halo flared, not in anger, she noted, but he took her by the hand and pulled. They turned south on Augentrostegasse, stopped for thirty seconds, then ran west on Orchisgasse, crouched behind a fence for two minutes, then ran south again on Strohblumengasse, narrow little lanes with smaller buildings, and more garden plots. At one turn, they saw the silhouette of a woman under a tree. *How?* The night was very quiet as Nate and Dominika walked past a boarded-up swimming camp with a log cabin and furled umbrellas—Strand Stadlau beach was a miserable grassy plot on the Danube canal, but the bare bulb over the cabin cast a shadow of a man standing stock-still, the toes of his shoes showing from around the corner. *Jesus Christ,* thought Nate, *for two hours we've been pushing an aggressive, stair-stepping foot route, turning corners, changing directions, and this guy is here* ahead *of us.*

It was getting colder. They could smell the river, and the mud, and the spilled fuel oil in the marshes ahead. They walked south on Kanalstrasse, then jogged west on Múhlwasserstrasse, heading toward the green and red lights of a rail semaphore about a half mile away. *Let them get around a rail yard,* Nate thought, but he was feeling a little nervous now, a little impatient—it's not panic unless you start screaming—and he hurried a bit more, listening for the sound of running, or the bumblebee buzz of a motorbike, or the squelch break of a radio. They high-stepped over a single set of rails, then two, then five, slipping on black tarry ties, the smell of diesel in their noses. Standpipes throughout the rail yard—curved pipes coming out of the gravel—vented dripping steam that was blown sideways in the rising wind, and they ran through the sour plumes, and over more rails, toward a group of warehouses in a row.

There was runny mud around the warehouses, and rusted engine parts, and tilted rolling-stock axles, and cracked iron wheels on their sides; they saw the black maw of an open warehouse door and ran up the sloped ramp and inside, then sat on a wet cement floor with their backs to a splintered wooden crate and eased their aching legs. Nate was thirsty and cursed himself for not thinking of bringing water. A leak in the roof dripped rainwater into a large puddle on the floor with a metronome *plop-plop.*

"How many of them?" said Dominika, her head back and resting. Her designer boots were muddy and scuffed.

"I don't know," said Nate. "More than a dozen. I've never seen anything like this."

"How are we going to get across the river?" said Dominika. Nate looked at her and thought wildly about making a run for the front gate of the US Embassy. No. Impossible. It would burn Dominika and be the end of the DIVA case. But at least they would be alive. *Jesus, no.* Nate could already hear Gable screaming at him.

"Gable told me something once," said Nate, sitting up. "What the Iranians did in Beirut, what they taught Hezbollah." Dominika was too tired to turn her head.

"They used surveillance to drive a target into a funnel—a street or an alley or a deserted square—where they could use a scope."

"What does that mean?" said Dominika, looking over at him.

"A rifle, a sniper, who has the position and range already dialed in."

"Do you think we are being herded?" said Dominika. "How could they?"

"Every turn we've taken since the apartment, we've gotten a hit. They're putting people in our way, and we've responded by moving away from them. In the direction they want."

"So where are they pushing us?" said Dominika. The clank of metal on metal came from outside. Dominika got to her feet and looked at the entrance to the warehouse, then motioned him to move. Nate followed Dominika to flatten against the warehouse wall, partially behind a rusted electrical conduit. They did not breathe. There was no moonlight, yet a faint shadow preceded the single figure as it walked up the ramp and stopped, hands on hips, to survey the dim, sprawling interior of the warehouse. Dressed in dark jeans and a nondescript jacket, the figure turned directly toward Nate and Dominika—they were invisible in the shadows—and started walking toward them. Nate reached for Dominika's sleeve to signal her not to move, but as the person drew even with them, Dominika's arm shot out in a backhand strike to the base of the nose with the sullen slap of a bat hitting a side of meat.

A surprised grunt morphed into a liquid gurgling as the man staggered back a few steps and sat down heavily on the floor, hands holding his ruined nose, now flowing with blood and swelling closed. Dominika squatted beside the choking man, grabbed a fistful of hair, and turned his head to look directly into her face. Beneath furry dark eyebrows, the man's wide-open eyes were jet black. His chin was covered in blood, mouth open to breathe. Dominika leaned close to him.

"*Hvatit,* enough," said Nate.

Dominika ignored him. "Her name was *Udranka,*" said Dominika, shaking the man's head by the hair.

The man knew. He looked at Dominika and whispered *Morder shooreto bebaran,* curse the person who washes your dead body, go straight to hell, as Dominika wrenched his head violently to one side, exposing his throat, and shivered the tip of the steak knife into the crook between his neck and collarbone, holding his head still. *Be about right,* thought Nate, *carotid artery, four seconds.* The man's eyes went wide, his legs twitched, and his head went back. Dominika took her hand out of his hair and let him fall backward to the floor with a thud.

Dominika straightened and looked at Nate. "Do not tell me anything," she said. "I do not care what you think."

The man's eyes looked up at the ceiling. "*Udranka,*" said Dominika again, looking down at him. Dominika bent and unzipped his jacket, flipped it open, and felt the man's pockets. She held up a phone, which Nate took, powered off, and tossed into the darkness. They could not speak or understand Farsi, and they didn't need to carry what was essentially a beacon to make it easier to track them. Dominika wiggled a small handgun out of an inner pocket and handed it to Nate. A German Walther, mag fully loaded; it looked like .380 caliber, what Gable would call a purse gun, but Nate checked the safety and put it in his pants pocket. Nate regretted interrupting this biblical moment, but he grabbed Dominika by the shoulder and pulled her away before she began sawing the Iranian man's head off with the steak knife for a trophy. She shrugged off his hand and glared at him.

They slipped out a broken back door and through a fenced supply yard, weaving through twenty derelict engine blocks tumbled widely in the mud like giant dice strewn in melted chocolate. The last warehouse in the row was close to a stand of trees, and they quickly got into the shadows and stopped to listen. They could hear the roar of the traffic crossing the Praterbrücke over the Danube; the hulk of the bridge loomed beyond the trees.

"When they find that man they will all come," said Dominika. Her face was ashen and determined. Nate peered into the night, looking for movement. She put her hand out to stroke his cheek, an unspoken apology. He was fighting to protect her, and she had been out of her head.

"I think we have to risk crossing the bridge," said Nate. "I thought we could wait, but we can't stay out here in the dark. We can't last out here." He put his arms around Dominika's shoulders. "We have to get into the city."

Dominika nodded.

"We work our way through the trees to the bridge," said Nate. "You say there's a walkway underneath?"

Dominika nodded, then looked up at him in alarm. "Neyt. No. That is where they will shoot. It is a straight catwalk under the bridge. It is lit with neon bulbs. Of course. It is a *zasada,* an ambush. They can shoot from either end, and there is no cover when crossing." It was then that they heard the sound of footsteps crunching on the forest floor, several pairs of footsteps, coming quickly. Had they found the man in the warehouse so soon? They were coming for blood. Nate gestured with his head and they both started running through the trees, around clumps of brush and vines, over forest litter, Nate all the time feeling the icy patch between his shoulder blades where the bullet would hit. Dominika was three steps ahead of him, running well, when she ran hip deep into a marshy patch and fell face-first into brackish water. She got up spluttering, and was about to grasp Nate's extended hand when she instead clasped her hand over his mouth and pulled him down among the tall weeds at the edge of the little bog. The stinking water seeped into their clothes, and got into their noses. Dominika held her lipstick gun out of the water, and Nate quietly shook his pistol dry. A misfire would kill them both.

"They are coming through the trees," said Dominika. "Two of them." Nate could see two silhouettes moving forward. There had been a plague of silhouettes tonight, phantoms all around them—on the street, behind buildings, under trees—herding them as delicately as a collie curls around a flock of sheep. It was getting late and Nate knew they were in considerable danger. The approaching silhouettes were spaced a small distance apart. By their size and shape, Nate estimated they were a woman and a large man, dressed in black jeans and dark jackets. He saw a glint of metal in the woman's hand. They approached with purpose, making enough sound to be heard, looking to the sides and behind—these two were driving them toward the bridge. Nate knew he and Dominika were running out of space—they had to begin moving in the opposite direction, maybe lie flat in the water and reeds and let these two walk past and try to break through.

Dominika's tactical solution was somewhat more Gothic. She whispered in Nate's ear, "I will eliminate the one on the left. Can you shoot the other one?" She looked at him as if she were discussing a recipe for raisin bread. Nate hefted the little automatic in his hand, then looked at the approaching surveillants, now about seven feet away, and tried to remember the precepts of shooting. *Combat pistol distance, focus on the front sight, lock the wrist, press the trigger, don't jerk it.*

In the instant before she moved, Dominika bizarrely thought of her father, and Korchnoi; she turned and looked at Nate, reaching out and squeezing his hand briefly. He was adjusting his crouch to time his jump to hers—he was intense, pale, determined. His purple aura pulsed with his heartbeat, and Dominika told herself she would not let him be harmed.

The woman in front of Dominika was wearing a motorcycle helmet, and Dominika lifted herself out of the cattails, streaming water. Smoothly and without haste she stepped forward and put the lipstick tube against the clear visor of the helmet and pushed the plunger. There was a *click* and the plastic instantly looked like the bowl of a blender processing tomatoes and tofu. Her frontal lobe now the consistency of summer gazpacho, the woman collapsed in a heap.

Meanwhile, Nate also stood up from behind the tall grass, raised the pistol in both hands, put the little white dot of the sight on the bridge of the man's nose, and squeezed the trigger three times. There were three indistinct *pops*—the little gun did not buck in his hand, and Nate was able to keep the barrel level. He looked up at the Persian. The big man shook his head and a knee began to buckle, but there was an ugly automatic in his hand coming up slowly, so Nate got down over his sights again and shot him twice more in the forehead. The man fell backward, arms flung to the side, reflexively squeezing the trigger twice, the rounds going into the night sky. "Lady's gun," Gable would have said. Nate walked over to the man with the pistol ready, but he was down.

Terrific. Now Nate had a story to tell some young case officer, just as Gable had told *him* stories about *his* shootouts. The Persian's face was marked by four small black dots ringed in red—two in one cheek and two in his forehead. Nate's hands were shaking, and he had an overarching sense of having screwed up—he could have run the SDR better, kept these people away from them, evaded them more cleverly. *Shut the fuck up,* Gable told him in his head. They had to defend themselves; this was not some cat-and-mouse surveillance in Moscow or Washington. This night was supposed to end with Nate and Dominika facedown in the marsh water, or flopping sodden over the downriver floor weirs, or crumpled backward on top of each other on the walkway under the Praterbrücke. And the evening was still young. There were more silhouettes moving around out there, and a shooter lying on a mat, smelling the gun oil on his hands, resting his chin on his arm, face green from the tritium-illuminated reticle in his scope.

Nate turned to Dominika and saw her lying facedown on the ground, arms underneath her, legs crossed at the ankles. Disaster. He rolled her over, wiped the dirt from her cheek, and roamed his hands over her body, the familiar contours, the sweet curves, looking for wounds, questing for pumping blood. Nothing. Her head lolled back, loose on her neck, and Nate shook her gently, frantically. She groaned. Nate supported her head and felt her skull; his fingers came away red and wet. Scalp wound. The 9mm round had creased her head, a matter of a millimeter from death, the width of the metal jacket on the slug. The contraction from the dead trigger finger of the man had clipped his agent, this blue-eyed gladiator, this passionate woman with uncommon courage and a volatile temper, the woman he loved. She could have been dead in his arms, but they'd had a little luck and he was going to get her to safety. He cradled her head and spoke into her ear. Another groan, and her eyes fluttered open.

"Domi," said Nate urgently, in Russian, "*Vstan',* come on, get up!" She looked at him vacantly, then her eyes focused and she took a deep breath. She nodded.

"Help me up, *dushka,*" she said, but she was slurring her words. He lifted her carefully and put her arm around his neck, stooping to pick up his TALON case and looping it over his shoulder.

"Come on," said Nate, "we can backtrack, get away from the river." Dominika stiffened up.

"Do not go near the big bridge," she slurred. "Another bridge," she said, pointing limply downriver. "Railroad, five hundred meters downriver. We can walk on the rails. We can reach my safe house. It is not too far. I can make it." She stumbled as she said it and slipped out of his grasp. She was on her hands and knees, head bowed, and Nate leaned over again and picked her up.

"Come on, baby," said Nate automatically. A fierce determination to save her welled up in him with exceptional clarity. If she were not hurt, she would have given him hell at being called baby. Nate took an oblique direction away from the bridge, paralleling the river. They pushed through the trees and the reeds, sloshing through unseen black water. When he stopped to listen, Dominika slumped against him, shaking from shock and the cool night air on her wet clothes. No more silhouettes, no snapping twigs—maybe they had broken out of the net, or maybe the Iranian team had pulled back, confident that the rabbits were headed to the bridge and were already stoppered in the bottle.

Nate trudged ahead, with the big Persian's heavy pistol in his belt. The TALON was banging against his hip, Dominika's arm was around his neck, and he held her by the waist. She was racked with fits of trembling, and periodically sagged against him. Nate sat her on a patch of dry ground and felt her hair. Sticky, but the wound didn't seem to be bleeding anymore. Dominika tilted her head up at him; in the starlight her lips looked black and were shaking.

"Neyt, take your tablet and go ahead," she said. "We have to protect the intelligence. I will meet you at my apartment." Nate smiled at her and brushed a strand of hair off her face.

"Domi, we go together. I'm not leaving you."

Dominika closed her eyes for a moment, struggling. "The Iranian information is too valuable," she slurred.

"You're too valuable . . . to me," said Nate.

Dominika opened her eyes and looked at him. The purple cloud around his head swirled and expanded. "Your color is so beautiful," she whispered in Russian, closing her eyes again.

Hallucinating, he thought. *Got to get her dry and warm fast.* "What are you saying?" he whispered back.

"So beautiful," Dominika mumbled.

He led her through another thicket—they had to step high as vines tugged at their ankles. The Danube marshes didn't want to let them go. Nate peeled the dripping-wet tweed coat off Dominika and put his thinner jacket over her shoulders. The hand that curled around his neck was icy cold. They had to get out of these woods.

They pushed through brush, and the stone-block pier of the railroad bridge suddenly towered above them. As they looked up, a flat-nosed, silver and blue S-Bahn train on the S80 line rumbled overhead, the arc-light snaps and pops from the overhead catenary lines lighting up their faces—Dominika's heavy-lidded eyes barely registered the passing cars. Nate led her up a slope to the rail bed and let her rest. He walked a little way out onto the bridge along the rails. The curved upper trusses of the bridge were close alongside the double tracks—inches of clearance on either side—with only a narrow structural girder running outside above the water. They would have to cross the entire bridge before another train passed; otherwise, they would have to step out onto the knobby, riveted girder above the black river and hold on until the train passed. Even odds that Dominika in her mazy condition would teeter and fall off. Once in the water, she would be gone as completely as if she had fallen overboard at night during a gale in the middle of the ocean.

Nate looked upriver. The Praterbrücke buzzed with late-night vehicular traffic. The pedestrian walkway underneath the roadway was a soft glowing gallery—contrasted with the darkly wooded left bank, where two bodies stiffened in the night air, and where a patient sniper in a hole waited for them to enter the neon-flavored kill box. For an instant, Nate wondered whether the sniper could cover both bridges from a shooting position somewhere in between the bridges, but that would mean dealing with traversing targets instead of a straight shot. There was no alternative in any case: He had to get Dominika inside and warm if she was going to survive.

They were halfway across the bridge when the box girders started vibrating and the overhead electric lines began humming—a noise like the one blowing across the mouth of a bottle produces—and the reflection from the big headlight came at them along the shiny rails like a fast-burning fuse, curving and speeding up. Nate helped Dominika under a slanted truss and balanced her on the girder, holding on to her with one hand while she gripped the steel with icy fingers. Their protruding heels hung over the flowing night-black river from which a bass note rose—millions of bucking brown Danube gallons racing to the Black Sea. The steel around them shook and Nate tightened his grip on Dominika as the pressure wave in front of the train buffeted them and then tried to suck them in, and the kinetoscope cabin lights as they whizzed by turned Dominika's face into a sooty-eyed, eldritch witch, but their eyes met and Nate smiled at her, and she started laughing, and he started laughing, and they hung on until the bridge stopped vibrating.

The kaleidoscope lights of the Prater in the distance called to them, offering cover and safety. The colder air over the river seemed to revive her, but halfway across the rail bridge, Dominika stopped, hugged a girder with white-knuckled hands, and leaned out over the roiling water. She vomited into the black, her body racked by tremors interrupted only by shivers. He held her close now, helped her walk over the rest of the bridge. Nate kept listening for the trains, but he also started surveying the approaching bank and riverside drive of Handelskai, looking for a dark lingering figure, or a stationary vehicle emitting a white plume of exhaust, or a fleeting glint of a scope over the blued barrel of a Dragunov sniper rifle. *All clear, until it isn't.* They walked through the park along Hauptallee to stay away from the river, Nate steering Dominika straight, occasionally boosting her up when her legs sagged.

They reached the amusement park as it was closing—it felt as if they'd been out all night—and they heard the sirens across the river. They walked along the esplanade, keeping out of the brightest pools of light so that no one could see the blood in Dominika's hair and on her shirt, listening to the music and smelling the food. Dominika wobbled a little. *Too much wine,* thought the old ladies in the stalls. The wobbling hid the shivering, which was coming in waves. Music from the rides and the wind rumble of the Ferris wheel was in their ears.

GAZPACHO

Blend country bread, ripe tomatoes, and seeded cucumber in a food processor with a splash of red wine vinegar, olive oil, salt, and cumin. Process until smooth. Push liquid through a medium sieve for a velvety consistency. Chill and served with diced green pepper, cucumber, and white onion.

11

They fell into the apartment, Dominika crawling on all fours while Nate secured the door with the striker-plate ratchet he kept in the bottom of his case. He picked Dominika up, carried her into the bathroom, and stripped off her sodden clothes. Her body was bruised, her back and legs and breasts icy to the touch. He laid her in the tub and started the tap, the hot water turning brown. She lay with her eyes closed as he washed her body and her hair and examined the hairline groove in her scalp. It had stopped bleeding. She opened her eyes once to look at him. Even submerged in hot water up to her chin, Dominika shivered. The surface of the dirty bath water vibrated.

"Zyuganov did this," she said, shuddering, as Nate sponged her legs, working down to her feet. It was totally, unpredictably natural: Dominika was naked and Nate was ministering to her—there was never a thought of embarrassment.

"He put an Iranian hit team on you?" said Nate.

"No. He would not go that far. But he deliberately blew Jamshidi to the Iranians."

"What happens when the MOIS tells the Center that they chased *two* debriefers tonight?" said Nate. He was drafting the cable to Headquarters in his head.

"The Persians will not report anything back to the Center," said Dominika, teeth chattering. "Our services do not share. Zyuganov has deniability. When I report what happened, they will attribute it to a counterintelligence investigation—the Iranians found a traitor—but Zyuganov will imply it was a tradecraft failure on my part. I know him."

"Do we still have a viable covert action?" said Nate, thinking out loud.

She shrugged. "Your people must do their work now, quickly. I will let you know what happens in Moscow," said Dominika, still shivering under the water.

She let him help her out of the tub, and he dried her body and hair gently with a towel spotted pink with the last of her blood, then he steered her to the bed and put her under the covers. She shivered and closed her eyes. Nate stood by the bed for a beat, looking down at her face turned sideways on the pillow, her neck long and elegant.

He went back into the living room, powered up his TALON, saw the titles, and opened the German- and English-language files: Wilhelm Petrs GmbH; Berlin assembly plant, Germany; KT550G Seismic Isolation Floor System; rated for III–IV MMI intensity; twenty million euros plus installation team costs. He knew they had what PROD needed. The lines scrolled past his eyes in a waterfall of data. Screen after screen. *Bingo*. A sound from the bedroom and he looked up.

"Is the information there?" Dominika said in Russian, standing in the doorway. "Did we get it?"

Nate nodded. "How much is Moscow charging Tehran for the floor?" he asked.

Dominika shivered instead of shrugging. "Over two billion rubles, I think; I'm not sure."

Nate tapped his TALON a few times and shook his head. "Over forty million euros. Double the purchase price."

"Of course, a lot of people will become rich," said Dominika.

"And the mullahs get a bomb." Nate put down his tablet.

"Then we are done," Dominika slurred, leaning against the doorjamb. Her hair was a tangled mess; it fell forward and covered half her face. A wave of shivering racked her body. Nate shut the laptop and hurried over to her. She had wrapped a blanket around herself, but her bare feet stuck out from underneath. He wrapped his arms around her inside the blanket. Her skin was dead cold—lingering shock, he thought—and he led her back into the bedroom. She held on to his wrist, a tight grip in those graceful fingers.

"You're still shivering," said Nate.

"*Gipotermiya*," said Dominika absently, closing her eyes.

"Get back into bed," said Nate. He covered her with the sheet, then a blanket, and unfolded the comforter over her. She shivered under the covers, her teeth showing through blue lips. Nate put his hand under the comforter and felt her hands, then her feet. Ice cold. He boiled water for tea, threw in four spoons of sugar, and made her drink it. She wouldn't stop shivering.

Nate didn't know what else to do. He quickly started unbuttoning his shirt, pulling it off his arms—he had to backtrack so he could unbutton his sleeves. He took off his pants and slipped under the covers, turning her on her side and fitting himself spoon-tight behind her. Her haunches fluttered against his thighs. She reached behind for him, grabbed his hand, and pulled it around her waist. Her whole body shivered, felt as cold as marble. *Cold as MARBLE,* thought Nate with a little shudder himself. Nate willed his body heat into her.

They fell asleep like that. An hour later, maybe two, Nate awoke; he didn't know what time it was. Her staccato breathing had smoothed out and her shivers had subsided. He moved slightly and she woke up, rolled over, and faced him, keeping her face close, eyes locked onto his. She was drowsy and blinked slowly. He could feel that her skin was warmer. Nate inhaled, drank her in. Everything was different—what they had been, what they subsequently became, what they were now. Surviving this night had shaken the mosaic of their relationship. Nate knew what was right, what was secure, but he now contemplated having broken every rule—sharing requirements, revealing the covert action, sleeping with his agent—with equanimity. This was something more important. As the familiar tightness began in his throat, he tried not to think of Gable and Forsyth.

They lay on their sides looking at each other. Dominika was dizzy and nauseated, but her body shivered—not with cold now but from desire, survivor's shock, her need for him—and she remembered the feel of his skin. She mashed her breasts against his chest and snaked her leg over his hip, kicking the comforter half off them. She reached to peel off his shorts. What had stalled between them she willed from her mind. Whatever happened tomorrow had nothing to do with tonight. She felt him move closer; they were kissing each other on the lips, the eyes, the throat, and his hands pressed against her back, against her hips. Her head swam—*idiotka,* she thought, *you probably have a concussion*—but she didn't care. His touch sent sparks up her spine and into the base of her brain.

Nate leaned forward and nibbled her bottom lip. "How do you feel?" he said. "Are you all right?" Dominika blinked at him.

"You know you don't have to go back inside," he whispered, his voice quiet, matter-of-fact; it was hard to talk and kiss at the same time. Dominika searched his eyes and put her hand behind his head, pulling him close for another kiss. His purple halo enveloped them both. She knew her secret sexual self was standing in the open doorway of her hurricane room. Will you come out or duck back inside?

"Do you think I will not return to Moscow?" she said. Her words were slightly slurred. "*Dushka*, now more than ever I must go back. You know it and I know it—we must both do our jobs."

"I'm saying you don't have to," said Nate. "Not after what happened tonight."

They stopped moving. His eyes searched hers, and his purple aura pulsed and glowed around his head. "Stop talking about work," she said.

And before the spell between them disintegrated, Dominika pushed Nate onto his back, swung her leg over him, and sat up, fighting the dizziness. Her eyes closed in concentration—it also helped to stop the room from tilting too much. Nate looked up at her half in alarm. Dominika's mouth was slightly open, teeth partially visible; she was breathing in little huffs. Straddling him, her hands splayed open on his chest, Dominika slowly raised up, moved forward, then back, delving for him, a Sparrow no-hands trick, until she trapped him, distending and electric, and her shoulders hunched in response. She started rocking—*jangha vibhor* came into her head, the erotic position implausibly translated from Sanskrit to Russian for the long-ago Sparrow handbook. She pushed hair away from her face, kitten grunts of exertion coming faster, eyes moving behind closed eyelids. Each flex of her hips stirred her insides; each time she dragged her mons across his pelvis, she felt her *klitor—what was it in English*?—thrummed up and down, like a light switch endlessly flicked on and off.

Nate put his hands around her waist to keep her from pitching to the floor when she started tilting a little. Even as he clenched his teeth and flexed his stomach under Dominika's genital onslaught, he suddenly, madly, flashed to the purring laptop out there in the living room loaded with secrets from the underground Persian centrifuge halls. Light slanting through the apartment blinds cast bent bars across Dominika's silver heaving chest, and Nate saw the strobe bars of neon lighting the catwalk under the bridge, saw the black bodies sprawled on the forest floor. He closed his eyes and saw the Persian man's eyes in the warehouse widen in shock, then fade out, pumping blood. Flashbacks. His own shock was bleeding off, too. *Jesus,* he thought, *concentrate.*

Something was happening, and Nate refocused. Dominika's eyes were still closed—she was rocking like Satan's baby on a hobby horse—her hands now up in front of her, clenched into fists, and she was hyperventilating. Her eyes popped open and she fumbled, frantic, for his hands, and she clapped them on her heavy breasts. She was hung up on the cliff edge, over the foaming sea, the rear wheels spinning in empty air, the chassis teetering one way then back. The hot-bubble sensation between her legs was fading, her slick, shivering ascent was breaking up. Exhaustion, concussion, hypothermia—she breathed a desperate moan. *"Pomogi mne,"* help me.

Help me? thought Nate. *You're the Sparrow, I'm just your peeled willow stick.* But he remembered what a lovely girlfriend in college liked, and Nate pinched Dominika's nipples, then held them firmly and pulled until he brought her down to him, her mouth plastered to his. He didn't let go. The sudden pleasure-pain took Dominika by surprise as she ground her mouth onto Nate's, and the car tilted the right way and slid off the lip of the cliff, and the familiar drum-head vibration started in her belly, and surged down her lateral lines to her feet and back again as her crotch seized up, three serious pulses, then two little ones, then the cartwheeling car hit the rocks at the bottom of the cliff and exploded, bigger than those before—combined. A stuttering moan deep from her belly wouldn't stop.

Amid the smoking rubble of her groin, Dominika dully registered Nate's arms now locked around her, and his breath in her mouth grew ragged. His arms squeezed her more tightly, the muscles of his stomach fluttered, his body shook violently, physically lifting her. Dominika's head bobbled and their teeth clicked together painfully. She hung on and rode his bucking body once, twice, three times, *Bozhe,* four, *Moy,* five, *my God,* and it impossibly started again for her, different this time, not an explosion but a resonance—B flat two octaves below middle C—that surged and receded and surged again inside her. This time she whimpered into Nate's mouth—she heard herself in her own head—and held on to him and twitched, and waited for someone to turn off the electricity.

They didn't move for ten minutes, listening to each other's heartbeats. She cleared the hair off her face and looked at him, then half slid off and lay beside him, found his hand, and held it in the darkness. She was still dizzy but not nauseated anymore.

"Cover us, *dushka,*" Dominika said. "I'm cold again." Nate pulled the comforter over them.

"Do you want water?" asked Nate.

Dominika shook her head. "I swallowed enough of the Danube tonight."

They held hands under the covers, his thumb caressing her palm, and once he turned to kiss her damp temple. Dominika was still and heavy limbed, filled with Nate in her head and in her swelling heart. He had saved her life tonight; he had bathed her body, had lain with her to share his body heat. Tonight's lovemaking was as if they had never been apart, as if they had never struggled with their passion. A rogue tremor fluttered her thighs, and she smelled him lying beside her.

Her thoughts drifted from the corporeal to spying. The immensely risky move of introducing Nate in the false-flag operation against Jamshidi nearly ended in disaster. They had been lucky. Dominika contemplated the treachery of Zyuganov. He was free now—with Jamshidi's brains decorating Udranka's canary-yellow kitchen—to assume primacy in Putin's procurement deal with Iran. *Khorosho,* very well.

She closed her eyes, her thoughts swirling. And her own future? She contemplated working in place for years, decades, as long as she survived. Would she end up like Udranka—how sorry she was for her, for all her friends, her *Rusalki,* victims of the system, the Kremlin's Mermaids. At best, she would see Nate once or twice a year, the rest of the time operating alone on the knife edge inside Moscow, stealing secrets, defying the *shakaly,* the jackals in the Kremlin and in Yasenevo, risking her life to stanch the moral hemorrhage of Russia. She was doing it for her father, for the general, for the man who breathed softly beside her, but mostly she was doing it for herself. She knew that, better even than her perceptive CIA handlers did. She glanced sideways at Nate, and he turned his head and smiled at her. Deep purple.

He had confided in her, had shown her CIA internal-intel requirements, had brought her into the covert-action operation and broken rules significantly more draconian than the nonfraternization protocols they previously had violated. But she saw that Nate had changed: He was willing now to run her on the denied area stage of Russia, to hang the albatross of impersonal handling around her neck. She could handle the dread and risk, knowing he was determined.

Nate felt his heart reattaching itself to the hard points inside his chest, beating more slowly, getting back to normal. His fingertips and toes were fuzzy numb, and he felt the bloom of her body heat next to him. He ran his thumb over her sweet hand, noted that her palm was slightly callused, as if she had been hauling on a rope, and a surge of emotion welled up in him. She was risking all, her existence, for him, for the Agency. It wasn't at all a matter of feeling sorry for her—it was instead a gut-filling tenderness for this brave, mercurial creature with brown hair and blue eyes and a hitch in her stride, Russian-stubborn and Russian-passionate. And she had calluses on those elegant hands.

They stared at the ceiling. Outside the window, the Prater was dark and still. The streets were quiet except for the whine of a garbage truck in the next district emptying bins with a roar of bottles and cans. The compressor in the little refrigerator in the kitchen kicked on with a rattle. Dominika's foot moved slightly and touched his. Nate looked at the luminous dial on his watch: 0400. The fridge compressor shuddered and stopped. They didn't look at each other.

"Of course I shall go back to Moscow," Dominika said in the dark.

The next morning Nate signaled Vienna Station for a meeting in a coffee shop a block off the Augarten and was surprised and delighted to see Kris Kramer, a former classmate from the Farm—they had begun calling him Krispy Kreme in the first week—quartering the block, checking his six, before sidling into the café and sliding into the booth. Kramer was short and dark and focused, had been first in their class, but they had not seen each other since graduation. In ten minutes Nate related what had happened the night before—Kramer took notes on a Hello Kitty spiral pad that belonged to his six-year-old daughter. "I was at home when you called, grabbed the first thing I saw," he said, daring Nate to give him shit about the pad.

When Nate finished, Kramer looked at him sideways. "Quite an evening," he said.

Nate shrugged, handed over his TALON, told Kramer the password, and asked him to get the downloaded intel to Langley immediately, with a drop copy to COS Forsyth in Athens. "When you forward the files, please send an ops cable. Just tell them that DIVA's okay and that I left the laptop behind so the Persians still think their secrets are intact. I'll tell the whole story again to Benford tomorrow." Kramer nodded, exited the café, and dematerialized around a corner.

It was eight o'clock in the evening when they met again, in the atrium café in the Hotel König Von Ungarn on Schulerstrasse behind the cathedral. They ordered beers and a small plate of croquettes with speck and Gruyère. Nate read the note from COS Vienna with instructions from Headquarters, specifically from Simon Benford, chief of Counterintelligence Division.

Benford would arrive in Vienna the next afternoon, and Marty Gable was coming from Athens—he was already in the air. The note was elliptical, but said they would discuss the next steps regarding DIVA's future and for exploiting the newly acquired information. Nate reread the note. He registered the silky feel of the paper and looked at Kramer, who nodded. Nate stuffed the water-soluble paper into his water glass. The paper fizzed and turned to the consistency of oatmeal in half a second. Kramer looked at him over the rim of his beer.

"You've been busy since Moscow," he said, popping a croquette and sipping beer. "All I hear is stories about Nash: working with Simon Benford, Restricted Handling cases, big recruitments, Athens fireworks, pursued by assassins in nighttime Vienna. And now this mysterious laptop download. I don't know the details, of course, but it would appear, nugget, that rumors out of Moscow of your demise were greatly exaggerated."

"Not so much," said Nate, blushing, and it occurred to him that the career torments of his early years were over, replaced by more serious stakes. He was working on projects other case officers would never know, had worked ops that did not normally develop in the space of five careers.

"Your favorite patron, Gondorf, is alive and well, you'll be glad to hear," Kramer said, sensing Nate's mood and trying to lighten it up. "He left Moscow Station a shambles, too scared to send anyone on the street. They gave him Latin America Division and he nearly destroyed that: Word is that on a visit to Buenos Aires, during a liaison reception with scotch-swilling Argentine generals, Gondorf ordered a drink that came with an umbrella—you don't recover from something like that. They sent him to Paris, where he is now, apparently insulting the DGSE in his high school French—you know how that service is."

Nate laughed.

"I should get going," said Kramer, eyeing the last of the croquettes. "I have to open up the house you guys are going to use tomorrow. Wait till you see this place. US Army used it for defector debriefings after the war, and now Station keeps it for contingencies . . . like when the great Nate Nash comes to town. Three stories, tower room, covered in ivy, in Grinzing, use the number thirty-eight tram."

"Krispy Kreme, thanks for all the help," said Nate. He knew what it was like, having to tend to safe houses for visiting colleagues.

"No problem, glad to assist," said Kramer. "I get vicarious pleasure watching you operate." His tone became serious. "Watch yourself, okay?"

VIENNESE CROQUETTES

Make a thick béchamel and add shredded speck (or prosciutto), grated Gruyère and nutmeg, incorporating well. Spread the mixture on a sheet and refrigerate. Form the stiffened filling into small balls, dip in beaten egg, then roll in panko. Chill breaded croquettes and then fry in hot vegetable oil till golden brown. Serve with aioli made with mayonnaise, pureed garlic, lemon juice, and smoked paprika.

12

Early evening and Nate and Dominika walked quickly from the next-to-last tram stop in Grinzing toward Heiligenstädter Park. The fluid move off the tram had not flushed any suspicious pedestrians, and their zigzag route—at one point they separated, then circled back on each other to look for a reaction—away from the station revealed no vehicles scurrying into position. Arm in arm, Dominika and Nate transitioned from "thick"—the bustle of touristic downtown Grinzing—to "thin"—the solitude of the park—and checked their status once, twice, a dozen times. They walked along the pathway, past a row of acacias with lamplight winking through the leaves. It was dead still as they turned into Steinfeldgasse—the street was gently curving and narrow, and it dead ended against the park. No coverage.

The house sat apart, close against the trees—massive, Gothic, covered totally in ivy, from entrance columns to the ragged slates on top of the square tower anchoring one side of the house. The ivy had been trimmed—hacked—from around some of the windows. The curtains were drawn and only a small light showed in an upstairs window. Nate expected to hear insane Bach being played on a pipe organ by the deformed monster in the turret. *Did the Agency employ deformed monsters?* he wondered. *I mean, apart from the emotional ones? I'll ask Gable.*

Nate thought of the desperate refugees, soldiers, informants, sympathizers, and defectors, who must have looked up at this façade before going in to be interrogated by US Army investigators in the months after World War II, with Vienna a moonscape of tumbled bricks piled two stories high, the city awash in poisonous bootleg penicillin. Now they were going inside to meet with Simon Benford, to discuss the future, to determine whether Dominika would survive a return to Moscow. None of them wanted to lose her, as they had lost General Vladimir Korchnoi, their prize snatched away by a single sniper's bullet; From Putin with Love.

The house had an overgrown yard, low spiked iron fence, and granite front steps worn to gentle scoops. The massive oak door had decorative wrought-iron straps across it. They stood for a second, listening to the street behind them, and to the house in front of them, then looked at each other: All quiet. They knocked and Gable opened the door, gray buzz cut fresh, eyes crinkled, forearms around each of their shoulders as he led them inside.

The lamp-lit living room was 1920s Austria—high ceilings, dark wood lintels, faded carpets, a milk-glass chandelier, and cracked leather armchairs. Heavy velvet curtains were drawn across leaded windows, blocking out the orange light from the streetlamps along Heiligenstädter Park. Stag horns were mounted high on a far wall. A log popped in the immense fireplace, taking the chill out of the cool night air. A sideboard with drinks ran against the wall, and there was a wax paper–lined box with what looked like baked buns. Benford pointed to them, said they were meat-filled and delicious.

There were only four of them in the room. Simon Benford, seeing everything, surprised at nothing, amused at even less. He was characteristically rumpled, his hair uncombed, and he sat in one of the ponderous armchairs blowing cigarette smoke toward the flue in a halfhearted attempt to keep most of it out of the room. It looked as if he had slept in his nondescript black suit. A pair of glasses was pushed up onto the top of his head: Nate knew that sometime during the evening he would start looking for them, cursing.

Marty Gable, square-jawed, just arrived from Athens, slouched on a matching leather couch, legs stretched out in front of him. He wore a short khaki vest with zippers and pockets. Dominika sat next to him, leaning back, her legs crossed, dangling a flat off one bouncing foot—her personal tell—nervous, excited, impatient, perhaps uncooperative; they'd have to wait to find out. She was dressed in a beige light wool dress with a wide lizard belt—it clung to her, softened her curves in the diffused lamplight. Her face was tired and drawn from the stress of the previous evening, but behind the fatigue Nate could see the luminance of emotion from their lovemaking.

It had been nearly a year since Benford had seen her: Dominika was proper and reserved in front of him, but Nate saw her eyes soften with affection when she greeted Gable again—*Bratok*, big brother. Nate was sweating it: Gable was looking at Dominika like the big brother he was to her. *Fucking Gable,* thought Nate. *He's picking up her postcoital glow*. Gable glanced at Nate across from him in the other armchair with a five-cornered look. Benford flipped his cigarette into the fireplace and leaned forward.

"We have a lot to discuss and scant time to do it," he said. "I would start with telling you both that I am relieved beyond measure that you survived the ambush by the Iranian team. I commend you." He lit another cigarette.

"I will continue by saying that Dominika's production has been superior, and we look for future reporting not only regarding her service but also on the plans and intentions of the Kremlin. Policy makers in Washington are struggling to understand the anatomy of the Russian Federation and President Putin's impulsions. Dominika, your evolving access can vouchsafe understanding, to the extent the hammertoes in the White House and on Capitol Hill are capable of understanding anything." He flicked cigarette ash on the carpet.

"I personally believe that the president has as his singular priority to preserve his position and exploit the emoluments that derive from his office."

Dominika looked at Nate. "Putin wants to stay president and continue stealing money," he said in Russian. She nodded.

Benford looked up at the ceiling. "Putin's domestic image is impeccable, flourishing in an atmosphere of ultranationalism and fading civil liberties. This is fueled by the quite charming Russian appetite for conspiracy theories about an inimical West, and is not at all threatened by either a besieged independent press or a battered dissident movement."

"Putin has no opposition at home," said Nate in Russian to Dominika.

"So as long as he is the popular lord of a quiescent nation," said Benford, "foreign misadventures, provocative sponsorship of rogue states, and warlike military gyrations—regardless of the outcome and irrespective of international condemnation—do not threaten what he holds most dear: maintaining power."

"He can do anything he wants as long as Russians do not complain," said Nate.

Dominika's foot bounced in agitation. "Gospodin Benford," said Dominika. "The only thing the president fears is angry people in the streets, like in Georgia, and in Ukraine. He does not want that, how do you say, *likhoradka,* in Red Square."

"Fever," said Nate. "He doesn't want that fever breaking out."

"Thank you, Dominika," said Benford, "for confirming my suspicions.

Whether it takes five years or fifteen, when it becomes too much for average Russians, they'll kick him out of the Kremlin."

"Dvorets v Izmene," said Dominika under her breath.

Benford looked over at Nate, one eyebrow raised.

"Palace of Treason," Nate said.

"Works for me," said Gable.

"Two issues now pertain," Benford said. "First, Dominika's security and her ability to continue operating inside Moscow. Second, the information on the Iranian's laptop, which is now being analyzed in Headquarters. Dominika by necessity does not need to know—cannot know—about the latter—"

"She knows," said Nate. He was strangely calm as Benford looked over at him.

"Nathaniel, your trademark grammar notwithstanding, I have asked you before not to speak in cryptograms. What do you mean 'she knows'?"

"I told her about the covert action. I also showed her the nuke requirements before we met Jamshidi." Dominika had stopped bouncing her foot and was looking at Benford.

"Dominika, apologies in advance," said Benford, who then turned toward Nate. "You briefed *your asset* on a covert-action operation?"

"Yes, sir," said Nate. "She had to know." Benford did not move and Nate felt the rush of stepping off a plank into the sea. "We were face-to-face with Jamshidi—thanks to Domi—and we both had to play the part. She knows the details of what they're hatching in Moscow to buy the seismic floor for Tehran. She's part of that; Putin talked to her about it personally. It's spectacular access. It's all in my report." Benford waved his hand in recognition. Nate plunged ahead, pointedly not looking at Gable.

"The Center is going to read about Jamshidi's assassination, and Dominika is going to have to explain why her operation blew up on her. We suspect with relative certainty that it was Zyuganov, but she needs a cover story about how the Persians went nuts, killed their own scientist, and made a try at her. She's skating right on the edge now.

"Zyuganov is treacherous," Nate said. "He already has an eye on her and if he hears anything from the MOIS about a second mystery man they chased around Vienna, she's in big trouble."

"The Persians will not communicate with the Service," said Dominika, "and the Center will not seek them out. Zyuganov will be focused on the business deal."

"The business deal we need to know about if PROD is going to be able to substitute flammable support beams for the floor," said Nate. "We all know this is an immense opportunity," he continued, sweating. Benford's face was a mask; he was giving nothing away. "I assessed the elements, and I tried to maximize the odds. Domi is risking her life for us, and I decided to tell her details. For her own security, she *had* to know."

The room grew silent. Part of the log fell off the grate in a shower of sparks. Gable got up, popped the cap off a cold beer, brought back two of the buns, and offered one to Dominika. They were *runza,* like Russian *pirozhki,* buns filled with savory ground beef, onion, and cabbage. Her foot bobbed up and down as she munched, watching the three Americans, reading their colors. No one spoke for a full three minutes.

"Nathaniel, you display an uncharacteristic intuition," said Benford. He got up from his chair and went to the sideboard. "I approve."

"That's it?" said Nate. Dominika looked over at him, eyes twinkling.

"No, it is not 'it,'" said Benford. "The stakes are bigger than ever. And there is a unique opportunity before us. As you may have divined, this procurement by Moscow of specialty construction material for the Persians is in fact a rare opening to massively affect Iran's nuclear program, because imports of embargoed equipment from Western sources are now routinely eschewed by Tehran. Technology supplied by Moscow would in consequence be accepted without hesitation or suspicion."

He ran his hand over the tops of a variety of bottles, deciding what to pour. "Dominika, you will be in double danger, I am afraid, because we are going to ask you to report on President Putin, on his plans to purchase the German floor system and circumvent the West's sanctions against Iran. That necessarily will require that we communicate with you inside Moscow, and that you transmit frequently." He turned toward Gable and Nate.

"I have directed a technical officer to be here, tomorrow morning at the latest. Dominika has to be trained on covcom; she has to be able to communicate instantly."

Dominika's foot continued to bounce. "Excuse me, Gospodin Benford," she said. All eyes turned toward her. "I understand the need for communications, and I will do it. But I would not like one of your satellite systems, the kind you assigned to General Korchnoi." Korchnoi had used satellite-burst transmissions to Langley right up until the day he was arrested. Letting the equipment fall into the Russians' hands had been part of Benford's plan to give credence to his capture, and to confer credit onto Dominika.

"Your concerns are understandable, but unfounded," said Benford. "These systems are immensely secure. I want to issue one to you." The two case officers—Nate and Gable—looked at each other: They would have gone in more softly, worked gently to get her to agree. They knew how Dominika reacted to authority.

"*Mozhet byt,* perhaps," said Dominika. "But our signals service—FAPSI—is now looking at your satellites and ways to intercept their transmissions; they are experimenting, how do you say, *treugol'nik*, throughout Moscow. Lines T and KR are focused on this. Korchnoi's arrest convinced them to concentrate."

"Triangle?" said Nate. "You mean they are triangulating?" Dominika nodded. *Another compartmented stream of counterintelligence intelligence—signals countermeasures in metropolitan Moscow,* thought Nate. From the expression on Gable's and Benford's faces, the same thought had simultaneously occurred to them. Benford stood and started pacing.

"We absolutely need you to communicate reliably," said Benford, an edge creeping into his voice. The blue halo around his head was intense. Dominika looked over to Nate for support.

"What about short-range agent communications?" said Nate. "Domi can send SRAC messages to Moscow Station, or to a base station, or to a ground sensor anywhere in the city. Two-way encryption, three-second bursts, low watts: If we do it right, the exchanges are impossible to anticipate, impossible to detect. She just has to get into line-of-sight."

Benford scowled at him, but he knew it was a solution. "What about it?" Benford said turning to Dominika. "Did you understand what Nate just said?"

Dominika shrugged. "Our Service has similar equipment, what you call SRAC." She pronounced it "shrek" instead of "shrack." "What I do not understand, Neyt will explain," she said. Gable looked at her, then at Nate, reading the pheromones. Fucking Gable.

"All right," said Benford, nodding to Gable. "Get the techs going on it.

We'll have to sweat the drop in Moscow, but I want her to have SRAC as soon as possible."

"You got it," said Gable.

"One thing more," said Benford. "I want you to stay up all night if you have to, work with Dominika on an exfiltration plan. We have another full day, no more, then she will be expected back at the Center. Tell Headquarters I want to issue her a secure exfil route. Tell them to send out the binder on Red Route Two. Brief her on it till she has it cold. I do not anticipate, nor will I accept, the possibility of an operational misstep, but if the unthinkable occurs, if she has to run, I want her to have the best escape route we own." He picked up a bottle and looked at the label, then looked down at Dominika.

"And you, Dominika, we need detailed intelligence from you the likes of which you've never reported before. We want to know about the finances of this Iran deal down to the last decimal point. We want to know how and when they're going to deliver this technology to Moscow and then to Tehran. I have prepared notes for you to consider regarding the ostensible covert delivery of the equipment to Tehran. You may have occasion to use it in front of Putin and garner credit for yourself."

Dominika bounced her foot. "Gospodin Benford, getting physically close to the president is not particularly difficult. He surrounds himself with cronies who do not challenge him. Being in his *confidence* is another matter. He is suspicious and envious."

"Fascinating. But can you do it?" said Benford.

"I think yes," said Dominika. "You remember I was trained in that sort of thing before I began work with you gentlemen." She smiled mildly without blinking at Benford.

Across the room, Gable looked over at a visibly uncomfortable Nate, pursed his lips, and raised one enigmatic eyebrow. "Whaddya think, Nash, good idea?"

The kitchen of the safe house was likewise right out of the 1920s, with a massive wooden table in the center of the room, heavy porcelain milk pitchers on the counter, a huge gray stone sink, and a black-and-white tile floor. Gable made sure the connecting door to the living room was closed.

"Simon, I want to talk to you about something," said Gable. Benford was washing his hands in the sink.

"Me and Nash both agree," said Gable. "Forsyth too. You know, it don't matter a damn whether she's good, or has the nerve, or whether we find the right sites for her in Moscow. Keeping her neck out of the noose is totally dependent on how good the Station officer putting down the freaking drop is. If they send a cherry out against the FSB—or worse, an idiot—we'll lose her in thirty days."

"Thank you, Marty," said Benford, turning off the tap. "I fully appreciate the situation." Gable threw him a dish towel.

"I'd just as soon disguise Nash as a Finn tourist and send him in to load the drop," said Gable.

"As much as it may surprise you, I considered that," said Benford. "But we could not with a clear conscience take that risk. We have to rely on Moscow Station to get her the equipment, and then manage the SRAC link."

"That slipknot Gondorf still isn't out there, is he?" said Gable.

"He has moved on to other challenges and is inflicting himself on the French in Paris."

"What about Moscow? Who's chief out there now?"

"Vernon Throckmorton," said Benford without inflection. His face did not move. Gable leaned wearily against the kitchen table.

"Are you kidding?" said Gable, "He's worse than Gondorf. A dreary son of a bitch."

"He has the favor of the division chief, and impressed the director enough to receive the assignment."

"Simon," said Gable. Not many people in CIA talked back to Benford. "He's a train wreck. The list of his flaps is a mile long. He compromises cases before breakfast, but the worst part is he doesn't know how bad he is. He thinks he's a fucking operator."

"That is your opinion, and it may well be, yet he is the newly designated chief of Moscow Station, with ultimate authority over his operations," said Benford, looking at Gable. "You get what you get." Gable, exasperated, tried one last time.

"I know this guy; he'll insist on going out on the street himself to put down Domi's package. He wouldn't see surveillance if it was riding in his backseat." Benford's face remained impassive. Gable extended his arms.

"Jesus, Simon, they'll pick him up three yards from kickoff: The motherfucker has a face like a bulldog licking piss off a thistle," said Gable. Benford did not react.

"You cannot put DIVA in his hands, you can't. We might as well pull her out and resettle her ass."

Benford shrugged. "I have considered an alternative. 'We are no longer operating in simple times, when history still wore a rose, when politics had not outgrown the waltz.'"

"What the fuck are you talking about?" said Gable.

"Prisoner of Zenda," said Benford. "It means we must contemplate desperate measures in desperate times."

"That's just great," said Gable, shaking his head, turning to go back to the living room. He stopped at the kitchen door. "What kind of alternative?" he asked.

"I will not unnecessarily jeopardize DIVA; there are too many risks already. To maximize her safety, I intend on placing my own penetration inside Moscow Station."

It was getting late, and a prattling Benford sat next to Dominika on the couch with an enormous world atlas open on his lap. He was using a squeaking felt-tip pen to trace a five-thousand-kilometer water route from the North Sea, through the Russian interior via the Volga Basin, to the southern coast of the Caspian Sea and the Iranian port of Bandar-e Anzali. "I trust your president will appreciate the advantages not only of maritime transport but also of covert delivery of the equipment to their clients," said Benford. Nate got up from the couch.

"Won't Putin become suspicious?" said Nate. "How is Dominika supposed to know about ship canals?"

"It will be all right, Neyt," said Dominika. "I will tell them I used to watch barges on the Volga when I was at Sparrow School. Besides, they all are drooling to make more money for themselves; they will never change. Never." She turned and looked at Benford beside her. *"Gorbatogo tol'ko mogila ispravit,"* she told him, smiling.

"Hell's that mean?" said Gable.

"Only the grave will cure the hunchback," said Dominika. Gable laughed.

Benford departed and Gable went out and came back with food. They worked through the evening. Nate and Dominika pored over maps and street footage of Moscow on Nate's TALON. The two of them picked a series of likely cache sites by which Dominika could receive her covcom equipment. She would have to case them on the ground herself. They would review the intricate exfiltration plan—Red Route Two—when the binder full of maps, photos, site reports, frequencies, and timing runs arrived the next morning. They could provisionally work out pickup sites in Moscow now. Hot-pursuit exfil, rolling pickup on the street: "As hairy as it gets," said Gable. He didn't add what happened to the agent when an escape plan unraveled. Nate fidgeted with the thought of Dominika vainly fleeing Moscow: He imagined the spotlights coming on, and the cars stopped sideways on the street, the grim men clustered around her.

The TALON's screen was smallish, so they sat close beside each other to look at the images. Nate could feel the heat radiating from her, could smell soap and shampoo. He watched her slim hands slide images on the TALON back and forth. She was totally engrossed. When Dominika went to the bathroom, Gable opened two beers and handed one to Nate.

"She looks good," said Gable.

"What do you mean?" said Nate, fastening his seat belt. He knew how Marty Gable came at things.

"I mean she looks okay after that close call with the Iranian team in the Vienna woods." He tipped the beer back. "You did a good job getting her out of a jam."

"Thanks," said Nate. He knew this was just the coda before the symphony.

"She's going to have to walk a fine line back in Moscow. This is a big deal."

"She can do it," said Nate. "It's why MARBLE picked her. He'd be proud of her." Gable nodded, finished his beer.

"Just so long as you don't send her back inside with your GPS," said Gable. Nate looked at him, then down at the TALON set.

"We're not going to give her—"

"I don't mean that; I mean your Guilty Penis Syndrome."

"What—?"

Gable pointed a finger at him. "Don't. Don't say a fucking word. I thought we talked about this."

"Jesus, Marty, I know what I'm doing. I wouldn't jeopardize—"

"You don't know apple butter from shit spread thin," said Gable. "What, you think that, if she loves you, she'll do anything for you?"

"What are you complaining about?" said Nate bitterly. "You just described the perfect agent."

"Yeah, I did," said Gable getting another beer. "Perfect until we get word she took one too many risks for you, and got caught, and they fed her alive feet first into a wood chipper." They stopped talking when Dominika came back into the living room, but she saw the two purple mushroom clouds above their heads and knew what they had been talking about—all of it.

They stopped working at 1:00 a.m. There would be another full day ahead with techs and SRAC and exfil planning. Jet-lagging Gable was asleep on the couch and Dominika covered him with a blanket while Nate placed another log on the fire. They walked up the curving staircase to the second floor and stood in the darkened hallway together, not moving.

"You okay with all this, so far?" said Nate. She knew he was worried, worried about her, and she was glad.

"*Konechno,* of course," said Dominika. "When I get back to the Center, I will tell them I had to stay inside for a day and a night after finding Jamshidi and abandoning the safe house. There will be no trouble." She was quiet for a beat, remembering Udranka.

"I want you to listen carefully tomorrow to the *spasitel'naya zateya,* the exfil plan. I want you to be able to bug out if something goes wrong."

"Yes, sir," said Dominika.

"I'm serious," said Nate.

"I am serious too, Neyt," Dominika said. "Do you think I will flee if I am in danger?" She brushed his cheek with her hand, almost feeling the purple halo around his head. "There is much I must do. They have to answer for Korchnoi." Nate took a step back.

"Terrific. Now you're on a jihad?"

"Do we have to talk about this now?"

Nate yawned. "All right. It's late. We should get some sleep."

Dominika looked at him through her lashes. "Shall I call you in the morning . . . or should I nudge you?"

"Domi. Gable's right downstairs . . ."

"Do you want me to fetch him?" she said, laughing softly.

"Charming," said Nate.

"I have something else charming to say to you," Dominika said. She leaned toward him, brushed her lips against his lips, then bent and put her mouth next to his ear. She breathed in his purple fog.

"I want you to make love to me," she whispered, pushing him toward his bedroom door.

Gable was downstairs, snoring quietly from the back of his throat. But he would know, and Benford would know, and then Forsyth. Dominika reached up and brushed a lock of hair off his forehead. Nate's purple fog was pulsing and she knew he was caught again by the old demons. She didn't care. Last night had cleared her head, and she knew what she wanted. She put a hand against his cheek.

"Neyt, I am inside the Center. I am placed in SVR counterintelligence. I am becoming close to the president, with access to information deciding one of the most important operations ever attempted by your service. I am back with you all now. I will report to you from Moscow. I know what to do, and how to do it. I know the risks. I know how to operate." Nate stared at her.

"What happened to us yesterday," said Dominika, "when we survived last night, and later on with you, I found something that was lacking from before. How do you say *ravnovesie*?"

"Equilibrium," said Nate. He saw where this was going, and it scared him, because he was thinking the same thing.

"Yes, equilibrium. Balance. I did not feel that before, but now we have it. *I need it.*" She put her hands on his shoulders, and dug her nails in softly. She looked coyly at him. "I need *you*."

"Last night. Last night was wonderful . . . ," said Nate. "But you can't work inside if we're having an affair. We need focus, calculation, a clear—"

"*Bozhe*, Oh God," said Dominika. "I am having an affair, I cannot go back inside. *Gore mne*, woe is me!"

"Keep your voice down, for God's sake," said Nate.

"*Dushka*, listen to me," said Dominika. "What we have, it makes things stronger, it makes *me* stronger. There is nothing wrong in this. Bratok is wrong, you all are wrong."

"How do you know what *Bratok* thinks?" said Nate.

"Because she's smart and you're a dumb ass," said Gable, standing beside them in the gloom, a blanket wrapped around him like a Plains Indian. They both jumped: Neither of them had heard him come up the creaky stairs.

"And I am right about what you think, *Bratok*?" said Dominika, unembarrassed, turning toward him and tugging the blanket more snugly around his shoulders. *Just like a little sister would,* thought Nate.

"You know what I think, and you both know the reasons why. No one can operate at peak performance with an emotional attachment to his agent"—Gable nodded to Nate—"or to her handling officer. Especially in a denied area like Moscow. You two think it over." He rubbed his hair and turned down the hall to his room. He suddenly stopped and came back to them.

"I want you both to be prepared for the black days ahead, maybe for the blackest day in your lives. Nash, I want you to be ready for the day we leave Domi behind in an airport terminal, or on a train platform, or at a border crossing, surrounded by FSB, without a backward glance, because we have to, because somehow, there're bigger stakes. And you"—he pointed his chin at Dominika—"I want you to be prepared for the day you knowingly let Dreary over here walk into a surveillance ambush in some provincial capital and get thrown in prison for twenty years because there's someone more important than Nash at risk and you can't tip your hand."

"*Bratok*, what did you call him?" said Dominika.

"Dreary," said Gable. Dominika looked at Nate.

"*Grustnyi*, melancholy," said Nate, shaking his head. Dominika laughed. Both Nate's and Gable's purple hazes floated in the low light of the hallway, a little alike, but different. Something in the house creaked. Gable hitched the blanket a little higher on his shoulders.

"I want you to be ready for the day one or both of you realize you won't see each other ever again, for the rest of your lives."

Dominika sighed. "All right, *Bratok*. Thank you for being *prepyatstvie*, how do you say this?"

"An obstacle," said Nate.

"You mean 'cock blocker,'" said Gable. "I can only hope."

"Jesus Marty, we didn't plan it, it just happened," said Nate. He felt stupid and lacking.

Gable shook his head. "I didn't say it was your fault; I said I was blaming you."

Dominika turned, opened the bedroom door, looked back at the two men, and went inside. She left the door slightly ajar, itself a message: *I'm here; it's your choice.*

"Come downstairs with me and have a brandy," said Gable. He nodded at the door. "Then you can do what you want."

Gable shrugged off his blanket, threw a log on the dying fire, and poured two brandies. He looked at his watch, a chunky Transocean Breitling, and rubbed his face. He pulled two thick black cigars out of the button flap pocket of his safari shirt, stuck one in his mouth, and tossed the other to Nate.

Gable nipped off the end of the cigar with his teeth, spit it into the fire—or pretty close to it—and puffed it alight with a battered stainless Ronson lighter, enveloping his head and shoulders in a greasy cloud of smoke. He tossed the lighter to Nate, who noticed it was embossed with a spear point insignia.

"Yeah, OSS logo, from World War Two," said Gable, puffing and looking at his ash end. "Some overwrought bureaucrat in Headquarters thought it would be romantic and adapted it for our clandestine service logo. Should've rounded off the spear tip and made it a butt plug."

Nate lit his cigar, which, despite the dark black wrapper, was surprisingly mild. His experience with cigars was limited, and he hoped he wouldn't keel over after the third puff. Neither said anything for a full two minutes.

"I know Forsyth has talked to you about this shit," said Gable. "And I'm blue in the face talking at you." Nate knew he was not supposed to say anything. Indeed, his job now, in this room, for the next hour, was to shut up.

"Nash, the most important person in your so-called professional life right now is upstairs in that bedroom, doing her kugel exercises under the covers, waiting for her lover-boy case officer to tiptoe through the door."

Nate blew smoke up at the ceiling as Gable had just done. Jaunty. "Marty, kugel is a noodle casserole. The word you want is 'kegel' exercises."

Gable stared at him, his cigar clenched between his teeth, and Nate resolved not to speak again unless spoken to. *"She is the most important thing,"* Gable repeated. "On one level, she's a valuable piece of property, an asset of the fucking CIA with nearly unlimited access, and we got to protect that asset and make sure she's productive, because this is all about national security.

"On another level, she's a smart, tough woman who's on a mission to ruin all those assholes who've fucked with her. She's a Russian, and a little volatile, we all know that, but she's committed. That's a self-propelled howitzer up there, and if you're a smart handler, you capitalize—no, you *exploit*—her motivations." He puffed twice and flicked the ash in the general direction of the crackling fireplace.

"MARBLE was the best, and Domi might be even better, if she survives. And her survival—that translates into her keeping focus, making the right decisions, not losing motivation—is materially jeopardized whenever the two of you take off your underpants and go at it like two angry camels in a tiny car." Nate willed himself to be still.

"We're starting a new phase in the operation, and DIVA is going to have to move in directions few Russian agents have ever tried. Unprecedented fucking access: Can you imagine an agent close to Stalin? Never. But Domi's caught the eye of Putin, and we want to know what that fucker has under his fingernails. And if we can screw up the Iranian nuke program, the stakes get even higher." Gable got up and poured another brandy, then held up the bottle. Nate waved him off, and Gable sat back down.

"So for instance, Domi goes back in and reports that Putin made a pass at her, wants her to spend a weekend with him at one of those dachas. What do you, her handler, instruct her to do? Tell me." Nate stared at him. The lead elements of cigar and brandy had arrived in Nate's head, and he tried to order his thoughts.

"Shut up," said Gable as Nate opened his mouth. "I'll tell you what you tell your agent. You review the intelligence requirements with her so she knows what tidbits to elicit in his bed. You let her read the bio profile on Putin by the OMS shrinks so she knows how many sugars he likes in his morning-after cup of tea. And you make sure she brings an extra pair of undies in case he rips the first pair." Gable took a swig of brandy and a puff of cigar, leaned forward, and lowered his voice.

"And when she comes home with the smell of his aftershave still in her hair, eyes puffy from three days of Vladimir, you're there to debrief her, and tell her what a shit-hot job she did, without a trace of irony, or judgment, or *inflection,* because she done her job, and you done your job, and there's more to do, so clear the decks and get busy." Gable leaned back in his armchair and puffed. "Sound like what you want to do, I mean, professionally?"

Nate closed his eyes. "I guess love doesn't come into it?"

Gable smiled. "Not with a valuable agent, it don't. It's old school, Nash—an old-time division chief, a real baron, once told me that case officers should never get married; too distracting."

"And you never got married?"

"I didn't say that."

"So what, you were married or not?"

Gable shrugged. "Yeah, for a little while."

Nate put down his brandy snifter. "And you're going to tell me about it?"

"Fuck no," said Gable.

"You've been wailing on me since I've known you," said Nate. "How about throwing a bone? Tell me." Two born manipulators, working on each other.

Gable stared into the fire. "Married young, both of us, thought she could handle the life, the travel, the nights out, but it was too much for her. She didn't get that the job swallows you whole—funny, because she was a pianist, playing was *her* whole life. I didn't know Lizst from Listerine, but the music was okay, when we weren't fighting. The second tour was Africa, and her piano wouldn't stay in tune until we lifted the lid and found a king cobra inside it; she wanted to live in Paris and Rome, but I dragged her to Manila and Lima instead, and she definitely didn't like the rape gate on the bedroom door or the shotgun in the closet. We fought like two scorpions in a brandy glass, trying to hurt each other, until she packed up and left, and we didn't get a second chance because back home she skidded on some ice and went off the road into a river, twenty-five years old, used to like listening to her play that Chopin, and two nights after she died, I was meeting a hitter from Shining Path in the port district of Lima, but the douche bag brought a knife to a gunfight, and I cancelled his ticket, and as I was going through his pockets a radio in a window somewhere was playing Chopin like she used to, and I stood over the guy and had to wait a couple minutes before my vision cleared, but that was a coincidence, because I don't think about her much anymore."

Marty Gable, Chopin, and Shining Path, thought Nate, *Jesus*. "I didn't know about that, Marty. I'm sorry."

Gable shrugged. "A long time ago, sort of where you are now. Only I didn't have a fucking sensitive mentor like you got. Now all you need is to listen to my goddamn wisdom, grow some brains, and act like a top pro."

"What happens to two scorpions in a brandy glass?" said Nate.

Gable flipped the soggy cigar butt into the fire, and drained his drink. "They can't get traction so they get face-to-face, lock pincers, and sting each other over and over. They're immune to their own venom. It's a fucking metaphor for marriage."

RUNZA

Sauté chopped onions and pureed garlic until soft. Season, add fresh dill and fennel (or caraway) seed. Add ground beef and brown, then mix in shredded cabbage, cover, and cook until the cabbage is wilted. The mixture should be fairly dry. Roll out bread dough into five-inch squares, cover centers with filling, fold corners over, and seal the edges. Bake in a medium oven until golden brown.

13

Director of the National Clandestine Service Dick Spofford sat at his desk on the seventh floor in CIA Headquarters. Floor-to-ceiling windows looked out onto the tops of the lush trees lining the George Washington Memorial Parkway and the Potomac River beyond. His office was modest—all the seniors' offices on the top floor were surprisingly small—with a couch and two chairs along one wall, a built-in bookshelf running behind the unprepossessing desk, and a small circular conference table in an opposite corner.

The third most senior officer in CIA, the DNCS—pronounced "dinkus"—directed the Clandestine Service and all foreign operations. His office was decorated with relatively inexpensive prints, mostly travel posters of the golden age of steamship travel, the Italian Lake District, and lighter-than-air dirigible service between New York and Berlin in 1936. An incongruous note was struck, however, by Spofford's displayed collection of small, plush animal figures—penguins, monkeys, starfish, buffaloes, leopards, puppies, a cross-eyed octopus—on the bookshelf behind him. Spofford was unaware of the furtive, incredulous glances as CIA's Five Eyes liaison partners—the Aussies, Brits, Canadians, and Kiwis—first noticed the cuddly menagerie.

Spofford leaned back in his ergonomic executive office chair—an Aeron, the model designated for Senior Intelligence Service rank of SIS-Four and above—and closed his eyes. His special assistant, Imogen, was tucked inside the kneehole of his desk, kneeling between his legs and moving her hand in a motion that recalled setting a handbrake. Spofford checked his watch: Leadership Committee in fifteen minutes. As it turned out, he didn't have that much time.

During a particularly energetic tug, Imogen's shoulder hit the underside of Spofford's desk—or, more precisely, the emergency alarm button under the desk drawer, which sounded a silent alarm in the nearby control room of the Office of Security, and which resulted in the immediate appearance in the DNCS's office of three Security Protective Officers and a two-person Emergency Medical Services team. The SPOs holstered their weapons as Imogen emerged from beneath the desk with cramping hands over her head. The woman on the EMS team privately noted that Mr. Spofford's handbrake might now benefit from a touch of the defibrillation paddles in her emergency kit. The cross-eyed octopus grinned from the bookshelf.

The precipitate retirement of Dick Spofford ("our work is not done; I will be with you all in spirit") set into motion a silent race for the DNCS position among senior officers who could reasonably be considered in line for the job: The three associate deputy directors (for Operations, Military Affairs, and Congressional Affairs) were leading contenders. ADD/O Borden Hood had his own public relations problems, recently having impregnated a young GS-11 reports officer during a foreign Stations inspection tour. The director passed on Hood.

The ADD/Mil, Sebastian Claude Angevine (French, pronounced On-je-VEEN, but widely known to subordinates as "Angina"), was tall and slim, with an enormous head topped by wavy hair, and a Roman nose down which he was accustomed to look. He had come up into the Clandestine Service through the security track—he started as a polygrapher, a career detail Seb Angevine took great pains to conceal. His frequent claim to have graduated from the Naval Academy was suspect. He ran Military Affairs badly—the Pentagon barely tolerated him. Imperious, self-absorbed, unaware, vindictive, and unloved, he expected the promotion to DNCS as head of Operations: It was his due.

The director hurried into the DCI's conference room, a folder in his hands. His executive assistant slipped in behind him, closed the outer door, and took a seat against the wall. The director looked around the table at his executive team: his deputy, the executive director, the line deputy directors—known as the DDs and including Ops, Intel, Science, Admin—and the other program DDs from Congressional Affairs, Military, and Public Affairs.

"Sorry I'm late," he said as he opened the folder. Angevine sat close to the head of the table, making sure the gold cuff links with embossed CIA logo—a gift from the director last year—were visible outside the sleeves of his suit.

"With Dick Spofford retiring," the director said, "we've had to move quickly to determine who will take his place. The ops chair is not one we can leave empty . . . not even for a little while." He flipped a sheet of paper in the folder, as if consulting notes. *Here it comes,* thought Angevine: When the director finished announcing that he, Angevine, would be the new DNCS, he would say only how much he appreciated the opportunity, how he acknowledged the trust bestowed on him, how greatly he looked forward to working with everyone around the table to accomplish the important mission that lay ahead. Or something like that.

He looked across the table at Gloria Bevacqua, ADD for Congressional Affairs, and smirked inwardly. What a hot mess: Asian slaw-stained pantsuit in primary colors with a knockoff Hermès scarf worn as a shawl. Feet bulging out of chunky-heeled Mary Janes. Legs by Steinway. Baked goods were always on a sideboard in the outer office of CA. DNCS, *yeah right.*

Talk in the seventh-floor executive dining room was that she was already bragging that she was going to be named DNCS, but rumors traded in the EDR were unreliable. This plus-sized fireplug had no significant experience in CIA, much less in operations: She had been brought over to Langley a year ago from Capitol Hill by the director. The thought of her heading the National Clandestine Service was laughable.

"The job of running the NCS has evolved," said the director. *He means he needs me, an experienced administrator,* thought Angevine. "The DNCS needs to bring in the entire Intelligence Community: Defense, NSA, NGA." *He's referring to my DoD account,* thought Angevine. "And managing Congress, the oversight committees, is arguably one of the most important components of the job," the director said. *What's he talking about?* "So while everyone around this table is eminently qualified and was seriously considered, I'm pleased to announce that Gloria will be taking over Operations. I'm confident Borden will support her in every way, as I'm sure you all will." Bevacqua looked around the table and nodded at everyone. She spoke briefly, saying how much she looked forward— *It was too fucking much,* thought Angevine.

Angevine sat still in his seat, a mild expression on his face, eyes glued to that motherfucking backstabbing cocksucker director. He didn't know that he had been passed over because the director—himself a hybrid, the former chief of staff for a senator—thought Angevine's "douchebagnitude" was too high, even for the DNCS position.

The DNCS job was mine, thought Angevine. *I was perfect for it.* He was constitutionally unable to contemplate that the director did not think Angevine was perfect for the job. For the next half hour, Angevine didn't see anything, didn't hear anything: His mouth tasted like zinc. The meeting broke up and Angevine was caught at the door with Gloria Bevacqua. He stopped to let her go first—they both couldn't have squeezed through together in any case.

"Congratulations," muttered Angevine. Gloria wore a hair clip on one side. Her hair was watery blond with competing peat moss–colored roots.

"Thanks, Seb," said Gloria with a sideways smirk. In a flash, Angevine knew that this had been cooked from the start—they'd known for weeks. More treachery.

"I'll want to reach out to Defense HUMINT in the coming months," said Gloria. *Why don't you bring them one of your twelve-inch pies?* thought Angevine.

"Yes, of course," said Angevine. Gloria knew that meant "Fuck you," but from her years on Capitol Hill she was used to dealing with recalcitrant pretty boys.

"Look, I know you wanted the job, but James wanted to go in a different direction," she said. *So the director is James now,* thought Angevine. He had a direction in mind for them all.

"How nice for you and James," said Angevine. He felt a rage welling up inside him and looked down at Gloria with contempt. She saw it and decided to rock this mincing beanpole in his place.

"Look, Seb," she said with a mocking smile, "don't take getting passed over too hard. Chicks still dig you." Angevine froze, actually froze at this towering insult from this . . . this sweaty *sagouine,* this slob. She walked away from him down the corridor.

Angevine sat at his desk looking blankly around his office, which was hung with pictures and commendations and awards—he had a decent vanity wall going. But now the framed exhibits mocked him. He turned his hate for Bevacqua over slowly in his mind. The other *pèdès,* those perverts on the seventh floor, were nothing. The director had betrayed him, but almost certainly with Bevacqua's encouragement. And now she was going to run the Clandestine Service? She was going to direct espionage operations and manage covert actions?

Over the next week, Angevine's rage bubbled and developed an edge like cheap Chianti in a plastic carboy. He wanted to damage them, to drag his hand across the icing of the pristine wedding cake, to tread through just-smoothed cement. He felt he owed the Agency no loyalty now—as if he had ever felt loyalty—and his petty spirit and mean motives set him to contemplate doing something monumental, really *staggering.* There would have to be a big payday too—very big.

Seb Angevine's late mother, Christine, had been an employee of the US Department of State, a career diplomat who specialized in the "consular cone," an expert in US consular law regulating, among other things, the issuance of visas to foreign citizens to visit or work in or immigrate to the United States. In the nature of most career officers in Consular Affairs, Christine was earnest and awkward, knew the Talmudic Foreign Affairs Manual (FAM) as if she had drafted it herself. She was short and slight, with bird-bone wrists and thin brown hair demurely done up in a bun. Christine was working on permanent spinsterhood: She essentially had given up on men.

Christine was in her late forties when she was posted to the US Embassy in Paris as consul general. The Consular Section had a large staff that Christine directed with her trademark introspective competence. Her young subordinates acknowledged her expertise and felt a little sorry for her, but did not particularly like her.

The allure of France was not lost on Christine, but she was at a loss as to how to find romance. Her two-year assignment was almost over; a return to Washington was imminent. It was a rainy fall afternoon, during a Consular Corps luncheon—dreary monthly events convened in elegant restaurants and attended by self-indulgent, foreign consuls general—when she met Claude Angevine. He was busy seating the arriving diplomats, unfolding napkins, and handing out menus when their eyes met. Claude bowed from the waist and smiled—a coal hopper of Gallic charm. Christine nodded at him and thought the moment *very Emily Brontë*. Claude's thoughts ran more along the lines of a K-3 visa (for a foreign spouse of an American citizen).

Claude was single, nearly fifty, tall, and dramatic, an ectomorph with a large head, long fingers, and a plowshare nose. He ran his fingers through impossibly wavy hair while speaking his sexy accented English. An intense courtship ensued—there were some initial awkward moments for Christine involving, well, the bedroom and sex, but he was charming, attentive, and told her he loved her. After three months Christine and Claude became engaged. Shortly thereafter they were married, transferred to the United States, and Christine got pregnant.

Their son, Sebastian, grew tall, looking very much like his father and, as a result of the latter's nose-in-the-air example, acting more and more like him. In both father and son, Francophile self-regard mixed with sedulous bad manners, a preoccupation with money, and the unshakable expectation that they were owed things in life. Father spoke to son in French, the better to sneer at others. The delicate Christine had never been able to cope with the lofty disdain of her husband, and suffered Sebastian's evolving adolescent disrespect in silence; father had taught son well. Then Claude abandoned the family and returned to France, now an expat US citizen—Sebastian was twenty—and Christine retired from State and wilted smaller and smaller, until she died.

Without support or a place to live, Sebastian graduated from college and joined the US Navy, went shakily through training, and evaded sea duty by applying to and joining the Naval Criminal Investigative Service. He found he did well chasing down bad checks, investigating rape cases, and tracking stolen supplies. He treasured the leatherette wallet with the NCIS badge, and he liked flashing it under people's noses. Then the position-vacancy call came out and he jumped at the chance to learn to be an NCIS polygraph operator—additional specialist credentials to brandish. A duty assignment to Annapolis on the security staff conducting clearance polygraphs for the Naval Academy plebes gave him the chops to claim "he had been at Annapolis"—not exactly a ring-knocker, an actual graduate, but close enough.

But the navy was for losers, he decided, and after getting out he applied to CIA's Directorate of Support, to the Office of Security, and the polygraph division. He was twenty-five. More prestige: first Annapolis, now Langley—never mind that he was a security investigator. CIA was the first string. Even the multiple insider euphemisms for the polygraph were cool. He started by "fluttering" new CIA applicants. He administered the periodic reinvestigation "swirls" on CIA case officers. He eventually was given an overseas trip to "box" a newly recruited asset.

He envied the laconic and sarcastic ops officers he met while abroad. He desired the cachet attached to operations and operators and the foreign field, but frankly wanted to avoid inconvenient and risky overseas assignments. He carefully began planning a safe and profitable career shift to the Clandestine Service: First a lateral assignment to an area desk, pure admin paperwork; then certification as ops-support assistant, tending asset files; then as a special assistant to a division chief, keeping his schedule; then a stint in Public Affairs, learning the art of saying nothing importantly; then hooking on to the coattails of an associate director, more staff work but breathing the air of the seventh floor; then into Congressional Affairs, where one meets future directors; until finally it happened and his patron was confirmed as director, and forty-year-old Sebastian Angevine, fifteen-year veteran of CIA's administrative track, formerly US Navy, was named CIA's new associate deputy director for Military Affairs and promoted in rank from GS-15 to SIS-Three with an increase in annual base pay from $119,554 to $165,300. His seventh-floor office soared above the treetops. The telephones on his desk were black, gray, and green. Access to a driver and a midnight-black SUV for getting to meetings at the Pentagon came with the job.

In less than a year, Seb Angevine was well-known on the seventh floor at Langley, around Pentagon conference tables, and in the National Security Council, though he was less well-known in CIA Headquarters on the operational floors and in the geographic divisions, where he rarely visited. The ambitious security officer morphed into a mid-level federal executive with airs. He wore Ermenegildo Zegna silk ties, Aldridge satin braces, and antique Carrington abalone cuff links. He ran long fingers through leonine hair carefully tended to keep the gray away from his temples. He flirted with women in the office—behind his oblivious back he was considered spotted and greasy, rather than interesting and urbane.

As he had learned during the formative years coming up, you really didn't have to sweat the work—it just sort of flowed around you, nothing but meetings, talking heads, and staff work delegated down the food chain. The other stuff was out of the senior manager's playbook: Once a year, either propose an amorphous new "program," or close down an existing program in a display of efficiency and fiscal rectitude; be sure to fire one or more struggling underlings each quarter to prove you're a leader; and know that there is no limit to obsequiousness and flummery when dealing with superiors. It was really quite easy.

The rest of it was gravy: access and privilege. Sensitive papers crossed his desk—CIA operational traffic, raw and finished intelligence. That was just the start. He was read into compartmented Department of Defense programs, hundreds of them, binders full of them; CIA and DoD shared a lot. In the Intelligence Community the gravitas of a bureaucrat was measured by the number of clearance designators behind his name: The longer the list, the bigger his *popol,* and Seb had more than a dozen clearances, including the rare Special Handling/Intelligence Techniques compartment, cynically referred to by secretaries and special assistants on the seventh floor by the acronym SH/IT. Angevine was in the know.

Okay, the government money wasn't great, and that rankled. He wanted nice things, perhaps an apartment at the Watergate, the new Audi, a girlfriend who could speak French with him. He liked going out to restaurants and bars, including unwinding at strip clubs such as Good Guys on Wisconsin Avenue. But that took money, and there definitely wasn't enough. He could trade his tepid federal salary for some big numbers in the private sector, but he wasn't ready for that yet—besides, they expected performance and results out there. (A lot of high-ranking chiefs in the Service landed big outside jobs at retirement, and most lasted only three years before being fired: You don't skate in the private sector, especially not with a front-office federal work ethic.) The solution was to stay in CIA for a while longer. So when Dick Spofford was caught making a deposit to his wank account, Seb Angevine had seen the future: He would ascend to the DNCS's job; the director was his ally and would confirm him. That had all changed now.

ASIAN SLAW

Cook soy sauce, fish sauce, and sugar and reduce to a heavy dark glaze. Add mayonnaise to the glaze to make a thick sauce. Pour over shredded red cabbage, diced scallions, red onion, chopped cilantro, and grated carrots. Season and further dress slaw with peanut and sesame oils, rice wine vinegar, red pepper flakes, and toasted sesame seeds.

14

It was a measure of Seb Angevine's pathology that his sudden bombshell decision to sell secrets to the Russians did not conflict with notions of loyalty to or betraying his country. He was apoplectic at being passed over—this did not happen to *him*. He idly tried rationalizing that passing secrets (and thus leveling the intelligence playing field) would create calm in the Kremlin, reassure Putin, and make Russian foreign policy less prone to global adventurism. *Yeah maybe,* thought Angevine, je m'en tamponne, *I don't give a shit.*

He was sliding down the slope toward espionage for two of the classic human motivations: money and ego. He wanted money, lots of it, and based on various counterintelligence summaries he had read, the Russians paid a lot better than they used to. And his damaged and galloping ego thirsted to repay the director; all the peacock deputies; that *morue, that codfish,* Bevacqua; and the entire CIA for ruining his life. The bitter contempt for his colleagues salved any guilt that might have intruded—none did—and focused him on what he really wanted.

The element that preoccupied Seb was how to pass classified information to the Russians and not be caught. During his training, the former NCIS polygrapher had learned a lot about past US espionage cases—Pollard, Ames, Hanssen, Pelton, Walker—and he knew how each of them had eventually been exposed: sloppy tradecraft, a pissed-off ex-wife, or a stupid accomplice, yes. But hands down, if you were an American passing secrets to the Russkies, you were most likely to be blown out of the water by an SVR officer *recruited and run inside by CIA,* a penetration agent who would report to Langley that the Center was running an American case—perhaps a name would be provided, perhaps not—and that's all the FBI needed to start an investigation.

Hanssen, for one, had gotten cute. From the first contact he had tried to stay anonymous to the Russians: He refused face-to-face meetings, identified himself only as "Ramon." But the Russians were also cute and tape-recorded one of Ramon's calls to his handler. *The actual audiotape was stolen from the file in Moscow Center by a CIA penetration of SVR and passed back to Langley.* Hanssen's thunderstruck Bureau colleagues had recognized his voice—he was in supermax ADX in Florence, Colorado, for life.

Therefore, the critical task was to find a secure conduit to the Russians that could not be tracked back to him. Seb spent the weekend thinking about the problem, exhausted and edgy, but nothing came to him. For dinner he munched absently on the *lumpia*—Philippine spring rolls—his housekeeper, Arcadia, had left in the fridge. Seb brooded alone. Then he remembered the OSI double-agent briefing on his calendar.

The Air Force Office of Special Investigations, known as AFOSI or simply OSI, was, like NCIS, more a law-enforcement agency dedicated to policing air force miscreants. A small counterintelligence section pursued leads, but if one of their cases really heated up, the "FEEBs" in the Hoover Building would take over, or CIA would swoop in for foreign-based cases. All that was left to try was controlled cases.

Seb Angevine knew that double-agent ops were a creaky anachronism of the Cold War. Generating (and approving) authentic feed material for passage to the opposition was an unending, crushing chore. Moreover, intelligence agencies around the world were all finely attuned to the threat of provocation from a dispatched volunteer: They had all been burned. Thus the opposition's requirements for bona fide intelligence were wickedly demanding—blockbuster intelligence, the kind that really could be considered a loss of national-security information, was the standard test for any agent. If intelligence production was meager, or inconsequential, or uncorroborated, a volunteer would not be vetted.

Angevine, as ADD/Mil, could ask for and receive detailed, classified briefings on any double-agent operation, and he called his contacts at the Pentagon to be more fully read into the new OSI project. Seb listened carefully to the description of SEARCHLIGHT, the code name for the operation. An air force major named Glenn Thorstad had been drafted as the double agent—a red-haired, green-eyed Lutheran from Minnesota; *a real squarehead,* thought Angevine. He was surprised to hear that Major Thorstad had already made contact with the Russian Embassy in Washington by slipping an envelope under the windshield wiper of a Russian diplomat's car at the National Arboretum on New York Avenue.

As Seb walked into the OSI briefing room in the Pentagon he saw Simon Benford sitting in a chair against the wall. Angevine was acquainted with Benford slightly—their professional worlds did not often intersect. He knew Benford was chief of CIA's Counterintelligence Division, and the enfant terrible of the Intelligence Community. Apart from that, Angevine was only faintly aware that Benford's universe was populated with moles and spies, a murky world of indications, clues, and intelligence leaks. Angevine did not like him—during the past year of high-level meetings on the seventh floor he could feel Benford's eyes on him, could hear the contempt in his voice when he spoke. But Benford was that way to everybody.

Angevine knew that veteran operations officers in the service (like Benford) discounted him. They all knew that Angevine had not earned his associate deputy director position in CIA by running operations in the foreign field. It was sweet irony that Angevine outranked them all—not that he could pull rank on any of them. In the strangely egalitarian clandestine service, and despite its patrician roots, even junior officers addressed seniors by their first names.

What was Benford doing at this relatively unimportant OSI meeting? He sat down next to him, the only two CIA officers in the room otherwise filled by blue uniforms and ribbons.

"Simon," said Angevine, staring straight ahead.

"Sebastian," said Benford, focused on the far wall.

"What are you doing here?" said Angevine. "A bit below your scope."

"I would have thought the same for you," said Benford. Neither had looked at the other once.

"I try to immerse myself in a variety of operations," said Angevine archly.

"Of course you do," said Benford, "being the ADD/Mil and all." Angevine ignored the sarcasm.

"And you?"

Benford turned to look at Angevine. "You know what I think of double-agent operations," he said. "Time intensive, dilatory, inconclusive. No serious service spends much capital on them anymore." Angevine turned and looked at Benford. "But you know all that, don't you, Sebastian?"

"Then why are you here, Simon?" asked Angevine.

"God Bless OSI," said Benford. "They are squeaky and enthusiastic and they try. And this operation of theirs—SEARCHLIGHT, I think they call it—seems to have drawn out the Bolshies. Quite remarkable."

"Bolshies?" said Angevine.

"Russians to you. The Washington *rezidentura* responded to the note that squeaky young air force major left on one of their cars. Directed him to a site in Maryland. Quite extraordinary; they normally turn volunteers away. The *rezident* may be under pressure from the Center to become more productive."

"Interesting," said Angevine. "Who is the head boy these days?" He was thinking ahead: Getting the *rezident*'s name could be useful in the future.

"It's the head *girl*, actually," said Benford.

Most interesting, thought Angevine. "Who is she?" he said.

"Yulia Zarubina," said Benford, tilting his head. "Name mean anything to you?"

A jolt of guilt ran up Angevine's spine. "No. Why, should it?"

"Yulia's grandmother was Elizaveta Zarubina, posted to Washington in 1940. While Hoover's FBI was chasing her husband around town, she recruited half the US atom spies in Moscow's stable. Oppenheimer, Gold, Hall, Greenglass. She was a legend, personally commended by Stalin."

"Never heard of her," said Angevine.

"Ancient history," said Benford. "Yulia kept the family name, presumably to continue the pedigree."

"So you're here to take a closer look at her," said Angevine.

"Indeed. She's a rarity in SVR. Highest-ranking woman in their service—she's around fifty-five. Only a few of them around.

"Coming up she did the usual rounds in the Foreign Language Institute and the Diplomatic Academy of the Ministry of Foreign Affairs," said

Benford. "Got her grandmother's genes: ten languages, cultured and savvy. Overseas tours in Paris, Tokyo, and Stockholm as *rezident.* Putin sent her to Washington as *rezident,* part charm offensive. But there's another side to our Zarubina. The reason I'm interested in this OSI stage show."

"Do tell," said Angevine, feigning uninterest, looking around the room.

"Yulia Zarubina is a recruiter. Got a talent for it. Source once reported that they call her *shveja,* the seamstress, like she sews up her targets." *Useful to know,* thought Angevine. *Benford just did my homework for me.*

"If she's coming out to play with our major over there," said Benford, "we'd like to take a closer look at her."

"It's all a bit melodramatic, don't you think, Simon?" said Angevine.

Benford tilted his head again. "It depends on your definition of drama, Sebastian," he said.

Angevine listened to half the OSI briefing on SEARCHLIGHT and slipped out the door, earning a heavy-lidded stare from Benford. He had heard enough. Every month OSI handlers, a production review board, and the deputy director of the A-2 Staff (Intelligence, Surveillance and Reconnaissance) would compile and review the proposed digital package assembled by OSI for passage to the Russians.

Angevine thought the operation idiotic and transparent. But the notion of photographing documents with a digital camera was interesting—perhaps something he could manipulate. He would append real secrets to the tail end of the OSI dross. He imagined the jaw-dropped Russians coming to the end of Thorstad's chicken feed to find additional images from another source, explosive images, dynamite secrets. No personal meetings, no exposure—he would be flying under the radar, using an approved channel. And the new source—Seb would have to come up with his own code name, that would be amusing—would be unknown and untraceable to him in Langley: If any suspicions emerged, Benford the mole hunter would have to comb through the thousands of USAF personnel files of those employees with access to classified information before looking elsewhere.

Two refinements remained: He needed access to the OSI flash card, and he had to receive his money. He thought furiously. He would insist that CIA's Military Affairs staff review the card before passage as a counterintelligence check—he would do it himself. As for the money: no bank accounts, domestic or offshore. Counterintelligence investigators could uncover those in an afternoon. No, the money would have to be passed via old-fashioned dead drops. But in this he was courting danger: The FBI followed Russian intel officers around Washington waiting specifically for such activity—loading and clearing drops. SVR officers in Washington were too hot. Except perhaps the urbane and effective Yulia Zarubina, Putin's poster girl for improved bilateral relations. It could work.

The courier from the Pentagon arrived with the zippered and locked portfolio, peeled off a copy of the receipt signed by Angevine's secretary, and left. He would return to collect the flash card for SEARCHLIGHT the next morning, after the mandated final review by CIA, specifically by the associate deputy director for Military Affairs. When CIA signed off on the contents, the card would be delivered directly to Major Thorstad, who would prepare to meet the Russians that night.

Angevine plugged the card into a stand-alone laptop on the credenza behind his desk and quickly scrolled through the air force feed material Thorstad would pass the next evening. *Ordure,* garbage. Ridiculous. The night before, in his locked office, he had used a lightweight Nikon to photograph a three-page classified cable off the screen of his Agency desktop—no hard copy, no print-job record, an anonymous photo and untraceable. Angevine chose an ops cable reporting the recent recruitment of a junior Russian military attaché in Venezuela. The Caracas Station cable was detailed, named names, listed the information the attaché was providing. The beauty of it was that Angevine had no connection to the Latin America Division, or to the operation—he simply had access to worldwide cable traffic.

Angevine knew that for the Russians there was no bona fides like telling them about an espionage case that involved one of their own. They relished catching their own traitors. Ames, by 1994, had been paid nearly $5 million for the names of twelve Soviets on CIA payroll, an immense payout by a normally stingy Moscow. Along with this info, Angevine had also written and photographed a single-page letter of introduction, the fourth image in his camera. He transferred the four images from his camera onto the OSI flash card and reviewed the results. The air force manuals, then three pages of a CIA ops cable, then his love letter. Angevine's images looked different—distinct metadata and .dox files—but that was fine; it highlighted the mystery. The letter was spare, muscular, all business. The Russians would shit when they read it:

> *I call myself TRITON* [Angevine had settled on the cryptonym with relish.] *In exchange for funds I propose to provide information that will be of interest to your Service. As an example, the preceding three pages detail a CIA operation in Latin America against your interests.*
>
> *I will not identify myself, nor will I describe my access or position. I require prompt payment in US dollars for this information and as good faith for future information, which I will pass via this channel. Emplace a waterproof package containing $100,000 at the site described below* [Angevine had drawn a map of a drop site in the Rock Creek Woods in northwest Washington] *in three days, which will be ample time for you to verify my information.*
>
> *I will instantly know if your Service attempts to identify me, or if word of my offer leaks out of your Center, in which case I will permanently break contact. TRITON*

Nine forty-five p.m. *Golly,* thought Major Thorstad, *this first meeting with the Russians was turning out to be a disaster.* He worried that he had misunderstood the directions he received: At nine o'clock in the evening, walk along the one-mile stretch of the unlighted Capital Crescent Trail in Bethesda, Maryland, between Massachusetts Avenue and MacArthur Boulevard. The former Baltimore and Ohio rail bed had been converted to an asphalt-paved hiking and biking trail, but at nine there were no hikers, and the dense woods on either side of the pathway were pitch-black. Thorstad had completed two circuits on the trail—almost by feel, it was so dark—and was nearing the yawning maw of the turn-of-the-century, brick-lined Dalecarlia Tunnel that passed under the nearby reservoir.

A man oozed out of the shadows at the mouth of the tunnel, his face and hands faintly discernible in the half moonlight. Thorstad slowly walked up to him.

"Tor-stud?" said the face, mangling his name. The major nodded. "Come close," said the man, with what Thorstad assumed was a Russian accent.

The major took a step forward. "I didn't know if I was in the right place. It's nearly an hour beyond what you—"

"Face wall," said the man, who lifted Thorstad's arms so his hands slapped against the rough brick. The interior of the tunnel was cold; groundwater dribbled from the arched brick roof, making a toneless *pock-pock* echo. The man expertly frisked Thorstad, taking his time with his crotch, back, and front. He stooped and passed a metal-detector wand around Thorstad's shoes and outer jacket. The man was a chunky, hard-faced mouth-breather. He reeked of alcohol—Thorstad supposed it was vodka—but he appeared steady on his feet. He grunted as he finished frisking Thorstad, who turned to look at him. The Russian took a penlight out of his pocket and flashed it twice, in both directions down the tunnel. No signal or response, but Thorstad realized in a rush that they were not alone, that Russian wolves had been watching him, the trail, and the forest since he arrived. He shivered inwardly at the thought of armed men in the gentrified woods of upscale Bethesda.

"Why have you contacted us?" said the man heavily.

Thorstad was eager to please, and OSI had coached him to be communicative, cooperative. "As I wrote in my note to you, I need financial help," he said. "I need money."

"Why not go to bank if you need money?" said the man. "Why come to us?"

"I have information of interest to you," Thorstad said lamely.

"Show me," said the man. Thorstad took the flash card out of his pocket and held it out in his palm, as if he were feeding a horse a sugar cube. The man took the flash card, turned it in his fingers as if he did not know what it was, then reached into his coat and stuffed it into a shirt pocket. Body odor mixed with the stench of vodka wafted up when he moved.

The man reached into another pocket and handed Thorstad a card with directions to and a line map of the next meeting site. "For next time," said the Russian, turning away to melt into the black, walking south through the tunnel. Thorstad watched him go. The Russian—a clunky SVR security man from the *rezidentura*—knew only that if, based on the American's information, the Center assessed that the volunteer was *dvurushnichestvo,* double-dealing, no one would be at the prescribed rendezvous. And the card, made of sodium carboxymethyl cellulose, would absorb ambient humidity and slowly decompose into a pulpy glob in a month's time.

Just plain rude, thought Thorstad, and he put the card into his pocket and walked on the path north, out of the woods, toward the lights of Massachusetts Avenue. He stared studiously ahead, intent on not looking for the night glimmer of Slavic eyes in the black trees on either side of him.

"And then what happened?" asked Benford. Redheaded Major Thorstad took a drink of water from a carafe in the middle of the conference room. Three OSI officers were taking copious notes, to Benford's obvious annoyance. The jubilant OSI guys didn't care: Contact with RIS—Russian Intelligence Service. In suburban Washington. The first encounter in three years. *Their* DA operation. It would be the shit-hot lead in the monthly activity report for the air force brass. Mr. Chips over there from CIA could kiss their asses.

"Well, I can tell you, the guy was quite rude," said Thorstad. Benford shifted in his seat and only at the last minute remembered this ginger snap was not a subordinate and therefore, technically, he could not bellow at him.

"He was forty-five minutes late in appearing," said Thorstad. "I walked the hiking trail *two* complete times." He held up two fingers to clarify for Benford. The OSI guys were taking down every word.

"They probably had people in the woods with night-vision goggles, looking at your approach, watching for coverage," said Benford.

Thorstad snapped his fingers. "You're absolutely correct, Mr. Benford. The man shined a flashlight in both directions down the tunnel. It was a signal of some sort." Benford suppressed a moan.

"I am gratified you agree," Benford said, his tone lost on Thorstad, who was trying to remember more details. Benford wondered if the major even considered that a different signal from that flashlight might have ended with him crumpled on the wet bricks of the tunnel.

"He took the flash card," said Thorstad, "and gave me this card with the next meeting site on it. In two weeks, in Georgetown."

Benford took the card, read it while feeling the satiny finish, and slid it to the OSI men at the end of the table.

"Water-soluble paper. Make sure you copy the instructions verbatim and put this in a glassine envelope. It'll decompose in three weeks if you don't keep it out of the atmosphere." The OSI officers looked at one another, unsure about "verbatim" and "glassine." Benford turned to Thorstad.

"Well, I suppose it went as well as we could expect," Benford said. "The unpleasant fellow—"

"I forgot to say that he reeked—*absolutely reeked*—of alcohol, apart from the rudeness," said Thorstad, interrupting.

"Yes, well, he probably has troubles of his own at home," said Benford. Thorstad looked a little guilty at being so unfair: He had not considered that the man might be having problems. Benford looked with clinical interest at the changing expressions on Thorstad's face. Where did OSI find this man-child major?

"He almost certainly was a low-level security officer from the embassy, perhaps from the *rezidentura,*" said Benford. "The Center would not risk sending one of their active operations officers under cover to this meeting."

Thorstad nodded. Benford turned to address the OSI men. "I would urge restraint in writing up this contact and predicting further progress," he said. "The likelihood of another meeting is exceedingly slim, given that the feed material is dated. The Russians are looking for exceptional intelligence. If they don't get it, they will conclude that the major is a dispatched volunteer and will simply turn the operation off."

The OSI men looked back glumly.

"I anticipate you will be left waiting at the next rendezvous," said Benford to Thorstad. "You should not be surprised at a no-show."

Benford rose and left the room. One of the OSI men flipped him the bird behind his back. Thorstad glared at him.

"At ease, sergeant. That's not the way we do things in the Air Force," Thorstad said.

ARCADIA'S LUMPIA

Dice cabbage, carrots, onion, scallion, and garlic and sauté in oil with soy sauce. Brown ground pork and combine with the vegetables. Wrap filling tightly in large wonton or lumpia wrappers. Fry in vegetable oil until crispy and golden brown.

15

Locked in the wood-paneled study of his house, Seb Angevine finished transferring the nine digital frames he had photographed directly off his office computer screen onto the SEARCHLIGHT stick being prepared for the second contact with the Russians. OSI had loaded twenty-three carefully edited frames of performance parameter documents for the F-22 Raptor, a stealth-fighter program that had been discontinued due to cost overruns and contractor disputes. Air Force CI analysts argued that the information would be tantalizing to the Russians and would keep the ball rolling. Angevine barely looked at the OSI feed material. His nine frames would be the main course and his "love letter" in the tenth digital frame at the end of the dump requested another $100,000 be cached in Rock Creek Woods. Angevine had no doubt the Russians would pay.

He had picked up the first payment early on a Sunday morning at the cache site without any trouble, though he nervously had given the Russians an extra day, in case they needed more time. But he was worried for nothing. The forest was dense along Oregon Avenue NW, and there were plenty of quiet suburban streets in the Barnaby Woods neighborhood to park his car without problems. The day was fine and the air still. There were no cars moving, and the woods were empty. Though he was confident that the Russians would not jeopardize their new case by trying to surveil the cache site, Angevine kept his eyes open, not only for the suspicious early morning loiterer but also for likely places the Russians could have set up a motion-activated camera. They wouldn't risk it, but he would be cautious.

The sunny paved trail led conveniently to a massive, hurricane-felled oak tree whose exposed root ball created a natural pocket from which Angevine with trembling hands extracted a bread-loaf-sized package wrapped seamlessly in blue packing tape. The loamy heft of the package was impressive. A hundred Gs. A Porsche Carrera. That Rolex GMT-Master II.

So he told the Russians to load another hundred Gs. They must be shitting themselves in the *rezidentura* up there on Wisconsin Avenue, wondering who the fuck TRITON was, what kind of mastermind he was, where he worked. Someone had included a plain typed note in the money package addressed to "dear friend," with a phone number for him in case he needed to talk. *Yeah right,* va t'en faire foutre, *go fuck yourself.*

Angevine noted that the Russians of course had been reserved and cautious in their message of greeting and references to future contact. They still did not know what they had in TRITON, but already the information about the Caracas recruitment would be incontrovertible proof that they potentially had a colossal asset. TRITON: monarch of the sea. Anonymous. Monumental.

The Russians would be patient, solicitous: They were confident in the expectation that eventually they would find out who he was. *No chance,* thought Angevine. TRITON would emerge from the sea foam, wave his trident, and call up a howling gale, then slip beneath the waves, untouchable. And that *pouffiasse,* that bitch Bevacqua, could sit behind her desk and try to figure out what was happening to her Clandestine Service.

The Russians already had his first dump: the counterintelligence lead from Caracas. Now it was time to pass something even better, even more explosive: Nine images of two separate Restricted Handling cables sent by Athens Station to Langley reporting two lengthy debriefing sessions on sensitive Russian military research and development conducted by a Russian-speaking CIA case officer with a source identified only as LYRIC.

Ten p.m. Major Glenn Thorstad stood in shadow in the little ornamental public garden on Grace Street NW, off Wisconsin Avenue, overlooking the C&O Canal. He was dressed in civilian clothes, a jacket over an open-necked shirt. He wore a wide-brimmed suede hat with a leather band, not quite a cowboy hat—that would have been too conspicuous—more like an Indiana Jones number, to cover his red hair. He checked his watch for the fifth time in the last thirty minutes.

Not counting his contact with the Russian security thug in the tunnel, this would be his first face-to-face meeting with a Russian intelligence officer, something he had never contemplated in his entire career with the Air Force. He had been working in TransComm—Transport Command, a *vital* cog in the Air Force machine—and had risen through a series of important jobs in coordination, scheduling, and finance. He had been spotted and drafted by OSI for his demonstrable access to an immense range of classified information. He sailed through security clearance, for he had nothing to hide—shoot, he didn't even drink. Thorstad originally had been flattered that OSI planners approached him to suggest he play a double agent, and the briefings and practice sessions were exciting and different. But now, on the street, waiting for the SVR, he wasn't so sure.

Thorstad had been coached on what to say, on what questions the Russians would throw at him to test him. OSI briefers told him the Russians would assume he was a double until and unless he proved to them that he was not—through unimpeachable feed material and authentic behavior.

"What's authentic behavior for a double agent?" Thorstad asked his training team at the same meeting. The OSI men looked at one another—no one had actually asked them that before. A fussy voice had come from the corner of the room, from a rumpled man with mussed hair and the intonation of a Latin teacher racked with gout.

"There is no such thing, so don't waste time thinking there is," said Benford, who had come uninvited to this briefing of Thorstad on the eve of his first potential substantive contact with SVR. "Act the way you feel: scared, guilty, mistrustful. You're an Air Force major who's betraying his country."

Thorstad swallowed hard. *This uncomfortable fellow again?* "That's right, you're a traitor," said Benford, "and the Russians will take your information and give you a bit of money, and when your access dries up, or the FBI apprehends you, Moscow will shrug their shoulders and go away until the next Major Thorstad appears at their door."

Thorstad stared at Benford, who had just stood up and was pacing a little. "It's all right to feel shitty; the Russians will see it and be reassured." Benford turned to look at the OSI men, who shifted uncomfortably under his gaze.

Major Thorstad replayed Benford's words as he stood in the shadows waiting for his contact to appear. He was expecting another seven-foot brute in a leather jacket to materialize, spin him around, shove him against the brick wall of the garden, and brusquely frisk him for a wire. He didn't know what to expect. He checked the flash card in his pocket for the eleventh time: F-22 Raptor. His second pass of intelligence to the opposition.

From over the low garden wall the sounds of a party drifted in the night air from a canal barge making its way down the waterway. Thorstad looked down at the fairy lights reflected off the water. He wished he were down there instead of here. A soft voice beside him startled him.

"Are you Glenn?" A low female voice. Thorstad turned. A woman with blond hair stood with her hands in the pockets of a light coat. She looked about fifty-five, short and somewhat heavyset. The lights from the buildings across the canal illuminated a round face with wise brown eyes and a mouth crinkled at the corners. She wore her hair up in a bun. She smiled politely at him. Librarian, personnel counselor, hospital administrator. She didn't even look Russian. She spoke fluently in a singsongy voice, with a trace of a foreign accent, like Dutch or Norwegian. Thorstad didn't know what to say.

"Air Force Major Thorstad?" The woman smiled taking a step closer. "Born 1979 in Farmington, Minnesota?" Thorstad swallowed and nodded. "From the name I suppose your family is Swedish?"

"Third generation," mumbled Thorstad. He sounded idiotic.

"*Talar ni svenska?*" she said. "Do you speak Swedish?"

"Only a few words," said Thorstad.

"*Charmerande,*" said the woman. "How charming. I remember my travels in Sweden fondly. *Gillar du kroppkakor,* do you like potato dumplings? So light and delectable." Thorstad could only stare at this merry matron as she rambled on about Swedish food.

"But I suppose we should speak English, don't you agree?"

Thorstad nodded again.

"Will you walk a little way with me?" said the woman. She actually stepped up to him and hooked her hand through his arm, like an aunt out for a Sunday stroll after dinner.

"My name is Yulia," said the woman as they started walking down the dark, narrow street. Brick buildings on either side were closed and quiet. They came up to a smaller street—narrow and brick-paved—that ran downhill toward the Potomac and the waterfront park. There was no one else moving and their footsteps were muffled as Yulia turned them into the dark lane—Cecil Place NW—by gently tugging his arm in the direction she wanted to go. If Thorstad had had some street training he might have noticed a shadowy figure standing still at the top of the street, watching the two. Another silhouetted figure stood beside a lamppost at the bottom of the lane watching them approach. A half block away on Water Street, in the shadow of the elevated Whitehurst Freeway, an indistinct face peered out the windshield of a parked van. The man periodically checked the mirrors. Yulia Zarubina, SVR *rezident* in Washington—*shveja,* the seamstress—had brought her boys out tonight.

"I am glad you contacted me," she said, still holding Thorstad's arm, but looking down at her feet. "I'd like to help you any way I can."

Thorstad again didn't know what to say—the OSI guys had prepared him for a spittle-flecked tirade from an overgrown head-knocker.

"Tell me a little about yourself, Glenn," Yulia said, looking up at him.

Golly, he thought, *even though she's RIS, she's* courteous. He didn't feel the seamstress's chain stitches begin to envelop him.

In the space of two minutes, Zarubina determined to her satisfaction that Thorstad was who she thought he was—*nevinnyi,* an innocent—and almost certainly not the author of the "extra material" on the first stick. She smiled again and started building her own *maskirovka,* her deception. She gently chided the major for the outdated intelligence in his first exchange. "The Raptor program, for goodness' sake; can't you find something a little more current, Glenn? After all, you are in such an important position. I have high hopes for us."

Thorstad was surprised, for this was not what he had been told to expect. "What do you have in mind?" he asked, remembering at the last minute that his OSI support team had told him to elicit information and requirements from the Russians. Yeah, *elicit.* Zarubina looked out at the nighttime Potomac, at the fairy lights of Rosslyn, and at the dark trees of Roosevelt Island.

"These things are so technical," said Yulia, squeezing his arm as they walked slowly along the waterfront. Her eyes caught his and she smiled, a grandmother about to repeat a recipe for cookies. "But it would be lovely if you could bring me any information—current diagnostics, flight-test data, design analyses—regarding the problem of wing buffeting in the F-35. That really would be lovely." She looked up at Thorstad and her eyes crinkled at the corners.

"The thirty-five?" said Thorstad. It sounded as though she knew a lot.

"Yes, I believe you call it the Lightning II. I hope you can find something. I was so excited when you contacted me." Zarubina seldom used the words "Center," "Moscow," and "Russia," and always kept it personal. There would be time for the relationship to be *utverdivshiysya,* institutionalized, by the Center, when it was too late to stop.

The Americans, thankfully, were predictable. She was relying on this American naïf to go back to his handlers—she correctly assumed this was an OSI initiative—and report that the Russians were interested, really interested, and that the DA op was on its way. Zarubina's personal involvement testified to that, and she hoped the Air Force CI officers would concur. She must continue meeting with this Thorstad creature, feign interest and patience, continue asking for information the Air Force would never agree to pass. Whoever this TRITON was, he needed the channel kept open and active.

There might be some opportunities for *aktivnye meropriyatiya,* active measures, disinformation, in the intelligence requirements levied on Thorstad, thought Zarubina. She had once asked a French military attaché—another double agent—for operational manuals on the Mirage 2000N, volumes one through twelve and fifteen through twenty-two. When the goggling Frenchman asked her why not volumes thirteen and fourteen (the books describing the three kiloton ASMP—the French acronym for "medium-range air-to-surface"—nuclear missile carried by the 2000N), Zarubina had patted her hair and ignored the question—as if uninterested in something she already possessed—triggering a two-year French mole hunt in the Ministry of Defense, and a constitutional crisis in the Élysée Palace regarding the continued viability of France's nuclear deterrence policy. That active measure had been inspired.

Her exceptional mind was running on this third track even while she spoke to Thorstad in soothing tones. With one ear she listened to her countersurveillance team working around her on the earpiece on the side she kept away from Thorstad. She had Thorstad's thumb drive in her pocket and was eager to see if the mystery source TRITON had again appended anything. Zarubina had an intuition that this was the beginning of a major case.

At the end of their walk, she watched Thorstad in his ridiculous wide-brimmed *shlyapa* trudge up Thirty-First Street NW toward the lights of M Street. Zarubina hoped this TRITON was intelligent. It didn't reassure her that he had chosen a code name for himself—a worrying possible indicator of the ego of an epic megalomaniac. Besides monarch of the sea, "triton" in Russian meant "newt." *Not exactly the most heroic cryptonym for an agent,* thought Zarubina, *but perhaps naming oneself after a squirmy amphibian will prove to be apt.*

"She was courteous and attentive," said Thorstad. He was sitting at a table in a Pentagon conference room surrounded by OSI agents and two officers from A-2 counterintelligence. Benford sat quietly at the end of the table, looking up at the ceiling as if he were thinking about what to have for dinner.

"She asked me about myself. I told her I needed the money, like we rehearsed. I admitted I liked to gamble," said Thorstad.

"And how did she respond?" asked Benford. The OSI agents weren't listening because they were all busy taking notes—*second contact with RIS, contact with the Washington chief of SVR, specific requirements on the F-35.* Their DA op named SEARCHLIGHT was catching fire. They would draft another lead item in the next monthly report—no, a separate memo to the Secretary of the Air Force, maybe even SecDef. They looked over at Benford. This dipstick from Langley said it would be a no-show. Some expert.

"She said we all occasionally have difficulties," said Thorstad. "She was, like, really understanding. No hard-line stuff, nothing."

Of course, thought Benford, *you just had a pleasant evening stroll with an old lady,* a shveja, *a seamstress.* But Benford's three decades of low-crawling through the wilderness of mirrors told him something did not add up. In matters of intelligence collection, the Russians were—had always been—greedy, covetous, rapacious, suspicious, impatient, avaricious, extorting, brutal. But never stupid. Benford knew the feeling, felt the familiar bolus in his throat, when contemplating some as-yet-unknown Russian action. In due course the plot would become apparent, like a sheep's head floating up from the bottom of the stew pot, staring and grinning. But by then it would be too late.

KROPPKAKOR-POTATO DUMPLINGS

Fry salt pork and onions until golden brown. Into cold mashed potatoes mix egg, black pepper, nutmeg, and flour and work into a dough. Cut and roll dough into balls, make a cavity in each, and fill with the pork/onion mixture. Crimp dumplings closed and boil in beef broth until cooked through. Serve with sour cream.

16

Vern Throckmorton, the difficult chief of Station, sat scowling behind his desk in his tiny office in Moscow Station. Even with the laminate pocket door opened, the closet-sized space had no chairs, so Hannah Archer had to stand uncomfortably under Vern's avocado glare. Hannah was the newest case officer in Moscow—she had been at Station for three days—and this was the first time Throckmorton had called her in, or even acknowledged her existence.

"Metrics," said the chief. "You know what metrics are?" Vern was a large man, broad shouldered and big bellied, with a double chin, bushy eyebrows, and thinning brown hair slicked flat in one piece with mousse across his beach-ball head. Hannah imagined that if one were able to get a fingernail delicately under an edge of the stiffened hair, it would lift off the top of his head like the lid on a tin of ship's biscuits.

"I don't know, Chief," said Hannah. "Isn't metrics a scale to measure things?" Hannah was twenty-five years old, just out of IO training—"sticks and bricks," they called it—internal operations for running agents in denied areas like Moscow. Hannah was pretty and a little lean—she liked her nature-girl figure—with curly blond hair and full lips. Hannah knew her eyes were her best feature, if unusual: the luminous green of the Caribbean, flecked with gold around the pupil. She wore dark-framed hipster glasses and a simple blouse and skirt. Lacrosse through high school and college had given her slim, strong legs. She knew people thought she had a smart mouth—from growing up with brothers—but she had tried to keep it shut during training. She stood still but for a tapping foot out of the chief's line of sight. Too much nervous energy—she had to work on that.

COS Moscow looked at her closely: The kid radiated intensity, and smarts, and brass, goddamn it. The evaluation cable said she had been one of the best students in IO training: She could detect coverage on the street like an instructor, had smoked a twenty-car FBI surveillance team during the course's final exercise, had pulled off an MCD right under their noses.

Vern huffed. The moving-car delivery—one of the most screamingly dangerous agent-to-handler exchange techniques in the book. *Hot shot,* he thought.

There was a further complication: Before this golden girl's arrival at Station, Throckmorton had gotten an "eyes only" cable from Counterintelligence Division—direct from Simon Benford—essentially ordering *him,* COS Moscow, to designate soon-to-arrive case officer Hannah Archer to be the action officer to deploy the SRAC network in support of a sensitive asset, GTDIVA. The cable perfunctorily mentioned only that Archer had received additional training in such systems. *Bullshit,* thought Vern. *I should be the one involved in this compartmented case.* He had immediately written back, stating his intent to handle DIVA personally, but received a call on the encrypted line from Gloria Bevacqua, the new DNCS, telling him to shut up and follow orders. He was still pissed.

"No," said Throckmorton, leaning back in his swivel chair. "Metrics is what I use to send case officers back home when they don't produce." He waited for a beat to read Archer's face, which was impassive—the kid kept the cork in the bottle.

"I got a cable designating you as the action officer for DIVA. So, I expect you to do that, under my direction. And if you think I'm not qualified, you can drop that idea," said Vern puffily.

He didn't advertise the fact that he had dodged IO training before coming to Moscow as chief—he had loftily declared he was too busy with other preparations, but in truth there had been no way he was going to risk washing out of the devilishly demanding course: Student attrition traditionally was 25 percent. He sat back in his chair behind the modular desk. On the corner of the desk was a dummy hand grenade mounted on a wooden base. The plaque on it read COMPLAINT DEPARTMENT. PULL PIN FOR FASTER SERVICE. It had been left by a former COS Moscow, now forgotten, but Throckmorton liked it, liked the message it sent.

"My first tour I served in Bucharest," said Vern, noticing that this Archer kid looked him straight in the eyes. "I'm one of the *original* denied-area specialists. I pulled off car tosses right under the nose of surveillance, and let me tell you, the *Securitate* were animals."

"The Golden Age of Internal Ops," said Hannah, with no inflection, but she instantly regretted it. *Smart mouth, shut the fuck up.* COS did not seem to register the crack, actually seemed to like it. *Denied-area specialist,* thought Hannah. Benford had told her that in the seventies one of Throckmorton's poorly executed car tosses along the number 3 highway through the Padurea Pantelimon, the dense forest of pine and oak outside Bucharest, had been observed by the *Securitate.* A thuggish team had waited for three weeks in the rain, and actually dropped four poplars across the road—two in front and two behind—with detcord to block any escape when the agent rolled up to the site in his car. *One of the original specialists,* thought Hannah.

An instructor had told her she assessed people well—something you don't think about until you go through fricking spy school and they tell you some nonsense about yourself—and she sniffed at her new COS's ego, clearly born of envy, and saw his chronic suspicion, doubtless fueled by self-doubt. And what a burden that oversized head must be walking into a room. Or putting on a sweater.

Hannah took a breath and looked down the length of the empty Moscow Station, which was essentially a soundproof trailer—bigger than a sea-land container. No windows, one entrance door, a little claustrophobic. Thick felt panels of muted blue covered the walls, and a durable carpet of the same color was underfoot. On either side of a narrow central pass-through, a half dozen modular desks were tucked along both walls, illuminated by recessed lamps that cast small pools of light on each desk, above which hung a credenza, the only place to store personal gear. The case officers otherwise had to "hot bunk" the desks—sit at whichever was free to read incoming traffic or draft cables. Under the desks huddled stumpy, two-drawer steel safes, gunmetal gray and dented. *More room in the 777 coming over. This is your home for the next two years,* thought Hannah. Moscow Station. The Real Steel. The Game.

The main door to the container swung open with a hydraulic whine, the brass finger-stock gasket ringing the massive frame—which guaranteed acoustical integrity around the door—gleaming in the light. Irene Schindler, deputy chief of Moscow Station, walked into the trailer. Without looking she swatted the oversized red button on the wall that caused the door to grind ponderously closed with a hiss. About thirty-five, Irene was tall, gray-skinned, sunken-cheeked, with hair cut short in a Prince Valiant. The top of her head brushed the low ceiling of the trailer as she looked wordlessly at Hannah, her narrow beaky nose pointing in her direction, then turned toward the opposite end of the enclosure and opened another pocket door. The deputy's office. Irene entered the little space and slid the door closed with a click. A faint astringent whiff hung in the air behind her.

Jesus Christ, thought Hannah, *my first tour and I end up inside the Addams Family's double-wide, sandwiched between two misanthropes.* And with about three thousand Russian surveillants outside on the street, salivating for her to come out and play. And DIVA, who was waiting for Hannah to deliver her lifeline.

Hannah had been used to Wonder Bread normal all her life: big family, all steady, Episcopalian, New Hampshire, lacrosse in the fall and spring, sailing in the summer. Her parents taught her to earn her own money, so she learned to flip burgers and fry clams during school breaks. Say what you do and do what you say. Tell the truth and stand up for what you believe. Necking with sunburned boys with crinkly eyes and freckles; drinking ice-cold shandies out of aluminum tennis-ball cans; steering a jeep with no top in lazy eights on a moonlit meadow.

A taste of the genteel South during four years at Washington and Lee University, then two more at Virginia to finish graduate work in philosophy and cognitive science—though she found UVA subjacent to W&L. It was interesting, but she wanted something else; *she had to get going in life.* Then, seriously, joining CIA was a commitment that mattered: service, sacrifice, contributing. Not exactly patriotism, but protecting her country came close.

Hannah was accepted and went to Langley. There she stepped from her polished mahogany world hip deep into a slack-water cypress swamp—thick with fusty methane bubbles and squishy underfoot. Central Intelligence Agency. She met people she never knew existed—seemingly with DNA strands identical to the antediluvian fish that crawled out of the ocean, grunted oxygen, and sprouted legs. Oh Lord, but this was a workshop for cognitive science, this rogue's gallery: droll skeptics; conflict junkies; bipolar egotists; indolent browbeaters—the sly inquisitors who relished causing distress as a gourmand relishes a mousseline.

And before Hannah concluded that she had mistakenly entered through the back door of an asylum, she began picking out people she thought of as the Worthies: the managers and engineers and analysts and assistants with good hearts and kind dispositions, who tithed their lives to the mission and to their country, and who all seemed to believe that the only enduring legacy in the service was to mentor and develop and support subordinates, to leave behind future leaders who would in turn become mentors to others. (Later, she wondered whether Simon Benford was a Worthy, or whether he was simply a demented ecstatic.)

As training started in earnest, observant Hannah began to know the operations folks—the field officers, men and women—who accomplished heroics from the depths of the shadows, who stole inaccessible secrets and skirted physical danger and manipulated the odds, and who in their anonymity seldom received credit for their secret successes but invariably shouldered the blame for their public failures. Hannah's sturdy mind knew who she was, and she knew what she wanted to be: an ops officer.

She worked hard at the Farm, passed with top marks, and expected to be picked up by Africa or Latin America Division—she was ready for the rough-and-tumble world of operations in the Third World; the mission appealed to her. But a mid-level manager with the sloping forehead and jutting mandible of a Neanderthal insisted, for no reason other than he could, that Hannah be assigned to Europe Division, where he was serving as the executive officer (EXO) to the chief. Hannah therefore was ordered to report to EUR Division. A respectful visit to his office to plead for reconsideration of assignment resulted only in the nettled EXO summarily postponing Hannah's first overseas posting and banishing her until further notice to the Iberian desk, amid the endless cubicles under the buzzing fluorescent lights. He petulantly told her she would be running name traces and drafting talking-point memos—she would learn her lesson for questioning his authority.

As she contemplated tendering her resignation from CIA, finding a schooner, signing on as cook, and sailing around the world, Hannah saw a face looking at her from over the partition of the adjoining cubicle. "I take it you just got out of the Farm," said a woman's voice. Only the top of her head and blue eyes were visible. Her voice was slow and smooth.

"And ended up in the third subbasement," said Hannah hopelessly. "I thought I was getting an assignment, but the EXO had another idea."

"Yes, the EXO," said the woman softly. "He's quite the wet orchard."

"Wet orchard?" said Hannah.

"Drippy. Smelly and unpleasant," she said. The woman's eyes scanned her, took in her shoes, and swept over her cubicle, cataloging everything. Hannah had no doubt that this woman could then write from memory everything she had seen in the last blink of an eye.

"How long have *you* been on the branch?" said Hannah.

"You're Hannah Archer, correct?" said the woman, gliding around the partition. She offered a warm dry hand, and her grip was surprisingly strong. "Name's Janice, Janice Callahan."

"Hi, I'm Hannah. How did you know my name?"

"Care for a walk?" said Janice.

"Sure," said Hannah. "Janice, do you always answer a question with a question?"

"What do you think?" said Janice.

Janice was over fifty years old, a honey-redhead with bedroom hair boyishly swept to the side, and crinkly blue eyes over a sharp nose and strong chin. Her mouth seemed to be in a perpetual grin, as if she knew the answer before the question was asked. When she smiled there were dimples. She wore a dark-turquoise silk blazer with Chinese buttons over a black pencil skirt; hints of a voluptuous figure were unmistakable. *Whoever she is,* thought Hannah, *regal just met sultry.*

They had lunch together in a corner of the cafeteria, then took a walk around the Headquarters building. Janice walked quickly, light on her feet, and her eyes never stopped moving: *She has swivel eyes like a freaking tree chameleon,* thought Hannah. *She can see in two different directions simultaneously.* They looped around the ornamental fish pond, then beneath the massive SR-71 Blackbird spy aircraft, displayed on a pylon as if in flight, the legacy of a former director from the military who blithely conflated fifty years of American espionage with an air museum. And they walked past the three mounted cement panels of the Berlin wall, one side raucous with Western graffiti, the other side unmarked and untouched by human hands.

Janice frequently ran her fingers through her untamed hair, perhaps stirred by memories of past spies and lovers. Her nougat voice enveloped them both as she told Hannah about her career. Only the old-timers remembered her now, she said with some indifference, and a lot of the old-timers remembered her exceptionally well.

Janice loved ops. She had the distinction—unique in the CIA—of having had successive assignments in every Cold War Eastern European capital. No other man or woman had done it. Never married, the nectarous Janice had gone from posting to posting, besting in turn seven inimical intelligence services—red-toothed and red-clawed, all vassals of the Soviets—the Polish SB, the East German Stasi, the Czech StB, the Hungarian AVH, the Serbian SDB, the Romanian Securitate, the Bulgarian SD. Voluptuous and distracting, Janice had faked the central European thugs out of their socks, without removing their shoes, for twenty years. She had handled sources, serviced dead drops, copied Warsaw Pact documents, and exfiltrated doomed agents to safety across a rust-red Iron Curtain limned from the Baltic to the Black Sea with plastic bags, scarves, and woolen caps caught on the barbed wire, flapping in the wind.

Hannah listened with rapt attention. "It's like the most perfect circle ever," said Janice, describing to Hannah the feel of a successful operational act while under surveillance, from kickoff to getting black to meeting the agent and returning with the intel, an empyreal cycle of action. Her eyes blazed in the remembering. Was this something that interested her? Hannah was intrigued, and she asked Janice to tell her more. She did better than that. The next day, Janice took her to meet Simon Benford, chief of Counterintelligence Division. CID was a mazelike windowless space, office after office, all closed, cipher locks on all the doors. In a far corner, Benford's office was a dimly lit burrow, spilling over with papers and files and newspapers. Benford sat behind a desk with approximately one square foot of clear space in front of him. On that clear space Hannah could see an orange personnel file with her name printed on the side tab. Benford was reading it carefully. Hannah looked over at Janice, who nodded slightly as if to say "watch your hands and feet."

"It appears you excelled in your basic training," said Benford finally, without raising his eyes from the open file folder. His voice was soft, his tone pained and impatient. "You logged especially good marks in street exercises. Your evaluations are topflight." Hannah thought, *Huh.* It looked as though they were reviewing her background, as if Janice had been talent scouting. She shrugged.

"I liked all my training," said Hannah. "I just want to get out of this wet orchard and get an assignment." She thought the argot would sound slick. Janice looked over at her with a grin that said *don't.*

"I'm sure you do," said Benford, now looking up. His hair was uncombed and a lock fell across his forehead. "I have a proposal to make to you. Listen carefully, for your response could affect the direction and nature of the rest of your career, however long or short it turns out to be."

Hannah did not move.

"There is an urgent need for an officer, specially trained in denied-area operations and covert communications, to deploy overseas to support an ongoing, sensitive case that is producing remarkable intelligence," said Benford. "I am looking for a first-tour case officer who is not widely known to the opposition. I am looking for an officer with intuition, nerve, judgment, imagination, calculation, and—pardon, Janice—the balls to operate securely against considerable hostile pressure on the street. I would like to consider you for this internal-ops assignment." He flipped Hannah's file closed and stared at her.

"I will not tell you where and with whom you will be working until you have successfully completed IO training. If you do, you will have additional training, some with Janice here—she is the best there ever was—as well as technical training. If by then you have not stubbed your toe, you and I will sit down to discuss additional sensitive refinements to this first assignment, the nature of which includes the likelihood of your violating internal CIA regulations and most likely making you subject to disciplinary action, if not civil prosecution."

"What's the downside?" said Hannah. Beside her, Janice did not look at her. *Tree lizard peripheral vision,* thought Hannah. *She doesn't have to turn her head.*

"Endeavor not to be clever until and unless I tell you to be," said Benford.

Hannah blushed.

"I want you to be completely clear about this," said Benford. "I am proposing that you become a specialist in internal operations like the person standing beside you." He indicated Janice with a languid wave. "After this current assignment, there will be more assignments like it. There are always more. By then you will have been diverted from the normal career path of a working case officer in the Clandestine Service. Your choice of foreign assignments may be affected, as will your promotion rate. You might balance this against the prospect of belonging to a small group of elite officers who can do things no other line officer in the Clandestine Service could even remotely contemplate." Through lowered lashes, he appraised the young woman with—he'd just noticed—celadon green eyes, which were locked onto his. She looked back without blinking.

"If you need time to consid—"

"I accept," said Hannah.

Benford thought he could detect her vibrating like a tuning fork.

After Hannah left, Benford rocked back in his chair and put his feet up on an overturned wastebasket. He moved the dusty gooseneck lamp on his desk and blinked at Janice, who had managed to move file folders to clear enough space on the small couch to sit. "What do you think?" Janice said.

Benford shrugged. "I sense resolve and spirit," he said. "On paper she's better than our other choices. That muscular kid from the University of Delaware . . ." He shook his head. "Anyway, I like this Hannah Archer. Nice job, good pickup."

Janice leaned back and stretched her legs, a move that would have distracted normal men. "She's going to have to learn to control the sass," Janice said.

"Nonsense," said Benford. "This place needs all the sass it can get." He twiddled a pencil. "Do you think she has the starch?"

"You never really know until they hit the bricks," said Janice. "I've seen star students in training disintegrate during a real op. But I think yes."

I think yes, too," said Benford tossing the pencil down.

"And the fact she's a woman?" Janice asked, running her fingers through her hair, mussing more than combing it. A Chinese button on her blazer had popped open.

Benford was oblivious to the simmering solar storm sitting five feet away from him who, for her own part, was not even remotely trying to flirt. "Means nothing. The years of housewife cover are gone; the Russians suspect everybody. The FSB will try to rattle her. Get her ready for the rough stuff, Janice."

The redhead nodded.

"When we tell her about DIVA, I want her to connect with the asset. God willing the two will never have to meet face-to-face, but I want her to feel she's trading covcom shots with her fucking sister. I want them to have a blood bond."

"Blood bond," said Janice.

"I'm sure you heard me. Let's make sure. Get Nash here immediately to mentor her through training."

MOUSELLINE SAUCE

Put a saucepan in a low-heat bain-marie and whisk egg yolks and progressive amounts of melted butter until a glossy, thick sauce is achieved. Whisk in lemon juice and salt, then fold in unsweetened whipped cream. Serve immediately.

17

She had a surveillance instructor named Jay, goateed, sixty years old, spry, and wry, a guru sitting on a mountaintop, who showed her how to find the answers for herself. With Nate observing, Jay and Janice ran Hannah on the Washington, DC, streets twelve, fourteen, fifteen hours a day. They set teams of five, ten, a dozen cars on her—she was expected to identify them and bring back license-plate numbers. She dragged surveillance foot teams of a dozen, fifteen, twenty people around metropolitan Washington, down alleys, up stairwells, across skywalks. She was required to calculate her status on the street precisely, unerringly, without doubt. She had to identify and remember faces. Benford monitored her progress from his cave in Headquarters. Moscow would be a thousand times worse, a million times more deadly.

Jay knew what Hannah was talking about when she told him about the tingling on her arms and the backs of her hands, how the air felt cool on her neck when the hairs stood on end, when she felt the coverage before she saw it and began to count the cars, filing away the faces. He helped her refine the witchcraft so it complemented the science. God, she was tired at night, and she started *dreaming* about surveillance, of the two minutes before hitting a site, of the rushing noise and the tunnel vision as she worked the gap—the three-second interval when surveillance couldn't see her hands.

The presence of the young case officer observing her training initially was unsettling. Hannah knew who Nash was; she had heard his name and the rumors about him in her homeroom at the Farm. On the street, during her surveillance-detection runs, he always appeared ahead of her, clearly observing the way she managed timing stops, the way she came at sites, the way she used double corners. As an instructor-evaluator, he was aware of her planned routes, but Hannah still could sense the ease with which he worked the street.

The first time she actually spoke to him was during a midnight debrief at the end of an exercise that had lasted eight hours. The ten-car surveillance team had retired for the night. In the parking lot of a supermarket on upper Wisconsin Avenue, Jay was reviewing a route map spread out on the hood of his car, Janice was flipping the pages of a wrinkled steno pad, and Nate was sitting on the fender of his car, hair matted with sweat. It had been a steamy Washington summer night, hours of exertion, and Hannah could feel her skin creeping under her shirt. A hundred moths dive-bombed the mercury vapor lights in the lot, casting wiggly shadows on the windshields of the cars. Nobody spoke for a while, the only sound the rustling of pages from Janice, whose light denim shirt was wet between her shoulder blades and under her arms. She had tied her hair back, but a few errant strands stuck to her neck.

It had been the first time Hannah failed during a run: She incorrectly assessed a car parked at one end of a scenic overlook on the GW Parkway as a casual, not surveillance, based chiefly on the fact that the couple inside the car had been necking. Tired, impatient, and determined to complete the dead drop, she disregarded the quivering hairs on the back of her neck, bent over the low stone fence, and emplaced the agent package in the cavity formed by a missing stone in the wall. The amorous couple had been surveillance, and they saw it all. A busted run.

"In Moscow," said Nate, "they would have stayed still until you left, then put cameras on the overlook, waited a week, a month, a year, and gotten the agent's license number when he came to unload the dead drop." Not accusatory, not critical, just fact.

Hannah paced up and down. "I didn't like that car from the start," she said. *Stupid comment; shut up.*

Nate looked at his watch, a black Luminox with a rubberized band—the face glowed in the low light. "Twenty years ago they would have arrested the agent right away and shot him in the Lubyanka," said Nate. "Today they'd run him against you for twelve months, identify more station officers, sites, and agents, and finish by setting up a splashy ambush for Russian TV. *Then they'd shoot him.*"

Hannah tamped down her anger. She'd take this from Janice or Jay, but this guy wasn't much older than she was. "I know," she said with a little edge. *"I got it."*

Jay's head came up at the tone of her voice. "That's why it's called training," he said gently. "You learn from tonight. In the field, even if you've been black for sixteen hours, if there's someone on the site when you get there—a drunk, two kids humping in the bushes, a herd of llamas—you abort the drop and we try it another evening at the alternate site. Your agent is inconvenienced, but he's alive."

"You have to be right one hundred percent of the time," said Janice softly. "The opposition has to be right only once."

Hannah stopped pacing and looked at Janice. "Loud and clear, Janice. When's my next run? Day after tomorrow? I'll be ready."

Jay and Janice left in one car. *Wonder if they're doing it,* thought Hannah.

Nate was still sitting on his fender looking at her. "You okay?" he said.

At the last minute, Hannah decided not to bristle at this patronization. "Yeah, fine," she said. "A little tired."

"I don't suppose you want to have a drink, unwind a little?" said Nate, looking at his watch. "District Two Bar up the road is open till two."

"It's pretty late," said Hannah, realizing she sort of wanted to go.

"When I was going through the course, I could never sleep right after an exercise."

"I know, right?" said Hannah. "The mainspring is still too tight."

"Jay used to say the flywheel was still spinning." An insider observation shared between colleagues in an exclusive club. Hannah felt it.

At the bar, they both ordered beers and split a plate of fries with Russian dressing, not quite Brussels-style, but appropriate, Nate noted. Hannah took off her light jacket; she was wearing a tank top, and Nate noticed her toned arms, then her long skinny fingers when she ran a hand through her curly blond hair. Her hipster glasses were smudged.

Hannah didn't want a second beer, but let Nate splash some of his into her glass. "That was a stupid fuckup tonight," said Hannah, then quickly, "I'm not fishing for sympathy; you don't have to say a thing."

The way she said "don't have to say a thing" reminded Nate of Dominika. "Look," he said, "no one goes through the course without tripping up once or twice. Better here than over there."

Hannah shook her head. "No, it was stupid. When Benford hears about it I'm toast."

"Benford's not like that," said Nate. "Besides, Jay and Janice saw something tonight."

Hannah waited for it.

"You didn't fall apart, you didn't make excuses, and you showed them you want to get right back up. That counts for a lot."

Hannah put a French fry into her mouth. "How do you know what Jay and Janice saw?"

"Because I saw it too," said Nate.

The hell continued: The unseen instructor staff broke into Hannah's car, and into her apartment, to harass and unsettle, to test, to try to break the sassy blonde who burned their surveillance teams night after night. Get her ready for the rough stuff, Benford had said; let her feel what it'll be like in Moscow. So the little games began: anchovy oil on her car's hot engine block; petroleum jelly on her windshield wipers; her mother's delicate gold chain taken out of her dresser drawer and cruelly knotted; her refrigerator unplugged for twelve hours, the contents dripping on the floor; a fulsome memento left floating in the toilet all day; a gritty boot print on her pillow. Hannah drove with the car windows down, peered through a greasy windshield, mopped up in the kitchen, held her nose and flushed the brown swan, flipped the pillow over, and fell into bed exhausted but exhilarated.

Nate had gone with the entry team into Hannah's basement apartment once, to observe and to provisionally check that she had not left route maps or notes lying around, a common student error during training. They all knew the Russians would pillage her quarters in Moscow surreptitiously. As the team ranged through Hannah's apartment, Nate had gone down the hall and stood at the threshold of her bedroom, leaning against the jamb, not moving. The room smelled citrusy. The shade was down on the only window in the little room. Her bed was messily made and a shirt hung off the back of a cane chair in the corner, two black pumps lined up underneath. Neat, but not a fanatic. The door to a small closet was partly open and something black and lacy hung on a hook. A lacrosse stick leaned against a corner, the handle wrapped in jock tape, black with her sweat. Nate resisted the impulse to step inside and check the drawers in both bedside tables—the entry team would do that.

Near the end of the course Nate saw that she was running hot and cool, the misstep of that early week not forgotten but left behind, the demons tamed. She was transforming herself into a prophet, a seer; she was feeling the street. Better, she was expanding her power, reaching back and getting into the teams' head. She began knowing what they'd do and where they'd be even before they did.

It was time then for the final exercise—time to go up against the FEEBs. The FBI foreign counterintelligence surveillance team—informally called the Gs and the best in the business—got ready to teach this hotshot blond spook twat some manners. At the start of the twelve-hour exercise, the massive FBI team flowed around the solo officer in her little car—the interior of which still reeked of cooked anchovies—vectored unerringly by an orbiting, fixed-wing spotter plane with an immense lens, a gyroscope-stabilized monocular that could keep Hannah in the crosshairs wherever she went, unseen and unheard. No one from the FBI told Jay or his staff that they were putting an aircraft on Hannah until the run had started and she was on her own. Fuck fair play; this was war, they said. Surrounded by snickering FEEBish instructors, Nate listened thin-lipped to the coverage on the radio net, praying that Hannah's sixth sense would kick in. He needn't have worried.

Smirks from the Aqua Velva–filled control room vanished when the blond spook twat purposely drove around Washington National Airport, forcing the spotter plane to shear off to avoid commercial landing patterns and resulting in the far-back FEEB team temporarily losing the eye. Hannah then quickly crossed the Fourteenth Street and South Capitol Bridges and disappeared into southeast Washington. The Gs found Hannah's fish-stinky car—they had put a beacon on it—an hour later near the Frederick Douglass house in historic Anacostia. Hannah was long gone—on foot, in disguise, disappeared. In the six hours remaining in the exercise, she successfully loaded a drop, cleared another, and met and debriefed an FBI special agent—one of their own—who was role-playing a penetration asset inside the Bureau. The irony was not lost on the feds.

The FEEBs were apoplectic, then rueful, then collegial, as they bought Hannah beers and pizzas late that night. Benford claimed never to have eaten a calzone and ordered one with leeks and mushrooms. Benford, Nate, Janice, and Jay, sitting at the far end of the long table, watched Hannah at the other end, surrounded by youthful Gs, being backslapped and trading high fives. At one point amid the hilarity, Hannah looked at Benford and nodded—for an instant the two of them were alone together in their cobwebby world. *Satisfactory,* thought Benford.

Nate now took the lead in the remainder of Hannah's training. They began reviewing DIVA's file. Nate described the asset Hannah would be handling and for whose life she would be responsible. They pored over the massive database of impersonal communications sites in Moscow—called GOLD NUGGET—which contained casing reports on dead drops, car-toss sites, cache sites, brush-pass sites, moving-car delivery sites, brief-encounter sites, and signal sites dating from the 1960s, when agents like Popov and Penkovsky were saving the world from atomic war. When the Soviet Union collapsed, GOLD NUGGET had been unplugged, deleted, and discarded in a fit of fashionable reform because, according to the helium-filled Russian Ops Division chief at the time, the Russians were "now our friends." A few secret anarchists in ROD had saved a backup disk of the data and, Russia having inevitably reverted to type, eventually reconstituted the database, now immensely expanded, synapse-quick, and interactive.

They worked in a disused conference room in CID—disused because Benford's counterintelligence subterraneans never gathered together in conference. This was partly because they worked on respective cases in isolation, but mostly because CI mole hunters were uncomfortable in crowds. Hannah, expressionless, assessed Nate's mountainous knowledge of Moscow—how could she ever hope to emulate him—and coolly noted his commitment to the asset DIVA. Hannah had not yet been told her true name, but she saw with a woman's eye that Nate was dedicated to her. There was no other word. Dedicated.

"You will be under the direction of chief of Moscow Station," said Benford to Hannah. "As you will discover, he has a forceful personality, and can be demanding and inflexible. He, oddly enough, is an adept politician, and has won the approval of the director." Benford looked over at Nate, and they both thought of a previous COS Moscow, Gordon Gondorf, an epic mismanager, now ensconced as COS Paris.

"It pains me to tell you," continued Benford, "that in matters operational the current COS Moscow is a botcher—is that a word?—a chronic muddler who, through inattention, ignorance, misplaced self-confidence, and blockheadedness, has left a smoking trail of flaps, ambushes, counterintelligence exposures, and, by my count, the lives of two and possibly three agents in his wake. You will not repeat this ever."

"Probably eats pie with a knife," said Hannah, recalling what her mother used to say, New England code for a hayseed, then remembered, *Oh God keep your mouth shut*. Benford rolled his eyes at her, but from the other side of the table Nate looked up, delighted: curly blond hair, glasses, smart, saucy—hot.

"Yes. Quite," said Benford. "The most hair-raising aspect of COS Moscow's career—apart from his inexplicable avoidance of accountability for his mistakes—is that he is *unaware* of his incompetence. He has no *sentient appreciation* of his deficiencies. He is Mr. Toad behind the wheel of a motorcar."

"Mr. Toad?" said Nate.

"*Wind in the Willows,*" said Hannah, chuckling. She was freshly showered, hair brilliant, face alight at having gotten through IO training, and flushed with excitement at now entering into Benford's confidence. She liked working with Nate, felt that she was part of his club, liked his loose-limbed approach, and was fascinated with what she privately called his *controlled fanaticism* to denied-area operations and to DIVA.

Hannah wore a pearl-gray suit and black heels (*the look is too old for her,* thought Nate; *she should wear something more casual*), no jewelry, and a sports watch with a bezel and a clunky metal-link band. He liked her heavy-framed glasses—brainy hiding beneath bubbly. For the first time Nate noticed her straight nose and her green eyes, and she caught him looking at her and smiled, and he smiled back. She wore nature-girl pink lip gloss. Benford started speaking again.

"While you will outwardly be under COS's command, you are working for me. You know the requirements and the priorities." He paused.

"What are you saying?" said Hannah.

"This stays in this room," said Benford. "What I am saying is: As long as COS does not interfere, or alter, or manage your mission parameters, fine. The minute he in any way jeopardizes your goals, you are to disregard his orders and proceed on your own recognizance."

"Jesus, Simon," said Nate.

Benford waved him to stop. "If the situation becomes untenable, go to the Station communicator and send me a cable in JOLT privacy channels, without COS release."

"Jesus *Christ,* Simon," said Nate. "You're directing her to mutiny? She's your illegal penetration of the Station?"

"I will not allow DIVA to be subjected to unnecessary risk, much less mortal danger born of stupidity. Hannah will successfully deploy comms to DIVA. Vernon Throckmorton will not fuck this up." Benford swiveled toward Nate. "So perhaps your own well-known custodial concern for Dominika is now not so misplaced."

Silence in the room. Agent's true name spoken. Never done.

"It's a nice name," said Hannah, smiling, anxious to break the silence. *These guys are invested in ways I'll never know,* Hannah thought. *So now I'm invested too. Her name's Dominika: Hello, my sister*. The young officer had no way of knowing that the crenellated mind of Simon Benford would not make such an inadvertent slip, nor could she have fathomed that Benford purposely had done so expressly to begin to create the metaphysical bond between this little blond gladiator and the former Russian ballerina, five thousand miles away.

The next morning, Benford wanted to talk some more.

"Your evaluations for the last two weeks of technical training were satisfactory," said Benford, "just as the last three months of your street training were. I commend you."

Hannah fiddled with her hands and blushed. She had practiced emplacing the short range agent communications (SRAC) sensors—they were called RAPTORS—at Cane Island in the Santee Coastal Reserve, two hundred acres of US government-owned tidewater scrubland somewhere south of Georgetown, South Carolina, under the guidance of a tall, rangy tech named Hearsey, who Hannah thought looked like a cowboy senator from Montana. The remote sensors—eight inches across, slightly convex, made of gray, scored fiberglass, and somewhat heavy—resembled oversized mushroom caps that had to be buried several inches beneath the ground. These sensors would receive DIVA's SRAC bursts and store them, and could be interrogated on command by a passing Station officer. They in turn could be preloaded with a Station message for DIVA that would be exchanged in a two-second "handshake" whenever the agent activated a sensor with her handheld unit. They essentially were electronic mailboxes filled and emptied remotely.

"Obviously," said Hearsey, drawling his words, "in the case of the RAPTOR equipment in Moscow, emplacement has to be done during the summer months when you can dig earth." He fingered the specially designed hand trowel that in one motion would excavate the dinner-plate-sized cavity for the sensor, allowing the soil or sod to be replaced and stamped flat.

"You can carry the three sensors in this pack," Hearsey said, handing her a nylon pouch with shoulder straps. "There are aluminum panels in the pack, treated with barium sulfate."

"Stop," said Hannah. "Tell me why the pack is lined."

Hearsey looked hurt. "The sensors run off a small source of strontium-90," he said. "Not enough annual sunlight in Moscow for photovoltaic power—solar, that is—so we developed a mini radioisotope thermoelectric generator to power these units. Half life of eighty-nine years. Your agent's *grandchildren* will be using these babies when—"

"Stop again," said Hannah. "The phrase 'half life' reminds me of nuclear zombies in apocalypse movies."

"These sensors are perfectly safe," said Hearsey, running his fingers through his sandy hair.

"Hearsey," said Hannah. He avoided looking at her.

"They're sealed, totally shielded. Still . . ."

"Still?" said Hannah.

"Don't carry them below your belt, near your fallopian tubes or anything. Why take chances?" Hearsey smiled at her.

At the end of training, Hannah was astonished when Hearsey bent down, gave her a hug, and said, "Wish I could go with you, you know, to help."

"And so it starts," said Benford. "You are assigned to deploy the RAPTOR short-range agent communication sensors for GTDIVA at selected sites around Moscow. You know the requirements: First the agent package is placed in a short-term drop. I need not remind you that this phase is a critical life-and-death operation. Then you must emplace the relay receivers—

how many are there? yes, three—as well as prepare the principal and mobile base stations."

Nate looked at Hannah. "That first drop to DIVA—if you whiff it, she's dead," he said, totally serious.

He was wearing a navy-blue blazer, gray slacks, blue-striped shirt, and a navy tie with thin pink stripes. *On spring break from prep school,* thought Hannah. She swallowed the "tell me something new" on her lips and nodded. Last night over burgers he'd talked about Moscow, about working as a US diplomat dip cover—from the embassy, about the city and its pulses. Hannah had recognized the voice of "I've done that" and listened hard.

"You have been trained in the RAPTOR system nearly to the level of expert," said Benford to Hannah. "I cannot augment your knowledge in this. Nash here will continue to brief you on FSB surveillance and on DIVA—I want you to begin understanding her life, her predilections, her idiosyncrasies. And her unambiguous and critical importance to the United States."

He stood and walked to the door of the conference room. "I will see you tomorrow, and we will briefly review everything we have discussed, and then I will send you to Moscow. Period." He nodded to them both and walked out.

LEEK AND MUSHROOM CALZONE

Dice onion, garlic, and washed leeks, then sauté with shiitake, cremini, and oyster mushrooms until cooked through and glossy. Add spinach and cook until wilted. The mixture should be dry. Place filling on rolled-out pizza dough, add cubes of feta cheese and a pinch of fennel seed. Fold one edge of dough over, and crimp seam. Bake in a high oven until golden brown.

18

They went to dinner on Capitol Hill at the Hawk 'n' Dove on Pennsylvania Avenue, close to Hannah's apartment. "She's temperamental, but loyal," said Nate, picking at a piece of salmon. "DIVA's been through a lot. She's seen the worst of her system."

Hannah took a sip of wine and read his face.

"Because of all that, she wanted out," said Nate. "It got pretty rough. Then, when MARBLE was shot—he was like a father to her—she got crazy angry and put herself back into harness. A year later she hands us this Iran thing."

Hannah listened. She had finally read all eight volumes of the DIVA file. "Tell me about the ambush in Vienna," she said.

Nate looked down. "Not much to tell. We got lucky. It was unreal—a dog-pack manhunt in modern-day Vienna."

"I don't know how I would react," said Hannah. She took another sip of wine. "There was something I wanted to ask you from the file. You wrote the ops cable about Vienna, about that night. You said that DIVA 'struggled for control' in that warehouse."

Nate shook his head. "Yeah, that's right. Domi was out of her mind over the murder of her Sparrow, the Serb girl." *Domi,* thought Hannah. *Huh, pet names between handler and agent.* Hannah saw that he was holding back.

"Struggling for control, out of her mind; what's that mean, exactly?" asked Hannah.

"I never really reported it. She executed one of the Iranian surveillants," said Nate quickly. "She severed his carotid artery with a steak knife."

Hannah put her fork down. Nate waited for the hands to the face, the shocked whisper, the pale face, but she didn't blink.

"I would have done the same," said Hannah without emotion.

Nate looked at her hard, reassessing this golden nature girl. Green eyes stared back unwaveringly. "It was life and death; it was a giant surveillance team. They kept showing up, driving us to a bridge, and probably under the sights of a sniper. I just wanted to get her out of there," said Nate.

He's protective, thought Hannah. *He cares for her.* "I can understand that."

"Yeah, well, it's important to keep her safe," said Nate.

He really *cares for her,* thought Hannah.

They paid the bill and looked at the time. It was too early to go home. They walked down Pennsylvania Avenue a few doors to a nearby bar, sat in a pair of overstuffed leather chairs in the back, and kept talking—about Moscow, surveillance, casing sites, DIVA. Two drinks later, they started discussing assignments, careers, the Agency, life. Conversation between them was easy, but she instinctively steered away from their love lives. Hannah thought Nate was thoughtful and a little shy; Nate thought Hannah was perceptive and spirited. They liked each other—as colleagues, as people—and shared a unique life, a unique vocation. They had spent a lot of time together recently. It felt strange, but it also felt good.

They left the bar, crossed Pennsylvania Avenue, walked around Seward Square and up Sixth Street SE, toward Hannah's apartment—a basement sublet in a row house a block from Eastern Market. Hannah's last two gin and tonics had numbed her nose, and she stepped carefully on the uneven sidewalk. The rearguard of multiple beers likewise had just arrived in Nate's head, and he had to tell Hannah—just had to—a Putin joke, first in Russian, but then in English when Hannah put her arm into Nate's and yanked, telling him she didn't speak Russian.

Stalin came to Putin in his dream and told him how to rule Russia. "Destroy all the democrats without mercy, then eliminate their parents, and hang their children, and incinerate their relatives and their friends, and kill their pets, and paint your Kremlin office blue," said Stalin's ghost. "Why blue?" said Putin.

"I don't get it," said Hannah.

"Come on," said Nate. "The only thing Putin asks, the only thing that doesn't make sense to him, is the color of his office?"

A snort came out of Hannah, then they both started laughing, and she held on to him to keep from stumbling. They stopped after a while, staring at each other and, subconsciously, scanned the other side of the street—spook habit. Hannah suddenly looked serious.

"Can I tell you something?" said Hannah. Nate blinked through the beer and tried to focus.

"Sure," he said.

"I'm a little scared about all this," said Hannah. "I didn't dare tell Benford, but I'm worried about that first run in Moscow. I mean, will I have the nerve? Will I see coverage if it's on me?"

A gout of tipsy tenderness welled up in Nate's chest. *Poor kid, she's fighting this alone.* He stepped up to her and held her head in his hands.

"It's normal to be scared. But you're a natural, one of the best I've seen. Everyone thinks so, or they wouldn't be sending you to Station. The first time, the hours right before you go out, is a bitch. But once you're on the street you'll start feeling the vibe and they won't be able to touch you."

Hannah hiccupped. "Shakespeare, are you actually holding my head in your hands?" She giggled.

Nate blushed and took his hands away, and she thought she had embarrassed him.

The streetlamps emitted a gassy haze filtered through the leaves of the trees along the sidewalk. The tension and fatigue of training boiled over, and she stepped up to him—*Don't stop now, idiot*—put clumsy arms around his neck, and they were kissing, a little unsteadily, but she felt his arms around her waist, and her pulse was racing, and they kept kissing, and she slid her hands down his back.

When Hannah kissed him, Nate was genuinely surprised. This talented woman had by all accounts maxxed the most demanding operations course in the Agency. She had, with aplomb, tied up the entire counterintelligence apparatus of the Washington FBI—on their home turf. She had been selected by the demanding and irascible Benford to service the drops and manage the covcom shots in Moscow in support of CIA's premier Russian penetration asset, DIVA.

More to the point, they had gotten along during these last training days—really gotten along, without all the usual territorial, glandular spraying between two ops officers—and Nate had genuinely celebrated her success. And now, unless this block of Sixth Street SE was leveled in the next two minutes by a fuel air explosive, it seriously appeared as if they would be making love. His head swirled as Hannah—tasting of lime and tonic—kissed him again and, like a guilty puppy who will not look at his scolding master, he stuffed the thought of Dominika behind the curtain. Hannah was smart and brave and sweet and confident and desirable, and perceptive, and sassy, and they were partners, in a way, in this risky undertaking. And, damn it, was he going to reject her on the eve of her seriously nervy assignment? He was prepared to rationalize this forever—but her arms were around his neck, and her mouth was yielding, and unless there was someone else on the sidewalk behind him those were probably Hannah's hands moving around; her tongue flicked at his lips, and then they were inside the neat, spare efficiency apartment, a few books on the bookshelf, two pairs of running shoes lined up by the door, and Nate almost blurted that he'd already been inside but caught himself. Her arms were around his neck again.

Oh God, suddenly she could feel she was wet between her legs. They kissed again, without urgency but deeply, and Hannah closed her eyes and felt a knot in her stomach—*What are you doing, are you crazy?*—and she pulled her sweater up over her head, and pulled his sweater over his head, and they were on her bed, on the blue-and-white quilt her mother had made—*thinking about Mother now?*—and they kept kissing, wordlessly, kicking off shoes and pulling off clothes, and Hannah put her glasses on the bedside table, and closed her eyes and his skin felt hot against her body, and she didn't stop kissing him while she reached for him—*God, he'll think I'm a real slut*—and steered him inside her, sweet and full, and rhythmically he moved, back and forth like a sexy tectonic slip plate, back and forth and back, thighs friction-hot, eyes locked on each other, mouths open, straining, and Hannah felt something stirring—she loved that gathering first tremor in her belly—and she levered her trembling legs out from under him and wrapped them around his waist and dug in her heels—*God, I should have put moisturizer on my feet, too much running*—and she held him by the shoulders and pulled him to her as her head went back on the pillow, and he nuzzled her arching neck, and the little tremor became a series of them, and she climaxed hard, *Babe, so good, it's been too long*, and felt that flush of wet underneath her and Nate was still moving and the sensation was glorious, and she opened her eyes, and put her fingers on his lips and pulled them to her, and she kissed him as he kept moving, *Dude, do not stop now*, and she didn't want him to stop.

Nate thought Hannah had a different touch than Dominika, somehow less primal—Hannah was a honeyed topaz to Dominika's fathomless sapphire; silent Hannah vibrated while vocal Dominika shuddered, and blond curls looked different against the pillow than chestnut tresses—he was going to drive himself crazy. Then he felt the hot wet bloom of Hannah's orgasm, different than—*Shut up for Chrissake*—and she clamped her mouth on his and she gripped him tighter, but silently, and they kissed again, more tenderly intimate than twenty minutes ago, lovers now, and he lay on the wet spot on the blue-and-white quilt as they dozed in each other's arms.

It was still dark and the streetlights were slanting through the windows when Hannah got up for two glasses of water. Nate watched her cross the shadowy single room to the sink and come back and he couldn't stop himself from noting that she was *shorter,* and her buttocks were *flatter,* and her legs were *skinnier,* and the nipples on her small breasts were *darker,* and between her legs she was blond and downy—*Fucking stop it, you* absolutely *will not imagine them side by side.* She saw him looking at her and put down the water glasses, and it started again and Hannah vibrated and this time quietly moaned his name with a shaking voice and they both collapsed and ended up falling asleep on the vastly expanded wet spot on the quilt.

As the sky through the little barred window was getting lighter—Hannah whispered in Nate's ear that the Mohammedan distinction between night and day is the moment one can distinguish a black thread from a white one—she put her chin on his chest and looked at him. Her glasses were on a little crooked. Her hair had been combed by an eggbeater, flyaway strands catching the rising light in the room. Nate could now distinguish her green irises—the Nash distinction between night and day. She kept staring at him.

"I'll keep her safe," Hannah said quietly. Nate searched her eyes.

"You love her, don't you?" said Hannah. "DIVA. I mean . . . Dominika."

Nate didn't move his head.

"I can't imagine how it feels," she said. "The worry, the not knowing." Nate didn't know what to say. She was silent for a moment.

"I'm glad we did this," said Hannah, smiling. "I'm glad I know you. And I won't let anything happen to her."

Nate felt a wave of affection for her well up inside him, supplanting for an instant the rising contrition blocking his throat.

Hannah rose up and leaned forward to kiss Nate, but he shot upright off the pillow and grabbed her by the shoulders.

"What are you doing?" said Hannah, looking wide-eyed at him.

“What do we have today?” said Nate, alarm on his face.

“Ten o’clock with Benford for training review,” she said. “What’s the matter with you?”

“Come here,” said Nate, pulling her off the bed and across the room to the little mirrored coatrack near the front door. He steered Hannah in front of the mirror and turned her jaw to one side. “Is it too hot to get away with a turtleneck?” he asked.

“Oh, fuck me,” said Hannah, looking at a hickey on her neck the approximate shape of the Republic of Romania.

Their affair charged the air like a thunderstorm building over a still wheat field, the thunder-rumble moment before the deluge when the grasshoppers on the stalks stop buzzing. Their days together were coming to an end and it spawned an urgency between them. They spent edgy, tick-tock days now, reviewing the files, studying the pictures, sitting together at the hastily organized, survival-Russian language lessons so she could at least read the street signs. Lovers’ tradecraft was hasty and ridiculous, but they couldn’t stop themselves: the spooks in them refused to look at the wall clocks; consciously they did not sit at the same cafeteria table; they waved theatrically as they left Headquarters and walked to their cars at opposite sides of West Lot. They pulsed with anticipation for dusk, and for the moment when the front door opened, and for the taste of each other, an eternity apart—well, twelve hours anyway. Like stoats, they baptized every room of their respective apartments—kitchen, living room, closets, window seats—and they talked into the dawn until one of them had to go; it felt as if they had known each other forever, and their shared secrets bound them together. Nate gave her a corny gift of a baby-blue woven cotton bracelet, which Hannah soaked in hot water to shrink it snug on her wrist.

He didn’t talk about it, but Hannah instinctively knew what Dominika was to Nate, and she resolved, in a way, to be case officer to them both. Her job was to protect and support DIVA in Moscow. She would do that with every fiber of her being. She would also adore Nate as much and as deeply and for as long as she could. She knew she had no cause to expect that there was a fairy-tale ending in any of this. For the time being, she savored both the mountainous challenge of operating in Moscow and the sweet ache of loving Nathaniel Nash.

Loving Hannah Archer affected Nate in a way he neither expected nor could adequately explain. Dominika was his life, CIA asset or not; her passion, courage, and determination in all things enthralled him. But as elegantly explained over the years by Forsyth, and somewhat less elegantly by Gable, their future was going to be a series of long, dark railway tunnels, out of which the train would periodically emerge into the sunlight before plunging back into another tunnel. More ominously, Gable said that their relationship was a threat to Dominika's security, both emotionally and practically. Dominika discounted that peril, but Nate wasn't so sure. His loving Dominika could kill her.

Nate didn't know what to think, even as he began wondering about what a life with Hannah, a fellow case officer, would be like. Tandem couples—spouses both inside CIA—worked together and covered each other. Nate shook himself like a dog. Life without Dominika was unimaginable. A surveillance-detection run with Hannah would be like having *two* Beethovens at the keyboard. Dominika's Parthenon profile in the lights of Prater Park came to him, then morphed into Hannah's cool fingers running through her mop of hair as she laughed. *Jesus.*

The thunderstorm broke the day Hannah was occupied with a preassignment physical. *Could a doctor tell if a woman had been making love last night on a coffee table?* Benford had commanded Nate to lunch in the Executive Dining Room (EDR) on the seventh floor of Headquarters, a long, narrow space with a panoramic view of the Potomac and primarily patronized by senior-grade Agency lawyers, congressional liaison mavens, and ambitious staffers with Caesar dressing on their ties. Benford—known, feared, reviled—made his way past the white tablecloths and clinking stemware, ignoring tentative greetings from other diners, to a small table at the far end of the room. Nate felt eyes on him as he walked behind Benford, and remembered Dominika's long-ago report about her lunch in a private dining room at the Center. Dominika. Nearly midnight in Moscow. *Sleep well.*

Benford waved off the menus and told the waiter to bring two bowls of crab bisque, turning to Nate without apology to tell him the bisque in the EDR was excellent.

"It must be a really excellent soup," said Nate.

Benford tore a dinner roll with his hands and munched bread. "Some things—chowder, bisque, denied-area operations—should be prepared perfectly, or not at all. Possibly including chili con carne."

"I agree with you, Simon," said Nate, going for ironically urbane, "including chili."

"Then why are you sleeping with Hannah Archer on the eve of her departure to Moscow to assume handling duties for DIVA, whom you are also fucking?" Benford tore another piece of bread. "Do you think this is the way to make a proper bisque?"

The waiter came and placed a bowl of thick, glossy soup at each place. Nate got one quavering spoonful into his mouth. He could taste nothing; he put his spoon down.

"I'm not going to try to excuse myself," said Nate. "With Dominika, it was the recruitment, with Hannah it was the training, being thrown together."

Benford slurped his bisque. "And you wanted bookends?"

Nate bowed his head, took a deep breath, and started talking to Benford, who was concentrating on his soup but listening to every word. Nate told him of his struggle with loving Dominika, of talks with Forsyth and Gable, of the nightmare ambush in Vienna and the aftermath. Now in Washington, mentoring Hannah through IO training, the affair had happened. Benford reached across and took Nate's soup, switching it with his own empty bowl. He resumed spooning bisque as Nate told him about his dark thoughts, his unworthy thoughts, about contemplating life with either Dominika or Hannah.

Benford wiped his chin with a napkin and sat back. "Nash, you're fairly fucked up," he said. "But I empathize with you."

"This never happened to you," said Nate.

"Let me continue the Sisyphean task of expanding your vocabulary. One feels empathy when one has been there; sympathy when one has not."

"You?" said Nate.

"Do not expect me to relate a mewling anecdote with a pithy moral at the end. What I want you to hear is that you would have been separated from the service long ago if you had not been ably handling MARBLE and DIVA, two Cadillac assets, and now LYRIC, who's immensely important, and but for the incidental reason that you are an excellent officer in matters not involving your dick. Forsyth and Gable have been steadfast in their support for you. But this bacchanalia cannot continue."

Benford pushed away from the table. "What a pleasant lunch. I want you to go away and think about this, then come back, and tell me what you want to do. My only requirement is that you do not ruin DIVA as an asset, and that you do not break Archer's heart on the eve of her assignment. That son of a bitch COS Moscow will do that to her soon enough."

BENFORD'S CRAB BISQUE

Sauté finely diced onion and carrot until soft. Separately mix butter and flour to make a light brown roux, then add chicken broth and whisk into a velouté. Add the onions and carrots and simmer. Incorporate heavy cream, sherry, lemon juice, Worcestershire sauce, cayenne, salt, pepper, and shredded crab meat. Garnish with sour cream and chives.

19

The tritium face on Hannah's watch read five minutes after midnight. She had been on Moscow streets for thirteen hours and was marshaling her flagging reserves as she chewed an energy bar. She was in the park, at the staging point for loading the last sensor site. Moscow summer light lasted late—at the height of the solstice there was never full darkness. She had run a complicated surveillance-detection route—the SDR had been planned meticulously, down to the last turn and the last minute. COS Throckmorton had looked over her shoulder the whole time, his Jerusalem artichoke nose inches from her ear, and hadn't said a word when she finished drafting the plan in Station.

Nate had been right: The minute she was out onto the street on an ostensible shopping tour, backpack slung over her shoulder, her senses lit up and she moved with confidence. She had done her homework: She knew Moscow streets as if she had lived there for years. She thought she might have had coverage in the first hour out of the embassy, but time over distance had stripped away the "possibles" one after the other. A loop to the north beyond the ring road in her sweet little Czech-made Skoda—the new-car smell was better than anchovies—ended with a turn to the west and a series of planned provocative moves, culminating in her stashing her car in the massive parking garage under Vremena Goda shopping mall. Parking underground was a precaution: A signal from any beacon emplaced on her car by the FSB would not reach the street from beneath the building. She had not seen any discernible surveillance indicators: no running pedestrians, no hastily averted looks, no revving engines, no car doors chunking closed, no *feel* of pressure on the wings, or behind, or ahead. You never know completely—that's where instinct and nerve take over—but as dusk approached, Hannah Archer *felt* the street and *knew* she was black.

Hannah sat in the gloom of the park, leaning against a tree trunk, her blond hair tucked under the hood of a light nylon jacket, the backpack between her legs. She wore black jeans, a moisture-wicking tank top under the jacket, and soft-soled shoes. Besides the pack, she was traveling light:

a dry magnetic compass, two-inch tactical flashlight with red lens, mini multitool, Hearsey's digging trowel. The black jacket was reversible to light blue, and would change her profile slightly. The summer night had a slight chill. Her body ached, her legs throbbed, her glasses were fogged around the edges, and she saw her hands shaking with fatigue as she unpeeled the last half of the energy bar. She felt sticky and longed for a shower. Her head, however, was clear, her brain processing everything, her senses alert. Now it was time to listen. The park was completely still, absolutely empty, utterly dark. She waited for the minute squeak of cheap shoe leather, the scratchy static of a radio squelch break. She was part of the Russian night; she was one of those Russian sylphs drifting through the air, she was— *Why don't you gambol through the park sprinkling fairy dust, you idiot?* Concentrate.

She put her head back against the trunk of the tree and closed her eyes. *Half a bottle of water left,* she thought. *Finish this and move to the signal site. I'm on schedule, should get back to the car when the mall opens at—* She suddenly bolted upright and frantically swung the backpack away from her crotch and to the side. *Christ, strontium-90 and you have it jammed against your freaking womb; won't need a night-light ever again.* The prospect of just having irradiated her vaginal canal prompted Hannah to think about Nate, then about the faceless woman who would be depending on these sensors she had hauled in her pack. They would be DIVA's lifeline to the Agency. She flashed briefly to images of beautiful, naked Nate in the slanting light of her little Washington apartment.

The last days in Washington with Nate had been strange: He seemed remote and unsettled. Hannah's blithe nature-girl intuition sensed he was struggling with their relationship in the context of Dominika Egorova, the woman she knew Nate loved. With New England equanimity, Hannah had not pushed herself on him physically, which was really too bad—she had planned on jumping his bones every night until the day of her departure. To fill up the reserve tank, she told herself, because she expected that Moscow was going to be a long dry spell in the jumping-bones department for a single woman in the US Embassy with a nonfraternization rule, which, in other words, meant American diplomats couldn't sleep with non-NATO lovers.

On their last night in her little apartment she broiled a steak and Nate made a salad, and they opened a bottle of wine. Hannah set the little table with a bowl of flowers, lit a candle—a little corny, but it looked nice in the darkened apartment—and turned the volume down on José González's "How Low"—exactly how she felt—while they ate and looked at each other. The whole thing sucked because they were both uncomfortable—*you will* not *start crying*—and she put her hands in her lap so he wouldn't see them tremble. Dissecting Moscow operations any more seemed stupid, and talking about Dominika was *out,* and discussing *their relationship* seemed flinty and pointless. She had seen how Nate was keeping the lid on—case officers can read faces—and she got up to pour him the last of the wine, and he had put his arm around her waist, more big brother than lover, and she tried to ease away but he pulled her back and kissed her, and kissed her again. Like a moron she was still holding the empty wine bottle, and he took it out of her hand and walked her backward to the bedroom—*dude, I mean, really*—and she heard herself say his name in the dark, over and over.

She shook her head. *Let's go,* she thought. Hannah was on the edge of Gorkogo, a huge wooded park that ran along the Moskva River in the Central Administrative *Okrug,* at the upper end of a grassy slope that ran down from the trees to a long set of stairs ascending from the river. Glass-globed lamp poles were spaced evenly along the stairs. Along the southern edge of the park, traffic on the elevated eight-lane Tret Transportnoye Kol'tso, the TTK, roared out of a tunnel and across the Andreevsky Bridge. Hannah's slope was visible from vehicles in all lanes, moving in either direction, and there is where she'd bury sensor number three, on the slope. In a car, DIVA would have line-of-sight to the sensor for the requisite two seconds, and would be able to initiate an undetectable SRAC burst as she drove by. A Station car similarly could load and retrieve messages to and from DIVA by driving past on the TTK.

Hannah checked one more time and slid halfway down the grassy slope in darkness, a ninja invisible in her black clothes. She knew exactly where to bury the sensor so its receiver/transmitter would be in electronic line-of-sight from the highway—which at this hour was only three-quarters jammed with careering cars, belching buses, and overloaded trucks. Hearsey's special trowel cut into the sod smoothly and she levered up the grassy patch, held it up like a scalp, dug sensor number three out of the pack—*Good-bye, you bastard,* thought Hannah, *I hope you're not the one who gives me a tumor*—and seated it in the earthen cavity. She replaced the sod, pressed it firmly in place—the sensor's slight convexity, Hearsey had explained, would prevent a noticeable depression over time as the earth settled around the device—and from a package the size of a sugar packet she sprinkled a green-tinted, granular seed mixture around the edges of the cut sod to promote additional grass growth. The next rain would let the seed—researched and developed by agrostologists from the US Department of Agriculture to exactly match the park's indigenous Russian wild rye grass—sprout and totally camouflage the edges of the patch.

Hannah scuttled back up the slope and into the trees. She stayed motionless for two minutes, listening for the scratch of a match, a muffled cough, the nearly imperceptible musical note of night-vision goggles. Or the panting and nose whining of a tracker dog. Silence. That was it. She had done it. She now knew what Janice had meant about the "perfect circle" of an operational act. She imagined Benford's face when he received her cable saying "all packages emplaced." She hoped he would be pleased; perhaps he would cable Nate in Athens to let him know. She hoped Nate would also be impressed. He would understand how it felt. *She would have a week of leave in a few months, maybe Athens?* Hannah inexplicably thought then of her family, and about how proud her parents would be if they knew what their daughter was doing, how her mother's eyes would sparkle, how her father would grin, how her two raucous brothers would thump her on the back. She could never tell them.

She shook herself out of the daydream. She still had to make a signal to DIVA, retrieve her car, then reappear at the embassy compound as if she were coming to work a little late this morning. The three sensor sites Hannah loaded that long night—substantially separated in different sections of the city, stealthily buried, all near arteries with a high volume of traffic—were, most important, away from any Western diplomatic installations (all of which were ringed by electronic burst detectors that could alert the FSB that an agent SRAC exchange had just taken place).

The most important drop—the package with DIVA's SRAC equipment—had been the first operational act a week ago. That night, Hannah's nine-hour SDR was executed through blustery squalls from the east. The heavy raindrops were the lashing tears of impotent rage from the ghosts of the old politburo who were watching a *woman*—blond, American, fearless—commit espionage in their Moskva, the ancient name, the city of "dark and turgid waters." If Hannah knew they were looking down on her, she would have waved and told them to chill.

DIVA's equipment package—in the textile district of southeastern

Moscow—was buried in the dirt of a pocket park under the highway bridge that took Volgogradskiy Prospekt over Lyublinskaya Ulitsa. After Hannah reported to Headquarters that the cache was loaded, the site had been monitored by satellite coverage for seven days to determine whether there was any extraordinary activity around the park, whether there were new tire tracks in the dirt, whether an out-of-place maintenance shed had been erected nearby. Or whether an FSB team was going to surge out of spider holes when Dominika walked under the abutment.

Benford made the final determination, to COS Throckmorton's fussed annoyance. Pointing his globoid nose at her, Throckmorton read Benford's cable to Hannah, not letting her read it herself. The cache was safe. Proceed. Tonight, the three sensors were down. Proceed. Benford directed Hannah to signal "have loaded" to DIVA, the last time a physical mark would have to be made.

The fatigue was affecting her vision a little, but Hannah slogged on foot northwest to the Dorogomilovo District, near DIVA's state-provided apartment on Kastanaevskaya Ulitsa. No one was on the street; the broad boulevard was empty. Hannah spritzed three bars of an iron fence behind a bus-stop shelter using a small spray bottle. The chemical in it was a delayed action marking system, DAMS for short, that was colorless and undetectable but would react hours later to the UV light of the morning sun and turn rust-colored in a matter of minutes, an indistinct slash of dye on the bars noticeable only to someone who knew where to look. The fence and bus stop were on DIVA's route to work, and she could check with a glance for a "have loaded" signal every morning and evening.

Two days later sensor number two was automatically interrogated by DCOS Schindler as she drove around Moscow on an ostensible trip to area antique shops. She returned to Station and with a trembling hand—she smelled like gin in the afternoon—put the SRAC receiver on Hannah's desk, and walked away. Hannah connected a cable, the screen of her computer blinked, and DIVA's burst message in English appeared.

MESSAGE 1. PACKAGE RECEIVED. EQUIPMENT SATISFACTORY. PREZ PRESSING FOR IRAN DEAL. WDC REZIDENT Z VISITING SOON, REASON UNKNOWN, RUMORS NEW US VOLUNTEER. INFO COMPARTMENTED BUT DEPUTY KNOWS DETAILS. WILL PURSUE. olga.

Hannah noted the correct lowercase o and punctuation in the signature, the duress indicators that told her DIVA was not being forced to send the message from the basement of Butyrka prison in north Moscow, surrounded by SVR technicians, their salami-greasy hands resting lightly on the nape of her neck. *All good things, sister,* thought Hannah.

Nate had told Hannah that DIVA herself chose the Olga pseudonym for her messages, after Olga Prekrasna, Olga the Beauty, the medieval Slav warrior queen who destroyed an enemy capital by releasing hundreds of sparrows with sulfur-soaked strings attached to their feet. At dusk the wheeling birds nested throughout the city—under eaves, in attics, inside barns, in haystacks—and the smoldering sulfur eventually combusted and started hundreds of fires simultaneously, incinerating the city. *The sparrow bringing fire and destruction,* thought Hannah. Olga Prekrasna, the Beauty.

Line KR Chief Zyuganov rode down the elevator from the executive fourth floor of SVR headquarters in Yasenevo muttering to himself. He had just briefed the director on the emergence of the new American source, identified only by his self-bestowed code name TRITON. Zyuganov snorted: *Triton,* a newt. TRITON's first report compromising a CIA recruitment of a Russian was ingeniously and deeply buried at the tail end of feed material passed by an oafishly transparent US Air Force double agent. It was all Line KR needed. The young attaché in Caracas who had agreed some months earlier to spy for the Americans against his own country was recalled to Moscow on an administrative pretext.

There had been no interrogation, at least not yet. The officer had been given a no-account job, kept under observation—in the old days he would have been shot in the Lubyanka basement, in the room with the hooks and the drains and the far wall lined with massive pine logs to prevent ricochets. This lesser administrative fate was a *Potyomkinskaya derevnya,* a Potemkin village, a false façade, concocted with the sole purpose of protecting the new source, TRITON. Later, with the blurring of months, the sentence would be carried out. The young *perebezhchik,* the turncoat, was already dead and he didn't even know it. Neither did CIA.

That Line KR could bag a traitor with such swiftness, with such ruthless efficiency, was a feather in Zyuganov's cap. The idiot director did not understand the salutary effects of having an omniscient counterintelligence machine hovering over the Service: No one would dare betray the Center with Zyuganov in charge. No, this politician-turned-director would never understand the *nyuans,* the nuance of the Game, but there was someone who did understand, a former intelligence officer, someone infinitely more important than the director. President Putin would know.

Zyuganov was in an exquisite position: he had cauterized the Caracas traitor, he was working the Iranian energy deal on the president's behalf, and he and Zarubina would manage TRITON (whose access almost certainly originated in the White House, the NSC, or in Langley). It would be colossal. Putin's unstinting patronage would follow. The future was rosy. Zarubina was nearly universally considered to become the next SVR director when she returned from Washington, the first female director ever. And there was an unspoken understanding with Zarubina that Zyuganov would ascend close behind her. Quite a partnership: The Seamstress and the Executioner.

The only *prepyatstviye,* impediment, in his career plans was his subordinate Egorova. With the intuition of an interrogator, Zyuganov knew that Putin was intrigued with her, knew she could be a challenge to Zyuganov's success. She had not been damaged at all by the collapse of her Iranian case. It was relatively simple: He could let things ride for a while and trust in his own abilities. Alternatively, he could arrange another accident. The latter option was infinitely more attractive, not only because it was malicious and violent but also because Zyuganov recently had made an important discovery.

The one remotely social activity the misanthropic Zyuganov indulged in was an occasional visit to SVR Department Five, the "wet works," to keep up with a handful of officers he had known during the Lubyanka years—the last remnants of a battalion of "special tasks" assassins and saboteurs from happier times. He felt marginally at home among these stolid, expressionless professionals, some nearing retirement, some younger ones still trying to make names for themselves. At any rate, he liked them better than the new crop of SVR dilettantes in Headquarters who spoke English and knew how to order wines. No, the "wet boys" were his people.

Zyuganov had been sitting in the Department Five lounge when a woman approached him, stood with heels together, and asked in a whisper if she might speak with him. She was of medium height, about forty, dyed blond hair cut short, figure heavy but not fat, with the shoulders of a man. A broad, flat nose ended above a razor-cut mouth and an overly strong chin. Zyuganov normally would be in no mood to speak with anybody so clearly soliciting favors, but he noticed the gray eyes behind the wire-rimmed spectacles, eyes so purely gray they looked artificial. They were red-rimmed and held Zyuganov's gaze unblinkingly. Some primal divining rod in his brain started quivering, a sociopath sensing a kindred spirit.

The woman was dressed in an inexpensive long-sleeved cotton dress, also gray, buttoned at the neck. Too-long arms stuck out of her sleeves. There was some indistinct lumpiness that hinted at substantial breasts, or perhaps just mattress stuffing. Nervous hands picked at the side seam of her dress, and Zyuganov noticed the fingers were stained yellow.

"What is it?" Zyuganov spat. He noticed she did not flinch, but kept staring at him.

"I would like to work for you," said the woman, still whispering.

"Impossible. What do you mean by asking such a thing? Selection into Line KR is exceedingly competitive." He looked away to terminate the conversation.

The woman did not move. "I don't mean in Line KR," she said. "With the other."

As Zyuganov made a dismissive gesture with his hand, the chief of Department Five walked in and the woman, after another lupine stare, turned and left the lounge.

The chief of Five didn't like Zyuganov, didn't like when he visited his department, didn't like the wormy little troll and his wormy little reputation. He was a reformer, a careerist, not an old *palach,* an executioner. "What are you doing talking to Eva?" the chief asked.

"I wasn't talking to her," said Zyuganov.

"Well, take my advice and give her a wide berth," said the chief.

"Who is she?" said Zyuganov.

The chief filled a glass with hot tea from a hissing samovar on a side table, deciding how to describe one beast to another. "Evdokia Buchina, her friends call her Eva for short—if she has any friends; started as an SVR corporal in Saint Petersburg, transferred to Moscow, then put in an administrative position here in Department Five. My department. It's been a year and I've tried to get rid of her since she arrived."

Zyuganov tried not to look interested. "What's wrong with her?"

"Nothing much," said the chief. "Disciplined for aggression in the office. Transferred for abusing prisoners."

Zyuganov's ears pricked up. "What do you mean, abusing prisoners?"

"Beating them to death in their cells. One in Petersburg, one in Moscow."

"Accidents happen," Zyuganov said.

The chief shrugged. "You want her transferred to your office? Wonderful. I'll send you her personnel file. I don't even know what half the words in her medical profile mean."

Zyuganov had been noncommittal. Eva said she wanted to work "on the other." He wondered whether he had found someone special. Her file was rich with tantalizing words, some of which Zyuganov had to look up: Androgyne. Pansexual. Schizotypal.

A personal interview with Eva was inconclusive: She answered in monosyllables, shook her head, and mumbled. But those eyes the color of wet cement never left Zyuganov's face. Following his instincts, he took Eva one evening to Butyrka prison to observe the interrogation of a jailed activist, a member of the political performance-art group *Voina* who, during a street demonstration to protest the policies of Vladimir Putin, threw a jar of green paint on an undercover officer of SVR. It was the young rocker's misfortune that this automatically became a matter for SVR's Department for Protection of the Constitutional System, which essentially meant he would be answering to Alexei Zyuganov and, in a debut appearance, Evdokia Buchina.

She broke six of his fingers, dislocated his left shoulder, crushed the small bones of his right foot, and fractured his condyle mandible, all before midnight. Zyuganov watched, fascinated, as Eva worked, methodical, lithe, patient, graceful, strong, her breathing steady, shooting him glances, the hellhound looking for approval, the schoolmarm spectacles glinting in the overhead lights. It was like sitting in Brahms's music room, watching him compose. Zyuganov had found his *izverg*, his Belial, his monster.

Hurting Egorova. Clipping the Sparrow's wings. Zyuganov left the idea in the wet locker of his brain. No, for the time being, he instead had resolved to starve Egorova of information in the matter of the deal with Iran, to compartment the relevant KR files so she would not meddle and steal his heat. He additionally needed to tie her up with useless work; he needed an *otvlekayushchiy manevr,* a distraction, a red herring.

The next morning fortune smiled on him.

Shaggy Yevgeny handed him a new cable from Zarubina's Washington *rezidentura* reporting the latest nighttime meeting with US Air Force Major Thorstad. Buried again at the end of the double agent chicken feed was another bombshell report from TRITON—fifteen frames. The anonymous newt had photographed three separate cables detailing an exchange between CIA Headquarters and the CIA Station in Athens on an intelligence source code-named LYRIC, who recently had been debriefed on Russian military intelligence (GRU) operations to acquire US military technology. Zyuganov's eyebrows went up: Based on the summary, the information passed to CIA was clearly from an insider deep within GRU, a source with firsthand access.

Pust'. So be it. *Another spy to ferret out,* thought Zyuganov, *another dumpling to gobble up.* The Americans apparently had been tireless in recruiting Russians recently. And in one stroke TRITON would neutralize their gains. He looked at Zarubina's cable, deep in thought. This LYRIC had to be someone on active duty in Moscow, sitting in an important position with heavy-duty access, not a functionary assigned to an embassy. That the debriefing occurred in Athens was only marginally important, he decided. Greece was a popular and inexpensive summer vacation destination for sun-starved Russians. The traitor GRU officer likely had gone on holiday with his family, contacted CIA while there, had been debriefed and paid, then finished his vacation and was probably already back in Moscow. It would be a straight mole hunt here in the capital, a matter of checking military-leave and international-travel records. A handful of likely GRU candidates would be rounded up, there would be a series of interrogations, and the *predatel svin'yu,* the swine traitor, would be revealed.

More interrogations. Zyuganov licked his lips—he had acquired a corneal trephine from the SVR ophthalmologic unit that he wanted to try out on someone. Then the thought occurred to him: He could use the Greece venue as a pretext to send Egorova to Athens on a "counterintelligence inspection tour," to interview officers in the *rezidentura* and embassy. She could cool her heels there for two weeks on a futile snipe hunt while he unmasked the mole in Moscow.

He sourly regarded his deputy, who looked back at him from the doorway. He gave him instructions: Tell Captain Egorova there is a counterespionage lead in Greece. Do not mention Zarubina or TRITON's report regarding LYRIC. She is to go to Athens and discreetly interview SVR, GRU, and embassy personnel and look for anything out of the ordinary; she should not return until she has interviewed everyone, two weeks or more.

"Interview everyone?" said Yevgeny. "On what pretext? How do we explain to the Athens *rezidentura*?" He knew his boss; it wouldn't do to push too much. Whatever, Egorova would be kept busy.

"Tell her it's a routine inspection. Tell her everyone has to do it," said Zyuganov. "Now get out of here. And get Zarubina on the secure line."

Yevgeny Pletnev looked across the desk at Captain Egorova and first thought that he had never seen such blue eyes in his life, then estimated the heft and feel of her breasts underneath that blouse, and then, transported, imagined himself in bed with her. He scratched himself under the arm. He had smoothly passed along Colonel Zyuganov's instructions to her in her smallish office in Line KR spaces, while she sat expressionless. He watched her carefully, curious—she already was a storied member of the Service. Yevgeny was the only officer in Line KR other than Zyuganov who had access to everything the department did, and in the iron-clad hierarchy of SVR, he owed allegiance to no one besides Zyuganov. But Egorova's celebrity intrigued him; he sniffed at her influence, assessed her cool detachment. Today she was dressed in a dark suit with a light-blue blouse, her hair pinned up, and she wore no jewelry except for a small watch with a narrow velvet band. Her blue eyes held his as if she were reading him. Graceful hands rested on the leather blotter. Her classical features were serene. She seemed different; he didn't know what to expect. Yevgeny was used to toxic outbursts from invidious sociopaths.

"Thank you, Yevgeny. I will make preparations to travel," said Dominika. Ironic: Zyuganov thought he was cutting her out, but he had just given her a two-week window to meet with CIA—and for her to see Nate again. She could not have imagined they would be together again so soon after Vienna. She mentally began drafting the SRAC message she would transmit this evening.

A golden opportunity. She looked at the grimy yellow halo around Yevgeny's head, the color fading in and out. A plotting toadeater, Zyuganov's sycophant, but with information she needed. And not dialed in quite right with the ladies, no matter how much he daydreamed about skirts. Dominika looked at this weird creature and shuddered.

Udranka was sitting on top of a file folder, her legs crossed. Get on with it; you don't have to like it, you just have to do it.

Yevgeny Pletnev had been drafted into SVR after graduating from Moscow University with an undistinguished degree in computer science, the result of patronage from an uncle who was a deputy in the State Duma, the Federal Assembly of Russia, and the head of the Commission for Legislative Support for Anti-Corruption. His uncle's influence, however, stopped at the imposing front doors of Yasenevo and the new employee—he was twenty-five at the time—found himself directed to the administrative side of the Service in personnel, logistics, and support. It was not long before the hairy young man calculated that advancement was more reliably attained by avoiding the messy and politically dangerous operations directorates.

Yevgeny spent the required dreary years in personnel until there was a vacancy for an administrative assistant in Line KR, the shady office that dealt with counterintelligence and surveillance of Russian citizens abroad. Despite warnings from colleagues, Yevgeny saw an opportunity and applied for the position. Three years in the Line KR staff room spent improving the antiquated computer network and cleaning up the files got him noticed by the horrid, diminutive chief of Line KR, Alexei Zyuganov, who ordered him to move to his personal staff, first in the outer office, then as associate staff chief, then as his personal aide-de-camp, then, last year, as Zyuganov's deputy. Yevgeny knew it was risky in the extreme—suicidal—to even contemplate hooking on to Zyuganov's coattails. *Chort poberi,* to join the demon. But the then thirty-five-year-old Yevgeny calculated that Zyuganov was powerful, irreplaceable, whispered about. Better still, his boss's serrated and fear-inducing reputation would rebound to him.

"This position is sensitive," said Zyuganov on Yevgeny's first day as number two, looking sideways at him, like a turtle. "You will see everything I see, read everything I read. You will have access to my files. Loyalty and discretion are required. I have approved of your work since you arrived in Line KR, but any deviation from these standards will result in immediate disciplinary action. In other words, I personally will bring you to the cellars and strap you to the table. Do I make myself clear?"

Yevgeny had nodded, and for a year worked fourteen-hour days. He was the model of efficiency, a paragon of discretion. He began anticipating his boss's moods, began recognizing the onset of the dark days, the *bezumiye*, the madness, and saw how the trips to the cellars would lift his mood, how his brow would be clear when he returned to the office with the charnel house smell on his clothes, and in his hair, and on his breath.

For six months, the little sociopath stayed suspicious, but eventually grew accustomed to Yevgeny's slavish and proper obedience. Zyuganov finally decided the hirsute young man could be trusted—to a point. The only human he ever brought completely into his confidence—the only other human accorded such access—was his mother. In any case, Yevgeny was deputy chief, and there was important work to be done: They had a mole to catch.

BAKED JERUSALEM ARTICHOKE

Mix heavy cream, pureed garlic, lemon juice, tarragon, and grated Gruyère, and season well. Add peeled and thickly sliced Jerusalem artichokes, then pour the mixture into a casserole. Top with bread crumbs and grated cheese, drizzle with olive oil, then bake in a high oven until the artichokes are tender and the topping is browned.

20

It was the beginning of Dominika's remarkable, precarious, audacious recruitment operation—Nate and CIA would have lost their minds if they knew what she was doing—to penetrate her very own SVR department by suborning her creepy deputy chief. And she had limited time to do it before she departed for Athens. No operation can be rushed before time, for it is to invite catastrophe, a flap, and exposure. But there was no choice.

Dominika knew she had to seduce Yevgeny and steal the secrets of her own office—Line KR—from him. She needed to know about Zyuganov's progress with the Iranians and about the notorious Washington *rezident* Zarubina, who had something on the stove; perhaps she had developed a source in Washington, something CIA would want to know, really want to know. Then there was this matter of a CI investigation in Athens. She needed details to bring to Nate.

She tamped down a grim revulsion when contemplating using Sparrow School blandishments on the woolly Yevgeny—a nightmare backslide into a chapter of her professional life that had been forced upon her. She heard Gable's warning in her head; she could see the expression on Nate's face.

When Udranka wasn't hovering, it would be Marta sitting at the foot of her bed, tossing her hair and blowing smoke at the ceiling, telling Dominika to get on with it, so she set her guts and clenched her jaw.

At first, Yevgeny was conscious only of Captain Egorova when she stood in front of Zyuganov's desk, or when she walked down the interior corridor of Line KR. As he did with other women in the office, Yevgeny liked to maneuver himself to the side, so he could look at Dominika in profile, from the elegant chin and throat to the jutting chest, around to the flat swoop of the buttocks, and then to the shapely legs and ankles. Dominika knew when the little squirrel was gawking at her, his yellow bloom pulsing, but she gave him no indication. Yevgeny did not register that, in the next days, Captain Egorova began to contrive an increasingly frequent series of encounters with him: Delivering a memo to him for the fourth floor; sitting beside him at the conference table; bumping into him in the cafeteria or outside on the sunny terrace during lunch; riding by lucky coincidence the number six metro from Yasenevo, then the transfer to the number three line together most evenings, Egorova to the Park Pobedy stop, Yevgeny farther on to Strogino.

"Strogino," said Dominika one evening, holding on to a strap in the swaying metro car, which was nearly empty at that late hour. It was safe to talk. "That is where Korchnoi lived," she said matter-of-factly. Yevgeny looked at her, eyes wide. He licked his lips.

"*That* Korchnoi?" he whispered.

Dominika looked at the canary-yellow flash around his head and shoulders. "It's quite a distance from Strogino to that miserable little bridge in Estonia," she said grimly. "A long way to go to pay for his betrayal." It physically hurt her to refer to Korchnoi like this, to dishonor his memory. She tamped down the rage in her throat. Yevgeny leaned toward her.

"I've heard about the case. There's an old file, incomplete, redacted. You know the inside story. *You were there at the swap*. Will you tell me sometime?"

"The Kremlin was well pleased," said Dominika, shrugging. "I was able to elicit the information that exposed Korchnoi. The president was very complimentary, but it's a little embarrassing," she said airily.

"I hear the stories," said Yevgeny. "The president likes you, you're *zolotoj*, a golden girl." He looked at her again. "You're clearly in good standing."

Dominika smiled at him. "Here's my stop," she said, standing in front of the doors. "See you in the office tomorrow." Yevgeny stared at her back through the glass panels.

They fell into the habit most evenings of talking in the relative anonymity of the metro car. With Yevgeny, there was no thought of comradeship, of developing any sort of friendship. Egorova was the teddy bear in the window he wanted to squeeze, and his bituminous thoughts ran from the soft, wrinkled soles of her feet to the rather severe mouth, from which he wanted to hear her begging him for love, or something like that. Yevgeny was loyal to Zyuganov, and he understood that Egorova was to be shut out of the secrets of Line KR, but his dreams of lying with Egorova did not conflict with any of that. Besides, he wanted to know the story of the traitor Korchnoi, of the woman who unmasked him. He *needed* to know about her connection to Putin. It was irresistible. He was a wasp hovering over a dish of sugar water.

"What's he like, the president?" said Yevgeny one night on the metro.

"Everything you've heard about him, it's true," said Dominika enigmatically. "Here's my stop." She had timed the conversation for just this effect. Yevgeny bent to look out the grimy window of the metro, the brakes of the car squealing, as the elegant Park Pobedy station, gorgeous with its curving ocher granite walls and glowing chandeliers, came into view. His face worked nervously.

"Look," said Yevgeny, "why don't I get off with you, if you're not busy? We could have a drink." The car jerked to a stop and the doors slammed open.

"You'll lose your train," said Dominika, listening for the klaxon warning that the doors were about to close. Yevgeny slung his briefcase strap over his shoulder.

"They run all night," he said. The klaxon sounded.

"Come on then," said Dominika, dragging him out of the car just as the doors hissed to a close. Yevgeny stood on the platform, intense, breathing through his nose, lips together in a half smile. He was getting what he wanted; he just didn't know he was feet away from a leaf-covered snare.

Some days later, the rain beat against the glass of Dominika's bedroom window and the ivy around the frame outside whipped in the wind. In the kitchen a steam kettle whistled. "It's preposterous," said Dominika, shrugging on a short robe to go fetch the tea. "This unidentified source, what did you call him . . ." She went into the kitchen.

Marta was sitting at the table smoking. You're doing fine. Rough in bed, gentle in his head, she said. Dominika shushed her.

"He calls himself TRITON," said Yevgeny sleepily from the bedroom. He looked like a chimp, the hair on his arms running into the dense thatch of hair under his arms, which were tucked behind his head. His chest and stomach were also heavily covered with dark hair, as were his legs. His *khuy* lay flaccid on a riot of crotch hair like a mouse on a potholder. When she first saw Yevgeny naked, Dominika had thought there would not be enough wax in Russia to strip away the hair on his body.

Two consecutive nights after work had sufficed to set the foundation, establish rudimentary bonds of trust, throw him a bone by describing work abroad, then get him talking about himself. Yevgeny was not stupid, so Dominika had to proceed carefully, but even the most introspective mind cannot resist talking about himself. Recruitment, seduction, persuasion, all began with listening, watching those blubbery lips moving, first snatching at food, then growing confident, then moving inexorably closer, still moving, slick and wet, then the liverish feel of them on her own lips—she remembered the feel of Nate's lips—and her secret self was barricaded in the hurricane room, the door trebly bolted.

Then *Bozhe pomogi mne,* God help me, there had been Yevgeny's notions of lovemaking, which hovered somewhere between the equine and the porcine. Nothing new to a Sparrow, but Dominika positively had to separate her mind from her body, to block out the feel of his endlessly molting chest hair on her breasts, as if a burst egg sack of baby spiders were crawling over her. She set her teeth and began to make him forget the rules and start him talking. She could not turn her face away; she could not hide her eyes or shut her ears to the grunts. It was the horrid, familiar hellish swamp They had thrust her into before, and she had sworn to make Them pay, but now she revisited the same bog by her own volition, for the Americans' sake, and for Nate. There was not a moment's thought of infidelity; Yevgeny was not shafting the same body that she gave to her lover, not at all the same.

"How can we be sure he's not part of the controlled operation run by the Americans?" Dominika called from the kitchen. She waited a double beat as she stirred strawberry preserves—an old Russian custom to sweeten tea—into two ceramic mugs decorated with folk-art birds. *My Sparrow cups,* thought Dominika. The prattle continued: The deputy of Line KR, having just slept with his beautiful subordinate, was now talking shop. Nothing could be more natural.

"The *rezident* believes he's genuine," called Yevgeny from the bedroom. Dominika walked back holding the two mugs. "Zarubina is not about to make a mistake. She's determined to become director after her Washington assignment." He propped himself up on one elbow and took the mug. "Besides, TRITON has already exposed the Caracas case," he said. "The Americans would never burn one of their recruitments willingly."

Dominika thought about her double life. *Never say never,* she thought.

She sat crossed-legged on the bed next to Yevgeny as they sipped their tea. Dominika ran her fingers, heated by the hot mug, along Yevgeny's furry thigh. *No. 45, "Apply extremes of heat and cold to enhance nerve response."* Yevgeny looked at her from beneath thick eyebrows. He was still trying to quantify his good fortune at having seduced the stunning Egorova—he could never look at her again in the office without seeing the undraped ballerina's body of the last thirty-six hours.

"Bona fides are essential in a case like this," she said, drawing hot circles on his leg. The rain rasped against the window, Yevgeny's breathing rasped in his throat, and the mouse on the potholder stirred.

Dominika looked up again. "You are quite attractive like that, trembling the way you do." She heard her own voice, saw her reflection in the darkening windowpane. *Vorobey, shpion, konets.* Sparrow, spy, slut. *Shut up. Focus.*

"Operational validation is critical," Dominika continued conversationally, as if she were not peeling Yevgeny's brain like skin off a scalded tomato. "Zarubina presumably has tried to identify TRITON?" She leaned forward and rested her chin in her hands, to give him a dose of blue eyes and perfume. Her little kimono parted an inch.

Yevgeny blinked. "No, nothing. She and the colonel don't want to scare him," he said shakily. "They think he's too valuable." He peeked at Dominika, who looked at him through her lashes as if he were a Polish rum cake. "Zarubina is going along with the double-agent charade to keep the channel open for TRITON."

"I'd still worry, just a little bit, that TRITON is a *maskirovanie,* camouflage for something bigger," said Dominika. "Our Service is not the only one that can play this game. CIA has their own grand masters."

"I am not an operations officer like you, Captain, but—"

"Considering the circumstances, Yevgeny," said Dominika, "I think you could call me Dominika in private."

Yevgeny fought the overload. "I was saying that, while I'm not a trained officer, it seems to me that the second TRITON report is incontrovertible proof that he's genuine. He's even passed CIA's own cryptonym for another source . . . LYRIC."

"The lead in Greece?" said Dominika.

"Not Greece," said Yevgeny. "Here in Moskva. The colonel thinks the leak is here, someone with access." He looked guiltily at her. Dominika moved closer to him, eyes searching his face, as if to identify the one feature that made him so irresistible to her and to, well, all women. She gripped his bristly chin in her hand, mock serious.

"Then tell me, please, Zhenya," said Dominika, already sure she knew the answer, "why am I going to Greece?" The use of the affectionate diminutive of his name added to the poignancy.

"I don't know," said Yevgeny.

He's telling the truth, Dominika thought. His yellow halo may have indicated galloping lust, and careerism, and unreliability, but its steadiness suggested that the *izvrushchenets,* this furry pervert, was likely telling the truth.

"I originally thought the colonel was simply covering all possibilities, sending you to Athens to investigate. But then he specifically told me not to mention TRITON or LYRIC or Zarubina to you . . ." His voice trailed off as he looked into her eyes.

Dominika saw a shadow flit across his face, felt a tremor run the length of his body. His yellow aura flickered, faltered. Dominika knew he had just realized the enormity of the infractions he had committed (telling her official secrets), of what he currently was doing (sleeping with her), and of the possible ramifications (Zyuganov's rage and the cellars). Thank God he did not realize the worst: He had just provided content for her report to Nate and Gable. *Congratulations, lover,* Dominika thought, *your first report to Langley.* Now she had to give him a little *muzhestvo,* a little courage. Otherwise, she would have to hit him in the throat with the tea kettle and bury him in the garden. This next stage—anchoring him—was immensely dangerous.

"Listen to me," she said, still holding his chin. "I know what you're thinking, but get such thoughts out of your mind. You're helping me, and you're helping yourself. Zyuganov does not reward loyalty; he is incapable of gratitude. You're at risk working for him, whatever you do, however loyal you are. I'm equally at risk. It's only a matter of time before we fall under his thumb. So we both fight and survive. You and I will help each other, watch each other's back. All right?"

Yevgeny didn't move. The ivy stems scratched at the windowpane—*or was it one of the* Rusalki, *her mermaid friends?*

"Zhenya, *think,*" said Dominika, tugging at his earlobe. "The only thing he cherishes is his own career. He's keeping information from me, sending me off to Greece, because he is afraid of the inevitable: that Putin will favor me in these matters, like in the Iran affair. I see the way the president looks at him. He dislikes him; he is repulsed by Zyuganov's history in the cellars." *Truth be told,* thought Dominika, *blue eyes probably admires him for all that.*

"I'm coming with you two to the Kremlin tomorrow," said Dominika. "The director will be there, energy officials, ministers." Yevgeny's brow was beaded with perspiration. "So see for yourself, watch how Putin treats the little colonel." She wiped the sweat off his upper lip with her fingers. "And watch how Putin greets me, then make up your own mind." Yevgeny laughed a little at that. Dominika knew he invariably reported any gossip, dissension, scandal, or plot immediately to Zyuganov. But now Yevgeny himself was guilty of the massive infraction of having rutted with a subordinate, the very subordinate Zyuganov had directed him to keep in the dark. Yevgeny's yellow halo was pulsing; he was calculating the consequences. Dominika swallowed as she leaned forward to kiss him, and the baby spiders tickled her arms and legs.

How long would his nerve hold? All but the most monumental human recruitments required constant firming up. Well, she would firm him up, then. Yevgeny would see how Putin reacted to her during the Kremlin meeting; he'd see that she would be the better ally. She intended to manipulate the outcome tomorrow, but it would be risky. Monstrously risky on several levels. She was ready to employ Benford's plan, the one they had discussed in Vienna. Last night the latest SRAC message—also obviously from Gospodin Benford—had validated the plan. Benford was pushing her toward Putin, she knew, trying to get her imbedded under the president's skin. But Yevgeny—she would have to keep an eye on him. Her ultimate safety now resided somewhere between his heart and his balls.

"So we protect each other, agreed?" Dominika said. His yellow halo quivered. "And we advance together." Yevgeny reached up and stroked Dominika's hair. *You're a remarkable woman, do you know that?* thought Dominika.

"You're a remarkable woman, do you know that?" said Yevgeny.

The Sparrow laughed. "I know I'm going to fetch some ice cubes from the kitchen. Do not move."

The meeting hall of the Russian Security Council was in building number one—the Senate building—in the Kremlin citadel. Close to the private working office of the president, the medium-sized room was opulent, overwhelming, imperial. Half columns of black marble were spaced along the outer walls, their gilded Corinthian capitals reflecting the bright light of a massive two-tiered crystal chandelier. The room was soaked in light—Dominika noticed there were no shadows cast on the gleaming parquet floors. The massive table ran down the center of the room: leather blotters lined the edges, and a burled-wood strip dotted with microphone pickups ran down the center. A dozen straight-backed wooden chairs decorated with inlaid ivory darts, each with green cushioned armrests, were arrayed along either side of the table. Extra chairs were lined up against the cream walls for aides and note takers.

At the head of the table was a wide-backed chair—a throne, its back higher than the rest—covered in watered silk. Behind the throne, on the wall, hung a gorgeous tapestry and a scarlet shield with the double-headed golden eagle of the Russian Federation. Dominika stood in the doorway as senior government officials—ten of them—filed down the sides of the table. *The double eagle of the Romanovs had been black—ironic that modern Russians were no better off than the serfs of Tsar Ivan Grozny, the Fearsome, the Terrible,* thought Dominika. As if on cue, President Putin entered the room through a side door, trailed by two aides. The men around the table remained standing until the president was seated, then tumbled into their chairs.

This was an Iran planning session, not a Security Council meeting, Dominika knew. That council had lost influence and standing during the first and second Putin regimes—it was now an elephant graveyard for soon-to-be retired military and intelligence officials, the current SVR director being one of them. Accordingly, Zarubina in Washington was positioning herself to unseat him. As the most junior participant in attendance, Dominika was seated at the far end of the table, beside an agitated Zyuganov. The SVR director, a full member of the council, sat woodenly halfway down the table.

Dominika scanned the other faces, pinched in tight shirt collars, suit coats stretched across bellies, lank gray hair spilling over glistening foreheads. Putin's insiders, the new politburo. Yellows and browns and blues swirled around their heads, a palette of greed, sloth, pride, lust, and envy. And gluttony. Govormarenko of Iskra-Energetika was halfway up the other end of the table, picking his teeth. Dominika recognized the only other woman at the table—Nabiullina, one of the president's closest allies and recent surprise pick as chairman of the Russian central bank—unsmiling and sitting at Putin's left elbow, surrounded by a dirty yellow fog.

Then it happened. Putin scanned the assembled faces and the menthol blue eyes fixed on Dominika. He was dressed in a dark suit with a white shirt and an aquamarine tie that positively shimmered in the movie-set light of the room. "Captain Egorova," he said, his voice cutting across the table. "Come and sit here," he said, indicating with a wave the chair to his right. On stumps that had moments before been her legs, Dominika got up, walked through the unfolding black bat wings of Zyuganov's insanity and past a frozen Yevgeny sitting against the wall, a notebook balanced on his knees. Eyes followed her down the silent room, knowing smiles on the faces of the wisest among them.

"*Initsiativa. Talant,*" said Putin looking around the room as Dominika sat down. "Talent was critical in the matter of the Iranian procurement. And initiative. Our intelligence service brought this opportunity to light; Captain Egorova . . . and Colonel Zyuganov were instrumental." He nodded down the table at Zyuganov, but the dwarf might as well have been sitting at a bus stop in Kazakhstan.

"And now we are in the final stage. The funds are available," said Putin, looking over at Nabiullina, who moved her head imperceptibly. "And the seismic floor is being assembled as contracted."

Down the table, Govormarenko held up three stained fingers. "Assembly completed in three months," he said. *That will be the lead sentence in tonight's SRAC shot,* thought Dominika.

"And the Germans will deliver the equipment as arranged," said Putin. These were not questions, they were edicts.

"The cargo will be loaded on a Sovkomflot freighter in Hamburg," said a man with bushy eyebrows. "The equipment will be off-loaded at Bandar Abbas in the Persian Gulf approximately one month later." Putin's blue eyes were unblinking.

All right Benford, just as we discussed. Dominika took a quiet deep breath. "May I make an observation?" she said. Putin turned to her and nodded, his eyes locked on hers. "I know nothing about sea transport, or heavy machinery, but officers in our Service know some things very well."

She didn't dare look at their faces around the table, especially not at Zyuganov's or the director's.

"Cover," she said. "Security. Stealth."

The room was silent.

"As I understand the transaction, the Iranians have agreed to our proposal because they will receive the flooring—embargoed equipment—in secret. For them it is the most attractive part of the transfer, and they are willing to pay double for it."

Putin kept staring at her.

"For a Russian freighter to transit from Hamburg to Iran would involve passage through the English Channel, the Strait of Gibraltar, the Mediterranean, the Suez Canal and the Red Sea, the Gulf of Oman, then the Strait of Hormuz in the Persian Gulf."

"Correct," said the man from Sovkomflot.

"A route that includes some of the most closely monitored international bodies of water on the planet."

"Also correct," said Sovkomflot.

"And the ship would be off-loaded at the port of Bandar Abbas."

"Yes."

"I would be surprised if Western navies did not quickly document the arrival of a Russian ship with a massive piece of machinery, not to mention satellite coverage of the main Iranian port," said Dominika.

"Unavoidable," said the Sovkomflot man, nettled at being told his business.

"Unavoidable is not acceptable," said Putin, turning to him. "The Persians will know all this, they will complain. The transaction could be jeopardized. This government would be embarrassed." *You mean* my *transaction could be jeopardized,* thought Dominika. *And one does not embarrass the president,* she transmitted to the clueless official.

"And how else would you get a multiton cargo from Germany to Iran?" snorted the Sovkomflot man.

Please God, Benford, let your facts be right, she thought. "Like we do in the Service," said Dominika. "Unseen, through the back door."

"Riddles—" said the Sovkomflot man, stopping when Putin put up his hand.

"Tell us," said Putin.

"Instead of heading south, our freighter proceeds north from Hamburg to Saint Petersburg and off-loads the equipment. Completely routine and innocent," said Dominika. "The shipment is then transported through Russia to a minor Iranian port on the south coast of the Caspian Sea."

"Improbable," said the Sovkomflot man. "Land transport would require a massive trailer. This cargo is bulky, as big as a house, weighs *over* forty tons. Even the military does not have equipment that capable." A few cronies spoke up, more to participate than to assist.

"A transporter-launcher for a ballistic missile might be modified to accommodate—" began a bald man.

"That would take months, and road quality is uneven the farther south—" said another.

"Are you mad? Through the heart of the country?" said Sovkomflot.

"Weather would have to be factored in—" said Govormarenko, still picking his teeth.

Putin held up his hand. Royal-blue pinwheels of light flashed behind his head and shoulders. He did not glance at his barnyard geese around the table. Dominika saw that *he knew* she had the answer; he just didn't know it came from Simon Benford. "Captain Egorova?" he prompted.

The room was silent.

"I looked at a map last night," answered Dominika. "I had an idea." A murmur came from the end of the table, which Putin ignored. Dominika didn't dare look away from him. "From Saint Petersburg through the lakes, Ladoga and Onega, across Rybinsk Reservoir into the Volga canal, to the Volga, all the way downriver through the delta at Astrakhan, then traverse south on the Caspian to Iran and the northern Persian port of Bandar-e Anzali." She looked at the faces and turned again to Putin. No one around the table would say anything until they were told by the president himself what they should think about the proposal.

"Waterborne, discreetly delivered directly from sovereign Russian territory to Iran," said Dominika. "The entire route is established: canals, lakes, inland seas, used by motorized barges that have the capacity of hauling three times the weight. They already haul timber, steel, coal, and gravel, including in darkness and all kinds of weather." The corner of Putin's mouth was twitching. "And Tehran pays, secrecy is preserved, and along with it Russia's reputation is, again, advanced," said Dominika. *Meaning of course that President Vladimir's place on the world stage is augmented as is, not incidentally, his bank account.*

The square-faced Nabiullina sat back in her chair. It was said she was brilliant, a Putin ally, protective. She was fifty, had shoulder-length auburn hair and bird-wing-shaped wire-rimmed eyeglasses. She wore a rust-colored jacket over a flowered bow-tie blouse. Her voice was like melting ice cream. "As you said, Captain," said Nabiullina, "you have no experience in shipping or transport. How is it you came up with this quite remarkable plan? How did you think about our internal river and canal system? Officers in your Service admittedly must be imaginative and flexible, but this is a remarkable performance." The message read: *It's a little more complicated than shaking your tits, missy; this is the Kremlin, and that's the president whom you've just given a presidential boner.* Nabiullina crossed her hands and smiled at Dominika, who smiled back.

Thank you, Benford, thought Dominika, *for being so smart.* He had anticipated the challenge and had suggested the correct answer.

"I thought of the river because I remembered seeing commercial traffic on the Volga near Kazan," said Dominika, "when I attended the Kon Institute. You may have heard of Sparrow School?" Dominika looked at Nabiullina steadily, fighting the anger swelling in her throat. It was excruciating to bring this up publically, but Benford had predicted the effect. "We were brought to the institute by hydrofoil on the river, and we used to walk along the Volga between training sessions. I always saw barges on the river. That's what reminded me." The reply read: *I have my own credentials,* sestra, *sister, and don't think for a minute I cannot handle dour economists or Vladimir's* stoyak.

Nabiullina stared at Dominika for a beat, reading the reply, acknowledging the psychic challenge. Putin was delighted with the exchange, the corners of his mouth threatening to lift in a smile. He stood up, pointed at the Sovkomflot representative as if to say "get going" and then nodded all around the table. That was enough of a prompt. As participants rose and milled, waiting for the president to leave the room, Putin stopped for a second and nodded again to Dominika, then exited the hall, Nabiullina and two aides in his wake. The side door closed with a click and people started filing out.

The director mopped his face with a handkerchief and quietly shook his head. Yevgeny avoided looking at her—he had certainly gotten an eyeful, seen the future. Zyuganov oozed up beside her and moved his mouth in a rictus of controlled fury.

"Very nicely done, Captain," he said. "The president was quite impressed."

"Thank you, Colonel," said Dominika, watching black parabolas arc out from behind his head. "The president is giving the Service all the credit. It is deserved. Bringing our officials together with the Persians—you have done much in a short time. This is your project."

Zyuganov looked at her with a slightly tilted head, as if he were deciding where he would start on her with the dermatome, to flense fillets of skin off her back and belly. Their footsteps rang off the marble floors of the Senate building corridor, then were swallowed up as they descended the richly carpeted grand staircase. Yevgeny was listening, close behind them.

"I would have preferred that you briefed me on your suggestion beforehand," said Zyuganov, looking up at her.

Of course you would have, you bedbug, thought Dominika, fantasizing about putting a hand at his back and trapping the toe of his shoe with her foot. He would be down the staircase on his face. "I did not expect the quite embarrassing invitation to sit at the head of the table. Believe me, Colonel, I never would have ventured to suggest—"

"When do you leave for Greece?" Zyuganov asked. There was a spot of spittle on his lower lip.

"In several days, Colonel," said Dominika. "I would welcome your views and guidance on this investigation."

"Yevgeny can give you what you want," said Zyuganov, turning back to his deputy to see if he had heard. Yevgeny's face was shiny with sweat. *Indeed he can,* thought Dominika.

"Thank you, Colonel," said Dominika.

Athens. Back with her friends. Back with CIA. Dominika would relish telling *Bratok* Gable about this meeting—she decided she would, with a straight face, offer to romantically introduce him to Nabiullina. Forsyth, quiet and wise, would focus on the Iran transaction. Benford of course would want to discuss TRITON, LYRIC, Zarubina. He would be pleased with the new intel, the leads. She would send multiple SRAC messages tonight as previews. Then, with a gulp, Dominika wondered how she would explain Yevgeny's "recruitment" to Nate.

In the car on the way back to Yasenevo, Udranka was sitting in the rear-facing jump seat, leaning back with her long legs stretched out and her hands behind her head. I wouldn't tell him, she said, no matter how much you want his forgiveness. You know what you did and why you did it. Who's to say you can't have a secret?

BABKA RUMOWA-POLISH RUM CAKE

Cream butter and sugar until light and fluffy, then blend in eggs. Add flour, baking soda, milk, and vanilla and mix well. Pour the mixture into a fluted tube pan and bake in a medium oven until an inserted toothpick comes out clean. Perforate the slightly cooled cake and pour over a syrup of sugar, water, lemon and orange zest, vanilla, and rum, soaking the cake completely.

21

Athens Station. Gable and Forsyth sat in the ACR in silence, waiting for Nate. Sitting two feet from each other without speaking was preposterous—no, creepy—but you didn't talk when the door was opened, ever. A minute later Nate stepped into the secure acoustical room carrying a metal in-box full of files. He dogged the door with a twist of a friction lever that was, like every other piece of the twenty-foot trailer, made of clear Lucite. Their ears popped as the door gaskets squeezed the last of the freely circulating air out of the room. Soon the atmosphere would be thick and coffee-heavy.

"How was LYRIC last night?" said Forsyth.

"Like rolling a boulder uphill," said Nate. "He brought his ego, as usual." He started taking folders out of the tray and laying them on the table.

"Did he bring the budget documents for the Ninth Directorate?" asked Forsyth. "DoD has been asking."

"Budget time in Washington," said Gable. "Cake eaters want to justify their own budgets."

"Nope," said Nate. "When I asked, LYRIC said he brought something better." Nate opened one of the files and took out a bound, one-inch-thick booklet and slid it over to Forsyth.

"What the fuck is this?" said Gable. Forsyth was riffling through the booklet.

"It's a classified report on the clandestine technology acquisition by GRU Ninth Directorate of the frameless canopy from the Chinese J-20 stealth fighter," said Nate, reading the Russian title on the cover. "LYRIC said the Russian air force is going to use it on their T-50. Better visibility, better heads-up display, survivable pilot ejection at higher speed."

Forsyth looked at Gable. "The Air Force will love this crap," he said, sliding the book back. "We're not going to refuse this sort of intel."

"A good sign, him bringing this out now," said Gable to Forsyth.

"What do you mean, 'a good sign'?" said Nate, looking at them both.

"No other issues, no other twitches?" said Forsyth.

Nate felt his scalp creep in alarm. "What are you guys talking about?"

"DIVA sent three separate SRAC messages last night. Came in late, after you had kicked off your SDR for LYRIC. You know the Moscow case officer out there?" said Forsyth, handing over the Moscow cables for Nate to read.

"Yeah, Hannah Archer," said Nate. "She's solid." *Hannah naked, hair wildly mussed, her feet on his shoulders, yeah solid.* "Three messages?"

"Five total. This Hannah cabled that there are two more SRAC bursts from DIVA coming tonight," said Gable. "She's cabling the texts as soon as she retrieves 'em and gets back inside the embassy." Gable ran his hand over his brush-cut hair. "Two runs in two nights. That cowgirl has some balls. We should get her assigned to Station when she finishes in Moscow."

Jesus, thought Nate, *that would be just perfect,* and studiously did not look up as he read. Halfway through the first cable Nate did look up. "The Center knows about LYRIC?" Nate said. "What does Benford say?"

"There's a rat up the drainpipe," said Gable.

"The Russians are talking to somebody code-named TRITON, who's gotten wind of LYRIC," said Forsyth. "It's in the second cable there. We normally wouldn't be read in to a CI case back home, but since DIVA generated the intel, Benford wants Station to know." Forsyth shook his head.

"So Benford's got a problem," said Gable, "and the Russkies know they got a problem, and now we, or more precisely you, got a problem. A Restricted Handling asset, your agent, in the crosshairs."

"Russia Division is worried," said Forsyth. "Benford told me they may have lost another case. Some Russian was called home from South America."

"This shit usually happens in threes," said Gable. "Seen it a million times."

"And DIVA could be in considerable jeopardy," said Forsyth. "She's been the frequent subject of a lot of spectacular cable traffic, from Athens, Vienna, Langley. God knows how many people have read about her."

"And bagging this third ear, this TRITON asshole, isn't going to be easy," said Gable. "Headquarters sends LYRIC's shit only to about a thousand fucking talkative dickheads," said Gable, nodding at the booklet Nate had collected last night. "Pentagon, Air Force, contractors, White House, the committees."

"Benford is going to be busy," said Forsyth.

"We have to pull them both out," said Nate, already three steps ahead, trying to slow down when all he wanted to do was hop in his car and go get LYRIC. "We can get the general out of Athens right here, right now. Digging Domi out of Moscow is going to be—"

"She's coming to Athens in a week," said Gable. "Thought I'd tell you so you can get a haircut."

Nate flipped through the cables, got through DIVA's brief mention of Line KR and her counterintelligence trip to Athens.

"She's done a spectacular job since she went back inside," said Forsyth. "Top-secret Kremlin intel, moles, counterintelligence leads, the whole Iran thing."

"We got to talk to her about risk, though," said Gable, looking at the slight vibration of the cable as Nate held it in his hands. "Judging from the variety of her reports, my guess is she's recruiting subsources inside her own directorate who have different access. Wonder how many she's sleeping with. Fucking nervy."

Nate looked at him and laughed thinly. "We can introduce LYRIC and DIVA on the plane," he said. "They can learn to ride horses together in Wyoming."

"Slow down," said Forsyth. "We don't know what we have yet. DIVA's in Line KR and sounds like she's got at least one subsource. We'll walk this back carefully with her, see what we have. Benford's coming out to talk with us and her next week."

"And LYRIC?" said Nate. "He's exposed. His reporting is pretty specific."

"They think LYRIC is in Moscow. As long as they don't call him back, we can wait a little," said Gable. "But get ready for the midnight boogie if we need to exfil him. Sites, safe houses, safety signals."

"I got all that. But I have a problem."

"Apart from your afflicted appearance?" said Gable.

Nate ignored him. "My problem is that I asked LYRIC to bring me the budget documents. This is the third meeting I've asked for them. It's not like he doesn't have them—he's the frigging GRU attaché in his embassy."

"You tell him you'll kick his ass next time?" said Gable.

"Sure, and all the rest of it. Langley's trust in him, memory of his kids, getting back at Putin. He understands it all."

"You think they already got to him?" said Gable.

"No, the old guy is still bringing stuff out in shopping bags. Productive as hell. And getting better each meeting," said Nate. "It's just that he does what he wants, when he wants."

"You've got yourself a Russian agent who's a general-rank officer. Used to doing things his own way," said Forsyth. "He came to us in crisis, but you're now his life; you've done a good job with rapport, and he's blooming again, feeling his oats. Control him, especially now."

"That's the problem," said Nate. "He's got an ego as big as Red Square; it's like he's forgotten how low he was when we popped him. I'm not sure he'll agree to bug out if we tell him to defect."

"Well, start talking to him, gently," said Forsyth. "Don't spook him, but get him ready."

"One thing for sure," said Gable, yawning and stretching his arms over his head. "If they call him home to the Aquarium—that's what they call GRU Headquarters—for any reason, like consultations, or to take a prestigious new job, or to sit on a six-week promotion panel, or because his great-aunt Natasha just fell down the stairs, and he walks through the front door of the Aquarium, that'll be the last we see of him."

Two nights later, Nate was walking with LYRIC along a marble-paved walkway in the modest Glyka Nera neighborhood on the darkened east slope of Mount Hymettus, away from downtown Athens traffic, a world away from where any official Russians would conceivably live or shop. They walked slightly uphill through pools of light cast on the marble by streetlamps with white globes, and passed unexpectedly through an unseen puff of incense coming from the open door of the little Church of the Metamorphosis. They continued in silence, up the deserted path, among the pines, the incense giving way to a fragrant fog of wild oregano.

LYRIC was dressed in a dark suit with a white shirt and black tie, a contrast to Nate's dark slacks and nylon shell. Nate had run an extralong surveillance-detection route that night—DIVA's intel that the Center was now aware of a CIA asset encrypted LYRIC had rocked him. He was determined that he arrive black at the nonsked meeting with the general, and hoped the nonscheduled call out had not spooked the old soldier. Not likely with LYRIC. Nate had waited on a bench among the pines, sighting through the branches, to observe LYRIC's arrival. No pedestrians at this late hour, no loitering cars filled with dark silhouettes and cherry-red cigarette tips. Black. Now business.

As they walked, the general's soft steps did not hesitate for even half a beat when Nate told him that the Center might be aware of a CIA reporting source, a GRU source with access to intelligence on military acquisition of foreign technology. LYRIC cocked his head at Nate while lighting a cigarette. "What exactly do they know?" said LYRIC.

"We will know more in several days' time," said Nate. "Right now we believe the identification lacks details." He knew he sounded pretty lame.

"No specific information on directorate or rank?" said LYRIC. His hands were behind his back, cigarette in his mouth. Out for a stroll.

"No specific information on directorate or rank, no," said Nate, "but the Center is aware that Athens is a possible venue. That could narrow the search and move the investigation dangerously close."

LYRIC waved his hand dismissively. "*Kto sluzhit v armii ne smeyetsya v tsirke,* he who has served in the army does not laugh at the circus. I am too familiar with the clowns in the counterintelligence staff in GRU. They could not catch a tethered goat." LYRIC rakishly blew smoke up into the night air.

"What about FSB or SVR?" said Nate. "Would they be involved in an investigation?"

LYRIC shrugged.

"SVR perhaps, if they need to investigate overseas," said Lyric. "FSB if in Moscow. But GRU will resist any attempts to steal primacy. Everybody is clamoring for advantage, pecking for morsels; they are like a flock of pigeons." They had reached the top of the walkway and looked up. The ridgeline of Hymettus was silhouetted against the glow of city lights on the other side of the mountain. They turned to walk slowly back downhill—there was no seven-minute time limit for personal meetings now. No Moscow Rules—yet. But there was every bit as much danger lurking around the corner. The hot-oil aroma of crispy fried fish and *skordalia*—garlic dip—from an unseen tavern down the hill drifted up through the pines, suddenly strong, then fading.

"General, I want you to consider travel to America if the investigation appears to be getting too close," said Nate.

LYRIC looked at him sideways. "You mean defect? Flee to the West?" He stopped and faced Nate. The garlicky air was perfectly still; nothing stirred in the pine tops. "I did not start all this with you to flee," he said. "Besides, it is safe. You will see."

Nate put his hand on the general's arm. "There is no thought of flight. I'm talking about an honorable retirement. A peaceful and comfortable life."

"Out of the question," said LYRIC, lighting his fourth cigarette.

"We would value your continued expertise, to continue to advise our government in military and scientific matters," said Nate, thinking, trying to sell the LYRIC retirement plan. Next he'd throw in cabana privileges at the Fontainebleau in Miami.

"I will assist and advise your organization regardless of where I am. I have been pleased with our collaboration, and I have been pleased with your professionalism. Well pleased."

LYRIC's lofty assuredness and ego were unshakable. Nate felt like popping the soap bubble. "We would not be able to continue if you were in *Chyorny Del'fin*, the Black Dolphin," said Nate softly. The casual mention of the worst prison in Russia, Federal Prison No. Six, near the Kazakh border, made LYRIC's head snap up. Nate knew he didn't have to mention that life in prison would be the least of the punishments LYRIC could expect.

"I'm asking you, General, to consider what I am saying to you. There's no need for undue alarm now, but you and I must prepare for the necessity of a new life, a new start. There's nothing dishonorable in it."

LYRIC looked at Nate and shrugged his shoulders noncommittally. *As valuable as he is,* thought Nate, *this agent is no MARBLE. I'll never call this guy* dyadya, *uncle.*

"I will consider what you say," said LYRIC. "But I have no wish to flee from my country. As they pay for what they have done, I am still loyal to the *Rodina*, my motherland."

Nate kept still—this was classic agent rationalization, a balm to the tortured conscience that contemplates treason in the still hours before sunrise. LYRIC went through the familiar routine of fieldstripping his cigarette. They were nearing the bottom of the path, where they must separate. Nate wearily contemplated several more hours of an outbound SDR, walking and riding three buses to get clear of the area and make his way to his stashed car. LYRIC stopped and faced him.

"As you report my continued willingness to operate with you, I want you also to please convey to your Headquarters my disappointment over this security lapse. But we will continue."

"Thank you, General," said Nate, a little weary of his star agent. It was time to separate and get out of the area. "Do you still have the local number to request an emergency meeting?"

LYRIC nodded.

"Do you remember the drill? Call from a clean phone, a hotel, a restaurant, a bar. And no speaking."

"I remember what you told me," said Lyric. "I will tap on the mouthpiece with a pencil. Tapping means Solovyov"—LYRIC patted his own chest lightly—"code name BOGATYR, is calling for an urgent meeting. Somewhat primitive methods, I must say. GRU officers use advanced frequency-hopping mobile phones to communicate with sources."

"*Prostota,* General. Simplicity—landlines and nonverbal signaling—is the best security," said Nate. *My friend, your GRU would shit if they knew how the FBI and the NSA were crawling up their frequency-hopping asses,* thought Nate.

"Call for any reason," he said, putting his hand on LYRIC's shoulder to get him to concentrate. "I'll be here at the usual time, and for three consecutive nights, as we agreed."

LYRIC nodded.

"And General, don't fool around with this. Please do it carefully. For me. Any summons to Moscow, for any reason, you tell me instantly. Okay, General?"

LYRIC patted Nate's hand. Nate kept it where it was and looked him in the eyes.

"*Okay, General*?" he said.

"Da ladno," LYRIC said, I get it already. Nate shook his hand.

"Stupay s Bogom," said Nate, go with God, and turned for the street.

"Podozhdite minutu," wait a minute, said LYRIC, taking an envelope out of his suit pocket. "Computer disk, Ninth Directorate budget, per your request." He smiled at Nate.

A point in time, the pendulum swinging; the will of the agent in the moment acknowledging the authority of the case officer. But for how long?

COD FRITTERS WITH SKORDALIA

Process water-soaked bread, abundant pureed garlic, ground pepper, olive oil, and red wine vinegar into a thick dip. Serve alongside chunks of quick-fried cod coated with a batter of flour, eggs, beer, white vinegar, and a drop of ouzo.

22

She had scant hours before leaving for Athens. But this morning there was something going on in the Line KR corridors in Yasenevo. Fussed junior officers were scuttling in and out of the large conference room at the end of the hall. Dominika looked in. The dusty and chipped birch conference table was being wiped down, and four heavy glass ashtrays were spaced down the middle of it. Oxidized aluminum carafes were arranged on a sideboard. The walls of the room were lined with dingy gray-blue felt, a worn blue carpet covered the floor, and water-stained acoustic tiles ran along the ceiling. *The Line KR conference room really is a dump,* Dominika thought. Not electronically soundproofed like the director's elegant conference room on the fourth floor, and certainly not as grand as the formal ground-floor auditorium off the Yasenevo lobby.

But this grubby little room had its own history. Dominika knew that the eleven SVR illegals officers arrested in and expelled from the United States—they had been imbedded in their deep cover lives from Seattle to New York to Boston—were debriefed in this room upon their ignominious return to Moscow. Afterward they had joined hands with then–Prime Minister Putin and sung patriotic songs as they contemplated the rest of their ersatz careers and lives in the bosom of the *Rodina*.

Looking around the room, Dominika briefly wondered whether that would be her legacy: Remembered as a despicable traitor now fled to the enemy West, with an in absentia sentence of twenty-five years imprisonment for treason and desertion—some still called it *Staliniskii chetvertak,* Stalin's quarter century—or maybe she'd end up like others before her, consigned to an unmarked grave.

A junior officer noticed Dominika in the doorway and stood up straight, heels together. No one in Line KR had seen much of the new captain with the blue eyes, though there were the usual Yasenevo rumors: foreign operations, priceless documents stolen from the Americans, arrested in Athens, and an exalted deliverance from CIA captors. Other whispered stories were darker, could not be discussed openly: She had killed men,

Russians and foreigners alike; she had been through the Kon Institute—the shadowy Sparrow School; she had been imprisoned but had survived the interrogators in Lefortovo. Rumors or not, you didn't toy with those blue lasers.

"What is happening?" said Dominika. At her voice the other two junior officers stopped what they were doing and faced her.

"Captain, good morning," said the first junior officer. Green light swirled around his head, the green of apprehension leavened with fear. Dominika vaguely registered—not for the first time—that people were afraid of her. It was what this tar-black Putin regime did to them all. What a waste her Russia had become.

"Good morning," said Dominika. The three young men weren't blinking. No one spoke. Dominika looked at them, then at the conference table, then back at the first officer. She caught his eye and raised an eyebrow, for the practice of it. The young man jumped as if shocked.

"Oh, pardon, Captain. The colonel instructed us to prepare the room for a meeting at noon." Dominika would not ask this underling with whom the meeting was scheduled. It didn't matter; she already knew, thanks to Yevgeny. She sourly noted that Zyuganov had told her nothing about it. She nodded at the three officers, left the room, and walked down the corridor painted light yellow with three decades of black scuff marks along the baseboard from the wheels of mail and equipment trolleys.

She knocked once sharply on Zyuganov's office door and pushed through. He looked up from the papers on his desk. Yevgeny was sitting in a side chair bathed in a satisfied horn-dog halo of yellow that flared when she walked in the door. Last night with him had been a trial: She had had to shake her sheets out the window to get rid of the curly hairs after he left her apartment.

Looking at smug Yevgeny slumped in the chair sparked the familiar cocktail of resentment in Dominika's chest, constricting, pulsating, migrating upward to stick in her throat. What she was doing with Yevgeny would otherwise be unthinkable for her—for any woman with free volition—who loved and lusted healthily with her whole heart. The *siloviki,* the bosses, had done very well by her, had trained her to close her ears to the whistling nostrils, to close her nose to the sour-drain smell behind the ears, to glaze her eyes and ignore the silver thread of spittle hanging from eggplant lips. They had taught her to slip without a ripple into the sewer. It was not love, it was not sex, and it was not earthy, exhilarating rutting with a naughty lover. It was *rabota*—work, labor, a job, duty.

Dominika took a sliding step to the side of Yevgeny's chair and hit him with a fore-knuckle strike in the temple, aiming for a spot an inch inside his skull. His eyes rolled up and his head flopped to the side. Without a break in her step, she rounded the desk and dug her nails into Zyuganov's teapot handle ears and mashed his face down against the desk, once, twice, then shifted slightly to skiver his eye socket into the corner of the wood. Ocular fluid squirted over the blotter. She let go of the ears, and Zyuganov's ruined face slid beneath the desk.

"Good morning, Colonel," said Dominika, clearing her head and straightening her jacket. He looked down at the papers on his desk, then back up at her. There was something wrong with Zyuganov's hair this morning. He had apparently pomaded it and it was lopsided. With the acuity of a bipolar sociopath, Zyuganov saw Dominika looking at his head. The black bat wings swelled a fraction. Yevgeny continued smirking.

"Egorova," Zyuganov said. Nothing else.

"Colonel, I noticed preparations in the large room. Is there a meeting scheduled for today?"

Zyuganov sat still and looked at her, as if deciding whether to respond. Yevgeny shifted slightly in his chair. Last night he had briefly told her about the conference and who would be attending. But Dominika had to ask about it—she could not hint that she knew the details, nor could she plausibly feign uninterest. Zyuganov fiddled with a six-inch stainless-steel bone chisel—one of a number of tchotchkes that littered his desk.

"The *rezident* from Washington is in the Center today," said Zyuganov reluctantly. "She arrived last night."

Yulia Zarubina, shveja, *the Seamstress,* thought Dominika. The legendary operator and Washington *rezident,* a product of the Foreign Language Institute and the old KGB, educated, multilingual, a hybrid too well connected for any *nadziratel,* any Kremlin overseer, to interfere with. Decades of spectacular operational successes, recruited target assets sewn up tightly like the cloth undertaker sacks used in villages in the Urals, with minute, precise stitches. Putin had sent her to Washington last year. The directorship was now within her grasp. *And she was back in Moscow to discuss a new case.*

"And the meeting?" asked Dominika. "Is there an issue for our department?"

"Zarubina will be making a report on the state of the *rezidentura* in Washington. She will review the counterintelligence atmosphere, and offer an assessment of political developments." The little bastard was being coy. No senior *rezident* returned to the Center for mundane briefings. He was not going to tell her anything. She looked at Yevgeny. *Do you see who your patron is?* she telegraphed him. Yevgeny avoided her eyes.

"What time will we start?" said Dominika, daring him to exclude her.

"At noon," said Zyuganov.

"Thank you, Colonel," said Dominika. Zarubina. Washington *rezidentura,* Line KR. *Forsyth and Benford will be interested,* she thought. And then she thought about Nate and how she ached for him.

All the faces around the table were turned to the conference-room door. Line R (analysis), Line T (technical support), Line PR (political), the Americas desk (General Korchnoi's old seat), they were all there. Zyuganov stood at the door greeting the visitor, washing his hands and showing his teeth. *Rezident* Zarubina entered the room, nodded at everyone, and walked around the table, shaking hands with those she knew, greeting those she did not. Dominika watched her as she worked her way around the table toward her.

The woman appeared to be over fifty, short and bosomy. She had honey-wheat hair pulled back in a matronly bun framing a full face that was lined around the eyes and mouth. There was an occasional flash of uneven, dark teeth, typical of her generation. Loose skin under the chin and a hint of jowls softened the image. Zarubina's almond eyes were hooded—there must have been ancestors from the steppes—and they gleamed with intuition. In the space of ten seconds Dominika saw how Zarubina looked steadily at whomever she was addressing, a sweet, slight smile on her lips, but every third second her eyes would dart to one side or the other, or over the shoulder, more watchful than any roe deer in a Siberian pine forest.

She was coming closer, talking to someone but fixing Dominika with her eyes. Closer. A pressure wave of air preceded her and then the golden light of Zarubina's aura engulfed Dominika, yellow, more than yellow, rich, velvet yellow tinged with pulsing swirls of toxin, deceit, subterfuge, *zasada,* ambush, *zakhvat,* entrapment. Now the eyes took her in, roamed across her face for a millisecond, calculating, weighing. *She's breathing me in,* thought Dominika, *searching the air for the* russkiy dukh, *the Russian scent of a foe. If anyone can tell I read colors, this* Baba Yaga, *this spell-caster, can.*

"How do you do?" said Zarubina, taking her hand. Her voice was smooth and low-pitched, right out of a warm kitchen with a stew bubbling in the pot. Her palm was soft and warm. "I have heard about you, Captain. I congratulate you on a brilliant start to your career." Resisting the old Russian urge to cross herself, Dominika smiled her thanks, feeling the familiar tightening in her throat. *More of the same, only this is a she-wolf with a different pelt. What is your project, Seamstress?* Dominika thought. *What are you sewing? Come, Grandmother, and tell me your secrets.* Then a pause, a click in Dominika's mind. *Can you guess* my *story? Do you know who I am, what my icy heart holds?* Even to think such things at this close range was folly.

Zyuganov stepped up and mumbled something about starting, and Zarubina turned to follow him after the X-ray plate behind her eyes recorded a last image of Dominika. She sat at the head of the table.

In that soft voice, with those mesmerizing eyes, Zarubina briefed the people around the table about the operational environment in Washington: The streets were loose with only intermittent coverage; the FBI were preoccupied. The American administration was floundering in resetting bilateral relations with Moscow; policy makers at all levels were eager for their own Russian Embassy contacts. Zarubina's case officers as a result had full developmental slates. More significant, the freeze in federal salaries—including those of CIA, FBI, and defense employees—was a resented hardship and was creating openings for SVR recruitment approaches to disgruntled American officers across the board. Finally, the *rezidentura* was engaged in *aktivnye meropriyatiya,* active measures, public propaganda to ensure that the White House would not again contemplate the establishment of a defensive missile shield in Eastern Europe, or support grassroots democracy protests from the Baltic to Ukraine. Of course, Zarubina left out operational details that were too specific—there was no need for them to know. She needed their assistance in production, analysis, and technical support. She turned to Colonel Zyuganov. "And Line KR's best counterintelligence reviews."

Zyuganov nodded. "I will attend to the requirement personally." Dominika saw that he already was imagining himself first deputy chief of SVR under this soft-talking woman.

Zarubina rested her plump spotted hands on the conference table in front of her. Her fingers twitched occasionally, the only outward sign of internal ecstasies. The yellow-gold bloom around her head was a diadem. She spoke softly, requiring total absorption from those around the table—they could feel their pulses settle in time with hers. Comrades, things were going well. Moscow was strong; Kremlin policies and global goals were syncopated; uninterrupted foreign successes were being realized. The Russian intelligence service was still the very best, the envy of nations and—a nod to Zyuganov—the scourge of opposition services. There was no mention of the glory days of the Soviet Union—*there needn't be*, thought Dominika. These words equally would please Tsar Vlad when digitally replayed for him.

Faces around the table, some otherwise very wise, were transfixed by the honeyed words. Sitting opposite Dominika, Yevgeny was staring at the mild grandmother who would be the next director. He felt Dominika looking at him and turned his head. Yevgeny slowly focused on Dominika's face, and she read his eyes instantly. The dingy yellow cloud of his lust had been shaken by Zarubina; it was now washed out, overlaid by doubt, guilt about what he had done with Dominika, panic about what he had told her. Dominika felt a momentary flash of alarm, fear that a repentant Yevgeny could come forward and admit all. It would not be overwhelming evidence of her espionage for the Americans, but it would be a short jump to the same conclusion for minds such as Zyuganov's and Zarubina's. Dominika was interested to note that she was not frightened at the prospect of trouble but darkly determined—Korchnoi must have tasted this high-wire thrill till the end of his days. She would have to try to settle Yevgeny down. Otherwise . . . what? Not even at Sparrow School did they instruct the girls how to fuck someone to death. Zarubina was looking at the faces around the table, a pleasant smile on her face. Zyuganov stood up.

"That will be all for now," he said. "Line OT, please stay behind."

Those officers excused began filing out, including Dominika. Yevgeny stayed in his seat at Zyuganov's left, taking notes. Zarubina chatted amiably with an officer on the other side of the table, but Dominika saw her eyes flitting around the room at the departing personnel, checking for resentment at being excluded, cataloging faces, assessing expressions, sniffing for trouble. Zarubina's golden halo was steady and strong; this was a creature with no doubts, no hesitation. Her only appetite was for the hunt, and the kill, and the feeding.

Whatever she was planning for her Washington *rezidentura*—the presence of the technical officers from Line T strongly suggested that the Seamstress intended to enhance agent handling for her new source, TRITON—details of her plan would be screamingly critical for CIA to know. Dominika resignedly told herself that she would have to endure one more night with Yevgeny before her trip.

Marta and Udranka were sitting in her office when she got back. Marta was smoking, as usual. Stop feeling sorry for yourself, Sparrow, said Marta. Fifteen minutes with that orangutan between your legs and you'll have the best present imaginable to bring your beautiful lover.

Dominika was leaving for Athens tomorrow morning. She told herself she should have been drafting and transmitting another SRAC message, or packing her suitcase, certainly ordering her thoughts for the inevitable marathon CIA debriefing, and checking a street map to get to the first meet with *Bratok* and Nate at a safe house, the address for which had been sent to her via SRAC exchange. Instead Dominika stood in front of the shower-fogged mirror in her bathroom, wiping her breasts clean with a washcloth. Yevgeny had tiresome predilections.

In classic Sparrow style, Dominika had navigated across Yevgeny's bow in the office late in the day, catching his eye, returning his lopsided smile, suffusing her face with an embarrassed blush at his inevitable and lurid suggestion for a good-bye hump to hold him over for the two weeks she would be gone. At least she was spared the tedious coquetry of suggesting it herself. She fed him, poured vodka down his gullet—alas, not enough—and had to lie with him, watching him sweat, whispering *ugovarivaniye*, coaxing encouragements, helping his body follow his mind, and purr convincingly as, finally, he hunched over her chest, shoulders shaking.

Then the next skin-crawling half hour cuddling the woolly caterpillar, faces inches apart, with his *huile de Venus*–oil of Venus they had called it at Sparrow School—drying on her chest, whispering to him about their shared secret, about his future, about the golden promise of a career with Zarubina in charge of the Service. Now Dominika played it stern, with his stubbly face in her hands: Your welfare is what I'm thinking about; there's nothing to feel guilty about. Don't throw it all away. Coming forward and what, confessing, would be the end, an unforgiveable transgression in their eyes. It would be the end of this, *of us*.

The smile was coming more frequently, staying longer on his lips, Yevgeny was reassured. His hand—those fingernails were marginally clean—trailed down her belly. *Ni khuya sebe, no fucking way,* thought Dominika wearily, and held his wrist. Instead she moved her own hand lower, and looked him in the eyes, which grew wider, then wider still. *Is this what you want?* Dominika thought dryly, moving her hand. *Is this sufficient*? *No. 96, "Chairman Mao's Chopsticks"*: After hours of practice at Sparrow School, it wasn't the hand or wrist that gave out, it was the electric ache in the shoulder, until you couldn't raise your arm, until you couldn't look at another oiled cucumber. Dominika still could not go near *Okroshka,* cold cucumber soup.

Yevgeny's lower lip quivered as if he were going to weep. Dominika had to slow her insidious hand so he could talk.

"God . . . knows," he said, concentrating. "Madame Zarubina was the one who made the request to discuss using an illegal to handle TRITON."

Throw the bone in the wrong direction. "Interesting but illogical," sniffed Dominika. "What could Zarubina want with someone like that?" Fast then slow.

Yevgeny closed his eyes and his breath caught. "Zarubina anticipates that she will be able to identify TRITON in the near future, and that he will agree to be handled personally. She says it's inevitable, whether in a week or a month. When that time comes she will meet him and settle him down. But then long-term handling must be by an officer not assigned to an official Russian diplomatic installation. Safer that way." He expelled a breath in a long sigh.

"An illegal?" said Dominika, almost sitting up, protesting to draw him out. "They cannot contemplate using someone without diplomatic cover with someone as potentially valuable as TRITON."

"Why did you stop?" said Yevgeny dreamily, looking down at her hand. If Dominika had an ax handle under her bed, she would have resumed with that. "Zarubina—wants to meet TRITON—herself at first," stuttered Yevgeny. "Yes, that's better—keep going. Zarubina said she eventually wants a faceless illegal—an expert in operating inside America—to assume handling. All traces of the case will evaporate." *And Benford will have no chance to catch him,* thought Dominika.

"The illegals cadre was decimated when the deputy in Line S, the illegals directorate, defected," said Dominika, thinking furiously, multitasking. "The identities of most illegals in S were blown to the Americans. The cupboard is bare."

Yevgeny shook his head. He spoke with an effort. "Zarubina said there is another illegals school, not the main one at Teply Stan, another one, not even a school, just a program, very small, just one or two students a year. It was not under Line S management, so it was not compromised. It belongs to the Kremlin." *What a coup it would be to get inside this program,* thought Dominika, *to identify illegals before they ever deployed to America.*

"What is the Kremlin thinking, directing such operations?" said Dominika, already knowing the answer. Russia's blue-eyed president-for-life and former KGB flunky wanted to keep his hand in the Game, but not to revel in the clandestine geometry of dispatching spies and saboteurs to impose his designs on the world. Putin's servants were all fungible and dispensable to him. No, this was another display of His Highness the Tsar's *muzhestvennost'*, his Russian virility. Yevgeny winced—in her anger, perhaps Dominika had yanked the wrong way. "Zarubina seems to know a lot about things," said Dominika, slowing down.

"How she knows about all this, I don't know."

"Perhaps Zarubina will be this new illegal's patron," said Dominika almost to herself, already mentally drafting another report, this one for Benford. Mentor one of Putin's *khor'ki,* one of his hot-eyed ferrets, and Zarubina would be rewarded—the directorship of SVR.

"Zarubina doesn't mentor anyone," said Yevgeny vaguely, looking down at Dominika's hand with heavy-lidded eyes. "Don't stop."

When would the new illegal be sent to America? Have they identified a specific person? How far along in training is he? Man or woman? What city will she live in? What is her occupation? What is her legend? "Feel good?" said Dominika, watching Yevgeny's flaring, bushy nostrils.

"Zarubina is a woman possessed," said Yevgeny, closing his eyes. Dominika thought he was more right than he knew. "She's insisting on absolute security. She will meet TRITON for as short a time as possible, then assign the illegal to TRITON to be totally clandestine. Line T is researching secure communications. All of this is to be outside Line KR. No one is to know, not even you. Zyuganov's orders."

Dominika smiled at Yevgeny. "I won't tell a soul in the Center," she said. She moved her arm more quickly—*martellato,* a little hammer in her hand.

"I know," said Yevgeny distractedly. He was breathing faster now.

"You're so sexy like this," said Dominika, thinking irony came naturally in the bedroom. Yevgeny suddenly started trembling. He fell back and ground the back of his head into the pillow, groaning. It was thirty seconds before he opened his eyes and his breathing slowed.

"It will be a long two weeks apart," panted Yevgeny.

Two weeks will be over before you know it, said Udranka from the corner of the bedroom.

"Two weeks will be over before you know it," said Dominika.

OKROSHKA—COLD CUCUMBER SOUP

Process peeled and seeded cucumbers, green onions, chopped hard boiled eggs, fresh dill, sour cream, and water to make a soup of granular consistency. Optionally add cubes of cooked ham. Season, chill, and serve garnished with dill or mint.

23

Hannah Archer had been busy. For four nonconsecutive days in the past week she had made careful surveillance-detection runs of five, six, four, and three hours, not only determining her status—that is, whether she had trailing surveillance that day—but also quantifying with eyes and instinct increasingly honed on the street *what sort* of surveillance might be on her. It was a good bet that she was still low on the FSB priority list, but since her arrival she had seen a slight incremental increase in coverage on her. Some FSB desk officer had probably picked her file and thrown it into the "check activity" pile in the "foreigners" box.

To COS Moscow's annoyance, Hannah regularly cabled detailed descriptions to Headquarters of what she saw on the street. Vern Throckmorton thought he should be doing the reporting on security conditions, but Hannah deferentially paid him no mind and filed weekly cables to Benford, per the latter's instructions. COS brooded about it but let it go, wary of the savant's mercury-switch temper. Never mind, both Benford and Hannah knew that surveillance activity was a delicate barometer of counterintelligence danger—whether the Russians' tails were up, whether they were on the scent, whether they were pulling on a string—and Benford now had to worry about DIVA.

Even if her operational act for a given day was simply to drive by and load/unload one of the SRAC receivers she herself had buried around Moscow, she had to know what sort of ticks were on her, what sort of gap they were giving her, whether they were tired and bored or riled and skittish. Passing an invisible SRAC site under trailing surveillance was nothing like meeting a source face-to-face, but Jesus, you still had to do it perfectly, still had to keep your shoulders square, look straight ahead, snap-check your mirrors, then fire the precisely timed shot with a hand casually inside the bag, remembering not to jackrabbit away after passing the site, and it was very preferable not to rear-end the Muscovite car ahead of you—little things that tech-savvy surveillance teams watch for, one lane over and three cars back, looking inside your vehicle with binoculars.

God, she loved the street, basked in the rhythms of it, kept her window down despite the cold to hear the sounds of it. On several nights she experienced what Jay, her internal-operations instructor, had told her sporadically occurs in case officers under surveillance: a state of grace where she became one with the grim, unshaven, unwashed men in the cars with the radios hot under the dashboards. On those nights, her transported spirit rode silent in the musk-ox backseat with them, listened to the clicks and squelch breaks, heard the muted profane comments, understood how they followed her that night.

One foggy evening she would hear the tire squeals of parallel coverage, glimpsing the telltale sidelights of cars on flanking streets keeping pace with her. Another night she would see—no, feel—them leapfrogging, her mind riffling through the growing catalog: *There's Oscar and Mustache Man, you switched off your left headlight, naughty, the bread truck we saw last week, boys, wipe the smudges when you take off the roof rack, coming up to the intersection and . . . there you are Matinee Idol, you should have waited behind the bus, never mind, I love you guys, come on, I'll go home early tonight so you all can rest.*

And the worst nights were when they weren't there, when the boys had abandoned her for another rabbit, and Hannah was fitful and lonesome. Those were the days when she gripped the wheel: *Okay fuckers, are you using the Doomsday Maneuver, so perfect that no one can fathom how you do it, no one can see it to beat it, and you're trying to catch DIVA, and kill her, and all that stands against your unshaven, flat fucking Slavic faces sinking your mandibles into the agent,* my agent, *is my gas pedal, and the narrow rippled mirrors on this chirping little hatchback, and my strontium-fortified cooz, and you guys* cannot *have her, it's not going to happen.*

Hannah knew that this shit, unrelieved, made you a little twitchy. Just look at Janice and Benford at Headquarters. She noted to herself that Nate wasn't twitchy at all, at least not in the bad sense. She thought of him all the time, but there was no question of sending him a friendly email, even a secure internal message. Too ex-lover, too possibly misunderstood.

She needed a friend: The catechism was to stay away from the other officers in the station—preservation of cover, avoid contamination, compartmentalize your individual activities. There were some workmates from

State, from her consular cover job in the embassy, but no real social prospects. Moscow was a nonfrat post, so unless she wanted to bench press an eighteen-year-old, off-duty American Marine security guard, it would be evenings in the embassy housing compound, sitting on kilim pillows around a coffee table eating cheese and crackers with six earnest State Department third secretaries listening to the new commemorative Joni Mitchell CD and wondering why the hostess, an overly dramatic thirty-seven-year-old global-studies major from Mount Holyoke named Marnie, wore a beaded peasant necklace with an oversized wooden *M*.

Stop it. Eighteen months left in this Moscow tour, with a hinny mule of a COS on one side of the office trailer and a tipsy, nicotine-saturated DCOS Schindler hanging upside down from the ceiling on the other. And scores of lynx-eyed FSB surveillants waiting for her to come out and play on the street. Hannah had accomplished what Benford asked her to do: DIVA had SRAC and could talk to CIA securely in Moscow, a towering if jeopardous triumph. At the end of her first year, Hannah would be due an R&R break. Rest and relaxation, at a location of her choice. Certainly home to New Hampshire, but maybe somewhere else, say, Greece, for a bit of sun and sea. And a bit of Nate?

"Hi, Dad," said Hannah, sitting in her darkened apartment, bathed in the light of the computer screen. The jumpy images of Hannah's mother and father in their sunny New Hampshire kitchen smiled back. It was morning back home in Moultonborough.

"How are you, Hannah?" said her mother. "Keeping warm over there?"

"I'm fine, Mom," said Hannah. "I bought a big brown furry hat. It's dreadful—muskrat I think—but warm."

"Are you eating well?" said her mother. She had mailed a box of cookies last month.

"Don't worry," said Hannah. "The commissary has everything: peanut butter, bologna, Velveeta." She dug her fingernails into the palm of her hand. This ghastly prattle was the best she could do: Before leaving for Moscow she had told her parents on no account to refer to or ask about her job. Never. They knew where she worked. Her parents had stared at her, unhappy and aghast, when Hannah said the Russians were always listening. Tonight the FSB techs would be watching the same images of her parents, hearing the same conversation. But not to use Skype as every other embassy employee did (with abandon) would be unexplainable and interpreted only one way: *She's a spook; deploy more surveillance.*

"Aren't there restaurants over there?" asked her father. Hannah smiled. He was role-playing the goofy New England hick. *Careful, Daddy,* she thought.

"Oh sure," said Hanna. "A bunch of us go out and try local dishes. It's a lot of fun. There's a dish with lamb and eggplant called *chanakhi,* and it's pretty good." Hannah wondered if the transcribers would note that the Georgian stew had been Stalin's favorite.

"It sounds heavy," said her mother. God. Hannah ached to tell her father what she was doing, how she had been selected and trained to beard the Bear in his own lair, about what she had accomplished. She knew he loved her and was proud of her. But her triumphs could not be celebrated. "Get used to it," Benford had said before she left. "Self-abnegation builds character." Whatever that meant.

"I should sign off now," said Hannah. "It's pretty late here." Her hand twitched on the mouse to click the disconnect icon.

"I hope you're getting enough sleep," said her mother. "Do you need anything, a warm nightgown, snuggly slippers?" The eavesdropping, slack-jawed louts with the earphones would be making jokes tomorrow about snuggly slippers.

"Nope, I have everything I need," said Hannah. "I'll talk to you guys next week," she said. Her mother blew a kiss, got up, and moved off camera. Her father stayed still, looking at her through the screen. *Careful, Daddy,* Hannah telegraphed.

"Good talking to you, baby girl," he said. "You take care over there. Love you."

"Bye, Daddy," said Hannah. *He means give 'em hell,* she thought. *That's just what I'm doing, Daddy.*

In Headquarters, Benford read Hannah's cables, icily impressed. She had performed well, he knew, and DIVA's SRAC system was working beautifully, full-out. Hannah had cased superior sites, her surveillance-detection runs were nearly perfect, and she was a brick on the street. So natural, so cool, in fact, that FSB surveillance apparently assessed her to be a low-ranking functionary in the embassy, a junior officer in personnel, and accordingly had deployed only sporadic "check-up" coverage on her. Most nights she was black—she was sure of it. And thank God that hammerhead COS had not interfered with her. Benford would keep his eye on Throckmorton.

The DIVA reporting (via SRAC bursts) about the mole TRITON and Russian attempts to discover the identity of LYRIC had torn away the rotten wainscoting to reveal a mass of termites. Big CI trouble. Benford looked dyspeptically at the Moscow cables again. If TRITON was inside the Agency, he would not see these DIVA reports—Benford had hurriedly invoked a dedicated compartment to limit distribution to himself, three officers in CID, and the new chief of ROD, Dante Helton.

With sandy hair, wire-rimmed glasses, and the wry look of a dissolute academic, Helton was relatively young for a division chief, having started his career in communist Eastern Europe as a junior officer. Helton once told Benford that ops in the former East Bloc in the Wild West days were every bit the challenge of Moscow, with the added dimension that your host-country adversaries—from intel-service chiefs and planners all the way down to surveillance personnel—were the inheritors of brilliant national patrimonies from Poland (Chopin) to Czechoslovakia (Freud) to Hungary (Teller) to Romania (Vlad the Impaler). They were devilishly smart as well as committed. Helton had operated in Warsaw under murderous pressure—his hostile surveillance team, eventually driven into a rage by Helton's endlessly smooth manipulation of them, had one December night in 1987 flattened the roof of his Polski Fiat 125 level with its doors with coal shovels. The next evening he fucked them all over again.

Benford sat in his littered office with Helton and Margery Salvatore, a CID maven whose Sicilian ancestors, Benford was convinced, must have included the Fisherwife of Palermo who in 1588 claimed to have flown on goats with local witches. Margery could figure things out, complicated things, and Benford wanted her insights. He likewise had summoned Janice Callahan. She had not yet arrived, to Benford's annoyance.

"If it's all right with you two, I will offer preliminary comments until Janice arrives." He bellowed through the door to his secretary, the one with the fluttering eyelid. "Tell Callahan to come instantly. If she is en route, tell her to begin running." He looked at Dante and Margery for any sign of disapproval or unease, and saw none. Benford registered that he was known as a temperamental crank, but was agnostic about it.

"I am going to Athens in several days to consult with Station and to participate in the debriefing of DIVA," said Benford, running nervous fingers through his unruly salt-and-pepper hair, inadvertently creating a modified Mohawk ridge on one side of his head. Normal: Dante and Margery did not blink.

"Only a few agents—all of them retired or dead—in the pantheon of Russian operations have been able to report with the scope and potential that DIVA is displaying. The fortuitous upcoming opportunity for a personal meet will, I expect, provide abundant detail." The door opened and Janice, ice-tea cool in a leopard-print wrap dress and Jimmy Choo black mules, ambled in. Benford scowled at her. "What took you so long?" said Benford. Janice looked around for someplace to sit—Dante and Margery had cleared the two frayed chairs of newspapers and boxes. The only other perch—a small swaybacked couch—was brimming with more files.

"If I run, my dress falls off and these shoes come off my feet, Simon," Janice said absently, running a hand through her hair and looking around. "I keep forgetting to bring a camp stool when I come to your office." Benford watched her as she cleared a space for herself. A small avalanche of files hit the floor. She leaned down to pick them up, her cleavage revealed exponentially. Helton studiously looked away.

"As I was saying, DIVA is a fitting successor to MARBLE, as well as a testament to his farsightedness, God rest him," said Benford. The room was silent. Every one of them had come up the ranks by reading the MARBLE omnibus.

"We now have to consider several matters," he said. "At this time I will not discuss DIVA's contribution to the Iranian nuclear covert action, nor her success in coming to the favorable attention of the Russian president."

"Now that you mention it, getting chummy with the president is a contact sport," said Margery. "We could jeopardize her continued access and well-being if he loses interest in her and sidelines her. Even Vladimir's wife, Putina, eventually got the heave-ho."

"The prospect of DIVA becoming a favored confidante to the president is enormous," said Benford.

"'Favored confidant.' Simon, what's that mean exactly?" said Dante. "You want DIVA to seduce the president?"

"Calm yourselves," said Benford. "We will exploit what we can with due consideration to protecting our clandestine reporting source." He glowered around the small office. It's why he liked these officers; they gave him shit. He began again, his clockwork mind driving without pause the pinions and keys and ratchets in his brain.

"Let's review. One: We know that the Russians have begun receiving truncated reports from someone code-named TRITON. Two: The Russians do not yet know TRITON's identity. Three: TRITON has reported to the Center that CIA has recruited a GRU source on military/scientific intelligence, and has provided *our internal* cryptonym—LYRIC. Four: SVR *Rezident* Yulia Zarubina continues to meet a transparent Air Force double agent to enable intel exchanges with TRITON. Five: A recently recruited SVR source was suddenly recalled from Caracas. That agent's status is unknown." He looked around the room.

"Does anyone outside CIA know the LYRIC crypt?" asked Margery. They all knew internal cryptonyms were sacrosanct, but they also knew that they were often mentioned in interagency settings.

"With the wide readership of LYRIC's reporting, and the frequent community meetings about his intelligence, it is possible, perhaps likely, yes, that the LYRIC cryptonym is known outside this building," said Benford.

"And DIVA has reported that this TRITON is using the US Air Force double-agent operation as a conduit to Zarubina?" said Helton.

"Correct. I hope to learn more about how this is done when we speak to her," said Benford.

"Okay," said Helton. "But that means TRITON could be in the military, here in Langley, in the White House, on the NSC, on the Hill, or an aerospace contractor in California."

"Also correct," said Benford. "The hunt for this mole would by necessity begin on quite a broad scale. Manpower constraints would be a consideration."

"We could be working on this for months," said Margery, imagining the task forces, the damage assessments, the production reviews. A mess.

"Years," said Benford.

Helton looked at Margery. "That's not the worst of it," he said. "If the Caracas recall is because of TRITON, that would suggest he's inside this building. The recruitment is too new; that case wasn't known outside Headquarters."

"Well, unless we hear that our Caracas agent is on a meat hook in Butyrka prison, we won't know," said Margery.

"And we do not have the luxury of time," said Benford, fidgeting with a pencil on his desk. "If TRITON is among us, and well-placed, and reading material across distinct disciplines—military, political, scientific, geographic—he could hamstring the entire operations directorate."

"And kill scores of agents," said Margery. She had worked in China operations in the early years and knew the list of agents "not returned, no contact, presumed compromised" by heart. She still thought of some of them occasionally. They all did.

Benford looked over Helton's shoulder at Janice Callahan, sitting quietly with mahogany legs crossed, arms outstretched along the back of the couch.

"Anything to add?" said Benford.

"Obviously," said Janice, "we have to find this unpleasant traitor as soon as possible." Benford's fuming silence was more appalling than his usual red-faced rants.

"Thank you, Janice," Benford said with elaborate irony. "How do we do it?" There was that *tick-tock* silence in the room, the second before the thermobaric vapor cloud ignites.

Janice lifted one leg and examined her shoe. "It might be easier than we think," she said. Benford stilled an impulse to rise from behind his desk, pull his hair, and gyrate. He instinctively cut Janice—all of these friends—some slack: Janice too had walked down dripping alleyways in rusty iron cities with the footsteps echoing behind her.

"How. Do. We. Do. It?" said Benford.

"Starve a cold and feed a fever," said Janice, looking at him through her lashes and flashing her trademark smile.

CHANAKHI—STALIN'S GEORGIAN STEW

In a heavy Dutch oven (or tagine) brown cubes of lamb that have been rubbed with salt, pepper, oil, paprika, and red pepper flakes. Add sliced onions and garlic and sauté until soft, then add chopped basil, parsley, and dill, followed by stewed tomatoes, their liquid, and red wine vinegar. Nestle cubed eggplant and cubed potatoes into the stew, and add water to cover. Put the lid on and simmer on low heat until the lamb is tender, the vegetables are soft, and the juices are thickened. Garnish with chopped parsley.

24

"Starve a cold and feed a fever?" said Benford quietly. "Please have the goodness to explain to me why you are quoting the Farmer's Almanac." Helton turned in his chair, smiling. He had the scent, just a whiff, and waited for Janice to explain.

"Simon, if TRITON cannot use the Air Force DA op to get his info to Zarubina—if we starve the cold—he'll get so anxious about his money, or his stroked ego, or whatever motivates him—we feed those fevers—he'll have to risk meeting Zarubina face-to-face."

"And we'll have a chance at getting a look at him," said Margery.

"Zarubina is no pushover," said Helton. "She'll be difficult to trip up on the street."

"Easier than trying to dig TRITON out of the long grass once he's been assigned an illegals handler," said Janice. "We all read DIVA's SRAC message. The Russians are getting ready to assign a clean illegal to meet him. We'll never find him then."

They all looked at one another. An illegal would mean big trouble. Since the beginning of espionage, a foreign spy with civilian cover, posing as a native-born citizen of the host country with a meticulously prepared legend, speaking fluent, colloquial language, and living an unremarkable life with a humdrum job, had been the perfect faceless solution to handle a sensitive asset in enemy territory. No official status. No diplomatic installation. No intelligence-service connection. No profile for the mole hunters to search for. And everyone in the room knew the Russians prepared and deployed illegals better than anyone.

"Janice is right. Terminate the Air Force double agent op," said Helton. "They'll scream bloody murder, but you can go over OSI's head and get some general to spike it."

"And our boy will have a dilemma," said Margery. "Without the DA op, TRITON has three choices: Find another anonymous way to commit treason, stop spying, or come out of the closet and deal with Zarubina in person on the street."

"And we make that nice old lady in the *rezidentura* come out and play, we elevate her heart rate a little, and we see," said Janice.

"I'll do this myself," said Benford, already thinking about the possibilities. "The Air Force is going to be enormously unhappy. And Major Thorstad will no longer have to endure the rigors of espionage. He will have to content himself with watching his videotape movie collection at night."

Janice got up from the couch and twitched her dress into place. "It's Blu-ray and streaming video now, Simon," she said. "VHS is gone."

"Gone? What are you talking about?" said Benford.

Seb Angevine sat in the black SUV returning to Headquarters after a meeting at AFOSI Headquarters in Quantico, Virginia. He was lost in thought as the vehicle sped north on the George Washington Memorial Parkway, the budding trees that lined the Potomac a blur. An hour ago, he'd had to suppress his panicked reaction when he was informed by a thin-lipped Air Force colonel that SEARCHLIGHT, the double agent operation featuring Major Thorstad, had been terminated on the orders of the deputy chief of staff for Intelligence of the Air Staff.

The colonel explained that, despite the operation's solid start and hopeful results in engaging with Russian intelligence, the decision to terminate the DA op was made because SVR requirements levied on Major Thorstad increasingly were zeroing in on classified programs and technology that could under no circumstances be approved as feed material. The potential tactical gains from dilatory contact with the Russians were eclipsed by the significant potential intelligence losses. Major Thorstad was to break contact and rebuff any attempts at recontact by SVR.

The working-level OSI planners and counterintelligence officers fumed: Their golden DA op was being canceled; it was rampant risk aversion. A notebook was thrown to the floor, and the word "chickenshit" was muttered by one person as he stormed out of the room. Red-haired Major Thorstad stood up to tell his colleagues that even though the decision from the Pentagon (he used the term "big house") was disappointing, strategic considerations took precedence. It had been an honor to have been involved in the operation, he said, and he was convinced that the continued collective efforts of the Air Force and the US Armed Forces would amply defend our national security in the future. He sat down when an unidentified voice said, "Blow it out your ass, Ginger."

Angevine had nodded at the OSI officers on his way out, keeping his composure. This was a catastrophe. Without the periodic exchange of chicken feed, he had no ready way to pass information to SVR. And if he could not pass information to the Russians, they would not pay him. He needed the money. And he still had a score to settle: He had to look at that *goinfre,* that hog Gloria Bevacqua, the new head of operations, during executive committee meetings, choking on the outrage of her having his job. His job.

He had to decide on a course of action. He had to balance the extreme risk of getting out on the street to meet Zarubina against his continuing—and increasing—need for money. Buoyed by the three Russian payments, Angevine had already splurged a little and bought a new Audi S7 (fifty-seven grand) and a Breitling Chronomat 41 wristwatch (twelve grand), and made reservations for a dive vacation to Belize (five grand). His government salary at the SIS-Three level simply wasn't going to cut it. *Merde.*

Getting to the Russians would be like stumbling through a minefield. He couldn't walk in or throw a package over the fence: The white-stone Russian Embassy on Wisconsin Avenue and the four-story Russian Consulate on Tunlaw Road were under constant FEEB surveillance from lookouts scattered throughout the neighborhood. He couldn't call in: Russian Embassy phone lines—dozens of them—were monitored around the clock. He couldn't knock on an apartment door: Only selected high-ranking Russian diplomats—such as Zarubina—lived outside the embassy compound, but those apartments were covered, including the Russian ambassador's downtown beaux arts mansion on Sixteenth Street NW.

What about a bump, on-the-fly contact on the street? A supermarket, bookstore, restaurant? Too risky. FBI surveillance of known and suspect SVR officers was random and rotated from target to target, making it hard to plan. Angevine knew this threadbare coverage was a result of agency cuts mandated during the annual congressional budget drama. The FBI's Foreign Counterintelligence Division (FCI) could field only reduced surveillance coverage and otherwise had to depend on limited technical means to get an inkling of which Russian intel officers were active, when they were operational, and with whom they were interacting. Down deep, the FCI experts grimly knew SVR was aware of exactly how little was arrayed on the street against them—Moscow could read the US budget news in the newspapers too. The Russians knew exactly how weak the Americans were.

A slim advantage for him. Still, thought Angevine, you could not predict when or on whom FCI surveillance would deploy. Consequently, trying to make public contact with any Russian was to spin a loaded cylinder and play roulette. He brooded the rest of the day, then drove downtown to the Good Guys Club on Wisconsin Avenue to watch the dancers, get a beer, and try to think.

From the street the club was marked by a neon sign on an otherwise plain brick front of a narrow row house built in the 1820s—just a hint of its former elegant federalist façade remained—in a now-dilapidated commercial district of pizza-slice kitchens and sushi takeout, grocery stores and nail salons. He left the pigeon-and-asphalt world as he pushed into the club, leaving for the time being the dilemma of his stalled career as a Russian mole. The single-room club—*Who was he kidding,* Angevine thought, *it's a strip joint*—was narrow but deep. Angevine nodded to the jaw breaker sitting on a stool by the front door and headed for the back of the room. The place was tight even on a weekday: all three small elevated dancing stages, spaced evenly down the room, were in action. Angevine weaved between the long tables and bench seats filling the length of the room. Each elevated stage had a Lucite floor illuminated from below in soft white light—decadent Weimar Berlin shadows were cast on the bodies of the girls—a Lucite pole refracting light up its length, and a full-length mirror on the wall. The only other lights in the club came from the tracked overhead spots in red, orange, and brilliant white. The stages were lit brighter than any movie set, and the names of the dancers scrolled endlessly on an LED ticker tape above the bar. Multiple speakers filled the club with stripper rock from the 1980s and '90s.

Angevine sat down near the back and ordered a beer and one of the small sandwiches available during happy hour, this one a surprisingly good hamburger on toast. One of his favorite dancers was finishing up on stage two and would be rotating to stage three, which was closest to him. She had seen him from down the room, with the acuity of all working girls who dance naked in front of strangers. Angevine appraised her under the spotlights for the hundredth time— she did something to him, those green eyes. And that body didn't hurt.

Sitting at the table next to Angevine was a portly man with a big head and an epic comb-over sweating in a shapeless suit—had to be some slumming GS-15 from HHS or HUD—accompanied by a nervous, blinking younger man. Fatso's neck bulged out over a cheap blue shirt collar with what looked like a miniature-palm-tree pattern. *Definitely HHS,* thought Angevine. The stripper lights in the ceiling over stage three caught the worn sheen of the shoulders and elbows of his dark suit coat as he hung it off the back of his chair.

Angevine's dancer (he liked to think of her as his), whose stage name was Felony, stepped up onto stage three and made an elaborate show of cleaning the full-length mirror behind her with a spray bottle of glass cleaner and a paper towel, bending straight-legged at the waist to wipe the lower half of the glass. This was preliminary Kabuki for every new girl: The mirrors were covered in handprints and lipstick kisses after each set.

Porky Pig at the next table laughed at Felony's mirror-cleaning routine and pointed at her buttocks and G-string. Not done. *Worse than HHS,* thought Angevine. *He could even be IRS.* Porky elbowed his scrawny companion as "Hotel California" came on and Felony hoisted herself on the Lucite pole halfway up its length, then started sliding headfirst to the floor slowly, infinitely slowly, as smoothly as any mechanical lift. Earthbound again, Felony began dancing for Porky, who had stopped pointing and grinning and was now staring and swallowing. Angevine watched his face shining under the lights as Felony spun on the pole and laid down a cloud of scent—White Shoulders eau de cologne.

Near the end of the set another Eagles song, "James Dean," came on and Felony turned on the afterburners. Angevine, astonished, watched the fat guy get up and start dancing like Boris Yeltsin, hunching his shoulders and shaking bunched fists. He began bellowing what sounded like "*Cheymes Dyeen*." The bouncer at the door all the way at the other end of the club started to get off his stool, but Felony waved him off. The young companion pulled at Fatso's arm, and he sat down. After her set, Felony shimmied into her merry widow, discreetly shifting her breasts to fill the cups, and went over to sit between the two men. Off-duty dancers always worked the crowd to soften them up for bigger tips in the next set.

Angevine could see the younger man doing most of the talking, but Felony kept a long-nailed hand on the inside of Fatso's thigh, pretty far above the knee. She had an instinct about who the important one was. After the requisite five-minute "meet and greet" and a not-so-discreet tip of a folded bill stuffed between her breasts by Porky Pig, the two got up, shrugged on suit coats, and left the club.

Felony came over to Angevine, who stood, and she shook his hand—the stripper world was regulated by an idealized protocol of respect and chivalry (and men keeping their hands to themselves). Angevine bought her a ginger ale for champagne prices and smiled at her. "Great dancing, as always," he said. He knew the girls seldom accept outside dates with customers, so there was no pressure. Besides, she couldn't stay too long at any given table.

"Those two guys were Russians," Felony said, jerking her head sideways. "From their embassy up Wisconsin. The fat guy didn't speak much English, so he brought the little guy along. Gave me a twenty."

Angevine looked up at her sharply. "How do you know they were Russians?" he said over the music. The Russian Embassy compound was two-tenths of a mile up Wisconsin Avenue in the next block. His scalp started creeping over his skull. Felony reached into her stocking top and handed him a calling card: *S. V. Loganov, Minister-Counselor, Embassy of the Russian Federation.*

"That's the fat guy; did you see him dancing?" said Felony, pointing at the card with the nail of her little finger. "But the little guy gave it to me, like he didn't know what to do, whether he should or not." She looked up at the LED sign. "Got to get changed. You staying around?" Angevine looked at her blankly, lost in thought.

He had been racking his brain for a way to connect with SVR for days, and now, here, this sweaty tub of suet had fallen into his lap. Of all the places to bump into a Russian without being spotted by the FBI, he had never considered the Good Guys Club. But no, it was impossible, insecure—someone might see him. Shit, there could have been FBI special agents in here tonight, covering the Russians, looking at any citizen who had talked to them.

Angevine told himself that this was not the way to get a recontact note to the Russkies. If Fatso was approached amid the strippers and music and liquor, he would suspect an FBI or CIA provocation, a blackmail ambush; he would fear a potential setup in any sealed envelope handed him. But what else was possible? Some desperate attempt on the street? If he screwed up, he'd be as fucked as if he had shown up at the front gate of the Russian Embassy with a "Hi, my name is TRITON" name tag on his lapel. *Ce serait mauvais.* That would be bad.

Felony came out of the dressing room in a hot-pink baby doll, garters, and platform heels, winked at Angevine, and weaved her way through the tables on her way to stage one across the room. She stopped frequently to greet familiar customers, her hands in constant motion, patting cheeks, mussing hair, trailing across shoulders. The other dancers were all doing the same thing. Angevine laughed soundlessly to himself. Dieu pourvoira, *God will provide,* he thought.

It was the start of Sebastian Angevine's combination recruitment operation and covert action. He was in a hurry, so it was going to be quick and dirty. He wasn't an ops guy, but he knew a lot and read a lot, and the ladies always liked his style—admiring the wrought silver links on his French cuffs and fingering the lapels of his cashmere jacket.

He set out to recruit Felony as a middleman—if he had known case-officer lexicon better he would have used "cutout"—to contact the Russians right there in Good Guys. If horny, wiggly, moist old Loganov came to the club with any regularity, Felony could give him a sign-of-life note for passage to the *rezidentura* informing that TRITON was ready for *reactivation,* or whatever they called it, and designating a meeting site. And comrades, bring money.

And if the FEEBs were observing Loganov that night, so what? They would be sitting a table away in the darkness, with their sports coats over their laps to hide their boners, watching the show, periodically glancing over, making sure no UNSUB—unknown subject—had any contact with Fatso. But the dancers? They circulated everywhere, sat with everybody, were forever stuffing bills in their bras or garters, putting fragrant hands on patrons' arms and shoulders—Felony could hand Loganov a *fucking toaster* without the FEEBs seeing a thing. And Angevine wouldn't even have to be there.

There was the small matter of recruiting Felony quickly. She accepted his invitation for dinner—it was made marginally less tricky by the fortuitous timing of the recent breakup with her latest boyfriend, a person she referred to only as Fernandez, who was prone to bouts of depression caused by chronic erectile dysfunction stemming from his glue sniffing. After six months, Felony had thrown him out of her apartment, a modest two-bedroom on Benton Street N.W., in Glover Park. She was ready for a real gentleman friend.

Angevine's eyebrows went up when Felony mentioned her address. It was, incredibly, a half mile away from the back wall of the Russian Embassy through leafy neighborhoods of single homes and low apartment blocks. Felony's apartment could be, with luck and a little finesse, a secure meeting site, or a timed drop, or a signal site, or an electronic letter box, unknown to the feds and with no connection to Angevine. Now Felony's successful recruitment was trebly important to him.

At the end of that first date, she told him her real name was Vikki Mayfield. Vikki was twenty-nine, a little old for a stripper, but her stomach and legs rippled when she hoisted herself on the pole. She was tall and had pixie-cut blond hair—she thought it made her look younger—careful green eyes, and perhaps a too-strong jawline. It was a little strange and a little sexy to see her in street clothes, because Angevine had seen her any number of times without a stitch on.

She did spray-on tan because tan lines were old school. She had Memory-Gel High Profile implants because massive beach-ball boobs were no longer industry standard. She'd been dancing for eight years, knew the business, and could pick the big tippers out of the audience—she could instantly assess the men who would tip a fin, or a dub, or sometimes a yard. She had explained the patois (five, twenty, a hundred dollars) to a delighted Angevine, and she thought he was sophisticated and well dressed, and she decided she liked him.

She was off the next night, so Angevine pressed for another dinner, during which he made good progress. Vikki was smart, had seen life, and knew the difference between a redneck boyfriend and a big-city suitor. She liked to talk, and Seb was willing to listen. She came from tidewater Virginia, not from trash, but she had to work nights. She did a little college—got an in-state ride to the University of Virginia but dropped out (too many mama's boys who wet their pants) and tried Haverford College up there in Pennsylvania but dropped out (too many weepy, sensitive poets)—then drifted south to Washington, DC. She started nude dancing, amazed at the money—fistfuls of it—and moved in with a succession of guys who slapped her, or wanted her to deal drugs for them, or wanted her to moonlight as an outcall, and she'd had enough and found her own apartment. She still had to deal with loser boyfriends, but at least she could kick *them* out.

She had seen Seb at the club numerous times and thought he looked prosperous. At first Vikki expected to find that he was a hot-to-trot middle-aged guy into Nuru massage and pegging. But French-speaking Sebastian was a good listener, he ordered the wine, he worked for the State Department or something, he didn't try to grab ass, and he was funny when he wanted to be. After the third date (she danced two days on and three off), she invited him to her apartment after dinner and they kissed a little, but he'd had too much wine and she floated a blanket over him and went to bed alone after looking at him asleep on the couch. He woke her up in the morning with a cup of instant coffee, all sweet and stuff, and they took a shower together and did it on the living-room floor, listening to the neighbors clumping down the stairwell, going to work.

Day six. It was clear that Vikki still had a hidden reserve of wariness about boyfriends, but Seb brought a bottle of wine and she cooked dinner: a steak, Irish mashed potatoes like her grandmother made, store-bought apple pie. He talked a little about his job; he was a pretty senior guy over there at State Department, sort of a diplomat and a specialist or something on Russia, it wasn't clear exactly. They made love again, this time in bed, and she had her first non-battery-powered orgasm in years—that was a *very* good sign, she thought. He could be a little goofy for sure, a little stuck up with waiters, and he spent a lot of time combing his hair, but it was better than her former boyfriend Darryl's motorcycle chain soaking in a bucket of kerosene by the front door all week. To thank her for dinner and sex, Angevine gave her a silver cuff from Eve's Addiction. It was mail-order jewelry, but Vikki wasn't going to say no.

The next morning he was leaning against the vanity in the bathroom, watching her sitting on the rim of the bathtub shaving herself, when he casually said he wanted to take care of her rent, which ran to $2700 a month.

"Why would you want to pay my rent?" asked Vikki. "I mean, that's very sweet, but I make enough."

Angevine smiled. "I just want to do something for you," he said. He wanted to move forward and contact the fucking Russians. This was taking too long. "I really like you, Vik."

"I like you, too," said Vikki. Maybe he just wanted to be nice.

Angevine pushed off from the vanity and bent over to kiss her. "I love watching you shave," he said, trying to find something naughty to say.

"Why don't you sit down and I'll shave you?" Vikki said.

"What?"

"Come on," said Vikki. "It feels so sexy."

"I don't know," said Angevine, imagining himself in the Headquarters gym shower room with shaved groin and bald *couilles.* "It's different for men."

"I'll be careful," said Vikki, reaching out her hand. She looked at him playfully. "I'll do anything *you* want, if you let me."

And Angevine made sure that she did.

It took a week for Loganov to show at Good Guys, and breathlessly Vikki called Angevine to tell him the Russian had reappeared and to get his ass down there. At the last minute Angevine had decided to be there when Vikki passed him the note: There was no danger that he could be identified in the crowded room, and he didn't want to leave the envelope with Vikki for her to possibly open and read an inexplicable message signed by a mysterious TRITON. As it was, he had described it as a fun game: He concocted a bullshit story for her about a "reach-out program" from the State Department to selected Russian diplomats, inviting them to private sessions where important global issues would be discussed. Angevine explained that the invitations had to be discreet—delivered in a men's club by a half-naked stripper, for instance—so the Russian officials would not be "punished" by Moscow if they participated.

Utter nonsense, of course, and Vikki looked skeptically at him, saying she didn't want to do anything illegal (which Angevine glumly registered as her probable unwillingness to be totally co-opted as his witting subagent) but she sat next to Loganov and took the small envelope out of the flowing sleeve of her black satin kimono and slipped it into the Russian's shirt pocket while leaning in and wrinkling her nose at the sweaty-cooked-cabbage-stinky-trousers bloom of him. From across the room, Angevine could detect nothing of the delivery. Vikki had been as smooth as a top pro.

There was another reason he wanted to be there. Angevine wanted to observe the Russian's reaction when he felt Vikki slide the thing into his pocket. Thankfully, the Russian did not react—maybe he didn't feel the note against his man boobs—but maybe he had been briefed not to react to notes passed to him. His expression would be priceless, however, when, back inside his embassy, he opened the envelope to find the second envelope with DELIVER TO ZARUBINA written on it. No employee of the Russian Embassy in Washington—not even the ambassador—would hesitate for a minute to deliver the note.

The ball was rolling. Angevine's spirits were soaring later that evening as they clinked champagne flutes in Vikki's apartment, and he scooped her up and danced her around the living room when Michael Bolton's "You Wouldn't Know Love" from his *Soul Provider* album came up on Soft Rock 97. The Russian money would be starting again—he already had additional info for Zarubina about continuing debriefings of a GRU officer in Athens. He looked into Vikki's eyes and kissed her. Maybe with more money he'd meet someone with a little more savoir faire, but tonight, right now, her hard dancer's body was pressed against him, and she kissed him back, her arms around his neck. His body stirred, but the stubble was growing back on his crotch and he had to stop two-stepping and scratch.

The night was pitch-black as Angevine sat on a wooden bench and waited. The forested slash of Little Falls Park enveloped him, blocked out the city glow, and muffled the traffic noise on nearby Massachusetts Avenue. He sat hunched over, lead ingots filling his stomach, and closed his eyes, listening to the small snaps and rustling noises that come from a forest, even at midnight. A few lights from houses in Westmoreland Hills winked through the trees. Thank God it was too late for someone to be walking his dog. *Tu es con,* he thought to himself, you're an idiot. He checked his watch.

Angevine was waiting for the Russians at the site he had included in the note, which he had cased in preparation for the resumption of his brilliant career as a dashing operative. He was sitting in a small grassy depression, part of an artillery fort called Battery Bailey, one of scores of crumbled, overgrown Civil War sites dotted around Washington, DC, now mostly just smooth hillocks or sweeping greenswards, some with a HISTORICAL SITE sign, most of them anonymous and forgotten. He knew the Russians would appreciate the chain of old forts for what they were: Sixty-five miniparks, little oases of darkness and quiet inside the bustling capital city, not fenced and never closed, not patrolled by police, with access from and egress into the quiet grid-square neighborhoods they had protected from Confederate attack in 1864. And now, as the new Cold War proceeded, they were perfect venues for meeting clandestinely in suburban Washington.

"Hello?" said a soft voice from the darkness on the other side of the grassy earthwork. "Is anyone there?" Angevine got up and walked to one of the artillery embrasures and looked out into the inky black. A small woman was standing on a lower dirt trail that snaked around the outside base of the battery walls, barely visible. She looked up at him.

"I took the wrong path and now can't seem to get up to where you are." She wore a light coat and a floppy hat, as if she were expecting rain.

What the fuck is this? he thought. *This is Zarubina? Who the fuck else could it be at midnight?* Angevine held up his hand and whispered, "Wait there; I'll come down." He walked around the far break in the wall, found the steep little trail, and in a second was standing beside her in the gloom.

"Mr. Triton?" said the pleasant old lady. "My name is Yulia. How nice to meet you finally."

COLCANNON-IRISH MASHED POTATOES

Peel potatoes and boil until soft. Vigorously mash with butter and cream until smooth. Separately sauté sliced garlic, chopped leeks, and shredded kale in butter until the vegetables are wilted. Season with salt and pepper. Fold the vegetables into the mashed potatoes and top with melted butter.

25

A late afternoon rainstorm lashed the awnings of the shops along Arkadias Street, turning the fine layer of marble dust that perpetually coated Athens streets and sidewalks into gunmetal library paste. A second line of squally showers scoured the city, replacing the baked-earth smell of the day with dusk's sweet air and, to Dominika, a trace of lavender. She stood under the awning of her apartment hotel, the Lovable Experience 4, in Ambelokipi, the commercial Athenian neighborhood almost equidistant between the embassy of the Russian Federation in leafy Psychiko and the safe house TULIP, which was maintained by CIA in the tony Kolonaki district, where she was to meet Nathaniel and Gable tonight.

Dominika checked her watch and waited another minute for the last of the rain to stop. She didn't have an umbrella—she wouldn't have used one in any case; no one in Athens did. Evening traffic was picking up and lights were coming on: She calculated that her foot route through the dusty neighborhoods of Nea Filothei and Gkizi to check for coverage would take a minimum of ninety minutes—more if she started to get repeats. The area was full of long stairways, one-way streets, and cut-throughs; she would fillet any vehicular team in these back streets, and if they put foot coverage on her, she'd see the transition and could abort. She had purposely worn a dark gray sweater over a navy skirt to avoid the splash of color that helps a team keep the eye while working at discreet distances.

Dominika didn't take anything for granted: Both her Russian colleagues and her American handlers were more than capable of surveilling her, albeit for different reasons and with radically different potential results. The Americans might decide to cover her approach to TULIP to check her status. Validation of an agent doesn't stop after recruitment, Dominika knew. In some ways they tested the continuing loyalty and veracity of their established reporting sources even more assiduously.

Surveillance from the *rezidentura* in the Russian Embassy was a different matter: The *rezident*—an accomplished senior officer widely known in the service as a *yubochnik*, a skirt chaser—might want to keep tabs on her for general CI reasons. More likely, she thought grimly, Zyuganov could order discreet surveillance on her during her time in Athens to see if she did anything he could use against her later. This Athens trip was a rare and priceless opportunity to meet the Americans—denied-area, internal assets everywhere dreamed of such a chance to reestablish contact with their handling services. But her own countrymen's inclination always to suspect their own made recontact with CIA dangerous.

The pines on Likavitos Hill smelled fresh in the night air, especially after the vehicle-exhaust fog she inhaled at street level in Filothei. Through the dark trees she could catch glimpses of the fairy lights on the summit, and the lighted Saint George Monastery. Her surveillance-detection route had flushed nothing—no repeats, no demeanor errors, no evidence of leapfrogging or parallel coverage.

Now it was very dark and she stepped off the road and waited, listening. No cars rolling past, no motor scooters buzzing. A light breeze through the pine tops mingled with the faint buzz of the city below. She was on sked, with ample time for the casual stroll down into expensive, hilly Kolonaki and to the safe house. She smoothed her hair self-consciously, imagining the apartment door opening, seeing the familiar faces alight with greeting. She stepped back onto the road, turned downhill on Koniari, then on Merkouri. Narrow meandering streets were dimly lit, the electric-blue flashes of televisions from inside the apartments visible on the interior ceilings. Piano music came from an open window.

Dominika crossed the street and checked her six, not focusing close behind her but looking a block back, surveillance distance. She used the cars parked thick along Kleomenous as a screen, moving smoothly, still watching for bobbing heads and shoulders. She suddenly smelled cinnamon and eggplant in the air—someone was baking moussaka. Her pulse was up a little as she turned right, uphill, on Marasli, then left for a half block on Distria Doras, came to the last apartment building before the start of the pine forest again, and waited a beat in the shadows, listening. She looked up at the roof line and at the one across the street, then scanned the darkened windows. No movement, no glint of a lens, no parted curtain. The front door squeaked when she went in.

With a lurch, the little elevator groaned upward, until it stopped with a clunk at the top floor. There was a small landing and a single substantial-looking door. Safe house TULIP. No sound came from inside. The overhead bulb on the landing turned off as the timer ran out, plunging her into utter blackness, and Dominika couldn't find the switch to turn the light back on, or anything that looked like an illuminated doorbell button. She ran her hands over the wall, blind. *Idiotka,* she thought, *knock on the door.* But was this the right apartment? Had she gotten the street right? She felt her way through the darkness to the door and put her ear to it, straining to pick up a voice, the clatter of dishes, music. Nothing.

The overhead bulb came on and Gable stood behind her, his beefy face a foot from hers. She had not heard him or felt his presence in the dark. Dominika willed herself not to jump.

"*Bratok*, you move well for someone your age," whispered Dominika, straightening up, fists on her hips, debating whether to clout him with the bag holding her shoes. Before she decided, or before Gable could give her his customary bear hug, the apartment door locks began snicking and clacking—one, two, three—and the door opened and Nate stood in silhouette, backlit by a dim lamp inside the house.

"I see you've met the doorman," said Nate.

"Does he always sneak up on people?" said Dominika.

"He has to," said Nate. "Otherwise they run if they see him coming."

Dominika stepped inside, following Nate into the apartment. Behind her, Dominika could hear Gable locking the three deadbolts again. They walked down a short corridor—English hunting miniatures hung in a row on either wall. The living room was white, subdued, with a gray-and-white marble floor. A large beige sectional couch and armchairs in the same material formed a central group in the middle of the room. Soft golden light came from several large ceramic lamps on end tables. It was the tastefully decorated living room of a wealthy lawyer, banker, or television personality, thought Dominika.

She turned and noticed that the beige drapes along two walls were automatically parting to reveal floor-to-ceiling sliding-glass doors that opened out onto an enormous sweeping terrace that wrapped around the entire roof. Couches, chairs, and potted plants were arranged outside, too, dimly lit by recessed bulbs along the walls. Dominika stepped onto the terrace to look out over the winking grid of nighttime Athens and the distant illuminated butte of the Acropolis, which rose out of the city like a boat on flat water. Behind her, around the other corner of the terrace, the pine forest of Likavitos rose sharply up the summit. She heard Nate ease up beside her, felt his hand on her shoulder. She turned and he pressed his mouth on hers, the familiar sweet lips, the taste of him. *My God, right here?* But she didn't want to stop.

Nate pulled away, smiling. "Gable's in the kitchen, but he'll be out in a minute. Do you want something to drink?"

She shook her head. "I missed you," said Dominika. She put her hand on his arm, and Nate covered it with his own hand. In that wordless moment, they were back where they had left off.

Marta leaned against the balcony railing. It's worth the wait; it always is.

"You've been busy," said Nate. "Benford, Forsyth, all of us, we're impressed. Your reporting has been remarkable . . . so are you," he whispered.

Dominika searched his face, read the purple bloom around his head, to be sure about him, then laughed. "You know how to flatter a woman, *dushka.* I've got a lot to tell you all."

Dominika had long ago decided not to tell her handlers—Nate or any of the others—about seducing Yevgeny. She had done nothing she was ashamed of; it was her job, and she would do anything it required—anything—but despite her resolve, Dominika did not seek their approbation, and didn't want to deal with their knowing looks. She would say only that Yevgeny feared and mistrusted Zyuganov and they had forged an alliance. Make it sound all dark-Russian-conspiracy and they would nod their heads acceptingly. Except maybe intuitive *Bratok*, or wise Forsyth, or that *mag,* that magician Benford, or maybe Nathaniel's heart would read her soul in about three seconds.

"How long do you have tonight?" asked Nate. Gable was wheeling a stainless-steel drinks cart out onto the terrace.

"I'm staying at the Lovable Experience Four," said Dominika. "Despite the quite remarkable name, it is adequate. The embassy doesn't know the hotel. I insisted on anonymity, behaved like a typical inspector from Line KR on an investigation. Zyuganov did us a favor sending me to Greece. We have all evening, most evenings, for two weeks, as long as I don't have to be in the *rezidentura.*

"Zyuganov thinks the GRU leak is in Moscow," said Dominika. "He wanted me out of the way to pursue the case."

Gable and Nate said nothing; handlers never discussed one reporting source with another agent.

"The night before I departed, Zarubina filed a report from Washington. Zyuganov doesn't realize I know about it." Dominika took a glass from Gable and raised it. *"Na Zdorovie,* to your health."

"What did Zarubina say?" said Nate. The CIA officers dreaded the answer they could guess at. A slight breeze stirred the pine tops.

"Zarubina has made contact with the source called TRITON. He must be someone inside your service."

"What was in the cable, Dominika?" said Nate. She saw his purple halo pulse with agitation.

"They now suspect the source you call LYRIC is here in Athens," she said. The worst possible answer.

A noise from inside the apartment made her turn. Benford stepped out onto the terrace; he had been in the kitchen when she arrived. He was dressed in a dark suit, tie askew, a kitchen towel over his shoulder. He carried a plate of *dolmades,* grape leaves stuffed with savory rice, glistening with olive oil, which he put on the drinks cart. Dominika shook his hand.

"Good to see you, Dominika," said Benford. "Are you well?"

Gable poured another glass of wine. "Domi was just telling us—"

"Yes, I heard," said Benford, turning toward Dominika. "Did Zarubina describe how TRITON got in touch with her?" *With the double-agent channel now unavailable to him, TRITON must have found another way to establish contact,* thought Benford. *Our boy is resourceful . . . and hungry.*

"I do not know," said Dominika. "I did not see the cable." She knew what was coming next.

"How did you collect the information?" said Benford. All three of them looked at her.

"Yevgeny Pletnev, Zyuganov's deputy in Line KR, told me," said Dominika.

Benford, without knowing he was remorseless, continued remorselessly. "You wrote in one of your SRAC messages—the sixth transmission, I think—that Zyuganov was keeping you in the dark," Benford said. His infernal memory recalled everything. "Surely his deputy would hew to his superior's wishes that he not tell you anything."

"But I got him to tell me," said Dominika casually. "Yevgeny fears Zyuganov. I convinced him we could protect each other." She knew she sounded lame. Benford's blue cloud was steady. She didn't dare look over at Nate.

"Yevgeny also saw Putin's favorable impression of me, especially after I suggested your water-delivery route to Iran, Gospodin Benford," said Dominika. "He has chosen sides; he wants my protection. All Russians know *vysluzhit'sya,* how do you say it?"

"Brownnosing," said Nate. He was looking at Dominika sideways.

"You took a chance recruiting this lover boy," said Gable. "It exposes you a little."

"He is not my lover," Dominika said too quickly.

"No, I meant you took a chance, recruiting this guy," said Gable.

"He will not confess anything to anyone," said Dominika, swerving. "He has already told me too much. He is afraid."

God this is awful, their faces showing nothing, their colors steady, their eyes seeing everything. Udranka laughed, showing teeth. You don't owe them anything, no explanations, no apologies.

"All right," said Benford. "We will discuss security later. Please come inside and sit down; there's much to do."

Dominika had quietly taken off her oxfords and slipped into her pumps, but now even these were off as she and the CIA officers sat around the marble coffee table, papers spread out, and worked by lamplight. If they had looked, they would have seen a sliver of moon rising over Mount Hymettus to the east. To an outside observer, the four of them could have been colleagues working on a sales campaign or a public-relations plan. Dominika was the recruited Russian source, but she had morphed into a member of a nameless team, specialists all, working against the odds to accomplish the impossible, to gain access to the inaccessible, to prevail against the unassailable.

The CIA men took notes. The quiet conversation was businesslike but cordial. There was an occasional chuckle. Nate recorded everything on his TALON tablet. Benford led them through the entire concerto, including current intel on SVR operations and SRAC reporting—he reminded Dominika that she had to keep her message numbers straight. They discussed Zyuganov, updates on the Iran deal, President Putin, Zarubina, and getting an ID on TRITON. She listened when they told her about the suspicious matter of the recalled military officer from Caracas, and she told them she'd try to find out. Nate spoke to her about possibly adding more SRAC sites for geographic flexibility, and they looked at a map to find contingency backup personal-meeting sites, in case of mechanical failure with the equipment. Personal meetings—a Russian asset meeting a CIA officer in Moscow—were the ultimate risk. For one brief-encounter site Dominika pointed to the massive wooded park on the Luzhniki bend of the Moskva River—*Vorobyovy Gory*, Sparrow Hills—looking out over all Moscow. It was accessible, close to teeming Moscow State University, and there were a thousand ways in and out. *Sparrow Hills*, thought Nate. *You couldn't make this up.*

Gable brought out the book on Red Route Two, the exfiltration plan for Dominika, in case she had to bug out of Russia. They studied it for an hour, and she memorized the timing, routes, and sites. Red Two came with a small equipment package that Gable opened and showed Dominika—they would have to deliver it to her hand-to-hand at the meeting site in Sparrow Hills Park once the location was validated. Nate sweat thinking about an unknown case officer rattling around in those woods with Dominika's life on the line, until he realized it would be razor-sharp Hannah Archer who was the action officer. *Hannah.* He blinked, uncomfortable, and shifted in his seat.

Benford sat back on the couch, eyes half-closed, listening to Dominika as she talked and the night air stirred the drapes. After the first two hours, Nate went into the kitchen with Gable to get more glasses. "She's something else," said Gable. "Most agents have one complete report and parts of a second. She's bringing out the fucking kitchen sink."

"If she's right, she also just saved LYRIC's life. The general has to listen to me now. We have to get him out."

"What do I keep telling you?" said Gable. "The best operational security comes from a penetration of the opposition."

"Miraculous getting that info out of that Yevgeny guy," said Nate, leaning against the kitchen counter, looking at Gable.

“You getting all huffy now?' said Gable. “She's been trained to get info out of men. What do you want from her?”

“Nothing,” said Nate. “She just took a big risk, popping him like that.”

“You gonna ask her if she fucked the guy?” said Gable. “You're her case officer; you should know everything about her—what she knows, how she got the info, what position he likes best.”

Nate stared at him. “Marty, if you're trying to piss me off you're doing it just right.”

“Yeah, well I hope Yevgeny didn't give her a dose.”

“Fuck you, Marty,” said Nate.

“What did I tell you, rookie? You get involved with her, you invest emotional capital, and it's going to be a black day when one or both of you have to do your jobs—maybe like she did back there in Moscow. But you don't listen to me.”

Gable picked up the tray. “Make up your mind whether you're gonna be the insightful case officer handling his agent with perceptivity and skill or the spoony little choirboy chewing his quivering lower lip.”

Nate followed him through the door. “Golly, Marty, the way you put it, it's a tough choice.”

COLD DOLMAS

Thoroughly combine white rice, parsley, dill, mint, finely chopped onion, and golden raisins. Roll a teaspoonful of rice filling in blanched grape leaves. Line the bottom of a Dutch oven with loose grape leaves, and pack rolled dolmas tightly in layers. Just cover with water, drizzle with olive oil, and dot with butter. Place a heavy plate atop the dolmas, cover, and cook over medium-low heat until the rice is cooked, about one hour. Serve cold with lemon.

26

Twenty-one hundred hours and Zyuganov sat in the backseat of a Lada Niva, a small utility vehicle belonging to the Moscow police. A police driver dressed in civilian clothes sat behind the wheel smoking, and beside him sat Zyuganov's new protégée, Evdokia Buchina, unmoving, looking straight ahead down the dark street at a dimly lit door about a block in front of them. Eva was in a light warm-up jacket and pants, and under the unzipped jacket was a white T-shirt stretched tight by her mezzo-soprano's bust. The sergeant behind the wheel had offered Eva a cigarette earlier in the evening, but she had not looked at him or even responded, so he left it alone, sensing something wrong with the mannish woman. If he only knew what was percolating under those dark roots, or behind those granite eyes, or between those track-and-field thighs, he would have gotten out of the jeep and smoked his cigarette by the rear fender.

Zyuganov looked at his watch. Five more minutes, then they would go through the door and up the narrow staircase of the dingy four-story building in the northeastern Golyanovo district of Moscow to the apartment where Madeleine Didier, second secretary for cultural affairs of the French Embassy—she was in fact the chief of the three-person station of the *Direction Générale de la Sécurité Extérieure* (DGSE), the external intelligence service of France—was meeting a Russian man who worked in the scheduling department of *Sevmash*, Russia's largest shipbuilding company. The DGSE had been developing the young Muscovite for a year, not, as was usual practice, to steal military secrets on the Russian navy's next-generation ballistic submarine, but rather to collect commercial intelligence on *Sevmash* to better position French shipbuilders like STX Europe to sell French-built warships to Moscow on advantageous terms.

The CI lead had started small, as it always does, then it got worse. One rainy afternoon the FSB followed an incautious Didier to a restaurant meeting with the *Sevmash* employee, then to another, and to the one after that. FAPSI had intercepted DGSE cables documenting operational progress with the target, who by then had himself been covered in cotton wool—total surveillance coverage—at home, at work, at play.

Zyuganov had no appreciation for the nuances of commercial espionage. All he knew was that a foreign intel service was spying in Moscow, and that President Putin had turned to SVR Line KR counterintelligence *and him,* to handle the situation. In an exhilarating ten-minute personal interview (Zyuganov promised himself there would be many more personal interactions with the president in his future) Putin told him he wanted the matter handled in a *specific* manner, to send a message to the French that Russia was not stupid, that with a *swipe of a paw* the bear could shatter their operation and, particularly, that the long-honored convention between spy services of not using violence against one another's officers *did not apply.* Putin directed Zyuganov to create shock and fear and to break the French of their *garlicky arrogance* so they would come to the table to sell ships *on Russia's terms,* which really meant on Putin's terms, which really meant a closing commission deposited in a sheltered account. Zyuganov stopped listening at "shock and fear" and made careful arrangements to bust the next clandestine DGSE meeting.

Eva had been shaping up nicely since her coming-out performance in the prison cellar, but Zyuganov wanted to test her in the more fluid atmosphere of the street, to see how she would perform against an opponent who wasn't zip-tied to a chair or strapped spread-eagle on a table. "Eva," Zyuganov said softly, and the woman opened her door, slid out of the jeep, and came around to stand next to him, her granny glasses catching the light from the streetlamps. They walked to the door of the apartment building, entered, and quietly climbed the dim stairwell. Eva led the way and Zyuganov, without a prurient thought, noted how her gluteus muscles flexed under the fleece warm-up. She trailed a bloom of animal earthiness, of horses and hay and barn.

The third-floor landing was nearly pitch-black, but Eva walked silently to an apartment door near the end of the hall and squared her shoulders to it. She glanced at Zyuganov, who nodded, and then she knocked softly twice. Zyuganov approved, a light tap from a neighbor to borrow some butter, not the pounding of the *militsiya.* The door opened a crack and a man's face appeared. "I need to telephone," said Eva in Russian, her voice cracked with urgency, close to crying.

Before the man could answer, Eva shouldered the door open, tearing the chain out of the wood and catching him in the face with the edge. Zyuganov followed her inside in time to see her pick up the dazed man off the floor, step behind him, put one hand on his forehead and the other on his chin, and violently snap his neck, letting him fall to the floor like wet laundry. Another man came out of the kitchen; he wore a jacket over a shirt, and he reached under it for a gun, but Eva crowded him and held his wrists and pushed him backward into the kitchen. Zyuganov heard dishes breaking and a bellow, and Eva came out of the kitchen with blood on her face, spitting on the rug. Zyuganov looked into the kitchen and saw the man sitting on the floor, holding his neck, with blood squirting through his fingers across the room onto the opposite wall. A short linoleum knife with a bird's beak curved blade was on the floor beside him. Zyuganov had not even seen Eva take the thing out of her pocket.

So much for French security guards providing cover for the meeting. They had been in the apartment ten seconds.

Eva's glasses glinted as she shrugged off her arterial-speckled warm-up jacket and wiped her face with it. Zyuganov clinically noted that she was not breathing particularly hard, but that under the straining T-shirt, her nipples stood out. He put a finger under the line of her jaw and felt a rock-steady pulse. Zyuganov held up his hand—*Softly, follow me*—and tiptoed down the little corridor. Light was coming from under the bedroom door. Zyuganov drew an MP-443 Grach auto out of a formed leather holster at his back. As he turned the knob a French voice inside said, "*Qu'est-ce qui a fait ce bruit,* what made that noise?" Zyuganov pushed the door open. Madeleine Didier, in a white shirt and navy skirt, was sitting on a straight-backed chair beside the bed, taking notes on a steno pad. The Russian man was on the bed, sitting up against the headboard. Both of them froze when they saw the nightmare pair of *Petrushka* puppets—one a troll with a gun too big for his hand, the other a gray-eyed reform-school matron with nipples like safe dials—come through the door.

Eva slid behind the Frenchwoman and lovingly slipped a forearm around her throat, stood her up straight, and held her still. Zyuganov stepped up to the Russian man, put a pillow over his face, and shot him in the head through the pillow. The muffled shot made no sound, but the pillow started smoldering from the muzzle's discharge gases. Didier looked on, horrified, as the pillow fell away to reveal the sightless stare of her source and the wall behind his head dripping applesauce. The traitor's death sentence carried out, Zyuganov moved to the next page of President Putin's programme: to complete the horror, to violate the gentlemen's agreement among spies, and to send an unambiguous message back to the French. Zyuganov nodded to Eva, who had been watching him while keeping mild but unyielding pressure on the Frenchwoman's throat. They had been in the apartment for ninety seconds.

Madeleine Didier was forty-six, a married mother of two. She had risen through the administrative ranks of an unapologetically chauvinistic DGSE with a combination of smarts, good looks, and the willingness to challenge the overstuffed croissants in her service who tried to sideline her, or deny her promotion, or put their milk-fed hands on her knee. Sharp-featured, with liquid brown eyes and shoulder-length black hair, she had unexpectedly landed the plum Moscow posting and was determined to make her mark in operations, as she had done in the management track. The *Sevmash* case had excited the analysts at the Swimming Pool (*La Piscine*, the nickname for DGSE Paris Headquarters because of its proximity to a nearby swimming federation pool) and Madeleine knew that continued production from her source would give her even more political leverage on her return to Paris next year.

Even as she was being stood on her toes by this carnival creature, the elegant Mme Didier did not fully comprehend that her heady foray into the glittering, champagne-bubble world of international espionage and intrigue had been interrupted by two cloven-hoofed, elemental beasties the likes of which not many in the sunlight-basking world could imagine existed. Brutal Moscow was one planet too far for Madeleine Didier and the DGSE. So it was with some disbelief and rising French indignation that she was thrown facedown on the bed and roughly, impossibly, had her shirt, skirt, brassiere, and *culottes* (Chantelle) yanked off, and her Saint Laurent patent leather Escarpin pumps (460 euros) pulled off her feet and thrown into the corner of the room. Real alarm rose in the Frenchwoman's mind when her hands were tied together behind her back.

As Zyuganov watched, Eva pulled Didier to her feet and put a strangle-knot loop of electrical cord around her neck and strained it tight, cutting off the protests that quickly morphed into short screams of panic and, with the increasing constriction, rasping gasps for air. Eva pushed Didier back against the bedroom door, grabbed her around the hips with one arm, and lifted her two inches off the floor. With her free hand, Eva flipped the loose end of the electrical cord over the top of the door and wound it around the doorknob on the other side. Eva then let Didier go. The cord stretched, the hinges crackled with the extra weight, and the knob creaked in protest, but Madeleine Didier's toes were now an inch off the floor, and her heels started beating against the door, her bound hands scrabbled at the wood, and the cord bit into her neck, forcing her head to a lopsided angle as saliva dribbled out one side of her open mouth. Eva stood close to her and watched her through her wire-rimmed glasses as the shuddering in the feet and shoulders started, and Madeleine's eyes stopped blinking and went wide in the amazed horror that this was happening to her, the head of the French service in Moscow, in a civilized world, with her husband waiting for her at home and her expensive still-warm shoes tossed in the corner of the room.

It had been four minutes since Zyuganov and Eva entered the apartment.

Eventually the involuntary tremors stopped and Madeleine was still. Eva tilted her head to look at the blackened, slack face, then turned to Zyuganov, who was collecting Didier's notebook and phone. He emptied the contents of her purse on the floor so the police would find her identification, and, looking at the dead Russian man again, he signaled Eva to follow him. Didier's body swung as they opened the door, which slowly drifted back from the weight on the hinges, and a lock of hair fell across her face. They stepped over Monsieur Broken Neck in the front room, and Zyuganov, avoiding the blood pool in the kitchen, lifted the lid of a warm pot on the stove. It was Russian red lentil soup, his favorite, and he took the pot and two spoons to the couch, where they took turns taking sips. *It's good, but not enough cumin.* Eva, his genetically contorted engine of vengeance, spoon poised above the pot, deferentially waited for Zyuganov to take a spoonful before she dipped in.

"Go on," he said, paternally. "Eat your soup."

Zyuganov reviewed Egorova's first report from Athens. She was methodically interviewing officers from every department of the Russian Embassy, and sending her anodyne reports through encrypted channels from the *rezidentura. She could flail around in Greece for as long as she wants,* thought Zyuganov, *while I narrow down the suspects here in Moscow and bag the GRU traitor who's talking to the Americans.*

Things were going well with the Persians too: Zyuganov had gotten energy sector big shots like Govormarenko together several times with dreary Iranian nuclear representatives from AEOI, and details about the purchase, transport, and delivery of the seismic floor were being hammered out. Zyuganov was sure this progress was being reported to Putin, to his credit. At one Moscow meeting he had taken the Iranian secret-service rep, Naghdi, aside and outlined his concept of transporting the cargo via an internal water route through Russia and the Caspian to ensure secrecy. He presented the plan as chiefly his own, saying only that other officers had "discussed its feasibility." The Persian scowled at him, but looked impressed nevertheless. Zyuganov daydreamed about letting Eva give the bearded Persian a deep-tissue massage with a carpenter's adze.

Eva. And Egorova. That would be quite a dance. Zyuganov rolled the idea around in his head of sending Eva to Athens to arrange an accident. He knew he couldn't whack Egorova outright: Putin liked her and had his eye on her. But Eva could push Egorova into traffic, or throw her down the stairs, or snap her neck in a slippery bathtub. It could also be a nice touch if Egorova disappeared completely. His Line KR would be the very section to investigate the possibilities: kidnapping, accidental drowning, defection. He could keep the ball rolling for years.

A wet job on Egorova was still risky in the extreme, especially with Putin's patronage of her growing. He would, of course, not discuss this with his hairy deputy, Pletnev, who increasingly seemed to be attracted to Egorova—at least he salivated more around her than he did with the other women in the section. *No, not with Yevgeny,* thought Zyuganov. He pressed a button on his phone.

Eva came in two minutes. She wore her usual gray reform-school dress, opaque nylons, and clunky black tie shoes with a thick heel. Her blond hair lay close on her skull. She walked splayfooted and leaned forward a fraction, as if she would break into a run in the next few steps. She entered Zyuganov's office and stood with her heels together, as usual looking at him just as a performing seal looks for the smelt in its trainer's hand.

Zyuganov leaned back in his chair. "Eva, sit down," he said sternly. She eased into the chair beside the desk, but sat upright, yellowed hands in her lap.

"I have been pleased with your work, Eva, very pleased," said Zyuganov. Eva nodded her head but said nothing, her eyes not visible behind the glint in her glasses.

"Have you ever traveled outside Russia, Eva?" Zyuganov asked. She shook her head no. *Bozhe,* God, it was like talking to a primate through a symbols keyboard.

"There may be need for you to travel to a nearby country in the future. Nothing for sure yet, but I wanted to speak to you about it."

Eva bobbed her head again. "I can be ready to travel when you need me," she said. "Where do you want me to go?"

"Nothing for sure yet," repeated Zyuganov, being careful. "You don't have family to take care of?" he said, imagining dinnertime at the Buchin household.

Eva shook her head.

"A man in your life? A boyfriend?" said Zyuganov. He might as well find out a little about her quadruped habits.

"I knew a man once," she said vaguely. It was unclear whether she had been acquainted with a man, or had been intimate with him, or had simply eaten one. She shifted slightly in her chair, perhaps moved by the memory.

"Well, there's plenty of time to meet new friends," said Zyuganov, wondering for an instant what he would do with Eva when he became deputy director of the Service.

"Thank you, Eva," said Zyuganov. "I'll let you know."

Eva stood and smoothed her dress in an approximately feminine way. "I'm ready to travel when you want," she said again, leaving his office.

If he fired that prehistoric cannonball downrange to destroy Egorova, Zyuganov's only regret would be not being present to see her die. He made a mental note to explore ways to film the assassination with a stationary video camera. Oh, and he'd want audio with the images too.

RUSSIAN RED LENTIL SOUP

Sauté chopped onions, minced garlic, and diced apricots till soft. Add red lentils, cumin, oregano, diced tomatoes, honey, salt, and pepper, and cover with chicken stock. Bring to a boil, simmer, and then process to desired consistency. Serve warm or at room temperature, with mint and sour cream.

27

For the second meeting at safe house TULIP, Nate picked Dominika up at dusk at a CPU—car pickup—site in Ambelokipi after his own hour-long SDR. He checked his watch to make sure he hit the four-minute window, then sighted down Fokios—no trailing coverage on the narrow street—as he slowed to make the turn onto Levadias. A parked car at the intersection had its front wheels turned out, a tell of staked-out surveillance, but an old lady was loading boxes into the trunk, and Nate saw no reaction as he passed. As he slowed to turn into the *Y*-shaped intersection with Levadias, Dominika stepped out from under a green canopy in front of a neighborhood pharmacy and, ballerina smooth and strong, slid into the passenger seat of the still rolling car, swinging the door shut as Nate moved away. She bent forward, reached under her seat, and came up wearing a long blond wig and a huge pair of tinted glasses. The elegant Slavic beauty with pinned-up hair had changed in four seconds to a bottle blonde with questionable fashion sense, perhaps on her way to dinner with a paramour. Nate looked over at her as she pulled the seat belt across herself.

"I never thought of you as a blonde," he said. "You look pretty sexy." He had been about to teasingly say "slutty" but thankfully his brain worked faster than his mouth this time. Gable's words from the night before hung in the hot air of the dusty little car.

Dominika smoothed the wig a little and laughed, glancing at him, checking. Steady purple. "Thank you, Neyt. Perhaps I will dye my hair blond. No one in my embassy would recognize me."

"They won't wonder where you are every evening?" said Nate.

"No. I will attend a party at the *rezident's* house in a few days, and an evening concert at the embassy next week. It will be enough. Besides, no one is going to ask Captain Egorova of Line KR what she is doing in Athens."

"Well, I'm glad Captain Egorova of Line KR is spending this evening with us," said Nate. "Everyone will be at the apartment tonight. Benford spent all day with Forsyth and Gable. He's hatching something."

"You were not there?" said Dominika.

She was lightly kidding, but it required an evasive response. Nate had been trying to meet LYRIC, to get him ready to defect, but the general had been a no-show. Mule-headed old soldier. But he couldn't tell Dominika about him.

"I had to help out in the political section all day. We have to play nice with our embassy colleagues." Nate dully registered the interchangeability of the concept of "cover story" and "lie."

"Do you think it will be a late night?" said Dominika.

"Probably. I brought stuff in for dinner." There were food packages on the backseat. "Why? Do you have to get back early?"

"No," said Dominika. "I was just curious."

Nate turned onto six-lane Alexandros Boulevard to begin a stair-step route around the back of Likavitos Hill and through Neapoli to park somewhere quiet and walk in the rest of the way.

"I was wondering," said Dominika, glancing over at him, "when we could expect to be alone." They were in the middle of a block of stopped traffic four lanes wide and ten cars deep, waiting for the light to change. Motorbikes wobble-walked between the rows of cars to gather at the front, under the light, like settlers lining up for a land rush. Nate checked his mirrors instinctively, then leaned over and put his face close to hers.

"Alone? What did you have in mind?" Nate said. Dominika brushed a bit of blond wig from her eyes and ran her fingers along the side of his face. Nate leaned closer, their lips nearly touching. Dominika closed her eyes.

"Additional SRAC training," said Dominika. "That means short-range agent communication, no?"

"How short-range?" said Nate, brushing his lips across hers.

"Certainly not *too* short," said Dominika, hooking his head and bringing their mouths together.

The light changed and the night erupted into an Athenian hysteria of forty cars honking, each one at the *malaka,* the silly jerk-off in the car ahead, to get moving.

Chief of Athens Station Forsyth opened the safe-house door and pulled Dominika inside by the wrist. They exchanged the requisite three Russian kisses on alternating cheeks, then Forsyth put his arm around Dominika's shoulders and led her into the living room, leaving Nate to juggle an armload of food parcels, shut the front door, and throw the locks. The rest of them were in the living room, standing around the drinks tray. Her team. Her family. Nate came in from the kitchen. And her lover. She could still taste him on her lips, still feel the tingle.

Something was up, something had happened. As Dominika smiled, shook hands, and accepted a drink, that ensorcelled mind of hers took in the scene. Aurae filled the room. The CIA case officers' shoulders were stiff. They were quiet and smooth, but too quiet; she could hardly tell something was wrong, that's how good they all were. Forsyth, in a light-gray suit with a navy tie, bathed in his artistic blue haze, ran his fingers through his salt-and-pepper hair; *Bratok*, dear brother Gable of the passionate purple halo, his shirtsleeves rolled up his thick forearms, was looking at her the way her ballet coach used to; Benford, tie askew, with flyaway hair and a wrinkled dark suit, was miles away, ablaze in the deep-blue atelier of the master watchmaker, tweezing clockwork gears, pins, and wheels in place, just so; and Nate, in a blazer and open shirt, trim and spare of movement, the man she loved, was mixing a drink, also purple, steady and bright—his passions included her. He looked up and his smile was relaxed.

Dominika was dressed in a simple navy cotton dress and black leather flats. Her hair was up and she wore only a light lip gloss. Usually she didn't wear jewelry, but tonight she had put on a single strand of pearls. She sat at one end of the couch, crossed her legs, dangled a shoe, and started bouncing her foot. The CIA men sipped their drinks.

"I will make a dash for the terrace and escape through the pine trees if you do not tell me what is going on," said Dominika, looking across at Benford, then at the rest of them, one by one. Gable was sitting closest to her on the L-shaped couch.

"Atta girl," he said, turning to Forsyth. "I told you. The first five minutes."

"Dominika, I want to applaud the remarkable work you have done since you returned to Moscow," said Benford, leaning forward in his armchair. "We have all of us been discussing the confluence of intelligence you have generated. It is a perfect storm of precious counterintelligence leads, a positive intelligence windfall, and a precarious but potentially epic covert-action opportunity. All thanks to you."

Gable leaned over and squeezed her arm in congratulation. "You keep listening to me, and you'll be a star," he said. Dominika looked at him deadpan and shook her head sadly, as if there were no hope for him.

"All this operational movement unavoidably multiplies the risk to you, Domi," said Forsyth. "We have to balance your continued safety against exploiting these openings. We want to propose something that will boost your standing and improve your security posture."

"Forsyth," said Dominika, though it came out closer to "*Fyoresite.*" Using his last name was the closest Dominika could get to the affectionate Russian use of the patronymic. "You all know that I will weigh risks and play the system, the system I know best. But I will not stop."

"With a resentful and barbarous superior like Alexei Zyuganov, you have a formidable enemy," said Benford. "We want to fortify you against him. You're too valuable to us."

"And there's an opportunity just now, but it's a little tricky," said Forsyth.

"She can do it," said Gable. Nate shifted in his seat, not knowing what was coming. Dominika tried to sit still, but her foot still bounced.

"What?" she said. "Tell me."

"Do you know Lieutenant General Mikhail Nikolaevich Solovyov, of the GRU?" asked Benford. Dominika felt all their eyes on her. Nate, in a flash, knew what Benford was thinking. He otherwise would never, ever, have revealed one agent's identity to another.

"He's in the military attaché's office at the embassy," said Dominika. "A one-star senior man in a junior position, kicked out of Moscow. I've interviewed him, he's old-school army, bitter, hates Putin, a real dinosaur—" Dominika stopped and looked at the CIA men. Utter silence in the room. "Solovyov is LYRIC?" she whispered.

"Atta girl," said Gable, getting up to unwrap the food.

They passed around plates of eggplant salad, feta cheese, grilled sausages, boiled zucchini in vinegar, flaky spinach pie, Greek beans, and toothpick meatballs. Dominika drank ouzo with ice and water along with Gable, while the others drank a dry white Moscofilero. Benford had flakes of phyllo crust on his tie.

"Thanks to you we know that LYRIC was fingered by TRITON, an incomplete identification," said Benford. "TRITON's last report to Zarubina reveals for the first time that LYRIC is reporting *from Athens,* not from Moscow, and we can anticipate that Zyuganov will move quickly. Ironically,

Dominika, he sent you here to get you out of the way, but Zyuganov inadvertently put you right on top of the target." Dominika put down her plate and stared at Benford. Forsyth was observing her intently.

"So it appears we will lose LYRIC as an active source sooner rather than later," said Benford. "You're on a counterintelligence inspection for Line KR. If, based on your interview of General Solovyov, you send a cable to the Center reporting his inconsistent behavior, evasiveness, and resentful attitude, and recommend Solovyov's recall to Moscow for interrogation based on suspicion of espionage, you will have uncovered yet another CIA mole."

Silence in the room that Nate estimated lasted twenty endless seconds.

"I won't do it," said Dominika quietly. "I will never again be responsible for the death of a decent man fighting alone against the *chudovishcha,* the monsters in my country. I won't."

"Calm yourself," said Benford. "The day the recall cable arrives from GRU Headquarters in Moscow, LYRIC will disappear, defected to the West, incidentally validating your CI recommendation to investigate him."

"LYRIC is retired in safety and Domi, you've got another feather in your cap," said Forsyth. "Zyuganov won't be able to mess with you."

"You will smuggle Solovyov out of Greece and to the United States?" said Dominika, looking at their faces.

Forsyth nodded.

"I have to be sure," she said, clenching her jaw.

"He will never again set foot in the Aquarium. He will be gone," said Benford. "Nathaniel has made the preparations."

"Don't spook her, for Chrissake," said Gable.

The moon over Hymettus was blood orange from the pall of urban exhaust over the city, even after midnight. Everyone had left the safe house except Dominika and Nate, who would leave together last and drive out. The others had staggered their departures, vectoring away in different directions to avoid contaminating TULIP in the unlikely event they were spotted by hostile surveillance—Russian security, Greek cops, Hezbollah scouts trolling for trouble. Athens was a dangerous, mixed-up city: part Balkan, part Mediterranean, part Beirut.

Nate darkened the living room, then opened the curtains to the terrace, and they stood outside, close together in the Athens night, smelling the black pines on the hill behind them. Dominika's head was bent in troubled thought, the clasp of her pearls visible on the back of her graceful neck. Nate knew she was struggling with the prospect of throwing the noose around LYRIC's neck. She didn't know General Solovyov at all, but she recoiled from the Judas touch. Nate knew she trusted them to exfil him in time, but she was still nervous about turning him in. Nate stepped closer behind Dominika and snaked his arms around her waist. She covered his hands with her own but didn't move.

"I know you're worried," said Nate quietly. "But he'll be out of the country two hours after we initiate the escape plan." Dominika patted his hands as if to reassure a child, then turned to face him.

"Do Boga vysoko, do Tsarya daleko, God is high up, and the tsar is far away," she whispered. Anything can happen, and there's no remedy.

"Of course the tsar is far away," said Nate. "Is there a situation Russians don't have a proverb for?" He pulled her closer, crushing her body against his. She smiled, relaxing a little, and put her arms around his neck, but really there was no remedy for the accumulated ice in the soul, the fatigue that only the best agents can live with year after year. She looked into Nate's eyes and saw the swirl of purple behind his head that never changed. She knew he was concerned about her. And he could read her moods as well as she could read his colors.

She wanted him, she needed him, and they had all night in an anonymous apartment, insulated from danger. She walked with him into the penthouse and sat on the couch, which held the lingering scent of Gable. Goddamn Gable. His odorant molecules swirled around them, and even as they kissed, Gable wouldn't leave them alone.

"I don't care," said Dominika, intuition telling her Nate was struggling. "Whatever happens, we have each other. Nothing else is important. Not what I do, not what you do. Not what we will do." They each had their own blinky thoughts: Yevgeny-Hannah, Hannah-Yevgeny.

Udranka and Marta, sitting in two chairs, applauded. Go away you sluts, Dominika told them. But her Rusalki mermaids lingered, watching and smoking.

They sat close, seeing each other for the first time. It was always like that with them, a heady discovery, more the start of something primal than the resumption of it. Dominika drank him in: She registered that her loose-limbed boy had changed in the last two years. He was thicker in the shoulders, wiser in the eyes. His purple aura still blazed steadily; it never changed. She took his hands and kissed the tops of them. These hands had changed too—they were less delicate, somehow rougher. She kissed his palms and leaned in to mash her mouth on his, breathing through her nose when he put his hands on her breasts. She pulled away when he started fiddling with the zipper on her dress and stood up in front of him. "*Terpeniye yest' dobrodetel'*, patience is a virtue," she whispered.

Dominika unzipped her dress and let it fall off her body. In the glancing moonlight, Nate noticed the curves and contours of her thin body as if he had never seen her before, the swell of her breasts in her brassiere, the slow expansion of her rib cage as she breathed, the silver-shiny diagonal scar on her thigh from a battle long ago. Her face was sharper, more elegant than ever, with a hint of stress around the eyes and at the corners of her mouth. She looked at him appraising her and held his eyes as she knelt between his legs, running her hands along his thighs and pushing him back as he made to sit up.

"You do not have permission to move," said Dominika, her eyes never leaving his face, even as she snaked the belt from around his hips and tugged down first his zipper and then his khaki pants and showed him, slowly, a little of *No. 17, "Stamens and pistils,"* blue eyes locked on his, one strand of hair in front of her face.

She was a glutton for the smell and taste of him, and with one hand she lifted his shirt and raked her nails along the two similar, tallow-wax shiny scars that crisscrossed his stomach from that same once-upon-a-time battle. What she was doing to him was in fact warping her own mind—never mind that Nate was flexed with head back and eyes closed—and Dominika trailed her free hand unseen between her own legs. She flashed to *No. 51, "Battre les blancs en neige, beat egg whites until stiff,"* and soon her eyes fluttered and closed and she groaned and stopped moving, her face partially covered by more of her hair that had fallen into her eyes.

When she got her brain back she blinked at him, wiped her upper lip, and giggled. "Am I *nekulturny,* not waiting for you?" said Dominika.

"Worse than uncultured," said Nate. "I give up trying to keep up with you. No man could hope to." Dominika started touching him again, her hands together as if holding an ax handle, insidious, persistent.

"Do not try to keep up," she said conversationally. "That is my advice to you." She kept moving and his legs started trembling. Nate felt those familiar leather straps tightening inside him. Dominika was staring at him, watching the havoc she was creating, as if she were a bystander. The now-vibrating straps in Nate's groin were getting tighter. "*Dushka*," whispered Dominika, coaxing him. "*Dushka, dushka, dushka*." Then the couch started spinning, and the walls collapsed, and the picture windows exploded, and the roof caved in. Dominika blinked at him, watching him regain consciousness.

"*Les rubyat, schepki letyat*," she whispered, *when you chop wood, woodchips will fly.*

Groaning, Nate sat up and they kissed. He brushed a strand of hair out of the corner of her mouth, and she wiped her face with her hand. The old line came to mind. "Why didn't you tell me I was in love with you?" said Nate. Dominika started laughing.

Udranka and Marta, sitting across from them, looked at each other and rolled their eyes.

Wearing his shirt, Dominika boosted herself onto the kitchen counter and watched as Nate, radiating purple and wearing only his boxer shorts, sliced an onion and garlic and sautéed them in fragrant green olive oil. He sliced roasted peppers into thin strips and added them to the pan. He opened a can of peeled tomatoes and squeezed them beneath the surface of their juice to avoid squirts. The hand-smashed tomatoes went into the pan—with a pinch of sugar—to start bubbling with the rest. Nate held a bushy branch of dried oregano over the pot and gently crushed some leaves into the stew. He reached for a square tin of paprika.

"Paprika," said Nate, holding up the tin. "Have you ever tasted it?"

"What a strange word, 'paprika,'" said Dominika, deadpan. "No, we did not have such things in my village, living alongside our pigs in the living room." Nate smiled and added a dash. "Another strange word is '*tupitsa*,'" said Dominika. "Do you know it?" Nate knew it meant "dunce"; he shook his head that he didn't understand, but Dominika knew he did.

The pan was simmering, and Nate turned on the little oven and put slices of country bread on the upper rack. When they were golden he rubbed each slice with a clove of garlic.

"All this garlic probably reminds you of the village," said Nate, not looking at her. Dominika tried not to smile.

Nate made three indentations in the simmering stew and cracked three eggs into the spaces. He slid the pan into the still-hot oven until the eggs were set, then carried the pan out to the terrace. Dominika followed with the toasted bread and two bottles of cold beer. They sat on the terrace floor—the marble was still slightly warm from the afternoon sun—the steaming pan on a low table between them, and dipped the toasted garlic bread and ate forkfuls of peppers, tomatoes, and runny egg yolk. At the first taste, Dominika looked up at Nate, a question on her face.

"Pipérade," said Nate, "from the Basque part of France."

"And where did you learn this?"

"College summer in Europe," said Nate. He dipped more bread.

"Very romantic," said Dominika.

"Yes. Yes, I am," said Nate.

"You are your biggest devotee," said Dominika, leaning over toward him. She kissed him lightly on the mouth. "May I ask about the officer Benford wants to send to meet me? Do you know her?"

Nate nodded, determined not to feel, act, or look guilty.

"She's young, but one of the best street operators I've ever seen. Benford thinks so too."

Dominika noticed his purple halo was pulsing.

"I observed most of her training. She's unbelievable," said Nate. More purple pulsing. He was conscious only of delivering his good-natured endorsement of Hannah Archer.

"Did you tell her about me?" said Dominika idly, dipping a piece of bread. Nate recognized that when a woman casually asks a man whether he has described her to another woman, there is considerable, imminent danger: the first puffs of oven-hot wind before the squall descends; the twenty pricked-up ears of the lion pride pointed at the stalled Land Rover; the rustle of monkey's wings in the trees on the road to Oz. Considerable danger.

"She has read your file," said Nate noncommittally. "She knows about the work you do. She admires you." Knowing this woman had read her file and "admired her" nettled Dominika. *Control yourself,* she thought. *You're not a jealous schoolgirl.* But Nate's halo was still pulsing.

"What is her name?" said Dominika, picking up empty bottles and leftover bread. Nate carried the pan of *pipérade* into the kitchen.

"Hannah," said Nate, hearing the shadow in Dominika's voice.

"Khanna," said Dominika, with a guttural *h.* "It is a good name, an ancient one. We know it in Russia." She was standing at the sink, running water and making a mound of suds. She scraped the pan, immersed it in the sink, and began scrubbing, head down, shoulders hunched. Nate stood behind her and put his arms around her waist.

"Domi, she's your contact on the street," he whispered. "She put down all your SRAC sensors. She's twenty-seven years old. She's an officer of our agency."

"Do you like her, as a person?" Dominika asked, changing the subject.

"Yeah, she's great. More important, you'll like her," said Nate. He felt Dominika's shoulders come down an inch, relaxing. *Jesus,* he thought. *She's so damn perceptive, though, like a mind reader.*

"Besides, you should be worrying about washing this pan," he said. "You're splashing water everywhere." Dominika turned and splashed a handful of water on Nate's chest. He reached around her, dipped his hands in the suds, and wet her shirt. They splashed some more water until her front was a clinging, transparent mess, her breasts visible through the sopping fabric. His boxers were in no better condition.

She turned her back to him, reached into the sink, and started scrubbing again. "I'm not finished with this pan," she said.

"Keep scrubbing," said Nate, lifting her shirttail and rhumba-stepping out of his shorts. Nate's initial movement from behind pushed Dominika forward and she had to catch herself, arms in suds up to the elbows. Subsequent movements caused a slopping wave action, which apart from creating a syncopation of slapping sounds, resulted in an ample amount of water splashing on their legs and feet.

Sometime later, they looked like the last guests at Caligula's house party, sitting on the kitchen floor in a pool of water, backs against the cabinets, waiting for their hearts to slow down. Nate's shirt was a sodden knot in the center of the floor and his shorts were under the small table across the kitchen. An occasional errant drop of water from the counter around the sink would drip onto one of their shoulders. Dominika's chest was white with dried dish-soap bubbles, and a tendril of her hair hung in her face.

"Thanks for helping with the dishes," said Nate.

Nate drove Dominika home through empty, predawn Athens, ghosting through intersections colored by flashing traffic signals. The car hissed through water on the streets from the crews who hosed down the sidewalks at night. Nate would drop her off a few blocks from her hotel and she would walk in.

"You'll send your report to the Center soon?" said Nate. His voice sounded funny to his ears, as if another person were speaking. He was tired.

"I'll recommend General Solovyov be summoned to Moscow for investigation," said Dominika. "That's how it's done. They will write that they want him at the Aquarium for something nonalerting—consultations, promotion panel, to sit on an advisory board."

"How fast will it come after you send your recommendation?" said Nate.

"Very fast," said Dominika. "You must be sure to get him out of Greece immediately. Zyuganov will want to reel him in right away, to embarrass GRU and to earn credit with the Kremlin. I will report to Hannah through SRAC on what the reaction is to his defection." She smiled. "And how many medals they will give me." The casual mention of Hannah, suddenly now a fixture in their professional lives, jangled in the air. Nate was sure Dominika mentioned her on purpose. "I'm looking forward to meeting her," said Dominika.

Nate wanted her to focus. "Zyuganov will be furious with you for having identified the traitor ahead of him," he said.

Dominika shrugged. "What can he do?"

"You forget the last time Zyuganov was upset with you," said Nate. "I was there. I seem to remember a Spetsnaz killer, a nasty-looking knife, and a lot of bandages."

"It is different now," said Dominika. "Zyuganov could not risk such games." She put her hand on Nate's arm. "Just be sure to get the general out. Do not fail me."

Dominika's flash precedence message from the Athens *rezidentura* requesting the immediate recall to Moscow of GRU Lieutenant General Mikhail Nikolaevich Solovyov on suspicion of espionage hit the Center like a bomb. Those few senior officers on the restricted list who days before had read the latest TRITON report knew Captain Egorova—who was not cleared and who *had not* read TRITON's reporting—was absolutely correct and consequently had scored a tremendous counterintelligence coup. The added benefit was that Solovyov had been unmasked as a result of a straight CI investigation, which automatically protected TRITON as the source.

This brilliant officer was a hero, and nothing less, they all said. The director, ministers, and President Putin himself all wanted to see her when she returned, and rumors of promotion to the rank of major began circulating. Egorova would stay in Athens for a few days to wrap up her interviews, but really to keep an eye on Solovyov and create the illusion of a routine investigation winding down, so he would respond to the recall without suspicion. Once the general was behind bars in Moscow, official praise could be heaped on Egorova.

Zyuganov had trouble focusing on a printed copy of Egorova's cable because the paper shook in his hand. His professional standing had been expanding, his position with the Kremlin was becoming stronger each day, especially in the matter of the Iranian shipment. And Putin had telephoned him personally on the encrypted *Kremlovka* line after the action against the French: He had seen police forensic photographs of Mme Didier, the Russian traitor, and the two DGSE security men in the ruined apartment. A hysterical Élysée had lodged a howling protest, and the DGSE had withdrawn its officers from Moscow. A phlegmatic Putin breathed one word over the phone, *Maladyets,* well done. Zyuganov swelled up like a toad with pride.

But the glow of these recent successes was now eclipsed by Egorova's triumph in Greece, a triumph that specifically reduced his stature. No one in Headquarters was talking about anything but that pneumatic prostitute. In the privacy of his office, Zyuganov had gone into a paroxysm of silent rage, convinced that Egorova was working to ridicule, denigrate, and mock him. She had her eye on his present job, he was convinced, and she would see to it that his chance at becoming deputy director was derailed. Zyuganov's bat-cave soul swelled with thoughts of murder.

He stewed at his desk, working things out. An accident, even one properly staged, would now be too coincidental. The notion of Egorova defecting to a Western service a day after exposing another traitor would be ridiculous. If Egorova simply disappeared, failed to return to Moscow, the theories, rumors, and suppositions would multiply by the dozen. Then an idea came to him, a crawly idea from under a damp log, with the promise of chaos, deceit, and misdirection to insulate him from detection and Putin's ire. He pushed the button on his phone.

Eva sat down in front of him as she had done before. Zyuganov slid a file across the desk, Egorova's personnel file. Photo, service record, training in *Sistema* hand-to-hand fighting, Sparrow School. Eva breathed the pages, nostrils flaring, memorizing the spoor. She finished reading, closed the file, and gave it back. She didn't need notes; she wouldn't forget. Zyuganov pushed another smaller photo, passport sized, to Eva. It was a visa photo of Madeleine Didier. Zyuganov leaned forward, held Eva's eyes, and whispered.

"Strangle her and leave this under her body," said Zyuganov, pointing at the snap. "No gun, no knife; use electrical cord. And take her clothes."

A hot *jeton* of comprehension in Eva's brain fell into the slot and she made the connection: Egorova's death would look like a reciprocal action by the French service to avenge Didier. She looked at Zyuganov for confirmation that she had it right.

He nodded.

It was intensely interesting to Zyuganov, one sort of monster, to see Eva, a derivative miscreation, put her head back and laugh, with the sound of a bag of cleavers bouncing down a flight of stairs. *Voskhititel'nyy,* delicious.

PIPÉRADE—BASQUE PEPPER STEW

Sauté sliced onions and garlic in oil until soft. Add thin strips of roasted red peppers and crushed peeled tomatoes, season with salt, pepper, oregano, and paprika, and simmer until incorporated. Break eggs onto the top of the sauce and finish in the oven until the eggs are set but the yolks are still runny. Serve with grilled country bread or as a side dish.

28

Benford had traveled incognito to Berlin to approach the SBE, the *Spezialle Bundestatigkeiten-Einheit*, the Federal Special Activities Unit, a discreet civilian intelligence outfit of twelve officers that reported directly to the office of the president. No one outside the German president's office was aware of the SBE, which was charged with managing operations that were either so sensitive or so politically risky that it was preferable the larger federal intel services like the BND or BfV not be involved.

Smelling baked bread as he walked through the pleasant Mitte neighborhood to Robert Koch Platz, Benford entered the unguarded front door of the *Bibliothek der Akademie der Künste*, the Library of the Academy of Arts, and rode the shuddering elevator to the disused fourth floor, where the offices of the SBE were concealed behind a plain door enigmatically labeled "*Werkzeug*," Utility. He was greeted by Herr Dieter Jung, the chief of the SBE, a man of average height and thinning hair, with a large nose and round glasses, who was skeptical, perceptive, and droll beyond his fifty years. It was also clear to Benford that Herr Jung was a consummate politician. Perfunctory introductions to a handful of SBE officers were made—two were attractive women in their thirties—and Benford was given coffee and cake.

Without preamble, Benford outlined the requirement and asked Herr Jung for assistance in aiding a technical team to gain unescorted access to the Wilhelm Petrs factory on Puschkinallee in Alt-Treptow, southwest of the river. He omitted most of the technical details, but he did tell Jung that this operation had the potential to set the Iranian nuclear program back five years. Benford airily said he needed a discreet escort for the team to and from the facility.

"I'm sure you do," sniffed Jung in fluent English, lighting a cigarette and then delicately picking a speck of tobacco off the tip of his tongue. "But it's out of the question."

Benford pressed, invoking Euro-Atlantic amity and the NATO alliance. Herr Jung was a picture of Olympian detachment, sitting with his arms crossed over his chest. Benford plunged on, now bringing in the Berlin airlift, John F. Kennedy, Marlene Dietrich, and David Hasselhoff. Stony silence, but slight wavering. Benford made to get up from his chair but paused, and then quietly suggested that he could share reporting on Russian intelligence activity in Germany.

"That information would be of mild interest," said Jung distractedly as he looked out a window.

Benford knew that despite SBE's protected status, Jung always needed operational successes to justify budgets, maintain presidential favor, and improve his prospects of promotion out of this library attic and into a Minister's office. He leaned forward and summarized a specific report detailing the recent SVR recruitment of a male Bundestag member from the Green Party, a recruitment based chiefly on the parliamentarian's weekend predilection for steam baths and birch branches.

"An interesting lead," said Jung, twirling a pencil, "if true." But Benford knew he was hooked.

The two attractive female SBE operatives were assigned as liaison officers for the team, which consisted of the whip-thin tech Hearsey and the two PROD engineers Bromley and Westfall. Marty Gable was included, primarily to manage operational equities, which essentially meant he would handle the two SBE officers, Ulrike Metzger and Senta Goldschmidt, to ensure no flaps occurred.

In the very early hours of a chilly fall morning, the SBE officers drove the CIA team to the closed rear gate of the Petrs factory and watched as Hearsey leaned over the lock in the sally door and fiddled for two minutes before straightening up and easing it open. A wave, and the German officers were gone—they would wait around the corner in the van until the team signaled for a pickup.

Hearsey opened the inner employee door to the main factory building in ninety seconds, and the four proceeded silently through an entrance hall. Bromley and Westfall wore backpacks and each dragged a large, wheeled, black canvas duffel bag.

"No cameras?" asked Gable.

Hearsey shook his head. "German employees' union won a national lawsuit to have security cameras taken out of all canteens and break rooms. EU privacy laws. Not bad."

"Guards, alarms?" whispered Gable.

"Door alarm on the main office door only. Not even a watchman. Not so many secrets to a seismic isolation floor," said Hearsey.

They walked down a corridor past a cold café that still smelled of coffee and rolls, and stopped before turning the corner of the hallway.

"They leave the factory floor unguarded?" asked Gable.

"Not quite," said Hearsey. "Final hurdle."

Hearsey put his mouth next to Gable's ear. "Last stretch of corridor before the factory floor," he whispered. "Motion-detection sensor at the end."

Gable watched as Bromley and Westfall took a series of telescoping plastic tubes out of their packs and quickly fit them together in a frame six feet square, over which they stretched an opaque gauzy fabric that they clipped at intervals around the frame.

"Stay close together," whispered Hearsey, holding one side of the frame up in front of him while Westfall held the other. Bromley, grinning, stepped up to Gable, put her arm around his waist, pulled him close, and eased in tight behind the two others. They all had done this before, Gable noted. Bunched together, arms around shoulders as if in a rugby scrum, bent behind the gauzy barrier, they rounded the corner and started shuffling slowly down the corridor, medieval siege troops approaching the castle wall, air full of arrows.

"Slow," whispered Hearsey to Westfall.

"The barrier absorbs infrared, microwave, ultrasonic. No Doppler if you move slowly," whispered Bromley, squeezing Gable's ribs and smiling at him. *As close to tech foreplay as you're going to get*, thought Gable.

Then they were past the sensor and into the factory. It was a cavernous assembly hall that was dimly lighted by single orange safety bulbs in cages set high on the ceiling. A colossal bridge crane, motionless on its rails, loomed over their heads. There was no sound, no movement in the plant. The occasional headlights of a vehicle moving down Puschkinallee—not many passed at two in the morning—would wash over the floor-to-ceiling glazed windows that ran the entire length of the west side of the hall.

The bulbs created diffuse pools of light in the otherwise darkened plant. Sections of honeycomb panels rested on cradles in the center of the hall—floor assemblies being fitted and tested. Farther down along the white-painted brick walls were thick polymer blocks suspended from square aluminum frames by heavy-gauge springs—shock dampeners. At the end of the hall, on stainless-steel shelving gleaming in the orange overhead light, were scores of numbered plastic trays. In each tray lay five four-foot-long aluminum struts side by side, a small piezoelectric cell affixed to one end of each.

They walked silently in single file past the plastic trays, comparing lot numbers, verifying the project code and shipping designator labels, all provided by DIVA from Moscow. The duffel-bag wheels thumped softly in the still factory. Bromley took digital photos of the shelves with a miniature camera using an invisible infrared flash. These aluminum beams, nestled in trays in this immaculate German factory, would eventually support the eighty-thousand-square-foot floor of the cascade hall in the uranium enrichment facility buried in the Iranian desert in the shadow of the Natanz Mountains. Gable picked one of the struts out of a box.

"Don't look like much," he said.

Bromley took an identical strut out of the duffel. "Trade you. This one is the devil's matchstick—forty percent white phosphorus." They started unpacking the bags.

An hour later, Gable and Hearsey made a last quiet security check. It was otherworldly that no sound—no whir of machinery, no click of cooling metal, no ticking of clockwork—was generated in such a place. Hearsey tapped Gable's arm and moved slowly forward in the gloom, keeping an eye on the striped tape markings on the spotless floor delineating safe walking lanes through the elephant graveyard of floor components, milling machines, aluminum blanks, and component bins.

Bromley was finishing repacking her bag. "You get everything done?" asked Hearsey.

Bromley nodded. "Westfall and I decided to keep the replacement beams together rather than spread them out. Looking at all those beams convinced us to concentrate the WP. We want to create a big hot spot right away."

"Once the fire starts, what about suppression?" said Gable. "The Iranians gotta think about that."

Westfall shook his head. "White phosphorus burns underwater, and when enough of the aluminum catches, there's not enough foam in Iran to put it out."

"And the mullahs will be running around like raccoons in a room full of disco balls," said Gable. The two techs looked at each other, trying to remember whether raccoons were indigenous to Iran.

Westfall double-counted the beams they had substituted to verify that the numbers matched. Checking the photos she had taken, Bromley made sure the plastic trays were aligned with the edges of the shelves as they had been when they came in.

Hearsey checked his watch. "Ten minutes early. Let's wait by the door." The duffel wheels thrummed in the night air as they made their way back. The team sat on the floor, backs against the wall, listening for the sound of the van pulling up outside the gate.

Gable wanted a cigar, but he knew he'd have to wait. "One thing bothers me," he said to Hearsey. "Say these turkeys put the floor in, but before they get the centrifuges installed, there's a quake and the strain gauges spark and ignite our beams, and the whole thing goes off too early. We can't put a delay timer in the control panel—the Persians would find that. We can't fuck with the software—they're gonna rewrite all the code themselves. We can't control the timing, so, what, we just hope for the best in this clambake?"

"Yeah, essentially we're taking a chance. Lots of discussion about that back home," said Hearsey. "We get a big quake too early, they have a fire in an empty room. It'll slow them up, but they'll just dig a new hole for Hall D."

"It's still a good chance," said Westfall. "We tried to calibrate for that. The strain gauges won't spark with tremors, or even with minor quakes in the two-point-oh-to-three-point-oh range. We need a bigger event, with sustained S waves."

Gable put his head back and looked at the dim overhead safety lights. "Okay. And what happens if there's no quake for five years? Iran gets the bomb?"

"Unlikely in that part of the world," said Westfall. "Nationally, they average five shocks a day—little ones, all over the country. Statistically, they have a good S wave event every seventeen months. That's why they want the floor, and that's our window."

Bromley looked over at Gable, knowing what he was thinking, feeling defensive about the covert action. "It's not perfect," she said. "No one's saying it is. But we have no other way of getting something inside their program. If it works, we get a cascade crash and meltdown. Everything inside the Natanz fence line will be hot for twenty-five thousand years. It's worth the risk . . . At least, it is to me."

Gable looked at her earnest face, the light catching the braces as she spoke. Kid had guts. And was claustrophobic. And came up with a technical operation to send white phosphorus into Iran. She was all right.

They quietly left the hall five minutes later. They waited in the interior courtyard of the plant, hugging the wall in the predawn shadow of the building's overhang. Incongruously—at least, it was incongruous for the exhausted CIA technical team—a bird chirped in a tree somewhere beyond the factory walls. The sound of an engine grew louder, a vehicle stopped outside the sliding metal gate, and the pedestrian sally port opened. SBE officer Ulrike Metzger stuck her head in the door and waved them forward. She was an ash-blonde and dressed as if she had just come off her favorite corner on Oranienburger Strasse, wearing fishnet stockings, stiletto heels, and a tight leopard-print jacket beneath which could be seen a sliver of the black, lacy cups of a bustier. Gold hoop earrings caught the reflection of the streetlights above the courtyard wall. She waved again to hurry them up.

They piled into a black VW Routan idling at the curb with only its sidelights on. Bromley and Westfall climbed into the third rear seats, slinging their tool kits ahead of them. Gable and Hearsey got into the rear seats, and Ulrike slid the rear door closed, then climbed in beside Senta Goldschmidt, the driver, another blonde dressed just as outlandishly as the first. From behind, Gable could see her purple jacket in raw Thai silk worn with a popped collar over which dangled antique chandelier earrings with amethyst drops. The van was swirling with three or four competing fragrances: the women's perfumes, one sandalwood, the other roses; someone's peppermint body wash; and pine air freshener coming from a plastic dispenser stuck on the dashboard. Gable could hear Bromley—she was allergic to everything—wheezing in the rear seat. He cranked his window down an inch.

Dawn was showing in the eastern sky when the minivan dropped Hearsey and the two junior techs at their hotel, and then Ulrike and Senta told Gable they could drop him at his separate hotel, the Cosmo near Checkpoint Charlie, or he could join them for *katerfrühstück*, a hangover breakfast, at the Café Viridis in Kreuzberg, across the river. The girls had been up all night, waiting on the street for the CIA officers to finish, and they were hungry.

Gable accepted the invitation; he liked these two SBE cowgirls who were young enough to be his daughters, and he approved of their easy familiarity and narrow-eyed professionalism. They had followed directions exactly, drove their routes with precision, and watched the street like pros. Gable's practiced eye estimated they carried pistols in their oversized hooker bags. And they did not once ask why the SBE had secretly enabled the surreptitious entry at one in the morning by four Americans with tool kits into the state-of-the-art assembly plant, unescorted, for three hours.

Senta inspected Gable out of the corner of her eye as they parked and walked to the café. Gable felt her studying him. His ops instincts were humming—a case officer never turned them off—and there was no such thing as a friendly liaison service. The SBE ladies ordered coffees, cognacs, and *Obatzda*, a smoky Bavarian cheese spread spiced with paprika and cumin. They all sat on a worn leather couch in the corner of the café, Gable in the middle of a cyclone of perfume, swinging earrings, and fishnet thighs.

The two of them talked nonstop, often at the same time—no way were they eliciting. Gable assessed away and watched them eat, looking for the various tells and tics revealed when humans feed themselves. Exuberant, boisterous, confident—what else? Curious, clever, covering their full mouths to laugh. Gable tried throwing a long pass, asking a nosy question about pay scales in their service to see who would answer, who would defer to whom. Both answered at once, laughing, complaining about their low pay. *Huh. Same rank. Coequals.*

"You guys did great tonight," said Gable. "I appreciate your assistance." Ulrike smiled, pleased. He had them laughing, telling war stories.

"I love the hooker getups, too," said Gable looking at them both. "Perfect for waiting in a parked van at night."

"What hooker getups?" said Ulrike.

"I want to ask you a favor," Gable said quickly, bailing. "We need to keep track of when the seismic floor is totally packed, and when it ships. Can you cover that?"

"The *Bundeszollverwaltung* will alert us ahead of time," said Senta. Her Thai silk jacket had a plunging front, and, as far as Gable could see, she wasn't wearing anything underneath it.

"Who will alert you?" asked Gable.

"Our Federal Customs Service," said Senta.

"Learning of the date of shipment will be no problem," said Ulrike. "It will be in the newspapers and on television. Three years ago the company shipped a huge package to a laboratory in Istanbul. They used a truck with one hundred and twenty tires to move it to the port. It took them thirteen hours, they go so slowly. It will be on television for nights."

"And there will be more coverage of them loading it on a ship," said Senta.

"I'll let our guys know," said Gable. "Thanks." They sipped the last of their coffee. Gable refused another brandy. They were at a "mile marker" moment in the conversation, when the subject would change or the evening would end. *This is when the first puffs of a cold pitch would come,* thought Gable, *but it can't happen, not here, not from these gals.* As if they read his thoughts, the SBE officers stood up, smoothed their minis, and slung their saddlebag purses over their shoulders. Ulrike signaled to the sleepy barman and left euros on the bar.

Outside the sky was a shade brighter, the underside of the clouds red with a rising sun not yet above the horizon. City traffic was still light. Ulrike said she had to return the van to the motor pool before 0600—strict rules—but that Senta would get Gable a taxi and see him safely back to the Cosmos Hotel. Gable, amused, said absolutely not, it had been a long night, he wasn't going to inconvenience them further, and he certainly could get back to his hotel on his own because, after all, Berlin wasn't Beirut or Vientiane or Khartoum, no offense, so he'd say good night and thanks for covering them.

Ulrike looked at her watch and said she had to go, kissed Senta on two cheeks, shook hands with Gable, and walked away. Senta flagged a taxi, yanked open the door, and slid in across the backseat. Gable got in and pulled the door closed while Senta fired directions at the driver. She sat back and looked over at Gable to see if he was angry. She spoke quickly, apologetically.

"Martin, I know you can get back to your hotel yourself," Senta said. They had not passed around names the evening before, but the SBE could be expected to read hotel registers like any other service. Per Benford's guidance and to display goodwill to their hosts, the entire team had traveled to Berlin in true name.

"You understand, you are a professional with much experience," said Senta. "Our chief, Herr Jung, is very *stur*, very stubborn, and he gave instructions to see you safely home. Perhaps he wants you Americans to pass along praise to the president for our efficiency. Perhaps he doesn't want a CIA *Kopfgeldjäger* running around Berlin unescorted. Perhaps he just likes barking orders."

"What's a *Kopfgeldjäger*?" said Gable, looking out the window.

"A headhunter," said Senta, smiling.

Gable smiled back. He guessed she was about twenty-five, with blue eyes and an upturned nose. The blond hair fell loosely to her shoulders, framing a ready smile with even teeth. *Not a knockout like DIVA,* he thought, *but she's got confidence and smarts, and she's not afraid of an old CIA buffalo like me.*

"How about you?" said Gable, kidding around. "You ain't nervous riding around alone with a Yank headhunter?"

"*Aren't* nervous," said Senta, laughing. "No. I have a gun in my purse to protect me."

Her handshake in the lobby was correct and firm, and Senta's heels clicked as she walked away with a backward wave. *Good legs,* thought Gable. *Shaddup, you're as bad as Nash. But she has a cute stern; you're tired, get some sleep.* He had a couple of hours before the car was to take him to the embassy for a full fucking day of writing cables to Benford about last night and listening to Bromley and Westfall ordering gluten-free lunches.

Upstairs, in his room, his face in the steamy mirror of his bathroom looked tired, and he ran fingers through the buzz-cut hair that looked grayer than he remembered. A sharp *clink* sound came from the bedroom, and Gable bent his head and listened. Someone—maybe—was moving out there. Chambermaids always tap on the door. So, what? At seven thirty in the morning in a four-star hotel in Berlin? Hotel thief? Some sort of comeback from the Germans? Russians? The worst answer, had they found out about the factory entry? LYRIC? They always were brazen in Berlin, habits from the old days.

Gable straightened up, wrapped a towel around his waist, and, with a practiced eye, inventoried the bathroom for weapons in three seconds. Damn little: toothbrush handle into the hollow of the throat, hair dryer cord garrote if he could get close, astringent mouthwash into the eyes. All bullshit if the threat was real, if there was a top pro in his room. He took a big bath towel from the rack, knotted the end, and plunged the whole thing under running water. He had seen a knotted wet rope used as an arm's-length distance weapon in Manila, an ugly little fight in a back alley swept by wind gusts during a tropical deluge. His agent had told him about *Sayaw ng Kamatayan,* the martial art of the islands that used whipping weapons. Okay, the knotted end of a sopping bath towel. Gable opened the bathroom door and stepped into the bedroom, ready to start the overhand swing.

Senta Goldschmidt lay on his bed, covered by a sheet drawn up to her eyes. One eyebrow went up when she saw Gable with the dripping towel in his hand. He shook his head, tossed the wet mass into the tub, and sat on the edge of the bed. Senta lowered the sheet to her chin.

"Did I frighten you?" she said.

"What are you doing here?" said Gable softly, taking one of her fingers gently.

"If my chief knew, I would be fired before lunch," said Senta. Her blue eyes searched his.

"And so?" said Gable.

"You interest me," said Senta. "I was attracted to you—"

"I'm not exactly in your age—"

"You know a lot, you've seen a lot—"

"And you're too pretty to be with—"

"And your eyes are *empfindlich,* sensitive," said Senta.

"Listen," said Gable, "I was guarding the Fulda Gap before you were born."

Senta looked at him and wrinkled her upturned nose. "What is a Fulda Gap?" she said.

Gable squeezed her hand. "Cold War? East German border? The two valleys where the Russians would attack west when World War Three started? Any bells?"

Senta laughed and slowly pulled the sheet off her body. She was wearing only fishnet stockings and her pendulous earrings. "That's history." She pouted, moving her legs. "Is there a modern Fulda Gap?"

OBATZDA—BAVARIAN CHEESE SPREAD

Mix room temperature Camembert with cream cheese, soft butter, amber beer, finely diced onions, paprika, cumin, salt, and pepper until smooth. Serve with red onion or chives on dark bread or with pretzels.

29

Dominika had two more nights in Athens before her flight back to Moscow. Benford had returned to Washington the day before, the day Dominika filed her recommendation to the Center to recall LYRIC. Nate had met the general and once again prepped him on the exfil drill. Everything was on a hair trigger.

Safe house TULIP: There was always a sense of edgy urgency during the last meetings with a source who was going back inside. The CIA officers pushed hard for hours, knowing she could handle it—and also aware of the probability that Dominika could not travel out of Russia again anytime soon. It could be years before they saw her again.

"When you get back to the ranch," Gable said, "put the hurt on that bug-eyed riverbank freak Zyuganov. Keep him off balance. Take credit for a counterintelligence victory. You solved it."

Having understood fully one half of what Gable just said, Dominika smiled at him. Steady, rich purple swirled around his head.

"And when President Vladimir calls you to the Kremlin to pat you on the fanny, wear something nice," said Gable, winking at her. "Real high heels, so you tower over him."

Dominika rolled her eyes.

"Domi, taking credit and improving your position with Putin comes with a risk," said Forsyth. "As long as you're a favored subordinate you will have influence. But you also will be resented by others, inside the Kremlin and out. And if you slip out of favor the fall could be a long one." Forsyth's halo was bright blue; he was concerned.

"There's another risk," said Nate. "If Benford catches TRITON, the Center is going to be looking at why their case crashed. You have to distance yourself." He was thinking of Yevgeny—he was a traceable link, and if he was interrogated, he could put Dominika in real danger. Nate ignored the image in his head of a faceless Yevgeny in Dominika's arms.

Gable poured her another finger of ouzo and filled the tumbler with water. "You got two, maybe three, personnel meetings with our officer coming up," he said. "I want you to use maximum caution—you see something you don't like, get the hell out of there."

Dominika patted his hand.

"Do you want to review the Sparrow Hills meeting site?" said Nate.

Dominika shook her head. "You have told me this officer who will meet me is very good," said Dominika. "I believe you all, but I will make up my own mind when I see her on the street." She was still deciding whether to build up a serious case of grudge against this twenty-seven-year-old woman.

"Make it a quick look," said Gable. "The meet should be four minutes, max. Our gal will have the equipment package for your contingency exfil kit." Gable ran his fingers through his brush cut. "You two will have plenty of time to get acquainted later," he said.

"She'll have everything you need," said Nate. "She'll be all trained up."

"Why do you call her she, instead of Hannah?" said Dominika, impatient.

Forsyth and Gable looked casually at Nate. They were exceptional readers of human emotions and, with the instincts of twitchy dogs in earthquake country, understood the situation. Jealousy, mistrust, and competition had no place in a denied-area operation, regardless of gender, ego, or personality. Forsyth made a mental note to suggest to Benford that another Moscow case officer be assigned to meet Dominika in Moscow, even though he expected Benford would refuse. He knew Hannah Archer was Benford's young star, handpicked and performing magnificently.

Gable, more earthy and cynical, suspected the worst. He looked at Forsyth and telegraphed that he would be giving Nash a high colonic the next morning in the Station, a service euphemism for scaring him shitless. Nate, sitting at the end of the couch and no slouch himself in reading signals, knew he was seriously in the red. And he was furious—with her and with himself. Dominika stood apart and watched the aurora borealis display of their respective haloes collide and separate, thinking that Tchaikovsky would be suitable accompanying music, all cannons and cymbals.

Her CIA men were too good to air internal problems in front of her, but Dominika knew she had just put Nate into the *banya*, the steam bath, and that, judging from the look on Gable's face and his swirling purple halo, he would be waiting for Nate tomorrow with the eucalyptus switch. She didn't know why she did it, but Dominika felt unsettled, a little twitchy. *First it's your temper, now you've become a green-eyed* klikusha, *a hysterical jealous demoniac,* she thought. Idiotka, *concentrate on your work. Focus on the Gray Cardinals in the Kremlin; reserve your spite for them.* She looked furtively at Nate as the men gathered their papers and filed to the door.

Dominika kissed Forsyth on opposite cheeks three times as he left. She hugged Gable, smiling into his eyes. "Will you give me a ride to my hotel?" she said, not looking at Nate. A contrary streak was building up in her, and she reserved the right to be petty about this Hannah. So she would leave, not stay behind with Nate. She did this for Nate, letting Gable see they wouldn't be together tonight. She ached for him, ached to feel him inside her, but she gave up loving him tonight because she loved him so much. She looked back at Nate as she left.

"Do not worry," she whispered. "I am all right."

Udranka was in the corner of the room watching the entire drama. Do what you want, she said, but don't expect me to agree.

Nate never got his high colonic the next morning. At the opening of business, the ops phone behind Margie's desk rang, and when she picked it up she heard a low quavering whistle, repeated twice. Margie stuck her head around the corner of her boss's office door, then into the office next door. Forsyth and Gable together walked through the interior network of rooms to Nate's little office, nearly at the end of the row, where he was drafting a cable to Headquarters on the safe-house meeting last night. Gable looked down at Nate and briefly mimed whistling. Outside the secure room, they would not speak DIVA's cryptonym aloud, nor would they refer to her bird-call telephone signal, triggering an emergency meeting—Nate checked his watch—in one hour.

Gable and Nate arrived at the safe house separately fifteen minutes apart. There was an empty tumbler from last night on the low table in the living room with a faint trace of lipstick. Gable and Nate saw it at the same time—they were racked with concern for her. They did a quick check of the apartment, then Gable went back down to the street to set up and watch her walk in.

Nate heard the elevator clunk to a stop on the landing, the squeak of its door, then Gable's key in the lock. Dominika stormed into the safe-house living room with pogrom and pillage on her face. She was wearing a light beige sweater, pleated navy skirt, and black leather flats. Her hair was messily up and she wore no makeup, which Nate always thought suited her classic features. Not this Visigoth morning though. Nate willed himself not to stare at DIVA's nipples showing under her sweater—less sexy than threat display. Gable walked in behind her, and both CIA officers waited, cataloging ashtrays and table lamps that could turn into projectiles. Dominika stood in the middle of the room. Her voice was flat but her eyes were animal eyes, shifting from Nate to Gable and back.

"The recall cable from Moscow arrived last night," she said. "There would have been no trouble. Solovyov had a day or two to prepare for travel. But this morning the old fool comes into the office and tells me proudly that his service has offered him the directorship of a highly classified project. He is convinced that he has been vindicated and is returning to a position of influence and prestige."

"We told him a hundred times he's under suspicion," said Gable. "He said he was ready to bolt the minute we rang the bell."

"Well, *Bratok*, he seems to have forgotten your words," said Dominika. She started pacing three steps one way, three steps the other, her arms crossed in front of her. "He is a lotus-eater; he believes they want him back!"

"Did he say when he was leaving?" said Nate. "Did he mention a flight?"

Dominika looked at him sideways as she paced, clutching herself. "I sat there, listening to him—I couldn't blink—knowing he was headed straight into the cells. What could I say? 'General, you might remember the words of your CIA officer that you are under suspicion, that this recall is a ruse, and that your escape to America is arranged?' I had to sit there and nod."

"Domi, when did he say he was leaving?" repeated Nate.

"He told me the one o'clock Aeroflot was full, so he was looking at something earlier," said Dominika. Nate looked at his watch. She stopped pacing and squared off in front of Nate and Gable.

"He's gone," she said. "The GRU security officer will drive him to the airport and stay with him until he boards. So forget it. He's in the Butyrka cellars and he doesn't even know it." She walked to the couch, sat down, crossed her legs, and started bouncing her foot. Then she got up again and paced to the window, parting the curtains to look out briefly. Gable looked at Nate and gestured with his head, then went into the kitchen and started opening cupboards and clinking glasses. Nate stood in the middle of the room.

"Dominika, come over and sit down," Nate said, gesturing to the couch. She looked at him over her shoulder.

"Of course," she said. "Let's review the next name on the list you want me to eliminate."

"Domi," said Nate softly, "will you sit down or would you like me to kick your butt to the couch?"

Dominika's head snapped around and she saw dragon tails of purple behind Nate's head. She flashed to a battered Nate dragging her through the Danube swamp and across the bridge in Vienna. He'd had the same expression that time as he did now. Dominika swallowed the bile in her throat, came around the back of the couch, slumped in the single armchair, and glared at him.

"If you think you can kick—"

"Don't try me," said Nate. "Will you shut up and listen to me?" Gable came out of the kitchen with three glasses of ouzo and a store-bought food container he had found in the refrigerator. He set the tray on the table in front of the couch.

"You might want to listen to him, sweet pea," said Gable, looking at Dominika. "This is bad, really bad. LYRIC is his agent. Just like *you're* his agent."

Gable had hit her over the head with it, and Dominika was furious.

"You told me Solovyov would be taken to the United States," said Dominika. "You all told me that you had the escape plan settled with the general. Now he's on a plane to Moscow and they will be waiting for him at the airport."

"Do you think we want it this way?" said Nate.

"Whether you want it or not, once again you bastards have made me responsible for putting a good man in his grave," said Dominika. She crossed her legs as she sat and started bouncing her foot again.

"Yeah, well a lot of good men—and women—get screwed in this game," said Nate. "Maybe the point is we protect a lot of others in the balance."

"Did you know this would happen?" said Dominika. They had made love on this couch, and again standing up at the kitchen sink, and he had known all along.

"Listen, Dominika," said Nate, "this is not a plot. We didn't use you to put the general away. He was our asset."

"You wanted me to expose him, to improve my position," said Dominika. "I never should have agreed."

Nate shook his head. "You heard Benford," he said. "The general—LYRIC—was already exposed by that son-of-a-bitch mole in Washington. LYRIC knew it—I told him, and he took it calmly. He was all set to resettle in the United States. He was always headstrong, an old soldier who was grieving for his lost kids, but still a patriot at heart. He *made* himself believe his people wanted him back. He wanted to go back. Maybe a little part of him knows the truth, but the Russian officer in him wants to believe otherwise."

"Get it out of your mind that this was some slick move," said Gable. "It's TARFU. We'll be answering questions from Washington for weeks. Forsyth and me, as chief and deputy, but especially droopy over there, as LYRIC's handler. No one likes to lose an agent."

"What is this TARFU?" said Dominika. Gable sometimes spoke in tongues.

"It means Totally and Royally Fucked Up," said Gable, pouring more ouzo.

"You will be censured?" said Dominika, looking at Nate.

"They'll second-guess him for months," said Gable. "But we gotta keep doing our jobs. Just like you." Dominika slumped in her chair, arms crossed. She hadn't thought of the implications for Nate—now she felt doubly responsible.

"And that means—look at me—that means you have to keep doing *your* job," said Nate. "And you have to stay safe. And part of that means staying strong against Zyuganov. And if it means in two days you have to go down into the cellars and slap LYRIC across the face, you fucking do it."

Dominika had not thought of the very likely possibility that Zyuganov would drag her to sessions in the prison with LYRIC. One CIA mole would be interrogating another, knowing the truth, with the poisonous dwarf looking at both their faces. If her expression did not show her unease, the shiver that would run through her certainly would. The CIA men saw it instantly.

"I will not do that," she said.

"You remember what I told you both in Vienna?" said Gable. "That someday you're gonna have to make a decision that'll make you taste your stomach behind your teeth, but you got no choice, and maybe it even means hurting someone you respect and trust. Well, it happened today and it'll happen again tomorrow, and the next day." Gable looked at his watch. "It's almost one o'clock. You hungry?"

Dominika shook her head. Gable peeled the foil off the aluminum container. Three small eggplants, stuffed with tomatoes and glossy with oil, lay in a row. Gable looked at Nate. "You want one?" Nate shook his head. Gable pushed the container away. He got up and shrugged on his coat.

"Whatta we doing now?" said Gable. "You going back to your embassy?"

Dominika nodded.

"Then we see you tonight as usual?" said Gable.

Dominika nodded. "I leave tomorrow on Aeroflot," she said.

"Anything you need?" said Gable.

Dominika shook her head.

"Okay, give me ten minutes to clear the street," said Gable. "See you tonight."

"Good-bye, *Bratok*," said Dominika. They didn't hear the elevator—he had taken the stairwell. They sat across from each other, not saying anything. Nate's purple halo was incandescent; it pulsed with energy. Dominika wanted to sit down next to him and put her arms around him, but she would not: LYRIC's disastrous decision, her lingering resentment, and her imminent return to Russia had settled on her like a heavy blanket. She had heard *Bratok*, and she now knew what bile tasted like behind her teeth. Dominika checked her watch and stood.

"I'm going now," she said.

"See you tonight," said Nate. "Same car site as yesterday?"

"Same time?" said Dominika. She wondered if the evening would end with them in bed.

They both would have been immeasurably sad had they known then that they would not be able to say good-bye to each other.

IMAM BAYILDI—STUFFED EGGPLANT

Slit small eggplants to make a pocket, then bake until soft. Sauté thinly sliced onions, garlic, and thin wedges of tomatoes, salt, sugar, dill, and parsley. Stuff the pockets of the eggplants with filling and drizzle with olive oil. Add water, sugar, and lemon juice to the bottom of a pan, cover, and cook over low heat, basting occasionally until the eggplants are nearly collapsed and the juice in the pan is thickened. Cool and serve at room temperature.

30

Dominika returned briefly to the embassy to see if she could pick up anything else on LYRIC, but there was nothing new: The old fool had departed on an early-morning flight. He expected to be met at Domodedovo airport by a young protocol officer and driven to GRU Headquarters in a black Mercedes. Instead, the attentive officer would escort him to the hospitality lounge off the main terminal, where five men in suits would seize his wrists and his ankles and there would be an arm around his neck to hold him still, and they would unbutton his shirt and take off his shoes, and welcome him back to the *Rodina*. He was lost.

Dominika stayed a while longer at the embassy, swallowed a wedge of Russian vegetable pie from the embassy canteen without tasting it, and then walked to her hotel. It was midday and the sun was hot on her head. She was dulled and numb over the LYRIC situation. They had done it to her again or, rather, she had done it to herself. She knew the CIA men were out of their minds with concern: They had just lost an agent, partly through bad luck, partly thanks to an old man's obstinacy, partly through inattention. But she was back in the familiar tar pit, up to her hips in it. *Welcome to the life you chose.*

She daydreamed, walking head down on the dusty sidewalk of Ambelokipi toward her hotel, about escaping. How would she frame it, how would she tell Nate she wanted him to take her to America, right now, and put her in a house near a lake surrounded by pine trees, a house with a fireplace, and make slow love in the mornings? *You're a little genius,* she thought. *A real dreamer. Who are you kidding*? This deep-freeze existence of hers would continue until she died, exposed by a traitor, or shot by a sniper, or butchered by a maniac assassin.

Marta walked beside her, smoking and looking at the young men on the sidewalk. Clear your mind, she told her, concentrate, love your man, and don't be afraid.

Love your man. Dominika cleared her mind as she got her room key from the desk and walked up the narrow stairs, dark and cool compared with the heat of the street. She wanted to change out of her sweater and dress for the evening reception at the embassy, from which she would then slip away to see Nate and Gable at a late-night meeting. She decided she would tell them both she was sorry tonight. Dominika had bought a sheer black body shirt from the Wolford lingerie store in Kolonaki that she would wear under a short jacket and skirt—not formal, but slutty professional. You could see through the gauzy material and she (or Nate) could open the crotch snaps with one hand.

She didn't recall having drawn the shades in the little sitting room, and something came grunting at her from the little bedroom on the right, a blur, and a shock, and the feel of steel arms around her waist, and Dominika twisted to her left while stepping wide, but the arms didn't let go, and she was picked up bodily and slammed against the wall with demonic force and the person was an indistinct shadow but not a man, not with that scent, not with those chest pillows, and Dominika hit the blond head with her elbow while reaching low with her other hand and driving a stiff-ridge hand strike between her legs, and got a chuffing noise for her effort, and the arms came away from her waist, but then snaked around her throat, and the woman put a knee in the small of Dominika's back and tried to pull her to the floor, but Dominika scrabbled at a little ceramic lamp with a seashell pattern on the shade and reached around, and smashed it against the side of the bitch's head, and the arms let go and Dominika turned to look at her, she was holding her cheek, dressed in a T-shirt and wrap-around skirt, and had big shoulders, big legs, eyes the color of slate, and that blond hair lying tight on her skull, and without warning she exploded from a standing start and drove her shoulder into Dominika's stomach, driving both of them backward onto a glass coffee table, which shattered, and the woman kept driving with her legs, pushing through broken wood and glass, getting a purchase and hitting at Dominika's head, and her ribs were on fire; she put a thumb into one of those river-stone eyes, but the beast just grunted and shook her head, and Dominika knew she could not beat this woman for sheer strength, and she fought a wave of desperate fear, thinking wildly about screaming for help as the face pressed closer to her, showing her teeth, and Dominika felt broken glass under her hand and she swiped a shard across the woman's face from above her left eyebrow diagonally downward across the fleshy nose to the lower right cheek, a pirate scar, and the woman rolled off, holding her face and wiping it with the T-shirt, braless breasts visible when she lifted the shirt, large dark-brown nipples, and then the woman exploded forward again like a wounded Cape buffalo, blood streaming down her face, and Dominika was hunched over, holding her ribs together and trying to breathe, when the banshee threw a looping punch that landed above Dominika's left ear with white light exploding in her head, and real rage came then and Dominika ignored her ribs and threw a snap punch, then another, at the woman's face with no effect and they both went backward onto the couch, legs intertwined and holding on to hair and clothes, each one trying to get on top, and the couch jumped a little off its legs with the thrashing around, and the beast heaved up on top of her, turned Dominika on her stomach, mashing her face into the couch, and Dominika could feel dripping blood on her cheek and got a blocking hand up between her throat and the cord before it was strained tight, but she could still pass out with enough pressure—thank God it wasn't piano wire—and with a lurch borne out of desperation Dominika rocked violently twice, sending the couch over on its back with a crack of wood, dumping them both against the wall and Dominika knew if she wasn't first on her feet in that confined space she was dead, so she put both hands under the woman's chin and a foot in her stomach and pushed, then rolled away and got to her feet, the cord still loosely around her neck but the beast was wiping her face again, her breasts glistening pink in the dim light of the room, and she was stepping casually over the upturned couch, and Dominika backed away, bracing for another buffalo charge, and on a whim said, *Suka ty zlo'ebuchaya,* you're a fucking bitch, to goad her, because Dominika had about one move left, and when Blondie came, arms reaching for her throat, Dominika ducked and took the left arm over her shoulder, did a quarter turn, and pulled down against the hinge of the elbow, separating the distal humerus from the radial head and splintering the olecranon, the point of the elbow, with a sound like a cracked walnut shell, and the woman barked once with the pain but kept coming, with a low moan from her chest, one arm swinging free, one eye blinking away the blood, and Dominika could barely raise her arm to pull the blood-soaked T-shirt to swing the woman in a flat circle and lift a foot to kick her behind the knee joint, and the sodden T-shirt tore down the front as the woman toppled, unable to break her fall with her limp broken arm, hitting the rug with her cheek, her head bouncing once on the floor and Dominika bent over the stirring woman, flipped her over, took three turns with the cord around her neck, and got out of range of that one good arm by scurrying above the woman's head, putting her feet on her shoulders, and pulling with her arms, she kept pulling the electric cord, the only way she could stay away from those hands and teeth, the only way she could exert enough pressure, both feet braced, leaning back with the ends of the cord wrapped around each fist, and Dominika pulled, turning her head to vomit a little, whimpering with the exertion, and the waves of pain in her ribs were worse, and the woman's blood-streaked face slowly tilted back to look at Dominika upside down and the flattened breasts shuddered and the saliva and blood ran the wrong way up her face and Dominika kept pulling, and the woman's good arm scrabbled at the treble-wrapped cord cutting into her neck and her bellow of dying rage came out as a rasping gargling, and the legs started kicking and the woman bucked twice, breasts flopping, and she kept pulling, but the air was full of buzzing sounds, and Dominika kept pulling, and her vision was tunneling now, black-rimmed and fuzzy, and she came back, five minutes or twenty-five minutes later, she couldn't tell, and the woman was still staring at her, and Dominika took her feet off her shoulders and knee-walked around her, looking sideways at the corpse in case she started moving again, but there was no rise and fall of the chest or diaphragm, and her skirt was wet from waist to hem and her feet were cut from the glass, and one elbow was bent too far one way, and Dominika could barely take a breath, but the virago was dead. She had killed it.

The blonde's leather wallet had some euros, a phone card, and a visa photo of an attractive brunette with a wry smile. No identification, no nationality. The clothes and the shoes didn't tell her anything and the wire-rimmed glasses were neutral. Who was she? Dominika set her jaw, leaned over the staring eyes, and opened the mouth wider and saw the signature of bad Russian dentistry—a mouth full of oxidized steel fillings, brown decay in the margins between enamel and mercury, and the scalloped pockets on the gums. So this was most certainly a deputation from Moscow. She did not have the slightest doubt from whom, but he must have had a plan to cover himself. Dominika stuffed the little photograph into her purse. She sat shakily on the couch and stared at the woman on her back, still showing off her fillings.

As she sat doubled over, Dominika had the quite startling epiphany that during the ten minutes of fighting this termagant, she had seen no human colors around her head, not even the black bat wings of pure evil.

The pain was worse now, radiating around to her back. Breathing hurt. She knew she had no other option than to return to her embassy. She needed discreet medical attention and she needed assistance in getting out of the country immediately. When the hotel staff found this strangled gorgon in her hotel room the police would search for her, she would be arrested, there would be damaging publicity and immense displeasure back home. She had to disappear from Greece. She would say only that she had been mugged by an unknown assailant. Only she and Zyuganov would know the truth, and it would be their mortal shared secret, the sheathed knife on the table between them.

When Dominika did not appear at the safe house that night, Gable and Nate closed up and CIA went into the familiar mode that was the default strategy when an internal asset misses a meeting: Maintain a low profile; wait for recontact. Athens Station reviewed possible reasons Dominika would be a no-show—embassy event, sudden orders from Moscow to return, trouble on the street. Nate had been shaken by the LYRIC fiasco, and now his other agent was unaccounted for.

"She can take care of herself," said Gable in the Station, unconvincingly. "We finished all our business, checked her out again on Red Route Two and the transmitter; she's got the meeting sites down and her SRAC net back home is working. We got a capable case officer to meet her in Moscow. The last evening was gonna be rapport building and a few drinks, unless of course Johnny Fuckfaster was planning something more."

Nate ignored him. "I'm going to do a flyby of her hotel, just to check."

Forsyth was sufficiently worried that he nodded okay. "Quietly," he said.

Nate did more than a flyby. He found the right alley, slid a square of stiff plastic past the service door latch, went up the back stairs of the Lovable Experience 4 until he saw the crime tape on the third-floor landing, found the room with more tape stretched across the doorjamb, eased open the door, and saw the blood and broken furniture and gouges in the walls.

The Station obtained a grisly autopsy photograph from a cooperative Greek cop, so at least they knew it wasn't Dominika in the refrigerated drawer downtown, but all agreed that little Zyuganov had tried another hit on their agent with an assassin who, judging from the morgue photo, may or may not have been a woman. Protracted discussion in restricted cables and over the secure phone included suggestions: Pull DIVA out now (Nate); give her a small squeeze bottle of Red Katipo spider venom to squirt into Zyuganov's tea mug (Gable); and multiple suggested drafts for SRAC messages to warn her (Forsyth). In the end, Benford overruled everyone, insisting that Dominika knew very well the dangers and a torrent of conflicting messages would only distract her. Benford said his go-to girl Hannah would be briefed on the situation so she would know the issues when the two women met on the street.

In a final call to Forsyth, Benford admitted to the chief that he was worried. "Goddamn it, Tom, DIVA's poised on the threshold of getting inside the Kremlin and developing significant new access, but the blade keeps swinging closer and closer. I don't know how long she'll survive."

"You want to consider pulling her out?" said Forsyth. "It's what Nash recommends."

No," said Benford. "Keep her alive as long as you can, but we have to play the game regardless of the cost."

"Simon, that's a little stringent, even from you," said Forsyth.

"Yeah, you'd be stringent, too," said Benford, "with that motherless TRITON somewhere in this building."

All DIVA traffic was in a highly restricted cable compartment with a BIGOT list of a dozen cleared readers, maintained as a counterintelligence-accountability document. Not even the CIA associate deputy director for Military Affairs, Seb Angevine, was privy to operational traffic on DIVA caroming between Athens, Moscow, and Headquarters. But he did attend the daily deputies' meeting in the director's conference room on the seventh floor, and he did hear the hoggish Gloria Bevacqua, the deputy director for operations, whispering to the director during the sycophantic milling at the end of every meeting that LYRIC had ignored warnings and returned to Moscow, almost certainly to be arrested, and that she *had not concurred with the plan to turn him in.*

Back in his office, Angevine pondered this. *The plan to turn LYRIC in*? He wrote a note, photographed the item because it had something to do with Russia, and included it in his dead-drop package that week for Russian *rezident* Yulia Zarubina. The *rezident* forwarded this latest TRITON report to the Center, eyes only Line KR, which was read by Zyuganov and his deputy, Yevgeny Pletnev, the former with a solar flare of suspicion, the latter with a douche of fear.

The only way the Americans could know about Solovyov is if they had another mole. And the "plan to turn him in," was that a garble? Egorova had returned miraculously from Athens and immediately requested to go on sick leave, claiming she had been attacked on the street and slightly injured. Quick recovery, they said: The CI analysts wanted to talk to her; the director wanted to see her; the Kremlin had summoned her. It all stank to Zyuganov.

When Zyuganov eventually heard that Eva Buchina had been found dead in the Athens hotel room, he was truly amazed that she had been bested in a struggle. How could thin, elegant Egorova manage to beat her? Did the skinny ballerina have someone with her for protection? Nothing would be said about it again; it had to be that way. Whatever happened, Eva had missed, and now, as useful as she had been, her demise was in one way welcome. Eva was uncontrollable: She would have been the pet snake, growing in length and girth, that one day starts looking at you through the glass of the terrarium as if you were the mouse.

Egorova would have praise heaped on her, and Zyuganov would wait, and watch. He was counting on TRITON to tell him what he wanted to hear.

RUSSIAN VEGETABLE PIE

Sauté diced onions and mushrooms in butter until slightly brown. Add shredded cabbage and sauté until wilted. Season mixture aggressively with thyme, tarragon, oregano, salt, and pepper. Spread cream cheese on the bottom of a pie shell, cover with a layer of sliced hard boiled eggs, and sprinkle with chopped dill. Add the cabbage-onion-mushroom mixture and seal the pie with the pastry top. Bake in a high oven until the pastry is golden. Let cool before serving.

31

Brief-Encounter Site TORRENT. The hard-packed dirt trail ran downhill until it doglegged with another trail coming up from the river walk. The lamp pole at the *V*-shaped intersection of the two trails was out—the glass globe was broken—and the area was dark; the only light coming obliquely through the tree canopy was from the lights along the river. They twinkled through the autumn-bare branches, which by now had lost almost all their leaves. Leafy or bare, the forest of *Vorobyovy Gory*, the horseshoe-shaped Sparrow Hills Park on the Moskva River, was dark and spooky. Hannah Archer, sitting against the trunk of a smooth-barked ash tree, shifted her aching legs and checked the luminous dial on her watch, then tucked it away under the sleeve of her black hooded hard-shell jacket.

Time. Hannah stood up slowly, not making a sound, and dug the Scout PS24 out of the shell's side pocket, a thermal imaging monocular with a rubber eyepiece at one end and a lens aperture at the other. Hannah set the lens on "white hot"—a (human) heat source would show up as a ghostly white image against a totally black background—and scanned a hundred-degree arc in front of her in the direction of the ascending trail. *Come on, DIVA,* thought Hannah, *what's keeping you, girl?*

At the very bottom of the curving trail Hannah saw a phantom coming up through the trees. The figure looked like something ghost hunters photograph in a farmhouse attic, floating and disembodied. Hannah watched her come along the trail, but she now concentrated on the path behind the ghost. No one coming up behind. Hannah smoothly pivoted to hose down the woods on either side with invisible infrared light. Clear. Hannah kept her feet planted and twisted her torso to check the black uphill forest behind her. Nothing. She refocused on the ghost, noting the imperceptible hitch in her stride—not quite a limp, but just noticeable if you looked for it. DIVA.

Hannah stowed the PS24 and swung her backpack over one shoulder. She stepped out from behind the tree and onto the trail just as Dominika came up. Hannah was a dark shadow, a forest druid in a hood, and she held up her hand.

"Captain Egorova?" she said softly. "I'm Hannah." She pulled the hood off her head and the curly blond hair spilled out, the eyes crinkled with intensity, and the guileless smile lit up the woods. With the smile came the candy-red bloom of dedication and appetite and resolve. *And passion?* As tall as Dominika, perhaps slighter, certainly fit—she vibrated with energy and operational adrenaline. With a nod of apology, Hannah brought out the thermal scope and did a three-sixty scan of the forest.

She would have handed it to Dominika to try but Moscow Rules included the requirement that the American case officer have no physical contact with the foreign agent for fear of pollinating the Russian source with *metka*, spy dust, a sticky, colorless fine powder—a compound of nitrophenylpentadienal, also called NPPD—which the FSB surreptitiously spritzed everywhere: on American doorknobs, car handles, floor mats, steering wheels, and in overcoat pockets. From a handshake or unwrapped item, a polluted Russian agent (if under suspicion) would fluoresce like a neon Samsung billboard above Tverskaya Street.

"Course you have to be careful with it," whispered Hannah, lowering the scope. "The IR is visible to a simple night-sight goggle, so you have to take short looks." *That smile would be visible to night-vision devices, too,* thought Dominika.

"Come on, let's walk," said Hannah and they took the longer uphill leg, deeper in shadow with less ambient light. They quickly set the time for their next brief encounter, always the first piece of business, in case of a sudden interruption and a busted meeting.

Dominika was impressed. Hannah was fast, complete, and ordered. "They want me to tell you they know why you didn't show up the last night in Athens," said Hannah. "They know about the blond woman, the assassin. Are you okay?"

"Taped ribs, bruised knuckles, sore throat. I told the Center I was mugged. There's no problem now," said Dominika. "My boss looks at me like I'm a witch."

"They want to know whether you are in danger from your supervisor. They instructed me to tell you that they will pull you out if you request."

Dominika looked at Hannah, with that guileless face and the red of passion swirling around her head. "Please thank them," she said. "I am in no danger and am making progress." *You sound a little old and stuffy next to this nature child,* thought Dominika. *I wonder if Nate thinks so, too.*

"That's a relief," said Hannah. "I could tell Nate was worried." *Indeed.* Dominika said nothing. Hannah moved right through her checklist.

"Here's the equipment kit for your exfil plan," she said, pulling out a small duffel wrapped in a larger plastic bag. She held it open so Dominika could lift it out. "Checked and totally clean. You already know what's in it; you practiced with the same kit. If you have any questions, I can talk you through them via SRAC. Okay?"

Efficient, confident; she knows what she's doing. How old? Nate said Twenty-seven? *Bozhe,* God. "I remember the plan," said Dominika, feeling like a foreign asset being briefed by her case officer—which is exactly what she was. "I have several things," she continued. "Please tell them that I have determined where LYRIC is. He is still alive. In fact, the old *morzh* has confessed to nothing. I saw him in his cell, but he did not see me. Zyuganov is sweating that he won't get a confession; the interrogation has gone on too long. Now they are worried about his heart. LYRIC is under house arrest in his Moscow apartment, waiting for the second round of interrogation. He won't make it past Level Two." Hannah looked over at Dominika, a serious look on her face. "Did you get all that?" said Dominika.

"Yes," said Hannah, patting her backpack. "I'm recording everything. I don't want to miss anything. But what's a *morzh*?"

Dominika didn't know the English word and tried to explain what a walrus was, and even tried a snorty grunt to illustrate. Hannah covered her mouth with her hand and Dominika started laughing too, and they were in the midnight woods, committing espionage, listening for the fatal snap of a branch, laughing like sisters.

"You'll be careful of that recording—my voice—won't you, Hannah?" said Dominika, resisting the impulse to ask whether Nate would hear it. *Of course he would.*

"I won't let anything happen to it," said Hannah, serious again. "Besides, if anyone tries to play it back without pressing the right buttons, it scrubs the entire digital file in two point three seconds."

"You seem to have all the right equipment," said Dominika.

"We have a lot of toys, sure," said Hannah, "but the most important thing is your security. That's my only job."

Dominika could even hear the cadence of Nate's words as Hannah repeated the cant. *They trained together, how lovely. And now I'm standing in the forest with this little gladiator, who's telling me she'll take care of me.* Dominika thought an uncharitable thought. "I feel safer with you already," she said, talking to the recording device, talking to Nate.

Hannah looked at Dominika for a second. *She's perceptive too,* thought Dominika. *Is that bitchy enough for you?*

"There's more," said Dominika. "Tell them that Yevgeny is still cooperating, and he will tell me anything I want to know." *Did you hear that, Neyt?* "Yevgeny just told me there was a request from Zarubina for satellite imagery support to survey a proposed meeting site in Washington, DC. Yevgeny was preparing a formal memo to the Space Intelligence Directorate at Vatutinki. He showed it to me . . . for a kiss." *Stop it, enough.* "I copied the coordinates." Dominika handed Hannah a slip of paper. "I assume Zarubina intends to use it for TRITON." Hannah looked at the paper and read the coordinates aloud for the recorder, then tore the paper into pieces and stuffed them into a small bottle of clear liquid that she shook violently. Acetone to destroy the handwritten note, Hannah explained, smiling. *Cute smile,* thought Dominika. *Smart girl,* she thought.

Marta sat on a fallen tree trunk, shaking her head. Really, now, jealousy does not become you.

"Captain Egorova, this is huge," whispered Hannah. "Nathaniel is going to freak. This could lead us to TRITON." Hannah's young face was alight.

It's Nathaniel now, thought Dominika, looking at her face. *There's not a false bone in her body. Candy-red halo, powder and strawberries, and those Roman curls.* Hannah pulled her sleeve up and checked her watch.

"We're past our time limit," said Hannah. "Is there anything else? Do you need anything? Is your SRAC gear okay?" Dominika nodded. She tamped down the urge to ask about her and Nate—she would not appear *nekulturny.* Hannah scanned the woods around them again and shook her head—negative, nothing moving.

"I'll see you again at site SKLAD—it's 'warehouse' in English. You remember?"

Dominika nodded.

Hannah looked down at her feet, then up into Dominika's eyes. "It was great to meet you," she said. "You're an amazing person, doing an amazing job."

Dominika searched her face for the fissure of sarcasm or toadying. Her halo held steady. "It is good to meet you too," said Dominika. "We will work well together. Please pass my regards to Nathaniel and the rest of them. You're doing the same job now that he did."

"I read the whole file," said Hannah. "Nate's a fantastic case officer. He helped me prepare for this assignment. He helped me a lot."

Dominika saw the emotion, saw how quickly she swallowed it down. She couldn't make herself dislike this woman.

"He's totally dedicated to supporting you," said Hannah suddenly. "*Totally.* We all are." The chemical message on the Pheromone Channel was unambiguous: *Whatever may have happened, for whatever reasons, he loves you. It doesn't matter what I feel, he's yours.* Hannah almost took Dominika's hand and shook it, almost impulsively reached out to give her a quick hug, but she stopped herself. She turned, flipped up the hood of her jacket, and walked uphill, swallowed by the shadows, leaving DIVA immobile for a second until she turned and headed downhill toward the river.

Udranka walked down with her. Kak tebe ne stydno, *she whispered, shame on you.*

Yevgeny left his hairy thigh draped over Dominika's haunches as he panted for breath. She had turned onto her stomach, partly to furtively mop her face but primarily so she wouldn't have to look at the forested ears and nostrils, the corrugated toenails and torn cuticles. *Bozhe moi,* my God, even his *khuy* was feathered in downy hairs like a Kamchatka brown bear. Sparrows used seduction to further the strategic goals of the homeland—sexpionage was the combination of the two oldest professions—but Dominika was having sex with bottle-bristle Yevgeny to keep herself alive: He was her only source of information about how the TRITON case was progressing.

She had been back to Line KR for a week. Zyuganov was the same: swirling black clouds of envy and deceit. The interservice counterintelligence board had been abuzz over Dominika's uncanny performance in detecting something fishy about General Solovyov and recommending his recall from Athens, a brilliant piece of intuitive tradecraft. Zyuganov, frantic with jealousy and Putin-envy, was now sweating to get a confession out of the old soldier, so far without results. Yevgeny said it was for this reason the general had been put under house arrest in his small apartment in the northwestern suburb of Khimki. A live-in guard watched the old bachelor—where was he going to go without a passport? Give him a month's rest, then start again.

Yevgeny had missed her while she was away. He had come over after work, and they sat in the living room of Dominika's little apartment and munched on *kotlety Pozharskie,* minced chicken cutlets fried to a golden brown with spicy *ajvar* sauce. As they ate, Dominika pulled on Yevgeny's strings with delicate fingers to get him talking. There was a lot, but Yevgeny could talk and eat at the same time.

Zarubina was now managing TRITON by means of personal meetings. She had flattered, complimented, suggested, cajoled, and directed TRITON to collect increasingly spectacular intelligence from the very heart of CIA. Yevgeny called her a genius, an artist. At the top of the list: Zarubina had been directed to task TRITON with discovering whether there was another American mole *inside* the Center—a mole who filled the gap when the traitor Korchnoi had been eliminated. The Blue-Eyed Serenity in the Kremlin had ordered his intelligence services—all of them—to find out. They all grimly noted the unmasking of the Caracas recruit. And the recall of the GRU general from Athens had caused a furor. The Americans were busy again, they told themselves, and they knew, just knew, that there were even worse enemies out there. *They're looking for me,* thought Dominika.

There was more, but Yevgeny's pilot light was on, and Dominika led him coquettishly into her tiny bathroom, where she hosed him down with the handheld shower like a draft horse and played a sexy game with the soap bar and rubbed him dry, then took him into the bedroom and turned her mind off and raked his back with her nails and put her heels on his furry butt, and closed her eyes and felt the sweat on his face drop onto her forehead and lips.

She almost started crying then, thinking about Nate and how they had quarreled, and how things had gone wrong with LYRIC, and something started in her mind, a wispy thought that she couldn't catch yet, so she filed it away and timed her faked orgasm to Yevgeny's barnyard finish—she went with the side-to-side tossing head and a big groan—after which he collapsed onto the bed with a ham-hock leg still cocked across her. When his breathing slowed, Dominika started pulling the string again.

"It did not escape Zarubina's notice that you were called again to the Kremlin to be congratulated," said Yevgeny, still breathing hard. "You know, Zarubina is going to be the boss someday, and she's got her eye on you. You're set," said Yevgeny, patting Dominika's buttocks. "Just don't forget your friends."

Udranka sat incongruously atop the armoire in the corner of the bedroom, swinging her legs. It really is too much, isn't it? But you don't have to like it, she said, you just have to do it.

The summons came from the president's secretariat two days after her return, but the car that had been sent for her careened past the Kremlin Borovitskaya Gate and continued another kilometer into the swanky Tverskoy District, past the display windows on Tverskaya filled with the sorts of shoes, clothes, and leather goods that do not exist in Mother Russia outside the MKAD ring road, and pulled into a broad, immaculate alleyway marked SHVEDSKIY TUPIK, Swedish Blind alley. Building No. 3 was a modern eleven-story brick-and-glass high-rise, incongruous amid the Soviet baroque buildings in the neighborhood, and clearly someplace special judging by the Federal Guard Service security booth outside the main entrance.

An aide was waiting to take Dominika up in a soundless elevator with no buttons. The doors opened to a luxurious living room with parquet floors and elaborate moldings on the walls and ceiling. At the end of the room President Putin was standing at a sideboard, talking on a telephone. He was dressed in a khaki sports shirt under a leather vest with zippered pockets. Three other people—two men and a woman—were on nearby brocade couches and chairs, all of them sitting in a funky yellow cloud. Dominika walked across the parquet, her heels clicking on the wood. She remembered what Gable had said about wearing heels the next time she saw the president. She wore a dark navy suit with dark tights. As usual, her hair was up in the regulation service style. The people had stopped talking and were watching her cross the room, ballerina smooth and statuesque. Enveloped in his usual Arctic blue, President Putin put down the telephone, shook hands, and then took her arm to walk Dominika away from the guests and back toward the waiting aide and the still-open elevator doors. In her heels, Dominika was taller by a head.

"Captain, thank you for coming," Putin said. "I congratulate you on another fine piece of work." Putin's cupid-bow mouth moved slightly, perhaps indicating pleasure, or even mirth. "It seems like Athens is lucky for you." His eyes locked onto hers, and Dominika, not for the first time, wondered if he could read her mind.

"Thank you, Mr. President," said Dominika, the only possible response in this insane moment.

"I regret I have to leave shortly; otherwise I would offer something and introduce you to some people," said Putin, nodding to the group on the couches and chairs. "I am hosting a conference at the state complex at Strelna for the next ten days. Do you know the Constantine Palace?"

"I visited as a child with family from Saint Petersburg," said Dominika, remembering the magnificent baroque palace and formal neoclassical gardens stretching to the sea. The grander Peterhof and Oranienbaum Palaces were on the same stretch of coast, south of Petersburg.

"Of course. Your family was from there," said Putin. *Yes,* thought Dominika, *my grandmother hid in a well as the Bolsheviks burned the house.*

"Well, you are overdue for another visit," said Putin. He was inviting her. But surely not as the only guest? *What do I do, Forsyth? Benford?*

"One of the cottages is prepared for a private gathering, people you should be introduced to," said Putin, gesturing for the aide to escort her back to the lobby. "You already know Govormarenko."

Sure, the energy-czar pig who's helping you siphon off profits in the Iran deal, thought Dominika. *God grant there is no hot tub in the gym.* "You're too kind, Mr. President. I may take advantage and visit relatives in the city at the same time." She shook Putin's hand—dry and firm—and stepped into the elevator.

"Make sure the captain's name is at the gate," said Putin to the aide. The elevator doors closed but Dominika could still feel his eyes on her.

KOTLETY POZHARSKIE—CHICKEN CUTLETS

Soak bread in milk and combine with ground chicken, butter, salt, and pepper, and incorporate into a paste. Form into small patties, dip in egg wash, and dredge in bread crumbs. Fry lightly in butter until golden brown. Serve with pureed potatoes and ajvar sauce.

32

Benford was late for his own meeting. He had been at a briefing downstairs in PROD on the progress of the W. Petrs seismic-isolation floor on its surreptitious water odyssey through continental Russia to Iran. The German SBE had alerted Berlin Station that the massive machinery had left the factory. The National Geospatial-Intelligence Agency in concert with CIA had been tracking it via a third-generation INDIGO EYE optical-imaging satellite that from its elliptical polar orbit two hundred miles up could read the name on the square stern of the barge that was plowing through the lakes north of Saint Petersburg, then southeast, down the Volga on its way to the Volga River Delta at Astrakhan to the Caspian Sea.

In a darkened room Benford was shown projected photos of the massive cargo, shrink-wrapped in white vinyl, covered across its girth with a dun-colored tarp, and secured Gulliver-style with dozens of interlaced straps. An insufferable imagery analyst from NGA with bullfrog eyes explained that orbital drift known as precession—Benford's glare stopped him from explaining Kepler's Third Law—meant that the bird's observational corridor would be pushed westward with each subsequent orbit. That meant, the self-satisfied analyst continued, the low earth-orbiting INDIGO EYE would lose the barge once it entered the Caspian. Benford continued staring at this unpleasant person, who hurriedly added that coverage accordingly would be assumed by a stealthy SOLAR FIST surveillance drone launched from the US Air Force base at Incirlik, Turkey, which could transit the five hundred kilometers of Azeri and Iranian airspace undetected and loiter for five days over the fetid Caspian, making lazy eights at an altitude of twenty kilometers.

At the end of the session, the goggle-eyed briefer—*How appropriate that an imagery officer has bug eyes,* thought Benford—smugly offered that drones would replace operations officers in five years. Benford stiffened. PROD officers in the room fell silent. "Thank you for your unsolicited comment," said Benford to the briefer. "No doubt you can look down a man's pants with your drones from a great height. But your drones cannot divine what he *intends to do* with his prick, with whom, and when."

He left and hurried to the alchemist's cave he called his office. Sitting in chairs around a desk mounded with papers were his trusty savants in CID, Margery Salvatore and Janice Callahan. Benford sat down and scowled at them. They knew not to speak. Benford was a man possessed, knowing that a mole reporting to the Russians was inside CIA.

"Pardon my language," said Benford, "but fuck. Since we became aware of the mole in CIA, we have curtailed the OSI double-agent operation to deny this TRITON a channel to the Russians. In so doing, we aspired to flush TRITON out into the open, and into personal contact with SVR *rezident* Zarubina. From DIVA's reporting we know that this has happened, but alas, fucking FBI coverage of Zarubina has revealed nothing. She is cautious on the street, aborts when she doesn't like the vibe, and is unpredictable. It is damn difficult to cover her discreetly."

"Let's shut her down with heavy coverage on the street," said Janice. "Make her make a mistake."

"Might work," said Margery. "But if they see too much pressure it's as likely the Center will put TRITON on ice until they dispatch the illegal to the United States to begin handling him."

"At which time the case goes underwater and TRITON works undisturbed for thirty years," said Janice. She had handled agents in communist Eastern Europe whose actuarial life expectancy as spies was eighteen months.

"Janice is depressingly correct," said Benford. "We have a narrowing window during which TRITON is still being met by a Russian intel officer whom we can follow. Zarubina uses aggressive countersurveillance; she regularly manipulates FBI coverage into traps."

"In all the years, in all the cases, there's always been the unpredictable, minute element that changes the course of an operation, breaks a mole hunt, anchors a recruitment," said Margery. "We need that now."

"Here is a penny, Margery," said Benford, sliding a coin through the detritus on his desk. "Throw it into the wishing well out front of the building."

"Margery, save that penny," said Chief/ROD Dante Helton, walking into Benford's office. He lifted a stack of files off a chair and dragged it to sit beside Margery. "Simon, look at Moscow 2584; just came in."

Benford sighed. "Dante, I appreciate your taking time to attend this gathering, which began about twenty minutes ago."

Dante pointed at Benford's monitor. "Look at it right now."

Benford found the cable, brought his half glasses down off his head, and leaned in, reading. "Hannah Archer had her first personal meeting with DIVA in Moscow at the Sparrow Hills site." said Benford, turning to look at the three. "Janice, your protégée performed splendidly again." He read on. "What is more, DIVA provided . . . holy fucking shit."

Benford put his finger on the monitor, reading slowly. "Thirty-eight degrees, ninety-two minutes north, seventy-seven degrees, zero three minutes west," he said, finally turning again to look at each of them.

Though unreservedly loyal to Benford, Margery had long predicted his sudden descent into eccentric senescence—the time had come, apparently. Margery proposed displaying Benford in his dotage for a fee in the ground-floor library as a way to raise money for CIA Family Day.

"Stop what you're thinking, Margery," said Benford. "DIVA got this from her deputy in Line KR, Pletnev. I think she's doing the Sparrow thing with him. She's got starch, that woman." Benford extracted a Washington, DC, map book from under a pile of newspapers, triggering a small avalanche of them onto the floor. No one moved to gather them up.

"Zarubina requested overhead imagery of these coordinates," said Benford, flipping the pages of the book. "The Russians case sites the same as we do. Downtown DC, Meridian Hill Park, in Columbia Heights, between Fifteenth and Sixteenth Streets." Benford found the page and looked at it.

"Margery, you are a prophet, a Sybil, a haruspex. Zarubina just gave us the site where she's next going to meet TRITON."

Seb Angevine had met Zarubina five times since he had gotten back in contact, and he emphatically didn't like being out on the street with her. Too exposed. He didn't know shit from tradecraft, but had to admit she picked some pretty cool, out-of-the-way places—urban lanes, alleys, courtyards—that he didn't even know existed. But he recoiled at the risks of meeting out in the open with the known SVR *rezident,* and he was jackrabbit nervous the whole time, usually waiting and watching from a concealed position, checking to see she arrived alone, ready to beat feet if there was trouble. Zarubina knew he was doing it, and once had gotten all grandmothery on him, the way she did, and hugged him and said he was a dear to be concerned about her. *Fuck you,* he thought. *I'm concerned about* my *balls.*

It was the money that kept him coming back. The Russians were paying big bucks now, meaty cash bundles in a backpack, plus hefty alias account deposits in foreign banks. Zarubina told him they had passed the two-million-dollar mark. Angevine knew they were feeding his ego and his venality, but they were welcome to manipulate him all the way to the teller's window. Zarubina didn't let up; she was relentless. And after five meetings, despite the grandmotherly exterior the imaginative Angevine saw the ancient Soviet venom of show trial and gulag, of politburo and mass graves in birch forests.

Things were going great with Vikki, thank God. She refused his suggestion to quit stripping, but they had taken some nice vacations together, and he was picking up her rent and expenses. The sex was great too, athletic and bendy. Thinking he had built up some frigging equity with her, Angevine once coyly suggested she get one of her girlfriends from Good Guys to come over for a three-way, but she'd had a fit and wouldn't see him for a week. *What's the big deal?* he thought. He had bought her a pair of gold earrings at Market Street Diamonds on M Street, and they had make-up sex, but she was still pissed at him.

Seb was using his position as a "senior" in CIA to read ops traffic he otherwise would have no access to. Lots of it. He never downloaded anything, never copied anything—too many forensic computer and print-run checks all the time. Zarubina had been impressed that he was taking photographs of cables off his internal CIA computer screen and had given him a remarkable miniature camera—a Chobi Cam from Japan—that was as big as an India rubber eraser and weighed half an ounce. It had better resolution than his iPhone (which wasn't allowed in Headquarters anyway).

"Of course Line T has better cameras," Zarubina sniffed, "but this one is available immediately." Meaning that the Japan-made minicam bestowed deniability for SVR were Angevine ever caught.

"Put it on video mode, dear," said Zarubina, "and scroll your screen as fast as you can. We can retrieve the images." His thumb on the "page down" key, Angevine was now photographing a cascading blur on his monitor of so many cables, memos, and briefing papers that he didn't even know what he was passing. They worked with three cameras—nicknamed Alpha, Beta, and Gamma—swapping them in rotation each meeting. They were emptying the vault.

At the last meeting Zarubina had sweetly reminded him that they still needed him to look for the CIA-run mole in Moscow. Angevine, for the third time, explained that there was a small percentage of cases that were so restricted that readership was limited to three people. Intelligence produced by these cases was so thoroughly edited for source-protection reasons that the name, gender, and nationality were unknowable. Sugary Zarubina asked him to keep trying.

It was at another weekly deputies' meeting with the hated Gloria Bevacqua that Angevine discovered the way around the compartmentation firewalls into the identities of restricted assets. In the middle of one of her feckless perorations, the sow tangentially complained about the red tape in the Office of Finance, which, she said, maintained a roster of *true names* used for making deposits into the alias bank accounts of agents, a bureaucratic requirement for federal monies allocated to intelligence sources. It was an unintended gap in the system. No one even registered Bevacqua's comments, except Angevine. As deputy director of Military Affairs, Angevine found he qualified for access to that top-secret finance database—all he needed was to reference a military reporting case to cover his request for the database. It was dangerous: It would leave a trail, but it could be done. Once.

He waited till the end of his nighttime meeting with Zarubina before mentioning it, to amp up the drama. "It's a one-time deal," he had told her. "And it's going to cost a million." Zarubina took Beta from him and handed him Gamma, the camera that at the next exchange would have the true names of CIA's most sensitive foreign assets, including any Russian names. CIA penetration operations in Moscow would be over. Zarubina patted Angevine on the shoulder, called him a wonder, and without hesitation said that the dollars, or euros, or krugerrands, or *blood diamonds,* whatever he wanted, would be deposited instantly on receipt of camera Gamma at the next meeting. Angevine literally licked his lips.

"I'll see you at RUSALKA, site Mermaid, in two weeks," said Zarubina, patting his arm. "Take care, TRITON." She returned to the *rezidentura* to draft the thunderclap cable that would galvanize the Center. Images of her sitting behind the SVR director's desk in Yasenevo, the direct Vey Che phone to the Kremlin at her elbow, flashed behind her eyes.

Bozhe, another nail-curling evening of his sweat dripping on her face and his chest hairs in her mouth. Dominika lay in her bed after Yevgeny had left, listening to her heart beating. His latest gossip from Line KR had nearly made her vomit with the shock. In two weeks TRITON would be delivering a list of assets' names—her name certainly included—to Zarubina. Benford could not protect her. The wolves were drawing close. Dominika strangely felt no fear, simply a rising determination to survive, for the sole purpose of destroying Their corrupt world.

She had two weeks to live. That realization, and Putin's silky invitation to the seaside mansion on the Gulf of Finland, finally had been the trigger to feverish thought that morphed into a plan—impossible, suicidal—she knew she would carry out: Ruin the *piyavki,* the leeches that attached themselves thick on the belly of the country. She would do it, if it was her last act. She could feel the urgency in her chest. She punched in two SRAC messages and went for a drive to transmit them to one of the sensors, thinking about blond Hannah. *Pass the word,* sestrenka, *my little sister.*

MESSAGE 35. URGENT. ZARUBINA REPORTS TRITON WILL DELIVER NAME OF RUSSIAN MOLE, HIGH DEGREE OF CERTAINTY, AT MEETING IN TWO WEEKS AT SITE RUSALKA. NO OTHER DETAILS. olga.

MESSAGE 36. INVITATION TO STRELNA BY PREZ IN NEXT TEN DAYS. WILL USE TRIP TO DELIVER LYRIC TO EXFIL SITE EARLY MORNING 12TH. INITIATE RED ROUTE TWO. olga.

The two SRAC messages from DIVA hit Moscow and Athens Stations and Langley insanely hard, "like the deaf ring a church bell," said Gable. Benford was on the secure phone to both Stations, issuing instructions like a man possessed, which he was. He asked for Forsyth's concurrence to bring Nate back to Washington: He needed a street operator to manage his nascent plan to prevent—at all costs—TRITON from making the meeting with Zarubina and passing that name. He drafted the SRAC message replies to DIVA himself, and ordered Hannah to load them into the sensor system.

MESSAGE 35 REPLY. PRESUME RUSALKA IS AT COORDS PREVIOUSLY SENT. CAN YOU CONFIRM LOCATION AND EXACT DATE?

MESSAGE 36 REPLY. UNDER NO/NO CIRCUMSTANCES ATTEMPT TO EXFILTRATE SUBJECT. IMPERATIVE YOU RESERVE RED ROUTE TWO FOR YOUR EXCLUSIVE USE. REQUEST EMERG MEETING AT SITE SKLAD TOMORROW. ACKNOWLEDGE.

COS Moscow Throckmorton, inflated with the urgency of the crisis, telephoned Benford that he would personally make the rendezvous with DIVA to tell her to stand down. "This requires gravitas, a senior hand," he said to Benford.

"Vern, you will do nothing of the sort," raved Benford, knowing that this red-assed baboon would lead half the FSB to the meeting. "You let Archer do this. It's why she's out there. Am I clear?" He got a mumbled assent.

The SRAC messages were being exchanged rapidly now. DCOS Schindler had to forego her afternoon gin-rocks to drive past sensor three to unload DIVA's fractious reply—the famous message 37:

MESSAGE 37. MEETING AT SKLAD TOMORROW ACKNOWLEDGED. WILL NOT ABANDON LYRIC. WILL NOT STAND DOWN ON EXFIL. HE AND I WILL BE ON EXFIL BEACH MORNING OF 12TH. BE ADVISED HE CANNOT WALK ON WATER. olga.

Hannah was sitting at her little desk in the Moscow Station enclosure, munching on a pastrami sandwich from the embassy cafeteria. The Russian cafeteria cooks managed to mangle most of the American items on the menu with the addition of inexplicable ingredients—pickle relish in the lasagna or blanched walnuts in the mac and cheese—but for some reason produced a delectable pastrami sandwich. Perhaps the Slavic love affair with salamis, sausages, pickled beef, cured hams, and peppered salt pork fat stirred them to treat pastrami the right way. The sandwich was rich with cheese and scallions and vinegary coleslaw. A plastic condiment cup of peppery orange *khrenovina* relish came with the sandwich—the cooks behind the cafeteria counter called the sauce *vyrviglaz*, yank-out-the-eye—but Hannah didn't even open the container. The last thing she needed was to begin feeling the volcano effects of *khrenovina* in the fourth hour of tonight's SDR. This was a screamingly critical meeting, a make-or-break, as a tense-sounding Benford had explained to her over the secure phone.

"Hannah, talk her down off whatever messianic high she's on," Benford hissed over the phone. "For fuck's sake, she *will not* jeopardize herself in this way. I don't care how you do it, lie to her, tell her the maritime assets are not available, tell her the site is compromised—shit, tell her I had a heart attack and am in intensive care. The last may not be an untruth in twelve hours."

"I don't give it that long," said Hannah, trying for a combination of confident airiness and reassuring familiarity. *Shouldn't have said it.*

"Hannah Emmeline Archer," said Benford, after a systole-thumping silence. *How did he know my middle name, and why was he using it like Daddy used to?* "I have always appreciated your youthful enthusiasm. I commend your performance in Moscow. But from today, do not endeavor to make a joke unless I specifically indicate that you should do so by saying 'be funny.' " *Just like Daddy,* thought Hannah. Her sandwich was half eaten, and would remain so.

"Simon, you picked me for this assignment," said Hannah. "You didn't make a mistake. I'll talk to her."

"Thank you, Hannah," said Benford. "The appropriate benediction is the one case officers in our service have said to one another for more than sixty years. *Good hunting.*" There was a pause. "And God bless," said Benford, the agnostic misanthrope who prayed before his own triptych of lying, cheating, and stealing. The connection ended with the hollow, rushing-water noise of the secure line.

Nearly time to kick off. She had budgeted eight hours for the SDR—the meeting was for eleven—and she had to get this balls-on right. Get black, stay black, and no mistakes. No such thing as an abort tonight. Hannah came back to her desk, reviewed the SKLAD site report and photographs, looked over the SDR route she had plotted months ago and which had been reviewed and approved first by COS (not that he ran SDRs), then at Headquarters. She could run it in her sleep. She was dressed in dark slacks and a cable-knit sweater, and she swapped her flats for woolen socks and low rubber-soled boots. She sanitized her pockets, emptying cell phone, house keys, and wallet into the credenza above the desk. She took only the small diplomatic identification booklet issued by the Russian Foreign Ministry and her car keys.

It was too cold to go with her hard-shell outer jacket—after sunset it was turning seriously frosty—so Hannah slipped on a heavy Russian-cut, wool-lined black coat with a black wool collar and cuffs and big buttons down the front. Once clear of the embassy and into her SDR, Hannah would tie a dark scarf on her head babushka-style, to break the profile and hide her blond hair. She slipped the sausage-shaped thermal scope into an inside pocket of her coat. Final check, ready to go. *Dominika, you* have *to listen to me,* Hannah thought. *It's my job to keep you in one piece.*

Hannah squeezed past two modular desks and knocked on the plastic sliding door to COS's office for a quick word before she kicked off her run. Per Benford's instructions, she had been unwaveringly deferential to the fustian Vern Throckmorton, despite the growing evidence of his incompetence and his chronic failure to realize what a mooncalf he was. He realized that Hannah was in his Station per Benford's direct orders and at first did not challenge Hannah's ops plans. Increasingly, however, Throckmorton began conflating Hannah's successes with his management of the Station, and had become obstreperous. Hannah patiently dealt with him and did not complain to Benford, thus sparing COS the bureaucratic equivalent of a rigid sigmoidoscopy with a triangular endoscope. *It might still come to that,* thought Hannah. *This crash dive with DIVA is giving COS a woody—he wants to be a hero.*

"He's gone," said a voice from the other end of the trailer. DCOS Irene Schindler was standing in her office, having slid the door open. Hannah turned and walked the length of the room toward her.

"Irene, will you tell him I had to kick off before he got back? I'll leave the box of tissues on the rear shelf of my car in the parking lot to signal you guys thumbs-up when I get home." Schindler leaned against the frame of the door and blinked. *She's half toasted,* thought Hannah.

"He went to meet DIVA," Schindler said.

"What do you mean he went to meet DIVA?" said Hannah. A shocky wave ran up her back, over the crown of her head, and down her arms.

"He said what DIVA needed was plain talk. He was—"

"Irene, shut the fuck up," said Hannah. "How was he going to get to the site? He doesn't even know where it is. What car is he driving? What route is he taking?"

Schindler put up her hand. "He read the site report. He has his own route. He's been doing this for years," said Schindler.

"Irene, I have to go," said Hannah, now in a panic. "Listen to me. You have to get on the secure phone to Benford. His number is on my desk. Listen! Tell him what happened. Tell him I'm going to try to beat COS to the site, to warn DIVA away. Are you listening?"

Schindler nodded. Hannah looked at her, took two steps up to her, inside Irene's aerosolized gin bubble, and took her by the shoulders. She could feel the balsa-wood bones under her hands. Hannah fought for control, resisted the impulse to shake her head off her shoulders.

"Irene, you have to do this immediately," Hannah whispered. "We have to protect DIVA, you and me, okay? You used to do this shit right. Dude, dredge up whatever you have left and help me." Hannah looked in her eyes. "I've got to go." She kept her hands on Schindler's shoulders for a second longer.

"Get your hands off me," said Irene. "I have to make a phone call."

EMBASSY GRILLED PASTRAMI SANDWICH

Put lean pastrami slices in a hot skillet and quickly toss until the edges are slightly crispy. Cover with asiago cheese and grilled scallions and cover with a lid until the cheese melts. Pile the pastrami on grilled country bread spread with mustard and topped with vinaigrette-based coleslaw. Drizzle Khrenovina sauce (processed slurry of tomatoes, horseradish, garlic, salt, pepper, paprika, sweet bell pepper, vinegar, and sugar) on top.

33

Hannah broke about a dozen rules for a proper SDR, pushing her little Skoda hard, pulling provocative move after provocative move to flush coverage. There was nothing, and she had to trust she was not on the list tonight—she was black. She vectored east through heavy evening traffic, then south, entering Lyubertsy, a desolated district of warehouses and truck parks. She used her mirrors to mark cars that turned when she did, stripping "possibles" one by one until she was alone. Hannah waited in silence for fifteen minutes, then dumped her car in a deserted construction site and set off on foot. Maybe the car would be there when she got back—it was fifty-fifty. She had another forty minutes to walk.

Site SKLAD was along a fenced-in walkway that skirted a darkened warehouse. In the opposite direction, the walkway ascended in a rusty steel-and-rivet staircase to cross above the electric wires over tracks for the *elektrichka* commuter train. Cavernous warehouse after warehouse stretched into the darkness, a grid square of oily access roads between them creating a maze of muddy lanes illuminated by the few mercury vapor lights that weren't burned out. Dogs roamed the warehouse grounds and they howled at the shrill whistle of a locomotive as it rumbled through, shaking the tin roofs of the warehouses. It was a muddy, rusty, decrepit, barbed-wire-wrapped, paint-flaking, ramshackle Gomorrah—in other words, suburban Moscow.

The air was still and crackling cold as Hannah ghosted past dark warehouses smelling of machine oil and iron filings. She stopped at the corner of one of the buildings and used her scope to scan up the road, then back behind her, then down the two side lanes. Empty. No engine noise, no acrid whiff of a cigarette, the scope registered only the faint thermal bloom of the lamps on the sides of the warehouses. She proceeded to the next corner and checked the four points of the compass again. Clear. She checked her watch and wondered if her COS was coming in with a horde of surveillants on his ass. With luck, he had gotten lost and was leading the opposition in circles on the ring road.

Hannah got to the walkway and silently ghosted up the steps to the elevated span over the tracks. Another dark-green train rumbled beneath the walkway, the overhead power lines zinging and snapping arc-light flashes. The steel walkway swayed as the train passed, and Hannah squatted, holding on to the rusty handrail. From the elevated walkway, she could see for some distance over the cruciform length of the four lanes between the warehouses. There was no moon, and it started raining softly, dimpling the oily pools on the ground.

It happened in a rush, the curtain going up on a nightmare tableau that Hannah watched with disbelief. A lumbering figure was coming up the side lane directly in front of her, a pigeon-toed shuffle she recognized as Throckmorton's. He had studied the site report and come straight to it. He was bundled in an overcoat and wore an enormous Muscovite fur hat on his head, big as a holiday fruitcake. His head was down, hunched into his shoulders, hands in his pockets, as he carefully stepped around puddles in the dirt. *Oblivious.* At a distance behind him, the hood of a blacked-out car peeked around the corner of a warehouse. *Dude, you dragged them here.* Hannah looked down the right-hand lane and saw another darkened car slow to a stop, and two dark silhouettes got out to stand in the shadows. Beyond a farther warehouse, another dark figure hugged the building to look around the corner. He started moving forward slowly—the others hung back. *Big team.* Hannah could feel her heart hammering in her jaw.

The nightmare got worse. With the instincts of an internal-ops officer, Hannah knew where to look next. Three buildings down on the left she saw another figure—thinner, head erect—walking slowly toward the intersection. *Jesus. It has to be DIVA.* Hannah watched, frozen, as the three figures—Throckmorton, DIVA, and the foot surveillant—converged in the night. They would arrive at the intersection simultaneously. More black silhouettes appeared on the wings. The hood of another car eased out around the first corner, and two more men—indistinct, wearing hats—stood behind it, watching.

Even as she moved silently down the stairway toward the muddy intersection, Hannah flashed to her father—not to Benford, or to DIVA or to Nate, she consciously marveled—and emerged at the end of the walkway, her head covered in her scarf, fur collar turned up. She was keyed up, breathing hard, yet icy cool in knowing what she was going to do. She waited a beat, until Throckmorton saw her and drew up with a start. He was instantly swarmed by two men who rushed from behind and tackled him facedown in the mud, their knees on his neck, their hands wrenching his arms behind him. COS Moscow started a high, keening wail and flailed his legs until another man sat on them.

This had taken two seconds, and in the third second Hannah turned and sprinted to her right, up the muddy road, in the opposite direction of DIVA's approach. The man coming in from the right yelled something and tried to cut her off, but Hannah had a step and got past him as he slipped in the mud and went down. More shouts—they were bellows of rage, of the hunt—and the sound of racing engines and the whine of mud-slick tires started up all around her. Throckmorton kept up his stuck-pig squeals. *That's it boys,* Hannah thought, *make as much noise as you can.*

The sound of footsteps was behind her, but they weren't getting closer. *Just so they think they've flushed the Russian agent, come on you turkeys, don't lose the rabbit.* She thought she might even get away, over a fence and across some tracks, rub their noses in the shit. The thermal scope was bumping her chest inside her coat; the more time they spent chasing her, the more time she would buy for DIVA.

The surveillance car—a muddy Volvo C30 with wipers going full tilt—came too fast out of a side alley between two warehouses and hit Hannah on the right hip with its left front bumper, throwing her twenty feet in the air and against the corrugated side of the warehouse on the other side of the lane. The car slid to a stop at an angle in the mud and the passenger got out and walked over to Hannah. The driver stood at the open door on his side, as if afraid to go near. The wipers slapped back and forth. Another car eased up to the scene, and four men ran up on foot. The rain had stopped.

Hannah had felt only an enormous blow on her side, and a flash, but woke on her back looking up at a circle of sweaty faces—eyebrows, Slavic cheekbones, moles, knit caps. She felt the pressure of the dirt beneath her body, but couldn't feel her legs. She tried to find her hands, and thought she moved some fingers, but couldn't see them. She tried to take a breath, but it felt like sucking air through a collapsed straw. The breathing part wasn't the worst—she felt something loose inside. The silent, grave faces looked down at her, and she stared back at them. She wasn't going to let them see her cry.

Dad, I saved her, I did. You would be proud of me, Daddy. I won't let them see me cry, but come and bring me home.

The surveillance-team leader bent down and loosened the scarf from under Hannah's chin and gently pulled it off—her head flopped to one side. The blond curls partially covered her peaceful face.

Dominika waited for an hour in the abandoned warehouse, looking out a cracked window down the muddy lane. There were two groups of people down the muddy street, both lit by the headlights of at least four vehicles that had appeared out of nowhere. The first group was holding a man who was bellowing something unintelligible as he was pushed into the backseat of a car. The second group of ten or a dozen men farther down the street were standing in a circle around a shape on the ground. It was too far to see, but when one of the men bent to take off a scarf, Dominika thought she could see a woman's hair.

She had been two warehouses from the actual meeting site spot—not more than one hundred meters—and had flattened herself against the wall when she heard the shouts and engine noises. She saw running figures moving away from her, but the number of car noises all around shocked her, and she squeezed through a gap in a broken chain-link fence and crawled into the corroded bucket of a steam shovel that probably had last been used to excavate the Moscow Canal in 1932. Men and vehicles passed back and forth for about fifteen minutes with Dominika huddled in a ball in a slurry of rainwater and flaking rust. Things quieted down and Dominika was able to peek over the lip of the bucket. She wasn't going anywhere for a while: FSB would leave a car with two men—silent trailers—in the area to see if anybody moved after things quieted down.

Marta and Udranka sat on packing crates near the door. You treated that young American a little hard, Marta said as Udranka tapped her foot. You see how everybody loves you?

Dominika shivered in the bucket and closed her eyes. She didn't know what had happened, but Hannah was supposed to have been there, and Dominika had a dreadful intuition that Hannah was the figure on the ground. The FSB would not knowingly harm a diplomat, but these surveillance men were feral pack hunters when they got the blood scent in their nostrils—the dogs were capable of anything.

Speaking of dogs. From around the corner of the warehouse Dominika saw two red eyes looking at her. They moved closer and became the black muzzle and hunched shoulders of an enormous dog—half dog, half wolf—which no doubt had slipped his leash somewhere in hell. The dog looked at Dominika, its visible breath drifting around its head in the cold air. A bark, a growl, much less an attack, would bring the FSB in a flash, but it was still, watching her with lowered head. Dominika remembered her childhood and what her father used to do with their little dachshund, Gustave, and she held out her hand. The massive dog hesitated and came closer, then closer, and sniffed.

What is your life, you devil? Dominika thought, keeping her hand still. Men's voices echoed off the warehouse walls. *Do they beat you and starve you? Do you hate them as I do? Do they fear you?* The dog looked into her eyes, turned, and shuffled into the darkness, looking back once as if to tell her *S volkami zhit, povolchi vyt,* to live with wolves, you have to howl like a wolf. Dominika silently thanked *Satana*'s dog. The devil had just told her what she had to do.

Benford could not move, could not think, could not speak. He had raved for twelve hours after receiving the call from DCOS Schindler alerting him that COS had gone out on the street to meet DIVA, and Hannah had gone after him. Nate arrived in Washington from Athens that evening in the middle of the crisis. He now sat on the couch in Benford's office, jet-lagged and unshaven. Janice Callahan ferried in cups of coffee and tea, and Margery Salvatore brought containers of homemade *soupe au pistou*—hearty vegetable soup with basil puree—which would hold them over until the cafeteria downstairs opened. Benford's lair filled with the smell of the Provençal comfort food, but no one was comforted—no one could eat.

They waited for word of disaster, for the exultant news on VGTRK, the All-Russia State Television and Radio Broadcasting Company, that the counterintelligence organs of the Federation's intelligence services had unmasked another traitor, a criminal paid by the Main Enemy to betray her country—*Comrades, let's revive the apt Cold War labels, for that is what the Americans are: Russia's Main Enemy*—and was now in custody waiting for the investigation to conclude and the trial to begin. Benford had spoken several times to a shaky-sounding DCOS Moscow asking for updates, but there were none: Neither COS nor Hannah had returned to the embassy; both were now seriously overdue. No news about DIVA. Schindler had prevailed on the consul general to make inquiries with the Russian Foreign Ministry concerning the missing diplomats, but there had been no response.

It had been rough lately for Nate Nash—he was turning the mental pages of an enormous photo album with "This Is Your Seriously Fucked-Up Life" embossed on the cover: He had lost LYRIC (through no fault of his own, but the agent was still lost); his bifurcated lover/agent relationship with Dominika was demented; he had slept with Hannah Archer, the case-officer colleague now missing in Moscow; DIVA had announced her suicidal intention to exfiltrate LYRIC from Russia's Baltic coast despite the fact that the latter was under house arrest for suspicion of espionage; he had been designated by Benford to take charge of an as-yet-unspecified operation to somehow prevent an unidentified mole inside CIA from passing DIVA's identity to the SVR *rezident* in Washington, a grandmotherly necromancer who appeared to be unbeatable on the street; and his Athens DCOS Marty Gable had asked him to reserve some time for a protracted counseling session when Nate returned to Station to discuss his lack of professionalism, his disregard for instructions, and, in Gable's words, his being "a dumbassador from the Republic of Stupid."

Five thousand miles east, Alexei Zyuganov also fumed at his desk in Line KR in Yasenevo. Those swineherds in FSB had blown it last night at the last possible moment—an additional second of restraint and they would have reeled in the Russian skunk the Americans intended to meet in that dismal warehouse district. He was sure of it. And chances were that it would have been the mole, the big fish they were all looking for. Instead they had a diplomatic incident on their hands: The accidental death of the American woman would cost more than one man on the surveillance team his job, and he personally would see that prison time would be tacked on. The blond American was nothing to him—unimportant. But on getting the word, he had hurried to the police morgue in Lyublino in the Southeastern Okrug to examine her belongings—he found only her dip ID card and the commercial thermal scope. A blue, woven cotton bracelet had been cut off her wrist. No meeting notes, no pocket litter that might provide a clue to who she was meeting. He checked the lining and seams of her clothing. He cut into the heels of her snow boots, ripped out the insoles. Nothing. They had lifted the sheet to show him the blue-black, caved-in right side of her body, and he instead looked at the face and had a microsecond of bat-wing doubt: a young woman such as this, operating in the capital, stealing their secrets, recruiting Russians. How many others like her? What sort of opponent was this?

Zyuganov checked his watch. The Foreign Ministry would be informing the American Embassy about Blondie in an hour, after they finished screaming at and slapping the fat face of the CIA chief who had been kept in an FSB office for nearly six hours, covered in dried mud and with snot dripping out of the armadillo he called his nose. His weeping, cringing performance was filmed, including when he made a puddle under his chair. It would play well in a future television documentary. To his credit, he had not admitted anything to the interrogators, and certainly did not confirm what they already knew: that the young girl on the gurney was a CIA officer. The whole evening was a waste.

Messy, inconvenient, incompetent. Zyuganov instinctively knew, however, that this incident would not ruffle the president's feathers. In fact, he would insist on press play. Any evidence of perfidious CIA violating the sovereignty of Russia played into Putin's domestic narrative. Russia must stay strong against the predations of the West. The Cold War never ended. Rebuild Russia's former power and majesty. Putin himself liked to tell the story:

It is discovered that Stalin is alive and living in a cabin in Siberia. A delegation is sent to convince him to return to Moscow, assume power, and restore Russia to greatness. After some reluctance, Stalin agrees to come back. "Okay," he says, "but no Mr. Nice Guy this time."

Zyuganov, in fact, was secretly glad the FSB had not successfully sprung the trap. He wanted to wrap up the mole himself, based on the name TRITON was going to provide to Zarubina in five days' time. He wanted to drag the traitor in chains to Putin only slightly less than he wanted to strap the swine to a table and listen to the hiss of escaping perfumed air as he perforated his thoracic cavity with a surgical trocar. Besides, Zyuganov had become preoccupied with a nascent theory about the mole. A small, niggling idea, delicious to contemplate, impossible to let go of. He was still forming his theory. He would be like a speckled *karakurt*, the venomous steppe spider, tightroping along the web, laying more silk, tips of his little feet on the signal line, waiting for a vibration.

Captain Dominika Egorova, of the elegant stride and blue-eyed ice. She had a spectacular ops history—you might say it transcended luck. She had survived—improbably—attacks by a Spetsnaz assassin, Department Five mechanics, and Eva Buchina. She miraculously had developed the information to nail Korchnoi. Quite remarkable. Her performance regarding the Iran deal—the suggestion regarding the water route through Russia had pleased Putin—to Zyuganov's pinched mind hinted at some sort of coaching. Who knew such geography? And her remarkable intuition about recalling Solovyov from Athens was implausible. Really? On the basis of one interview?

And more recently there were other gossamer tugs of the web. The Athens *rezident* had cabled Line KR congratulations on Egorova's successful investigation. A fawning *rezident* wrote Zyuganov that he regretted he didn't have the opportunity to entertain the captain more, but he understood the preferences of a counterintelligence inspector. Curious, Zyuganov had called Athens on the secure phone to discover that Egorova had chosen to stay not at the compound, but in an unknown outside hotel. With the exception of a few Russian Embassy reception evenings, Egorova had been out-of-pocket every night for two weeks. Not an infraction, but irregular. *How could one explain all the suspicious factors? What was this busty ex-ballerina doing every night? Should he ask her? No, better not to telegraph his interest. TRITON and Zarubina would supply the answer soon enough.*

There was another stone in his shoe. Zyuganov caught a fleeting interaction between Egorova and his deputy, Yevgeny, in the corridor outside his office. Egorova was leaving the conference room and Yevgeny made way for her in the doorway, bowing slightly at the waist in comic-opera butler style. That was not so much—Yevgeny was a hairy clown in front of women—but Zyuganov was interested, very interested, to see Egorova flash a smile at him. Zyuganov knew nothing about flirting, or courtship, or seduction, but other synapses fired, inky thoughts that his busty celebrity employee was working on Yevgeny, that he was being flanked, that she threatened him.

Egorova's most-favored status with Putin was the ultimate screaming outrage. Zyuganov gnashed his teeth at the thought of it. He had rounded up spies. He had handled the Persians. In fact, he had done as much to secure the Iran deal as anyone. Govormarenko had said so himself, had mentioned it to Putin. So why was she favored? When he became Zarubina's deputy director in SVR, he would be shown more respect. *And by the time I become deputy,* he thought, *Putin will have moved on from Egorova, and then her fortunes will be what* I *decide: SVR advisor to the Northern Fleet at Severomorsk; intelligence administrator in Grozny, Chechnya; adjutant at the Kon Institute, back to Sparrow School. Let her spend the rest of her career demonstrating fellatio to hayseed students from the republics.* Then he remembered: *If she turns out* not *to be the mole.*

Zyuganov would have been apoplectic if he had known about Putin's invitation to her for some sort of power weekend near Petersburg. He would have been additionally outraged if he knew that Dominika had persuaded Yevgeny—Sparrow style—to sign an authorization chit for a pool car for Egorova to drive the six hundred kilometers to Strelna on the M10. Yevgeny increasingly was seeing the light: Having Dominika as an ally was the smart bet, so he took the risk of not telling Zyuganov.

Word came to Benford and his coterie simultaneously from the Ops Center and State Department wire in a treble rush of body-blow news. The Foreign Ministry informed the consul general of the US Embassy in Moscow that First Secretary Vernon Throckmorton had been detained by Federal Security Service officers on suspicion of espionage but had invoked diplomatic immunity. He was free to return to the embassy, but the Ministry was issuing PNG expulsion orders designating Mr. Throckmorton persona non grata. He was given forty-eight hours to leave Russia.

The second piece of bad news was in fact the absence of news: DIVA had not responded to three separate SRAC messages loaded by a dyspeptic DCOS Schindler urgently calling for a sign-of-life reply. She could be home sleeping, recovering from what must have been a nightmare evening of a busted meeting—Janice, Dante, and Nate had lived it, knew the freezing cold gripping the legs, felt the sweat running underneath the layers of clothing, remembered the sound of men and vehicles coming closer from behind, the sides, and all around. Or DIVA could be in a chair in some overheated office with sooty venetian blinds carelessly canted, handcuffed, and stripped to her underwear, while a rotation team of FSB officers—little sly men, or brutal brawlers, or wet-lipped matrons—softened her up before the vertigo ride in the back of a van to Lefortovo or Butyrka for the real pros to begin. These would include the alligator-clip, car-battery fraternity of interrogators, chemists, doctors, and psychologists, a *Matryoshka* collection of tormentors, like wooden nesting dolls, each monster emerging out of the previous monster, each succeeding horror worse than the previous one until the final horror. Which, Benford knew, would be Zyuganov.

The third piece of bad news was the worst. Dante was summoned to the Ops Center after midnight to pick up a statement off the wire—impersonal, dismissive, with the familiar trace of Soviet irony—from the protocol department of the Russian Foreign Ministry: *Third Secretary Hannah Archer of the US Embassy died in a traffic accident late in the evening of the 10th. Due to inattention on her part, she was struck by a vehicle in rainy conditions. The US Embassy is requested to inform the Ministry regarding the disposition of the remains.*

Dante sat with his head in his hands. Margery and Janice were silent, red-eyed, sniffling. Benford sighed. "She was an exceptional young woman," he said softly. He looked up at Nate. "What are you prepared to do?" he said. Everybody in the room turned toward him.

"I'm going to make it rain on Zarubina," said Nate quietly. "She's not getting Domi's name." Benford stared at him in silence, and Nate looked him right back in the eyes.

"Simon, spin up Red Route Two," said Nate. "DIVA's coming. And no one's going to stop her."

SOUPE AU PISTOU

Heat olive oil and sauté diced onions, leeks, and celery in a Dutch oven. Add trimmed chard or kale leaves, cooked white beans and chicken stock to cover, bring to a moderate boil, then add chopped tomato, diced potato, small pasta (anelli or ditalini), diced zucchini, and chopped stems of chard or kale. Simmer until the ingredients are cooked and tender. Season aggressively. Spoon pistou (process garlic, salt, basil leaves, chopped tomato, olive oil, and grated Gruyère or Parmesan cheese into a thick sauce) into the soup when serving.

34

Yevgeny told Dominika at the morning staff meeting about the young woman—suspect CIA officer Hannah Archer—who had been struck and killed by a surveillance car in Lyubertsy District the night before. FSB was keeping the accident quiet for the time being. Dominika's mind clicked off as she collected her files, and she heard herself say something offhand, like "I hope they roast the stupid idiot who did it" and got back to her office, sat down behind her desk, fought tears, and tried to breathe.

Udranka called to her from the corner of the room. We're all the Kremlin Mermaids, dushka, *we're all with you. And Hannah walked through the door and smiled at her.*

She had always been able to control her outward emotions, even as she built, refined, and polished the soaring rage that had become part of her. The death of Hannah rocked her as much as Udranka's murder had, but with the added pain of knowing the spirited, devoted, brave little nature girl had saved her life last night. She closed her eyes and asked Nate for help, asked why she, Dominika, brought death. And there was an old soldier waiting in his apartment for the interrogations to resume, a process most certainly to conclude with *vyshaya mera,* the highest punishment. She had put him in the cellars, and she was going to get him out—tonight.

As Dominika left work, a new image came to her, gentle and fair, yet terrible and deadly. She thought of her grandmother's stories about the *Rusalki,* the mythic Russian water nymphs, the lovely, long-haired mermaid demons who were the spirits of young women, dead before their time. They would sit along the shore and sing, and lure men close, to drag them to the bottom.

Dominika knew she would have the spirits of Marta, Udranka, and Hannah riding with her. *We'll sit on the shore, sisters, and sing, and then you'll be able to rest.* Then she thought, *Hurry up, you're losing your mind.* And the sweet nymphs in her mind's eye turned into something with canine red eyes living in the freezing coal-black of a warehouse. *And you can come, too; we all go together.* Whatever was going on in that overheated brain and anguished breast, Yevgeny saw it in her face and did not say good night, much less suggest a farewell session of slap-and-tickle before she left. Zyuganov also saw her walk past his office door, and his schitzy receptors registered that she looked different—suffused with something—another tantalizing anomaly for his Egorova-the-mole theory, another furry fact for the dung beetle to roll back to the brood hall and munch on.

Nine o'clock. Her hands shook as she washed the single plate and teacup with painted sparrows on it. She couldn't exactly remember packing the small overnight case, but somehow the high heels went in, along with the dress with the plunging neckline. She checked the tool kit for Red Route Two and the test lights winked green; she looked around her apartment wondering if she would ever be back, and saw her bed, neatly made—she hated what she had done in it—but she was going to pull this off and send them to hell. The dark-blue Lada Priora from the motor pool had a stick shift and smelled like hulled pistachios; Dominika ground the gears until she got the feel for it. Kutuzofsky Prospekt was crowded, but the MKAD was a belching, streaming mass of evening traffic and she couldn't roll the windows down to breathe—she couldn't remember breathing—but she got off onto M10 and then onto Yubileynyy, then took a right turn onto Lavochinka, LYRIC's street, and found the building directly across from Dubki Park and the golden domes of the Church of the Epiphany in Khimki, walls walrus-tusk white, and found the apartment block with the covered cement entrance painted a faded pink. Dominika went up the stairs, past apartment doors, listening to the televisions and the crying babies, her heart pounded in her mouth, her jaw throbbed, and her vision was a gray cone as the door opened. The bored police officer guarding the old man had a flat, ugly face and lank dirty hair and wore a track suit. LYRIC was visible in the living room behind him, in old felt slippers, sitting on a couch, newspapers on the floor. Dominika's arm moved before her brain willed it, aiming at the hollow of the meaty neck, and the policeman staggered back one step, clutching his smashed trachea, then collapsed. Dominika stepped over his strangling blue face, and General Solovyov, looking shrunken, put on some pants, shoes, and topcoat—no discussion—and her voice was someone else's, and she shook him then pulled him, ignoring the slack-eyed stare on the floor, down the stairs. She dragged the seat belt across the old man's chest, smelling sour fear, and she had to backtrack, then got onto M10, sometimes four lanes, usually two, the trucks had trailers with bald tires, the bastards didn't ease over to let her pass, so peek and floor it, engine whining, over and over and over. The general was silent, not asking, looking straight ahead, her responsibility now, eleven o'clock and the muddy little towns, Zelenograd, Solnechnogorsk, Klin, Novozavidovsky, Tver, and Dominika asked him how much time; they probably had another hour before the relief guard discovered the body. The general started rambling, honor and the Red Army and Russia, and he called himself a fool, he knew it now, an old *zhopa,* an old asshole, and he asked who she was, and cried remembering his children, and thanked her over and over, and his panicked green words filled the dark of the car, with the center line painted not exactly straight, and the oncoming headlights filled her eyeballs, and the rearview mirror was clear and dark, and the towns stopped; now came the vastness of the *Rodina*, spruce and pine trunks in the headlights, flashing metronome steady, midnight and the land flattened to the horizon, the floor of the sky, stars like dust, and Dominika's eyes started to blur. She shook her head, and the hound loped on the road in front of her, looking back at her with red eyes, and she heard Udranka laughing somewhere out there in the dark fields, and red dog eyes became the flashing red lights of a GAI traffic militia on the shoulder, the undercarriage of a truck visible in the ditch, a cop waving them through, no radio alerts yet. The road kept unpeeling itself into the black vastness ahead; she looked at the general and Hannah was sitting there instead, with her hands in her lap and the wind in her hair, and Dominika caught it before they drifted into the trees. The general helped her stay awake, with cold night air and Soviet patriotic songs, "*Katyusha*" and "*Svyaschennaya Voyna* (The Sacred War)," sung in a roaring bass, then hiccups from singing so hard, then laughing, two spies hurtling through the night with wet cheeks and the King of Hell's dog in the headlights, loping tirelessly as they ghosted through Veliky Novgorod, at one o'clock, two hundred kilometers to go. Then the singing and remembering were too much, he wanted to turn around, sniffling, then silence and the city glow of Saint Petersburg, where the roadblocks would be. Two o'clock, and Dominika got off the M10 onto the KAD to avoid going into the city, the early morning ring road was empty. Now she had to watch her mirrors; it would be here, jeeps across the roadway, they'd both be cooked now. Three o'clock, and the little blue car was on the Petergofskoye, the A121, along the tsar's long-ago palace coast; there were glimpses of the Gulf of Finland and tang of ocean, and they were past the lighted gates of Constantine Palace—the president was in—then the darkened Peterhof Palace, massive white in the distance, then the domes of the Oranienbaum Palace—nothing in the mirrors—now under the KAD causeway. She checked the kilometers—exactly two point four said Benford—and the marshy coast opened up on the right, water flat as silver glass, and she turned at a squat billboard onto the pitch-black beach road, windows down and headlights playing over the riprap boulders and the stony beach and the sea grass. Now she turned the lights off, pulled the hand brake to crunch to a stop; it was nearly four o'clock. And where the water was clear up to the beach, opposite the boulder with two vertical slashes in red paint, was the start of Red Route Two.

General Solovyov—and his interrogation and conviction for espionage—was Zyuganov's responsibility. The relief guard had called in at midnight reporting that Solovyov's apartment was empty except for the corpse of *starshina* Bogdanov—the sergeant's windpipe had been crushed. Zyuganov was informed an hour later and came as close to losing his mind as he ever had. He was in his office within a half hour, raving into the phone about CIA action teams loose in Moscow. He screamed high-pitched at the SVR watch center duty officer to issue Moscow-wide bulletins describing Solovyov to police and *militsiya* units throughout the city. Yevgeny, unshaven and sleepy, was told to connect with Moscow Police's Main Office of the Interior for Transport and Special Transportation and *this instant* order a 100 percent watch at Domodedovo, Sheremetyevo, and Vnukovo International Airports and at Bykovo regional airport. Zyuganov woke up the director of the FTS, the Federal Customs Service, and demanded that his Department of Contraband Control at the airports X-ray without exception all large outgoing diplomatic pouches from the American, British, Canadian, Australian, and New Zealand embassies (the Five Eyes allies had been in league against Russia since the October Revolution in 1917). When told by the Customs director—himself a former KGB crony of the president—that diplomatic pouches were inviolable, Zyuganov impoliticly threatened to smash his testicles with a Moscow telephone book, and the director said, *Idi na khui,* fuck off, and hung up.

Zyuganov was breaking crockery all around town, issuing orders and making threats; the *siloviki* wire, the crony network, even at this hour started buzzing about the missteps, the potential colossal failure of the little SVR ghoul whom no one liked or trusted anyway. Careers—and not just careers—were in real jeopardy when such gossip floated up and eventually reached the Kremlin, like an embolism reaching the brain. Zyuganov knew he was making a show of himself, but he couldn't let Solovyov escape. He was already exhausted, but the sandstorm in his head abated for a second and he could think. It wasn't the local CIA station; they had lost one of their own and were leaderless at the moment. No, CIA would direct one of their *assets* to spirit Solovyov out of Russia. Would they risk their best asset—the Mole—to save this old man? They might: The Americans historically had gone to great and expensive lengths to rescue lost assets, something his own service did not bother about.

And what kind of person could deliver such a devastating blow against a trained police officer—Bogdanov had been a shot-put champion in the police league—killing him without a struggle? Egorova, trained in *Sistema;* Egorova, who killed Spetsnaz operatives and the unbeatable Buchina; Egorova, the ballerina who was mesmerizing the president. Egorova, his nemesis. He screamed for Yevgeny, ordered him to call Egorova at home and tell her to report to the Center instantly, but his hirsute deputy would not look him in the eye. Something was going on. Zyuganov recalled Egorova smiling at Yevgeny—was he covering for her? As Yevgeny sweated in a chair in Zyuganov's office, an assistant called Egorova's apartment—no answer at two thirty in the morning.

Ten minutes of roaring questions at a terrified Yevgeny netted no results, but the interrogator in Zyuganov sensed that there was much to find out. The dwarf's instincts, already aroused, now stood on hind legs and howled at the moon. Taking a steel spring baton out of a bottom desk drawer, Zyuganov wheeled on Yevgeny. The panicked assistant in the outer office quietly left her desk and ran down the hallway—she had no desire to hear the coming attractions. Zyuganov was aware only of an itchy impatience to learn what was happening—he was aware of a clock ticking down, of criminals making their escape. He swung and brought the barrel of the baton down on the chair's armrest, splintering four of the five long metacarpal bones in Yevgeny's left hand. The hairy baboon screamed like, well, a hairy baboon, clutched his ruined hand, and doubled over. Zyuganov yanked him upright and brought the black steel spring down on the top of Yevgeny's left thigh, creating a greenstick fracture of the femur just above the knee. Yevgeny grunted like a beast and collapsed off the chair onto the floor. Like an insect that can lift ten times its own weight, Zyuganov bodily hauled Yevgeny back up into the chair, where his protégé sat with spittle on his chin, his head lolling. Zyuganov brought his face close to Yevgeny's, inhaled the familiar, delectable scents, and whispered, *Pora spat', polnoch; skoro zapojut petuhi,* it's time to go to bed; it's midnight and roosters will sing soon. The Lubyanka Lullaby.

Through the spittle and tears and snot, Yevgeny talked. "We were intimate," he said.

Zyuganov shook Yevgeny's head by the hair. "Pig. Intimate with who?"

"Captain Egorova. Dominika," whispered Yevgeny.

Of course, thought Zyuganov. "What did you tell her?"

"Office matters. She was in Line KR, after all."

Zyuganov used the shank of the baton to lift Yevgeny's chin. "*Mudilo,* motherfucker, what office matters?"

Yevgeny stared at Zyuganov, not speaking, daring to resist, and the baton was snapped on Yevgeny's cheekbone, one-quarter force, just enough to get the ears ringing and the eyes watering. "What office matters?" he repeated.

"Zarubina," panted Yevgeny, "TRITON, Solovyov's house arrest."

More came out. He had authorized a car for her to drive to Saint Petersburg to visit family—fearing additional demonic ministrations, Yevgeny did not mention the invitation from the president. Zyuganov straightened, exultant. This was as good as confirmation for him that she was the mole, that Solovyov was with her, that she probably intended to hand him over to CIA officers in Petersburg—there were cruise ships, ferries, trains to Finland and the Baltics, innumerable flights. He left Yevgeny sobbing in the chair, picked up the phone, and called the SVR dispatcher. It was a matter of seconds to establish which pool car Egorova had been issued. Zyuganov barked orders to activate the transponder in the vehicle via encoded phone—all staff cars had tracking beacons installed to prevent their unauthorized private use (unless of course the dispatcher's palm had been greased).

Zyuganov then called the Big House—the Saint Petersburg SVR regional office—and forced the duty officer to wake up the chief. It was three in the morning, but Zyuganov did not apologize: Moreover, he was taking an immense bureaucratic risk in demanding all the resources for a full-out sweep search for Egorova's vehicle. He was almost certain she was heading to Saint Petersburg. The chief, another Putin crony, agreed reluctantly—a spy case was nothing to fool with, so he'd comply—but he resolved to report Zyuganov's unhinged behavior to the director in Moscow and, given the opportunity, to the president during the breakfast reception at Strelna later this morning.

In the meantime, police and *militsiya* mobile units would be alerted by radio, the car, plates, and passengers' descriptions broadcast widely. Additional teams would roll the minute the drivers reported for work and, most important, two stubby, twin-boomed, twin-tailed Kamov Ka226 militia helicopters would be airborne within thirty minutes. The midnight-blue aircraft were equipped with standard receivers that could detect the beacon signal from Egorova's vehicle at a distance of two miles and an altitude of one thousand feet. It would take time for them to quarter the city airspace, to cover the urban sprawl around the horseshoe-shaped Neva Bay, but once locked onto the beacon signal, moving or stationary, vectoring ground units could converge in a matter of minutes. Zyuganov closed his eyes, picturing blue lights all around the car, Egorova and Solovyov facedown on the roadway, hands cuffed behind them.

Zyuganov asked the chief to keep him informed. He declared that this manhunt was the culmination of a protracted and highly classified mole hunt that would ultimately conclude with the arrest of two dangerous traitors. And Saint Petersburg would share in the credit, and foreign enemies would be thwarted, and the Federation would remain strong and inviolate, under the inspired leadership of the president. The Petersburg chief purred something into the phone, an exchange between them of *vranyo,* the Russian bureaucratic lie—the chief knew Zyuganov was lying, and Zyuganov knew he knew, and both of them didn't blink an eye. Zyuganov hung up the phone, incrementally placated. He might have all this under control.

Yevgeny was sitting tilted in his chair, head forward, a thread of saliva from his mouth to the floor. Yevgeny's disloyalty to the Service and to his country was monstrous, but his betrayal of Zyuganov personally stirred up in him all the noxious, misanthropic, adult-diaper issues that his mother—SVR doyenne Ekaterina Zyuganova, now political advisor in the Paris *rezidentura*—had palliated in his early career by tucking her son into the Lubyanka job. But he was chief now, chief of Line KR, and on his own, responsible for the imminent capture of two CIA agents in Russia. He was partner with the genius Zarubina in the conduct of the massively productive TRITON case. He wondered whether Egorova had reported about the case to Washington. No matter, once an illegals officer began handling TRITON the Americans would never find him.

And he would be running SVR with Zarubina, and the Service would multiply and prosper, and the Main Enemy would thrash hopelessly against them, and other enemies would quail, and fractious former republics would come back into the fold, and a new Russian hegemon would be born with Vladimir Putin in charge, stronger than before, and traitors—he looked down at the back of Yevgeny's wooly head as his doubled-over deputy quietly retched on the carpet—*traitors like this,* thought Zyuganov, hearing his own shrill voice as he brought the baton in a singing arc down on the back of Yevgeny's skull, *pig manure like this will be eliminated.*

They ate in moonlight off the hood of the car, soft *pyrahi* buns with blood-red savory beet filling. *Nathaniel would tease about the beets,* she thought. Dominika then registered that this would be the last authentic Russian meal LYRIC would ever have, and it would be her last *nonprison* Russian meal too, if the United States Navy did not appear in approximately twelve minutes. At exactly seven minutes after four in the morning, she dug the radio out of the pack and stood on the boulder above the water, a statuesque *Rusalka* mermaid (despite the black jeans, sweater, and black running shoes) about to serenade the moon. The empty sea was a slab of smooth slate, the horizon in the gulf a silvery line. Dominika's elegant hands with square-cut nails—the same hands that six hours ago had snapped the hyoid bone in a Moscow policeman's throat—held the radio and depressed the transmit button of the jet-black, cigarette-pack-sized AN/PRC-90 modified by CIA, transmitting an encrypted very-low-frequency (VLF) trinumeric code to the British Ministry of Defense's Skynet 5 satellite in geosynchronous earth orbit at fifty-three degrees meridian east, twenty-two thousand miles above Franz Josef Land archipelago in the Barents Sea. DIVA did not know any of this.

When the Red Routes Two, Three, and Four operational exfiltration plans were being formulated three years earlier, Simon Benford had reluctantly agreed to partner with the British MOD and Secret Intelligence Service (MI6) to take advantage of UK satellites' footprints over Russia's northern tier and Arctic latitudes. After all, the Brits exfiltrated agents too; allies could share capabilities. But negotiations had stalled in London when Benford demanded nothing less than *instantaneous* message relays from the Brit satlink, dryly noting that MI6's performance during previous crisis operations recalled "a dead heat in a dirigible race." That prompted the patrician Oxonian who looked after operations at "Six" to call Benford a tossbag, but since Benford did not know he was being called a fuckhead, the exchange was forgotten and the liaison negotiations were successfully concluded.

Skynet 5's microprocessors received DIVA's trinumeric blast, read it, reencrypted it, and transmitted a different trinumeric code in 1.6 seconds. The VLF transmission from the satellite arrived simultaneously in the Doughnut—Government Communications Headquarters (GCHQ) in Cheltenham—where automated equipment instantly forwarded the "execute" code to MI6 London Headquarters in Vauxhall Cross and to CIA Headquarters in Langley, Virginia, then to the thirty-five-meter buoyant wire antenna trailed behind the forty-foot US Navy shallow water combat submersible (SWCS) ghosting at a depth of five fathoms, one thousand yards from where Dominika and LYRIC were standing on the beach.

In two minutes, as if to heighten the drama, the minisub surfaced smoothly, directly in the shimmering path of moonlight. It was motionless on the dead-calm sea: The SWCS looked like the smooth gleaming back of a sleeping baby whale; only two feet of freeboard showed above the surface. Dominika dug into her pack and took out a plastic square the size of a matchbox, flipped a tiny toggle, and set it on the rock. The Pegasus cube began showing brilliant infrared light, invisible to the naked eye, in intermittent green-flashing and steady-on modes. Dominika looked through a short IR spotting scope and saw lightning-bright green flashes from the submarine. She handed the scope to LYRIC, who looked through it at the submersible and grunted, impressed.

A smaller dark blob separated from the SWCS and silently headed toward them—the inflatable's bow pushed a white curl of water that chuckled under the raft, the only sound it made over the nearly imperceptible whine of its electric trolling outboard. A single hunched figure sat in the back of the craft. It would take several minutes to reach the beach, so Dominika got busy: She packed the transmitter and the IR scope into the backpack, along with the IR beacon light; all this equipment would go with LYRIC into the submarine. There would be no trace of General Solovyov; the *Rusalki* would have carried him forever beneath the sea. The little raft was still a ways off, and Dominika had a dread feeling that it was taking too much time. Every minute saved would be critical—she had to dress for the president's weekend garden party—so she walked back to the trunk of the car, unlocked it, opened her suitcase, shucked off her shoes and socks, yanked off her sweater, and peeled off her jeans. She shivered in the night air, barefoot and in her bra and panties. Then she heard the sound of a helicopter somewhere to the southeast.

PYRAHI—STUFFED BUNS WITH BEETS

Bring milk, shortening, and butter just to a boil, then cool. Mix sugar and yeast in water and let stand. Beat eggs, salt, and sugar and incorporate with the cooled milk and yeast, then add flour to form a soft dough. Flatten the dough into small rounds, spoon filling (grated beets, sugar, and salt sautéed in butter) into the center, and fold up the four corners of dough and pinch closed, leaving a small slit on top. Bake in a medium-high oven until golden brown, and serve with melted butter, sour cream, or yogurt.

35

Zyuganov sat in his office with three officers from the SVR administrative and security sections. The shrouded body of Yevgeny had been carried out on a canvas stretcher a half hour ago, and Zyuganov had foamed at the mouth while describing to the men how Yevgeny had been in league with the CIA mole he, Zyuganov, was minutes away from apprehending. Yevgeny was doubtless a subagent dishing information to the opposition and, when confronted by Zyuganov, had panicked and made a move to attack his boss.

"Attack? With what?" said one of the security men. Not even Zyuganov's reputation as a wet-boy executioner, inheritor of the speckled majesty of the *Vozhd,* the multilimbed monster that lent its name to Uncle Joe Stalin, could confer immunity in the case of unjustified murder committed inside the walls of the Center. To be sure, justification could come in the space of a fifteen-second exculpating phone call from the Kremlin, *or in the microsecond after the triumphant arrest of the CIA mole in their midst,* thought Zyuganov.

"With this instrument," said Zyuganov, holding up a half-inch, curved surgical needle. "He was trying to slash me."

"How is it you have such a thing in your office, sir?" said one of the men.

"What difference at this point does it make?" said Zyuganov, pounding his fist. The white phone on his desk trilled—the secure high-frequency Vey-Che line. It was the SVR chief in Saint Petersburg calling to report that one of the militia helicopters reported a signal to the southeast of the city, in a vector essentially along the line of the M10 from Moscow. Zyuganov checked his watch: four thirty. It had to be Egorova coming up from Moscow; they'd have her in the bag within the hour. Zyuganov barked orders that police and militia vehicles be directed to converge on the M10, setting up on all exits to the A120, the outer ring road just after the town of Tosno. He put the phone down and looked at the three *zadnitsi,* these three admin assholes, knowing they'd heard every word, and told them to get out of his office. They hesitated, then rose to leave, but one security man mumbled something about continuing the interview at another time. *Yes, your dismissal-from-the-service interview when I'm deputy chief,* thought Zyuganov, his brain buzzing with excitement.

He had not considered before now that as deputy of SVR he would be able to compile and maintain a list of people who displeased, angered, or otherwise annoyed him. He could have video feeds from the cellars at Lefortovo and Butyrka piped into his office. He would be driven to the Kremlin to have tea with the president. He shivered deliciously as he recalled the sound of dropped melon and the yielding resistance of bone when he hit Yevgeny with the steel baton. He thought of the sights and sounds that would accompany the upcoming interrogations of Egorova and Solovyov. Then the phone trilled again.

"Goose chase," the Petersburg chief said over the phone. "The air unit went right down on the deck as signal strength increased, and almost got sucked into the pressure wave of the Sapsan high-speed train from Moscow. The bastard runs at two hundred and fifty kilometers an hour."

Zyuganov swore. "What about the signal?" he said.

"No cars on the road," said the chief. "I woke up the Rail Ministry; the engine has a transponder in the nose to track the train. The helicopter was homing in on that. Lucky they didn't fly into—"

"What the fuck is the train doing on the track at four in the morning?" raved Zyuganov. "It's supposed to be in Petersburg at midnight."

"I asked about that too," said the chief. "Five-hour departure delay in Moscow. Something on the tracks in the middle of nowhere. It's bad luck. The helicopter is returning to the field to check for damage. I can tell you the pilot was really shaken."

"Fuck the pilot," yelled Zyuganov. "I want that bastard to continue to search. Find that car. I know she's out there." Zyuganov banged down the phone. *Sapsan,* a peregrine falcon chasing a Sparrow; *eto prosto pizdets,* this is totally, elementally, fucked up.

When Dominika heard the helicopter thrashing around in the night sky somewhere to the south she dropped everything, ran around the car, and stuffed the last of the equipment into the kit bag. She took the docile general by the elbow and helped him over the rocks to the small sandy beach, willing the rubber raft to hurry, hoping that the old man would get off this beach, willing the helicopter to stay away. According to the exfil drill, Dominika helped the general off with his topcoat, which she also stuffed into the kit bag. In Athens there had been discussion of leaving LYRIC's shoes and coat on the beach, eventually to be found and to suggest that the desperate fugitive had committed suicide by walking into the sea, but Dominika had convinced Benford that this would be *inostrannyy,* too foreign, un-Russian. Better that he should dematerialize without a trace.

The rubber raft grounded on the beach, the man stepped over the rubber gunwale, and Gary Cooper walked toward them—at least that's what the six-foot-two Navy SEAL looked like to Dominika. Petty Officer Second-Class Luke Proulx of SEAL Team Two was dressed in black Nomex overalls and carried a stubby matte black MP7 submachine gun across his chest on a one-point sling. As he approached Dominika and the general he pulled a knit watch cap off his head. *Of course he would have blond hair,* thought Dominika. And a red halo that turned the color of chilled rosé in the moonlight. *Naturally.*

"General. Ma'am," said Proulx in unaccented Russian. "Good morning." *Perfect Russian, and of course he would also have blue eyes,* thought Dominika, only then realizing she was in her underwear—Simone Perele from Paris, but still . . . The SEAL didn't give the faintest indication that he saw her nakedness.

"I heard a helicopter a minute ago," said Dominika, resolved not to be embarrassed. "You must leave immediately." Petty Officer Proulx nodded, put his cap back on, and took the kit bag from Dominika.

"Ready, sir?" he said, shifting his weapon and moving to the rubber raft. Without his coat, General Solovyov was shivering in the cool night air. He turned to Dominika, stood straight, and saluted. He silently mouthed *Spasibo,* thank you, then turned and climbed into the raft, which the SEAL had pushed off the sand and was holding steady in shallow water. Luke Proulx looked back at Dominika, smiled, and whispered *Udacha,* good luck. He bounded into the raft, started the silent motor, and headed out for the wallowing black log of the submarine in the moon path. Dominika was shivering now too as she watched the silver bow wave spread in a vee across the flagstone sea. She was astounded to register a "Hey, wait for me" stuck behind her lips, but knew she would never be able to go.

"Stupay s Bogom," she whispered. Go with God. She turned quickly and clambered over the rocks, then dove into her suitcase in the open trunk of her car. Dress over her head—a gray scrunched tunic-drape cocktail number—pointed toe Fendi stilettos onto her feet—she had to wipe her soles clean of sand—a string of onyx stone beads around her neck. She slammed the trunk and got inside the car, smoothing her upswept hair and putting on a touch of lipstick. She wanted the effect of arriving at the Strelna mansion as if she had been driving all night, dressed somewhat inappropriately for a breakfast buffet, or whatever beastly Fall-of-Rome entertainment these *kabany,* these tusker boars who ran her country, who lounged and ate and drank and stole Russia's wealth out of the mouths of her people, had in mind—provided, of course, that the Tsar approved.

She looked out at the empty ocean; the silver sea was flat. The vessel had slipped beneath the waves; the *Rusalki* mermaids had gotten their man. Perhaps now the spirits of Udranka and Marta and Hannah could rest—how Hannah would have enjoyed this early-morning operation on this pebbly beach. Dominika gripped the steering wheel and fought fatigue, emotion, longing. She longed for Nate, to see him and talk to him, and to have him take her in his arms and just hold her—at least for a while before they fell into bed. The sound of helicopter rotors was audible somewhere in the distance, growing louder, and Dominika started moving fast down the beach road—headlights out, *Don't clip one of the boulders, I hope it's too dark to see a dust plume*—and squealed onto the A121 back toward Petersburg, past the dark palaces, no traffic at 5:00 a.m. and her mirrors were clear.

The rotor noise was louder as she pulled into the entrance to the Constantine Palace and Strelna conference facility. The gate guard looked into the sky as he walked around to her window and shined the light in her eyes.

"Get that light out of my face," snapped Dominika. "Captain Egorova of the *Sluzhba Vneshney Razvedki*, SVR. I'm expected."

Sitting in the SWCS was like being a fragile and somewhat insignificant component in a cramped steel tube stuffed with conduit and pipes and cable ties and digital displays. Petty Officer Proulx had helped LYRIC squeeze through a hatch on the dorsal surface of the SWCS and eased him into a nylon webbing seat, buckled a harness over his shoulders and across his stomach, then released a latch and slid the seat on tracks backward to click and lock against stops in the third position. After pulling the sea cocks on the raft—once inflated it could not possibly fit back into the submersible—and watching it settle underwater by the heavier stern, Proulx slipped through the hatch and into the second seat, putting the MP7 on safe and stowing his weapon in a scabbard beneath his seat. He stuffed the bag with the exfil equipment in a side locker, then hit a toggle to close the hatch, which he then manually dogged with a hand crank. Their ears popped as the hatch sealed shut and the cabin pressurized.

Proulx turned in his seat—no easy feat in the cramped space—and took a pair of headphones off a small hook and handed them to the general. He put on his own headset and adjusted the bud mike across his cheek.

"You okay, sir?" said Proulx. The general nodded and whispered "Da" into the mike. Proulx passed a plastic squeeze bottle he took out of a becket on the side of the seat. "Here, sir, drink this. It gets pretty hot and dry in here." The mildly fruit-flavored water had a low dose of benzodiazepine to reduce anxiety, relax the muscles, and make sleep possible. The "benzo cocktail" was standard kit for maritime exfil ops.

"Better than the motherfucking wet-pig boats we had to drive before," said Master Chief Petty Officer Mike Gore over the headset, sitting ahead of Proulx in the nose. The hulking and dyspeptic Chief Gore was at the controls. "C'mon, let's get out of here; shallow water gives me the shits," he said. The men were sitting like a three-man bobsled crew, in single file, legs slightly bent, knees against the backs of the seats ahead. There was a sound of gurgling water that enveloped them, and a slight sensation of sinking. The only ghostly light in the stuffy compartment came from LED displays.

"General, you want to listen to a little music?" said Proulx into his mike. "How about some Tchaikovsky?" It had been Benford's suggestion that they have Russian classical music on hand, music that could be silenced if the boat's sonar detected surface units anywhere nearby. The SWCS perceptibly started moving forward, a small hum came from the engine compartment bulkhead behind their seats, and the entire submersible suddenly banked like an aircraft and took a steep vertigo-inducing downward angle.

Fifteen minutes later, Proulx glanced at a small piece of polished metal attached to the overhead like a rearview mirror and saw that LYRIC's head was back against the padded headrest, his eyes closed. Proulx switched off LYRIC's headset and reached forward, tapping Master Chief Gore on the shoulder.

"So the landing zone is clear and this angel in her underwear is on the beach with the old guy—I mean Ingrid Bergman meets Jane Russell. Couldn't be true, Master Chief; shit, I expected Spetsnaz to come out of the sea grass." Gore grunted into his mouth mike.

"Proulx, the next hop, you sit offshore, and I'll take the inflatable in. Fucking CIA running porn stars in Russia. I gotta get a job with them." The two SEALs were silent for a few minutes. "The old guy okay?" said Gore. Proulx nodded.

"Yeah, he's out," said Proulx.

"Okay," said Gore. "Enough of Pyotr Ilyich; give me some ZZ Top."

Five hours later the SEAL SWCS eased up astern of the US Navy amphibious landing ship LPD-24, the USS *Arlington,* which was participating in a US Sixth Fleet antisubmarine warfare exercise with the Estonian and Latvian navies. The *Arlington* was slowly steaming in a racetrack ASW course west of Suursaari Island in the Gulf of Finland, 120 kilometers west of the exfil beach. The SWCS was floated into the *Arlington*'s flooded well deck during a prolonged squall that reduced visibility to zero. LYRIC was out and safe.

Dominika followed the guard jeep with the rotating yellow light down a broad avenue, the palace looming to the left, then in a wide curve past administrative buildings and the multistory hotel that accommodated conference attendees, through a park of trees and well-tended lawns, a fountain, a baroque gingerbread house with a double-eagle medallion on the peak of the roof and through another gate with the candy-cane barrier already raised. They passed modern, boxy two-story mansions with light-green mansard roofs, one after another. Dominika counted ten or twelve, and there were others behind these, all of them dark and sitting naked in a park devoid of trees and crisscrossed with cement walkways. These were the VIP cottages reserved for heads of state during international gatherings at the Palace of Congresses State Complex, right on the shore. The Gulf of Finland was visible in the growing light, and Dominika wondered what President Putin would say if he knew there was a US Navy minisubmarine out there under the surface, carrying a Russian military officer to safety in the West, a two-star general who had been a reporting source of CIA. Would he break a bloodstained canine gnashing his teeth?

They pulled into the circular drive of the last of the cottages—it was brightly lit. A dozen other cars were parked in a small contiguous lot. Of the eighteen mansions, this was the closest to the sea. A butler in white coat came out of the house to take Dominika's pitiful suitcase inside. Another attendant stood to park the car. Dominika dully realized that the ripple-soled shoes in her bag most likely had beach sand on them, as surely did the floor mats of the car. Nothing she could do about it now. As they climbed the shallow steps of the mansion a stubby blue helicopter roared overhead, the range lights on its belly flashing, then banked sharply over the water and came back to buzz the mansion.

The vast entrance hall was marble and gilt trim and frescoed ceilings. Russians living in the mean little towns between here and Moscow slept in single rooms with dirt floors, but the *praviteli,* the lords of the country, swathed themselves in rococo splendor. Dominika's heels clicked on the travertine, echoing in the space, producing a doomsday clockwork *tick-tock* sound. A side door opened and a majordomo approached. An obsequious welcome and the suggestion that perhaps the captain would like some light refreshment after her long drive. *You have no idea, Tolstoy,* thought Dominika. She was exhausted. He led the way through tall glass doors that opened onto a sprawling terrazzo patio with a sweeping view of the ocean. Radiant heating units negated the morning chill. A sideboard groaning with chafing dishes, crystal decanters, and silver bowls filled with flowers stretched along the side wall. Dominika took a flute of juice.

She walked to the railing to look down on a lower-level terrace with an enormous swimming pool lit by aqua-colored underwater spots, bright even in the rising morning light. Steam rose from the heated water. Two men in dark suits—blobs of brown around their heads—stood at either end of the pool, watching the president of the Russian Federation swim laps. Putin was using a punishing butterfly stroke, coming up massively in the water and with clenched fists hammering the water in front of him. There was nothing of the silky dolphin undulation of the expert butterfly swimmer—Dominika had seen Nate swim fly with virtually no splashing. Each time Putin came up to breathe, water streamed from his face and he would blow like a whale, throwing out a mist cloud in front of him, tinged aqua either by the pool lights or by the aura around his head and shoulders. After a full length, he showed no sign of tiring and Dominika turned away. At the other end of the terrace was a grouping of chairs—a single man was sitting with his back to her. He turned as he heard her approaching footsteps.

It was Govormarenko of Iskra-Energetika, the crapulent Putin crony who had negotiated the seismic-floor deal with the Persians. She remembered the dark comma of eyebrows over the hooked nose, the wavy white hair of the debauchee. He rose as Dominika approached, wiping his mouth with a linen napkin. There was a full plate of food and a half-empty flagon of beer on the low table in front of him. He was dressed casually, in black slacks, a peach sweater, and white leather Gucci driving moccasins.

"Captain Egorova, welcome," he said, smiling. Despite the napkin, there were crumbs clotted at the corners of his mouth. *He remembered my name,* thought Dominika. *Either I'm on the agenda or he wants to share a hot tub.*

"Gospodin Govormarenko," said Dominika, nodding.

"What an early arrival," he said, "but a pleasure to see you again." He gestured to a chair.

"I drove last night from Moscow," said Dominika, sitting on a separate armchair. It would do no harm to establish her cover story about last night. "I plan on visiting family in Petersburg." She looked out at the sea. The rising sun was coloring the small whitecaps pink, and the sky promised to be cloudless. The terrace was still and comfortable, despite the frontage on an open coast: Spotless glass panels around the terrace railing blocked the wind.

"My God, no one drives from Moscow; you're lucky to be alive," said Govormarenko, flirting. "You should have told me. I would have sent my plane to fetch you."

Fetch me a vomiting basin, thought Dominika. It was certain that Govormarenko's private jet would have love stains on the couch and thumbprints on the windows. "Perhaps next time," she said. She tried to switch him off. "Gospodin Govormarenko, you are up early," said Dominika. She would have guessed that he would be a reluctant riser, preferring the warmth of his sour, hoggish bed. He reached for a plate of golden *draniki,* folded one of the potato pancakes in half—rich mushroom sauce oozed out the end—and stuffed it in his mouth.

"Captain, I insist you call me Vasili," he said, chewing. He looked at a ponderous Breitling wristwatch with a toffee-colored face. "The president rises early for a swim. He wishes to discuss progress regarding the Iran deal. Have you heard the latest developments?"

"I trust the news is good," said Dominika, trying not to look at the daub of mushroom sauce on the front of Govormarenko's sweater.

"It's better than good," said Govormarenko. "The powered barge transporting the cargo has cleared the Volga delta canal at Astrakhan. Transit of the Caspian to Bandar-e Anzali should take four days, weather permitting. Tehran has already deposited four hundred and fifty million euros in the Central Bank, and the remainder will be paid on delivery in five days. Nabiullina is arriving today to make a report on the transfers."

Dominika did not look forward to seeing the chairman of the Central Bank again, the suspicious Putin favorite who questioned Dominika on how she had conceived of the water delivery route through Russia. *Suka,* bitch.

Govormarenko folded another pancake and swallowed it whole. "Thirty-seven billion rubles," he said. "You will not have to drive to Saint Petersburg ever again, Captain." Govormarenko sat back in his chair and looked at Dominika.

"I'm not sure I understand you, Vasili," said Dominika.

"I'm sure you know exactly what I mean," said Govormarenko. "Earnings for you could come to eight and a half, nine million rubles. If you want to shop in New York, that would be a quarter of a million dollars." *Earnings. He can calculate like a machine, convert currencies in his head,* thought Dominika. *How many ways would they cut up the Persians' money? How big would the president's share be? It would be interesting to know where they stashed their money abroad.*

"The Iran deal was an excellent example of behind-the-scenes intelligence work supporting a commercial deal that helped Russia," said Govormarenko, lifting his mug of beer and draining it. "We supported an important client state, we extended influence in a strategically important region, and we have boosted the prestige of the *Rodina* in the world." There it was again: *Vranyo,* the Russian Lie.

"Helped Russia?" said Dominika. Govormarenko ignored the irony with a wave of his hand.

"You are a member of the consortium of creative partners that made it possible. And you should profit from your participation—you *will* profit. And there will be other commercial endeavors. We'll need someone in the Service on our team."

"And what would the director say about such an arrangement?" said Dominika.

Govormarenko shrugged. "He's retiring soon. And Zarubina will either come in or stay out. She's brilliant, but old school. It's her choice." He reached over to pat Dominika's knee. "It's enough to know that we have a brilliant protégée in the Center." *This warthog is recruiting me as the oligarchs' penetration of the Service,* thought Dominika. *Certainly with Putin's blessing. Benford, what do you think of that? And he just confirmed that Zarubina will become the new director on her return from Washington.*

"And Colonel Zyuganov?" said Dominika. "He worked with you closely to achieve these wonders. Is he part of the team?"

"It is a little different with Zyuganov," said Govormarenko, confidentially. "The colonel could do with a course of charm school." *It couldn't be clearer: Zyuganov is not part of this cabal; he's excluded. He won't last forever,* thought Dominika. *What a useful look inside the cave—Nate and Benford would value this information.*

In the next instant, three things occurred simultaneously: The majordomo rushed out onto the terrace, leaned over, and whispered into Govormarenko's ear; four men in *militsiya* uniforms filed through the glass doors and walked up to the table; and President Putin, followed by his two mastiffs, came up a flight of steps from the pool level in his swimsuit. He was shirtless and had a towel draped around his shoulders. He looked at the policemen, then at Govormarenko, then with a slight lifting of one corner of his mouth—indicating runaway mirth, or perhaps the first heave of towering rage—he nodded to Dominika. *He's shirtless in a wet bathing suit and I'm wearing a cocktail dress,* she thought wearily. *And this morning a Navy SEAL called me ma'am while I was in my bra.* The sun was up now, and the ocean had turned from gray to blue, matching the pulsing blue annulus around the president's head.

"What is the meaning of this?" said Govormarenko, speaking instead of the president.

The lead *militsiya* officer came to attention. "Orders from Headquarters, sir."

Govormarenko stuffed another pancake into his mouth. "What orders?"

"A full search bulletin on a vehicle traveling from Moscow. A police air unit tracked it here, sir."

"Whose car is it?" asked Govormarenko.

"It's probably mine," said Dominika, sipping juice from her glass. "It's from the motor pool in Yasenevo." The *militsiya* officer darted a look at the other cops. *Shit, she's SVR, and the president is standing three feet away.*

"And why was the bulletin issued?" said Govormarenko.

The cop shrugged. "I don't know sir, just that Headquarters said the order was from Moscow."

Finally the reedy voice, short and sharp. "Never mind why; *who* issued the order?" said Putin.

The cop was sweating now. "I don't know, Mr. President."

Putin glanced at Dominika, who was trying to lounge casually in her chair. Dominika saw that he already knew everything. "I really don't think Captain Egorova is a fugitive," Putin said quietly. "You men are dismissed."

Seb Angevine put his feet up on the desk and admired his Crockett & Jones oxfords from London, £350, $600, hand-stitched by some Bob Cratchit specifically for him. His suit coat hung on a hanger behind his closed office door, charcoal-gray lightweight wool by Brioni, £4,500 or $6,000, which was accented admirably by his dark-blue seven-fold silk tie from Marinella in Naples, $200.

Seb was killing time before his secretary left for the day so he could set up the little Chobi Camera—this one was Gamma—and fast scroll cables on his desktop monitor while the camera was recording on high-res video. Tonight would be special: He would capture a finance office payment roster with the *true names* of the most sensitive assets in the CIA stable. Angevine didn't care who they were—they all should know there was risk being a spy; they had to take their chances. Hell, *he* was taking a risk spying for the Russians. But the only really important name, the one Zarubina would pay him a million dollars for, was the Russian name on the list. After Muriel poked her head in to say good night, Seb took out the segmented, bendy minitripod, screwed the camera onto the mount, made sure the camera was oriented correctly, and started the video function. Angevine fast scrolled about fifty cables, then stopped. On instinct he swept the tripod and tiny camera into an open desk drawer just as there was a knock on his door and the elephantine face of Gloria Bevacqua, the director of the Clandestine Service, peered around the corner.

"Am I interrupting anything?" she said, stepping inside the office. Her dirty-blond hair in a short bob showed dark roots and was sticking out in back. She wore a tangerine pantsuit of Orlon or rayon with dirty sleeves and a dried stain high on the left shoulder, as if she had been burping a baby that spit up milk.

Yes, I've been copying hundreds of classified cables off the Agency's secure cable system to deliver to Moscow tomorrow night for a seven-figure payment, the result of which hopefully will destroy your ability to manage the Clandestine Service. "No, Gloria," said Angevine. "What can I do for you?"

Bevacqua left a few minutes later, huffy that Angevine had declined to serve on a newly formed administrative review panel she was organizing. She needed senior-officer filler to serve on the commission and thought asking Angevine personally would compel him to agree. *No such luck, you slob,* Angevine thought. Allez au charbon, *go back to your sty.*

Angevine set his camera up again and started scrolling. He left the finance asset roster for the last, and scrolled down at normal speed, reading it carefully. There it was, his million-dollar baby. He checked twice; it was the only recognizable Russian name. *Huh, a woman,* he thought. *Can that be right?*

Dominika Vasilyevna Egorova. Angevine memorized the name. *Wonder if she's hot. Not for long, after Zarubina gets the name.*

DRANIKI—POTATO PANCAKES WITH MUSHROOM SAUCE

Grate peeled potatoes and onions, then add raw egg, salt, and flour to make a thick batter. Spoon a small dollop of batter into hot oil and fry until golden brown. Serve with mushroom sauce made by processing sautéed diced onions and mushrooms with sour cream and heavy cream. Simmer the processed puree (do not boil) with additional heavy cream and garnish with chopped parsley.

36

Nate and Benford sat alone in the secure conference room in the new Washington Field Office of the FBI in northwest Washington, DC. Benford had complained about having to drive downtown to Swampoodle, the long-forgotten name of the nearby nineteenth-century Irish shantytown razed to build Union Station. Benford further noted that the WFO relocation from gritty Buzzard Point on the Potomac was a requirement so that the FEEB cowboys would be closer to the Government Accountability Office, which was diagonally across G Street from the new field office.

Benford had worked closely with the Bureau for years and disliked them generally, but he had a few close FEEBish friends, like Chief of Foreign Counterintelligence Division Charles Montgomery, with whom they were to meet. As they were waiting, an annoying, mustached special agent known to Benford stuck his head into the room.

"The spooks are in the house," he yelled, cupping his hands around his mouth. Benford looked at him with an expression of distaste. The FEEB had bushy hair and a mustache that looked like a basting brush.

"McGaffin," said Benford, "why aren't you on a stakeout? Aren't there still bank robbers roaming the capital?"

"It's under control," said McGaffin. "What're you guys doing down here?"

Benford looked significantly at Nate.

"There's new intelligence from Moscow that the Center is running a mole inside the FBI and we have come to submit a request to the FISA court to review your personal Internet-use profile. I personally expect to find materials both puerile and prurient."

McGaffin shook his head, said, "Speak English," and withdrew.

Benford again looked meaningfully at Nate. "And perhaps you now understand my misgivings in coming here to partner with these white-collar G-men," said Benford.

Nate shook his head. "We've got one shot to bust up Zarubina's meeting and identify TRITON," he said. "If these guys have an idea, we should listen."

Special agent Montgomery came into the room, walked around the table, and shook Benford's and Nate's hands. He was fifty, slim with premature white hair, half-frame glasses at the end of his nose, and gray cop's eyes that missed nothing.

"Sorry I'm late," said Montgomery, sitting on the other side of the conference table. "Still getting over jet lag. London conference went on forever." He rubbed his face.

"But at least there's the British cuisine," said Benford.

"Yeah," said Montgomery. "I'd never heard of haggis before. Scottish, not British. Ate a plate before our hosts in MI5 told me it was innards wrapped in sheep's stomach. I'm serving Rocky Mountain oysters next time they come here."

"I always assumed testicles—whether bovine or other—were a favorite on the FBI cafeteria menu," said Benford.

"Simon, the Brits would call you a 'prannock,'" said Montgomery, deadpan, opening a file folder. "That's an objectionable person."

"May we proceed?" Benford said. Montgomery nodded. He was one of a few FBI officers who knew about the TRITON case.

"Look, we've discussed this. Zarubina is meeting your boy sometime in the next seven days," said Montgomery. "We've stayed off her butt at your request so she won't see coverage and abort." Montgomery had argued that the FCI surveillance team—called the Gs—could cover Zarubina without spooking her. "I still think we can take her," said Montgomery.

Nate shook his head. "Charles, we can't take the chance. Your guys are good, but if Zarubina sees anything on the street, she aborts the meeting, and the Russians switch handlers to an anonymous illegals officer we'll never be able to identify."

Montgomery rubbed his face. "Well, that's what I want to talk to you guys about. We have an ace," said Montgomery, flipping a sheet of paper. "We know the Russian meeting site is in Meridian Hill Park."

"A thin advantage," said Nate. "SVR will be looking very carefully at the park for days in advance, especially during the nighttime hours before the meeting. They're going to see a big team staked out, no matter how good they are. A squelch break on a radio, someone with binoculars, it's unavoidable."

"Okay, I'll accept that, but I've been thinking about a solution," said

Montgomery. "We have two guys on the Gs. They've bounced around a little—"

"Bounced around, meaning what?" said Benford.

"Different jobs," said Montgomery.

"Why?" said Benford.

"They have authority issues," said Montgomery, folding his hands together on the table.

"Meaning what?" said Benford.

"Meaning they speak their minds," said Montgomery.

"As in . . . ," said Benford.

"As in telling their supervisors to pound sand," said Montgomery.

"And you want to saddle us with these unstable Gemini twins in a critical operation that could cost an agent's life exactly why?" said Benford.

"Because I believe they are the best street operators I've seen in twenty-five years," said Montgomery. "If Zarubina is a clairvoyant witch on the bricks, Fileppo and Proctor are warlocks."

Benford looked over at Nate, who nodded slightly. "The three of us in the park, no one else, no radios. We bag TRITON before he can talk to Zarubina," said Nate.

"That's what I was thinking," said Montgomery. "Put the three of you in loincloths and give you blowguns. Might work."

Benford shifted in his seat, thinking. "When can we meet these warlocks of yours?" he said.

"They're waiting outside," said Montgomery, and went to the conference room door.

Fileppo and Proctor came in and sat on either side of Montgomery. Both were dressed casually in jeans and Clarks low-top desert boots. The one on the left wore a plain black sweatshirt, the other a zip-necked fleece pullover.

"This is Donnie Fileppo and Lew Proctor," said Montgomery. Nate reached over the table and shook their hands. Both had serious grips. Nate estimated that Donnie Fileppo was around twenty-five, with close-cropped brown hair, a high forehead, and eyes that flicked from face to face. Lew Proctor was slightly older, with laugh lines around his eyes and a buzz cut. They both sat slumped in their chairs and looked with feigned disinterest at the CIA men.

"So it's Donnie and Lew?" asked Benford.

"Yeah, his full name is Donatello," said Proctor, leaning forward to look around Montgomery at Fileppo. He kept his features serious, but his eyes laughed. "It's mostly a girl's name in Italy." Fileppo did not look at Proctor.

"Have you guys ever worked solo surveillance?" said Nate. "We have a big problem and we need two foot soldiers to help me cover a park downtown."

"What park?" said Fileppo.

"Who against?" said Proctor.

"You don't need to know until we consent to your participation," said Benford. Nate didn't look at him, but recognized the tone: Vintage Benford, being disagreeable to test his interlocutors. Fileppo shrugged.

"We can't help you with your scary-big problem if we don't know the frigging target and park," said Proctor. Montgomery shifted in his seat.

"Special Agent Montgomery said you guys are pretty good on the street," said Nate.

"Good enough," said Fileppo. "What street you come up on?"

"Moscow," said Nate.

Proctor nodded.

"That's why this is so important," said Nate. "It has to go right or someone dies in Moscow."

"Not to mention that a fucker American traitor working for fucking Moscow gets away with it for a fucking long time," said Benford.

"We fucking can't have that, can we, Donatello?" said Proctor.

Nate went out on the street with Fileppo and Proctor. Montgomery had not exaggerated: They were smooth, fast, physically conditioned, used barely noticeable hand signals, and could change their profiles with the flip of a hoodie or the change of a jacket to its shucked-inside-out material. Fileppo even did parkour—urban freerunning. He could run at a twelve-foot wall, take two steps on the bricks as if walking up it, and leap the rest of the way to the top.

Dinner breaks were instructive: Neither man drank during duty hours. After-hours beers were limited to two. Conversation was raucous and profane, but Nate recognized the ticks of top surveillance pros who worked well together: They finished each other's sentences, looked over the other's shoulder, and signaled something of interest by a minute jerk of the chin. Each knew what the other was going to do before he did it. Nate ran them along Connecticut Avenue—their backyard—and it was like watching two Cape hunting dogs work in tandem. They covered practice rabbits—unsuspecting civilians—up close, then dropped back, anticipated turns, and got ahead of them or followed from across the street. They supported each other flawlessly.

Fileppo used his baby face to get past doormen. Proctor could play the downtown urban courier and roam freely through office buildings. Both could read mail in eleven-point type upside down on receptionists' desks. They were rogues, pirates, Visigoths. After two days Nate told Benford it was okay—the three of them were going to cover Meridian Hill Park for the next five consecutive nights.

The park was a twelve-acre wooded hill in the Columbia Heights neighborhood, two and a half miles north of the White House. Set on a steep hill, the park had twisting pathways, statuary, and graceful cement stairways. The centerpiece of the park was a two-hundred-foot Italianate cascading fountain with thirteen descending basins—each bowl filled and then emptied into progressively larger bowls, increasing from five to twelve feet wide, eventually flowing into a graceful curved reservoir at the bottom. Top to bottom the decline in elevation was a mild terraced drop of fifty feet. Broad cement aggregate stairways ascended on either side to meet at an upper pool and columned terrace at the top of the cascade.

Nate, Fileppo, and Proctor split up and covered the upper level of the park—a grassy mall bordered by linden trees—then rotated to case the lower level, including the cascade. They couldn't know whether the Russians had people periodically out, security scouting, so the plan was to then exit the park separately and walk two blocks past stately row houses on W Street to a sandwich shop called Fast Gourmet. Nate looked for Fileppo and Proctor as he walked over, but they were nowhere in sight. They were playing with the CIA guy with the Moscow creds, to show him they could.

Fast Gourmet was a modest shop, with display case, counter, and two tables, in the back of the cashier's building in a gas station on the corner of W and Fourteenth Streets. Fileppo was already inside ordering three

Chivito sandwiches on soft rolls. Proctor walked in two minutes later. No one talked while they waited for their food. Nate had not exactly bonded with the two FBI guys, but they shared an unspoken collegial regard for one another—they recognized skills and appreciated fellow top pros.

"It's going to be the terrace at the top of the cascade," said Proctor finally, sitting at one of the little tables. "Two entrances on the west side off Sixteenth, still lots of foliage."

"Definitely," said Fileppo, pulling up a chair. "It's the only logical place. Forget the upper mall. The terrace is screened from above by the wall, and you can see all the way down to W Street. Nothing's coming up those stairs unobserved." Nate was looking dubiously at his *Chivito*, piled high with grilled steak, cheese, boiled egg, and marinated onions, and oozing an unidentified sauce.

"*Escabeche*," said Fileppo, following Nate's look. "The onions are marinated in vinegar."

"From Uruguay," said Proctor. "Best in DC."

Nate took a bite and had to confess that it was magnificent. He wiped his mouth with a napkin. "Okay," he said, "you're Zarubina. How do you come in? Where do you put your CS, your countersurveillance? From what direction is TRITON coming?"

"Russians like to control the meeting site. It's their MO," said Proctor. "She'll pop in by one of the side stairs to the upper terrace and watch our boy come up one of the stairways either side of the cascade."

"If she brings CS, they're going to be in the trees, and in the park above the fountain," said Fileppo. "They're going to be watching outward for a big team, for cars and radios. They're there to call an abort and to protect their old lady."

"She's supposed to be unreal on the street," said Nate.

Fileppo and Proctor looked at each other. "*We're* unreal," said Fileppo, and Proctor nodded. They put down their sandwiches and bumped fists.

"Jesus, before you guys move in together, tell me how we set up on this site," said Nate.

He got two blank looks from Fileppo and Proctor, which lasted a noticeable three seconds. "Here's our gut feel; tell us what you think," said Proctor. "Donnie and I will be at the bottom of the cascade. We move around separately, screening behind the reflecting pool, the balustrades, hedges, and walls. If it's before ten, there's gonna be some casuals in the park. If it's after ten, the Russians will have to deal with park police making sure the place is empty."

"And if your mole-man is on those stairs going up, we'll rush him before he gets halfway," said Fileppo.

"How are we going to know a guy on the stairs is mole-man?" asked Nate, watching these two work out the details.

"Hundred percent Zarubina uses a simple safety signal—flick a lighter, take off a scarf, put a white paper sack on the railing," said Proctor. "Positive signal, something he can see even in the dark. *She'll* be telling us when he comes."

"And that's when we stick him," said Fileppo. "No way the two of them are gonna say one word to each other, much less pass anything."

"Yeah, Donnie gets spun up during takedowns. But you're going to wait for me, right?" said Proctor to Donnie.

"I don't get 'spun up,'" said Fileppo. "Where do you get that shit?"

"You always do," said Proctor.

Jesus, they sound like an old married couple, thought Nate as he concentrated on his sandwich.

"Okay, you guys are down below," said Nate, "and I want to be right up Zarubina's ass, real close. Any ideas?" He was okay with asking these experts their opinion: Nate's specialty was detecting and defeating hostile surveillance; these guys *were* surveillance and it would pay to listen to them.

"There's only one place," said Fileppo. "The wall of the upper terrace behind the upper pool has three deep alcoves with a candle-jet fountain in each—you know the fluffy columns of water about three feet high. You gotta stand in ankle-deep water at night, but with dark clothes, squatting behind the bubbles, and the noise of all the water—fountains, cascades, basins—you're invisible. You just gotta wade across the upper pool and you're right behind her."

"Maybe wear a pair of knee-high rubber boots," said Proctor.

"I scare her shitless coming out of the dark, speaking polite Russian and not letting her leave," said Nate. "You guys put flex cuffs on dickhead, then you hit the button and call everybody in, right?" said Nate. Benford and Montgomery had arranged for a dozen Washington metro police units, three FBI vehicles, a van, and an ambulance to be in holding positions in a ring four blocks away from the park. On receiving an electronic signal from Proctor's SHRAPNEL message unit—essentially an encrypted pager developed by CIA—they would light up Columbia Heights. No other radios, cell phones, or electronics—the Russians listened as well as watched.

TRITON would be arrested. Zarubina, with her diplomatic immunity, would be courteously detained until the Russian Consul from the embassy could spring her. Per the well-known Cold War drill, he would serenely maintain that Zarubina had been walking in the park to take the night air. Then he doubtless would rave about fascist American police procedures. A PNG expulsion—persona non grata—would follow and Zarubina would return to the bosom of the *Rodina* to answer questions from a pair of blue eyes over a mouth pursed in annoyance.

And Dominika would avoid the cellars yet again, thought Nate. *She would be safe.*

URUGUAYAN CHIVITO SANDWICH

Stack a soft roll with thin slices of caramelized, grilled flank steak, melt mozzarella over the meat under the broiler, then add boiled ham, fried pancetta, diced green olives, sliced hard-boiled egg, thin-sliced onion marinated in vinegar and sugar, lettuce, tomato, and aioli. Cut the sandwich on the bias and serve.

37

Time check. 2219. 10:19 p.m. If something was going to happen, it could be now: Neither CIA nor SVR clandestine meetings were ever set exactly for the hour or half hour—too predictable. Despite the cool evening, Nate sweat under a black plastic hooded poncho and rubber boots as he crouched in the pitch-black of the fountain alcove behind the upper pool. The floor of the alcove was slick with algae, and the shin-high water smelled metallic and toxic. Looking through—around—the bubbling column of fountain water, Nate could barely see the empty terrace and silvery cascade basins below. Beyond the cascade the park was dark, backlit faintly by orange city-glow.

The damn fountain jets were fouled or something, and the water column pulsed irregularly, high then low, splashing Nate's poncho, which was keeping him only moderately dry. Nate worried that the water would make a noticeable rattle off the plastic, but there was a lot of covering noise—the three echoing and splashy alcove fountains emptying into the upper pool, arpeggio waves spilling into cascade basins below. Two previous nights of waiting in this stinky water wonderland had made him wish he had assigned either Fileppo or Proctor to the fountain alcove—let one of them squat for hours in a recirculated, copper-pipe-rancid ribollita, with green things floating around his boots like Italian veggie soup. But he knew he had to be here up top: He had to freeze Zarubina, and FBI personnel had to be the ones to lay hands on an American citizen arrestee for legal reasons. *Okay, TRITON, you fucker, come on in.*

Some vestigial Paleolithic instinct made Nate's scalp creep—there was someone directly above his alcove, on the grassy mall level. There was no moonlight and no shadow; there were no voices. All was silent. But he could feel it, a scalp-crawly sense of a person approaching. A minute later, peering through the damn bubbling water, Nate saw a short figure glide soundlessly in front of him onto the terrace from the right. He held his breath and hoped he was invisible in the clammy black. It was Zarubina—Nate recognized her from the hundreds of photos in the FBI mug book on her.

She wore a camel-hair outer coat, a scarf knotted loosely around her neck. Her honey-blond hair was up in a bun, and sturdy legs beneath the hem of her long coat ended in clunky midheel shoes. Zarubina stood quietly by the balustrade above the first of the basins and looked to her left, then turned to the right. She was slowly scanning the reaches of the empty park below her. *You urban Apaches better be as good as you say you are,* thought Nate, telegraphing to Fileppo and Proctor out there in the dark. Zarubina finished her turns and stood still, head down, a seriously spooky sight, some ancient priestess on the elevated altar, calling in the bat-winged gods. *She's listening, she's feeling the vibe,* thought Nate. *Is she feeling the electrons coming out of the tips of my fingers? Jesus, this grandmother can kill DIVA tonight. No she won't; it will* not *happen.*

Zarubina turned to look up at the top of the wall at mall level—brilliant black eyes, slightly hooded, passed over Nate's alcove—and nodded once. Her team would keep looser watch—she had signaled the all clear. She moved closer to the terrace balustrade, put both hands on the cement, and leaned forward like a dictator on a balcony giving a speech to the masses below. She reached up and loosened her scarf from around her neck and draped it over the balustrade so that a discreet corner of it hung down. Safety signal. *Wait, wait, wait,* Nate telegraphed to the men down below.

Nate didn't move for two minutes—120 seconds that felt like two hours—and then he saw the head and shoulders of a tall angular figure come up the stairs from W Street. He moved slowly, and started up the left-hand staircase along the cascade. *Are you TRITON?* The man held his head down, his hands jammed into his pockets. Nate strained to see his face, to identify him from the halls of Headquarters. *Come on.* The man stopped climbing the broad stairs a third of the way up and raised his head to look at the upper terrace and Zarubina. He saw her darkened figure and took one hand out of his jacket and raised it briefly. *Yeah, wave hello.* Zarubina did not respond, but the man resumed trudging up the steps. He was half-way up now.

From the bottom of the stairwell the shadow of a spirit, a winged ogre, flew out of the thick border hedge, planted hands on the brick wall at the bottom of the stairs, vaulted onto the bottom step, and started running up the stairs. Fileppo. At the same instant—how had they timed their moves so closely?—Proctor materialized from inside a privet hedge bordering the opposite stairwell, glided over the steps, and walked, arms outstretched for balance, along the lip of a lower basin to cross the cascade. It looked as though he were walking on water. This took four seconds. Zarubina bellowed like a man as the two figures converged on TRITON, who, with amazing quickness, ran up two steps then sideways straight into a hedge, which swallowed him up amid great crunching and snapping of branches. Proctor and Fileppo both broke right—one into the gap plowed by TRITON, the other through a break in the hedge two steps below. The Cape hunting dogs were on the impala.

On the fifth second of the action, a flashlight started shining on the lower part of the stairway, a voice called, and the light started coming up. Nate saw the silhouette of a flat-brimmed campaign hat—the lemon squeezers worn by frigging US park rangers. The ranger obviously had heard the sound of exploding foliage and the buffalo trumpeting of a Russian intelligence officer and appeared in order to chase away what he thought were kids. There was no time for this. Nate came out of the alcove, swung down to the pool, caught his poncho liner under one of his boots and went down on his hands and knees in the elbow-deep water. He got up, pounded to the edge, and swung his legs out—his boots were full of water. He shucked them off and looked for the old lady. Zarubina was gone, the terrace was empty. She hadn't moved either to the left or right. Then he heard the splashing. Caught between Nate splashing like an asshole behind her, and the park ranger coming up at her, she had vaulted the balustrade and was sloshing down the cascade, one basin at a time, to evade contact. It was impossible to see her in the darkness, but she was noisily displacing a lot of water.

Nate vaulted the balustrade and started down after her. *How hard is it going to be running down a fifty-five-year-old woman?* The floor of the top basin was slimy and Nate skidded, then caught himself on the lip. He swung his legs over and lowered himself into the next, slightly larger, basin, a three-foot drop. *Eleven more.* He could barely see the cascade by the city-glow in the sky, but he could hear splashing below him—Zarubina was down there. He wondered about Fileppo and Proctor and imagined them on top of TRITON, pushing him facedown in the dirt. He could imagine the cricket zip of the flex cuffs as they secured his wrists. Nate slithered over the lip of the basin—*ten more*—and wondered where they were. *Where are the sirens?*

They *had* to bag TRITON. He knew Dominika's true name.

The night was brisk and quiet, even peaceful. Angevine had parked Vikki's car—a ridiculous candy-apple red Kia Rio with a feathered Navajo dream-catcher talisman hanging from the rearview mirror—a block from the park, against a wrought-iron fence on Ecuador Alley, a typical Washington alley-way used by garbage trucks that ran behind apartment buildings and the garages of row houses. He could cut unobserved through backyards, get to Fifteenth Street, and enter the park as the Russians had instructed him, from the W Street end. Vikki had asked him why he wanted to borrow her car when he had a perfectly good BMW—a sweet new gunmetal-gray M3, seventy-two thousand MSRP that he bought when he got tired of the Audi S7—but he could hardly explain that he wasn't parking a BMW in a Wash-ington alley while he went to meet the Russians.

He was looking forward to seeing Zarubina tonight. He had rehearsed a dramatic little speech about the immense value of the name he was about to provide, and how the bonus for the information should be commensu-rately large. He dallied with the idea of haggling over money before actually handing over Gamma. But haggling would serve no purpose; the Russians already had paid him handsomely and would continue to do so. Maintain-ing good will was important, especially since Zarubina had told him Pres-ident Putin himself had sent respectful greetings to TRITON. Angevine imagined himself being hosted by Putin in some luxurious snow-draped dacha during a surreptitious visit to Moscow. A roaring fire, ice-cold vodka, and a long-legged Ukrainian beauty on a bearskin rug. There would be plenty of those—Putin liked fucking Ukrainians.

No, he'd hand over Gamma right away and save the daydreams for later. He rolled the memorized name around in his head, practiced saying it. *Dominika Vasilyevna Egorova.* Apparently the idiots in Operations were reduced to recruiting women now. He'd utter the name personally to amp up the drama, and Zarubina's sweet, cake-baking grandmother's expression would melt into the vulturine face of the Soviet raptor anticipating the kill. Angevine had seen that face.

He could hardly wait. All the money in the world, plus paying back the donkeys in the Agency who didn't see fit to acknowledge him. He was across the park and starting up the stairs. There she was, a dark blob behind the balustrade, and the tail of the light-colored scarf just discernible against the stone. There was a quiet scuffling behind him, and a rustling of hedge to the side. He turned and saw a banshee ape bounding up the stairs and another faceless nightmare approaching from his left. A bellow from Zarubina sent voltage up his spine, and Angevine moved before the conscious thought registered. He leaped up two steps, then plowed through a hedge to his right, feeling branches volleying against his outstretched arms and his face.

He exploded out of the hedge and ran through a stand of trees, hearing footsteps and the chuffing of a sprinting athlete behind him. His lungs were about to burst and he expected to feel arms around his legs in a flying tackle. Running with the desperation of a fugitive, Angevine dug into his pocket and took out CYCLOPS, a three-inch aerosol dispenser developed by CIA for the Second Gulf War containing a fine, pink powder compound of phenacyl chloride and dipropylene glycol methyl ether—intended as an alternative to pepper spray—which, if sprayed into the mucus membranes of the eye, caused severe pain and a temporary loss of sight. Angevine had palmed two CYCLOPS units after a laboratory demonstration he had attended as CIA associate director of Military Affairs. As the pink fog puffed out of the little dispenser, Fileppo's exceptional reflexes saved him at the last minute: he ducked and only a few grains of the powder hit his face, but the pain was intense and his left eye shut down like an out-of-focus telescope lens. Fileppo grunted and toppled over, holding his eye. Angevine jammed the little aerosol into his pocket and kept running.

He was being chased like a common purse snatcher. Sobbing, Angevine vaulted over the low brick wall onto the sidewalk on Fifteenth Street, sprinted across the street, and cut behind a building. Tasting the phlegm in his throat, he crouched behind a Dumpster in the alley and listened. No footsteps. Was he clear? Normally he'd wait, but he had to get away from there. His hands and face were scratched and bruised. He crossed the alley, stepped over a low chain-link gate, skirted a building, and came out right where he had parked Vikki's car. With shaking fingers he unlocked the door, started the engine, and drove down the alley with his lights off. He made himself drive slowly. At a dogleg in the alley he turned on his lights and saw a face, crimson in his taillights, growing in his rearview mirror. Someone running faster than he was driving—and gaining. Angevine floored it, came out on Fourteenth Street in a squealing turn, and barreled down the street, turning right then left, then right again. Whoever it was had been close enough to read Vikki's license plate.

Zarubina saw movement and understood in a flash of professional clarity. Her bellow was one of rage, of the *impossibility* that her will was being challenged. In the instant she saw TRITON crash through the hedge, she also heard splashy movement from behind, then spotted the bouncing beam of a flashlight coming up the far staircase. Yulia Zarubina, *Shveja,* the Seamstress, did not hesitate. She swung her legs painfully over the balustrade to drop into the uppermost basin. She was going to wade downstream, split the seam, and slip between them. As she moved forward, she shucked off her already waterlogged coat—it sank and hung suspended under the surface. Zarubina swung her legs over the rim and lowered herself into the next basin, losing her grip and sitting down in the water with a squishy bump. Ponderously, she got up and slogged forward. There was a moving pulse of pain—like a rose thorn being dragged across her inner wrist—and her hand felt numb. The sound of splashing from above made her move faster, to the basin rim, and over, and to the next, and over. Her shoes had come off and her matronly dress, buttoned up the front, was soaked and clung to her ample bosom and around her stubby legs. Her breathing was hard; her chest felt as if it were compressed.

She kept hearing splashes behind her, prodigious amounts of water were cascading ahead of her, and she slid off another basin rim and waded forward. She was getting the rhythm of sitting, pivoting the legs, and easing down into the next basin. The flashlight had passed her and continued up the stairs—one threat evaded, but the sloshing noise from above was growing. Sit, pivot, slide down. Try to breathe. Two more basins to go, and then she would come to the lower pool, then the park exit to the right, where her surveillance team would swoop in and pick her up, alerted by all the noise. Zarubina trudged through the water—the basins were larger the farther down she got—when she felt a hammer blow of pain in her left arm. She put her hand under her armpit to ease the ache, which was seeping up her neck to her jaw.

Zarubina felt dizzy as she sat and pivoted her legs to slide into the last basin before the bottom pool. Her walking was unsteady and her breath came in shallow gasps. The park, and the trees, and the fountain, and all this damn water—everything was moving—and the orange glow of the night sky was pulsing. Zarubina sat heavily on the last basin rim and swung her legs around, but couldn't slide down. She sat, legs dangling, fighting the pain that was coming in waves, just like the sheets of water sliding under her thighs and around her legs. She could taste the pain. Her left arm hung numbly at her side. She heard a terrible rushing sound in her ears and looked up again at the night sky, now crossed by pinpoints of light, and a new surge of pain exploded in her chest.

Zarubina's head went back, eyes staring and mouth open, and she slowly pitched forward and belly flopped into the bottom pool. She floated face-down, arms underneath her, the softly falling water rocking her stocking feet. Her hair, knocked loose from its bun, fanned out in the black water, a Soviet Ophelia sadly not to be mourned by her blue-eyed prince in the Kremlin.

Nate slid down into the last basin. She was gone. Impossible; he had been seconds behind her. Then he saw her floating in the bottom pool. He vaulted the rim, splashed his way to her, and picked her head up out of the water. She stared at him with small black eyes. Her mouth was slack, and a strand of green weed was stuck to the side of her face. Nate tried to hold her weight and drag her to the edge of the pool to haul her out and get her on dry pavement. There was the sound of running footsteps and Fileppo appeared out of the dark, a hand over one eye. He helped Nate haul Zarubina out and they started working on her. Nate clenched his hands and began pushing her chest—the metronome beat of the pop hit "Stayin' Alive" was the required 103 beats a minute. *Ah, ha, ha, ha, stayin' alive.*

"Get some air into her," said Nate, pumping. A cupful of dirty water spurted out of Zarubina's mouth.

Fileppo looked at Nate. "Dude, you speak Russian," he said.

"You're not conjugating verbs, Donnie; blow into her mouth." As Donnie bent forward, Nate saw his red-rimmed, swollen eye. He kept compressing Zarubina's chest.

"What happened to your eye? Tell me you got him," said Nate. Donnie came up from Zarubina's mouth.

"Fucking guy sprayed me with some kind of fucking blinding agent," he said, leaning down again. Nate kept pushing. Zarubina stared up at them.

"Tell me you got him," said Nate again.

Fileppo turned his head to speak. "Lew chased him into an alley."

"Why didn't you light up the troops? They should have swarmed the area," said Nate. Blue-lipped Zarubina listened to the conversation while staring at the sky, her head rocking slightly as Nate pushed at her chest.

"I don't know," said Donnie miserably. "Proctor had the SHRAPNEL unit." He bent down again and blew into Zarubina's mouth, and her cheeks puffed out.

It got crowded suddenly. Proctor appeared from the W Street entrance, drenched in sweat and panting. The park ranger, flashlight in hand, came breathlessly from the other side of the cascade. She was a slight girl with black bangs in a Park Service parka, wearing her campaign hat with the strap under her chin. She shined her light on Zarubina's blue face.

"What's going on?" she said, looking at the men.

"Mouth-to-mouth resuscitation, Officer," said red-eyed Fileppo, coming up for air.

"We're G-men," said Proctor. "We're attempting to revive this woman." The park ranger goggled at him. *Do they actually call themselves that?* thought Nate.

"You have a radio?" said Proctor. The ranger moved her bangs.

"Call the DC cops, get an ambulance here." The girl moved fast enough and started talking into her brick, the stubby antenna quivering as she held it in shaking hands.

Proctor looked at Nate, who was still pumping Zarubina's chest, and his expression said it all. These street guys, like Nate, knew there were no excuses, not even when bad luck and fate went against you. "I lost the signaling unit when I went through the hedge," said Proctor bitterly. "Then Donnie got his ass kicked, and I chased the son of a bitch across Fifteenth following the sounds of flying garbage cans and dogs barking. Then I lost him, but there's something else," he said, explaining.

The sirens began softly at first, then filled the air like a discordant flooding tide, and the surrounding buildings, park fountains, treetops, and faces of the statues flashed blue-red-yellow as the sirens subsided with growls, and car doors began chunking and the squeak of gurney wheels grew louder. Nate and Donnie got out of the way as the EMTs popped Zarubina's dress buttons and put paddles on her and she flopped twice, but she wasn't coming back.

Montgomery and Benford finally appeared, looking like death. Proctor stepped up, grabbed Montgomery by the elbow, and took him aside. Benford, Nate, and Fileppo followed, walking away from the crowd gathered around Zarubina's body, her feet sticking out between their legs. Benford looked up at the sky and closed his eyes.

"You lost the signaling device?" said Benford.

Proctor nodded.

"And you were spritzed?" Benford asked.

Fileppo nodded.

"Could you identify him in a lineup?" asked Montgomery.

They both shook their heads.

"So the guy got away?" Benford asked. "TRITON, the Center's penetration of CIA, the man who knows the true name of our premier source inside Russia, is running loose?"

"Simon, the Russians have a saying," said Nate. "*Eto yeshshyo tsvyetóchki a yágodki vpyeryedí.* These are just flowers; berries will come soon."

Benford turned a baleful eye on Nate.

"Nathaniel, if this is how you wish to tender your resignation to leave federal service and pursue a career teaching Russian at Walden Online University, it is accepted immediately," said Benford, turning to Fileppo and Proctor. "And these colleagues no doubt will be able to find employment as choreographers for the Ice Capades."

"Mr. Benford, with all due respect," said Fileppo, "go fuck yourself."

"Everybody take it easy," said Montgomery.

"What I meant by flowers and berries," said Nate, "is that the best may yet be ahead. Proctor, tell them."

"I got the plates off a moving car in the alleyway," said Proctor. "The guy jackrabbited away when he saw me." Montgomery called a FEEB special agent over and Proctor gave him the plate number to run an urgent trace.

"It could be a civilian," said Proctor.

"Why'd he burn rubber?" said Montgomery.

"With that face approaching in a dark alley? Anyone would," said Benford. Proctor opened his mouth, but Montgomery put up his hand. Behind them, Zarubina was zipped into a metro-DC coroner's rubber bag and lifted with a thump onto the gurney. The SA came back after having called in the plate. Montgomery read off a notepad.

"Car belongs to a Vikki Mayfield," said Montgomery. "Lives in Glover Park, on Benton Street."

"That's a few blocks from the Russian Embassy on Wisconsin," said Fileppo.

Benford scowled at all of them. "Flowers before berries," he said, shaking his head. "Charles, may I suggest you do a full run-up on this Mayfield woman?"

Montgomery nodded.

"And now it's time for the Gs," said Benford. "A straight surveillance." He turned to Proctor.

"And before you leave for the evening, would you be so kind as to root around in those hedges to see if you could possibly retrieve the SHRAPNEL unit? It's worth possibly the equivalent of three years of your salary."

"Sure thing, Mr. Benford," said Proctor. "Where shall I put it when I find it?"

RIBOLLITA—TUSCAN SOUP

Sauté diced onions in olive oil and tomato paste until translucent, then add diced carrots, celery, zucchini, leek, and cubed potatoes, and cook until soft. Cover the vegetables with chicken broth, add chopped kale, chard, and cabbage, and bring to a boil. Add cannellini beans, salt, and pepper and simmer. Add cubes of stale Tuscan bread to the soup and mix well. Serve with a drizzle of oil and/or balsamic vinegar and grated Parmesan.

38

There was still a rust-colored spot on the carpet where something had leaked out of Yevgeny's head. Zyuganov sat at his desk, staring at the spot but not seeing it. Under his hands, on the desk blotter, were the cables from Washington reporting in detail every aspect of the disastrous events of the night before. Zarubina's CS team described what appeared to have been an ambush at the site—the source disappearing into the night, pursued on foot by two men, outcome unknown. Another cable recounted the scene at the bottom of the cascade, where medical technicians attended someone. Cable three was the consul's report of the death of *rezident* Yulia Zarubina, and his visit to the District of Columbia city morgue in southwest Washington to identify her. The remains would not be released to the Russian Embassy for another day, but the consul had been able to collect Zarubina's personal effects—wristwatch, overcoat, one shoe, pocket litter—to ensure there was nothing of operational value. The consul moreover elicited from the morgue physician that Zarubina's mottled face and purple lips strongly indicated a massive myocardial infarction.

Zyuganov was badly shaken: He had planned on riding the Zarubina elevator all the way up to the executive fourth floor at Yasenevo, but that *zastupnichestvo,* that patronage, was gone. Zyuganov's scaly amphibian instincts knew that, despite his oily efforts, he was not favored by Putin—in fact, he was barely tolerated. The fourth cable from Washington was an operational perspective: Until the status of TRITON could be verified, the *rezidentura* would make no attempt at recontact. After an operational flap like this, the likelihood of a possibly arrested source being directed against his former handlers was high. Unless and until TRITON began reporting "incompatible" intelligence—that is, information the Americans would never give up—the case was on ice. Zyuganov swore. Now this compounded his troubles: He could not prove that Egorova was the mole; General Solovyov had disappeared, possibly in the hands of the Americans; Zyuganov's grandstand play of tracking Egorova's staff car to Petersburg had led police to a presidential guesthouse *where she was being entertained by Putin himself.*

Zyuganov ominously had received no call about these setbacks from the president or the director—in Stalin's day the hollow cessation of communication from the top meant only one thing: Kiss the wife and kids goodbye. The one call he *had* received was doubly alerting. Govormarenko telephoned on the secure line—*Since when did a civilian use encrypted government communications? Since Putin handed him the receiver, that's when*—to curtly announce that his continued participation in the matter of the cargo now en route to Iran would no longer be required. Govormarenko mouthed the explanation that the deal was concluded, the last of the monies were being deposited, and the intervention of the Service could be brought to a close. Zyuganov knew very well what that meant: There would be no *vyplata,* no spoon of sugar—no payoff—for his work putting together the operation. It also meant that his connections to the *siloviki* around Putin likewise were being severed, like mooring lines on a departing ship, dropping one after another from the pier into the water.

Egorova. Zyuganov closed his eyes and saw her on the stainless-steel table in the Butyrka prison cellar as he worked his way up her body with an iron bar—feet, shins, knees, pelvis, stomach, ribs, wrists, arms, collarbone, throat. He would use a bent spoon on her eyes. She would flop like a screaming leather bag of broken glass. Investigators still wanted to talk about Yevgeny. He did not experience even a second of remorse about staving in the skull of his moronic deputy—Yevgeny had told everything he knew, but nothing that could nail Egorova. Zyuganov's options were narrowing, his career standing was tottering, his prospects were bleak. His career: *Bog ne vydast, svin'ja ne s'est,* God won't give it away, pigs won't eat it.

Mother. She had survived four decades in the Soviet grinder, a high administrative functionary successively in the NKVD, KGB, and SVR, through Khrushchev, Brezhnev, Andropov, Chernenko, and Gorbachev, through the dissolution of the Soviet Union, through the turmoil with drunken Yeltsin into the proto-Soviet moonscape of Putin. She had retired with honors and was now *zampolit,* political officer in the Russian Embassy in Paris, a ceremonial position, a reward for a lifetime of loyalty to the *Rodina.* She had brought him into the Service under her patronage. Maybe she could help him now. He picked up the secure Vey-Che phone and ordered the operator to connect him with Paris. He would tell her all the details. *Mamulya,* Mommy would know what to do.

Dominika had been at the guesthouse in Strelna for three days. She had no way of knowing what had happened with the TRITON meeting, and she expected and anticipated sudden exposure, the tramp of footsteps coming for her, the icy blue-eyed stare as she was led away from the madhouse charade of this power weekend. She was already surfeited with the cloying cream sauces, the endless ranks of chilled vodka bottles, the rose-scented sheets, the limitless views of the gunmetal sea, the piped-in patriotic songs—Putin's favorite was "From What Begins the Motherland"—for breakfast, lunch, and dinner. There had been a steady stream of guests—fat-bellied oligarchs, nicotine-fingered ministers, sloe-eyed models, and dissolute actresses—and they socialized together in groups in the salons, dining rooms, and terraces, then separated and came together again in different groups, in clouds of greedy yellows, fearful greens, or, occasionally, the blues of intellect.

Govormarenko, in a dingy yellow haze, early on took it upon himself to introduce Dominika to the arriving luminaries, transmitting with an arm around her waist a "she's with us" message, and the eyes would narrow and the heads would nod, and the women would appraise her jutting dancer's glutes, and the men would stare at her top hamper, and Govormarenko's hand would snake around her waist to steer her toward another introduction. Dominika initially planned to break the little finger of his encircling hand by bending it back to his wrist, but she quickly assessed this train of events and the opportunity it presented. She could not send a SRAC shot to Hannah—*Oh God, Hannah is gone*—but she knew what Nate would say, and Gable, and she could hear Benford's voice, so she smiled and joked with the men, hinted darkly about her work in the Service, and flattered the women with clotted foundation on their collars and salt rings under the arms of their blouses.

Dominika's magnificent radar registered the absence of sexual overtures from any of the men at the weekend retreat. To be sure, there were undisguised stares and furtive sidelong glances, but it was as if some invisible letter *Z* had been hung around her neck, *zapovednyy,* reserved, forbidden, hands off. But reserved for whom? After an initial and halfhearted flirtation from Govormarenko—his principal interest was food and drink—he did nothing more than paw at her waist and occasionally contrive to bump a shoulder against the side of her breast. It was clear that the only alpha male in the mansion had sprayed the tree trunk, and the lesser omegas of the pride could read territorial pheromones very well.

Udranka's spirit, sitting by the shore and singing the sweet song of the Rusalka, threw back her head and laughed. You're Putin's pussy.

Khorosho, very well. Dominika resolved to be CIA's penetration not only of SVR but also of Putin's wheeling circle of vultures in business, politics, and government. The president spoke to her whenever he saw her, a fact noted by one of the actresses who, by her dismayed expression, clearly had previously been one of Vladimir's wind-up toys. The president certainly was a dandy, dressed in open-necked shirts and fitted jackets. He had a jaunty sailor's roll when he walked. He was usually accompanied by a statuesque beauty who, it was whispered, had been a rhythmic gymnastics dancer—a Russian and Olympic champion. The rumor was confirmed on the second day, in the sprawling, mirrored basement gymnasium filled with machines and free weights, when the blonde, dressed in spandex, demonstrated some routines, including lying on her chest and bringing her legs back over her body so her toes touched the floor on either side of her head. The president, dressed in a heavy, woven judogi tied at the waist with a black belt, beamed at his soft pretzel.

Now the judo demonstration. To the delight of the overdressed guests who lined the enormous gym mat, Putin began grappling with a chunky man in his twenties, and threw him with great force each time they grabbed each other's lapels. The president was not thrown, ever—the young man knew how to fall and roll in this job. After one particularly violent takedown—Putin used *hane goshi,* the spring hip throw—a woman cried out in alarm and was shushed as if she were interrupting a pianist at a concert. After ten minutes, Putin straightened, wiped his face with a towel, and walked over to the nuzzling knot of sycophants, who politely applauded. Putin acknowledged the applause with Olympian modesty. His eye caught Dominika, standing in the back of the crowd.

"Captain, do you know judo?" Putin asked. Faces turned toward her.

"No, Mr. President," said Dominika.

"What do you think?" Putin said. Faces were swiveling between the two.

"Very impressive," said Dominika.

"I understand you were trained in *Sistema,*" said Putin. Faces turned again, expectant.

"Yes, Mr. President," said Dominika. She hoped she wasn't sounding like a cow.

"How would you compare judo against *Sistema*?" said Putin, draping the towel around his neck.

"It would be difficult to compare, Mr. President. For instance, I could identify only four ways to kill you during your sparring session." The nervous woman gasped again, and they all looked at Putin's face for his reaction. Putin's blue halo was pulsing, and the corners of his mouth twitched.

"The notorious reserve of the external service," said Putin to the crowd. He walked across the gym to the broad staircase leading up to the dining room, content to let the buzzing guests follow him and his blue aura like geese. The woman brushed past Dominika with her nose in the air, and a sweating industrialist mopped his face with a handkerchief and shook his head at Dominika, but she knew she had scored positive points with Putin. He was one-dimensional, primal, nationalistic, instinctive, afflicted with a world lens that registered only blacks and whites. But he was a natural conspirator who was concerned with only one thing—*sila*—power, strength, force. It was from having and keeping *sila* that everything else derived: personal wealth, Russian resurgence, territory, oil, global respect, fear, women. He consequently respected others who displayed strength. Dominika just hoped she hadn't overdone it.

That night, Dominika was on the terrace after dinner talking to a ferret-faced man from Gazprom who was predicting that, by controlling natural gas exports, Russia would reclaim the Baltic countries as integral republics in thirty-six months. Dominika imagined Benford's face when he read that. A white-coated attendant approached, stood with his heels together, and said that Captain Egorova was required in the president's study.

The first thing she saw on entering the room was that there were no armed men lined along the walls to take her away. Putin was sitting behind an ornate desk covered by green felt under a heavy piece of glass. He wore an open-necked shirt under a preposterous velveteen smoking jacket—his notion of what a *chentelman* wore after dinner. He motioned Dominika to a chair and stared at her in silence for ten seconds. Dominika willed herself to look back at him. Had TRITON delivered her name? Was the door going to blow in and security thugs fill the room? Putin's halo was steady; he did not appear outwardly agitated. He continued looking at her, his hands flat on the glass. How tiresome this Svengali act was; Dominika wanted to slap his blue eyes crossed.

"*Rezident* Zarubina is dead," said Putin. "She died last night during a meeting in Washington." *Was this a trap? She wasn't supposed to know about TRITON. Play dumb.*

Dominika kept her face closed down. "My God," she said. "How did she die?" *Satisfactory. But do they know my name?*

"Heart attack," said Putin, "while trying to escape from an ambush."

Too bad, Baba Yaga. I guess your broom couldn't fly you to safety, thought Dominika. "Ambush? How can this be? Zarubina was too good on the street," said Dominika, shaking her head. "But what about the source?" *Do you know my name?*

"Status unknown," said Putin, still looking at her. *Is this a game he is playing? Does he know something else?*

"Mr. President, this is a disaster. But in my work, when we speak of ambushes, we speak of foreknowledge, of setting a trap. Besides Zarubina and her team, the only two people in Line KR who knew the location of any Washington, DC, meeting sites were Colonel Zyuganov and Major Pletnev. Madame Zarubina kept very close control on such operational details."

"Pletnev is dead too," said Putin.

This time Dominika did not have to feign surprise. *Poor hairy Yevgeny, but now he's no longer a danger.* Her mind was racing, calculating, evaluating the risk of what she was going to do. "Pletnev dead?" said Dominika. "Did Colonel Zyuganov kill him?"

Putin leaned forward on the desk. "That's an interesting question," he said. "Why would you think that?" Putin smelled intrigue like a croc smelled a carcass in the river. And like crocodile Stalin, Vladimir Putin knew the value of keeping subordinates at one another's throats. Dominika registered his animated interest, took a deep breath, and told Putin about Zyuganov's boycott of information in Line KR, about how Yevgeny was frightened of him, about Zyuganov's fixation on and determination to uncover the mole.

"He is unsettled and imbalanced," said Dominika, as casually as she could. "He treated Yevgeny like a barn animal. Pletnev told me some of his troubles and, frankly, asked me for advice on operational matters." *It won't hurt Yevgeny now to say he talked out of school.* "And you have seen how Colonel Zyuganov tracked my vehicle, how he thought I was involved in the disappearance of Solovyov—*I*, who originally identified the general as suspicious." Dominika paused for effect. "The colonel is under immense strain. He has grown erratic." Mentioning Solovyov was safe; Govormarenko had gossiped about the general's disappearance.

"I have remarked on it," said Putin. "What do you make of him?" *Softly, obliquely,* thought Dominika.

"Mr. President, based on the little Major Pletnev confided in me, this all came to a head two days before Zarubina was reportedly to acquire a CIA mole's name. There is great turmoil. Zyuganov sends police to arrest me here, and now you tell me that he has killed Pletnev, and the *unbeatable* Zarubina is ambushed."

"What are you saying, Captain?" said Putin. Time for the *desinformatsiya,* the deception.

"These mishaps are nothing less than Zyuganov protecting himself, with the aid of the Americans. And who searches loudest and most noisily for the mole? The mole himself, Mr. President." Putin's blue eyes never left her face, but his cerulean halo pulsed, and Dominika knew he believed her.

That night in her bedroom at the mansion Dominika could not sleep. The medieval and massively heavy dinners continued: Tonight it had been carved roast beef, veal medallions, *buzhenina,* baked ham, roast duck and *patychky,* breaded Ukrainian meat skewers served with a fiery Moldovan *adzhika* pepper sauce. Cream- and butter-sauce boats sailed in formation between silver candlesticks. There were platters of herring, salmon, and sturgeon in dill and sour cream, and *kulebyaka,* salmon in puff pastry. *Pelmeni* and *vareniky* dumplings were ladled from tureens like hatchlings poured out in a fish farm. Chafing dishes of buttered vegetables; terrines of pork, salmon, and boar; and casseroles of mushrooms, truffle-laden, steaming when spooned out, covered the table. Govormarenko had joked loudly to Putin that delicacies from Ukraine, Georgia, and Moldova were all the more savory, to appreciative laughter from guests with full mouths. A yellow haze enveloped the table.

Dominika lay in the four-poster bed under a spectacular rose-colored goose-down comforter, listening to the ticking of an antique ormolu Empire mantel clock and the competing faint buzz of the sea outside her window. She had one more day in the extended weekend and was positively itching to get back to Moscow, to spin up her SRAC equipment, and to send a flurry of messages reporting everything that had happened. And it was certain that SRAC messages from Nate and Benford to her had been preloaded and would be waiting for the electronic handshake from her unit. She was on fire to know the status of TRITON, the circumstances of Zarubina's death, whether LYRIC was safe, and the small matter of whether *she* was safe. Hannah's spirit would be riding with her back to Moscow, she knew, and would be with her when she made her SRAC runs, working the mirrors, wide-eyed and laughing.

How she longed for Nate. The stress of the past days—the drive to Saint Petersburg, waiting on the exfil beach, watching and smelling and tasting this ghastly Putin menagerie—had exhausted her. She missed Nate's touch, longed to feel his lips. God, she wanted him. Dominika lay still under the billowing comforter and moved her hand between her legs. Grandmother's long-handled hairbrush—the tortoiseshell talisman that had helped her decipher her first adolescent urges—was in the luxurious tiled bathroom across the room, too far away. It didn't matter: She closed her eyes and saw Nate. Udranka laughed outside the window as Dominika's head pushed back deeper into the pillows, and her breath came in puffs through barely parted lips, and her eyes jounced around under closed eyelids, and the jolts started down her legs, to her curling toes. After a few delirious seconds her breath slowed and she blinked her eyes open, wondering for an instant where she was. Her thighs trembled with tiny aftershocks, and she wiped the dew off her upper lip. Then the impossible happened.

There was a soft rattle of the door handle and the door began to open. Dominika half sat up. The leading edge of a brilliant blue halo appeared slowly around the door. Bozhe moy! *My God,* thought Dominika, *it can't be.*

Marta, voluptuous, lush, abundant—with a mane of hair around her face—sat across the room on a couch, legs crossed, a cigarette dangling from her lips. Dominika's dead sister and fellow Sparrow blew a stream of smoke straight into the air, looked at the swinging door, and then at Dominika. What are you prepared to do? she whispered.

The president slipped into Dominika's bedroom—presumably knocking was not a consideration when Vlad had something on his mind. He walked slowly, passing through a shaft of moonlight from the ocean-side window that turned his blue halo turquoise. As he rounded the corner of her four-poster bed, Dominika hurriedly tried composing herself under the comforter—she had been thinking about Nate and her nightgown was gathered above her waist. Was the president's sudden appearance in her room the result of video coverage in her suite? Had the president watched grainy night footage of the stirrings of her trembling hand beneath the comforter? If he had, he moved quickly.

The president was wearing a plain dark-blue silk sleep shirt and pajama pants—Dominika drolly noted that there were no heraldic devices on the breast of the shirt, no Romanov double eagles, no hammer and sickle, no red star. Putin pulled up a delicate antique chair and sat beside the bed, close to Dominika, as if he were a country doctor come to take a patient's temperature. Dominika sat up and was about to pull the comforter demurely to her chin but instead let it drop to her lap—*What did it matter, she was Putin's Sparrow after all*—and reached to snap on the little coral-shaded bedside lamp. She saw the president's eyes flicker over the bodice of her sleeveless nightgown and the swell of her breasts under the lace.

Across the room, on the Recamier sofa the two of them—Marta and now Udranka—sat watching, her dead Sparrows there to give her strength. Hannah's ghost would not be here, not her, not for this.

"Good evening, Mr. President," said Dominika, casually, as if unannounced visits by the silk-festooned Sovereign of all the Russias to female guests' bedrooms in the Strelna guest mansion after midnight were perfectly common—which, Dominika concluded, they probably were.

"Captain Egorova," said Putin, not even remotely begging forgiveness for the intrusion, his eyes still on her cleavage. "I have been receiving a steady stream of communications concerning the subject we have been discussing. The most recent cable just arrived."

"Which subject is that, Mr. President?" said Dominika.

Udranka signaled she should do the discreet Sparrow Shrug and let one lacy nightgown strap fall off her shoulder. Devchonka, *you slut, be quiet,* thought Dominika.

"About Zarubina's source TRITON and the American mole in the Center," said Putin without a trace of impatience. "We received a cable tonight from the Paris *rezidentura.* TRITON attempted contact with the embassy there but the fools thought he was a crank and he was turned away by mistake. He left a local telephone number."

My God, thought Dominika, the man who could get her killed was already there and running free in Paris, a phone call away from contact. "So it is likely he escaped. Is the *rezidentura* going to try to find him?" she said. She would have to draft a dozen SRAC messages to Nate and Gable and Benford. They *had* to get after him. Putin did not answer.

"Colonel Zyuganov was informed of TRITON's appearance by an unauthorized secure phone call from Paris placed by his mother." Dominika registered that this meant Zyuganov's phone lines had been monitored. Her suggestion that he was the mole apparently had made an impression. Something else.

Putin leaned back in his chair. His blue halo pulsed. He was enjoying himself; perhaps he was imagining slipping under the comforter next to her. "Colonel Zyuganov was logged out of Vnukovo on a flight to Paris tonight. He has not checked in with our embassy. His whereabouts in Paris are unknown. His mother, Ekaterina, was found murdered in her apartment."

"Do you think he is gone, fled to the West?" said Dominika.

"Perhaps," said Putin. "But I believe he has gone to Paris for a desperate reason. I think he will call the local number TRITON left and ask for a meeting." Putin was thinking this through, dangerously so. Maybe he had doubts about Zyuganov's guilt. God, she had to transmit SRAC messages, to give CIA enough information to catch TRITON. If Zyuganov spoke to TRITON for even two minutes she would be finished.

"It is possible, Mr. President," said Dominika. "But what can he hope to accomplish?"

"Isn't it clear to you?" said Putin. "Zyuganov intends to eliminate TRITON, the source who can identify him as the Americans' mole."

"Mr. President!" said Dominika, feigning shock, but gratified that he had made a wrong assumption. Putin's blue halo positively glowed. The Russian in him was enjoying the chess game; the former KGB officer in him was savoring the maze of contradictions; the despot in him was relishing the mayhem. Something else in him was waking: He looked again at Dominika's breasts, at the hint of darker nipples under the dentelle lace. *Udranka clucked from the darkened corner of the room.* Putin leaned closer and put his hand on Dominika's hand.

"I want you to do something," he said, stroking her wrist. Dominika waited for him to speak, mentally cataloging the Babylonian possibilities. *Yes, or no, Benford? Nathaniel, will you understand?*

"I want you to go to Paris, this morning, without delay. You speak fluent French, yes?" The president's hand trailed up her stomach and lightly across her left breast. Dominika forced herself—*willed herself*—to stay still. She was conscious of involuntarily widening her eyes. Putin's X-ray blue eyes searched her face.

"You will arrange a meeting with TRITON before Zyuganov gets to him." His fingertips left the lace and traced a line on her skin between the swell of her breasts. Dominika was motionless. Could he feel her heart beating? Could he differentiate between the normal pulses of passion and the timpani pounding of revulsion? My God, was this stroking the preliminary to seduction, or was it more like what it seemed: Namely, the caress of a ravening collector handling an antique vase, the affirmation of ownership? Putin's halo enveloped her. His furry cologne—a ghastly rosewater- and cumin-infused toilet water from someplace like Sochi—got into her nose like a gnat. The president watched her face as his finger slipped under the material and made a slow circle around her left nipple. Dominika, the clinically trained Sparrow, knew the involuntary pilomotor reflex triggered by the release of oxytocin was contracting the skin beneath her nipples, but Vlad baby knew only that she was getting hard.

"After he tells you Zyuganov is the mole, I want you to dispose of TRITON," said the president. "He is blown, on the run, an embarrassment." *How charming,* she thought. *Hands on my tits and he orders me to commit statal murder; he wants me to kill for Mother Russia.* He was not content to bleed his country; now he would—once again—defame her. Dominika looked into his unblinking eyes. His lips were pursed as if he had nougat in his mouth. He was sitting very close to the bed, waiting, and Dominika, seized with an appallingly lurid intuition probably shared two thousand years ago by Messalina when she wormed an oiled hand under Claudius's toga, reached out and put her hand in the president's lap.

"Kill him?" whispered Dominika. So this was what it would be like as a member of the club. The president's nostrils flared as Dominika lightly felt around through the silk for the *laska,* the sleeping little weasel in his pajamas.

"And then I want you to clear up any misunderstandings remaining with Colonel Zyuganov," said Putin. Dominika's fingers detected something—it might be what she was looking for. Still sleeping.

"What do you—" The president softly squeezed her breast—his fingers were calloused—to silence her. Dominika thought a reciprocal squeeze would be appropriate. Nothing stirred in the silk forest.

"He need not return to Russia," said Putin. He took his hand away from her breast. Should she do the same? Not yet.

"We have men in Department Five who do these things," said Dominika, moving her thumb pad up and down. "Mr. President, I am hardly the best candidate." There was no reaction from between his legs. Was she losing her Sparrow touch? She'd been at the top of the class in what the matron instructors at Sparrow School had called monkey love.

In the corner of the room, Marta and Udranka looked at each other, shaking their ghostly heads.

"I want *you* to attend to it," said Putin. "As you will be promoted to chief of Line KR on your return from Paris, it is appropriate for you to manage this personnel action yourself." *Personnel action*—Stalin's venerable euphemism for wiping a human being from the face of the earth. This was the typical bear trap: Promotion. Kremlin favor. Profit sharing. And then she would belong to them, these black-mouthed reptiles throwing their coils around her chest to draw her close. It didn't make sense for her, specifically, to be sent to kill these two, but it didn't have to make sense. She recoiled at the oily orders given by this outwardly mellow potentate. Dominika knew that if she carried them out she would forever be under Putin's thumb. She thought it ironic, however, that Putin had for the last five minutes been under her thumb, with no appreciable results.

Chief of Line KR. She would be running counterintelligence for the entire Service. It would mean unparalleled access. Nathaniel and Gable and Forsyth and Benford would not believe her at first. And her blue-eyed, melon-headed benefactor had just given her the travel opportunity to meet them and tell them. But God, she had to get to Paris immediately and prevent Zyuganov from closing with TRITON. Dominika knew Nate would rush to Paris when she called her SENTRY number—they would find a solution to this together. Together.

Her sudden longing for Nate reminded her she still had her hand in the president's lap. His face was impassive, but there was some stirring, in fact quite a lot of stirring, as if Putin could on demand make the weasel come out of the forest. With practiced feel, Dominika estimated smaller-than-average dimensions, but it was quite firm. His hand reached out and caressed her breast again, lightly, just fingertips brushing skin. Dominika wanted to scream, but she lowered her eyes and smiled at him.

He looked back at her without agitation or emotion. "Are you willing to accomplish these things?" he asked her, the wakened weasel now noticeable under the pajamas. Dominika realized that giving the order to kill had been the stimulus, the turn-on.

Dominika balanced the prospect of a decades-long torrent of intelligence production for CIA against an abject and scurvy existence as a female member of this rat pack, the first scene of which she was now playing out, teasing the weasel of the president.

"Mr. President, I will do anything to help you and my country," said Dominika, with a look that might have also hinted *You don't own me.*

President Putin returned her look with a rare, small smile that said, *Sure I do,* and, as if to demonstrate his adamantine will, stood up, looked down at her, nodded, and left the room silently. Her hand still tingling, Dominika could only stare at the slowly closing door. Exhausted by the last seven minutes, she sank back into her pillows while Marta and Udranka applauded from the shadows. But now Hannah was in the room too; *Dude, get ready, we have a lot of work to do.* And Dominika was glad she had their spirits with her—and she would see Nate soon. The tiny clock on the mantelpiece, which had chimed the hour for the Grand Duke Constantine two hundred years ago, chimed now for Dominika, as if announcing the start of the race to Paris.

PATYCHYKY—MEAT SKEWERS

Thread meat cubes marinated in vinegar on skewers and squeeze together to form lumpy kebabs. Mix bread crumbs, curry powder, salt, and pepper, and coat the meat skewers. Roll them in an egg wash, then again in the bread crumbs, pressing to adhere and to compact the meat. Fry the skewers in oil until golden, then place them on a bed of butter and sliced onions and bake in a low oven until the meat is tender. Serve with salad and adzhika sauce.

39

Seb Angevine had to run his fingers through his hair and compose himself before opening the door to Vikki's apartment. He had driven away from the park in a panic, forcing himself to motor slowly through the city, shaken and looking in his rearview mirror for flashing red lights, taking Columbia Road south onto quiet Twenty-second, across Buffalo Bridge, stair-stepping through deserted Georgetown, then north on Thirty-seventh into Glover Park. As he drove he deleted the digital files stored in Gamma, and with shaking fingers pried out the tiny memory card. The little camera was flipped over the bridge into Rock Creek, and the memory card with 22GB of top-secret internal CIA cables—including the true names of CIA sources—went down a sewer grate on Q Street. No matter: He had memorized the name of Dominika Egorova. Ten minutes later, Angevine parked Vikki's car close to the back door of the apartment unit, partially screened from the street by a commercial Dumpster. He sucked at a bleeding knuckle and tried to think.

Putain de bordel, goddamn it, this was disaster, this was ruin, this *was exactly why* he had told himself he would not deal with the Russians in person. His new BMW was parked one car down, and its shark nose seemed to wag at him in condescending disapproval. He didn't exactly know how Vikki would take the news that he was a disaffected and invidious senior CIA official treasonously providing classified US information of national-security import to the external intelligence service of the Russian Federation in exchange for obscene amounts of money, and had narrowly escaped being swarmed this evening in a downtown park by unidentified law-enforcement officials—presumably FBI—who in all likelihood were driving to Vikki's apartment at this moment to arrest him. He hoped she could handle it all at once.

"You fucking asshole!" Vikki said.

"I only passed background material," Angevine lied.

"I helped you get that note to the fat Russian guy at the club," Vikki said. She was not dancing tonight and had been sitting on the couch in her underwear watching television and sewing a new costume. She was now standing squared off in front of him, hands on her hips. Angevine registered how good her body looked and the thought flitted across his mind that maybe he should include her in his hastily formed plan. *Nope,* he thought, *this bolt-hole was for one. Too bad, really.*

"No one got hurt," he said. "Nobody." He had forgotten about the attaché recalled from Caracas, and about the thirty days of counterintelligence interviews endured by General Solovyov.

"I'm an accomplice, you bastard; they could charge me for helping you," said Vikki. Her MemoryGel High Profile implants were heaving with emotion, and her hands were now clenched into fists.

"My information only provided insights that reassured Moscow we could be better partners internationally," said Angevine loftily, using the Aldrich Ames defense, though he sounded to himself like a United Nations delegate in a fez discussing global initiatives at a shrimp boil on Bayou Bartholomew.

"That's just freaking great," said Vikki. "Better partners."

"I need your help," said Angevine. "One last time."

"I'll help you, all right," said Vikki. "I'll help you pack your clothes and get the hell out of here."

"I'll leave, if that's what you want," said Angevine, "but I need you to drive me, just a little way, and that's all." This was going to be tricky, he knew, but he couldn't do it without her. He had read about the technique when he was still in NCIS, and never forgot it. But now he had to work on Vikki. He dangled the keys to his BMW.

"I'm giving you my car. I was going to surprise you over dinner," said Angevine. From her expression, it was clear that Vikki did not believe him.

"Look," said Angevine, "I'm not going to lie to you. I've fallen for you, fallen hard. I need your help getting out of the country, to get to France. Once I'm out, you're meeting me there . . . under the Eiffel Tower," he added for effect. Vikki crossed her arms in front of her—defensive, wavering a little—and shook her head.

"We have to hurry a little, baby," said Angevine. He walked over to the window that looked out onto the rear parking lot and peeked through the blinds. Nothing. Yet. He turned back to Vikki and put his arms around her, sliding them up and down her back. "We've been through a lot," Angevine cooed, "and the good times are all ahead of us."

"What do you want me to do?" asked Vikki slowly, surprised that she felt sorry for him, even though he was full of shit. And he was giving her the car. And she'd never been to Paris.

"Where's Agatha?" said Angevine, smiling and holding her at arm's length.

"In the closet," said Vikki. "What do you want with her?"

"You'll see," said Angevine.

Zyuganov hung up the phone, having listened to his mother for forty minutes tell him how *odurelnyy,* how colossally stupid he had been. She was losing her mind: She scolded him while stirring a pot of *Soupe a L'ail,* creamy garlic soup, she was making for her lunch. *Put down the spoon and listen,* he thought. She told him not to do anything rash, stop giving orders to everyone, and stay quiet. Attract no attention to yourself, she advised. *Nebylo u baby hlopot tak kupila porosya,* Ekaterina Zyuganova told her son, *a woman had no trouble so she bought a piglet;* you've asked for trouble. She would make a call or two, revive old contacts, and call him back. She told him his first duty was to the State, that the State would take care of him, that he owed his first and last loyalty to Russia. Zyuganov privately thought his mother was a throwback Bolshevik: He had forgotten how old-fashioned she was.

Ekaterina Zyuganova had known Zarubina and was shocked to hear she'd had a heart attack—the news of her death had rocketed around the Center and to worldwide *rezidenturi.* She told her son that she guessed that the fate of TRITON—and subsequently of the mole inside the Center—would not be known for some time but that, in her experience from the Stalin years, all traitors eventually were unmasked.

"Eventually may not be fast enough for me," Zyuganov had told his mother. The investigators looking into the "quarrel" that resulted in Yevgeny Pletnev's death had demanded that Colonel Zyuganov relinquish his service passport—it would be best if he did not contemplate foreign travel for the immediate future. A furious Zyuganov also had to sit still for an audit of his section—Line KR had been immune to such internal controls in the past. Interviews with all employees of Line KR were scheduled. Zyuganov knew the signs: For all intents and purposes he was under loose house arrest; his command of Line KR soon would be taken away from him; it would be a short step to arrest, trial, and prison. And Egorova—*he absolutely knew* she was the CIA mole—dined in luxury on the shores of the Gulf of Finland with the president and his guests.

Five vehicles from the Gs—the FBI's counterintelligence surveillance team—took up positions characteristic to this special kind of surveillance: They would monitor Vikki Mayfield with the intention of seeing who she was with. Coverage did not have to be discreet; the goal was to identify the man who had escaped from the park. Fileppo and Proctor provided whatever description of the man they could, arguing testily between themselves. They were in one car. Nate rode with another G named Vannoy, a phlegmatic twenty-six-year-old with a movie-idol profile and Popeye forearms. At the team's arrival, a blacked-out G vehicle ghosted through Vikki's building's rear lot, the passenger reading the numbers of the license plates of the parked cars into his radio. These would be traced instantly by FBI in federal, metropolitan, and national databases. The team dispersed into "fore and aft" positions, four cars to cover all possible directions radiating from Mayfield's building. Nate's car was coordinating rover. They settled in.

"I'm always on the other end of surveillance," said Nate. "It's the waiting that's hard; I never realized it."

Vannoy looked at him. "You get used to it," he said. "You were in Moscow, right?"

Nate nodded.

"They pretty good over there?" In the streetlight, he looked like a silent-film star.

"They go in pretty heavy," said Nate. "Unlimited resources and they don't have to answer to anybody."

He looked out the window for a second. "We lost an officer in Moscow a few weeks ago," said Nate. "They hit her with a car. Accident I guess."

Vannoy's eyes narrowed. "Her?" he said.

"Yeah, Hannah Archer; bigger balls than you and me combined," said

Nate. They were quiet for a minute. "And now she's got a star on the wall at Headquarters."

"I've seen that wall," said Vannoy. "Lots of stars."

"I've seen your FBI Hall of Honor too," said Nate. They fell silent, listening to the night sounds in the dark neighborhood. Dead leaves in the gutter rustled in the light breeze. It was colder now, past midnight. The radio, volume turned low, burped once.

"How long to run those plates?" said Nate.

"Takes a little longer at night," said Vannoy.

"I'm sure Fileppo and Proctor want to get their hands on this guy, whoever he is," said Nate. "Asshole dusted Fileppo pretty good."

"Proctor will help him ice it down," said Vannoy. Something in his voice?

"Those two are amazing on the street," said Nate. "Seriously, I never saw two guys work together like that."

Vannoy shifted in his seat. "They're good, maybe the best on the whole team," said Vannoy. "They piss off everybody, but they get results."

"It's like they know what each other is thinking," said Nate.

"They should; they've been together long enough," said Vannoy.

"What, like roommates?" said Nate.

Vannoy looked to see if Nate was fucking with him, saw that he wasn't. "Yeah, roommates," said Vannoy.

Nate opened his mouth to say something, but the radio hissed with three squelch breaks—someone moving—and Vannoy started the car. Vikki Mayfield's cherry-red Kia pulled out onto Benton Street. A woman wearing a hoodie was driving. A passenger sat tall in the passenger seat and wore a brimmed hat. Looking through binoculars, Nate could clearly see him—a man with a prominent nose—as he reached over to touch the driver on the shoulder. Vannoy let two cars slot in behind the Kia and took the third position. There would be no need for fancy tactics like handing off the eye or leapfrogging ahead of the rabbit. Just follow the Kia, period. Vannoy reported by radio as the team started rolling. Two minutes later, Nate's cell phone rang. Benford. Pissed. Seriously pissed.

"Nash, put me on speaker; your team leader needs to hear this," said Benford. "Special Agent Montgomery and I are sitting in the Ops Center of the Washington Field Office surrounded by a herd of wildebeests from the FBI's Office of General Counsel. A like-minded herd of gnus is sitting in CIA

Headquarters. We are, forgive the hyphenated word, video-conferencing in real time."

"Coming through loud and clear, Chief," said Nate, winking at Vannoy, who suppressed a chuckle. There was a brief hesitation. Benford's agitation was palpable.

"It is our belief that the man in the park, and the passenger in the vehicle you are following, is Sebastian Angevine, CIA associate deputy director for Military Affairs. It is his registered license plate on a car at Mayfield's building. We are reviewing Angevine's internal computer-access profile as we speak. An audit of his finances and accounts will begin tomorrow morning. Mayfield is employed as an exotic dancer in Washington and is, presumably, his paramour." Nate had a wisecrack in mind regarding "paramour" but wisely decided now was not the time.

"I am advised both by FBI and CIA counsels that at this time there is no *proof* that Angevine is guilty of espionage as described in either 18 U.S.C. 794 (a) or (b) or in 17 U.S.C. 794 (c). This may change if and when any compelling evidence surfaces. Accordingly, Nash, and listen carefully, there is no authority for stopping or detaining either Angevine or Mayfield. Please ensure that the team understands this. Special Agent Montgomery is telling me that 'it's an order,' which in FBI culture must mean that it's imperative."

"Understood, Chief; we'll make sure the team knows," said Nate into the phone. "We're leaving Glover Park and moving north on Wisconsin. She's driving moderately through light traffic. It's too early to predict direction. Maybe she's taking him home. I'm assuming he lives in Virginia?"

Benford's muffled voice asked a question to someone in the room. "Correct. He lives in Vienna, Virginia, off Beulah Road," said Benford. "Nathaniel, that these two are moving on the street past midnight in the same evening of a busted clandestine meeting with the now-defunct Russian *rezident* is, for us sentient nonlawyers, a significant suggestion of guilt. We have no way to know how Angevine assesses his situation, especially in the *context of proof.* He may be confident or panicked. It is therefore your only job to stay close and not let him out of your sight. If they go to a bar at this late hour take a table beside them. If he goes to the men's room, use the stall next door. If they go to his home, set up outside, making sure he cannot slip out the back door. Call it in and we'll make sure the Vienna police do not shoot you. Am I clear?"

Vikki was muttering to herself as she followed Angevine's directions on what turns to make. Wisconsin Avenue was nearly empty. Seb was sitting in the passenger seat with Agatha—a three-quarter-length dressmaker's dummy—on the floor between his legs. Vikki used the padded torso to design stripper outfits and showgirl headdresses; Agatha had a featureless, smooth, white plastic head. A coat was buttoned around the torso, and a beige plastic bag stretched over the head had been taped tightly around the neck. Vikki had complained when Angevine wrenched and twisted the metal stand out of the bottom of the dummy, but he told her she wouldn't be *making* dresses any longer—she would be *wearing* Chanel in Paris by Christmas, to which she replied "bullshit" but secretly hoped so.

He obviously knew where he wanted to go—he had cased this route ahead of time. An animated Angevine told her to go through Tenley Circle, then take Albermarle into American University Park, a neighborhood of streets in a tight grid square, with parallel alleys running behind houses. Vikki saw three sets of headlights follow at a respectful distance turn for turn. Angevine told her not to worry about them, and made her repeat exactly what she was to do when he exited the car. This was it. He barked at her to turn right, then quickly left onto Murdock Mill Road, a short one-way street that they entered the wrong way. As the following cars' headlights disappeared for a second around the double corner, Angevine tapped Vikki on the arm and she pulled the emergency brake to slow the car. Angevine shouldered the door open, jumped out, and ran into the shadows of an alley, skidding to a stop behind a row of garbage cans. He crouched and held his breath.

For a terrified amateur on her first time, Vikki nailed it. She released the brake and kept going without a check in speed, steering straight while she reached over, pulled the door shut, grabbed Agatha off the floor, propped her up on the passenger seat, and clapped Angevine's discarded hat on the dummy's head. *Who's the dummy?* thought Vikki, bitterly, now on her own and once again in the headlight glare of cars behind her. She continued east on Butterworth, around Westmoreland Circle to Dalecarlia, which would take her via Canal Road and Chain Bridge into suburban Virginia. Her instructions were to drive to Angevine's town house and straight into the attached garage. Vikki was to spend the night in the house with all the curtains drawn. She was to undress and stash Agatha in a junk closet in the finished basement. In the morning she could return to her house, leaving the FBI to wonder how and exactly when Angevine had disappeared into thin air.

Three cars back, Nate's instincts were jangling off the hook. The stair-step route through AU Park was bullshit, illogical. That prick was planning something and Nate asked Vannoy to tell the car with the eye to close up and watch out for a car escape. He didn't know whether Angevine even knew how to bail out of a moving vehicle under surveillance, but it was important that the lead unit regularly verified that two people were in the car. Nate was on the phone to Benford passing updates. Fileppo and Proctor were in the second vehicle, giving the rest of the team unmitigated shit, and Vannoy told them to shut the fuck up and take the eye. They immediately reported that there were two people in the car—the woman and the tall man with a hat.

Angevine had seen four or five cars pass his alleyway, and none of the cars had slowed, no one looked to the side—they had missed his escape. Now he needed time. It was all up to Vikki (and Agatha) to keep the ball rolling. He checked his watch. Nearly 2:00 a.m. He would have to hike out of the neighborhood, but the metro would be running by 5:00 a.m. He'd get to Union Station and grab the MARC to BWI—if they discovered he was missing they'd shut down Dulles and National airports first, then think about Baltimore/Washington International later. By then he'd be on the first foreign flight to anywhere—Mexico City, Costa Rica, Toronto; he'd buy tickets to his first stop with his credit cards and true-name passport, leave a trail, then disappear after a second flight into the European Union. He could get to Paris without a trace. Paris was the place: He spoke the language, knew the city, had relatives there. He had cash, and could eventually buy a black-market alias French identity document. And the Russian Embassy, a modern concrete-and-glass fortress near the Bois de Boulogne on the Boulevard Lannes in the sixteenth, would welcome him with open arms, especially if he arrived with the name of the CIA source inside the Russian Service. It was imprinted in his money-grubbing memory: *Dominika Vasilyevna Egorova.*

Angevine did not intend to retire in exile in some overheated defector's apartment in Moscow, like Kim Philby, or Ed Howard, or Edward Snowden, minded by dour FSB watchdogs, cooked for by a headstrong battle-ax, and serviced every ten days by third-tier slatterns with acne between their breasts and skin tags on their necks. No, thank you. All he required of the Russians was a retirement payout and access to his foreign account, which, by his conservative estimate, was somewhere around five million dollars. Money in hand, he would then disappear: A little house with a terrace shaded by flowering vines on one of the Aeolian Islands; maybe a penthouse on Avenida Atlantica along Copacabana Beach; or maybe a stone mansion on a hill in Tuscany, surrounded by his own vineyard. A girlfriend or two—those Brazilians girls were blazingly hot—but Angevine couldn't see Vikki fitting in. He wondered whether she would realize that when she tapped him on the arm to signal his rollout, it was the last time they'd touch. Well, she got the BMW.

As he walked down alleys, sticking to the shadows and thinking about the girls in his future, Angevine randomly and suddenly remembered how Gloria Bevacqua, the sow who had stolen the top operations job out from under him, had mocked him the morning of the announcement. *Chicks dig you, Seb,* she had smirked at him, and in his fury he had been launched on this, this *utterly insane,* this *utterly destructive* journey with the Russians, and now he was walking footsore and sick with worry in the night, a fugitive. He had narrowly escaped from those galloping night stalkers in the park, but there was no guarantee he'd even make it through the airport. He was not sorry for what he had done, but he felt sorry for himself. A sob caught in his throat and he cried silently as he walked. *Chicks dig you, Seb,* echoed in his head, the big spy, the big man. He wondered what Zarubina was reporting back to Moscow—probably that he was caught and arrested. They'd be amazed to see him surface in Paris. He brightened as he imagined how he'd coolly tell the Russian Embassy receptionist to telephone upstairs to the *relevant office* to inform them that TRITON was in the lobby.

Vikki had also been crying, gripping the wheel of her little car wondering whether she was going to jail for leading five ominous FBI cars behind her on a prolonged goose chase into the vastness of suburban Virginia, to give Seb time to get away. She might have been able to plead ignorance—he had lied to her, misled her, she didn't have anything to do with anything—but the stiff-backed presence of the dressmaker's dummy with the floppy hat propped on the seat next to her would be proof of her complicity. Vikki contemplated pulling into the next strip-mall parking lot and walking back to the cars and telling them everything she knew, which wasn't much. She wasn't guilty. With the instincts of a professional stripper, Vikki somehow knew Seb would never send for her to meet him in Paris. But she couldn't hurt him. In any case, the decision quite unexpectedly was made for her.

A drunk pulling out of an all-night fast-food drive-thru crossed two lanes of Route 123 in Vienna and narrowly missed Vikki's car, thanks partly to her violent swerving and locking of brakes. Behind her, Fileppo and Proctor likewise screeched to a stop, both of them braced for the thoracic thump of metal when cars collide. They slid to a stop inches from Vikki's rear bumper, but the kettledrum crunch came when the G car in position two collided with the rear of Fileppo's car, subsequently pushing them heavily into Vikki's car. The chain-reaction shock wave was transmitted through bumper and frame, with the result that featherweight Agatha was catapulted forward into the windshield, then backward against the seat and headrest, snapping off her plastic head, now hatless, which bounced and landed on the rear window shelf, where it rocked back and forth, a Cold War commemorative bobblehead. Vikki put her face in her hands. *This is all the time you're going to get, Seb,* she thought. Proctor and Fileppo walked up to Vikki's car. Fileppo leaned into the window, asked if she was all right, and told her to turn off her engine. She put her forehead on the steering wheel and closed her eyes

She heard another voice talking into a phone. "Simon," the voice said, "he used a JIB head, a goddamn homemade jack-in-the-box, and rolled out. Best guess is AU Park; no reason to have gone through there except for an escape. Probably forty minutes ago. Two cars are going back to sweep search the area, but if he's in a cab or in the metro, he's gone." Vikki looked up from the steering wheel and saw a young man with dark hair with a phone to his ear. He was listening carefully. He thumbed the phone off and turned to the other two guys—all three of them younger than she would have expected, but with grim faces. The first young guy said, "Everyone stays put until a special agent gets here. None of us has arrest authority." Nate leaned into Vikki's window.

"You okay?" Nate smiled.

Vikki nodded.

"Just off-the-record, you have any idea where your boyfriend is headed?" Nate had just potentially violated Vikki's rights.

"Dude, chill," said Fileppo. Proctor nodded. They knew about this legal shit.

"We've fucked this up several times, man," said Proctor. "Don't do it this way." Nate ignored them and looked at Vikki.

"I don't know what you know, or what he told you, or what you think," said Nate, "but if he gets away, a woman about your age is going to die by being fed alive, feet first, into a crematorium."

Fileppo looked at Nate, surprised. "C'mon, miss," he said, forgetting himself. "You can't let that happen."

"Not you too," said Proctor. "Shut the fuck up, both of you."

Vikki looked up at the three of them. "He said he's going to Paris. That's all I know," Vikki said, contemplating for the first time in her career the irony of her stage name at the Good Guys Club—Felony.

FRENCH GARLIC SOUP (SOUPE A L'AIL)

Bring chicken stock to a boil. Sauté abundant minced garlic in duck fat (or olive oil), add to the stock along with a bouquet garni, and simmer. Remove the bouquet and add beaten egg whites to the soup, let them set, and remove from the heat. Temper egg yolks, add them to the soup, and season with salt and pepper. Put a slice of day-old country bread in a bowl, sprinkle with Parmesan, then pour soup over. Egg whites can be cut into smaller pieces.

40

The morning after his escape, Angevine stood on the sidewalk outside the Russian Embassy in Paris. Traffic on Boulevard Lannes was Gallic insanity: Two lanes of the broad and normally graceful avenue became, during *pointe du matin*—morning rush hour—an untidy, four-lane mass of blue exhaust, honking horns, and overwrought Parisians. His escape had gone off without a hitch: No alerts had arrived at Baltimore/Washington International. He had compulsively decided to risk a direct flight from BWI to Amsterdam, and immediately went to the Central Station and took the high-speed Thalys train to Paris Nord. In the borderless European Union—thanks to the Schengen Agreement of 1995—there were no internal passport controls anywhere. The only record of his travel would be his name on the flight manifest from the Baltimore flight, but after arrival in Amsterdam, he was gone, disappeared. And based on other defectors' escapes over the decades, CIA moreover would assume he was already in Moscow.

Arriving in Paris, Angevine went directly to his aunt's dormer apartment on the top floor of the building at 11 Quai de Bourbon on the Île Saint-Louis, the lozenge-shaped island in the River Seine upstream of and connected to the larger Île de la Cité. His widowed aunt was his late father's sister, deaf and addled, but most important, the crone had a different last name. There would be no hotel-registration cards, no tracing him to this apartment. The apartment was cluttered but comfortable, bookshelves bursting with papers and ceramic figures. It smelled like cats and cabbage. From the grimy windows of the spare bedroom he could look out onto the Right Bank and, just over the trees, see the mansard towers of l'Hôtel de ville, city hall. Angevine listened to the hourly bells in Notre Dame Cathedral: He was home again—at least it felt that way—and he could *operate* here. And he wouldn't be surprised if tomorrow the astonished Russians changed his cryptonym from TRITON to LAZARUS.

That's what he had thought. Now he was on the sidewalk, nursing a bruised bicep, and looking back through the barred gate at a beefy embassy guard with no neck who had frog-marched him out of the consular section, past amused Frenchmen waiting for their visas, and out the gate with a shove. Angevine felt like screaming at the ape—they had no idea the mistake they were making—but people in a line outside the gate were staring, and he didn't want to attract attention. He had bellowed at the startled receptionist inside too, repeating his last name, spelling it, demanding to see someone with authority, claiming to have a professional connection to Madame Zarubina in Washington, DC. This all meant nothing to the young receptionist—she was the wife of a junior vice consul—but she was familiar with the type of *bezumtsy,* the madmen who often appeared in the visa office, drawn by the allure of a foreign embassy and convinced they were engaged in undefined but important missions involving, typically, either outer-space travel or spy work. The receptionist pressed the button under the counter while taking down the man's local telephone number to placate him until the guard appeared from a side door to throw him out.

The receptionist told her husband about this latest fruitcake over lunch of *blanquette de veau,* a silky, milk-white veal stew, at the nearby Brasserie Alaux on the Rue de la Faisanderie. The husband had heard the name Zarubina before, though he couldn't recall what it had been about, except it had something to do with *them* upstairs. When dealing with *them,* it always paid to be careful. After lunch, the vice consul retrieved the fruitcake's scrawled name and number from his wife's notepad and went upstairs to the grilled day gate of the *rezidentura* and pressed the bell. There was no movement in the corridor for half a minute, then the sounds of footsteps. The clunky matron Zyuganova—it was whispered throughout the embassy that she had been a favorite of Andropov's who had brought her with him from the KGB when he became general secretary of the Party—stood silently, looking at him through the screen. *A real Bolshevik, this one,* thought the young vice consul; *not many of them left.* In a brief sentence he explained what he was doing there, and handed her the scrap of paper through the mail slot.

"In case it is something important," he said, bowing a little at the waist.

"Thank you, comrade," said Zyuganova, with a face that betrayed nothing. *Who is she calling comrade?* thought the vice consul as he headed for the stairwell.

Zyuganova wrote the number in a steno pad, then took the original note to the *rezident,* who characteristically did not like discussing operational matters with this woman, this cast-iron Soviet throwback *apparatchik*—he had been saddled with her as *zampolit,* a political advisor from the Center—but he listened as she said the fruitcake visitor had mentioned Zarubina, and they had all heard about her death in Washington—gossip got around faster than intel reports—so it was probably important. Ekaterina Zyuganova smoothed her elaborate upswept hair last in style during the Khrushchev era, and argued that quick action was of the essence: The Paris *rezidentura* should attempt to contact this American and meet with him as soon as possible. She did not mention that she knew everything about TRITON and the mole hunt after talking to her son, nor did she raise the importance of all this to Alexei, who would be vindicated, exonerated, and restored if the American mole was identified.

The Paris *rezident* didn't like any of it. He was thinking of his own equities, and was nervous about the counterintelligence pressures he had been feeling lately on the street from the DST, the French internal service. He saw danger signals everywhere: No one knew what had happened in Washington, whether it was a flap and an arrest, but when someone like Zarubina dies, it probably wasn't good news. Now an unvetted madman miraculously appears in Paris, asking for contact with SVR. He wasn't buying it; this probably was a trap—the Americans were aggressive, probably in league with the French. He smelled ambush, provocation, a dispatched double agent.

Zyuganova recognized the signs of timorous careerism in the *rezident,* sweating behind his desk, but she was determined to spur Yasenevo to action: If the Paris *rezident* would not act, they could at least send a telegram to Moscow, with the details of the fruitcake's appearance, to let them decide. As a concession to her seniority and vestigial influence in Yasenevo, they drafted an urgent cable to the Center together. It might be as long as a day before Moscow responded. Zyuganova waited an hour, then called her son on the Vey-Che line and told him the whole story.

"I am coming to Paris," Zyuganov said. He wanted TRITON's Paris number.

"You'll do nothing of the sort," Zyuganova snapped. "You have been instructed to remain at work. You may not travel." She knew the perilous position sonny boy was in, and the importance—*the necessity*—of obeying orders and coming out of this affair in one piece. Survival in SVR was not easy: Ekaterina knew how the *chudovishche*, the monster, dormant under the surface, could, with terrifying speed, emerge and devour miscreants. During her forty years in the Service she had followed the rules and spouted the cant, out-Heroding Herod from her seats on the Collegium of the KGB, on the staff of the Central Committee, and in the office of the chairman of the Party.

So it was with a mixture of alarm and anger that Zyuganova greeted her son when he appeared at her apartment in the fashionable Parisian suburb of Neuilly a day later. He was ill-dressed in a cloth coat and baggy pants, and he was unshaven. His eyes had that certain glassiness the mother recognized as the augury of one of his Lubyanka moods, unpredictable and vicious. The Center had already sent an advisory to the *rezidentura* that Zyuganov was headed for Paris—he had departed from Vnukovo airport with his civilian passport, violating the restrictions of the ongoing investigation set by SVR inspectors. The Center instructed the Paris *rezidentura* to escort Zyuganov—if he appeared at the embassy—immediately to the airport and put him on the next flight back to Moscow. He wasn't officially a fugitive, but unless he returned immediately, Zyuganova knew, he would be ruined, whatever the outcome with TRITON. She resolved to save her son by turning him in.

Zyuganov was no longer thinking clearly, much less rationally. He was aware only of an animal need to uncover the name of the mole, and if skipping out of the country against orders and dangerously flitting into a possible American intelligence ambush was the only way to do it, then that is what he was going to do. His mother stood in the middle of her tasteful apartment speaking to him with that Central Committee tone of voice that, depending on the point she wanted to make and the height of her emotion, varied from a steely monotone to a full-throated bellow. She was bellowing at him now, furious at his stupidity, furious that her forty-something-year-old son had disobeyed her, had disobeyed the State. *Govniuk!* Shit for brains.

Ekaterina walked to the side table in the living room and picked up the telephone. Security from the nearby embassy on the other side of the Bois would be here in two minutes, to escort her son back home, stuffed in a wicker laundry basket if necessary. She identified herself to the telephone operator and asked to be transferred to the *rezident*. That's the last thing she remembered clearly. Zyuganov came up behind his mother, swung his fist, and hit her on the side of the neck. She groaned, dropped the telephone, and fell to the parquet floor. Shaking her head, she looked up and saw what countless prisoners in the cellars had seen—the freezing glower of a butcher at midnight—but what no mother wants to see reflected in the face of her *mal'chik*, her baby boy. Zyuganov ripped the phone out of the wall.

Ekaterina heaved herself to her feet and staggered into her bedroom holding her neck—another telephone was on the night table. Zyuganov was behind her and pushed her violently onto the bed. Ekaterina screamed at him, called his name, tried to break through the psychotic tantrum that blazed in his eyes. Her diminutive son leaped on her and his fingers brushed across a garment in plastic fresh from the *teinturier*, the dry cleaner, and he wrapped the billowing film around her head, once, twice, and strained it tight under her chin. Zyuganov's tooth-baring grimace was inches from his mother's face, and he watched her eyes go wide, and her open mouth sucked in plastic, and her head shook side to side, desperately trying to get oxygen. He pressed down on top of her and held on tight until her heaving slowed, her legs stopped kicking, and the familiar shudder—well known to Zyuganov—passed through her, and she stared at him through her shroud. He rolled off her, then went through her pockets. Too easy: He had TRITON's phone number. He knew he had to get out of the apartment immediately. He rummaged in drawers on his hurried way out.

As he walked away from the building, Zyuganov saw a Russian Embassy Peugeot pull up—the diplomatic plates on the car and the bullet heads of the occupants were unmistakable. They'd find his mother, but they could not positively connect him to that. The French police would want to question him. But it wouldn't matter, he told himself irrationally. He would return triumphant to Moscow with proof that Egorova was in the pay of CIA, and he would be vindicated, congratulated, promoted. Wild thoughts of bringing TRITON back with him—a gift for Putin's trophy wall—caromed in his head.

Zyuganov walked quickly past the shops and apartment buildings along Rue de Longchamp to the Pont de Neuilly metro and cleared the area. As he rode rocking into the center of Paris—he planned to call TRITON from one of the phone-card-operated booths in the Galeries Lafayette on Boulevard Haussmann—his distracted mind skipped over the vinyl long-play record of his memory. Events had come in a rush: The traitor Solovyov had disappeared; Egorova was a guest of Putin; the Washington meeting with TRITON had imploded; Zarubina was dead; TRITON appeared in Paris, asking for contact; his mother had called; he had come to Paris; and he had resolved outstanding issues with her. By tonight he would be talking to TRITON, and could return to Moscow triumphant. Troubles with Putin would evaporate, and recriminations involving Yevgeny would fade away.

What he didn't know was that the president of the Russian Federation had his own timetable.

BLANQUETTE DE VEAU

Boil peeled pearl onions and sliced mushrooms in water and butter until glossy and soft. Cover cubed veal, rough-cut onions, carrots, celery, and bouquet garni with water, bring to a boil, then simmer until the veal is fork-tender. Strain the meat, reserve the broth, and discard the vegetables and bouquet. Make a roux, incorporate the broth, and boil until the sauce thickens. Add pearl onions, mushrooms, cream, salt, pepper, and veal, and continue simmering. Temper egg yolks and whisk into the stew, but do not boil. Add lemon juice and serve with potato puree or white rice.

41

Dominika was free of the grimy-necked court of oligarchs at Strelna, free of the sucking noises as brittle-haired women cleaned their teeth after dinner with silver toothpicks, free of midnight caresses by her pajama-clad president. She landed at Charles de Gaulle International Airport on the first morning flight from Saint Petersburg and called CIA's SENTRY number, repeating her designator and telling the operator she was in Paris, the name of her hotel, and her newly purchased cell-phone number. It usually took Nate forty-eight hours to get there.

The last time Dominika stayed at the Hotel Jeanne d'Arc in the Marais she had been dragged to the cobbles and kicked by a long-haired *voyou,* a thug in a leather jacket, sent by Zyuganov to damage her. Dominika remembered the flat *click* of her lipstick gun as she put an expanding bullet into the chest of the second black-jack-wielding attacker. Now she had two such single-shot electric pistols in her purse—the only weapons she could travel with on such short notice—with real lip gloss inside each. One Russian red, the other nude pink. One for TRITON, the other for Zyuganov.

So now Dominika the Sparrow becomes Dominika the assassin, Vladimir's whore killer. This is totally perverted, she thought, looking at the malevolent little tubes on the hotel bed, the infernal instruments of her Service. She had killed men before, to save Nate and Gable, but this was different. Would Zyuganov be armed, traveling as he had, on the run? As much as she despised him, as much as *he* wanted to destroy *her,* could she press the lipstick tube against his temple and press the button? Could she contrive to walk past TRITON on the street, let him go by, then pivot and shoot him in the back of the head? She thought the answer was yes, she would kill to protect herself or Nate. She would be destroying everything she hated. But at what cost?

The rage against the *siloviki,* the bosses, against her Service, and against the blue-eyed judo man with the rolling gait, sustained her. Was her soul worth the spectacular access she would gain for her friends at CIA? Would Nate—wry, clever, passionate Nate—tell her nothing was worth losing her soul, not all the secrets in the world. Would he?

Udranka was in the corner of the room looking out the window. Why don't you ask him? she said.

There was a soft knock at the door. Dominika went to the door, slipped the chain, and opened it, keeping a lipstick down by her side. Nathaniel stood there, dressed in a light outer coat, collar up, hands in his pockets. His purple halo filled the corridor, then rushed into her room, swirling around her. He smiled at her, then noticed the lipstick in her hand.

"Is that what I think it is? Didn't the chambermaid bring enough towels?" Nate whispered in Russian. Dominika shook her head.

"*Parshiviy,* jackass, I was just thinking about you," said Dominika. She pulled him inside, closed the door, and tossed the lipstick onto the bed. She threw her arms around his neck and they kissed; her head swam with the feel of his lips, with the feel of his arms around her. They parted and looked silently at each other, then Nate put his hands in her hair and brought their mouths together again. Dominika pulled away.

"Stop for a minute. I want to tell you Hannah saved my life the night she died," said Dominika, blinking quickly to stop her welling eyes.

"I think I know," said Nate.

"She led surveillance away from me; I was a hundred meters away," said Dominika. "They got excited and hit her with a car, probably by accident."

"I went to the funeral in New Hampshire," said Nate. "The family was devastated." His eyes were shiny too. They looked at each other, and she telegraphed "I know about her" and he telegraphed back "I'm sorry" and they didn't say any more about it, for Hannah's sake.

"How did you get here so quickly?" Dominika asked.

"We knew Angevine was heading here the night he escaped. Gable and I have been in Paris for two days," said Nate. "Benford arrived last night. We're tearing the town apart. We've been sending SRAC messages to you nonstop."

"After delivering the general at the beach, I was stuck at Strelna. Is he safe?"

"A pain in the ass, but safe," said Nate. "Benford was seriously exercised that you disregarded instructions not to use the exfil plan. Now you have no contingency available."

Dominika shrugged. "Who's Angevine?" she said.

"TRITON to you," said Nate.

"I have TRITON's local cell-phone number, the one he gave the embassy," said Dominika quickly, remembering. "They gave it to me before I left Strelna." Nate immediately called it in to Gable, who was working on phone and name traces at the US Embassy.

"I am going to call his number, play a Russian from the Center, to try to get him to meet me," said Dominika.

Nate brushed a strand of hair away from her face. "To do what?" he asked, smiling. "Take him into custody?"

Dominika waited for him to stop fiddling with her hair. "No. To kill him." Nate stopped what he was doing. "And then I'm going to kill Zyuganov. He arrived here sometime last night."

Nate took her hands in his. "That's all a little ambitious, don't you think?"

"Do you think so?" said Dominika, taking her hands away. "Putin's orders." She briefly explained everything, including Putin's midnight visit to her room, his instructions to her, and his promise to promote her. Nate's halo flared and Dominika suppressed a smile.

"He had his hand underneath your nightgown?" said Nate.

"Do not tell me you're *revnivyy*," said Dominika. She put a hand on his arm. "*Dushka*, you are attractive when you are jealous."

An hour after arriving in Paris, Nate and Gable stood in Chief of Station's Gordon Gondorf's office. Gondorf's deputy, a long-suffering senior case officer named Ebersole, stood in the corner of the room, leaning against the wall. He knew Gable slightly from an Asian tour. Nate saw Gable shake hands and slap his back, Gable-code that he liked and approved of this officer. Gable's planet had two moons: He either approved of you or thought you were an ignoramus.

The chief was another matter. Nate had not seen Gordon Gondorf since Moscow, when Nate had been monstrously, unfairly, summarily sent home short-of-tour by his vindictive chief. Gondorf (universally known as Gondork) was perpetually in a state of hysteric professional trepidation. Everyone—superiors, subordinates, fellow chiefs of Station, host-country liaison officers—to Gondorf represented trouble, a potential rival who he knew, *just knew*, sooner or later would derail the shrill locomotive of his career.

He was short with a whippet's face and carefully combed thinning hair. He had gnawed cuticles, M&M eyes set too close together, and little feet characteristically shod in strange, high-sided loafers that officers in his Station called "pilgrim shoes." Typically, Gondorf was unaware of anything his officers thought, said, or did. More representative of Gondorf's virtuosity as COS was a large poster on his office wall of a kitten hanging by its forefeet from a branch with "Hang in There, Baby!" in large letters along the top.

Seeing him again, Nate remembered hearing how Gondorf had extirpated the entire South America Division with mismanagement, miscalculation, and neglect. He was infamous within the division for issuing preposterous edicts—Gondorf's Twelve Rules—regulating the conduct of Stations and chiefs to ensure there were no troubles, flaps, or scandals and, sadly by extension, no operational successes. After that divisional tour de force, Gondorf should have been locked head and wrists in a pillory and put on display in the Memorial Garden in front of the Headquarters building as was his due, but instead, in the inimitable custom of the Office of Personnel's senior-assignments staff, he was assigned as COS to prestigious Paris Station to keep him out of Washington (and derivatively to inflict him upon the French, who were finicky and obstreperous).

Briefing Gondorf on urgent and dangerous operations was always tricky, like sneaking up on a grazing deer: Too fast, too direct, and he'd bolt from any perceived danger. Nate told him about TRITON's escape to Paris, about the risk to a sensitive asset, but omitted specific mention of Dominika. Gondorf would have wet himself.

Nate paused after ten minutes. Gondorf was sitting behind his desk, fiddling with his fingers, and Nate thought he would be rolling ball bearings in his hand if he could. Nate shot a glance at DCOS Ebersole, whose face was expressionless—strictly Easter Island—doubtless learned behavior to survive in the underground-bunker environment of Gondorf's Station.

"So we need unilateral phone traces on Angevine's US mobile number," said Gable to Gondorf. "We don't want to go to the French and risk exposing our source. And we want to look for this guy ourselves, without the cops. And we have to do this fast."

"What you want and what's going to happen are two different things," said Gondorf. His voice was quivery, like a guinea pig's if it could talk. "I'm not risking pissing off the French just for your mole hunt. You shouldn't have let the guy escape." His eyes darted to the faces in the room, calculating pushback. He didn't calculate on Gable.

"It's time to listen closely, Chief," said Gable. "The life of an asset is at stake. Not maybe, not later. Right now." Gable stood up and leaned over the desk. "If you won't get the cement out of your ass, then I'm taking Ebersole here upstairs and we're going to run traces on the cell number and try to geo-locate the fucker's phone. If we get a hit, then Nash and I are going to draw two Brownings from your weapons locker, hit the street, and look for the guy. If I have to shoot someone—inside or outside this embassy—to save the agent, I fucking will." Gable's buzz-cut head loomed over Gondorf, who avoided looking at him.

Gondorf silently tabulated the half dozen serious bureaucratic infractions just committed by this lummox from Headquarters, not the least of which was a thinly veiled threat of bodily harm. "I'm ordering you two jerks to stand down," he said. "I want you both out of my Station and out of the country immediately." It was the best he could do, with this Rottweiler drooling over his desk.

Nate stood up. "Let's get out of here," he said to Gable.

"Simon Benford is arriving tonight," said Gable to Gondorf. "You can tell him what we can and can't do." He turned to the DCOS. "Can you take us upstairs and get us going?"

During the last five minutes Ebersole had also silently calculated the shift of tectonic plates. He knew what was right, what was necessary, what was righteous. If he was sent home by a vindictive Gondork, it would be a blessing. "No more Brownings in the inventory," said Ebersole, "but I have two nine-millimeter H&K P2000s for you."

"What holster?" asked Gable, stretching this out to fuck with Gondorf.

"Nylon Bianchi belt rig," said Ebersole. "The best."

"Let's go," Gable said.

As they filed out, a fuming Gondorf pointed at Nate. "Nash, you always were a fuckup."

It occurred to Nate that the immediate absence of anything close to hatred or resentment meant he was over Gondorf, over the anxiety of his early career. He was now fully invested in major-league ops the likes of which Gondorf would never fathom. He stopped at the door. "Gordon, I personally regret that our relationship has not grown since we last worked together," he said. "At that time I recall that you were afraid of the street. Nothing much has changed."

Nate patted the ridiculous poster on the wall as he left. "Hang in there, baby," he said.

They struck out on tracking a US phone but the next day, after running the local number of Angevine's prepaid French cell provided by Dominika, they logged a hit in fourteen minutes. The Station was able to geo-locate Angevine's instrument based on signal strength on the network downlink. They determined that his phone was, for most of the day, physically located somewhere on the Île Saint-Louis. They could not further pinpoint the location since the twenty-seven-acre island had no physical cell towers and moreover delineated the boundary of the fourth arrondissement with the fifth. There was a "soft" cellular zone on both islands in the Seine, but it was enough of a lead to know he was there. Quick traces in the reverse-directory did not reveal any Angevines in the neighborhood.

Île Saint-Louis. The bastard was somewhere close by, in an area the size of four carrier flight decks. The island was three streets wide, connected to either bank by five bridges, a discreet and exclusive enclave in the center of Paris, graceful seventeenth-century slate-roofed Baroque mansions sprung from the loamy fifteenth-century medieval roots of cow pastures, charcoal ricks, and royal falconry gazebos. Gable and Nate walked the narrow one-way streets twice, past louvered shutters and ornate oak doors with brass lion-head knockers, ducking under striped canopies that shopkeepers cranked down against the afternoon sun. They measured progress by counting quaint shop windows piled high with cheeses, or breads, or bottles of wine, stepping around early evening shoppers with string bags and holding baguettes under their arms. Angevine's face was stuck on the backs of their eyelids, and they looked for the frying-pan features of the five-foot-two Zyuganov—a photo had been found by Russian analysts at Benford's insistence.

Benford walked toward them dressed improbably in sunglasses, raincoat, and a beret he had purchased on the Île de la Cité from one of the dozens of gift shops along the north side of Notre Dame Cathedral. Gable told him he looked like the owner of a pornographic bookstore, which comment Benford chose to ignore. He was in a foul mood after a spirited exchange with COS Gondorf, which Benford characterized as like watching a salamander jettisoning its tail and wriggling under a leaf. "I intend to recommend he be withdrawn short of tour for cause," said Benford. "He can spend the rest of his career with Vern Throckmorton as a nautch dancer in Bollywood."

They sat at a wicker table inside a wine bar, Benford with his back to the window. "Where is DIVA?" asked Benford.

"Just got in. She's at her hotel across the river, in the Marais," said Nate. "Fifteen-minute walk." Nate told him about Zyuganov, Putin, and what the president had ordered Dominika to do.

Benford was quiet for a minute. "Unprecedented, once-in-a-lifetime access," he said. "But we're a thread away from losing it all, from losing her. If we cannot disrupt Angevine's meeting with Zyuganov, it's over. I'm not taking the risk of sending her back to brazen it out."

"You know she won't run," said Nate. "Absolutely not."

"Nothing is absolute," said Gable.

"This is," said Nate. "I know her. Despite all your collective ragging on me, maybe I've gained definite insights on what makes her tick. She won't do it."

"I know she won't, not of her own volition," said Benford. "Remarkable woman." He sat back. "By the way, we heard that a certain shipment arrived after a long sea voyage, was received by the purchasing party, made an arduous overland trip, and is being installed as we speak. You might pass that along to her; she made it all happen."

"She still won't quit," said Nate.

Benford dismissed it with a wave. "Nathaniel, rent a room on the island. She should stay off the street, but I want one of you to be with her at all times." They ordered beers and waited until the waiter had poured.

Benford took off his sunglasses. "We have tonight and perhaps tomorrow to stop Angevine. If we do not, I will assume her name is in Moscow, from the lips of the traitor. If that is the case, then one of you will sling her over your shoulder and carry her to the US Embassy, and we will fly her to safety."

Gable drained his beer. "And if we see Angevine and Zyuganov tonight, for instance?" he said.

Benford put on his sunglasses and got up to leave. "Then you carry out Putin's orders for DIVA."

Nate rented a room on the island at the Hôtel du Jeu de Paume—small, elegant, with polished wooden ceiling beams, first hewn to build a handball court for Louis XIII. Dominika looked at the four-poster bed significantly, but Gable had taken off his shoes and was stretched out on the couch.

"I'm going to take another lap around the island," said Nate, looking at his watch. "We didn't check the river landings and the little park at the east end."

Gable waved. "When you come back, I'll go back out. You got your phone?"

Dominika was shrugging on her coat, and Gable looked up at her. "Where are you going?" he said.

"With him," she said.

Gable shook his head. "Better you stay here with me. We don't want the Russkies seeing you with Americans on the street." He pointed at Nate. "Especially not with sexually ambiguous ones."

Nate flipped him the bird.

Dominika turned slowly to face him. *Oh-oh,* thought Nate. "*Bratok*, are you telling me I cannot go out?"

"Yep," said Gable, who was generally unaware of Dominika's fiery moods, and certainly was immune to them. "Until this concludes we have to stick together like summer underwear."

Dominika tilted her head like a puppy hearing a dog whistle, and turned to Nate. "Do you tell me the same thing?" she said.

"We can go out after it gets dark," said Nate. "We just don't want Zyuganov to see you with me. He knows my face from my time in Moscow, you know that."

Dominika crossed her arms.

"Don't take it personal, sweet pea," said Gable. "Benford's staying away too. TRITON knows *his* face. Look, we're here to stop these guys, to preserve your cover."

"The way to preserve *krysha*, my cover, is to let me find Zyuganov and finish with him. TRITON you can arrest and do whatever you want with him."

"And have him repeat your name during trial?" said Gable. "Not going to happen."

"So what are you going to do?" said Dominika.

Nate jacked the slide of his H&K P2000 with a slight musical ratcheting sound, flipped the safety on, and slid the pistol back into his belt holster at his right hip. "Be back in an hour," he said.

Nate came back to the room, tired, cold, and hungry. He had done three circuits, looking for the tall angular figure, the Gallic nose, the dramatic hair. Or the flat Slavic face and jug ears of the Russian psychopath. He had cased the paved ramps leading down to boat landings at river level, rough stones periodically awash as the Seine boiled around the island and through the channel separating it from the larger Île de la Cité. He had sniffed around the small park—Le Square Barye—at the east tip of the island, Lebanese cedars and willows scraggly in winter, and checked the broad steps leading down to the curved stone terrace against which the steel-blue river parted like water split by the bow of a ship.

Gable was still stretched out on the couch, reading a magazine. Dominika was lying on her side on the bed, eyes closed. She had been furious at being kept in the room, at being treated like a piece of property—which she knew, in some way, she was.

She discussed the situation with Marta, Udranka, and Hannah, all of whom sat on the bed with her, a Rusalka slumber party. They know what they're doing, said Hannah, the operator. Patience, said Marta, the wise one. Shut up, said Udranka, the passionate, you're lucky to have someone to love and who loves you.

As Nate came into the room, Gable's cell phone trilled, waking Dominika, who sat up in bed, blinking. Her hair was tousled and she pulled at her wool skirt. Gable got up and started jamming his feet into his shoes. "Benford from the embassy. He wouldn't say over the phone, but something's in from Headquarters, something we should know."

"Maybe new SIGINT on Putin," said Nate.

"SIGINT? Fuck no," said Gable, "not after Snowden went over. That loser gave the Russians all the keys. Moscow changed all the channels. We ain't collecting shit from the Barents Sea to the Bosphorus." He belted his coat. "I gotta get over there; don't know how long I'll be." He slipped out.

"Did you see anything?" said Dominika. She got off the bed and put her arms around his neck. Nate shook his head.

Dominika put her face close to his, brushed her lips against his. "Will my *tyuremshchik,* how do you say this, let me go out, perhaps take me to dinner? I'm hungry." She shifted her arms and slid her hands down Nate's back.

"I'm not your jailer," said Nate. "And get your hands off my pistol."

Dominika stepped back, smiling. "You are so clever Mr. Neyt, even though you are sexually ambiguous. Now will you take me to eat?"

Nate and Dominika took a discreet back booth at the Brasserie de l'Îsle Saint-Louis for dinner. They could not know that Angevine was sitting in his aunt's apartment two hundred meters from where they were, looking at a wall clock in his aunt's parlor.

Over *salade frissee,* earthy cassoulet, and baked Camembert with caramelized onions, they whispered about the idea that Dominika might very well have to come back with him directly and resettle in the United States. Dominika looked at Nate over the rim of her wineglass.

"And what would I do in America with a death sentence issued by Moscow over my head, with Department Five *chistilshchiki,* mechanics, looking for me?" said Dominika.

"You couldn't return to Moscow. Not with one or both of them running around," said Nate.

"Zyuganov is a wanted man. So is TRITON," said Dominika. "I would have time to strengthen my position."

"You're not making sense," said Nate. He took her hand, and his purple halo pulsed. "This is hard enough. If you keep working, okay, you're maybe the best agent in the history of Russian ops. But if you're blown and they kill you, it's all for nothing. No, Domi, if you have to bug out and resettle, then you clear your head and come out."

"It is not that easy, 'just come out,'" said Dominika.

"I'm just worried about how this is developing," said Nate. The aura around his head told her he was concerned.

"Please pay the bill," said Dominika. The argument would come later; right now it hovered between them.

They walked down the single main street, past darkened shops and galleries, Nate still searching the faces of the few pedestrians hurrying home in the chilly night. Inside the room, they had not yet taken off their coats when Gable called, sounding pissed. He would be back in two hours; hold down the fort. *With what news?* thought Nate. Pull her out? Let her go back inside? Nate could imagine the debate. Do not disturb the intel flowing from DIVA. Let her run as long as she can. Don't upset the case. *Let the lawyers and political appointees decide her fate.*

They looked at each other in their coats. Nate knew that adapting to a new life was a nightmare for defectors, an accumulated and unrelieved assault on the psyche of an alien culture, even for an experienced spy who had worked in the foreign field: elevator music from unseen speakers, the competing exhausts of a crowded mall, the taste of different tap water, the overload of colors in the cereal aisle in a supermarket. The wide screens, and iPhones, and tablets, blipping and beeping and winking. And his beautiful Russian, moreover, would have to adapt to a new life somewhere discreet and remote. Nate imagined her walking down Central Avenue in Whitefish, Montana, looking in vain for *solyanka, pirozhki,* or *pelmeni.*

He looked at her, recognizing the signs—flashing cobalt eyes and flushed cheeks. He made to take her coat from her, but she stepped up to him and pushed him gently into the single plush armchair, then swung her leg over and straddled his lap.

"Now I am going to explain how things are," said Dominika.

"No you're not," said Nate. "You're going to listen to your handling officer, and follow instructions." Dominika put her hands on his shoulders.

"What instructions?" said Dominika. Nate pulled on the lapels of her coat to bring their mouths together.

"Don't move," she said. She reached under her jacket, then her skirt, working through the layers of her clothing and his, shifting and rearranging, pulling and unbuttoning, tucking and unzipping, until the impossible happened and she felt him between her legs. They were completely dressed, down to their boots, but inextricably connected, several layers down, and

Dominika watched him with wide eyes as she slowly ground her hips on him. *She ignored Udranka in the corner.* The familiar pulses grew in her belly, radiating up to her chest, making it difficult to breathe. All she could do was bend at the waist toward him, her face an inch from his, keeping her seat, until her lips started quivering and she closed her eyes and laid her forehead against his and whispered, *Davai, davai, do it, do it,* and they both started shaking and tried not to fall off the planet.

"What instructions?" she said shakily.

BAKED CAMEMBERT WITH CARAMELIZED ONIONS

Take a wheel of Camembert out of its box and make a shallow X incision through the top skin. Insert slivered garlic and thyme sprigs. Put the cheese back into its wooden box, drizzle with olive oil (or white wine or vermouth), place on baking sheet, and bake in a medium oven until the cheese is runny all the way through. Serve with sliced onions caramelized in butter and balsamic vinegar.

42

They stirred again after several minutes. They were both stifling as a result of having just carnally coupled while wearing winter clothing, including sweaters and outer coats, in an overheated hotel room, the premises having been last used as a sweat bath in 1634. When Nate proposed a shower, Dominika countered with a suggestion that they go back outside into the cool night air and walk around the romantic little island, perhaps crossing a bridge into Saint-Germaine-des-Prés to find a late-night Left Bank bistro to have a glass of wine. Nate saw that Dominika was tense and keyed up—it wasn't just the usual sewing-machine legs after coition—and going back on the street was a subconscious tonic for her. The unspoken thought was that this life of espionage could very suddenly end for her, and she was prepared to have a fight about it.

Dominika put her arm into Nate's and they exited the hotel—as usual checking both ways down the length of the deserted main street. They turned right toward Île de la Cité—the cathedral would be lit, and they could cross the "Lovelock" bridge with hundreds of lovers' padlocks hanging from the railings. They were the only ones on the street as they neared the little square at the western end of the island. The bistros and brasseries were all dark, sidewalk tables and chairs stacked and chained together. It was near midnight and the air had grown cold. A river barge steamed down the left channel, blocking the reflected lights of the grand siècle lampposts along the embankment, its diesel thrumming.

Dominika suddenly spun Nate by an arm, took his head in her hands, and kissed him. Nate kissed her back but then began to pull away to say something smart, but Dominika wouldn't let go of his head and brought his face down to hers again. Her eyes were open and she shook her head slightly, still holding his head. Nate didn't move, but put his arms around her. He could see her looking at something out of the corner of her eye. He was conscious of someone walking by, but Dominika's hands blocked his view. She jerked her hands and shook her head again. Finally she broke free. Her eyes were wide.

"Zyuganov," she whispered, "that was Zyuganov." She turned and started moving in the direction the little shadowy figure had gone, along the Quai d'Orléans, along the southern side of the island. Nate reached out and grabbed her hand.

"Stop. I'll follow him and call in reinforcements," he said. "Gable will be here in fifteen minutes." Dominika shook her head and twisted her hand out of his.

"If he gets away, I'm finished," said Dominika.

"Not if you're back in the hotel," said Nate.

"*Zabud' pro eto,* forget it," she said. "He's trying to kill me, and I will not take a back door. Don't even think of trying to stop me."

"You mean take a backseat," Nate said.

Dominika shook her head. "There's no time," she said. "Zyuganov is moving. TRITON is on this island. They could slip into a building and we'd never find them." She started moving, looking back at him. "Come on," she hissed.

They walked tight against the wall of the buildings, pausing in doorways to let Zyuganov maintain his distance. His silhouette ghosted along the opposite sidewalk. He was not hurrying—he occasionally looked out over the water—and he certainly wasn't looking for surveillance. *Jesus,* thought Nate, *we cannot blow this.* Zyuganov's head and shoulders appeared, then faded, and then reappeared, as he passed through light reflected off the river. Halfway down the street, Zyuganov slowed and turned to walk down one of the broad ramps leading to the river-level landing, his head descending out of view. Nate and Dominika quietly crossed the street and peeked over the wall. Zyuganov was standing at the bottom of the ramp, leaning against a lamppost. River water swirled blackly past him.

"We wait for TRITON to show, or go now?" asked Dominika. Nate pulled her sleeve and dragged her back into a shadow cast by a tree growing out of the sidewalk.

"Zyuganov's not going anywhere on that landing. And TRITON has to come right by us to get down to him," said Nate. "We want them both." Dominika nodded, and took out two lipsticks. *Christ, the lipstick gun again,* thought Nate. *Russians.* They stopped talking and watched the top of the ramp. They were cold waiting two, three, five minutes.

They suddenly heard voices from the riverside platform. They peeked over the wall again to look down on the tops of Zyuganov's and Angevine's heads. Nate pulled up straight. *Fucker came around the other way along the lower river-level promenade,* thought Nate. Dominika was looking down at them and started tugging at Nate's sleeve. The two men were arguing, and their voices grew louder. Angevine reached out and collected a fistful of Zyuganov's jacket lapel. The dwarf pulled away angrily, turned, and started walking up the ramp. Angevine followed him, shouting as he caught up. Nate heard the word "euros" repeated twice. Zyuganov ignored him and continued walking up the ramp.

"TRITON just told Zyuganov my name," said Dominika, starting to move. *And Zyuganov just told him he had no money,* thought Nate, coming up behind her. *Maybe they'll kill each other.*

At the top of the ramp, Angevine spun Zyuganov around—the American towered over the Russian—then both men stopped as they saw the silhouettes of Nate and Dominika standing in front of them. They were five feet apart, looking at one another, frozen in place. Angevine passed his fingers through his hair. Zyuganov's face was crazed, his chest heaved.

"*Suchka,* little bitch," said Zyuganov, meeting Dominika's eyes. "I knew it was you," he said in guttural Russian. "Are you ready to come home to die?"

"I'm more interested in whether you know you will never set foot in the *Rodina* again," said Dominika. "The Paris pauper's cemetery is called Thiais, *zhopa,* asshole." Listening to the Russian, cool and deadly between them, Nate was once again reminded that the only people Russians hated more than foreigners were themselves. Then everything broke loose.

As if it were a starter's gun, a river barge sounded its air horn, and Angevine spun and ran back down the ramp, sliding on the uneven cobbles as he descended, and Zyuganov simultaneously darted to his right past Dominika. Spurred perhaps by their respective instincts, Nate and Dominika reacted simultaneously. Nate pounded down the ramp to chase Angevine along the landing. Dominika moved toward Zyuganov and tried a foot sweep, but the poisonous dwarf agilely skipped over it and sprinted down the darkened Quai d'Orléans. Dominika ran after him down the center of the midnight-empty street. She flashed that there were two spans of the Pont de Sully on the eastern corners of the island into either side of the city proper. She could not let him escape. Zyuganov knew she was the mole.

Zyuganov was surprisingly fast, and Dominika could not gain on him, even as she vaulted over the hood of a parked car to try to shorten the distance. Zyuganov sensed she had drawn closer and he veered wildly away from the bridge and instead vaulted the waist-high fence of the little Barye park, tore through hanging willow branches and blindly down the broad steps to the platform on the river. A hoarse call from a watchman sounded from the shadows. This was the eastern tip of Île Saint-Louis, and the Seine endlessly plowed into and flowed around the prow-shaped breakwater. Zyuganov stopped short and turned around. Dominika stood at the top of the stairs, breathing heavily. She was dressed in a dark pleated woolen skirt with tights, a sweater under an oiled jacket, and jogging shoes. Her hair was halfway down from the running, and she absently brushed it behind an ear as she slowly came down the steps toward him. She could still feel Nate on the inside of her thighs. She was immeasurably tired.

Rounding the corner of the landing, Nate slipped on a slimy cobble and went down hard on his butt, which saved him from the ten-foot pipe—one of several discarded scaffold stanchions that had been stacked against the wall—Angevine swung at his head, but which instead rang like a bell off the stone wall. Angevine swung it again like a broadsword, over and down in a log-splitting stroke, directly at Nate's head. Still on his back, Nate twisted to avoid the massive skull-caving blow and rolled into the freezing Seine, all sewer-sweet smell and bitter taste. He could immediately feel the scour of the water as it boiled past and he got his fingers and the toe of one shoe into a masonry seam before the current could pluck him off the stone and whirl him downriver—he'd be around the Orsay bend and past the Eiffel Tower in three minutes. That's if he wasn't sucked into some vortex or pinned under a dock and drowned. He tried a quick grab at the pistol in his belt but almost lost his grip and had to hang on as the river tugged at him.

Angevine stood over him, legs apart, seriously winded but lining up a final swing to smash Nate's face or shatter his clinging hands. "You fucks underestimated who you were dealing with," he panted, resting the pipe across his shoulder, as if he were waiting his turn in the batting cage.

"Yeah, you're right: You're a bigger traitor than *any of us* imagined," said Nate.

Angevine fumed at the insult, choked up on the pipe for more accuracy, and stepped closer. Nate risked being taken by the river as he reached out with one hand, grabbed Angevine's pant leg, and pulled. Unbalanced by the big pipe he held over his head, Angevine's feet shot out on the slimy blocks and he tumbled into the river, the stanchion bouncing off the stones into the water next to him. He came up spluttering beside Nate and reached for a handhold, but was a foot too far and was instantly swept away from the embankment, turning in the water, arms feebly paddling for stability. In three seconds he was in the middle of the channel.

One of the late-night *Bateaux-Mouches* boats—long, wide, gaily lit, and glass-topped—thrumming downstream sounded its whistle as the dot that was Angevine's head bobbed over the bow wave and down into the trough, bouncing along the hull until bobbing again over the stern wake, and with an audible scream was sucked into the foaming prop wash. His body disappeared underwater, then was thrown back up by one of the propeller blades, followed by his severed head. The frantic ship's horn kept sounding its bass note while Japanese tourists on the upper rear deck turned night into day with flash photography. Angevine's body continued floating downstream in the shimmer of embankment lights, eventually disappearing around the Île de la Cité.

With considerable effort, Nate scrabbled back up onto the landing, shivering, his clothes streaming river water. As he pounded up to the street, his thoughts raced. Angevine was gone. The prick never got his final payment for betraying his country, and now he was dead. Gable would kick Angevine's fished-out head back into the river and say, "Our grief can't bring him back." Then Nate flashed to Zarubina floating facedown in a fountain. Dominika. He sprinted down Quai d'Orléans, his breath ragged and his shoes squishing, the river stink in his nose. Down at the other end of the island there were lights and sirens.

As Dominika came down the steps toward Zyuganov, she knew she would kill him. Taking him back to Moscow in chains had been an appealing option—Putin would have been impressed—but not now, not after he had heard her name from TRITON's lips. She fingered a lipstick tube in her pocket, feeling for the end with the trigger plunger. She would walk to within an outstretched-arm's distance and aim for center mass. With the explosive bullet even a hit in the hand would vaporize it to the wrist and cause massive blood loss. A torso hit and the subsequent hydrostatic shock would turn the thoracic cavity into an inflated bag of sweetmeats.

Zyuganov stood watching her, darting glances to the left and right—there were no stairs or ladders, no other way off the platform. The river? He was not a strong swimmer and did not think he could survive a plunge into the water. Egorova had a reputation, had killed men, had gone through hand-to-hand *Sistema* training, but was she that good? As he waited for her, the diminutive Zyuganov experienced the old familiar sensation of the assassin's prickling impatience to get up close and stick pointy things into soft places. His instincts told him to wait, get her close, blind her, or cripple her, then finish her. Zyuganov wanted to see Egorova's face as she died.

Bat wings of black unlimbered behind Zyuganov's head—no gargoyle on the cornices of nearby Notre Dame could match these—as Dominika walked up to Zyuganov, slowly sliding her hand with the lipstick out of her pocket.

Marta and Udranka were on the riverbank, like two Rusalki mermaids, singing. Over the sound of her pounding heart, she heard Hannah behind her.

Dominika raised the lipstick tube, her arm straight and tense, pointed at his chest, and pushed the plunger. Zyuganov flinched and ducked. Then the world slowed, the stars froze in their orbits, the river stopped flowing. All that came out of the lipstick was a faint musical ping, as if a spring had snapped in a pocket watch. Misfire. Faulty electrical primer. Cracked component.

There was no time to dig around for the second lipstick tube. In a singular circular motion, Dominika threw the dud lipstick into the river, stepped slightly to Zyuganov's left, and grabbed his sleeve. He pulled back, and she continued stepping into him, swinging his arm in the direction he wanted to go, then suddenly back in an arc toward her, bringing her other arm up and across his neck. Before she could strike, Zyuganov somehow blocked her arm and stepped away from her. He moved with speed and skill. They stood looking at each other—black fog came out of his eyes and mouth, and he snarled at her. She would trap an arm and deliver another strike to the head, then fish out the second lipstick gun.

Zyuganov came at her in a strange loping gait, and Dominika stepped into him to use his momentum, but he put one arm around her neck and bared his teeth. Was the little cannibal going to bite her? Dominika pulled her head back and hit him twice, very fast, under his nose, aiming for a spot two inches inside his skull. Zyuganov's head went back and his eyes blurred, but he kept his claw around Dominika's neck, and with a jerk drew her to him, mashing her breasts against his chest. He smelled like vinegar and night soil.

Zyuganov's free hand brought up the eight-inch Sabatier fillet knife he had taken from his mother's kitchen and stuck it into Dominika's side, down low, just above her hip bone. The curved blade was thin and murderously sharp, but it flexed—as boning knives are predisposed to do—as it tore through Dominika's tough outer jacket and only three inches of the blade penetrated her body. Dominika felt a flash of fire in her side that radiated around her waist and up her stomach. She dug thumbnails into Zyuganov's eyes—got one but missed the other—as he shook his head in pain.

Zyuganov knew what flesh felt like and he pulled the blade out and stabbed back in, trying to get inside the coat, and this time felt sweater wool against his knuckles, but Dominika's hand clamped down on his wrist and he could get only an inch of the blade in. Wrenching the knife away, Zyuganov stabbed again, then again, reaching around to her lower back, trying for kidneys or the lower lobe of her liver. Zyuganov looked up at her face with one good eye—the other was blurred and weeping—and saw the bitch's mouth was open and she was panting, those blue eyes blinking rapidly, and her body trembled a little as she started sliding down the front of him; he let go of her neck and she sat down with a bump on the stones, leaning a little and holding her side.

Dominika was aware only of a belt of intense pain around her waist and the feel of the cobblestones as she lay down on her good side and the wet grittiness on her cheek. Zyuganov was close, enveloped in black, and he pushed her on her back—rolling was an agony because something inside her was adrift, hot and liquid. She heard a man's voice—*Nathaniel help me,* she thought—but Zyuganov screamed and brandished the knife and the voice—a night watchman's, *not Nathaniel's*—faded away. Zyuganov straddled her and sat heavily, causing more pain. He greatly regretted that he could not spend hours with Egorova, but this would have to do. That meddlesome watchman would call the police—he had a minute or two to spare.

The night glow of the City of Light filled her vision. The pain in her guts was rising in waves to her jaw, and the hand clamped over the first wound was sticky. She opened her eyes and saw Zyuganov leaning forward, silhouetted against the lights of the city, bat wings extended. She felt cold air on her belly and breasts, and realized Zyuganov had pulled her sweater up to her chin. *Not like him, the little asexual bug.* She then felt cold, questing fingers running along her rib cage, cold beetle fingers feeling for the space between the fourth and fifth ribs where he could shiver the knife in to fillet her heart and lungs.

He hadn't been flirting. His fingers stopped moving—he had found the hollow between her ribs, exactly where he could start the tip of the blade into her. Zyuganov leaned over Dominika—one of his eyes was swollen shut—and breathed into her face. Then he placed one hand behind her neck and lifted her head, as if he were about to spoon soup into a sick relative. He hoarsely spoke in Russian.

"A person can never know exactly when and where he will die, but you can know this now, Egorova: midnight in Paris, on a stinking embankment, tasting blood on your tongue, and smelling blood in your nose. I will cut off your clothes and roll you into the Seine so your American friends can find you downstream, swollen and splitting, with the river in your mouth, and it will be *pizdets*, an ending, for you." Dominika's eyelids fluttered, and she whispered softly. Zyuganov frowned and put his ear close to her mouth. He relished the dying declarations of people in pain, especially when he had personally administered the pain.

"Do you know when you will die, *svinya*, pig?" said Dominika. Zyuganov looked into her blue eyes—they were flat and dull from the shock. He smiled and shook her head side to side a little, chidingly, while whispering.

"Little Sparrow, you will not be—"

Dominika put the lipstick tube under Zyuganov's chin and pushed the plunger. The distinctive *click* was barely audible, followed by a wet melon-against-the-wall sound. Zyuganov's undamaged eye was open as he fell to one side, and his head hit the stones with a flat slap. One of his legs was lying across Dominika's stomach, and his face was pointed away from her. The back of his head—there was no aura around it—was a furry candy dish empty down to the start of his teeth. The night air stirred strands of his hair around the shattered rim of his skull.

With a shaking backhand toss, Dominika threw the lipstick tube over Zyuganov and into the river. The motion caused her great pain in her stomach and she tried pushing Zyuganov's leg off her. Her arms weren't working very well and her hands were numb. That further movement brought a fresh wave of pain in her chest and a rushing noise in her ears, which blanked out the rumble of the river, so she did not hear the running footsteps and was surprised to see a young face in an orange jacket lean over her. She could smell his aftershave. He was very handsome, not as lovely as her Nate, but he smiled and said, *Ne bouge pas,* don't move, and she heard the word "plasma" and she felt him lift her sweater and apply pressure to the stab wounds, and wondered whether they would release her body into the river, because there she could swim and sing with Marta and Udranka, and there was the whiff of alcohol and a pinch in her arm and she took Hannah's hand as they lifted her onto the gurney and carried her up the stairs away from the river, the night glow fading in her eyes.

Lights flashed off the façades of the buildings. There was a small crowd of gawkers, those already moving at this early-morning hour, and Nate pushed through them. He ran up to a policeman in boots and a helmet who turned with extended arms to stop him. Nate could think of nothing to say in French except *ma femme,* my wife, the irony of which almost made him choke with emotion. The policeman nodded and Nate walked a few feet and stopped at the top of the steps. The cobbled terrace looked like an invasion beach: Discarded medical packaging and two clumps of red-soaked gauze were strewn around amid two substantial puddles of black treacle—by lamplight blood appeared quite shiny and black—and Nate could see a knife on the ground, the gore on its blade in lacy streaks. Dominika did not have a knife. It must have been Zyuganov's. And the blood on the blade must be hers.

There was another policeman standing beside a body on the ground with a rubber sheet over it with more blood showing from underneath. An ambulance team was unzipping a body bag. A second policeman in coveralls and a garrison cap was writing on a clipboard. The cop signaled the medical personnel with a wave and they laid the bag next to the figure and dragged the rubber sheet off the body. Nate held his breath.

It was Zyuganov without the top of his head. *Lipstick gun,* thought Nate. Where was Dominika? Was she stabbed? *God, the river.* Nate imagined Dominika, having blown the dwarf's head off, clutching herself and trailing intestines, staggering blindly and pitching headfirst into the water. The gurney with Zyuganov's bagged body came up the stairs, the two policemen following. *Cremate the little bastard,* thought Nate. *Otherwise he'll crawl out of the crypt during the next full moon.*

The first cop signaled that Nate had to leave. Nate tried to ask a question, but his brain was stuck in Russian. All he could get out was *Ma femme?* again and the cop shrugged and said, *Hôpital* several times, then, *Elle était mourante,* and Nate got enough of it, and he could feel the blood drain from his face and he stammered, *Mort?* dead? but the impatient cop repeated, *Elle était mourante,* which Nate guessed meant not dead but dying. The cop looked at him with interest.

Nate sat down on a bench in the shadows and closed his eyes, his hands shaking, his clothes still dripping. Phone it in. *Encrypted cell phone, but be careful.*

Gable answered after the first ring. "What?" he said.

"We saw them on the island. I went after TRITON."

"You get him? Tell me you got him," said Gable.

There was buzzing and a thump. "Nash?" said Benford. "You're on speaker. What happened?"

"Simon, listen, your mole is dead; he fell in when we fought and was run down by a riverboat. The prop took his head off. I saw it. By now he's bumping against the flood walls along the Île aux Cygnes, the Isle of Swans, downstream from the Eiffel Tower."

"Where's sweet pea?" said Gable.

"She went after her boss, chased him to the end of the island."

"What the fuck were you two doing out of the hotel?" said Gable.

"We went out for dinner and were walking back. You can fire me later," said Nate.

"Never mind that," said Benford. "What happened? Where is the dwarf?"

"Missing half his skull. She did it, but Jesus, Simon, it looks like he stuck her; there's blood, a lot of it, and the medics took her away before I got there. I think the cop said she was dying."

"Maybe it was his blood," said Benford.

"There was a bloody fillet knife on the ground. The cop kept saying 'hospital.'"

"Did he say where?" said Benford.

"I don't know what hospital, but I'm going to find out and go."

"Negative, Nash. Stand down," said Benford.

"What do you mean stand down? She's fucking dying."

"Nash, did she have her dip passport with her?" asked Benford.

"Yeah," said Nate, holding his head.

"The hospital authorities will inform her embassy. When they hear her name, there will be a diplomat, a consular officer, and two security men in her room within thirty minutes."

"We don't know that," said Nate.

"Hey, dumbass," said Gable. "You see where this is going? You want to go visit her with a handful of daisies and bump into half her embassy?"

"We can't just leave her," said Nate, rocking back and forth.

"Stop talking and start thinking," said Gable. "She did what she was supposed to do; she completed her mission. She's a frigging hero."

"Maybe a dead hero," said Nate.

"Maybe, maybe not," said Gable. "Think it through."

"So we're withdrawing and letting her go through this alone?"

"And we hope for the best and we wait till we hear from her back inside," said Benford quietly.

"What do you mean hope for the best? What if she dies? She won't be around to answer her messages."

"If she comes through this her bona fides will be unassailable. Anyone who could hurt her now is gone. It's perfect," said Benford.

"Simon, listen to yourself," said Nate. "She's all torn up and you're talking about her cover?"

"I am concerned for her as much as you are," said Benford. "But she has excelled in the service of the State. She'll be untouchable."

"If she doesn't die in one of their shitty clinics," said Nate.

"Nash, I want to see you in twenty minutes at the hotel," said Gable. "I'll help you check out."

"Sure, *Bratok*," said Nate. "Some big brother."

"That's right," said Gable. "I'll do anything, no matter how difficult, to keep her safe."

"Abandoning her is your way to keep her safe?" said Nate, gripping the phone. *It's probably best we aren't face-to-face*, he thought.

"That's exactly how we're going to keep her safe," said Gable. "That dark day I told both of you about just happened."

Nate closed his eyes and saw Dominika with a tube in her mouth, her vital signs twerking on a green screen, one hand and arm wired with sensors and IVs, the other lying at her side; that's the one he would hold to his cheek, to let her know he was there. His eyes stung and he didn't speak.

"Nash, you there?" said Gable.

He didn't answer, looking at the river, blinking at the fuzzy lights.

"Nathaniel," said Benford. "Talk to her now. What would she tell you?"

"I don't know," said Nate.

"Yes, you do," said Benford. "Listen to her."

A chill went through him as Nate heard her voice, at once stern and sweet, with the lilting accent that went straight through him, and his name, Neyt, and she said, *dushka,* let me go, I will do this work and see you next time, and he asked her when, and she said next time, and Nate thought he could hear Dominika's Kremlin Mermaids singing on the riverbank.

He let out a shuddering sigh. "I'll see you at the hotel," Nate said brutally, and clacked the lid of his phone shut.

It was midnight, eighteen months later, two hundred miles southeast of Tehran. A musical note—like a ticker-tape bell—began dinging in the underground control room dedicated exclusively to Centrifuge Hall C at the Natanz uranium-enrichment facility. Two night-duty technicians roused themselves and looked at each other across the control console. They could feel movement in the floor, and their wheeled desk chairs swayed slightly. On the wall, a framed photograph of the Ayatollah Khamenei swung lopsidedly on its hook, and a glass of tea with a spoon in it chittered across the desk like a wind-up toy. The little bell kept dinging. Earthquake.

One technician casually roll-walked his chair to the barrel-shaped CMT40T triaxial broadband seismometer in the corner of the control room and made sure it was recording and sending MMI values to their desktops. He noted that initial seismic intensity readings were in the 4.0 to 4.5 range. Heavy, but not dangerous. At least, not now that they had the seismic-isolation floor under the machines.

Both technicians automatically checked digital and analog dials to verify cascade feedstock flow, rotor status, and bearing temperatures. All normal.

The Hall C cascade was operating perfectly; it had been absolutely *perfect* since its installation and testing a year ago. Seventeen hundred gas centrifuges were spinning at fifteen hundred revolutions per second, a speed of over Mach two. Now, six months of careful, measured production—kept secret from IAEA inspectors—was increasing stock and pushing enrichment up toward weapons-grade percentages. The late martyr, Professor Jamshidi—likely a victim of Zionist assassins—had built this. *It is his magnificent legacy*, thought the technician.

The earthquake bell continued dinging, but tremor values were decreasing. There might be aftershocks, but it was over. The two technicians flicked quick looks at the closed-circuit video of the cascade hall, dimly lit, cool, and quiet, a forest of tubes and spaghetti clusters of pipes above them, the soothing, steady hum of centrifuge rotors the only sound in the room. All normal, all running smooth and true. *Even through a four-point-oh tremor*, thought the tech.

It was the floor, the seismic floor, a true marvel of German engineering. The techs knew that the equipment was German—all the labels said so—but Russian technicians had assisted in the installation. *Who knows why? Don't ask.* The new display on their board was mesmerizing; you could look at it for hours. A graphic schematic of the seismic floor—the whole thing was computer-controlled—with hundreds—no, *thousands*—of LED lights representing subfloor pivots, pintles, and hinges. The dark-blue LEDs winked and flashed, sometimes singly, sometimes in blocks or rows or ranks, sometimes in vertigo-inducing waves, indicating the constant, individual, minute adjustments made by the mechanism beneath the pebble-grain aluminum floor. *Like the flashing marquees at the casinos and hotels in Las Vegas, enough lights to turn night into day*, thought the tech. *Like to see all that, preferably before we bomb New York.*

The LED display was active, lights blinking first on one side and then the other, showing the technicians that the floor was reacting to and dampening tremors they themselves could no longer feel through the control-room floor. Amazing. Then a single red warning light appeared on the master display, a light they never expected to see: *Fire*. The techs looked at the dials, then at each other. Short circuit? Negative. Mechanical failure? None indicated. Equipment racks? Air handlers? AC power? Nothing.

The floor display came alive as all the LEDs blinked on, flashed once, and went dark. Both techs simultaneously looked at the video monitor and saw a spot of blinding white light burning from beneath the floor, now visible among the rotors, growing arc-weld white, casting *Clockwork Orange* shadows of centrifuge tubes against the far walls. One of the techs dove for and slapped the red SCRAM button to stop the centrifuges, but a melting spot on the floor had created a minute imbalance in the third machine of the second row of the first cascade. It came off its bottom bearings, and with the vacuum broken, the spinning internal rotor first cracked the casing and then shattered it, sending whining shrapnel squealing into neighboring machines, beginning a deep, rumbling crash that increased in fury as rank after rank of dervish machines came off their rotor points. The bellowing destruction was overwhelmed only by the cacophony of the fire alarms howling in the hallways.

One tech had already hit the emergency radiation alarm, and the klaxon began braying outside the control room. The other tech picked up the phone and called IRGC General Reza Bhakti, the four-star Iranian Revolutionary Guard Corps commander of the facility. Screaming into the phone and cursing foully, Bhakti ordered the two technicians to stay in the control room until he got there. He put on his hat with the gold leaf on the bill and rushed in his Jeep to the aboveground adit to the Hall C tunnel. Both techs knew the drill and remained calm: they would stay in the sealed, windowless control room until the immediate crisis was over, then walk out dressed in the protective radiological suits hanging in the closet. This emergency procedure did not, however, take into account the accelerating white-phosphorus-and-aluminum-fueled meltdown whose next stop was, arguably, the center of the earth.

The techs watched the monitor as the picture went white from pixel overload, then to brown when the lens fused, then to black when the camera melted off its wall strut like candlewax. Had the camera still been working, the technicians would have seen the few still-upright centrifuge tubes melting like sand castles at high tide. With gaseous feedstock released into the superheated air, the conflagration became radioactive. The white phosphorus by that time had taken over the entire aluminum floor, and was now consuming the cement walls and the steel reinforcing beams in the ceiling, creating a supersonic, swirling annulus of fire that drew in air so violently that the Hall C blast doors buckled inward. The slanted, quarter-mile entrance shaft was turned into a wind tunnel, sucking equipment, carts, and loose construction materials down into the furnace at 100 mph. The Hall C air vents were likewise turned into jet nacelles, a phenomenon IRGC General Bhakti personally experienced when he parked his Jeep next to an aboveground air intake and was lifted out of his seat, slammed through the protective grate, and sucked down into the superheated vent, igniting halfway down like a kerosene lamp wick. His general's billed hat somehow remained on the floor of the Jeep.

It was getting hot in the control room, and the phone no longer worked. The dials were dead, the digital displays black, and air screamed down the tunnel, rattling the door. The techs swiveled in their chairs when they heard a hissing noise. A spot of fire had begun in a lower corner of the control room and soon elongated and climbed up the angle of the wall and along the line of the ceiling. The control room was constructed of concrete, which wasn't supposed to burn. The techs struggled into their protective suits as the fire spread along the join of the ceiling. The far wall was changing color as the magma in the cascade hall next door began to burn through. The swaddled techs hesitated at the door, not knowing whether to go out into the bellowing entrance tunnel. The tilting photo of Ayatollah Khamenei fell to the floor and spontaneously combusted.

A week later Ali Larijani, chairman of the Parliament of Iran, was instructed by Supreme Leader Khamenei to place a call to the office of the president of the Russian Federation. Larijani's previous position as secretary to the Supreme National Security Council and leading nuclear envoy made him well versed in the minutiae of Iran's nuclear program. His high rank, moreover, gave him sufficient gravitas to speak to the northern idolater frankly, informing the Kremlin of the suspension of diplomatic relations between the Islamic Republic and Russia, and of Tehran's intention to reestablish cooperative, unilateral contacts with Islamic groups in the Caucasus. Larijani ended his call by passing a personal message from the supreme leader to the president. *Eeshala tah akhareh ohmret geryeh bakoney.* I hope you mourn for the rest of your life.

43

President Putin sat at his desk in the birch-paneled president's office in the Kremlin Senate Building. He wore a dark-blue suit, a light-blue shirt, and a silvery-blue necktie. He drummed his short fingers on the desk as he read the urgent and sensitive blue-stripe SVR report about the fire and centrifuge crash that had occurred two days ago at the uranium facility in Natanz. Overhead imagery from the Russian Defense Ministry's YOBAR satellite was included in the folder. Infrared pictures revealed a miles-long tail of climbing, superheated smoke billowing southeast from the site. That was a toxic plume that would kill anyone downwind—Iranians, Afghans, and Pakistanis alike. Synthetic aperture radar on the bird saw through the pall of smoke to reveal a (radioactive) caldera where the roof of Hall C had melted and collapsed. A technical endnote equated the intensity of the Natanz heat bloom to that of the 2014 eruption of the Kelud volcano in East Java.

Kakaya raznitsa, *who cares*, thought Putin, flipping the folder closed and tossing it into an out box of white Koelga marble. He didn't give a shit; global imbalance, confusion, and chaos suited him and Russia just fine. Maybe this fire was the work of the Americans or the Israelis, or maybe those Persian *babuiny*, baboons, didn't know how to handle uranium. Well, he had long since received the money from Tehran for the shipment, and "investors' deposits" had been made—Govormarenko had already divvied up the euros. Never mind; when the Iranians were ready to rebuild, Russia would step up with equipment and expertise to assist. At à la carte prices.

And let them try to rile up the Caucasus—no chance, he had his domestic audience well in hand. Ninety-six percent of Russians approved of his recent military initiatives in Ukraine; ninety-five percent of them believed that America was goading fractious Kiev to persecute ethnic Russians in that country. Ninety-two percent believed—*no, knew*—that the same situation existed in Russian enclaves in the Caucasus, Moldova, Estonia, Lithuania, and Latvia. Opportunities would present themselves. They always did.

He would keep an eye on the oligarchs. They were rumbling about their money troubles in the face of Western banking sanctions. Nothing a few corruption trials and prison sentences wouldn't smooth out. Massive gas and oil deals with China, India, and Japan would take the teeth out of the sanctions soon enough. And he would continue to defame and stress the NATO weak-sister coalition. Conditions were right to shatter the Euro-Atlantic alliance once and for all, which would be redress for the dissolution of the USSR. With NATO razed to the ground, the Czech-Polish missile shield proposal would no longer be a worry.

As President Putin contemplated his suzerainty, his Slavic soul lifted. He regarded his opinions as revealed truth. He alone was keeping the barbarians at the gate at bay. Russia would be feared anew; Russia would be respected once again. He did not dwell on the stern measures that were required to achieve his goals—Ukrainian orphans had smoldered in the street before, and if necessary, they would do so again. This was his; it belonged to him. His soul took wing and soared over the crenellations of the Kremlin wall, past Bolotnaya Square where thousands had protested in vain, and then dipped its taloned wings and ghosted along the river and over the gray *V*-shaped roof of Lefortovo Prison, where Russian traitors went to die. Catching a draft, it soared higher over the Lubyanka, protecting them all with sword and shield, and, tilting, sailed over Tolstoy's roof in Khamovniki and over the Doric façade of the State Conservatory, where Sofronitsky, God's pianist, astounded mortals but was never allowed to play outside *Rodina*. An updraft carried Putin's soul over the Mednoye Forest, where Vasili Blokhin executed seven thousand men in twenty-eight days, and then over the Yasenevo pines to the glass and metal tower among the trees—SVR headquarters—spinning faster around the trees and then steadying, sailplaning up to and through a window with blinds drawn against the afternoon sun to fill the office with the breath of scything wings, Putin's soul come for a visit.

Unaware of the spectral visitor, the new Chief of Line KR brushed a strand of hair behind an ear and threw the report on the Natanz fire into the out basket on the corner of her desk.

ACKNOWLEDGMENTS

Writing a novel is a lonely job. What got me through the wilderness were the many people who advised, supported, reviewed, suggested, corrected, and contributed to the finished product.

My thanks to my literary agent, the transcendent Sloan Harris of International Creative Management, who continued as the unerring windsock of taste and class and grace in all aspects of the manuscript. His advice and counsel have been invaluable. Josie Freedman in Los Angeles translates the cuneiform tablets of Hollywood Babylon, and Heather Bushong tames the hordes. And my thanks to Heather Karpas for her unending support.

My editor at Scribner is Colin Harrison, and he is the best in the galaxy. He walked with me through the damp basement of the original manuscript, guiding and suggesting and encouraging, in a process that was much more than editing, much more than proofing. As he read and reread the book, his discerning eye missed nothing, equally pondering the historical arc of modern Russia or the science of uranium enrichment, while pointing out the tautological difference between "mud" and "sludge." The book would not have been finished without him.

Thanks, too, to the extended family at Scribner and Simon & Schuster, including Carolyn Reidy, Susan Moldow, Nan Graham, Roz Lippel, Brian Belfiglio, Katie Monaghan, Kyle Radler, Rita Madrigal, and Benjamin Holmes. Special thanks to the prescient Katrina Diaz, for endless hours of assistance. The support everyone showed during the protracted coordination process was greatly appreciated.

I must acknowledge colleagues on the CIA Publication Review Board and thank them for their assistance in getting final approvals for the manuscript.

My brother and sister-in-law, William and Sharon Matthews, read the draft manuscript and suggested changes and improvements. William sells commercial real estate, lectures on economics at a university, and somehow knows the difference between a surveillance satellite's low-earth orbit and a geosynchronous one. Inexplicably, my brother is moreover aware of the fortifying effects of scandium on aluminum. The combustible seismic floor in the novel is his invention. He encouraged the author and strategized with me on matters large and small. The book is dedicated to him, and CAJW would be proud.

I send heartfelt thanks to a former Cold War colleague, BB, who reviewed and massively corrected the Russian words and phrases used in the manuscript. He is a virtuoso operations officer, a scholar, and a legendary linguist. He added critical cultural comments about how Russians behave. I appreciate his help, and salute him.

Daughters Alexandra and Sophia continue to advise the author drolly in matters of popular music, clothing, and cinema with patience and good humor.

Despite all the input, I hasten to add that any error of fact or language or science is mine.

Last, but not least, I thank my wife, Suzanne, for reading the draft, twice, which is more than anyone should have to do, and for her discerning eye and steady hand, tempered by her own career of three decades in CIA. Over the years, we did a few of the sorts of things described in the book together, and she knows what's real and what is fiction. I thank her for her enthusiasms and for her patience as I wrote.

ABOUT THE AUTHOR

Jason Matthews is a retired officer of the CIA's Operations Directorate. Over a thirty-three-year career he served in multiple overseas locations and engaged in clandestine collection of national security intelligence, specializing in denied-area operations. Matthews conducted recruitment operations against Soviet–East European, East Asian, Middle Eastern, and Caribbean targets. As Chief in various CIA Stations, he collaborated with foreign partners in counterproliferation and counterterrorism operations. He lives in Southern California.

Turn the page for an excerpt from

The Kremlin's Candidate, the thrilling finale to

Jason Matthews's Red Sparrow Trilogy.

Coming soon from Scribner . . .

Colonel Dominika Egorova of the SVR—encrypted DIVA by the Central Intelligence Agency—considered the best US clandestine reporting source, ever, in the history of Russian operations, often referred to as the "jewel in the crown" of Langley's asset stable, was about to transmit her weekly electronic, short-range agent communications message to CIA's Moscow Station. She would simultaneously receive a return message on her SRAC receiver. As usual, she wondered whether Nate Nash, the CIA operations officer who had recruited her, and the man she loved, would read her ops note, limited by the miniaturized processors in the SRAC transmitter to fifteen hundred characters. She liked to think he would.

Dominika started walking south on Neglinnaya, feeling the ice water flow into her chest as she went operational. It was a transformation both mental and corporeal, the mark of a street operator, partly learned, partly instinctive. Her pulse quickened and she tamped down the adrenaline rush in her neck and shoulders. Dominika's vision became acute—crystal clear and focused on the middle distance. Her hearing likewise was tuned to the timbre of the street around her—she heard car engines, the hiss of tires on wet cobbles, and the shuffle of footsteps on the sidewalk. It was late; Moscow traffic, while never nonexistent, would be light. She had to determine her status: She had to know she was surveillance free, she had to get black.

Walk south on Neglinnaya, stair-step west, use the empty high-end Stoleshnikov Lane, luxury stores dark, surveillance would shy away from this funnel, this choke point, so look for the squealing, leapfrogging units hurrying to get ahead, *negative*, turn north on Bolshaya Dmitrova, cross street for a snap look, parked car with sidelights on, *negative*, past Muzykalnyy Teatr, its bas-relief columns illuminated, woman with shopping bag, second hit, but she's hurrying home, *disregard*, and cut through Petrovskiye Vorota, leafy walking path lined with empty weekend market stalls, *no flanker silhouettes under the trees*, get to the little car, parked under the sooty overhang of the Rossiya Theatre, no stakeout units, no finger smudges around the door locks, get in, pause, *smell* the car for the lingering reek of an entry team, *proceed*, check the trapped glove box, *tape still in place*, pull out in traffic, ignore horns, look for trailing units reacting, swerving to keep up, keep windows down, *hear the street*, north out of town on Tverskaya, change lanes, watch for reaction, keep speed slow, lull coverage, no turn signal, merge onto the M10, gradually increase speed, traffic sluggish, articulated trucks belching smoke, headlights slotting behind? *Negative*, Sokol District coming up, *pay attention*, take split onto Volokolamskoye shosse, lighter traffic, *goose it*, watch for reaction, *negative*, nearing timing point, black ribbon of Mosky Kanal, check time, Svoboda overpass coming up, reach into the oversize purse on the passenger seat, feel for the button under the fabric, light-rail overpass for number six tram coming up, *check mirror*, clear, *now*, two-seconds, low-power burst, one point five watts waking up the SRAC receiver buried six inches under the grassy rail embankment under the catenary lines, yellow light inside the purse winking green, electronic handshake, *message received*, message to Nathaniel, *Where are you?*, now the roar of the tunnel underpass, check mirror, *drifting, steer straight*, don't jackrabbit away, looping ramp to the elevated E105 ring road, traffic faster now, *your six is still clear*, past sleeping towns, Strogino where Korchnoi lived, and past Myakinino, and past Druzhba, the *Rodina* dark, Mother Russia in shadow, her countrymen snug in their homes, believing only what their blue-eyed tsar told them to believe, eating only what the tsar fed them, hoping only for what the tsar let them hope for, fatigue now from gripping the steering wheel for so long, *watch for the exit*, west on Rublevskoye, take it slow, left, right, left, natural reverses in the triangle formed by Rublevskoye, Yartsevskaya, and Molodogvardeyskaya, look for swirling coverage, *negative*, cross Rublevskoye and east on Kastanaevskaya, her building, no. 9, dark windows, half covered by ivy, bulb burned out over the entrance, dim staircase, she'd have to finger the key into the lock of her apartment door.

She rested her forehead against the steering wheel. Kastanaevskaya at this early-morning hour was completely lined with parked cars, both sides of the street. Cursing, Dominika had to cruise several blocks west before she found an empty spot near an all-night Almi pharmacy, its green neon sign coloring nearby trees and the scrawny grass verge in front, its front door reinforced with bars and opened remotely by the duty clerk. Trash paper swirled in the empty lot. Dominika locked her car door and started walking on the darkened sidewalk toward her building. The neighborhood was deathly silent. She clutched the oversize tote purse with the stiff bottom that was the concealment for her SRAC unit, antenna wires and transmit button sewn into the lining, standby and receive LED lights concealed as interior compartment snaps.

Once home, she would fit a thin lead into a port inside the bag to download the incoming message from CIA: intelligence requirements, or personal meeting skeds (schedules), or occasionally the rare operational requirement. Since her recruitment five years ago, she had met her CIA handlers overseas—sparingly and cover permitting—to participate in a recruitment, or in a false-flag approach, or a debriefing, all of them glorious, heady trips to meet these singular men: her lover and love Nate, crimson around his shoulders, dark and watchful, unmatched on the street; profane and purple-haloed Marty Gable, brush-cut hair and scarred knuckles, whom she called *Bratok*, brother in Russian; and rotund, unkempt Simon Benford, blue-shrouded and driven, the genius deceiver, the brilliant spy-catcher, head of CIA's Counterintelligence Division. Another reunion loomed: Last week's message had mentioned Istanbul, and Dominika anticipated new instructions.

She thought about Nate as she walked. *Bozhe*, God, loving him was against all the rules of tradecraft. Gable and Benford naturally had found out, and were going to eviscerate Nate if they didn't stop seeing each other. But Dominika wouldn't stop, and Nate couldn't stop. She had told them she was committed, she was not spying *against* Russia but *for* Russia, to flush out the Kremlin sewage farm, and send them all back to their filthy little beginnings. So, if she was CIA's irreplaceable agent, valued beyond all measure, and she wanted to love Nate, then they should shut up. *Pravil'no?* Right? She dreamed of kissing Nate again for the first time, in a taxi, or an elevator, or pressed hard against a hotel room door. His hands on her, and—

Dominika saw movement under the trees in front of the pharmacy, silhouettes coming up off the grass, one, two, three, like demons emerging from the underground. They began moving through the trees, parallel to the sidewalk, heads turned toward her. Dominika's first thought was that somehow the internal security service—the *Federal'naya Sluzhba Bezopasnosti Rossiyskoy Federastii*, the FSB, the spy catchers—had discovered her, knew she was spying for CIA, and had intercepted tonight's burst transmission to the Americans on Volokolamskoye shosse. Impossible. How? A mole in Washington? A breach of security at Moscow Station? A cracked cipher? However they did it, all the evidence they needed to bury her was sewn into the purse hanging on her shoulder. Could she resist, somehow get away? How many of them would swarm out of the night and overwhelm her? She'd soon find out. The only weapon in her purse was a key ring. Keeping an eye on the silhouettes, Dominika laced keys between three fingers of her right hand.

Dominika had been trained—and kept up weekly sparring sessions—in *Sistema Rukopashnogo Boya*, the hand-to-hand combat system used by Spetsnaz, the ferocious Russian special forces. *Sistema* was an amalgam of classic martial arts, ballistic hand strikes, management of an attacker's momentum, and devastating strikes against the six core body levers. She had killed trained assassins—with desperate luck—in hand-to-hand encounters. But she knew that in combat one slip, one missed block, sustaining a crippling strike, would be the end.

The three silhouettes stepped into the light, and Dominika breathed a sigh of relief. *Gopniki*. Not an FSB arrest team. A *gopnik* was a male street tough—head shaved, gap-toothed, perpetually slurry-eyed and red-faced on cans of alcoholic Jaguar energy drink. Invariably dressed in Adidas track suits, pointed-toed leather *tapochki*, and *gondonka* flat caps, they infested suburban Moscow street corners, bus stops, and city parks, sleeping, drinking, puking, mugging and beating up passersby. Their byword was *bychit*, to behave like a bull. They would want her purse, and would bludgeon her to death to get it. She would be just as compromised if these reeking gutterpups dragged the purse off her shoulder and found the concealed SRAC burst transmitter than if FSB did.

The three were whip-thin and malnourished, but Dominika knew they would be quick and able to absorb punishment. It would be critical to keep them off her. She would trap the lead attacker with a joint hold, and drag him in circles to keep him in front of the other two. She would use the keys to rake their eyes, then sweep their legs with her foot, and stomp a high heel into their throats or temples. That was the plan, at least.

"*Suka*, bitch, give me your purse," said Number One, stepping toward her, front right. They were indistinguishable from one another, simply incoming threats.

"*Blyad*, whore, did you hear?" said Number Two, coming in front left.

Dominika stepped slightly right as Number One reached out to grab her. She covered the top of his hand with her left hand and bent his wrist down and back. He howled as Dominika pivoted with him to the left, blocking Number Two, then continued pivoting to swing Number One, on his toes with pain, into Number Three in a tangle of legs and arms. She held on to Number One and turned him again into Number Two, foreheads clunking like coconuts. Number Three was coming in fast, his arm raised above his head. Knife. Leaning back, Dominika turned Number One into the line of the downward slash. The blade flensed down the side of Number One's shaved head and cut his ear off at the root. Dominika let the bellowing Number One drop to the ground holding his head, his neck black with spurting blood. She instantly stepped forward with a corkscrew punch, driving the three keys clamped between her right knuckles into the right eye of Number Three, feeling ocular fluid spurt over the back of her hand. She raked the keys out of the eye socket, across his nose, and into his left eye, a glancing blow. Maybe he'd still be able to see out of that eye later. Number Three collapsed shrieking *Suka*, and covering his bloody face with trembling hands.

It had taken three seconds, and two of them were on the pavement writhing amid gouts of spattered blood, but Number Two was almost on her, and she knew if he knocked her down all three would swarm her, maddened by their pain, and slam her skull against the concrete till they saw gray brains in the streetlight. Without thinking, Dominika dipped her shoulder as she grabbed the leather handles of her purse, and swung it in a flat arc into the left temple of Number Two. The four pounds of steel-bodied SRAC components sewn into the bottom of the tote bag hit skull bone with a flat metallic sound. Number Two wobbled, and sat down with a thump, cross-eyed.

Breathing hard, Dominika looked at them on the sidewalk, one facedown and unconscious, the other curled up and whimpering, the third still sitting up, staring but not seeing. These three pigs had come close to ruining everything, to exposing her, to sending her to the basement room in

Butyrka prison with the pine-log wall designed to catch ricochets, and the drains in the sloping, brown-stained cement floor placed to sluice away the fluids of the executed prisoners. Five years of unimaginable risks, of narrow escapes, of precious intelligence—*measured in linear feet*—passed to the Americans, of countless meetings in countless safe houses, only to be nearly unseated by three besotted *gopniki* two blocks from her apartment. This was another charming part of her Russia too, these louts who were as indolent, and cruel, and predatory as Putin's inner circle sitting in the jeweled halls of the Kremlin. They were the same cancer. She risked her life, and tonight they had almost ended it. She could be in a freezing cell awash with sewage, or dead and staring out of a cardboard coffin with a cloth tied under her jaw to keep her mouth closed, *these animals* . . .

In a rage, Dominika stepped up to the dazed punk, set her feet, and swung her stiffened arm under his chin and into his throat—a Spetsnaz killing stroke—fracturing the hyoid bone and rupturing the larynx. He fell backward, and began gasping, eyes staring at the top of the trees.

"*Ublyudok*, bastard," said Dominika, watching his legs jerk.

She was shaking so badly the sticky apartment key skittered over the lock before she could open the door with two hands. She left the lights off except for a small lamp near the front door. Her skirt was spotted with something dark and wet. The SRAC message downloaded to her laptop blinked once, flashed green for two seconds—she read the word "Istanbul"—then it went black, with the words "error 5788" appearing on the screen. *Chyort*, damn it! The *gopnik*'s head apparently was harder than the components. Now she would have to trigger a cringingly dangerous personal meeting with an officer from Moscow Station—*Why couldn't Nate come to meet her*?—to exchange the damaged equipment for a new SRAC set.

She left her clothes in a pile on the floor, kicked off her shoes, and looked at herself in the mirror. The knife scars from the fracas in Paris with that psychopath Zyuganov were shiny white over her ribs. She was sure that evil dwarf was burning in Hell.

The skin between her knuckles had been torn by the keys, and her hand throbbed. The little lamp cast a shadow over the curves of her body. Five years was a long time. Her figure was softer now, her rib cage didn't show, and her breasts were fuller. Thank God her stomach was still flat, and her hips had not spread to all points of the compass. The French bikini wax had been a silly impulse, but she was getting used to it. She was satisfied that her legs and ankles were slim and her calves were still knotted with muscle from her ballet years.

Her image suddenly deformed into someone else, an out-of-body wraith. An unbearable melancholy washed over her. She stifled a sob, momentarily overwhelmed by her situation, by tonight's danger, and by her whole existence as a spy. *Look at you*, she thought, *what are you doing? Who are you? A ridiculous fanatic fighting alone in the dark, overwhelming dangers arrayed against you, the odds of surviving slim, your friends far away, separated from the man you love. How long will you last? How did your mentor Lieutenant General Korchnoi—he spied for CIA for fourteen years—summon the will and determination to keep going?* Dominika blinked as tears slid down the cheeks of the revenant in the mirror. It wasn't her, it was someone else crying.